The Dream of X
and Other
Fantastic
Visions
5

The Dream of X and Other Fantastic Visions

Being The Fifth Volume of
The Collected Fiction of William Hope Hodgson

Edited by Douglas A. Anderson

Night Shade Books • New York • 2019

First Night Shade Books trade paperback edition 2019.

10 9 8 7 6 5 4 3 2 1

Library of Congress Cataloging-in-Publication Data is available on file.

ISBN: 978-1-59780-960-3
Hardcover ISBN: 978-1-892389-43-5

Interior layout and design by Jeremy Lassen

Printed in the United States of America

Contents

Contents

That Delicious Shiver

"It is pointless, though irresistible, to speculate upon what heights of Fantasy Hodgson might have scaled had the war not intervened."
—James Cawthorn & Michael Moorcock, *Fantasy: The 100 Best Books*

"A ghost story that is worth anything must be really thrilling. It must give us that delicious shiver down the spine, and it must possess mystery. Added to these qualities, it must cling to reality by some sort of explanation, however fantastic the story be, to be truly effective."
—William Hope Hodgson,
"The Writers of Ghost Stories" (an unfinished or lost essay)

THIS FIFTH AND FINAL VOLUME of the collected fiction of William Hope Hodgson is best if not, perhaps, considered as the ragged leftovers of the first four courses. Instead, I'd argue that we've saved the best for last; this is dessert, a sweet sampling of Hodgson's best—and strangest—work, a literary crème brûlée to savor and enjoy.

We begin this volume of Hodgson's fantastic visions with the evocative and heart-wrenching parable "The Valley of Lost Children," which originally appeared in *Cornhill* in February 1906. Sentimental, certainly, but "The Valley of Lost Children" does not shirk from the harsh realities of its day in its depiction of a fantastic realm beyond death. This is followed by the Swiftian conceits of "Date 1965: Modern Warfare," which imagines the battles of the future to be fought by knife-wielding butchers, with the flesh of the fallen quite literally going to feed the victors. Originally appearing in the December 24, 1908 issue of *New Age*, it presents a wry and winking examination of the soldier's lot in life.

"My House Shall Be Called the House of Prayer" (*Cornhill*, May 1911) and "Judge Barclay's Wife," (*London Magazine*, July 1912) might be excused as Hodgson's most devout explorations of Christian mercy. But to do so would be to ignore his gift for dialogue, and the intricate way in which he strives to capture the patterns of his protagonists' speech.

The gender-bending "The Getting Even of Tommy Dodd," which was later published as "The Apprentices' Mutiny" in *Sea Stories*, originally appeared in *The Red Magazine*, August 15, 1912. While this is a story that can be read for its entertainment value alone, the success that young Tommy Dodd finds in posing as his pretty "cousin," Jenny ("By George, youngster, you make a pretty girl!"), begs any number of questions about the shipboard world that Hodgson, a sailor and bodybuilder, spent much of his life in and out of.

"Sea Horses" from *London Magazine*, March 1913, is another tale of a doomed child in an uncaring world, but imbued with the same sort of hope and fancy (even while moored to the harsh ties of reality) exhibited in "The Valley of Lost Children."

The next batch of adventure yarns all appeared in *The Red Magazine*, a common venue for Hodgson's stories, including the D.C.O. Cargunka and Captain Jat tales. "How the Honourable Billy Darrell Raised the Wind" appeared in *The Red Magazine*, March 15, 1913. "The Getting Even of 'Parson' Guyles" appeared in the November 1914 issue. "The Friendship of Monsieur Jeynois" originally appeared in *The Red Magazine*, August 1, 1915. "The Inn of the Black Crow" originally appeared in *The Red Magazine*, October 1, 1915. "What Happened in the Thunderbolt" originally appeared in *The Red Magazine*, January 15, 1916. "How Sir Jerrold Treyn Dealt with the Dutch in Caunston Cove" originally appeared in *The Red Magazine*, May 1, 1916. "Jem Binney and the Safe at Lockwood Hall" originally appeared in *The Red Magazine*, October 16, 1916. "Diamond Cut Diamond with a Vengeance" originally appeared in *The Red Magazine*, January 1, 1918.

The explosive "Eloi, Eloi, Lama Sabachthani" originally appeared in *Nash's Illustrated Weekly*, September 20, 1919.

"The Room of Fear," much like "The Valley of Lost Children" and "Sea Horses," deals with a child's fate, as a young mother and her plucky son confront the dull thunder of childhood fears which may, of course, be more substantial than either one imagine. Suspected to be an early story, "The Room of Fear" was unpublished during Hodgson's lifetime. Another early and unpublished story is "The Promise," a supernatural tale of a sibling's love and the miraculous promise of resurrection.

The novel fragment "Captain Dang" imports its title character from "The Sharks of the St. Elmo," which appears in volume three of this series, but seems otherwise unconnected to it. Still, with lines like "There's poetry in canvas, laddie, when the wind gets into it," "Captain Dang" shows that even Hodgson's cast-offs hold an evocative power that ranks among fiction's best.

"Captain Dan Danblasten," Hodgson's tale of a lusty pirate's retirement and the strange will he leaves to a childhood sweetheart and her seven daughters, appeared in the May 1918 issue of *The Red Magazine*, published the same week as *The Times* ran Hodgson's obituary (April 19, 1918 is believed to be the date Hodgson was killed by a German shell).

From there, we move on to Hodgson's copyright versions, stripped-down abridgements of his best-known works, written to secure American copyright protections. Many of these have a "Cliffs Notes" feeling to them, particularly "The Ghost Pirates" and "Carnacki, the Ghost Finder." The title story, "The Dream of X," however, distills Hodgson's epic novel, *The Night Land*, down to its barest essentials, losing none of its power or poetry in the process. It is likely that these copyright versions were never intended by Hodgson to be seen by a reading audience, but "The Dream of X," perhaps best known due to the 1977 Donald M. Grant publication, with its breathtaking Stephen A. Fabian illustrations, stands as a testament to the shame that would have been. Also in this section are the stories "Senator Sandy Mac Ghee," "The Last Word in Mysteries," and "The Dumpley Acrostics."

Next, we present a spattering of alternate versions, including "An Adventure of the Deep Waters," "Captain Gunbolt Charity and the Painted Lady," "The Storm," and "The Crew of the Lancing." We'll leave it to the reader to determine what might have been. We close this volume with a pair of counterfeits, "The Raft," and "R.M.S. 'Empress of Australia.'"

In his introduction to the first volume of this series, Night Shade Books' Editor-in-Chief Jeremy Lassen makes the assertion "it goes without saying that William Hope Hodgson was one of the great fantasists of the 20th century." Regardless, Night Shade spent the next four volumes proving that point. Now, as we arrive at the final volume of the series, we believe we have fulfilled our goal, that in presenting our definitive edition of the collected fiction of William Hope Hodgson, we have ensured that Hodgson will be considered by the next generation of scholars, editors, publishers, authors, and readers. Considered, not just against the works of literary peers, from H. G. Wells to Bram Stoker to Wilfred Owen, but against those writers whose own works benefit from and build upon Hodgson's masterful imagination, from Lovecraft and Clark Ashton Smith to Jack Vance, Gene Wolfe, Greg Bear, and China Miéville.

Ross E. Lockhart
Petaluma, California
2008

Fantastic Visions

The Valley of Lost Children

I

THE TWO OF THEM STOOD TOGETHER and watched the boy, and he, a brave little fellow near upon his fourth birthday, having no knowledge that he was watched, hammered a big tom-cat with right lusty strokes, scolding it the while for having killed a "mices." Presently the cat made its escape, followed by the boy, whose chubby little legs twinkled in the sunlight, and whose tossed head of golden tangle was as a star of hope to the watchers. As he vanished among the nearer bushes the woman pulled at the man's sleeve.

"Our b'y," she said in a low voice.

"Aye, Sus'n, thet's so," he replied, and laid a great arm about her neck in a manner which was not displeasing to her.

They were neither of them young, and marriage had come late in life; for fortune had dealt hardly with the man, so that he had been unable to take her to wife in the earlier days. Yet she had waited, and at last a sufficiency had been attained, so that in the end they had come together in the calm happiness of middle life. Then had come the boy, and with his coming a touch of something like passionate joy had crept into their lives.

It is true that there was a mortgage upon the farm, and the interest had to be paid before Abra'm could touch his profits; but what of that! He was strong, uncommonly so, and then there was the boy. Later he would be old enough to lend a hand; though Abra'm had a secret hope that before that time he would have the mortgage cleared off and be free of all his profits.

For a while longer they stood together, and so, in a little, the boy came running back out of the bushes. It was evident that he must have had a tumble, for the knees of his wee knickers were stained with clay-marks. He ran up to them and held out his left hand, into which a thorn was sticking, yet he made no movement to ask for sympathy, for was he not a man?—ay, every inch of his little four-year body! His intense manliness will be the better understood when I explain that upon that day he had been "breeked," and four years old in breeks has a mighty savour of manliness.

His father plucked the thorn from his hand, while his mother made shift to remove some of the clay; but it was wet, and she decided to leave it until it had dried somewhat.

"Hev ter put ye back inter shorts," threatened his mother; whereat the little man's face showed a comprehension of the direness of the threat.

"No! no! no!" he pleaded, and lifted up to her an ensnaring glance from dangerous baby eyes.

Then his mother, being like other women, took him into her arms, and all her regret was that she could take him no closer.

An Abra'm his father, looked down upon the two of them, and felt that God had dealt not unkindly with him.

Three days later the boy lay dead. A swelling had come around the place where the thorn had pricked, and the child had complained of pains in the hand and arm. His mother, thinking little of the matter in a country where rude health is the rule, had applied a poultice, but without producing relief. Towards the close of the second day it became apparent to her that the child ailed something beyond her knowledge or supposition, and she had hurried Abra'm off to the doctor, a matter of forty miles distant; but she was childless or ever she saw her husband's face again.

II

Abra'm had digged the tiny grave at the foot of a small hill at the bank of the shanty, and now he stood leaning upon his spade and waiting for that which his wife had gone to bring. He looked neither to the right nor to the left; but stood there a very effigy of stony grief, and in this wise he chanced not to see the figure of a little man in a rusty-black suit, who had come over the brow of the hill some five minutes earlier.

Presently Sus'n came out from the back of the shanty and walked swiftly towards the grave. At the sight of that which she carried, the little man upon the hill stood up quickly and bared his head, bald and shiny, to the sun. The woman reached the grave, stood one instant irresolute, then stooped and laid her burden gently into the place prepared. Then, after one long look at the little shape, she went aside a few paces and turned her face away. At that, Abra'm bent and took a shovelful of earth, intending to fill in the grave; but in that moment the voice of the stranger came to him, and he looked up. The little bald-headed man had approached to within a few feet of the grave, and in one hand he carried his hat, while in the other he held a small, much-worn book.

"Nay, me friend," he said, speaking slowly, "gev not ther child's body ter ther arth wi'out commendin' ther sperret ter ther Almighty. Hev I permisshun ter read ther sarvice fer them as 's dead in ther Lord?"

Abra'm looked at the little old stranger for a short space, and said no word; then he glanced over to where his wife stood, after which he nodded a dumb assent.

At that the old man kneeled down beside the grave and, rustling over the leaves of his book, found the place. He began to read in a steady voice. At the first word, Abra'm uncovered and stood there leaning upon his spade; but his wife ran forward and fell upon her knees near the old man.

And so for a solemn while no sound but the aged voice. Presently he stretched out his hand to the earth beside the grave and, taking a few grains, loosed them upon the dead, commending the spirit of the child into the Everlasting Arms. And so, in a little, he had made an end.

When all was over, the old man spread out his hands above the tiny grave as though invoking a blessing. After a moment he spoke; but so low that they who were near scarce heard him:

"Leetle One," he said in a half whisper, "mebbe ye'll meet wi' that gell o' mine in yon valley o' ther lost childer. Ye'll telt hur's I'm praying ter ther Father 's 'E'll purmit thess ole sinner ter come nigh 'er agin."

And after that he knelt awhile, as though in prayer. In a little he got upon his feet and, stretching out his hands, lifted the woman from her knees. Then, for the first time, she spoke:

"Reckon I'll never see 'im no mor," she said in a quiet, toneless voice, and without tears.

The old man looked into her face and, having seen much sorrow, knew somewhat of that which she suffered. He took one of her cold hands between his old, withered ones with a strange gesture of reverence.

"Hev no bitterness, Ma'am," he said. "I know ye lack ther pow'r jest now ter say: 'Ther Lord gev, an' ther Lord 'ath teken away; blessed be ther Name o' ther Lord;' but I reckon 'E don't 'spect mor'n ye can gev. 'E's mighty tender wi' them 's is stricken."

As he spoke, unconsciously he was stroking her hand, as though to comfort her. Yet the woman remained dry-eyed and set-featured; so that the old man, seeing her need of stirring, bade her "set" down while he told her a "bit o' a tale."

"Ye'll know," he began, when she was seated, " 's I unnerstan' hoo mighty sore ye feel, w'en I tell ye I lost a wee gell o' mine way back."

He stopped a moment, and the woman's eyes turned upon him with the first dawning of interest.

"I was suthin' like yew," he continued. "I didn't seem able nohow ter get goin' agin in ther affairs o' thess 'arth. I cudn't eat, 'n I cudn't sleep. Then one night, 's I wus tryin' ter get a bit o' rest 'fore ther morn come in, I heerd a Voice sayin' in me ear 's 'twer:

" ' 'Cept ye become 's leetle childer, ye shall not enter into the Kingdom o' 'Eaven.' But I hedn't got shet o' ther bitterness o' me grief, 'n I tarned a deaf ear. Then agin ther Voice kem, 'n agin I shet ther soul o' me ter et's callin'; but 'twer no manner uv use; for it kem agin and agin, 'n I grew tur'ble feared 'n humble.

" 'Lord,' I cried out, 'guess ther oldest o' us 's on'y childer in ther sight o' God.'

"But agin ther Voice kem, an' ther sperret thet wer in me quaked, 'n I set up in ther bed, cryin' upon the Lord:

" 'Lord, shet me not oot o' ther Kingdom!" Fer I wus feared 's I mightn't get ter see ther wee gell's 'ad gone on befor'. But agin kem ther Voice, an' ther sperret in me became broke, 'n I wus 's er lonesome child, 'n all ther bitterness wer gone from me. Then I said ther words that had not passed me lips by reason o' ther bitterness o' me stubborn 'art:

" 'Ther Lord gev, an' ther Lord 'ath teken away; blessed be ther Name o' ther Lord.'

"An' ther Voice kem agin; but 'twer softer like, 'n I no longer wus feared.

" 'Lo!' et said, 'thy 'art is become like unter ther 'art o' one o' ther leetle ones whose sperrets dew always behold ther face o' ther Father. Look now wi' ther eyes o' a child, 'n them shalt behold ther Place o' ther Leetle Ones—ther valley wher' maybe found ther lost childer o' ther 'arth. Know thou thet ther leetle folk whom ther Lord teketh pass not inter ther Valley o' ther Shadder, but inter ther Valley o' Light.'

"An' immediate I looked an' saw right thro' ther logs o' ther back o' ther shanty. I cud see 's plain 's plain, lookin' out onter a mighty wilderness o' country, 'n et seemed 's tho' ther sperret o' me went forrard a space inter ther night, an' then, mighty suddin et wer', I wus lookin' down inter a tur'ble big valley. 'Twer' all lit up 'n shinin'; tho' 'twer' midnight, 'n everywher' wer' mighty flowers 's seemed ter shine o' ther own accord, an' thar wer' leetle brooks runnin' among 'em 'n singin' like canary birds, 'n grass 's fresh 's ther 'art o' a maid. An' ther valley wer' all shet in by mortial great cliffs 's seemed ter be made o' nothin' but mighty walls o' moonstone; fer they sent out light's tho' moons wer' sleepin' ahind 'em.

"After awhile I tuk a look way up inter ther sky 'bove ther valley, an' 'twer's tho' I looked up a mighty great funnel—hunder 'n hunder o' miles o' night on each side o' et; but ther sky 'bove ther valley wer' most wonnerful o' all; fer thar wer' seven suns in et, 'n each one o' a diff'rent colour, an' soft tinted, like 's tho' a mist wer' round 'em.

"An' presently, I tarned an' looked agin inter ther valley; fer I hedn't seen ther half o' et, 'n now I made out sumthin's I'd missed befor'—a wee bit o' a child sleepin' under a great flower, 'n now I saw more—Eh! but I made out a mighty multitoode o' 'em. They 'adn't no wings, now I come ter think o' et, an' no closes; but I guess closes wer'n't needed; fer 't must heve bin like a 'tarnal summer down thar; no I guess—"

The old man stopped a moment, as though to meditate upon this point. He was still stroking the woman's hand, and she, perhaps because of the magnetism of his sympathy, was crying silently.

In a moment he resumed;

"Et wer' jest after discoverin' ther childer's I made out 's thar wer' no cliff ter ther end o' ther valley upon me left. Inste'd o' cliff, et seemed ter me 's a mighty wall o' shadder went acrost from one side ter ther other. I wus starin' an' wondering', w'en a voice whispered low in me ear: 'Ther Valley o' ther Shadder o' Death,' 'n I knew 's I'd come ter ther valley o' ther lost childer—which wer' named ther Valley o' Light. Fer ther Valley of ther Shadder, 'n ther Valley o' ther Lost Childer come end ter end.

"Fer a while I stared, 'n presently et seemed ter me 's I could see ther shadders o' grown men 'n wimmin within ther darkness o' ther Valley o' Death, an' they seemed ter be groping' 'n gropin'; but down in ther Valley of Light some of ther childer had waked, 'n wer' playin' 'bout, an' ther light o' ther seven suns covered 'em, 'n made 'em j'yful.

"Et wer' a bit later 's I saw a bit o' a gell sleepin' in ther shade o' a leetle tree all covered wi' flowers. Et seemed ter me's she hed er look o' mine; but I cudn't be sure, cause 'er face wer' hid by a branch. Presently, 'owever, she roused up 'n started playin' round wi' some o' ther others, 'n I seed then 's 'twer' my gell righ enuff, 'n I lifted up me voice 'n shouted; but 'twern't no good. Seemed 's ef tar wer' sum-thin' thet come betwixt us, 'n I cudn't 'ear 'er, 'n she cudn't 'ear me. Guess I felt powerful like sheddin' tears!

"An' then, suddin, ther hull thing faded 'n wer' gone, an' I wer' thar alone in ther midst o' ther night. I felt purty 'mazed 'n sore, an' me 'art seemed like ter harden wi' their grief o' ther thing, 'n then, 'fore I'd time ter make a fool o' meself et seemed 's I 'eard ther Voice saying:

" 'Ef ye, bein' eevil, know how ter gev good gifts unter yer childer, how much more shall yer Father w'ich es in 'eaven gev good things ter them thet asks 'Im.'

"An' ther next moment I wus settin' up 'n me bed, 'n et wer' broad daylight."

"Must hev bin a dream," said Abra'm.

The old man shook his head, and in the succeeding silence the woman spoke:

"Hev ye seen et sence?"

"Nay, Ma'am," he replied; "but"—with a quiet, assuring nod— "I tuk ther hint's ther Voice gev me, 'n I've bin askin' ther Father ever sence 's I might come acrost thet valley o' ther lost childer."

The woman stood up.

"Guess I'll pray thet way 's well," she said simply.

The old man nodded and, turning, waved a shrivelled hand towards the West, where the sun was sinking.

"Thet minds one o' death," he said slowly; then, with sudden energy, "I tell ye thar's no sunset ever 'curs 's don't tell ye o' life hereafter. Yon blood-coloured sky es ter us ther banner o' night 'n Death; but 'tes ther unwrapping o' ther flag o'dawn 'n Life in some other part o' ther 'arth."

And with that he got him to his feet, his old face aglow with the dying light.

"Must be goin'," he said. And though they pressed him to remain the night, he refused all the entreaties.

"Nay," he said quietly. "Ther Voice hev called, 'n I must jest go."

He turned and took off his old hat to the woman. For a moment he stood thus, looking into her tear-stained face. Then, abruptly, he stretched out an arm and pointed to the vanishing day.

"Night 'n sorrow 'n death come upon ther 'arth; but in ther Valley o' ther Lost Childer es light 'n joy 'n life etarnal."

And the woman, weary with grief, looked back at him with very little hope in her eyes.

"Guess tho we'm too old fer ther valley o' ther childer," she said slowly.

The old man caught her by the arm. His voice rang with conviction:

" 'Cept ye become 's leetle childer, ye shall not enter into ther Kingdom o' 'Eaven."

He shook her slightly, as though to impress some meaning upon her. A sudden light came into her dull eyes.

"Ye mean—" she cried out and stopped, unable to formulate her thought.

"Aye," he said in a loud, triumphant voice. "I guess we'm on'y childer 'n ther sight o' God. But we hev ter be mighty 'umble o' 'art 'fore 'E 'lows us in wi'ther leetle ones, mighty 'umble."

He moved from her and knelt by the grave.

"Lord," he muttered, "some o' us, thro' bitter stubbornness o' 'art, hev ter wander in ther Valley o' ther Shadder; but them as 's 'umble 'n childlike 'n faith find no shadder in ther valley; but light, 'n their lost j'yfullness o'child'ood, w'ich es ther nat'ral state o' ther soul. I guess, Lord, 's Thou'lt shew thess woman all ther marcifulness o' Thy 'art, 'n bring 'er et last ter ther Valley o' ther Lost Childer. 'n whle I'm et it, Lord, I puts up a word fer meself, 's Thou'lt bring thess ole sinner et last ter the same place."

Then, still kneeling, he cried out: "Hark!" And they all listened; but the farmer and his wife heard only a far distant moan, like the cry of the night wind rising.

The old man hasted to his feet.

"I must be goin'," he said. "Ther Voice 's callin'."

He placed his hat upon his head.

"Till we meet in ther valley 'o ther 'arth's lost childer," he cried, and went from them into the surrounding dusk.

III

Twenty years had added their count to Eternity, and Abra'm and his wife Sus'n had come upon old age. The years had dealt hardly with the twain of them, and disaster overshadowed them in the shape of foreclosure; for Abra'm had been unable to pay off the mortgage, and latterly the interest had fallen in arrears.

There came a bitter time of saving and scraping, and of low diet; but all to no purpose. The foreclosure was effected, and a certain morning ushered in the day when Abra'm and Sus'n were made homeless.

He found her, a little after dawn, kneeling before the ancient press. She had the lowest drawer open, and a little heap of clothing filled her lap. There was a tiny guernsey, a small shoe, a wee, wee pair of baby boy's trousers, and the knees were stained with clay. Then, with about it a most tearful air of manfulness, a "made" shirt, with "real" buttoning wristbands; but it was not at any of these that the woman looked. Her gaze, passing through half-shed tears, was fixed upon something which she held out at arm's length. It was a diminutive pair of braces, so terribly small, so unmistakably the pride of some manly minded baby-boy—and so little worn!

For the half of a minute Abra'm said no word. His face had grown very stern and rugged during the stress of those twenty years' fight with poverty; yet a certain steely look faded out of his eyes as he noted that which his wife held.

The woman had not seen him, nor heard his step; so that, unconscious of his presence, she continued to hold up the little suspenders. The man caught the reflection of her face in a little tinsel-framed mirror opposite, and saw her tears, and abruptly his hard features gave a quiver that made them almost grotesque: it was such an upheaval of set grimness. The quivering died away, and his face resumed its old, iron look. Probably it would have retained it, had not the woman, with a sudden extraordinary gesture of hopelessness, crumpled up the tiny braces and clasped them in her hands above her hair. She bowed forward almost on to her face, and her old knuckles grew tense with the stress she put upon that which she held. A few seconds of silence came and went; then a sob burst from her, and she commenced to rock to and fro upon her knees.

Across the man's face there came again that quivering upheaval, as unaccustomed emotions betrayed their existence; he stretched forth a hand, that shook with half-conscious longing, toward an end of the braces which hung down behind the woman's neck and swayed as she rocked.

Abruptly, he seemed to come into possession of himself and drew back silently. He calmed his face and, making a noise with his feet, stepped over to where his wife kneeled desolate. He put a great, crinkled hand upon her shoulder.

"Et wer' a powerful purty thought o' yon valley o' ther lost childer," he said quietly, meaning to waken her memory to it.

"Aye! aye!" she gasped between her sobs. "But—" and she broke off, holding out to him the little suspenders.

For answer the man patted her heavily on the shoulder, and thus a space of time went by, until presently she calmed.

A little later he went out upon a matter to which he had to attend. While he was gone she gathered the wee garments hastily into a shawl, and when he returned the press was closed, and all that he saw was a small bundle which she held jealously in one hand.

They left shortly before noon, having singly and together visited a little mound at the foot of the hill. The evening saw them upon the verge of a great wood. They slept that night upon its outskirts, and the next day entered into its shades.

Through all that day they walked steadily. They had many a mile to go before they reached their destination— the shanty of a distant relative with whom they hoped to find temporary shelter.

Twice as they went forward Sus'n had spoken to her husband to stop and listen; but he declared he heard nothing.

"Kind o' singin' et sounded like," she explained.

That night they camped within the heart of the wood, and Abra'm made a great fire, partly for warmth, but more to scare away any evil thing which might be lurking amid the shadows.

They made a frugal supper of the poor things which they had brought with them, though Sus'n declared she had no mind for eating and, indeed, she seemed wofully tired and worn.

Then, it was just as she was about to lie down for the night, she cried out to Abra'm to hark.

"Singin'," she declared. "Milluns o' childer's voices."

Yet still her husband heard nothing beyond the whispering of the trees one to another, as the night wind shook them.

For the better part of an hour after that she listened; but heard no further sounds, and so, her weariness returning upon her, she fell asleep; the which Abra'm had done a while since.

Some time later she woke with a start. She sat up and looked about her, with a feeling that there had been a sound where now all was silent. She noticed that the fire had burned down to a dull mound of glowing red. Then, in the following instant, there came to her once more a sound of children singing—the voices of a nation of little ones. She turned and looked to her left, and became aware that all the wood on that side was full of a gentle light. She rose and went forward a few steps, and as she went the singing grew louder and sweeter. Abruptly, she came to a pause; for there right beneath her was a vast valley. She knew it on the instant. It was the Valley of the Lost Children. Unlike the old man, she noted less of its beauties than the fact that she looked upon the most enormous concourse of Little Ones that can be conceived.

"My b'y! My b'y!" she murmured to herself, and her gaze ran hungrily over that inconceivable army.

"Ef on'y I cud get down," she cried, and in the same instant it seemed to her that the side upon which she stood was less steep. She stepped forward and commenced to clamber down. Presently she walked. She had gotten halfway to the bottom of the valley when a little naked boy ran from out of the shadow of a bush just ahead of her.

"Possy," she cried out. "Possy."

He turned and raced towards her, laughing gleefully. He leapt into her arms, and so a little while of extraordinary contentment passed.

Presently, she loosed him and bade him stand back from her.

"Eh!" she said, "yew've not growed one bit!"

She laid her bundle on the ground and commenced to undo it.

"Guess they'll fet ye same's ever," she murmured, and held up the little trousers for him to see; but the boy showed no eagerness to take them.

She put out her hand to him, but he ran from her. Then she ran after him, carrying the little trousers with her. Yet she could not catch him, for he eluded her with an elf-like agility and ease.

"No, no, no," he screamed out in a very passion of glee.

She ceased to chase him and came to a stand, hands upon her hips.

"Come yew 'ere, Possy, immediate!" she called in a tone of command. "Come yew 'ere!"

But the baby elf was in a strange mood, and disobeyed her in a manner which made her rejoice that she was his mother.

"Oo tarnt ketch me," he cried, and at that she dropped the little knickers and went a-chase of him. He raced down the remaining half of the slope into the valley, and she followed, and so came to a country where there are no trousers—where youth is, and age is not.

IV

When Abra'm waked in the early morn he was chill and stiff; for during the night he had taken off his jacket and spread it over the form of his sleeping wife.

He rose with quietness, being minded to let her sleep until he had got the fire going again. Presently he had a pannikin of steaming tea ready for her, and he went across to wake her; but she waked not, being at that time chased by a chubby baby-boy in the Valley of Lost Children.

Date 1965: Modern Warfare

[Extract from the "Phono-Graphic."]

THE NEW WAR MACHINE, coming as it has so promptly after the remarkable speech by Mr. John Russell, M.P., in the House on the 20th of last month, will find the narrow path of Public Opinion paved for its way into actual use.

As Mr. Russell put the matter:—

"A crisis has come which must be faced. The modern fighting-man, soldier, butcher, call him what you will, has made definite representations that he must know in what way he benefits the community at large, by killing or being killed in the gigantic butcheries which follow in the wake of certain political 'talkee-talkees.' In fact, like the prisoners of last century, if he must tread the mill—in his case the mill of death—he is desirous of knowing that it is doing some actual work. He has become an individual, thinking unit—a unit capable of using the brain of which he is possessed. He has risen above the semi-hysterical fervour of the ignoramus of half a century ago, who went forth to kill, with the feeling that he was engaged in a glorious—nay, the most glorious vocation to which man can be called: a state of mind which was carefully fostered by men of higher attainments; though not always of higher intellect. These latter put forward in favour of the profession of human butcher, that the said butchery of their fellows, as the running of the same risk, were the best means of developing all that is highest and most heroic in man. We of this age 'ha'e oor doots;' though, even now, there be some who still swear by the ancient belief, pointing to the Nations of the Classics, and showing that when they ceased to be soldiers they fell from the heights they had gained by arms, and became soft of fibre and heart. To the first of these I would reply that in these days of high national intellectuality we are realizing that the killing of some mother's son does not help the logical solution of the question: To whom should the South Pole belong? More, that the power of Universal Law (the loom of which even now we can see) will usurp the place of the ancient butcher—in other words, that intellectual sanity will reign in place of unreasoning, foolish slaughter.

"To the second danger, that of becoming soft of fibre and heart, I will oppose the fact that to lead the life of a civilian in this present century of ours, calls for as much sheer pluck, heroic courage, and fortitude as was possessed by the most blood-drunken human butcher of the old days.

"If any have doubts on this point, let them try to imagine the ancient Roman soldier-hero facing the problem of 270 miles per hour in one of our up-to-date mono-rail cars; or, further, a trip round the earth in one of the big flying boats, at a speed of from 600 to 800 miles an hour, and they will, I think, agree that there is some little reason with me.

" 'Oh,' I hear the cry, 'that's because we're used to it. Let them get used to it, and they wouldn't mind.'

"True, my friends; but so were the Ancients used to slaughter; almost as much so as we're used to our mono-rail and flying boats. Yet there were cowards then, who shirked fighting, and never won free from their cowardice; for all that they lived in a very atmosphere of war. There are cowards today, who have never travelled above the puny rate of 100 miles an hour, and who never will; though all about them is the roar of our higher speeds; for the rest, the courage of the man of today is well suited to the needs of his time; far more so than if he were gifted with the sort possessed by some ancient hero.

"But to get back to our muttons, as an ancient saying has it. War is still with us. So long as nations remain separate, having separate and conflicting interests, so long will the profession of human-butcher remain a hideous fact, until the time when we are agreed to form a World-Nation, policed, instead of butchered, into order.

"A World-Nation is the cure for the causeless slaughter which obtains at the present date; yet it is a cure that lies in the future, and our aim at present is to make the best of that which we cannot escape. To this end I have two propositions to make; though they might both come under one head, and that is Economy.

"The first would deal with expenditure. It will be remembered that up to the summer of '51 the 'gay' uniform was not entirely discarded among the home regiments. On that date, however, it was finally abandoned, and universal brown became the accepted covering. Yet, in many ways this uniform is needlessly expensive, and I would suggest in place thereof the usual butcher's blue overalls. This only by the way. I would dismiss all officers, and appoint in place thereof, to each hundred men, a head butcher. This will be sufficient for the present. I will explain later other ways in which the expenditure might be still further cut down.

"The second portion of my proposals for economy deals with an innovation—Receipts! Yes, I would have receipts.

"Given the fact that there is, and seems likely yet awhile to be, a need for human butchering; then, in the name of any small fragment of common sense we may possess, let us put the thing on a saner, more business-like footing—And Save the Meat! (Loud cheers.) Aye, save the meat, economize; treat it as the business it is—and a nasty, dirty business at that. Like reasonable people, go to the best, the most direct way to get it done and over as quickly and efficiently as possible. We could, in the event of my suggestion being adopted, point out to the victims that they were, at least, not dying quite in vain."

Mr. Russell then went on to make suggestions:—

"War would, of course, have to be conducted on somewhat different lines than has been the case hitherto. Also, we should have to make International agreements that all nations should conform to the new methods of doing our killing. But no doubt it could be arranged. The item of economy would prove a mighty argument in its favour.

"As to the actual scheme, there are several which I have in my mind, any one of which would do. To take one. We will suppose that there is a matter in dispute between two nations, and we are one of them. Well, we would, according to my idea, have a committee to study its importance, size, risks, desirabilities, etc.—everything, in fact, except the morality of it; then we would refer to statistics of various 'kills' in former butcheries, and so—taking all the points into consideration—strike an average, and form an estimate of the number to be killed to make a sure thing of it. The other side would do the same, and neither would know the number of men the other had voted to the settling of the business. This would supply a splendid element of chance, well calculated to give opportunities for developing all the necessary heroic qualities which any man could hope to have.

"The next part of the work would be to pick the men. They would be chosen by lot; so many from each station— a method well calculated to improve their nerve, hardihood, manhood, stoicism, fortitude, and many other good qualities. As the last stand of those who uphold war has been its beneficial effect on the manhood of the nation, it will be seen that my proposition must meet with their approval; for, before a blow has been struck, a large proportion of the training has been accomplished.

"Having now picked our butchers (or victims), their numbers as per estimate of the Meat Office—I mean the War Office—we would turn them into a big pen along with the chosen number which the opposing nation had voted as being necessary to accomplish their purpose. Each man would be provided with a knife and steel, and—commencing work at the usual working hour of the country in which the butchering is effected—would proceed to the slaying with all the speed at their command. The survivors would, of course, be esteemed the winners. The slaying over, the meat would be packed and sold by the winning side to defray expenses, in this wise minimizing the cost of a somewhat unpleasant but—according to many learned men—a very necessary and honourable business.

"This meat should sell well; for I can imagine that there should be considerable satisfaction in eating one's enemy: moreover, I am told that it is a very old custom.

"I would suggest, in closing, that the butchers receive instruction from the Head Butchers in the proper methods of killing. At present they put far more science into destroying bullocks quickly and comfortably than in performing the same kind office for their fellows. If a man must be killed, at least let him be treated no more barbarously than a bullock. Further, they would have to learn, when killing, not to spoil the joints. Let every man understand his trade!"

Here Mr. John Russell made an end amid profound cheering from the whole House.

My House Shall Be Called the House of Prayer

(An incident in the Life of Father Johnson, Roman Catholic Priest)

"And the Great Deep of Life."

FATHER JOHNSON'S IRISH VILLAGE IS NOT IRISH. For some unknown reason it is polyglot. They are, as one might say, a most extraordinary family.

I took my friend, James Pelple, down with me for an afternoon's jaunt, to give the priest a call in his new house; for he had moved since last I saw him. Pelple knew of Father Johnson, by hearsay, and disapproved strongly. There is no other word to describe his feelings.

"A good man, yes," he would remark. "But if all you tell me, and the half of what I hear from others, is true, he is much too lax. His ritual——"

"I've never been to his place," I interrupted. "I know him only as the man. As a man, I love him, as you know; as a priest, I admire him. Concerning his ritual I know nothing. I don't believe he is the man to be unduly lax on vital points."

"Just so! Just so!" said Pelple. "I know nothing; but I've heard some very peculiar things."

I smiled to myself. Certainly, Father Johnson has some unusual ways. I have seen him, for instance, when we have been alone, forget to say his grace until, maybe, he had eaten one dish. Then, remembering, he would touch his fingers together, and say:— "Bless this food to me" (glancing at the empty dish), "an' I thank Thee for it" (looking at the full one in front). Then, remembering the dish yet on the stove:—"An' that too, Lord," and direct the Lord's attention to the same, by a backward nod of his head. Afterwards, resuming his eating and talking, in the most natural fashion.

"I've heard that he allows his church to be used for some very extraordinary purposes," continued Pelple. "I cannot, of course, credit some of the things I hear; but I have been assured that the women take their knitting into the church on weekday evenings, whilst the men assemble there, as to a kind of rendezvous, where village topics are allowed. I consider it most improper, most improper! Don't you?"

But I found it difficult to criticise Father Johnson. I was frankly an admirer, as I am to-day. So I held my peace, assisted by an elusive movement of the head, that might have been either a nod or a negative.

When we reached the village, and asked for the priest's new house, three men of the place escorted us there in state, as to the house of a chieftain. Reaching it, two of them pointed to him through the window, where he sat at table, smoking, after his early tea. The third man would have accompanied us in; but I told him that I wanted to see the priest alone; whereupon they all went happily. To have need to see the priest alone, was a need that each and all understood, as a part of their daily lives.

I lifted the latch, and we passed in, as all are welcome to do at any hour of the day or night. The door of his house opened into a short half-passage, and I could see direct into his little room, out of which went the small scullery-kitchen. As we entered, I heard Sally, his servant-wench, washing dishes in the little scullery; and just then Father Johnson called out to her:—"Sally, I'll make a bet with ye."

In the scullery, I heard a swift rustling and a subdued clatter, and knew that Sally (having heard that preliminary often before) was stealthily removing the handles of the knives from the boiling water. Then her reply:—

"Did y'r riv'rence sphake?"

"I did, Sally, colleen," said the priest's voice. "I'll make a bet with ye, Sally, you've the handles av thim knives over hilt in the hot water—eh, Sally!"

And then Sally's voice, triumphant:—

"Ye're wrong, y'r riv'rence, thim knives is on the dhresser!"

"Aye, Sally." said Father Johnson; "but were they not in the hot water whin I sphoke firrst?"

"They was, y'r riv'rence." said Sally, in a shamed voice; just as she had been making the same confession for the past seven years. And then the priest had a little fit of happy, almost silent laughter, puffing out great clouds of smoke; in the midst of which we walked in on him.

After our greetings, which the priest had met with that strange magnetism of heartiness that had left even the critical Pelple less disapproving, we were set down to a tea, which we simply had to eat, the priest waiting on us himself, and making the little meal "go," as you might say, with the abundance of his energy and humour—telling a hundred quaint tales and jests of the country-side, with his brogue making points of laughter where more formal speech would have left us dull and untouched.

The meal over, the priest suggested that we might like to accompany him down to his chapel, and see whether things were "kapin' happy," as he phrased it. As you may suppose, we were quite eager to accept his invitation; for, as I have made clear already, I had never been down to his place before, and I had heard many things—even as had Pelple—about his chapel and his methods.

We had not far to go. On the way, Father Johnson pointed with his thumb to a little stone-built cabin, very small and crude, which I learned was rented by a certain old Thomas Cardallon, who was not an Irishman.

"Tom's wife died last week," said the priest, quietly. "He's to be evicted to-morrow as iver is, if he cannot fhind the rint."

I put my hand into my pocket, with a half-involuntary movement; but he shook his head, as much as to say no good could be done that way. That was all, and we were past the small hovel in a minute; but I found myself looking back with a sudden, new curiosity at the little rough-built living-place, that, before, had been only one poor hut among many; yet was now instinct to me with a history of its own, so that it stood out in my memory, from the others, that were here and there about, as something indicative of the life-hope and striving of two poor humans. I put it badly, I know; but it was just such a jumble of vague thoughts and emotions as these, that stirred in my mind. I had reason afterwards to have further memory of the cottage and its one-time occupants.

We reached the chapel very soon; but when we entered, I stood for a moment, in astonishment, looking up the single aisle of the long, whitewashed room. There was not much noise; for, as I discovered, reverence and the sense of the Place, held power all the time; moreover, they were Father Johnson's people. I looked at my friend, smiling, I fear.

"Even worse than Rumour foretold." I suggested in a low voice; but he made no reply; for he appeared to me to be stifled by the excess of his astounded disapproval. The priest was a few paces before us, where we had made our involuntary pause in the doorway; and he, too, came to a stand, and looked at the scene, unobserved.

You will understand that there was cause for my astonishment, and even—as many will agree—with the strong disapprobation which my friend was feeling, when I tell you that there was an auction in progress within the House; for within the doorway to the left, was a pile of household goods, evidently from the cottage of one of the very poor. In front of the little heap was an old man, and round him, in a semicircle, stood a number of the villagers, listening intently to the old man's extolling of each article of his household gear, which he was putting up for sale.

" 'My House shall be called——' " I quoted softly and involuntarily; but less with any blame in my heart, than a great wonder, salted by a vague shockedness. The priest, still standing a little before me, caught my half-unconscious quotation; but he only said "Hush!" so gently that I felt suddenly ashamed, as if I were a child fumbling with the Garments of Life, which the priest had worn upon his shoulders all the long years.

For maybe the half of a minute longer, we stood staring at the scene, Father Johnson still a few paces before us into the chapel.

"Tom Cardallon," he said presently over his shoulder. "If he sold outside, the officers would confiscate. I showed ye the house av him, as we passed."

He beckoned us to join the group of villagers round the pitiful pile of household goods, which we did, whilst he went on up the chapel, speaking a word here and there to the many who were gathered together in companionship for the quiet hour that preceded the evening Rosary. Some were praying; a few were sitting quietly in restful isolation from the world of reality; many of the women, I noticed, were knitting, or sitting making butter in small glass jars, which they shook constantly in their hands. The whole scene, in the soft evening light that came in through the long narrow windows, giving me an extraordinary sense of restfulness and natural humanity.

I turned presently from my viewing of the general chapel, to the particular corner where I stood upon the skirt of the little group around the old man. I began to catch the drift of his remarks, uttered in a low tone, and found myself edging nearer, to hear more plainly. I gathered—as the priest had told us—that he had just lost his wife, after a long illness which had run them hopelessly into debt. Indeed, as you know, the eviction from the little hovel was arranged for the morrow, if the old man could not find the small sum which would make it possible for him to stay on in the old cottage, where he had evidently spent many very happy years.

"This 'ere," the old man was saying, holding up a worn saucepan, "wer' one as my missus 'as cooked a pow'r o' spuds in."

He stopped, and turned from us a moment, with a queer little awkward gesture, as if looking round for something that he knew subconsciously he was not in search of. I believe, in reality, the movement was prompted by an unrealised desire to avert his face momentarily, which had begun to work, as memory stirred in him. He faced round again.

"Eh," he continued, "she wer' great on chips in batter, she wer'. Me 'n 'er used ter 'ave 'em every Sunday night as ever was. Like as they was good to sleep on, so she said. An' I guess they was all cooked in this 'ere ole pan."

He finished his curious eulogy, rather lamely, and pulled out his old red handkerchief. After he had blown his nose, and furtively wiped his eyes, he used the handkerchief to polish the interior and exterior of the pan; after which he held it up once more to the view of the silent and sympathetic crowd.

"What'll ye give for it?" he asked, looking round anxiously at the many faces.

"Sixpence," said a low voice, and the old man, after a quick glance round the crowd, said:—"It's yours, Mrs. Mike Callan," and handed it across to a woman in the front of the crowd. The money was paid into his hand in coppers, as I could tell by the chink.

I looked towards the purchaser, feeling that I should like to buy back the saucepan, and return it to the old man. This way, I saw Father Johnson moving here and there through the little crowd, with a calico bag in his hand. From this, in a surreptitious manner, he drew something constantly—which I conceived by the faint chinking to be money—and distributed it to a man here and a woman there among the onlookers, accompanying each act with a few whispered words.

I understood much and guessed the rest. It was obvious that the people had little money to spare; for both their clothes and their little huts, all told of an utter poverty. This poverty, Father Johnson was remedying for the occasion, and his whispered words were probably hints concerning the articles for which to bid, and the amount to be bid for each. This, of course, is only a guess; but I believe that I am correct, in the main.

Once, I bid for a little old crock, offering double or treble its original value; but the old man took not the slightest notice, and continued to offer the article to bids that counted pence to the shillings of my offer. I was astonished, and began to see newly, if I may put it in that way. The man next to me, bid fivepence; then turned and put up his finger, shaking his head in friendly fashion, but warningly. Evidently, I was to be allowed no part in this function of neighbourly help, which was obviously ordered by rules of which I lacked a fundamental knowledge. A woman, near to me, made things somewhat clearer. She bent my-wards, and whispered:—

" 'E'd not take it back from you, Sir, nor the price you offered, neither. 'E's got a inderpendent 'eart, 'e 'as, Sir. Poor old man."

So the things were going to be given back, after all. I wondered how they would arrange the returning. It was evident that he had no conceiving of the intentions of his neighbours; for the emotion of distress was too plainly writ in his face, with each familiar article that he auctioned. I learned afterwards that he was detained in chapel by Father Johnson for a few "worrds," during which the household gear was replaced in his cottage.

When everything else had been sold, there remained only a poor bundle of something, done up in a faded shawl. It was as if the old man had put off, to the very end, the selling of this. Now, he got down clumsily on to his knees, and began to undo the knots, fumbling stupidly, and bending his head low over the bundle. He got the knots undone at last, and presently, after a little turning over of the few things, in a way that I perceived to be more a dumb caressing, than because he sought any particular article, he rose to his feet, holding an old worn skirt.

"This 'ere," he said slowly, "wer' my missus's best, an' she wer' very spechul 'bout it, these 'ere thirty year. I mind w'en she first wor' it." (His face lined a moment with emotion, grotesquely.) "She wer' that slim 's she hed ter put a tuck in ther waistban'; not that it 'armed it; she tuk pertickler care, an——"

I lost the old man's low-voiced explanation at this point; for I was suddenly aware that Father Johnson was almost at my side. I glanced an instant at him; but he was staring at the old man, with the oddest expression on his face. I noticed, subconsciously, that he was clenching and unclenching his hands rapidly. Then the old man's quaver caught my ear again:—

"It's fine an' good cloth, an' them stain-marks couldn't be 'elped. As she said, it wer' ther Lord's will, an' she mustn't complain. This 'ere one on the 'em wer' done fifteen year back——" Again my attention was distracted. I caught the sharp flip of a finger and thumb, and a man looked round and sidled out of the crowd, up to Father Johnson, in obedience to his signal.

"Sthop ut, Mike! Sthop ut this instant!" I heard the priest whisper, his brogue coming out strong, because he was stirred. "Offer ten bob for the lot, an' sthop ut; 'tis breakin' the hearts av us."

He handed the man some money, and Mike bid for the shawl-full. But, even then, it was horrible to see old Cardallon's fight, before he could relinquish the garments to the buyer.

The sale was over. The latter part of it had been attended by an ever increasing audience; from those who at first had been content to sit and talk and rest quietly on the benches; and who—coming from the outlying districts—were not intimate neighbours of old Tom. As they broke up to return to their seats, I saw one or two women crying openly.

James Pelple and I stayed for the service of the Rosary, in all reverence, though of another persuasion. Afterwards, as we stood in doorway, waiting for Father Johnson, I looked across at him.

"Well?" I queried, "a den of thieves?"

But Pelple, "the Stickler," shook his head.

"A wonderful man," he said, "a wonderful man. I should like to know him better."

I laughed outright.

"So you've come under the banner too," I said. "I wondered whether you would." And just then, Father Johnson joined us it his cassock, and we began our return journey to his house.

On the way, we passed the door of Cardallon's cottage, the upper half of which was open. The priest looked in, with a cheery word, and we joined him. The old man was standing in the centre of his hard-beaten mud floor, staring round in a stunned, incredulous fashion at all his restored household goods. He stared half-vacantly at Father Johnson, the tears running slowly down his wrinkled face. In his right hand, he held the little bundle, knotted round with the faded shawl.

The priest stretched a hand over the half-door, and blessed old Tom Cardallon in the loveliest, homeliest way, that stirred me, I admit frankly, to the very depths.

Then he turned away, and we resumed our walk, leaving the old man to his tears, which I am convinced were signs, in part at least, of a gentle happiness.

"He would not take the money from us," said the priest, later. "But do ye think the heart av him would let him sind back the gear!"

I looked across at Pelple, and smiled to his nod; for I knew that his last vague questioning was answered.

Judge Barclay's Wife

MRS JUDGE BARCLAY SHE WAS CALLED, and no one thought to call her anything less. And at the instant of this tale she sat in the crude, log-built cabin that did temporary duty for a court in the small township of Selville, which lay at the head of what was locally termed the "gold-creek."

Her husband, assisted by the sheriff and a number of his posse, accompanied by a number of miners, was trying a young miner named Jem Turrill, and the old Judge's face showed a strong tendency to mercy as he looked down from his raised seat of packing-cases at the sullen face of the young man before him.

On her part, Mrs Judge Barclay was trying to catch the Judge's eye, to "stiffen his back-bone," as she would have phrased it; for she had dealt with him often and bitterly concerning his undue tendency to mercy. A hard-faced, big-boned, childless woman of sixty she was, vigorous and a ruler of men, her husband in particular, except on this one point which pertained to mercy. Judge Barclay, however, had once been sheriff, and had practical knowledge that the capital sentence given in court was but the precursor of that dread scene where a rope, and too often a fine man, kicking his life away, formed a dreadful conjunction in his memory. Many and many a man had he seen pass outward this way; yet, with pleasure it may be told that such experiences had not brought callousness.

But Mrs Judge Barclay knew nothing of what I might term the practical side of Justice. She failed in Realisation. She attended constantly at the courts where her husband presided, and would listen with critical severity to her husband's "handling" of the case, and see no further than the given sentence. Too often, she would listen, with a sort of impatient half-contempt in her heart old Judge Barclay's constant tempering of Justice with good human mercy; and always after any special evidence of this trait in him, she would consider it her duty to "stiffen his backbone," as she termed it—a process which occasionally included the unloading upon the Judge of some rather brusque comments, bordering almost on the contemptuous.

As a result of his wife's constant attitude, old Judge Barclay had more than once found himself dealing out sentences that were sterner than his heart considered the needs of the case to require. This wife of his strung him up, as it were, to a sort of concert-pitch of austerity. But such stringing up was only temporary, in every case; and after the Court had ended the old Judge would have a bad time with his own kindly nature, the while, perhaps, that he would be walking back to his log hotel with his wife, nodding absently to her comments of somewhat grim approbation. Perhaps, once in a way, he would wake up to the whole meaning of the situation, with, maybe, something of a vague half-bitterness towards his wife, and a desire to show her somewhat of the things that lay actually "behind the sentence"—the human agony and shame and degradation of the poor human in the Machinery of Correction.

Once, indeed, he had made the attempt; had silenced her with a sudden sternness that had astounded her, and brought a certain novel respect for him into her general feeling of Proprietorship. But he had failed entirely, as he worked slowly and earnestly, striving to pull up for her inspection the deep roots (the principles) out of which grew the plant of his conduct in life. He had no particular gift of speech and had striven with logic, where only the wand of emotion might have helped him to reach down to the sunk wells of pity that lay so deep in the frozen womanhood of his grim and childless wife.

His effort merely earned the retort that "evildoers must take their physic, or else quit their bad ways," and further, that if he had not the "stomach for his duty," he would be better employed doing other work, "maybe nursin' babbies!" (What an inverted expression of the pain of her denied motherhood lay in this tilt at the Judge; though it is more than probable that the woman never realised it.)

And now she sat in the log-shanty court, and stared with cold eyes of complete condemnation from Jem Turrill, the prisoner, to her husband, the Judge, and so back again to the prisoner, her brain taking the evidence, piece by piece, and her stern reasoning breeding in her an impatient contempt for the look of compassion which old Judge Barclay occasionally turned upon the sullen and youthful Jem.

Jem Turrill was certainly a rather sullen looking young lout; but, for all that, he was possessed of a more wholesome heart and better abilities than a casual look at his face suggested; the poor effect he produced owing itself probably to his constant sullen expression, which put onlookers immediately out of sympathy with him. He was given to occasional heavy drinking-bouts, and he gambled inveterately, but also he worked hard, and he had a very real affection for his old mother, whose love for him had for so long been pitiful in its hungry anxiety to aid and coax him to steady ways, without angering him.

Her affection had brought her West, among the mining towns, that she might be near to him. She had come one evening, a few months prior to the event I am relating, and the son had welcomed her with a curious mixture of honest joy and equally honest shamefacedness, lest the other miners of his acquaintanceship should view the matter from the standpoint of the "maternal apron-strings." Yet the over-youthful Jem need not have troubled; his comrades neither thought nor cared one way or the other about the new arrival, except, it might be, to envy him the possession of a competent house-keeper and cook in his little, rough shanty. And, as I have said, though a wayward, sullen youth, his affection for his mother was genuine and curiously intense, after its own peculiar fashion.

But of all this Mrs Judge Barclay was unaware. It is to be doubted whether she even realised that the youthful thief and murderer (for these were the counts on which he was standing his trial) so much as possessed a mother—whether, indeed, such a dreadful creature could possibly have been born of woman! If she herself had borne children, she might have understood many things, and she would not have been sitting there. As it was, she sat there, calm and logical and utterly impatient of the "sentimentality!" of her husband's expression as he viewed the sodden-looking young reprobate before the Court.

And young Jem Turrill was in very sore trouble, indeed; though far less a guilty-souled man than the woman or the Court believed him. Indeed, by the woman and the Court, he was already foredoomed to condemnation; but Judge Barclay saw a little deeper, and was striving, somewhat inefficiently, to elicit such replies from the prisoner as should present his case in a less dreadful light. But young Jem only stood like a clumsy oaf, protesting with sullen earnestness his innocence to the old Judge who desired to believe him; and to the Court that entirely disbelieved him. Once, in the midst of his protesting of innocence he stopped, and looked suddenly at Mrs Judge Barclay—the one woman in the court—as if he had an abrupt thought that she perhaps might understand that he was innocent of the worst. The action was born of a sudden, rather hopeless instinct, that became instantly wholly hopeless, as his look met her grim, unfaltering gaze, as merciless as that of any man present. And with a hopeless little half-drunken shrugging of his shoulders he had turned from her, and once more faced the old Judge, whose leaning towards mercy he perceived dimly.

The details were brief enough. He had been up at the shanty of one Duncan Larsden, playing cards, during the past night (it was early morning still). Pistol shots a little before dawn had brought up the sheriff and a couple of his men, who found Larsden dead, with a bullet-wound in his head. Young Jem Turrill was gone, and with him, as was shortly proved, at least two hundred ounces of Larsden's gold. The sheriff took up the hot trail, and ran the young man down within two hours, and already he was in the Court, being tried for his life. Indeed, so speedily had events moved that his old mother at that very moment awaited him in the shanty with a newly cooked damper, and a freshly opened tin of salmon, all unaware of the dreadfulness that was falling.

As I have said, Jem sullenly but vehemently protested his innocence. When caught by the sheriff he was found to have on him a one hundred ounce bag of gold-dust, in addition to the nuggets of the dead man. The gold dust he was easily able to prove as his own property; at least, it had been his on the previous evening. His version was that Larsden had lost his two hundred ounces of nuggets to him, and had then staked his claim against the three hundred ounces of gold that Jem held. Larsden had won, but even as he declared himself winner, two aces had dropped out of his sleeve, and Jem had rounded upon him as a cheat—a swizzler. At the accusation, Larsden had drawn on him, but his "gun" had missed fire, and Jem had got home a good useful shot before the other man had time to pull the trigger a second time, and Duncan Larsden had slipped out noisily into the twilight of life. Jem had then got a sick fright that the affair might look bad for him, and, like a silly young fool, had proceeded to make it immediately ten thousand times worse by bolting with the gold. Possibly, if he had been more sober, he would have seen the folly of his action in time, but regrets were useless; he had bolted, and been found with the "stolen" gold upon him.

It is true that, in young Jem's favour, it was found that a miss-fire cartridge occupied one of the chambers of Larsden's revolver, but this was not exactly evidence; and against this one favourable item was the fact that the young man had gone off with the two hundred ounces of gold that had not been his the previous evening. This was the thing that condemned him; there was no thought of mercy on the part of the jurors; there had been far too much thieving in the township of late; it was a matter that vitally affected each and every one of them, for some had gold in their shanties or tents, and others hoped some time to be in a like pleasing condition. The result of such interests, dealing with such evidence, was a foregone conclusion—young Jem Turrill was sentenced to be hanged the next morning at dawn; the gallows a tree just outside of the north end of the township. It had been used previously for the same purpose, having a convenient bough.

As Jem was led out of the shanty where the Court had been held, he turned suddenly and stared fiercely at Mrs Judge Barclay; she was, as I have said, the only woman there.

"Hey!" shouted the sullen Jem, with an extraordinary flash of analytical inspiration. "You'm a hard-hearted old brute you be! Sittin' there an' thinkin' proper to have me murdered, you old hag!"

He was hustled away, for old Mrs Barclay was well enough liked, and thoroughly respected; and the only effect of the young man's outburst was to fix more firmly on her mind, and on the minds of all the others, that he was but a brutish creature, and better hanged soon than late. Even old Judge Barclay was conscious of a momentary flash of anger against him for his address to his wife.

And so the young man went out to the little log-built lock-up, where he was to fret away the hours that remained.

Meanwhile, someone told his old mother.

At daybreak next day, however, when the sheriff visited the lock-up with a number of his posse to lead young Turrill to his own grim version of under-the-greenwood-tree, he found the men he had left on guard comfortably ensconced within the lock-up, in a state of beatific drunkenness, but Jem, the condemned (but soul-guiltless) murderer, was distinctly not there.

Explanations from the guard were confused, and the sheriff twisted the key on him, in turn, whilst he organised search parties for Jem Turrill. The search parties were not a success, and it seemed that Jem had got safely away, but the sheriff was an obstinate man, and having arranged a hanging, was determined that a hanging there should be. He stuck, therefore, to the search, but adopted a new method; he watched the comings and goings of Jem's old mother.

Meanwhile, old Judge Barclay, having a day of rest before him, chose to go fishing, accompanied, as ever, by Mrs Barclay. He was in a restful and contented frame of mind. He was thoroughly, though secretly, glad that young Jem had escaped. He felt in his heart that, whatever the evidence, the man was less guilty than proof had shown.

It was in the late afternoon, just as old Judge Barclay was having an exciting moment with an exceptionally fine fish, that both he and his wife heard a woman screaming somewhere among the trees on their side of the river. The Judge handed his rod to his wife, and ran off in the direction of the sound. Mrs Judge Barclay consigned the rod to the river-bank, and followed him. The screams continued, and the old Judge began to run, breathlessly, and his wife also, with a sudden, new-born feeling of something that was worse than discomfort stirring peculiar emotions within her. They dashed on among the trees, guided by the screams, and burst through into a small clearing, in the midst of which stood a solitary oak; and so had view of a painful and dreadful sight—Justice, the Fetish of all perfect man, about to accept a victim.

There was a group of men under a great bough of the oak, and one of the men was trying to throw a rope up over the branch; and even as the old Judge and his wife ran across the clearing, he succeeded; whereupon several of the men ran and caught hold of the dangling end, and proceeded to haul the slack over the branch. Mrs Judge Barclay saw then, all in a moment, as it were, that the other end of the rope was fast about the neck of a man who had his back turned to her, and she experienced a peculiar little sick feeling, as Nature began to have birth in her. She was still hastening towards the group as she discovered these details, and in almost the same instant she discovered that the screaming came from a woman who was held by a couple of the men.

Her glance went again to the others. Several of them had stepped back a little from the noosed man, and had their Smith and Wessons in their hands. She recognised the sheriff, and knew that the man with the rope about his neck was Jem Turrill. She did not know that they were going to shoot poor Jem full up with lead as soon as he should have swung sufficiently to get the "taste of the hangin' into his heart." Nor, if she had realised the fact, would she have understood that mercy was really at the back of the men's intention—mercy with the cestus, instead of the gentle fingers of woman, but mercy nevertheless. And so came Mrs Judge Barclay to the group of men intent about their work.

The condemned lad (for he was scarcely more) stood pale and grimly silent, swallowing constantly and dreadfully at the dryness that seemed to fill his throat, and looking with wild eyes at the woman held by the two men, for it was his old mother.

"Help! Help!" she would scream, and fall into a sudden, trembling silence, quivering so that her quivering shook the two brawny men who held her, so callously determined. And again her scream would ring out madly, "Help! Help!" crying to any god that might be listening.

Mrs Judge Barclay stood a moment, looking at it all with wider eyes than she had ever opened before—seeing it, and at last beginning, with a horrible sickness in all her being, to understand something of what old Judge Barclay, her husband, had never been given words or skill to "make seen" to her.

The mother's crying broke out again, fierce and terrible in its white-hot intensity:—"Help! Help!" And she began to struggle like a maniac, with the two big men who held her. The dreadfulness of it all! ... It was she, his own mother, who had innocently led the posse to where her son was hid. They had watched her, as I have told, and had followed her, secretly, as she slipped away quietly through the woods, taking a towelful of damper and tinned goods to Jem's hiding-place. She it was who had managed the escape for him by conveying drink to the man on guard, and she it was who had found the hiding-place for him, and she it was who had brought him food; and now she had brought him to his death. She began to scream incoherent words and to give out scarcely human sounds, and her struggles became so fierce that her clothing was ripped literally into ribbons of cloth and cotton in the hands of the two unemotional, almost casually determined men who had held her off from going to her son.

Old Mrs Barclay stared, suffering at last in understanding of the stern and deathly intention that informed the group of men "about their business"; and with her heart sick with the horror of pain that seemed suddenly to emanate from that one plague-spot of tragedy, and fill all the earth. Her grim old face had grown ghastly under its pale tan colour.... This was Justice, the Justice that she had so constantly hammered into her husband the need of dealing, without shrinking.... This madly desperate mother, and this lad, barely out of his teens (she was seeing sanely at last), standing noosed within a few yards of her, and already, as it were, looking at his mother from the other side of the Eternity of Death.... And the sheriffs men (the Men of Death they seemed now to her) all around, so dreadly purposeful and obdurate to the Voice of Natural Pity that wailed at them out of the lips of the crazed mother.... This was what she—she, Anna Barclay, had urged her husband towards many and many a time; she had never known; never! Never—NEVER! ... She could almost have screamed her denial....

No wonder John (her husband) had been always so inclined towards mercy.... My God, were there often such scenes as these going on in the same world.... Was there often this weight of terror and complete HORROR bred into being by the deliberate doings of Man, for any purpose whatever— call it Justice or by any other name?... This dreadfulness. This dreadfulness that choked her. This ... and suddenly she found her voice:

"STOP!" she cried, with a voice as deep and hoarse as a man's. "STOP!" ... She waved her hands a moment incoherently, fighting to take control of the fierce passion of horror and agony of pity that beat through every fibre of her, possessing her. "Stop!" she cried again; and then:

"How dare you! ... Oh, how dare all you men be met together here to do this—to do such a thing! To do such a thing..." She stopped abruptly, and stared at the men, as if they were things incredibly monstrous, and they, on their part, looked round at her and the Judge, only then aware of their advent.

"Let him go at once!" said old Mrs Judge Barclay, speaking again, as her voice became once more a controllable possession.... "Let him go to his mother.... Let them both go."

Across the ring of men the mother had fallen suddenly to her knees; her mouth was gabbering breathless words of prayer, her hands outstretched at arms' length, her fingers twining and intertwining madly.

"Save ... him," came her voice at last, no louder than a hoarse whisper, yet having a strange quality that seemed to make the very leaves above them stir and rustle. And, with the two completed words, she pitched forward, out of the relaxed hands of the two men who held her, on to her face, with a little thump, her forehead and nose ploughing into the trampled mud beneath the tree.

There came a queer, little inarticulate cry from Jem, and he began to fight desperately, bound hands and feet as he was, towards where his mother lay on her knees and face; but the sheriff and one of the men caught him and dragged him back beneath the over-reaching bough. The sheriff signed hastily to old Judge Barclay, and the Judge put his arm about his wife to lead her away. But she tore from him, and faced the sheriff.

"It'll be all right, mum," said that man. "You go along quiet now with the Jedge. We ain't goin' to hurt Jem more'n the flap of a fly's tail. Don't ye worrit..."

"You're going to hang that young man as soon as I've gone!" burst in Mrs Barclay, very white-faced, but with now a strange shining in her eyes. "That's what you mean to do!"

"Yep," said the sheriff, scratching his head, and trying to catch Judge Barclay's eye. But Judge Barclay was looking only at his wife, with something that was new in the way of his look.

"Yep," said the sheriff again. "Jem's boun' to hang, sure, mum, but we ain't goin' to hurt him worth a mench. We'll turn 'm off nice an' easy. You go along of the Jedge now..."

But he never finished his piece of excellent and practical advice; for, with a bound astonishing in so elderly a woman, she came at him, and he gave back helplessly, not knowing how to cope with such an attack. Yet she had no meaning to strike him. Instead, before he knew anything beyond his bewilderment, she had opened his holster and twitched out the heavy Smith and Wesson; then, with a leap, she was back from him, facing the group:

"Hands up!" she screamed, her voice cracking and her old eyes literally blazing, "You shall not murder that boy; not so what he's done! HANDS UP! I say, or I'll surely shoot at you."

The old woman's expression was so full of a desperate resolve that the men's hands went up, though maybe a little hesitatingly and doubtfully. Yet, they had gone up, and up they remained, as the muzzle of the heavy weapon menaced first one and then another. For suddenly it was very clear to the men that the woman was wound up to such a pitch of intensity that she would shoot first and do the thinking afterwards. It is true that several of the men held their revolvers in their hands; but what could they do? They could undoubtedly have snapped off shots at the old woman, but they were not going to shoot old Mrs Judge Barclay; the thought was below their horizon of practical things. Neither would it have done to have attempted to rush her, for there would have been, most surely, one or two sudden deaths achieved in the operation, and the after situation also would have to be faced; so, as I have told, they kept up their hands, and watched the old woman with quite as much curiosity as rancour. They were very practical men.

Old Judge Barclay, however, failed to realise the entire earnestness of the situation, and, after a moment of stupefaction, began to run towards his wife in vast distress.

"Anna, Anna!" he cried out. "Anna, my dear, put that down and come away!"

But she ripped round at him:

"Stand back, John!" she shouted shrilly. "I shall shoot!"

But the old Judge still failed to realise, and continued to come towards her.

"Stand back, John, or I shall shoot!" she screamed. "I'm fair wound up, an' you'll make me do murder! Stand back, John!"

As she spoke, she fired the pistol to frighten him; and because she had never fired a pistol before, she had no suspicion that the reason her husband's hat flew off was that the bullet had passed clean through the crown of it, just grazing his bald, old head. If she had thought at all about the displacing of the hat, she would merely have supposed that his sudden start at the shot accounted for it.

The old Judge came to an abrupt stand, his face grown very white; but he said not a word more, and his wife took no further notice of him; not even insisting on his putting up his hands. She wheeled round sharply again upon the sheriff and his posse, and discovered the sheriff half way across the grass towards her; for he had thought to catch and disarm her whilst her attention was taken with the Judge. The old woman's eyes blazed as she saw how nearly he had succeeded:

"Back!" she screamed at him, and in the same instant fired. The sheriff reeled a moment; then steadied himself, and thrust his hands earnestly above his head. The bullet had struck him full in the stomach, but the huge buckle of his belt had turned it, so that it had glanced out through his shirt again harmlessly, a mere half-flattened little chunk of lead.

"Get back to the others!" ordered the old woman, in a voice high and tense. "Turn your backs, all of you!"

As one man, the posse faced about.

"Go off a bit from the young man!" said Mrs Judge Barclay. "Stop there. Keep there!"

She ran swiftly to the prisoner, whirled him round on his heels with one vigorous hand, and pulled out the sheath-knife, which had never been removed from his belt. She slashed at the thin rope about his wrists, and all the time she kept a strict watch upon the line of masculine backs before her. She cut the rope at last, and his hands also, but not badly; then pushed the knife into his cramped fingers, and the lad proceeded to cut loose the lashings about his ankles.

"Now, GO!" said old Mrs Judge Barclay, fiercely, as he stood free. "An' mind an' sin no more. GO!"

She almost shrieked as he stood and stared at her; and she pointed to the horses of the posse. He looked swiftly towards his mother; but the Judge's wife beat him with her free hand fiercely, pushing him towards the horses. And suddenly, he obeyed, and began to run stiffly towards the animals.

When he reached them he displayed a little of that sense and ability which I have hinted lay cloaked so securely below his somewhat habitually sullen expression, for, having freed all the reins, he gathered them into his hand, and mounted the finest of the horses, which belonged to the sheriff; then, leading the rest, he went off at a fast trot.

The line of silent men began to stir uneasily, and old Mrs Judge Barclay steadied them with her voice. For a space of fifteen minutes, timed by her old-fashioned gold watch, she stood on guard. At the end of that time the mother of Jem came-to, and lifted a muddy face, stiffening sharply into terror with suddenly returned memory. She hove herself up giddily on to her knees, and glared upwards and round her, expecting dreadfully to see something that swayed, writhing, above her from the great branch.

Said Mrs Judge Barclay:

"Your son's gone, ma'am. He'll be well down the trail by this."

Her voice began to shake curiously as she spoke; and suddenly she reached her breaking-point, and collapsed, settling all in a heap on the muddy ground. She never heard the dazed, crazy words of fierce gratitude that the other woman gave out as she bent over her, aiding the old Judge to lay her down straight.

Old Mrs Judge Barclay came round some minutes later, to find her mouth uncomfortably full of bad whisky, and her husband still anxiously loosening garments that Jem's mother had already loosed quite sufficiently. His clumsy old fingers shook as he fumbled, and she put up a sudden hand of tenderness, and caught the fumbling fingers and held them with an almost hysterical firmness. In a little she rose to a sitting position, and looked round at the ring of men, who stood, each with his whisky-flask in his hand, ready, as it might be thought, to insure that the supply of restorative should not run dry.

Presently Mrs Judge Barclay spoke:

"Now," she said, turning her white, plucky old face towards the sheriff, "if you must hang somebody, hang me; not a bit of a young boy like that!"

But they hanged neither old Mrs Judge Barclay nor young Jem Turrill; for the latter got clear away. And concerning the former, if the truth must be known, the sheriff and his men entertain for her a respect few women have ever screwed out of their somewhat rugged-natured hearts. Moreover, they kept the affair strictly quiet, for it was not one in which any of them was able to discover undue credit to himself. As for old Judge Barclay, he had nothing of reproach for his wife. In his heart he was unfeignedly thankful that young Jem had got away; and equally glad, in another fashion, that Providence or kind Chance had ordered it that his wife should witness the working of the unmitigated Justice that she had so often upheld.

The Getting Even of Tommy Dodd

"I BELIEVE THE YOUNG BEGGAR WILL, TOO!" said James, the eldest 'prentice.

They were in the glory hole of the "Lady Hannibal," and Dayrin, the youngest 'prentice, aged fourteen, and known aboard by the name of Tommy Dodd, had been expounding a plan "to get level" with everybody in general, it seemed; for Tommy had been tasting another dose of that gross injustice which is dealt out so liberally to the boys in some ships.

"I'll fairly make the old man a fool, you'll see," he said. "And as for that old bo'sun and the third mate and the steward, I'll make them wish they'd never been born. Fancy the pig breaking all the stops on the fore, main, and mizzen, just at eight bells as I was coming below to dinner, and then sending me up to put new ones on! It's taken me two hours, and now the beastly dinner's cold, and I've no time for a sleep, or anything. And he's done that every day this week for my afternoon watch below. I told him he was a bully when he did it again to-day, and look what he's done!"

And Tommy rolled up his trousers to show a great abraided bruise where the third mate had kicked him with his heavy boots. "I hit him twice in the stummick, but he held my hands, and kicked me till I was sick. Look at my shins!" And he showed his shins, cut and bruised in a dozen places by the third mate's boots.

James and the other 'prentice in the port watch bent and looked at the boy's legs, nodding their heads with a sort of savage sympathy.

"If Tommy tries that idea of his for the homeward passage, I guess I'll help him for all I'm worth," said James.

"I will say that for the old man," remarked Tommy; "he sung out to the third to go steady when he was kicking me. But all the same, he turned on me himself, and told me I deserved what I'd got. I was in such a wax I told him straight out that if I'd been even half his size

I'd have wiped the deck with both him and the third mate. He kicked me bang off the poop then, down the poop ladder on to the main deck, when I said that; but when I got to the bottom I told him that, after I'd wiped the deck with them, I'd make him kiss my feet to teach him to know a man when he saw one."

"You know, Tommy," said James, "you're a plucky kid; but you'll be murdered outright one of these days if you don't mind. I wouldn't have said what you said to the old man for the value of the ship."

"Anyway," ended Tommy, "the first mate likes me. I know that."

A few days later Tommy got across the bo'sun's hawse concerning the cleaning of the pigsty, which the bo'sun had set Tommy to do every morning watch for a fortnight past, and which, properly, should have been done by the hands when they washed the decks. When the bo'sun came forrard from washing down the poop, he found, to his pained amazement, that Tommy had not touched the pigsty except with the seat portion of one of his garments, for the boy was sitting calmly on the top of the sty smoking a cigarette, his bucket and broom reclining beneath him on the deck. The bo'sun expressed fluently his distress at this condition of affairs, and suggested, with the aid of the broom-handle, that Tommy Dodd should get to work at his accustomed dirty task.

"Clean it yourself!" said Tommy the instant the bo'sun had loosed him. "Clean it yourself, you old bully, if your back ain't too fat to bend!"

He avoided further acquaintance with the broom-handle, and, catching up his bucket of water, hove the contents in the bo'sun's face, then made a sprint for the poop, dodged the broom which the bo'sun threw, and returned the bucket as interest, cracking the bo'sun on the shin, and afterwards continuing at top speed to the poop.

The bo'sun arrived almost in the same instant, and Tommy Dodd would certainly have fared very badly but for the interference of the mate, who told him that he would deal with Tommy. Later, he gave orders privately to the bo'sun that he must ease up on the boy, or he, the mate, would have something to say in the matter.

Yet, in spite of the efforts of the first mate to keep Tommy out of serious trouble, the boy had several narrow escapes from real bodily injury, for the third mate and the bo'sun were by nature bullies, and the captain, though, as I have said, not a bad man, was very hasty-tempered and hard by nature, so that when all is said and done poor Tommy had a very rough and brutal time of it on the way out.

And hence, as I have hinted, Tommy's plot to avenge himself and the others, for it must not be supposed that he had any monopoly when rough treatment was being handed out. And of the plot and its workings you will have chance to judge, as you read on.

As Tommy himself put it: "I make a spiffing girl when I've the right togs on. I've acted often at home. You'll see if I don't fool 'em all!"

From now until the "Lady Hannibal" reached Melbourne there were long and secret conferences in the 'prentices' berth, or glory hole, during which the plan was fully matured. As James remarked:

"It should go off all right, you know. The skipper's an awful old fool over any girl he can get to talk to him, an' Tommy should be able to fetch him."

"The old man'll sure to want to kiss you, Tommy," said one of the 'prentices in the other watch. "What'll you do then?"

"I'll smack his face for him, good an' hard!" said Tommy, with gusto at the thought. "Guess I'll get square with him. And I'll fix the third mate, too. You'll see!"

When Melbourne was reached the 'prentices clubbed their spare cash, and thereafter took to frequenting milliners' and other shops dedicated to the daintying of woman.

At the conclusion of their purchases the whole six of the young rascals carted the bundles into the 'prentices' berth, and, having locked the door and covered the ports, Master Tommy Dodd went through an elaborate "trying-on."

At the end of his efforts, however, a queer silence possessed the glory hole; for Tommy, when finally dressed, from pretty shoes—which his slender feet and years allowed to be surprisingly small—to his mop of naturally curly, golden hair, made so dainty a girl that his fellow 'prentices felt all at once different towards him. He looked so like a girl. It was James who voiced the general feeling, when he said abruptly, "By George, youngster, you make a pretty girl!"

As James made the remark, there came a sharp rap on the berth door, and the voice of the third mate, demanding admittance. The lads looked from one to the other, in complete dismay; but Tommy perceived suddenly that the advent of the third mate might prove helpful, rather than otherwise; moreover, it was a good chance to test the efficiency of his disguise. And he whispered to the others to let the officer in quickly, before he began to suspect that something was up. This the lads now did, and the third mate burst in roughly, with a coarse remark, and looked suspiciously round. Then he saw the girl, standing demurely quiet by the table, and at sight of her quite extraordinary prettiness, he became suddenly so polite, that Tommy nearly burst out laughing. Instead, however, he took up his part in earnest, and looked at him with a primly disgusted look, that made the whole coarse bulk of the third mate abruptly realise itself, which cannot have been pleasant for him. Then Tommy turned to James, and said aloud, but in a nicely modulated voice:

"Well then, Mr. James, when you see my cousin, Mr. Dayrin, will you tell him, please, that his cousin, Jenny Dayrin, has been down to see him, and that I should like him to come up and spend a couple of days with us, if the captain will let him."

The third mate, staring foolishly at this dainty girl of apparently near seventeen years, realised suddenly that she must be cousin to Tommy Dodd, though he had forgotten, until that moment, that the youth was properly named Dayrin. He made a resolve that as soon as Tommy came aboard, he would be nice with him. He hoped that Tommy would not blacken him to this pretty girl, who called the youngest 'prentice "cousin," and had come down to invite him up, probably to some fine house. That was the worst of these beastly 'prentices, you never knew how to treat them, or where you had them, when you got into port—they had such swagger "people."

For his part, Tommy—as he explained to the others afterwards—had killed many birds with one stone. By the simple act of letting the third mate see him, as his supposed girl-cousin, he had slain at birth any suspicions which might afterwards have arisen at the likeness of the girl, Jenny, both in face and voice, to Tommy Dodd, the 'prentice. Further, he had insured a cessation of the third mate's bullying all the time that they were in port. He had also provided means whereby he could receive invitations—from himself—to spend the day ashore; and these invitations could be easily extended to the rest of the berth; for, as the girl-cousin Jenny, Tommy Dodd felt that be could easily persuade the captain to grant such relaxations as those he now proposed to himself. Later, as he hoped, he would see other means of utilising this new and delightful power which he had created. In the meanwhile, the third mate—as Tommy had already grown to expect—was "toning down" to the others, and finally asked James, in a low voice, to introduce him to Miss Jenny. This was achieved, and the third mate laid himself out in a grotesque effort to make himself agreeable to pretty Miss Dayrin; finally offering to show her round the vessel, which offer was accepted with demure quietness.

The third mate took the supposed girl around the poop, where the skipper was enjoying a stroll before going ashore for the evening. Here, seeing the chance of becoming introduced to the captain in his new character, Tommy evinced a quite extraordinary interest in the wheel, during which the skipper—perceiving that the girl was exceedingly pretty—strolled up within hearing, and finally joined the third mate—much to that man's disgust—in explaining the action of the steering-gear.

"Then this is the thing that makes the ship turn round?" said Tommy, in his clear voice, and pitching it a little near its ordinary compass, for the edification of the five other 'prentices, whose faces he saw craned round the edge of the port stairway, where it came up to the poop deck.

"Yes," said the skipper, looking at her with approving eyes. "I can see you're a clever young lady."

Tommy was aware that the watching faces had suddenly disappeared, and that there were sounds of smothered laughter down on the main deck, as his five berthmates, scuttered—shaking with wicked joy—into the glory hole, there to enjoy to their hearts' content the idea of their old "tough" of a captain telling his youngest 'prentice that he was a clever young lady—that same Tommy whom he had booted scientifically and indelicately but a few hours earlier.

Up on the poop, the skipper was still deep in explanations, which presently began to bore Tommy frightfully; so that he remembered suddenly that he must hurry home to tea. At this the skipper actually beamed, and, with a polite bow, asked the young lady whether he could not persuade her to honour his table with her presence. And Tommy consented so to do honour unto his captain, by condescending, for the first time, to eat some of the cabin delicacies. Truly, as Tommy thought, "this is all right, but"—as he remembered his toilet—I mustn't eat too much."

Meanwhile, the captain had called the steward up on the poop, and was busy laying the foundations for such a tea as Master Tommy had not eaten for many a long day. "And," thought Tommy, as he harked, "I'll get even with the steward before I'm done for all the gubbins he's done us out of, and for all the short whacks of sugar, and for that time he sneaked to the skipper when we threw spuds at him." And, indeed, for many another crime against the glory hole; for the steward was a disagreeable man, and the high spirits of the 'prentices' berth, which culminated in the body of Tommy Dodd, had always excited his ire and spite. Therefore, was Tommy joyful in contemplation, the while that the skipper personally conducted the remainder of his tour round the ship, having told the disgusted third mate that he could go ashore any time he liked.

Presently they came to the glory hole, and the skipper indicated the interior of the berth through the open doorway.

"Where my young gentlemen live," he said, adopting somewhat of a parental attitude to the youngsters who inhabited that gloomy but lively abode.

He was not aware yet that Tommy was claimed as cousin by the pretty girl at his side, but when this was explained to him he adopted an attitude that was even more indicative of kindliness and benevolence, which rose a wicked idea in Tommy's mind.

"I should think you are a very kind captain to them," he said, in the most girlish way possible. And the captain spared not of emphasis to insure this point being fixed in the mind of his newly-found girl friend, for he saw that along such lines lay the way to her liking and favour.

Tommy—the girl—stepped in over the washboard, and all the 'prentices rose and uncapped.

"What a quaint little place!" said Tommy, parodying a remark of his sister's, which she had made when she came down in London to see the vessel in which her brother was to sail. "And do they sleep on all those shelves? How funny!" Then, as if the idea had come suddenly: "Oh, captain, couldn't we have tea in here? We could all have it together; it would be so homely. And if my cousin comes back, he could join in with us."

Tommy clapped his hands, as if in ecstasy at the thought, and looked up at the skipper, very nicely from under the longest lashes in the world—or so that elderly reprobate thought at the moment.

"I—er—well—er——" said the skipper confusedly, and with the beginnings of a little irritation, that somehow was held in check by the daintiness of Tommy's attitude of request. "I—er—think the cabin will be nicer, Miss Jenny, don't you?"

"Perhaps you're right, captain," said Tommy thoughtfully, with his head of golden curls a little on one side, pondering.

"More room, too," added the skipper, brightening, as the danger seemed to be passing—"much more room."

"Yea," said Tommy, nodding and peering round at the gloomy little berth. "This is a pokey little place. Why don't you make your young gentlemen live with you in the cabin, captain? Then the steward could look after them properly. And it would be so nice to have them all with you."

James, away in the corner of the glory hole, nearly choked; whilst the captain turned to the doorway and got out on deck, hoping thus to change the conversation, which was becoming a practical difficulty for a sea captain troubled with paternal and benevolent instincts towards his "young gentlemen."

"Tea'll be gettin' cold, Miss Jenny," he said, and held out a large hand to help Tommy, which the boy took, to assist him over the wash-board. Then the boy turned and looked back into the berth. "Come along, all of you!" he said. "The captain says it will be nicer to have tea in the cabin, as there will be more room there. Be quick, the tea's getting cold! We'll all have a jolly tea together! Come on, captain!"—this last to the distracted skipper, who had halted, as if suddenly frozen, at finding this innocent but startling interpretation put upon his attempts at evading having to join his authority to the girl's suggestion to invite the whole berth to tea.

For their part, the five 'prentices stood as still and stupid as the skipper; but presently James terminated the suspense, by asking in so many words:

"Are we to come, sir?"

"Of course," said Tommy, laughing happily. "Didn't you hear the captain saying it would be nicer to have it in the cabin?"

But James still looked at the captain, who now saw that he could not possibly evade the invitation and still retain the high opinion which Miss Jenny had formed of him. He, therefore, with a fierce attempt to sound hearty, told the boys to follow, which they did, all more or less uneasy, because they understood perfectly the skipper's attitude in the matter, yet all of them wordless with astonishment and admiration at the way in which Master Tommy Dodd was "carrying it off."

As they all sat down round the cabin table, with the captain at the head, the steward finished setting out the additional tea-cups for the five lads. Tommy noticed the way in which he was doing it, and saw how to avenge the bitter disgust which was on the man's disagreeable face.

"Oh, steward," he cried out, in his clear voice, modulating the tone, so as to suggest only the astonishment of a daintily-nurtured girl, "you shouldn't put your fingers in the cups. And your hands are dirty, you know!"

The captain turned in his chair, and saw that Miss Jenny was only too correct. He had never noticed these details before, but now they seemed rank and dreadful before this pretty girl. He grew ashamed, through the action of his servant, and turned on him, his voice making the cabin ring.

"Steward," he roared, "go and wash yourself! Take all these cups, and bring clean ones! You're only fit for hog-feedin'!"

Tommy Dodd had scored one victory over an enemy of the berth.

Throughout the meal, as befits a privileged person, he ate cake only. He took moderate bites and little sips, and remembered in time that rigid but nameless article which held his small and muscular waist so stiffly. Because he remembered, he stopped in time!

All the weeks that the vessel was in port Tommy had the most glorious time. He received numberless invitations from himself, alias Miss Jenny Dayrin, which the captain allowed him to accept; for he could refuse nothing to the girl, who often paid him a visit on those days when Tommy had been allowed to accept an invitation ashore. This coincidence alone being sufficient to insure Tommy's never having a refusal of leave from the skipper. The berth also was invited on several occasions, much to the disgust of the third mate, who found himself excluded from such privileges; yet dared not vent his anger on Tommy, whom he suspected of having "told things" to the girl, lest, after all, he should be mistaken; for Miss Jenny took care not to drive him quite hopeless, but to utilise the situation to the best advantage, so as to punish the hulking brute as far as possible with the whip of jealousy, and yet to keep him hoping faintly, so that, in her more usual character as Tommy Dodd, she should have as free a time as possible from the bullying of that particular officer.

In time, the day came for the "Lady Hannibal" to sail for home, and the skipper paced the poop in an almost tearful mood, hoping to discover the figure of Miss Jenny on the wharf, waving a good-bye. Yet in this, as you may think, he was bound to be disappointed, as was the third mate, who now realised definitely that he had no more to gain from the friendship of Master Tommy, and therefore took the first opportunity of soundly kicking the boy. The assault of the third mate resulted in his getting rather hurt; for Tommy, desperate, pulled an iron pin from the wall, and hit the third mate on the head, stunning him for a moment. Then the first mate interfered, and sent Master Tommy into the berth, to be out of the way, warning him plainly to avoid the third.

A consultation was held in the berth, among the lads, and it was agreed that, all things being taken into account, Tommy had better do his disappearing trick without delay—that very night, in fact.

It was James who saw Tommy fall overboard, and gave the warning cry, which resulted in the vessel being hove-to for something like a couple of hours, whilst the boat plied round about in circles, trying to find the boy; naturally having to return without him, to the genuine grief of the first mate, and the sorrow of the third, who would like to have kicked Tommy soundly once more before his decease. However, it could not be helped, there were still left the five others, and he expended his sorrow conscientiously upon them.

And so the "Lady Hannibal" sailed onward—minus at last that bright spirit of mischief and pluck, Tommy Dodd!

Even as it was James who saw Tommy go, it was the same shameless lad who saw Miss Jenny Dayrin come; at least, he was the one who first drew attention to the soft and persistent knocking on the coamings of the main hatch, two days after Tommy had been lost overboard. They lifted a hatch-cover, and saw the pretty face of the girl, looking up brightly at them.

"I've got tired of being down here," she assured them happily, whilst the third mate nearly fell down the hatchway, in his astonishment, delight and surprise at this unexpected wonder from the gods.

News of the find was taken to the skipper, who blossomed suddenly with joy, and ran like a lad all the way to the hatch, where with his own hands he rigged a ladder to enable the dainty maid to ascend from the hold. And Tommy, thoroughly sick of the darkness, and able to have come up in a moment like any cat, had to fight down his impatience, and finally ascend in decorous fashion, with the third mate and the captain each vying with the other to give her much unnecessary assistance.

"I always meant to be a stowaway," she explained to the group of officers who now surrounded her. She looked at the captain. "I thought I'd come in your ship," she said sweetly. She held out a bundle. "See," she added, "I've brought some clothes, and there are some more down in that nasty place. Please, Mr. Third Mate, will you get them for me?" It was obvious that Tommy was enjoying himself, and that he had not been brought up with "elder sisters" for nothing!

Later, the captain took Miss Jenny the round of the cabins, so that she might take her choice. She chose the biggest, but remarked that it smelled fusty, at which—as Tommy had intended—the captain set the steward to scrub it out thoroughly, and wash the paintwork. Then, very well satisfied, Tommy returned to the poop, and sat languidly in the captain's deck-chair, whilst the captain and the third mate, rigged up a weather cloth to windward of him, to protect him from the wind.

Needless to say again, Tommy was enjoying himself. He enjoyed especially the efforts of the five other 'prentices to obtain surreptitious views of the poop deck. Finally, the third mate also became cognisant of these efforts, and went down on to the main deck to explain in his own fashion how unsuited they were to the manners of the "captain's young gentlemen."

Tommy, much trained by painful experience, had watched the departure of the third mate, and now listened keenly. Immediately afterwards, the sound of a scuffle, and a lad crying out, told him that the third mate was indulging his feet. The girl jumped from her chair, furious. Now she would reap the real reward of her position. She raced to the break of the poop, and looked down, and the skipper came quickly after her; for he, too, had heard the muffled sounds, and was perturbed by the swift action of this pretty maid, who was staring down now on to the main deck.

"Oh, you horrible, brutal man!" the skipper heard her say, in clear-cut, passionate tones of scorn, that could be heard fore and aft. "Fancy a great, ugly coward like you kicking a boy! I couldn't have believed it, if I hadn't seen it." She turned to the skipper. "Captain," she said, tensely, and looking very pale and likable, for Tommy was truly shaken with anger, "Captain, do you allow this sort of thing?" And the skipper, who had before now, as you know, been forced to interfere between the third and his victim, though hard himself of heart, found himself, in the position of the "paternal and benevolent" captain, forced to speak both didactically and morally. Moreover, he, himself, was very angry that the third mate should have brought about this scene. He stooped over the rail of the break, and looked down at the sullen and half-shamed third, where he stood, still holding the lad he had been hammering, whilst a little way off, waited a group of the 'prentices, looking tense and excited.

"Let go that boy, mister!" said the skipper. "I'm ashamed of you, Mister Davies. I won't have this sort of thing in my ship."

The third mate stared up furiously at the skipper. He felt that his superior was being gratuitously treacherous. Never before had the skipper posed as a stickler for tenderness to the boys.

"Go to blazes!" muttered the third mate, and flung the boy he held brutally against the hatch.

"Oh, captain!" said the girl's voice, shrill with horror and anger. And the man in the captain answered to the call; besides, he had been insulted before the girl. He came down the poop ladder in two jumps, his coat dropping on the bottom step.

"You need manners, mister," he said; and hit the third mate hard in the neck. Curiously, the girl on the poop gave out no scream at this fresh scene of brutality. She seemed to take a personal delight and zest in each heavy blow which the captain got home on the lumbering carcase of the third. Indeed, she danced excitedly from foot to foot.

"That's what he's been wanting! That's what he's been wanting!" she breathed ecstatically to herself, as the skipper laid the third flat with a strong punch in the face. And not an onlooker but echoed the thing in his heart. The third was certainly not beloved in the "Lady Hannibal," nor in any other ship where he had been allowed to make himself evident.

"Captain," said Miss Jenny, when the breathless, but triumphant, skipper returned to the poop, putting on his coat. "Captain, will you shake hands. That man deserved it." She held out her hand, and the skipper, a delighted conquering hero, grasped it, and shook warmly.

"I was afraid, Miss Jenny," he said, "you'd think I'd been a bit hard. But he needed it. I've had to speak to him before," he added virtuously.

"He certainly needed it," said Miss Jenny. "I'm sure you would never strike a defenceless boy." Tommy was thinking of that bucket the skipper had thrown, besides odd and sundry kicks received in person. But the skipper replied manfully:

"Never, miss." And, somehow the young lady pardoned him the lie without contempt. He had done her heart's desire that day, and she could forgive much.

It was the following morning that Miss Jenny learned the fate of Tommy, and returned from the 'prentices berth to the poop to play mourner to her own death. "What a dreadful thing, captain," she said. "And I believe the poor boy was driven to it by the brutality of the third mate. I can never sit at table again with that man. I shall always feel he is a murderer!"

And the skipper was sufficiently alarmed at this view of the matter, and his own possible responsibility in the case, not to remove any of the latter from the shoulders of the third mate; but made that much-hammered young man sit down later to his meals alone. Thus did Tommy go forward along the path of virtue, leaving vengeance unto those best able to dispense it.

In the meantime, he shifted his attention to considering the case of the bo'sun, who had been somewhat over-attentive in the days of Tommy's 'prenticeship.

Incidentally, while he was turning this matter over in his brain, he improved the condition of the 'prentices' berth by insisting on having his tea there every evening with the watch below, to which the reluctant captain found himself forced to give consent, and to add, privately, unusual dietary luxuries to the normal bill of fare of the glory hole, so that he should not fail to stand well with his young enchanter; Certainly the skipper was not coming off scot-free in the scheme of retribution which Master Tommy Dodd had introduced. As for the steward, he groaned in his soul, or his apology for that article, for in verity the boys in the 'prentices' berth were living almost as well as the cabin. Truly, Tommy Dodd was a great man!

One day, whilst Tommy and the skipper were pacing the poop together, the latter waxed paternal. Tommy had been speaking of the 'prentices—a common topic of his— for, when not with the captain, Miss Jenny was sure to be found in the 'prentices' berth.

"You mustn't let them boys be too free with you, Miss Jenny," said the captain.

"No," said Miss Jenny demurely.

"They've never—er—any of 'em tried to kiss you, or any nonsense o' that sort?" asked the skipper, a little hesitatingly.

"Never!" said Miss Jenny emphatically, which was in every way true.

"You just tell me, Miss Jenny, if anyone ever bothers you. I'll deal with 'em!" the captain assured her fervently. And Tommy thought he might venture to put the first spoke in the bo'sun's wheel.

"I—I don't like the bo'sun," said Tommy, in a shy voice. "He looks rudely at me," which was likely enough; for it is to be doubted whether the bo'sun had ever looked otherwise at any woman.

"I'll settle him—quick!" said the captain, and began to walk towards the break of the poop. "The dirty scum! I beg pardon, miss; but the very idea!"

"No," said Tommy simply, "don't touch him, please; but I do wish you'd make him clean out that pigsty forrard. It smells horridly whenever I go past. I've told him once. I told him he ought to get inside and clean it properly himself, instead of making the boys. Don't you think it's a man's work, captain? It needs such hard scrubbing, I should think. He was so rude when I told him."

"Come along forrid with me, miss," said the captain. "I'll just have a look at that pigsty. I'll learn him to so rude!"

The captain went forrard with the girl, and together they inspected the pigsty, Like most stys, it smelled on the "strong side"; but to the infatuated skipper this was sufficient. It smelled. He sent for the bo'sun, meaning to make the pigsty an excuse for letting off his wrath at the bo'sun because that man of tar and sin had dared even to look in the direction of his pretty companion.

"Get a bucket an' broom, smart now," said the skipper, harshly, when the man arrived. "Get some of the boys to fetch water along for you, an' give that sty a proper clean out. It's a disgrace to any ship, a foul, stinkin' thing like this. Makes the young lady sick every time she passes it. An' I don't wonder!"

The bo'sun glared angrily at the girl, for whom already he had achieved a strong antipathy; but he obeyed the skipper, in silence, for the skipper was a "tough," and notorious, at that, with his fists. When the water came, the man began to clean out the sty in the usual sailor-man fashion; that is, with buckets of salt water and a long-handled deck broom.

"Why don't you go in, bo'sun, like you make the boys?" asked Miss Jenny, quietly.

"You stow it, miss," said the bo'sun, nearly bursting. "You don't understand ship work, you don't!"

"Silence, you clod-foot" roared the skipper. "The lady's right; you get inside, an' do it on your hands and knees."

The bo'sun straightened up, and Tommy, to his joy, perceived that there was going to be bad trouble. The skipper saw it in the same moment, else he had never earned his title as a bucko, and he hit the bo'sun hard and solid in the wind, then bundled him, limp and gasping, into the iron-barred sty. He shouted to a man to go aft to the steward for a padlock, and with this he secured the iron-barred door, which closed the only entrance to the sty.

"Now, my lad," said the skipper, "I'll learn you to be civil; you stays in there, 'long o' the pigs, till you've scrubbed that sty out good on your hands and knees; an' if you wants water, here's water!" And he hove a dozen buckets of salt water over the cooped man.

And as Tommy went aft and ascended the poop ladder with the skipper, he heard the sounds of stifled mirth proceeding evidently from the 'prentices' berth, and be knew that joy reigned in the glory hole, for all the ship was aware that the skipper had locked the bo'sun in the pigsty.

From now onward, so far, at least, as the 'prentices were concerned, the voyage was very pleasant, for Miss Jenny held the skipper religiously to his "paternal and benevolent" attitude towards his "young gentlemen," whilst that same captain, though the father of a large family, grew daily more enamoured of his fair passenger. One morning, when the decks were being wet down, and Miss Jenny was paddling about gaily with bare feet in the cool water, the captain's affections got the better of his discretion, for having gallantly offered to hold Miss Jenny's shoes for her, whilst she sat and dried her feet, be so far forgot himself as to stoop quickly and kiss her "pretty toes," as he termed them.

At once Miss Jenny was all dignity, and rose from the captain's chair to display this new attribute to full advantage, being the better able to act with feeling because of the snigger from the man at the wheel that had followed the skipper's act.

"I'm ashamed of you, captain!" said Miss Jenny, with superb simpleness, and, taking her shoes from his now limp hand, she descended to the cabin.

"I'd said I'd make him," said Tommy, righteously to himself, as he entered his cabin. "And I guess I'm square all round now."

It was on the day that the "Lady Hannibal" entered London docks that Miss Jenny took the captain on one side, as it were, and made known the plain, unvarnished truth.

"I'd not have told you at all, captain," she said, "for you've really been a brick, the way you hammered the third and the bo'sun, but I couldn't have you writing home to my people that I was drowned; besides there might be other complications. All the same, if you like to shake hands, and be friends, I'll not tell a soul, then no one can laugh at you. But I guess I got level with you all."

And the skipper, dumb with emotion of a strong and varied kind, shook hands, speechlessly, with this pretty girl, who assured him that she was Tommy Dodd, his youngest 'prentice.

"The other fellows will see about my chest, sir," said Tommy, "and I'll change into my ordinary togs ashore; then no one here'll know."

The skipper nodded, still silent; and Tommy went up out of the cabin.

"Lord!" muttered the skipper, maybe half an hour later. "Good Lord!" He scratched his rough head. "An' I kissed his blessed feet!"

The Sea Horses

"An' we's under the sea, b'ys,
Where the wild Horses go,
Horses wiv tails
As big as ole whales
All jiggin' around in a row,
An' when you ses Whoa!
Them divvels does go!"

1

"HOW WAS IT YOU CATCHED ME ONE, GRANFER?" asked Nebby, as he had asked the same question any time during the past week, whenever his burly, blue-guernseyed grandfather crooned out the old Ballade of the Sea-Horses, which, however, he never carried past the portion given above.

"Like as he was a bit weak, Nebby b'y; an' I gev him a smart clip wiv the axe, 'fore he could bolt off," explained his grandfather, lying with inimitable gravity and relish.

Nebby dismounted from his curious-looking go-horse, by the simple method of dragging it forward from between his legs. He examined its peculiar, unicorn-like head, and at last put his finger on a bruised indentation in the black paint that covered the nose.

" 'S that where you welted him, Granfer?" he asked, seriously.

"Aye," said his Granfer Zacchy, taking the strangely-shaped go-horse, and examining the contused paint. "Aye, I shore hit 'm a turrible welt."

"Are he dead, Granfer?" asked the boy.

"Well," said the burly old man, feeling the go-horse all over with an enormous finger and thumb, "betwixt an' between, like." He opened the cleverly hinged mouth, and looked at the bone teeth with which he had fitted it, and then squinted earnestly, with one eye, down the red-painted throat. "Aye," he repeated, "betwixt an' between, Nebby. Don't you never let 'm go to water, b'y; for he'd maybe come alive ag'in, an' ye'd lose 'm sure."

Perhaps old Diver-Zacchy, as he was called in the little sea-village, was thinking that water would prove unhealthy to the glue, with which he had fixed-on the big bonito's tail, at what he termed the starn-end of the curious looking beast. He had cut the whole thing out of a nice, four-foot by ten-inch piece of soft, knotless yellow pine; and, to the rear, he had attached, thwart-ship, the aforementioned bonito's tail; for the thing was no ordinary horse, as you may think; but a gen-u-ine (as Zacchy described it) Sea-Horse, which he had brought up from the sea bottom for his small grandson, whilst following his occupation as diver.

The animal had taken him many a long hour to carve, and had been made during his spell-ohs, between dives, aboard the diving-barge. The creature itself was a combined production of his own extremely fertile fancy, plus his small grandson's Faith. For Zacchy had manufactured unending and peculiar stories of what he saw daily at the bottom of the sea, and during many a winter's evening, Nebby had "cut boats" around the big stove, whilst the old man smoked and yarned the impossible yarns that were so marvellously real and possible to the boy. And of all the tales that the old diver told in his whimsical fashion, there was none that so stirred Nebby's feelings as the one about the Sea-Horses.

At first it had been but a scrappy and a fragmentary yarn, suggested, as like as not, by the old ballade which Zacchy so often hummed, half-unconsciously. But Nebby's constant questionings had provided so many suggestions for fresh additions, that at last it took nearly the whole of a long evening for the Tale of the Sea-Horses to be told properly, from where the first Horse was seen by Zacchy, eatin' sea-grass as nat'rel as ye like, to where Zacchy had seen li'l Martha Tullet's b'y ridin' one like a reel cow-puncher; and from that tremendous effort of imagination, the Horse Yarn had speedily grown to include every child that wended the Long Road out of the village.

"Shall I go ridin' them Sea-Horses, Granfer, when I dies?" Nebby had asked, earnestly.

"Aye," Granfer Zacchy had replied, absently, puffing at his corncob. "Aye, like's not, Nebby. Like as not."

"Mebbe I'll die middlin' soon, Granfer?" Nebby had suggested, longingly. "There's plenty li'l boys dies 'fore they gets growed up."

"Husht! b'y! Husht!" Granfer had said, wakening suddenly to what the child was saying.

Later, when Nebby had many times betrayed his exceeding high requirement of death, that he might ride the Sea-Horses all round his Granfer at work on the sea-bottom, old Zacchy had suddenly evolved a less drastic solution of the difficulty.

"I'll ketch ye one, Nebby, sure," he said, "an' ye kin ride it round the kitchen."

The suggestion pleased Nebby enormously, and practically nullified his impatience regarding the date of his death, which was to give him the freedom of the sea and all the Sea-Horses therein.

For a long month, old Zacchy was met each evening by a small and earnest boy, desirous of learning whether he had "catched one" that day, or not. Meanwhile, Zacchy had been dealing honestly with that four-foot by ten-inch piece of yellow pine, already described. He had carved out his notion of what might be supposed to constitute a veritable Sea-Horse, aided in his invention by Nebby's illuminating questions as to whether Sea-Horses had tails like a real horse or like real fishes; did they wear horseshoes; did they bite?

These were three points upon which Nebby's curiosity was definite; and the results were definite enough in the finished work; for Granfer supplied the peculiar creature with "reel" bone teeth and a workable jaw; two squat, but prodigious legs, near what he termed the "bows"; whilst to the "starn" he affixed the bonito-tail which has already had mention, setting it the way Dame Nature sets it on the bonito, that is, "thwart-ships," so that its two flukes touched the ground when the go-horse was in position, and thus steadied it admirably with this hint taken direct from the workmanship of the Great Carpenter.

There came a day when the horse was finished and the last coat of paint had dried smooth and hard. That evening, when Nebby came running to meet Zacchy, he was aware of his Grandfather's voice in the dusk, shouting:—"Whoa, Mare! Whoa, Mare!" followed immediately by the cracking of a whip.

Nebby shrilled out a call, and raced on, mad with excitement, towards the noise. He knew instantly that at last Granfer had managed to catch one of the wily Sea-Horses. Presumably the creature was somewhat intractable; for when Nebby arrived, he found the burly form of Granfer straining back tremendously upon stout reins, which Nebby saw vaguely in the dusk were attached to a squat, black monster:—

"Whoa, Mare!" roared Granfer, and lashed the air furiously with his whip. Nebby shrieked delight, and ran round and round, whilst Granfer struggled with the animal.

"Hi! Hi! Hi!" shouted Nebby, dancing from foot to foot. "Ye've catched 'm, Granfer! Ye've catched 'm Granfer!"

"Aye," said Granfer, whose struggles with the creature must have been prodigious; for he appeared to pant. "She'll go quiet now, b'y. Take a holt!" And he handed the reins and the whip over to the excited, but half-fearful Nebby. "Put y'r hand on 'er, Neb," said old Zacchy. "That'll quiet 'er."

Nebby did so, a little nervously, and drew away in a moment.

"She's all wet 's wet!" he cried out.

"Aye," said Granfer, striving to hide the delight in his voice. "She 'm straight up from the water, b'y."

This was quite true; it was the final artistic effort of Granfer's imagination; he had dipped the horse overside, just before leaving the diving barge. He took his towel from his pocket, and wiped the horse down, hissing as he did so.

"Now, b'y," he said, "welt 'er good, an' make her take ye home."

Nebby straddled the go-horse, made an ineffectual effort to crack the whip, shouted:—"Gee-up! Gee-up!" And was off—two small, lean bare legs twinkling away into the darkness at a tremendous rate, accompanied by shrill and recurrent "Gee-ups!"

Granfer Zacchy stood in the dusk, laughing happily, and pulled out his pipe. He filled it slowly, and as he applied the light, he heard the galloping of the horse, returning. Nebby dashed up, and circled his Granfer in splendid fashion, singing in a rather breathless voice:—

"An' we's under the sea, b'ys,
Where the Wild Horses go,
Horses wiv tails
As big as ole whales
All jiggin' around in a row,
An' when you ses Whoa!
The debbils does go!"

And away he went again at the gallop.

This had happened a week earlier; and now we have Nebby questioning Granfer Zacchy as to whether the Sea-Horse is really alive or dead.

"Should think they has Sea-Horses 'n heaven, Granfer?" said Nebby, thoughtfully, as he once more straddled the go-horse.

"Sure," said Granfer Zacchy.

"Is Martha Tullet's li'l b'y gone to heaven?" asked Nebby.

"Sure," said Granfer again, as he sucked at his pipe.

Nebby was silent a good while, thinking. It was obvious that he confused heaven with the Domain of the Sea-Horses; for had not Granfer himself seen Martha Tullet's li'l b'y riding one of the Sea-Horses? Nebby had told Mrs. Tullet about it; but she had only thrown her apron over her head, and cried, until at last Nebby had stolen away, feeling rather dumpy.

"Has you ever seed any angels wiv wings on the Sea-Horses, Granfer?" Nebby asked, presently; determined to have further information with which to assure his ideas.

"Aye," said Granfer Zacchy. "Shoals of 'em. Shoals of 'em, b'y."

Nebby was greatly pleased.

"Could they ride some, Granfer?" he questioned.

"Sure," said old Zacchy, reaching for his pouch.

"As good 's me?" asked Nebby, anxiously.

"Middlin' near. Middlin' near, b'y," said Granfer Zacchy. "Why, Neb," he continued, waking up with a sudden relish to the full possibilities of the question, "tha's some of them lady ayngels as c'ud do back-somersaults an' never take a throw, b'y."

It is to be feared that Granfer Zacchy's conception of a lady angel had been formed during odd visits to the circus. But Nebby was duly impressed, and bumped his head badly the same day, trying to achieve the rudiments of a back-somersault.

2

Some evenings later, Nebby came running to meet old Zacchy, with an eager question:—

"Has you seed Jane Melly's li'l gel ridin' the Horses, Granfer?" he asked, earnestly.

"Aye," said Granfer. Then, realising suddenly what the question portended:—

"What's wrong wiv Mrs. Melly's wee gel?" he queried.

"Dead," said Nebby, calmly. "Mrs. Kay ses it's the fever come to the village again, Granfer."

Nebby's voice was cheerful; for the fever had visited the village some months before, and Granfer Zacchy had taken Nebby to live on the barge, away from danger of infection. Nebby enjoyed it all enormously, and had often prayed God since to send another fever, with its attendant possibilities of life again aboard the diving-barge.

"Shall we live in the barge, Granfer?" he asked, as he swung along with the old man.

"Maybe! Maybe!" said old Zacchy, absently, in a somewhat troubled voice.

Granfer left Nebby in the kitchen, and went on up the village to make inquiries; the result was that he packed Nebby's clothes and toys into a well-washed sugar-bag, and the next day took the boy down to the barge, to live. But whereas Granfer walked, carrying the sack of gear, Nebby rode all the way, most of it at an amazing gallop. He even rode daringly down the narrow, rail-less gangplank. It is true that Granfer Zacchy took care to keep close behind, in as unobtrusive a fashion as possible; but of this, or the need of such watchfulness, Nebby was most satisfactorily ignorant. He was welcomed in the heartiest fashion by Ned, the pump-man, and Binny, who attended to the air-pipe and life-line when Granfer Zacchy was down below.

3

Life aboard the diving-barge was a very happy time for Nebby. It was a happy time also for Granfer Zacchy and his two men; for the child, playing constantly in their midst, brought back to them an adumbration of their youth. There was only one point upon which there arose any trouble, and that was Nebby's forgetfulness, in riding across the air-tube, when he was exercising his Sea-Horse.

Ned, the pump man, had spoken very emphatically to Nebby on this point, and Nebby had promised to remember but, as usual, soon forgot. They had taken the barge outside the bar, and anchored her over the buoy that marked Granfer's submarine operations. The day was gloriously fine, and so long as the weather remained fixed, they meant to keep the barge out there, merely sending the little punt ashore for provisions.

To Nebby, it was all just splendid! When he was not riding his Sea-Horse, he was talking to the men, or waiting at the gangway eagerly for Granfer's great copper head-piece to come up out of the water, as the air-tube and life-line were slowly drawn aboard. Or else his shrill young voice was sure to be heard, as he leant over the rail and peered into the depths below, singing:—

"An' we's under the sea, b'ys,
Where the Wild Horses go,
Horses wiv tails
As big as ole whales
All jiggin' around in a row,
An' when you ses Whoa!
Them debbils does go!"

Possibly, he considered it as some kind of charm with which to call the Sea-Horses up to view.

Each time the boat went ashore, it brought sad news, that first this and then that one had gone the Long Road; but it was chiefly the children that interested Nebby. Each time that his Granfer came up out of the depths, Nebby would dance round him impatiently, until the big helmet was unscrewed; then would come his inevitable, eager question:—Had Granfer seen Carry Andrew's li'l gel; or had Granfer seen Marty's li'l b'y riding the Sea-Horses? And so on.

"Sure," Granfer would reply; though several times, it was his first intimation that the child mentioned had died; the news having reached the barge through some passing boat, whilst he was on the sea-bottom.

4

"Look you, Nebby!" shouted Ned, the pump-man, angrily. "I'll shore break that horse of yours up for kindlin' next time you goes steppin' on the air-pipe."

It was all too true; Nebby had forgotten, and done it again; but whereas, generally, he took Ned's remonstrances in good part, and promised better things, he stood now, looking with angry defiance at the man. The suggestion that his Sea-Horse was made of wood, bred in him a tempest of bitterness. Never for one moment to himself had he allowed so horrible a thought to enter his own head; not even when, in a desperate charge, he had knocked a chip off the nose of the Sea-Horse, and betrayed the merciless wood below. He had simply refused to look particularly at the place; his fresh, child's imagination allowing him presently to grow assured again that all was well; that he truly rode a "gen-u-ine" Sea-Horse. In his earnestness of determined make-believe, he had even avoided showing Granfer Zacchy the place, and asking him to mend it, much as he wanted it mended. Granfer always mended his toys for him; but this could not be mended. It was a real Sea-Horse; not a toy. Nebby resolutely averted his thoughts from the possibility of any other Belief; though it is likely that such mental processes were more subconscious than conscious.

And now, Ned had said the deadly thing, practically in so many naked words. Nebby trembled with anger and a furious mortification of his pride of Sea-Horse-Ownership. He looked round swiftly for the surest way to avenge the brutish insult, and saw the air-pipe; the thing around which the bother had been made. Yes, that would make Ned angry! Nebby turned his strange steed, and charged straight away back at the pipe. There, with angry and malicious deliberateness, he halted, and made the big front hoofs of his extraordinary monster, stamp upon the air-pipe.

"You young devil!" roared Ned, scarcely able to believe the thing he saw. "You young devil!"

Nebby continued to stamp the big hoofs upon the pipe, glaring with fierce, defiant, blue eyes at Ned. Whereupon, Ned's patience arose and departed, and Ned himself arrived bodily in haste and with considerable vigour. He gave one kick, and the Sea-Horse went flying across the deck, and crashed into the low bulwarks. Nebby screamed; but it was far more a scream of tremendous anger, than of fear.

"I'll heave the blamed thing over the side!" said Ned, and ran to complete his dreadful sacrilege. The following instant, something clasped his right leg, and small, distinctly sharp teeth bit his bare shin, below the up-rolled trousers. Ned yelled, and sat rapidly and luridly upon the deck, in a fashion calculated to shock his system, in every sense of the word.

Nebby had loosed from him, the instant his bite had taken effect; and now he was nursing and examining the black monster of his dreams and waking moments. He knelt there, near the bulwarks, looking with burning eyes of anger and enormous distress at the effects of Ned's great kick; for Ned wore his bluchers on his bare feet. Ned himself still endured a sitting conjunction with the deck; he had not yet finished expressing himself; not that Nebby was in the least interested . . . anger and distress had built a wall of fierce indifference about his heart. He desired chiefly Ned's death.

If Ned, himself, had been less noisy, he would have heard Binny even earlier than he did; for that sane man had jumped to the air-pump, luckily for Granfer Zacchy, and was now, as he worked, emptying his soul of most of its contents upon the derelict Ned. As it was, Ned's memory and ears did duty together, and he remembered that he had committed the last crime in the Pump-man's Calendar . . . he had left the pump, whilst his diver was still below water. Powder ignited in quite a considerable quantity beneath him, could scarcely have moved Ned more speedily. He gave out one yell, and leaped for the pump; at the same instant he discovered that Binny was there, and his gasp of relief was as vehement as prayer. He remembered his leg, and concluded his journey to the pump, with a limp. Here, with one hand he pumped, whilst with the other, he investigated Nebby's teeth-marks. He found that the skin was barely broken; but it was his temper that most needed mending; and, of course, it had been very naughty of Nebby to attempt such a familiarity.

Binny was drawing in the life-line and air-pipe; for Granfer Zacchy was ascending the long rope-ladder, that led up from the sea-bottom, to learn what had caused the unprecedented interruption of his air-supply.

It was a very angry Granfer who, presently, having heard a fair representation of the facts, applied a wet but horny hand to Nebby's anatomy, in a vigorous and decided manner. Yet Nebby neither cried nor spoke; he merely clung on tightly to the Sea-Horse; and Granfer whacked on. At last Granfer grew surprised at the continued absence of remonstrance on Nebby's part, and turned that young man the other end about, to discover the wherefore of so determined a silence.

Nebby's face was very white, and tears seemed perilously near; yet even the nearness of these, did not in any way detract from the expression of unutterable defiance that looked out at Granfer and all the world, from his face. Granfer regarded him for a few moments with earnest attention and doubt, and decided to cease whipping that atom of blue-eyed stubbornness. He looked at the Sea-Horse that Nebby clutched so tightly, in his silence, and perceived the way to make Nebby climb down . . . Nebby must go and beg Ned's pardon for trying to eat him (Granfer smothered a chuckle), or else the Sea-Horse would be taken away.

Nebby's face, however, showed no change, unless it was that the blue eyes shone with a fiercer defiance, which dried out of them that suspicion of tears. Granfer pondered over him, and had a fresh idea. He would take the Sea-Horse back again to the bottom of the sea; and it would then come alive once more and swim away, and Nebby would never see it again, if Nebby did not go at once to Ned and beg Ned's pardon, that very minute. Granfer was prodigiously stern.

There came, perhaps, the tiniest flash of fright into the blue eyes; but it was blurred with unbelief; and, anyway, it had no power at that stage of Nebby's temper to budge him from his throne of enormous anger. He decided, with that fierce courage of the burner of boats, that if Granfer did truly do such a dreadful thing, he (Nebby) would "kneel down proper" and pray God to kill Ned. An added relish of vengeance came to his child's mind . . . He would kneel down in front of Ned; he would pray to God "out loud." Ned should thus learn beforehand that he was doomed.

In that moment of inspired Intention, Nebby became trebly fixed into his Aura of Implacable Anger. He voiced his added grimness of heart in the most tremendous words possible:—

"It's wood!" said Nebby, glaring at Granfer, in a kind of fierce, sick, horrible triumph. "It carn't come back alive again!"

Then he burst into tears, at this dreadful act of disillusionment, and wrenching himself free from Granfer's gently-detaining hand, he dashed away aft, and down the scuttle into the cuddy, where for an hour he hid himself under a bunk, and refused, in dreary silence, any suggestion of dinner.

After dinner, however, he emerged, tear-stained but unbroken. He had brought the Sea-Horse below with him; and now, as the three men watched him, unobtrusively, from their seats around the little cuddy-table, it was plain to them that Nebby had some definite object in view, which he was attempting to mask under an attitude of superb but ineffectual casualness.

"B'y," said Granfer Zacchy, in a very stern voice, "come you an' beg Ned's pard'n, or I'll shore take th' Sea-Horse down wiv me, an' you'll never see 'm no more, an' I'll never ketch ye another, Nebby."

Nebby's reply was an attempted dash for the scuttle-ladder; but Granfer reached out a long arm, that might have been described as possessing the radius of the small cuddy. As a result, Nebby was put with his face in a corner, whilst Granfer Zacchy laid the Sea-Horse across his knees, and stroked it meditatively, as he smoked a restful after-dinner pipe.

Presently, he knocked out his pipe, and, reaching round, brought Nebby to stand at his knee.

"Nebby, b'y," he said, in his grave, kindly fashion, "go you an' beg Ned's pard'n, an' ye shall hev this right back to play wiv."

But Nebby had not been given time yet to ease himself clear of the cloud of his indignation; and even as he stood there by Granfer, he could see the great bruise in the paint, where Ned's blucher had taken effect; and the broken fluke of the tail, that had been smashed when the poor Sea-Horse brought-up so violently against the low bulwarks of the barge.

"Ned's a wicked pig man!" said Nebby, with a fresh intensity of anger against the pump-hand.

"Hush, b'y!" said Granfer, with real sternness. "Ye've had fair chance to come round, an' ye've not took it, an' now I'll read ye lesson as ye'll shore mind!"

He stood up, and put the Sea-Horse under his arm; then, with one hand on Nebby's shoulder, he went to the ladder, and so in a minute they were all on the deck of the barge. Presently, Granfer was once more transformed from a genial and burly giant, into an indiarubber-covered and dome-ended monster. Then, with a slowness and solemnity befitting so terrible an execution of justice, Granfer made a fathom, or so, of spun yarn fast about the Sea-Horse's neck, whilst Nebby looked on, white-faced.

When this was accomplished, Granfer stood up and marched

with ponderous steps to the side, the Sea-Horse under his arm. He began to go slowly down the wooden rungs of the rope-ladder, and presently there were only his shoulders and copper-headpiece visible. Nebby stared down in an anguish; he could see the Sea-Horse vaguely. It seemed to waggle in the crook of Granfer's arm. It was surely about to swim away. Then Granfer's shoulders, and finally his great copper head disappeared from sight, and there was soon only the slight working of the ladder, and the paying out of the air-pipe and life-line, to tell that any one was down there in all that greyness of the water-dusk; for Granfer had often explained to Nebby that it was always "evenin' at th' sea-bottom."

Nebby sobbed once or twice, in a dry, horrid way in his throat; then, for quite half an hour, he lay flat on his stomach in the gangway, silent and watchful, staring down into the water. Several times he felt quite sure he saw something swimming with a queer, waggling movement, a little under the water; and presently he started to sing in a low voice:—

"An' we's under the sea, b'ys,
Where the Wild Horses go,
Horses wiv tails
As big as ole whales
All jiggin' around in a row,
An' when you ses Whoa!
Them debbils does go!"

But it seemed to have no power to charm the Sea-Horse up to the surface; and he fell silent, after singing it through, maybe a dozen times. He was waiting for Granfer. He had a vague hope, which grew, that Granfer had meant to tie it up with the yarn, so that it could not swim away; and perhaps Granfer would bring it up with him when he came. Nebby felt that he would really beg Ned's pardon, if only Granfer brought the Sea-Horse up with him again.

A little later, there came the signal that Granfer was about to ascend, and Nebby literally trembled with excitement, as the lifeline and air-pipe came in slowly, hand over hand. He saw the big dome of the helmet, come vaguely into view, with the line of the air-pipe leading down at the usual "funny" angle, right into the top of the dome (it was an old type of helmet). Then the helmet broke the water, and Nebby could not see anything, because the "rimples" on the water stopped him seeing. Granfer's big shoulders came into view, and then sufficient of him for Nebby to see that the Sea-Horse was truly not with him. Nebby whitened. Granfer had really let the Sea-Horse go. As a matter of fact, Granfer Zacchy had tethered the Sea-Horse to some tough marine weed-rootlets at the sea-bottom, so as to prevent it floating traitorously to the surface; but to Nebby it was plain only that the Sea-Horse had truly "come alive" and swum away.

Granfer stepped on to the deck, and Binny eased off the great helmet, whilst Ned ceased his last, slow revolution of the pump-handle.

It was at this moment that Nebby faced round on Ned, with a white, set, little face, in which his blue eyes literally burned. Ned was surely doomed in that instant! And then, even in the Moment of his Intention, Nebby heard Granfer say to Binny:— "Aye, I moored it wiv the spun yarn safe enough."

Nebby's anger lost its deadliness abruptly, under the sudden sweet chemistry of hope. He oscillated an instant between a new, vague thought, and his swiftly-lessening requirement of vengeance. The new, vague thought became less vague, and he swayed the more toward it; and so, in a moment had rid himself of his Dignity, and run across to Granfer Zacchy:—

"Has it comed alive, Granfer?" he asked, breathlessly, with the infinite eagerness and expectancy of a child.

"Aye!" said Granfer Zacchy, with apparent sternness. "Ye've sure lost it now, b'y. Tis swimmin' roun' an' roun' all the time."

Nebby's eyes shone with sudden splendour, as the New Idea took now a most definite form in his young brain.

Granfer, looking at him with eyes of tremendous sternness, was quite non-plussed at the harmless effect of his expectedly annihilative news concerning the final and obvious lostness of the Sea-Horse. Yet, Nebby said never a word to give Granfer an inkling of the stupendous plan that was settling fast in his daring child's-mind. He opened his mouth once or twice upon a further question; then relapsed into the safety of silence again, as though instinctively realising that he might ask something that would make Granfer suspicious.

Presently, Nebby had stolen away once more to the gangway, and there, lying on his stomach, he began again to look down into the sea. His anger now was almost entirely submerged in the great, glorious New Idea, that filled him with such tremendous exaltation that he could scarcely lie quiet, or cease from singing aloud at the top of his voice.

A few moments earlier, he had meant to "kneel down proper" and pray God "out loud" for Ned to be killed quickly and painfully; but now all was changed. Though, in an indifferent sort of way, in his healthily-savage child's-mind, he did not forgive Ned. . . . Ned's sin had, of course, been unforgivable, presumably "for ever and ever and ever"—Certainly until to-morrow! Meanwhile, Nebby never so much as thought of him, except it might be as one whose bewilderment should presently be the last lustre of the glory of his (Nebby's) proposed achievement. Not that Nebby thought it all out like this into separate ideas; but it was all there in that young and surging head . . . in what I might term a Chaos of Determination, buoying up (as it might be a lonesome craft) one clear, vigorous Idea.

Granfer Zacchy went down twice more before evening, and each time that he returned, Nebby questioned him earnestly as to the doings of the Sea-Horse; and each time, Granfer told the same tale (in accents of would-be sternness) that the Sea-Horse was "jest swimmin' roun' an' roun'; an' maybe ye wish now ye'd begged Ned's pardon, when ye was bid!"

But, in his heart, Granfer decided that the Sea-Horse might be safely re-caught on the morrow.

5

That night, when the three men were asleep in the little cuddy, Nebby's small figure slipped noiselessly out of the bunk that lay below Granfer Zacchy's. He flitted silently to the ladder, and stole up into the warm night, his shirt (a quaint cut-down of Granfer's) softly flickering his lean, bare legs, as he moved through the darkness, along the barge's decks.

Nebby came to a stop where Granfer's diving-suit was hung up carefully on the "frame"; but this was not what Nebby wanted. He stooped to the bottom of the "frame," and pulled up the small hatch of a square locker, where reposed the big, domed, copper helmet, glimmering dully in the vague starlight.

Nebby reached into the locker, and lugged the helmet out bodily, hauling with both hands upon the air-pipe. He carried it across clumsily to the gangway, the air-pipe unreeling off the winch, with each step that he took.

He found the helmet too clumsy and rotund to lift easily on to his own curly head, and so, after an attempt or two, evolved the method of turning the helmet upon its side, and then kneeling down and thrusting his head into it; after which, with a prodigious effort, he rose victoriously to his knees, and began to fumble himself backwards over the edge of the gangway, on to the wooden rungs of Granfer's rope-ladder, which had not been hauled up. He managed a firm foot-hold with his left foot, and then with his right; and so began to descend, slowly and painfully, the great helmet rocking clumsily on his small shoulders.

His right foot touched the water at the fourth rung, and he paused, bringing the other foot down beside the first. The water was pleasantly warm, and Nebby hesitated only a very little while, ere he ventured the next step. Then he stopped again, and tried to look down into the water. The action swayed the big helmet backwards, so that—inside of it—Nebby's delightfully impudent little nose received a bang that made his determined blue eyes water. He loosed his left hand from the ladder, holding on with his right, and tried to push the clumsy helmet forward again into place.

He was, as you will understand, up to his knees in the water, and the rung, on which he perched, was slippery with that peculiar slipperiness, that wood and water together know so well how to breed. One of Nebby's bare feet slipped, and immediately the other. The great helmet gave a prodigious wobble, and completed the danger; for the sudden strain wrenched his grip from the rope between the rungs. There was a muffled little cry inside the helmet, and Nebby swung a small, desperate hand through the darkness towards the ladder; but it was too late; he was falling. There was a splash; not a very big splash for so big a boy's-heart and courage; and no one heard it, or the little bubbling squeak that came out of the depths of the big copper helmet. And then, in a moment, there was only the vaguely disturbed surface of the water, and the air-pipe was running smoothly and swiftly off the drum.

6

It was in the strange, early-morning light, when the lemon and gold-of-light of dawn was in the grey East, that Granfer discovered the thing which had happened. With the wakefulness that is so often an asset of healthy age, he had turned-out in the early hours, to fill his pipe, and had discovered that Nebby's bunk was empty.

He went swiftly up the small ladder. On the deck, the out-trailed air-pipe whispered its tale in silence, and Granfer rushed to it, shouting a dreadful voice for Binny and Ned, who came bounding up, sleepily, in their heavy flannel drawers.

They hauled in the air-pipe, swiftly but carefully; but when the great dome of the helmet came up to them, there was no Nebby; only, tangled from the thread of one of the old-fashioned thumbscrews, they found several golden, curly strands of Nebby's hair.

Granfer, his great muscular hands trembling, began to get into his rubber suit, the two men helping him, wordless. Within a hundred and fifty seconds, he was dwindling away down under the quiet sea that spread, all grey and lemon-hued and utterly calm, in the dawn. Ned was turning the pump-handle, and wiping his eyes undisguisedly from time to time with the back of one hairy, disengaged hand. Binny, who was of a sterner type, though no less warm-hearted, was grimly silent, giving his whole attention to the air-pipe and the life-line; his hand delicate upon the line, awaiting the signal. He could tell from the feel and the coming-up and going-out of the pipe and the line, that Granfer Zacchy was casting round and round, in ever largening circles upon the sea-bottom.

All that day, Granfer quartered the sea-bottom; staying down so long each time, that at last Binny and Ned were forced to remonstrate. But the old man turned on them, and snarled in a kind of speechless anger and agony that forced them to be silent and let him go his own gait.

For three days, Granfer continued his search, the sea remaining calm; but found nothing. On the fourth day, Granfer Zacchy was forced to take the barge in over the bar; for the wind breezed up hard out of the North, and blew for a dreary and savage fortnight, each day of which found Granfer, with Binny and Ned, searching the shore for the "giving up" of the sea. But the sea had one of its secret moods, and gave up nothing.

At the end of the fortnight of heavy weather, it fell calm, and they took the barge out again, to start once more their daily work. There was little use now in searching further for the boy. The barge was moored again over the old spot, and Granfer descended; and the first thing he saw in the grey half-light of the water, was the Sea-Horse, still moored securely by the length of spun yarn to the rootlets of heavy weed at the sea-bottom.

The sight of the creature, gave old Zacchy a dreadful feeling; it was, at once, so familiar of Nebby, as to give him the sensation and unreasoning impression that the "b'y" must be surely close at hand; and yet, at the same time, the grotesque, inanimate creature was the visible incarnation of the dire cause of the unspeakable loneliness and desolation that now possessed his old heart so utterly. He glared at it, through the thick glass of his helmet, and half raised his axe to strike at it. Then, with a sudden revulsion, he reached out, and pulled the silent go-horse to him, and hugged it madly, as if, indeed, it were the boy himself.

Presently, old Granfer Zacchy grew calmer, and turned to his work;

yet a hundred times, he would find himself staring round in the watery twilight towards it—staring eagerly and unreasoningly, and actually listening, inside his helmet, for sounds that the eternal silence of the sea might never bring through its dumb waters, that are Barriers of Silence about the lonesome diver in the strange underworld of the waters. And then, realising freshly that there was no longer one who might make the so-craved-for sounds, Granfer would turn again, grey-souled and lonely, to his work. Yet, in a while, he would be staring and listening once more.

In the course of days, old Zacchy grew calmer and more resigned; yet he kept the motionless Sea-Horse tethered, in the quiet twilight of the water, to the weed-rootlets at the sea-bottom. And more and more, he grew to staring round at it; and less and less did it seem a futile or an unreasonable thing to do.

In weeks, the habit grew to such an extent, that he had ceased to be aware of it. He prolonged his hours under water, out of all reason, so far as his health was concerned; and turned queerly "dour" when Ned and Binny remonstrated with him, warning him not to stay down so long, or he would certainly have to pay the usual penalty.

Only once did Granfer say a word in explanation, and then it was obviously an unintentional remark, jerked out of him by the intensity of his feelings:—

"Like as I feel 'm nigh me, w'en I'm below," he had muttered, in a half coherent fashion. And the two men understood; for it was just what they had vaguely supposed. They had no reply to make; and the matter dropped.

Generally now, on descending each morning, Granfer would stop near the Sea-Horse, and "look it over." Once, he discovered that the bonito-tail had come unglued; but this he remedied neatly, by lashing it firmly into position with a length of roping-twine. Sometimes, he would pat the head of the horse, with one great hand, and mutter a quite unconscious:—"Whoa, mare!" as it bobbed silently under his touch. Occasionally, as he swayed heavily past it, in his clumsy dress, the slight swirl of the water in his "wake" would make the Horse slue round uncannily towards him; and thereafter, it would swing and oscillate for a brief time, slowly back into quietness; the while that Granfer would stand and watch it, unconsciously straining his ears, in that place of no-sound.

Two months passed in this way, and Granfer was vaguely aware that his health was failing; but the knowledge brought no fear to him; only the beginnings of an indefinite contentment—a feeling that maybe he would be "soon seein' Nebby." Yet the thought was never definitely conscious; nor ever, of course, in any form, phrased. Yet it had its effect, in the vague contentment which I have hinted at, which brought a new sense of ease round Granfer's heart; so that, one day, as he worked, he found himself crooning unconsciously the old Ballade of the Sea Horses.

He stopped on the instant, all an ache with memory; then turned and peered toward the Sea-Horse, which loomed, a vague shadow, silent in the still water. It had seemed to him in that moment, that he had heard a subtile echo of his crooned song, in the quiet deeps around him. Yet, he saw nothing, and presently assured himself that he heard nothing; and so came round again upon his work.

A number of times in the early part of that day, old Granfer caught himself crooning the old Ballade, and each time he shut his lips fiercely on the sound, because of the ache of memory that the old song bred in him; but, presently, all was forgotten in an intense listening; for, abruptly, old Zacchy was sure that he heard the song, coming from somewhere out of the eternal twilight of the waters. He slued himself round, trembling, and stared towards the Sea-Horse; but there was nothing new to be seen, neither was he any more sure that he had ever heard anything.

Several times this happened, and on each occasion Granfer would heave himself round ponderously in the water, and listen with an intensity that had in it, presently, something of desperateness.

In the late afternoon of that day, Granfer again heard something; but refused now to credit his hearing, and continued grimly at work. And then, suddenly, there was no longer any room for doubt . . . a shrill, sweet child's voice was singing, somewhere among the grey twilights far to his back. He heard it with astounding clearness, helmet and surrounding water notwithstanding. It was a sound, indeed, that he would have heard through all the Mountains of Eternity. He stared round, shaking violently.

The sound appeared to come from the greyness that dwelt away beyond a little wood of submarine growths, that trailed up their roots, so hushed and noiseless, out of a near-by vale in the sea-bottom.

As Granfer stared, everything about him darkened into a wonderful and rather dreadful Blackness. This passed, and he was able to see again; but somehow, as it might be said, newly. The shrill, sweet, childish singing had ceased; but there was something beside the Sea-Horse . . . a little, agile figure, that caused the Sea-Horse to bob and bound at its moorings. And, suddenly, the little figure was astride the

Sea-Horse, and the Horse was free, and two twinkling legs urged it across the sea-bottom towards Granfer.

Granfer thought that he stood up, and ran to meet the boy; but Nebby dodged him, the Sea-Horse curvetting magnificently; and immediately Nebby began to gallop round and round Granfer, singing:—

"An' we's under the sea, b'ys,
Where the Wild Horses go,
Horses wiv tails
As big as ole whales
All jiggin' around in a row,
An' when you ses Whoa!
Them debbils does go!"

The voice of the blue-eyed mite was ineffably gleeful; and abruptly, tremendous youth invaded Granfer, and a glee beyond all understanding.

7

On the deck of the barge, Ned and Binny were in great doubt and trouble. The weather had been growing heavy and threatening, during all the late afternoon; and now it was culminating in a tremendous, black squall, which was coming swiftly down upon them.

Time after time, Binny had attempted to signal Granfer Zacchy to come up; but Granfer had taken a turn with his life-line round a hump of rock that protruded out of the sea-bottom; so that Binny was powerless to do aught; for there was no second set of diving gear aboard.

All that the two men could do, was to wait, in deep anxiety, keeping the pump going steadily, and standing-by for the signal that was never to come; for by that time, old Granfer Zacchy was sitting very quiet and huddled against the rock, round which he had hitched to prevent Binny from signalling him, as Binny had become prone to do, when Granfer stayed below, out of all reason and wisdom.

And all the time, Ned kept the un-needed pump going, and far down in the grey depth, the air came out in a continual series of bubbles, around the big copper helmet. But Granfer was breathing an air of celestial sweetness, all unwitting and un-needing of the air that Ned laboured faithfully to send to him.

The squall came down in a fierce haze of rain and foam, and the ungainly old craft swung round, jibbing heavily at her kedge-rope, which gave out a little twanging sound, that was lost in the roar of the wind. The unheard twanging of the rope, ended suddenly in a dull thud, as it parted; and the bluff old barge fell, off broadside on to the weight of the squall. She drifted with astonishing rapidity, and the life-line and the air-pipe flew out, with a buzz of the unwinding drums, and parted, with two differently toned reports, that were plain in an instant's lull in the roaring of the squall.

Binny had run forrard to the bows, to try to get over another kedge; but now he came racing aft again, shouting. Ned still pumped on mechanically, with a look of dull, stunned horror in his eyes; the pump driving a useless jet of air through the broken remnant of the air-pipe. Already, the barge was a quarter of a mile to leeward of the diving-ground, and the men could do no more than hoist the foresail, and try to head her in safely over the bar, which was now right under their lee.

Down in the sea, old Granfer Zacchy had altered his position; the jerk of the air-pipe had done that. But Granfer was well enough content; not only for the moment; but for Eternity; for as Nebby rode so gleefully round and round him, there had come a change in all things; there were strange and subtile lights in all the grey twilights of the deep, that seemed to lead away and away into stupendous and infinitely beautiful distances.

"Is you listenin', Granfer?" Old Zacchy heard Nebby say; and discovered suddenly that Nebby was insisting that he should race him across the strangely glorified twilights, that bounded them now eternally.

"Sure, b'y," said Granfer Zacchy, undismayed; and Nebby wheeled his charger.

"Gee-Up!" shouted Nebby, excitedly, and his small legs began to twinkle ahead in magnificent fashion; with Granfer running a cheerful and deliberate second.

And so passed Granfer Zacchy and Nebby into the Land where little boys may ride Sea-Horses for ever, and where Parting becomes one of the Lost Sorrows.

And Nebby led the way at a splendid gallop; maybe, for all that I have any right to know, to the very Throne of the Almighty, singing, shrill and sweet:—

"An we's under the sea, b'ys,
Where the Wild Horses go,
Horses wiv tails
As big as ole whales
All jiggin' around in a row,
An' when you ses Whoa!
Them debbils does go!"

And overhead (was it only a dozen fathoms!) there rushed the white-maned horses of the sea, mad with the glory of the storm, and tossing ruthless from crest to crest, a wooden go-horse, from which trailed a length of broken spun yarn.

How the Honourable Billy Darrell Raised the Wind

"POLLIE," SAID THE HONOURABLE BILLY to his young wife, "what were you christened?"

"Mary," she replied.

"Then who was the first idiot to call you 'Pollie'?" he asked.

"Everyone have called me that always," said the Honourable Mrs. Darrell.

"Asses!" declared the Honourable Billy. "I shall call you Mary in future, for ever. And remember, Mary, that it should be really 'everyone has.' Now, dinna forget, lassie!"

Mary Darrell—but lately Mary Ryden, mill-girl—sighed a little, and grimaced prettily. " Fine" talk held so many unsuspected entanglements; but she was learning swiftly, almost minute by minute, the ways and the speech of her young, and certainly lovable, lord.

"Mary," said the Honourable Billy, some minutes later, looking up from his bank-book, "we've just exactly five pounds and six shillings left in the bank. My Uncle John promised me a thousand pounds the day I married you, or else I'd never have had the cheek to ask you—"

"Husht! Dear, do husht talking like that!" interrupted Mary. "As if I wouldn't be proud to be your wife, so how poor you was."

" 'Were,' bless you," said the Honourable Billy, drawing her gently to him.

His wife nodded, and continued.

"You must be a sensible boy, and let me go back to the mill until your stories are selling better, dear," she said coaxingly. "I should feel such a proud girl."

"Never!" remarked the Honourable Billy, very quietly, but in a tone that told her it was hopeless to press the point; though, in her heart, she believed that necessity would presently compel him to let her go back to her mill-work, where she could earn from twenty-five to twenty-eight shillings per week—sufficient to keep the two of them comfortably.

The Honourable Billy went to the corner cupboard, and reached down a bill-file, which he brought to the table, and began to examine.

"Two pounds three and sixpence to Tauton," he muttered, jotting down the amount on an envelope.

"I could do without butcher's meat," said Mary. "I love potatoes, and we could save a bit that way, dear."

"Yes," said the Honourable Billy grimly. "We might feed you on good plain water, whilst I have a good steak to my dinner! Mary, if I catch you doing that sort of thing, there'll be trouble!"

He lifted several more bills off the file.

"Seventeen and six to Motts for redecoratin'," he read out. "One pound fifteen to Jenkins for groceries. Fourteen pounds to Tuttles for new furniture. Tailor—poor devil!—wants something on account. I owe him ten pounds. Thank God, anyway, you made me pay the rent out of that last cheque. There's half a dozen old accounts here, and the big bill of Williams's for the pictures I bought, depending on that thousand of my uncle's that he forgot about, and then went and bust, poor old chap!"

He stopped speaking, and totted up the whole of their debts.

"Sixty-three pounds sixteen and nine-pence!" he declared at last. "And we've five pun sax in the bank; no stories sold, and meanwhile we've got to live. Tell you what, lassie—I've just got to rustle, and let you see I'm not just such a piece of show-goods as I know you imagine in that quaint little heart o' thine. I guess I've got to raise the wind pretty sudden, an' I'm going to do it, too, even if I indulge in burglary!"

"Why not let me go back to the mill, dear, really?" ventured his wife once more.

"Mary," said the Honourable Billy, taking her on to his knee, " hold your tongue!"

Which Mary did, literally, until her laughter forced her to let go.

"It's so slippy," she explained, with sublime impertinence. "And, anyway, I know you'll have to let me have my own way in the end."

And in the same moment in which she concluded this prophecy, there was a knock at the front door. She returned, carrying an opened letter, set out in varying sized print, and the blanks filled in with spidery writing.

"It's from some people called Stubbs," she said, looking very white and frightened. "They say as we've to pay Williams's bill by next

Wednesday, or they'll summons us. And it was give to old George Cardman"—referring to the old weaver next door, who strongly disapproved of the Honourable Billy—"and now the whole Court will know"—meaning the Farm Court, in which their little cottage stood. "The postman ought to be more careful." And she fought to keep from crying.

"Cheer up, little woman!" said the Honourable Billy, taking the letter from her. "I'm going to raise some money jolly soon now. You'll see." Yet how this was to be achieved he had no distinct notion, and Pollie felt that this was so.

"Oh, let me go back to the mill, dear, until we're clear!" she begged him once more. "Do—do let me, dear! I should be so much happier, you don't know. I've always had such a horror of debt!"

"No!" said the Honourable Billy, almost fiercely. "You're never going back there again!"

And with that from her young lord and master she became silent, yet loving him queerly the more, even whilst her judgment made her feel impatient with him.

An hour later big Tom Holden called. He was the steam-lurry man at Grafter's mill, where Pollie had worked before she married the lovable but absurdly poor Honourable Billy. Tom, as it chanced, had been the Honourable Billy's rival, and had eventually fought with him concerning Pollie, with the result that he had found himself knocked out in something under a minute, much to his astonishment. He had eventually become the Honourable Billy's staunchest friend and admirer.

For a time Tom sat chatting quietly, but in a half-hearted fashion as if his thoughts were on the wander and his interest not truly in the topics raised. Eventually he caught the Honourable Billy's attention with a quick glance, and nodded meaningly towards the door, having first made sure that Mary was not looking at him.

From this manoeuvre the Honourable Billy gathered that Tom wished to speak to him privately outside; so that when, a few minutes later, the big driver rose to go, he reached for his cap.

"I'll come a few steps with you, Tom," he said. "I feel I want to stretch my legs." He turned to his wife. "Sha'n't be five minutes, dear," he explained, and followed Tom.

For perhaps a minute big Tom Holden walked at a rapid rate, wordless. Eventually he jerked out, apparently apropos of nothing:

"T' match at Jackson's Green is off."

"Oh!" said the Honourable Billy, immediately interested, for he knew that Holden referred to a boxing match that had been arranged between a local champion called Dan Natter, and Blacksmith Dankley, who worked a shoeing forge on the Longsite Road, and was reckoned the best man with his hands for many miles. "That's a beastly pity, Tom!" he added. "Why's it off?"

"Dan's sprained hisself—'s ankle or summat," replied Holden. "Doctor's sure's he con't fight, not for a three-month. I wor in Jackson's place t'-neet, an' he wor tur'ble cut up. He's like ta be, for he's bet big money 's he'll find a mon to lick t' feightin' blacksmith i' twenty roonds."

"Well," said the Honourable Billy, "why doesn't he get another man ? There's three weeks yet to the fight."

"He con't," replied Holden. "Dan's t' best mon i' these parts, an' a likely lad. Not but Dankley's the best mon to my thinkin'."

He relapsed into silence, and for some moments increased the speed of his steps, his actions suggesting suddenly to the Honourable Billy that he wrestled with some mental problem, or with a natural diffidence to say something that was in his mind. Abruptly he said:

"T' purse wor a hundred pounds, an' t' winner to share t' gate-money."

And again he fell to wordlessness and quick walking. Suddenly he brought out the thing that was in his mind.

"Happen tha'd be too proud to try for 't?" he said, with a queer little note of awkwardness in his voice.

"Me?" demanded the Honourable Billy, lost to all, save astonishment. "Good Lord!" Then, after an instant's pause: "I'm not half good enough. They'd never let me try."

"Tha' con ax 'em!" said Tom Holden briefly, and still walking.

"It'd be a godsend," remarked the Honourable Billy, after a further little space of thinking. "The way things are now I'd jump at it. Only, I tell you I'm not half good enough. Dankley's a thundering good man. He's an awful slogger, I've always heard; but he's got the science to back it. He'd be a first-rater if he'd only follow it up. I tell you, Tom, the Jackson crowd would just laugh at me if I put myself on offer."

"Happen tha c'ud try," said Holden, stopping and facing him. "Happen some o' them 'd laff t'other side the face 'fore tha was done. Tha's best man wi' tha hands 's a've seen; an' I knows wod I'm sayin', tho' I bean't no use to box mysen. Coom down wi' me t'-morrow neet, an' see Mister Jackson. He's fair mad to find a good mon to taake place o' Dan. Wilta?"

"Tom," said the Honourable Billy grimly, "if Jackson's fool enough to try me and risk his money on me, I'm game, you bet. And I'll, do my best for him, and that'll be for myself, too. I want the cash thunderin' bad."

" 'I," said Tom; "owd George Cardman wor sayin' summat 's made me think tha' wor short. Well, Aw'll call for thee t'-morrow neet at ha'-past seven. Tha'll do a-reet; tha'lt see. Good-neet. Don't say aught to Pollie." And with that he turned, and made off in the direction of his home without another word.

Said Pollie, when the Honourable Billy returned:

"What did Tom Holden want to say, dear? Was it anything important?"

"Why," said the Honourable Billy, "who said that Tom Holden wanted to say anything?"

Mary Darrell laughed, but asked nothing further; for she could trust her husband, and she would not force him into the position of having to fib, or else having to refuse blankly to tell her. Yet she half meant, in her way, to discover what it might be that Tom had been so palpably secret about.

The following day the Honourable Billy went off to see Williams, the man to whom he owed the big bill for pictures, and, after some talk, he managed to arrange things.

Then he went home to tell Mary that he had deferred the threatened fall of the sword for a month. But when he got home he found fresh trouble, for there, with his foot down to prevent the door from being closed, was a big, coarse-looking man, whose voice seemed to fill the Court.

"I'll ha' my money!" he was shouting to someone within the nearly closed door. "I'll ha' my money!" And he gave the door a shove with his great hand that forced it half open.

But it was immediately pushed to again, and a little, frightened voice from behind it was heard saying: "Go away! Go away! Go away! Go away! Oh, go away!" And then the sound of sobs.

"No; I'll not go away wi'out my money!" roared the man, thumping the door vigorously with each word to emphasise himself. "Tell that skulkin' toff that married thee to coom out an' pay his debts, 'stead o' loafin' ahind thy skirts like a great babby!"

"Go away! Oh, do go away, Mr. Jenkins!" said Mary's voice from behind the door, sobbing bitterly. "Oh, go away! Oh, go away!"

"Not I!" shouted the man. "I'll ha' my money! Send un out! I'll teach un! Send tha loafin' toff out!" And he thumped at the door till it quivered again; and poor little Mary Darrell, pushing desperately against it from behind, screamed piteously. "I'll teach un!" roared the big grocer. "I'll teach un!"

"Certainly!" said the Honourable Billy, at his elbow, in the quietest voice in the world. "Will you give the lesson here, Mr. Jenkins, or in the little field at the back? In any case, perhaps you will be good enough to stop bullying my wife." Then, as the man turned, half ashamed and blustering, upon him, "Oh, you hideous lout!" he said, with a flash of white-hot rage. And therewith he struck the big grocer with his open hand on the side of the face so hard that he knocked him down.

The burly grocer was doubtless a bully; though, possibly, he had not considered himself bullying in an unrighteous cause; but he had plenty of animal courage, and, moreover, he fancied himself somewhat with his fists. He got up, with an inarticulate roar, and hurled himself at the "toff."

"Urr! urr! urr!" he grunted, and with each grunt he drove a blow at the Honourable Billy's head. But the head refused to wait for the big red fists, and slid under them, swiftly and gracefully, or slipped to the side. Then the Honourable Billy shot his left hand in quickly, and broke one of the big grocer's short ribs; for he was uncommonly angry. And, because he was so uncommonly angry, he followed his left lead with his right fist with all his strength. There was a nasty, snicking, breaking sound, and the big man lay senseless on the floor of the Court with a broken jaw.

"My word! My word, sir!" said a quick voice behind the furious young man. "Knocked big Jenkins into heaven with a left and right, sir! My word, sir; but you're the man I'm looking for. My name's Jackson, sir—Jackson of Jackson's Bowlin' Green, at the back of the Black Anchor."

The Honourable Billy looked round, and found a small, rather dapper-looking man, with a somewhat Jewish kind of face, holding out a much-ringed hand to him.

"I'm Jackson, sir," repeated the little man, as if the name explained everything that might need explaining.

"Ye-es?" said the Honourable Billy, a little dazed still with the anger that had burned in him. He took the extended hand, and gave it a brief, unconscious shake, then dropped it, and turned to the man upon the ground.

"Allow me," interposed the little man, and knelt beside the big grocer, making a swift examination. "Broken rib; jaw broken and dislocated," he commented calmly. "You've got a good punch on you, sir—a rare good punch."

He put his hand over the man's heart, and afterwards pulled up one of his eyelids.

"Needs a doctor pretty bad," he remarked. "I've my light wagonette here; perhaps you'll give my man a lift, sir?"

He put his fingers into his mouth and whistled, and there drove in through the entrance of the Court a smart, light, sporty-looking wagonette, driven by a big, stout man in a light-grey top-hat, who chewed a straw and viewed the little group without any undue exhibition of emotion.

"Come and give us a lift, Marles!" said the little man briefly. "Be smart now!"

The man climbed down, and came leisurely across.

"Had his medicine good, Mr. Jackson, by the look of un!" he commented, stooping forward, hands on knees, and inspecting the man upon the ground.

"Take his shoulders," was all the reply his master made; and they set-to and got the weighty grocer into the wagonette.

"No, sir!" said Mr. Jackson, as the Honourable Billy made to follow. "You keep out o' this. Tom Holden mentioned you to me, and I was coming up to see you. After what I've seen I'm not going to have you gaoled, as you may be, for assault. Leave the whole thing in my hands, sir. I'll fix it up, if anyone can. You go home and stay there quietly until I come up and have a talk with you, sir. You'll know me—Jackson's my name, sir. Jackson!"

And with that he and his man got into the wagonette and drove off.

"He's right," muttered the Honourable Billy. And suddenly he remembered Mary. He rushed to his door, and found it closed. From within there came an indistinct sound of sobbing. He turned the handle and pushed, but was immediately aware that someone was pushing back. There came a little gasp of terror and hopelessness behind the door, and then his diminutive wife's voice frantically:

"Go away ! Go away ! Oh, go, go, go, go, go, go, go!"

And in the middle of this frightened and unstrung reiteration, the Honourable Billy pushed the door open and went in. He found Mary at the back of the door—a small, trembling, dishevelled figure, pushing and pushing, and sobbing desperately as she pushed—a thoroughly unnerved and terrified little woman.

"Oh," he said, with infinite tenderness, "my little defender of the castle!" And he caught her into his arms and carried her into the inner room. "Poor kiddy!" he muttered. "The brute has upset you."

"There—there—there's been—been three; one—one—one af-ter another," said Mary, unable yet to still her sobs. "They—they said such—such h-h-horrible things, and—and —and tried to come in-n-side. But I pushed against them; and—and—and then you—came in."

"Poor little woman," muttered the Honourable Billy. "No more answering the door when I'm out, remember; that is, not until I've paid all the brutes up. We'll never buy another shillingsworth from any of them as long as we live. The rotten brutes to bully you like that! If I'd caught 'em! If I'd caught 'em!" he added to himself, with a dreadful little note of savagery in his voice. Then, suddenly remembering the condition of Jenkins the grocer, he fell silent, troubled and bothered that he had hit so hard. Yet, in the same moment, fiercely sure that he would do the same thing again in like case.

Presently he had his wife hushed and assured, telling her that all would be well, and that he had found a method of earning enough money within a few weeks to pay off all their debts, and have something in the bank, if only things went right. But what was to prove this sudden road to wealth he was careful to hide from her.

Later, when Mr. Jackson returned to pay his promised call, the Honourable Billy ushered him into his little study, explaining to him, as soon as he had closed the door, that his wife must not hear a word of the match with Dankley, or she would be dreadfully upset.

Then Mr. Jackson got to work and proposed terms; yet, in the end, explained to the Honourable Billy that nothing could be signed until the committee who were running the affair along with him had signified their agreeableness for him to take the place of Dan Natter. Therefore, the Honourable Billy must call at the Black Anchor that night, where the committee were to meet in a private room, and discuss the situation, and choose some boxer to meet Dankley.

"And pretty glum they are, sir," said Jackson, gleefully rubbing his hands; "and so was I, for that matter, till I saw you paste big Jenkins. He's quite a tidy man with his fists, too, and a bit of a rough customer. We'll keep him quiet, though, till the match is over, even if we have to shanghai him, sir. You bet we will, as sure as my name's Jackson."

He stood up, and shook hands.

"You'll be down, then, sir, soon after eight to-night at the Black Anchor," he concluded. "Ask anyone, sir. Say you want Jackson's place; they'll show you. Ask for me. Good-night, sir,"

And with that he was off.

At seven-thirty, as arranged, big Tom Holden called for the

Honourable Billy, who promptly told him that Jackson had been up himself to see him.

" 'I," said Holden, composedly. "Aa thowt he might; for I cracked tha up proper to him. Aa'm reet glad tha went for Jenkins; he's a rough lot an' dirty-mouthed, he is that."

At a few minutes past eight the two of them reached the Black Anchor, where Tom—who seemed to know his way about—led the way down the corridor to a room at the end. He opened the door, and pushed the Honourable Billy in, saying:

"Aa've brought a mon 's 'll lick Dankley inter fits. Mr. Jackson, there, knows 's he's a good 'un."

The Honourable Billy looked round him. He was in a big, brightly lit room, in which a dozen sporty-looking men, generally on the wrong side of forty, were sitting round a table, smoking and drinking. Mr. Jackson was at the head of the table, and held an auctioneer's gavel, with which, from time to time, he pounded on the table. Otherwise he seemed to be taking no part in the conversation, that had been warm and general when the two entered the room. Moreover, he took no notice of the Honourable Billy, beyond the most casual nod, and certainly ignored Tom Holden's reference to his knowledge of the young man's capabilities. It was evident to the Honourable Billy that he knew what he was doing; and that there was rhyme reason behind this unexpected noncommittal attitude.

A quick and general silence had met Tom Holden's remark, and there was a turning of heads and craning of necks as those at the table moved to view the new champion so forcibly announced.

Then, in the silence, there came a loud, rough voice, from a big man sitting near Mr. Jackson: "Fetch un in, Tom! Fetch un in! Don't keep us all waitin'!"

There was a sneering note in the man's tone that made the Honourable Billy look the more particularly at him. Thus he saw that the big man was not staring at him, as were the others; but looking ostentatiously at the door, as though he supposed the man to whom Tom Holden referred must be still without.

"Here he be," replied Holden, pointing to the Honourable Billy, and looking a little puzzled.

"What!" roared the big man, whose battered face, thick ears, and broken knuckles told that he was a pugilist. "What! Ha, ha, ha, ha! Aa could eat un wi'out salt—a stuck-up bloomin' young torf as fancies hisself a fi'tin'-man! Yon's no sort o' use to us, Tom, as tha should ha' known. Us wants a man, an' a dommed good un, too. Yon's mebbe one o' them fancy, soft-glove chaps. Us wants a lad as'll put the fear o' God inter Blacksmith Dankley. An' us'll never find one; an' that's my bettin' any day!"

From other men at the table there came a murmur of protests, not against the rudeness of the big pugilist, but against Tom Holden for attempting to foist such an obvious impossibility upon them as the Honourable Billy—a "torf."

As silence came again on the room, Mr. Jackson spoke, in a quiet, emotionless voice:

"I'm inclined to fancy the looks of the young gentleman," he said.

"Ha!" snorted the big boxer. "Ha, ha! Tha'd lose tha money if tha put it on the likes of 'im!"

"I was going to add, Bellett, when you interrupted me, that I was prepared to back my fancy," continued Mr. Jackson, in the same even voice. "For a reasonable sum, and for the sport of the thing, I'll back him against you, Bellett, that he outs you in three rounds."

"What!" shouted Bellett, anger and astonishment expressing themselves as comrades of wounded pride. "What! I'll out un wi' my coat on in two twos!" And he jumped up from his chair, with a spring that told of the powerful muscles hidden by his loose clothes.

"One moment, Bellett," said Mr. Jackson, who had an unmistakable eye to the main chance. "We'll book the bets first, and then clear the room, and you shall go ahead in proper order."

"Aa back mysen for twenty pun that I outs the calf in thirty secs!" said Bellett loudly, and throwing down two ten-pound notes on to the table.

Very calmly, Mr. Jackson covered them, and proceeded then to book bets with most of the men round the table, who evidently considered that the "torf" stood no chance at all with the formidable Bellett, and staked eagerly on what they considered a "dead cert." They must have thought that Mr. Jackson was a bit above himself that night, and betting out of sheer obstinacy; for it was plain to them that he was bound to lose his money in a very few minutes. Yet they should have remembered that Mr. Jackson was not noted for coming out on the wrong side either of a bet or a bargain.

As soon as the bets were all taken, the room was cleared, and Bellett gave a spring into the middle of the floor.

"Come on, my lad, if tha bain't 'feared!" he called. "Tha'd best take off tha coat." he added, for the Honourable Billy, seeing that Bellett had not stripped, had stepped forward silently, fully dressed as he was.

"Thanks," replied the Honourable Billy evenly. "But I'm rather susceptible to draughts."

"Oh, come on, my pretty lad, an' be done wi' tha gab!" said Bellett, squaring up. "Tha'lt feel more nor draughts in half a sec!"

"Stop!" shouted one of the men. "Gloves! You've no gloves on."

"Gloves be dommed!" said Bellett. "We'm all friends 'ere. Oo's to know?" And with the word he drove off with his left at the young Honourable.

The Honourable Billy stepped back easily, just out of distance, and pushing up the right-hand blow that followed like lightning, stepped in under the big man's arms, caught him round the body, and patted his back twice with the flat of his palm, saying, "Be calm, Bellett. Be calm, I beg of you." And was gone from him with two quick, steps.

There was a half-instant of silent astonishment from the onlookers, which was followed by an approving shout of laughter. But Bellett was certainly in no laughing mood. He sprang for the young man, and drove in right and left, right and left, right and left, a dozen furious blows in as many seconds, most of which the Honourable Billy slipped or guarded; but at the end of the rally, when he had been driven once all round the room in this fashion, he let through a heavy lefthander, which fairly floored him.

"Ha!" shouted Bellett, gasping, and standing exultantly over him, waiting for him to rise. "Got tha now, lad!"

"Not—quite!" jerked out the Honourable Billy, and dived clean through between the big man's feet, turned a complete somersault, and landed, standing, in time to meet his opponent's rush.

Bellett swung a mighty right and left at him, grunting. Billy slipped the first, and the second he blocked, standing in close to the big man's body. Immediately afterwards he upper-cut him savagely with the right, and as Bellett reeled, head jerked backwards, he hit him, thud, thud, left and right, clean on the mark, sending him down with a dreadful grunt to the floor, where he lay untended long after he had been informally counted out; for everyone in the room was eagerly shaking hands with the Honourable Billy, and apparently willing to forget for the time being that he bore the stigma of "toff-dom," imprinted large and general upon him.

"Tha'rt a hply surprise, lad!" said Bellett's voice suddenly from the floor; and turning, they saw that the big pugilist was sitting up, looking rather sick and dazed, but otherwise apparently right enough.

He got to his feet, staggering a little, and came across to the Honourable Billy.

"Tha's best man, dom tha, lad, as ever Aa've stood up to! Aa've no ill-feelin', lad. But tha's queerest torf as ever Aa've come up ag'in! Tha'lt suit fine, Aa'm thinkin', to win us a pot o' money ower the fight wi' Blacksmith Dankley."

He turned to the rest, who signified their approval by shouts of "Ay, ay! Yes, yes!" Whilst Mr. Jackson nodded, contentedly smiling as he picked up the stakes. He had known both the men he had to deal with, and the opportunity, and had gone the right way to make the most out of both.

"Aa towd tha so!" shouted big Tom Holden, at this point, to the room in general. "Aa towd tha so! Aa con't box, but Aa knows a good lad when Aa sees one. What dost tha think, now?"

" 'E's a 'oly terrer!" volunteered a small Cockney; and the room once more echoed the coincidence of their opinion.

And so it was arranged that the Honourable Billy should go into training immediately for the big fight with Blacksmith Dankley, and a glad, yet somewhat anxious man he was; for so much depended on his winning it.

But to hide everything from Mary the Honourable Billy found impossible, for she worried about his sudden distaste for pastry and sundry other normal delights; so he explained to her that he wished to be pretty "fit," as he had on a friendly sparring match with an acquaintance, which was certainly a modified form of describing a prize-fight!

The Honourable Billy followed his own methods of getting into condition. He knew his own constitution, and had no intention of running himself stale. He lived his ordinary life of moderation, merely taking a little more consideration as to what he ate, and adding to his normal amount of exercise two smart bouts a day with the gloves and a little skipping.

This hardly suited the old-fashioned strict views of Bellett, who desired to act as his trainer; but the big boxer had to admit that the Honourable Billy was certainly, as the saying goes, fit to fight for his life, and so contented himself with no more than an odd, misdirected growl or two of vague disapprobation.

Meanwhile, the Honourable Billy and his wife were steadily dodging duns, and by the time that the week of the fight arrived, he had a nice little stock of summonses pending at an early date. The only effect these had on the young man, was to make him the more fiercely determined to win the fight, and so pay all their debts at one sweep. But the effect on poor Mary was to make her grow thin; and the Honourable Billy had a very serious and angry talk with her one day, when he found that she had been eating as little as possible, so as to save in every way. He assured her that, in all probability, their troubles would be over in a few days, but gave no more definite statement; so that his small wife put no great faith in his hopes, but went about her house-work silently, and listening nervously for knocks that might betoken some fresh dun, come to post in a sheaf of bills and insolent, though just, demands.

"What sort of a chap is Dankley to look at?" the Honourable Billy asked his trainer one day as he dressed himself after the practice bout. "I've heard heaps about him, but I've never seen him. He's mighty strong, isn't he, by all accounts?"

" 'I, he is that!" replied Bellett, nodding. "Theer's only big Farm'r Dikkun as cou'd throw 'un, to my thinkin', lad. Not but Farm'r Dikkun should, for he weighs summat like seventeen score, an' t' blacksmith bain't no more nor fifteen stone odd; but he's a terrible hard-made man. Tha's geet tha work cut out, lad, if tha's to win. So Aa'm tellin' thee."

"I believe you, Bellett," replied the young man, and made up his mind that he would cycle along the Longsite road that afternoon and see whether he could not get an "unofficial" look at his opponent to be.

This he did, and dismounted at the forge. He had meant at first to hide the reason for his visit by making belief that he had casually dismounted in passing to light a cigarette, but decided to go his natural way, which was to be absolutely straight. Therefore he leant over his bicycle, and nodded to the big smith.

"Good-afternoon, Mr. Dankley," he said. "I felt I wanted to see you."

"I don't do nowt wi' them things, lad," replied the smith, getting up from the anvil, where he had been sitting a moment, and coming slowly to the entrance of the smithy.

"I didn't mean that," replied the Honourable Billy, smiling. "I meant that I wanted to see you—I mean that I'm the man they're backing against you; and I've heard so much about you, I felt I must come and have a look. I thought I'd be frank, and then there'd seem nothing underhand about it. See?"

Very solemnly the big smith rubbed his great, bony hand on his leathern apron, and solemnly reached it out to the Honourable Billy.

"Shake hands, lad. I didn't know thee for him as is matched again' me. I heard as it were one o' the gentry, an' I like thee for thy straight way."

He had been slowly shaking the Honourable Billy's hand throughout the whole of this speech, and now, ceasing, he took the cycle from him, and leant it against the outer wall of the smithy, inviting the young man to come in and take a rest on an old chair, which he proceeded to polish with his cap.

"So thou art the lad?" he said, after he had gone back to his anvil-seat. And he sat for maybe a full minute, looking gravely at the Honourable Billy, whilst, at his back, his striker and apprentice both stared with keen interest at the man who was matched against their formidable master.

Meanwhile, the Honourable Billy took in the details of his future opponent, noting the enormously muscular hands and forearms, and the amount of bone that went to the making of the wrists and fingers.

"Like ramming my face against a chunk of iron in the glove, to meet all that with his weight at the back of it!" was his mental comment. "He's one of those big, lean men, who never look as big or as strong as they are. He's just leather and bone, from fingers to toes, and I'm blest if I know how I'm going to hit him hard enough to knock him out. It'll be like slogging at pig-iron."

Thus the Honourable Billy's thoughts, and a wave of depression came upon him, for the man was so much more formidable than he had supposed.

Very slowly the big smith shook his head, gently; and again looked the young man over.

"What do'st thou weigh, lad?" he asked, at length.

"Thirteen stones four pounds," replied the Honourable Billy; whereupon the big smith showed some surprise.

"I hadn't thought it, lad," he said. "Thee doesn't look it. But thou'rt a well-made lad, sure enough." And once more he ran his appraising glance over him from head to feet.

"What do you weigh, Mr. Dankley?" asked the Honourable Billy.

"Fifteen stone thirteen an' a ha'f pound," replied the smith quietly. "I can give thee two stone an' nine pound, lad. Too much, lad—too much."

"Um!" said the Honourable Billy, feeling disconsolate.

"But there's youth to thy side of the bargain, lad," the smith comforted him. "I be seven and forty—seven and forty!"

"May I be half the man at seven-and-forty," replied the Honourable Billy fervently. He stood up. "Well, I'll do my best on Saturday," he said; "I can't do more—"

"Tha'lt be lickt!" interrupted the striker suddenly at this point.

"Why, tha bain't more nor half so strong as I be; an' measter here he con outlift me wi' one hand."

"Hold thy tongue, Dave," said the big smith.

But the Honourable Billy took up the striker's remark, smiling.

"I'll try a lift with you, Dave," he said, catching up the name from Dankley. "Make your own choice."

The burly striker came forward, grinning, for he felt confident in his own very considerable powers, and had no conception of the muscular body that the Honourable Billy's well-cut clothes veiled so successfully into apparent average bulk.

"Aa'll lift tha' wi' fifty-six pun weights," he said, and brought out two from a recess near the wall. These, after rolling up his sleeves a little higher, he proceeded to lift, one in each hand, over his head, with a clumsy ease, holding them there for a few seconds, and then lowering them again to the ground.

"Theer!" he said, triumphantly. "See if tha con do that?"

The Honourable Billy made no reply in words, but, stepping forward, he pushed the two weights with his foot, until the handles came together. Then, stooping, he caught the two with his right hand, and lifted them with the greatest ease, without any jerk, clean up over his head with the one hand.

There came a little gasp of astonished admiration from the young apprentice, and the striker let out an oath of astounded disappointment, whilst even Dankley showed some surprise.

"Wait a moment," said the Honourable Billy, putting down the weights. He pulled off his coat, and rolling up his right shirtsleeve, displayed an arm that brought forth a second gasp of astonishment and complete admiration from the apprentice, but the sight of which reduced the burly striker to a state of stunned envy.

"Have you another weight the same as these?" asked the Honourable Billy; whereupon the apprentice ran across the smithy, and dragged one out from among some lumber, and placed it beside the two others.

"A piece of rope?" queried the Honourable Billy.

"Here, lad," said the big smith, courteously. And the Honourable Billy found that he had slipped his stout leather belt, and was holding it out to him.

"Thanks," said the Honourable Biliy, and buckled the three weights together. Then, taking the strap by the bight, he snatched the hundred-weight-and-a-half of metal to his shoulder with one hand, and pressed it thence easily to full arm's length above his head.

"Well done, lad! Well done!" said Dankley. "Thou art a strong lad, and no mistake. Go your ways now, an' don't come here again till after the match, lad, or there's them that'll say we had mind to cook summat. Good-arternoon, lad." And he shook hands once more with him. "Us shall see who'm best man on Saturday."

And so the Honourable Billy left him, feeling that, whatever happened, the man he had to fight was a thorough sportsman, and would box clean. But, for all that, he felt that the match would be bound to go to the big smith, if only his ring-craft were as good as rumour told, for the man's tremendous physique and calm, balanced assurance had impressed him very deeply, so that he was somewhat depressed as he pedalled home along the Longsite. This feeling was not eased when he reached his little cottage and found his wife weeping quietly in their combined study and sitting-room, and learned that there bad been two new summonses received by registered post whilst he had been out.

"By the lord," said the Honourable Billy, with tremendous earnestness, "I'll win! You see if I don't."

"Win what, dear?" asked his wife, quickly looking up at him through her tear-stains.

"It's a secret, little woman," said the Honourable Billy; "but I've got hopes of making some money soon. I shall know by Saturday night, and then we'll pay off all these debts and go away for a nice little holiday."

He nodded his head vigorously and patted her arm, but the memory of the gigantic blacksmith made him feel terribly unsure of winning.

"I will!" he said suddenly, aloud. "By the lord, I will!"

"What is it, dear?" asked his wife, looking up at him with a sense of vague fright. "Tell me what you are going to do? Tell me, dear? I'm bothered, and I shall only worry all the more if I don't know. Tell me, dear?"

But the Honourable Billy only gave her a hug, and told her there was nothing at all to worry about.

"I'll tell you on Saturday, dear," he said. "I shall know all about it then." And with that, seeing that he did not wish to say any more, she asked no further.

But she turned it over continually in her mind, with a slight sense of worry that grew, as she thought, putting this fact to that fact. Yet a day or two had passed before she had reasoned to the truth.

The following morning the Honourable Billy was chased into

town by a couple of his creditors, and had fairly to run for it.

"Tha's had a breather!" was Bellett's critical comment as he entered, breathless. "What hasta bin doin'?"

"I'm worried to death with those confounded duns! They're following me everywhere!" said the Honourable Billy. "It's sickening!"

"They can't do nowt," said Bellett, "so as you keep 'em from gettin' into the 'ouse ! They can't gaol you, not till you've bin through th' coort, an' shown contempt o' the order to pay!"

"Is that so?" said the Honourable Billy. "All the same, it's deuced unpleasant; and if I let them come close, and they sling any of their dirty abuse, I shall be plugging them! Then I guess I shall get gaoled quick enough for assault!"

"Tha's reet there, lad!" replied Bellett sympathetically. "Th' judge never shows no mercy on a fightin' man, not so how he've done his best to keep out o' trouble!" He spoke with deep feeling that told much to the Honourable Billy, who remembered Bellett's early attitude to him. "Wot tha's got to do." continued the trainer, "is to lick Blacksmith Dankley, an' thou'll ha' brass an' to spare, lad. But tha mun mind his left, lad; he've a turrible quick left punch!"

"You can bet I'll do my best," said the Honourable Billy quietly, as he drew on his gloves for the bout. "But he's the hardest-looking case I've ever set eyes on, and he runs two stone nine heavier than I, and not an ounce of waste on him!"

"He's older, lad," said Bellett reassuringly, "and he's slower nor thee on 's feet, an' a trifle slower nor thee wi' his punch. But he's a turrible good man, he is that, an' I guess he've the reach o' thee ; an' he'll take more punishment, I'm thinkin', than tha con stand, lad. But thee keep up tha pecker! Tha's a s'prisin' strong lad, an' thee strips as big agin as thee looks i' tha clo'es!"

And with that they began the usual bout.

That night, the fight being on the morrow, Bellett wanted the young man to sleep down at his quarters, for a number of reasons which he stated plainly. But the Honourable Billy declared that his wife would worry if he did not go home, and promised to get to bed early and come down in good time in the morning, so as to escape meeting any of his creditors.

This he did, and got down to the trainer's room without trouble, where Bellett met him, and looked him over with an anxious and critical eye, declaring at the end that he was fit to fight for his life.

"And I need to be, Bellett!" replied the Honourable Billy soberly. "Wait till you see Dankley in the ring!"

"Ay, I knows Dankley!" replied Bellett. "He's a tur'ble good fighter, but I b'lieves tha'lt out un. Tha's quicker an' cleverer nor 'im wi' thy feet; but he's wonnerful clever wi' his 'ands, an' a tur'ble good two-'an-ded fighter. Lucky for thee there's to be no clinchin' an' wrastlin', for Dankley 'ud do thee out i' no time that way, lad; he wou'd that!"

The fight was arranged to begin at three o'clock prompt that afternoon, and at two-thirty Bellett came in to help the Honourable Billy to get into his fighting gear, which consisted of short, loose black drawers, striped at the sides with bright orange silk ribbon, and belted with a light elastic belt of the same colour. On his feet he had light boxing-pumps, with very short-legged socks. Over all he drew on his dressing-gown, and at ten minutes to three he followed Bellett out on to the bowling green, where his appearance was greeted by a loud cheer. For seats had been built up roughly all round the green, and at least three to four thousand people were there, awaiting the great match.

In the ring the Honourable Billy saw that the big smith already waited, dressed in a huge overcoat. He was sitting contentedly in his chair, and seemed entirely without concern or excitement of any kind. Behind him stood his striker and another man, who were evidently to act as his seconds. On his part, the Honourable Billy was seconded by Bellett and—by his own request—big Tom Holden, the lurry-man.

The Honourable Billy climbed into the ring, and the big smith rose and bowed gravely to him, with a curious old-fashioned courtesy that surprised and pleased the Honourable Billy; then re-seated himself, and seemed once more to resume his calm meditation.

"The man's a born gentleman!" muttered the young man. "I've never met a man I could like better!"

The preliminaries were speedily arranged, and a Mr. Ritter, who was to act as referee, inspected the ring.

"One minute!" called the timekeeper. And the two principals rose from their chairs and took off their outer wraps, each looking curiously to learn how the other would "strip."

The blacksmith had his coat off first, and stood revealed in a pair of short, blood-red drawers, buttoned loosely at the knees. He wore a plain leather belt, and had on the regulation pumps.

As he showed himself, a murmur of admiration and astonishment came from the on-looking thousands; for the man was a kind of gaunt Hercules. I mean that, whilst spare of muscular tissue about the wrists, hips, knees, shins, and elbows, he was yet tremendously muscled, in such, a fashion as to suggest that his muscular system consisted of immense masses of muscle, gathered into compact, rugged heaps, and possessing very little taper to the sinews, which seemed to show covered only by the hard, brown skin for half the length of his forearms and lower legs.

The effect was that though enormously muscular, he yet gave to the eye, through his great bony wrists and legs, an impression of gauntness, which was not lessened by the huge, gnarled neck, entirely void of any "grace-flesh" to give it beauty.

"Like a blessed 'orse and a rock rolled into one!" said a man in the crowd; and this certainly expressed somewhat the sense of gaunt but huge strength that the big blacksmith gave.

Very easily the Honourable Billy slipped out of his long dressing-gown, and stood strong and beautiful in the sunlight. Like the enormous blacksmith, he was naked except for his loose black silk running knickers, and the short socks and boxing pumps on his feet. But the difference in the two men was extraordinary.

Where the blacksmith showed the great bones and massive sinews, seeming covered only by the skin, the younger man tapered by beautiful degrees from the working mass of his muscles down to the steel-like tendons into which they blended.

Yet, for all that this beauty of outline was his, there was no mistaking the marvellous development of the torso; of the deltoids of the shoulders; of the great biceps that bunched up grandly as he bent his arms a time or two; and of the huge triceps at the back of the upper arms, that rippled and stood out strangely as he straightened his elbows. Even Dankley nodded in commendation, and reproved his striker calmly for some apparently disparaging remark.

As the younger man had removed his wrap, there had been a murmur from the enormous crowd, which had grown almost instantly to a silence, as they looked him over in an ever-growing wonder of appreciation, that finally burst out into a roar of applause. And through the deep note of the men's voices it was possible to detect the shriller interest of the gentler sex in the young gladiator. And directly the air was full of yellow roses—this being his colour—which were showered into the ring; and which one of the attendants at once proceeded unemotionally to sweep out with a broom.

Dankley, on his part, glanced round at the onlookers with a touch of grim humour, for never a red rose had been thrown. They took the point, and there came a burst of cheers and laughter, and immediately there came a storm of red roses, with renewed cheers and laughter.

As the attendant proceeded to sweep the red roses after the

yellow, the crowd calmed down to an expectant silence and hum of undertalk, in which it was possible to hear odd remarks.

"T' blegsmith 'll out un sure!" the younger man heard one burly local assuring all within his vicinity; and directly afterwards Mr. Jackson's voice delightedly:

"Look at that abdominal development, sir; look at it! No waste weight there!" gleefully punning, and booking bets as fast as he could pencil them down.

"Sunshine trained, by the look of his skin. Looks like a blessed Greek god done in bronze," the Honourable Billy heard a tall, intellectual man remark to a friend; and suddenly realised that they were referring to him.

"Blacksmith Dankley's no beauty, but he's a heap stronger than the young chap," were the last words the Honourable Billy caught; for the next thing he knew the chairs and attendants were out of the ring, and he was shaking hands with the great blacksmith in the centre.

"Now, lad," said the big smith, as they gripped, "it's thee or me. An' God Almighty let the best man win!" he concluded, with a solemnity that was almost a prayer. Then they stepped back, and faced each other with their hands up.

For perhaps five complete seconds the two stood there, making no more movement than two statues of gladiators; the while they looked at each other, and tensioned each his nature to the first act in the rough game. Whilst round about them a tingling silence of suspense and fierce interest held the vast audience almost to breathlessness.

Abruptly the great blacksmith lowered his hands somewhat, and spoke to the Honourable Billy:

"Lead off, lad! Lead off!" he said. "My blood runs slower nor thine."

The Honourable Billy nodded, and stepping in swiftly, flicked Dankley twice on the right cheek with his glove, sufficiently hard to stir the big man's blood to retaliate. Then back out of distance. There came a touch of brightness into the older man's eyes, and a sudden alertness into his shoulders and knees; and the fight had begun.

The Honourable Billy circled swiftly to the right, and the other pivoted easily to cover him; then, like a flash, the young man stepped in. Smash! The Honourable Darrell found himself on his back half a dozen yards away.

He had altogether under-rated the speed of the big man's footwork. He had been thinking of the smith's notorious left, and had not conceived that he would attempt to block him off with his right; for he had edged so much to Dankley's left, that it had not appeared to him a possibility in the time, owing to the smith's method of standing. And, lo! the great blacksmith had pushed up his lead with his enormous wrist like lightning, and punched him off his feet with the right.

He felt like the veriest amateur; shame and pain and sickness all shaking him towards losing his balance to get out of his difficulty; for already the big smith was standing over him, waiting to give the knock-out the instant he should rise.

And somewhere to his left he heard dully, and seemingly at a considerable distance, the monotonous sound of a man counting—"three, four, five." And abruptly it came to him that it was the voice of the referee counting him out. "Six." In another four seconds the fight would be at an end, unless he could rise and avoid the waiting smith, and he would have lost—knocked out of time like some village youth standing up to a professional pug in a travelling boxing-booth.

"Seven." And the money that would be lost by those who had backed him. "Eight." And the creditors and his little wife—their debts, their—His chance to earn the money was almost gone. "Nine!"

His life and his wits came back into him suddenly with a kind of such fierce abruptness that in one instant of time he had passed from the inert, sagging, almost lifeless man upon the floor of the ring into a man almost mad with the fierce determination yet to win; and in that same instant he had bounded to his feet, and with one terrific upper-cut jolted back the big smith's head, following it with a left and right on the body that drove the huge man backwards, almost staggering. All round the ring the young athlete pursued his man, driving in right and left, like a madman, more than a trained boxer, hulling his man time after time, and pasting him severely about the face with three flush hits in succession. For he was in those brief moments almost above himself physically and psychically, with the enormous revulsion from total despair to bright hope; and his blows and his movements were scarcely possible to follow, so utterly swift and vehement were they.

Of course, it is easily understood that, normally, the big blacksmith would never thus have been taken off his guard, but he had so entirely considered his man "done out" that he had relaxed his watchfulness in the last moments of the count, and so had been utterly taken aback when the "miracle" occurred. Yet, though he was thus temporarily at a disadvantage, he was far too clever and practised a boxer to allow his opponent long to have it all his own way, and before many seconds had passed, and whilst still the excited shouting and yelling of the audience at the rally filled the green with sound, the Honourable Billy received a couple of "propping-off" hits that took a lot of steam out of his mad rush, and reduced him to something like sanity and a realisation of where he was and what he was fighting for.

There followed a short passage of cautious work on both sides, for the big smith had received some very punishing blows, and one of the face hits had puffed up the flesh around his left eye, whilst the young man, on his part, was a little distressed and shaken, both by the effects of the primary blow and the combined results of his mad boring of his opponent, and the heavy jolts with which the smith had propped him off.

Time was called, and both men went to their corners, breathing heavily, the smith marked in several places upon his iron-like body, in addition to the puffed-up flesh about his left eye, whilst the Honourable Billy had a great, angry red blotch upon his ribs below his left arm, where he had received the smith's right, in the blow that had so nearly knocked him out. But, apart from this, he had no other marks, though his head was singing a little from one or two half-escaped punches of Dankley's.

"Ee, lad, aa thowt tha' wor done that time, sure!" whispered big Tom Holden, as he helped the young man into his chair and whipped open his towel.

Bellett, however, was grimly silent, doctoring the "punch"; after which, as he plied the sponge, he gave way to terse and pointed comment and advice.

"Tha's geet thyself plugged proper, lad," said Bellett almost fiercely. "Maybe's tha'lt feight now, an' quit foolin'. Dost tha' think Dankley's a fule or a babby? Thee larn thy man afore tha' goes to close feightin', or thee's as good as licked now this moment. Now, mind thee what I says. Use thy feet an' thy brains, if so be as they bain't all addled. Not but you come out of it better than might be," he concluded, with a faint note of encouragement as the call came for seconds out of the ring.

And directly afterwards, "Time!"

The Honourable Billy walked swiftly to the centre of the ring, and faced the big smith, who suddenly took the offensive with a speed of movement truly astonishing in so big a man, for he circled the younger man twice, almost as nimbly as a great cat, and twice managed to get his left home on to the young man's face, owing to his greater reach. Thrice in almost as many seconds the Honourable Billy tempted his opponent by uncovering himself somewhat, and thrice the smith's ponderous fist came almost home, but always a little to the left, so that a swift movement of the head or the feet, as the case might be, carried him into safety; and the third time he countered with his right, making Dankley grunt suddenly.

This was the only blow that he got home that round, and the audience kept a rather disappointed silence as each man walked to his corner, for they considered it to have been rather a tame spell, though the few more knowing ones had followed the game with the most severe appreciation, and clapped warmly a somewhat diminutive applause to the young man.

"Tha's done reet weel, lad!" was Bellett's approving comment. "Aa'm proud of thee, lad! Tha's larnin' tha' man, an' aa con see as tha've foun' summat to help thee."

"Yes," muttered the Honourable Billy, as they tended him with sponge and towel, "he's as quick on his feet as I am, though you said he wasn't, Bellett. But he doesn't hit quite straight. He hits just a trifle to the left always, and also I'm pretty sure his timing's a bit off. I b'lieve I can hit quicker, an' I'll prop him off good if I'm right."

Bellett nodded intelligently, but warned him:

"He've the reach o' thee, lad. Mind what thee's doin'! If tha' mistimes tha' poonch he'll get thee first wi' yon long reach, an' out tha' like a bullock!"

And with this solemn warning there came the cry for seconds out of the ring, and then the call of "Time!"

The big smith was first to the centre of the ring, and met his man with a quick and skilful rush, which showed that he meant to force the fighting. He made the full use of his tremendous reach of arm, and kept the Honourable Billy hard at work on the retreat, trying both to avoid punishment and the ropes. Eventually Dankley got home a powerful left-hand punch that seemed to stagger the younger man, and immediately followed it with a tremendous right-hand swing at the jaw. But the Honourable Darrell was less harmed than he had allowed to appear, and slipped swiftly under the prodigious swing, at the same time driving home his own right with a fierce half-arm jab into the great smith's short ribs that made Dankley gasp suddenly.

On the instant the young man seized his chance, and let out hard with his left at the same place, getting home tremendously, and immediately tried for the point of the big man's jaw as his head came forward. But the great blacksmith was too hard and too clever, and guarded the attack, getting in a couple of quick but clumsy jabs at the Honourable Billy's face that drove the young man out from under his guard, and so evened things somewhat.

From the tremendous audience there came a sharp ripple of clapping hands, and a storm of bravos and party-calls, intermingled with howls of advice to each of the men to go in and finish the other. But this the referee checked, threatening to exercise his powers unless better order and manners prevailed.

Meanwhile, the two men had stood back mutually a moment for a breather, until the disturbance had ended; and now once more advanced, the big smith showing more of care than he had shown hitherto in his battle with the Honourable Darrell. Thrice he feinted at the head, and made as though to come in at the body with his right; and thrice the Honourable Billy "stood off," studying his man. Directly afterwards, the great blacksmith attacked suddenly with stupendous vigour; rushing his man to the ropes with a succession of heavy right and left blows, delivered at short range, and taking the odd punches that the Honourable Billy managed to return as if they were no heavier than slaps.

Yet, the quickness of the younger man on his feet, and his exceptional headwork, saved him at first, and he seemed like breaking away into the open ring; when suddenly the smith dropped his guard, and the young man, unable to resist the temptation, drove a hard, straight left at him, which appeared to be utterly disregarded. For in the same instant, Dankley countered with his right at the body, bashing the Honourable Billy slam into the ropes; and then, stepping into him, he drove in a right and left that the half-sick and dazed man was quite unable to avoid; so that he hung against the ropes, guarding stupidly and almost ineffectually the attack which seemed likely to end the battle quickly.

There was not a sound in all the green, except the dull, heavy thud of the blows, and the gasps of the younger man intermingled with the grunts of the smith as he sent his blows home. And then suddenly across the rather terrible silence there came a shrill scream, and a woman's voice shouting: "Stop! Stop! Stop!"

The voice seemed to pierce to the young man's senses, and he made a desperate attempt to rally; forcing himself up from the ropes, and striking out with a kind of wild hopelessness at the great blacksmith, who gave way calmly a pace, and hit him wherever he wanted.

From the surrounding people there came a curious murmur, through which pierced again the scream and the cry of: "Stop! Stop! Stop!" in a woman's voice. The murmur rose into a roar of remonstrance, through which ran a sharp peal of hand-clapping that grew louder and louder. The green was full of an excited shouting, and then came the woman's voice again, dimly through the enormous uproar.

On the Honourable Billy it seemed to produce an extraordinary effect. He appeared literally to galvanise into life and control of his forces. He slipped a tremendous right-handed drive of the smith's, and countered on the big man's jaw with his left. The blacksmith replied with a sharp, fierce rally of blows, and came into half-arm fighting, hitting the Honourable Billy once almost off his feet. The young man circled swiftly to the right, keeping out of distance, and Dankley followed him with a heavy left-hand drive, which the Honourable Billy slipped his head under, and immediately got home a heavy half-arm blow on the blacksmith's ribs, making him reel.

In the same instant the uproar outside of the ring was redoubled. There came a flash of skirts across the ring, and a little woman, exceeding white of face, darted between the two men, just as the cry of "Time!" came sharply. She sprang at the great smith, and set two diminutive hands against his massive chest, pushing him back fiercely. "Stop! Stop! Stop!" she kept reiterating, in a voice that was scarcely above a tense whisper of sound. "Stop! Stop! Stop! You shall not! You shall not! Oh, tha sha'n't! Tha sha'n't, tha gre't brute!" she ended in broad Lancashire, and burst into fierce crying; but ceased not to push the brawny smith backwards.

"Mary!" shouted the Honourable Billy, and leapt forward. "Mary—"

Whatever he might have said more was lost in the enormous babel of sound without the ring. Hoarse roars of anger at the interruption, constant pounding of benches, cat-calls, and through all the shrill, insistent sound of the referee's whistle, calling for order.

But for the moment order was an impossibility. Hundreds of people had left their seats, and were invading the ring, some to inquire what it all meant, some to protest angrily at the interruption, some to declare that the Honourable Billy's little wife was right, and that the fight should go no further. And the diminutive cause of it all was sobbing her heart out in the Honourable Billy's arms, whilst the giant blacksmith stood by, and patted one of her hands with one of his enormous palms.

Gradually the audience were got in hand again, and persuaded or hustled—as the case might be—back to their seats, whilst the referee informed them in pointed words that he would stop the fight unless perfect order were kept.

He then turned to the occupants of the ring, and held a short discussion—not only with the promoters, who had now entered the ring, but with the principals themselves—the end of which was that it was resolved that the fight must go forward either to the full twenty rounds agreed upon, or else to a knock-out.

The only dissentient was the Honourable Mrs. William Darrell, alias Mary, who declared with a white and determined little face, and a nose that was not unbecomingly red, that she would not leave the ring without her husband, and that, if she had but learned earlier of the fight, it should never have been allowed to commence.

At this unexpected obstacle—and a very determined and vital one it was likely to prove in the circumstances—the promoters looked somewhat blankly at one another, whilst the timekeeper and referee conferred with one another. All recognised the peculiar delicacy of the situation, in that the lady was the wife of one of the principals; so that no one dared voice the only obvious solution of the puzzle, which was to gently but firmly remove the diminutive obstruction. Meanwhile, the great smith set the case out to the Honourable Mrs. William Darrell.

"Nay, lass," he said. " 'Tis but a game, when all be said. Thee go home, like a wise lass, an' 'twill soon be over belike; an' thy lad maybe the winner, if thou leave him easy minded."

But Mary was deaf to the big man's earnest advice, and clung, white-faced and determined, to her husband, who, after a little time of careful thought, told her that it was his wish, and all for the best, that the fight should continue, and that he wished for her to put no difficulty in the way.

For some minutes he argued with her, pointing out that the match must be concluded; that, apart from the prize which he hoped to win, there was a great deal of money hanging on the event; and that it must simply go forward, whatever their own private feelings might be.

And this way, and just as the big audience was beginning to stamp with impatience, and clap encouragement, she consented, and allowed Mr. Jackson to lead her from the ring. She kept a brave face, and turned once to wave encouragement to her young husband, at which the audience cheered her, but as soon as she was well away, she burst into hopeless crying, that sorely disturbed the businesslike Mr. Jackson, who gave much pointless and disturbed comfort, assuring her constantly that her husband would win, as surely as his own name was Mr. Jackson. And it was with this final assurance echoing in her ears that he left her in one of the private rooms of the Black Anchor, where she sobbed hopelessly a while, until, suddenly, she discovered that on the couch opposite there reposed nothing less than the Honourable Billy's everyday clothes, this being the very room which he had used as a dressing-room.

She dried her eyes, and going over to the pile of garments, began tenderly but methodically to fold them; in the midst of which occupation she was suddenly disturbed by a storm of cheering, quite close at hand. She ran to the window and discovered with a vast shock that it looked right down on to the green; and that she was actually but a short distance from the fight. She stared in a sort of fearful fascination, and saw to her horror that her husband lay flat in the ring, with the great smith standing over him, ready to strike, whilst near at hand was another man, who seemed to be saying something as he stooped over her husband.

In a very agony of distress, she threw up the window, and thrust her head and shoulders out. She heard the man's voice now; he was counting—"seven—eight—ni—" She did not hear the end of the count, for suddenly her husband's still figure came to life, and dashed up at the great smith.

She saw the big man strike at her husband twice, and miss him; then again, and knock him staggering across the ring. She saw the smith leap at the staggering man, and strike a tremendous blow, but her husband ducked his head with strange quickness, and the next instant there came the dull thud of a blow, and she saw the big smith sag in suddenly at the waist, and her husband, close up to him now, standing, and hitting with both hands. There was a tremendous roar of hoarse shouting from the audience, and fierce cries of both execration and applause; and suddenly she commenced to dance up and down, with clenched hands, and fierce, bright eyes, and shout: "Hit him, Billy! Hit him! Hit him, Billy! The great brute! Hit him! Oh, kill him!"

She saw the great smith strike a wild blow, and saw her husband knocked backward a couple of paces; she screamed fiercely again to her husband, amid the noise of the shouting, to play the executioner. She saw her husband leap forward, as the smith struck at him again; they seemed to strike together, but surely the Honourable Billy must have timed his blow a hundredth part of a second earlier than Dankley's, for the blacksmith's grizzled head went upward, sharply, and he lurched backward, splaying his arms, and so came with a dull thump to the floor of the ring.

Mary stared out, wide-eyed now, though her fists were still clenched intensely. She saw her husband spring forward, and stand ready, near to the fallen man, saw the other man (the referee) stoop towards the fallen smith, watch in hand, counting. As in a dream she heard the count mounting up—"seven—eight—" Still the man upon the floor of the ring never stirred, and still her husband kept his tense attitude of watchfulness. "Nine"—and absolute silence from the audience, broken suddenly by a fierce shouting of "Get up! Get up, man! Get up!" "Ten!"

The match was won, and her husband had won the match. At first, Mary Darrell did not realise that the fight was ended, but when she saw her husband being clapped on the back by every man who could get near to him, and saw Mr. Jackson pump-handling one of his gloved hands excitedly, whilst Bellett, the trainer did likewise with the other, she came out of her dream, and stood there in the window, white and silent, and extraordinarily proud of her man, who had beaten the enormous smith.

But when the Honourable William Darrell came into the room presently to dress, he found his diminutive wife mechanically folding and refolding his garments, blindly, whilst she wept, utterly unstrung. The men who had followed him to his dressing-room, gave back and left them when they saw that his wife was there, and the Honourable Billy caught her into his arms;

"It's all over, little woman," he assured her, "and we can pay every penny we owe, and I'm all right, lassie; look up, look up, and see for yourself. It's all over and done with, dear."

"I—I know" whispered Mary, looking up at him through her tears, and fumbling for her handkerchief. "I—I saw. I wanted you to kill him—the great, horrible brute, hitting you like that!"

The Honourable William Darrell roared, though with somewhat painful laughter, for his features were more than a little tender and swollen, owing to the force of the big smith's punches. His body also was badly bruised in places, where Dankley's immense blows had got home; and as Mary dried her eyes, and was able to see with more clearness, her indignation broke out afresh. Yet, presently, being a thoroughly sensible little woman, she admitted that it was not fair to blame Dankley.

"But, oh! I'm so glad you knocked him down, too!" she said.

"What a bloodthirsty young madam I've married," said the Honourable Billy. "But I'll admit I'm jolly glad, too. You see, what you describe, dear, as a knock-down, was really a knock-out, and by that same knockout, all our debts are paid, and there'll be money in the bank as well. Now dance, you war-like fairy!" And with that, and part-dressed as he was, he insisted on waltzing gravely round the room with her, after which he resumed his clothes and sedateness together, and so hastened out to inquire after the well-being of the great blacksmith.

He found him dressed, and apparently very little the worse for his knock-out, for he rose at once to shake hands quietly with the young man.

"I'm proud, lad, to ha' foughten wi' thee," he said gravely. "The god o' battles ha' seen fit for thee to win, yet 'twas thy fight an' my fight, lad, while it lasted. But thou art a strong and clever lad, an' better for thy years I never saw, an' proud am I to own it, an' to give thee credit and wish thee God's luck.

"And to thee, lass," he added, stepping forward to Mary Darrell, "I give thee my respect, an' may God bless thee an' thy lad through the years; and see thou stand strong for him always, lass, in the trouble of life, as to-day in the game that is now done, and thou do likewise wi' her, lad."

And with that, he patted each of them seriously upon the shoulder, as though he gave them a blessing. And afterwards called to his striker, and the two of them went home, and so passed out of this tale.

Perhaps one of the Honourable Billy's greatest surprises of that day came to him as he was making a slow way through the immense crowd of his newly won admirers, with his wife upon his arm. For, suddenly, a big, dishevelled-looking man came scrambling and shouting huskily through the crowd, and stopped before the Honourable Billy. He had no hat on, and his face was all bandaged up.

"Hey!" he said, rubbing two great, red hands, with a kind of excited humility, " I ha' coom to beg thy pardon, Mr. Darrell, an' thy missus's. Tha'rt greatest boxer Aa've ever seed, Mr. Darrell, an' Aa'm proud to think tha have poonched my head wi' thy own hands, an' I ax thy pardon humbly for all as I said."

"Yes," said Mary Darrell, answering for her husband. "We forgive you, Mr. Jenkins, but you ought to be ashamed of yourself. We shall pay you every farthing we owe you, and perhaps you'll learn to know honest people when you meet them. You were a horrible man that day!"

"I am fair 'shamed, missus," said the big grocer awkwardly. "But Mr. Darrell gave me what for"—and he pointed to his bandages—"an' I'm coom now to beg pardon—"

"That's all right, Jenkins," interrupted the Honourable Billy, and delighted the grocer and made him his friend for life by warmly shaking one of his big red hands, there, in token of amity, before the onlookers.

I will take this opportunity to tell that within three days the Honourable Billy and his wife owed not a farthing to anyone, and could have had credit unlimited only that this was against the Honourable Mrs. William Darrell's ideas.

The Getting Even of "Parson" Guyles

I

"IS MR. MAGEE IN?" shouted a burly, thick-necked, very self-assured looking man.

The self-assured looking man rapped heavily with his stick on the counter of the small book shop, as he shouted; and at the same moment a door opened noiselessly, away among the shadows, at the back of the shop.

A lean, grim face, with clean-shaven mouth, and wearing a grey goatee, Dundrearys and blue glasses, stared out from the shadows.

"Is Mr. Magee in, confound your rotten business ways!" shouted the burly man. And beat angrily again upon the counter.

The man who owned the grim, clean-shaven mouth, came forward, with a curiously noiseless step, out of the darkness that lay in the back portion of the long, narrow shop.

"I'm Mr. Magee," he said, quietly. "Ye'll kindly stop that sort of noise in my shop."

"My time's money," said the stout man. "I can't wait all day in a hole like this, while you play dominoes in the back parlour. I don't wonder your business is rotten. Your methods are rotten. And I consider the offer I have to make you is far above the mark. I'm the agent for Mr. James Henshaw. I've been instructed to offer you £50 for your business, and your stock at valuation. If you like to take £100 down and clear out this week-end, I'll give you a cheque now, and you can sign this agreement."

The stout Agent drew a foolscap envelope from his pocket; but Mr. Andrew Magee intervened.

"The door, Sir," he said, quietly, "is to your left. I'll thank you to be going now."

"You mean," said the Agent, "that you'll fight, like a lot of other silly fools have tried to do. You know what that'll mean; we are opening a thirty yard frontage right next door to this hole of yours. Your potty business'll be dead in a fortnight. It's a present I'm offering you; that's what it is."

Mr. Andrew Magee came round the counter. He was tall, and had a lean, hard figure. He touched the other man on the elbow.

"The door, Sir," he remarked, gently, "is to your left—"

"Be damned to you and your door!" roared the Agent. "You smug, ignorant, unbusinesslike fool. Take my offer, or out of this hole we'll have you in a couple of weeks."

"I allow no man to call me that, Sir," said Mr. Andrew Magee, as he hit the Agent hard and solid on the side of the jaw. "That's not to give you the dope," he said; "but to teach you to mend your manners. Out of my shop!"

The last four words came with a queer metallic-sounding rip of cold passion, that somehow fitted well the grimness of face and figure of Mr. Magee. And the Agent stayed for no further argument. He rose, staggering; gripped the side of his fleshy jaw, and ran wordless out of the shop.

"Damn a' bloodsuckers an' them as useth their power to oppress!" said Mr. Magee, solemnly, as he stood by the counter. "Am I never to live honest, or must the sins of my youth wither always the chances of my age?"

Such phrases as these may be better understood when we realise that Mr. Andrew Magee's proper name was Andrew McGuyles, and that in his young manhood he had been a Presbyterian minister, and had never, despite his deviations from the "narrow path," ceased to have a deep feeling for all matters of religion. Many a time, had he fought to gain back to an honest life, and each time he had fallen, either when his own particular "devil" entered him, or because, as now threatened, the Fates were minded to deal him one more unkindly clout of misfortune.

"Professionally," Mr. Andrew Magee, or McGuyles, was known always as either "The Parson" or "Parson" Guyles. The title was a respected one on both sides of the water; for a cleverer safe-blower (i.e., safe-breaker) there had never been in either country.

II

The Agent was quite right, in the main, when he said they would run the "Parson" out of his shop, in quick time.

The Agent, and Millionaire James Henshaw (who had made his first money by curious methods on the other side, and was now increasing it by methods equally undesirable) had a few words about the dour

Scotsman, whose premises they wished to annex.

"Yes," said Millionaire Henshaw, when the Agent had told his story. "Run him out. Make an example of him, by all means. We can't let that sort of thing pass. We've got to put the fear of God into them, and then buy 'em out at skim-milk prices."

Parson Guyles did not get even a "skim-milk" price. He was ruined utterly within three months, by being totally undersold, until he did not have half a dozen customers into his little dark shop in a day.

The hour in which he put his shutters up for the last time over the little window, would have been a bad time for the Millionaire or his Agent to have met him. However, he had a little money saved, and he disappeared quietly, having paid all his debts; for Parson Guyles, when he was living honestly, lived honestly, because of the grim Puritan blood that was in him.

III

When Parson Guyles at any time ceased to be found at any address known to the Profession, it was generally concluded among his expert friends that "the Parson was on the honest lay again," and no attempt would be made to discover his whereabouts, until he chose to re-discover himself. Perhaps this consideration for what many of them must have regarded as nothing more than a recurrent peculiarity of the Parson's, may have been partly prompted by the complete and efficient unpleasantness that followed upon any intrusion, by his expert acquaintances, into what might be termed his "hours of honesty."

But now, three months after he had put up the shutters in the little book shop, the Parson appeared once more among people who knew and appreciated him for his record of "work accomplished"; and because of this, accorded him a welcome, that had in it a respect that rose above any criticism of his peculiar instincts for, and lapses into, what our spiritual advisers term the Narrow Path.

During the months which lay between the closing of the little shop and Parson Guyles' re-appearance, he must have put in a great deal of professional work, in the way of expert Inspection of Premises; for when he convened a meeting of three (John Vardon, engineer; Sandy Mech, expert "spade and shovel" man, and himself) the proposition he had to lay before the meeting, backed up by the very exact and appropriate information that he had to offer on all needful or disputable points, produced amazing, though professionally subdued, enthusiasm.

"You are sure the limit of Eternal Wonder, Parson," said Sandy

Mech. "Count me and J. V. in to the last snuffing. I reckon the Almighty—"

"We'll ha' na talk of the A'michty," interrupted Parson Guyles, sternly. "There's just John Vardon and you and me an' the De'il in this; not to mention yon Millionaire hog. The A'michty, I pray, will no interfere, an' that's as much as ma conscience can hope."

IV

"This is going to be a longish job, ye'll understand" said the Parson, as they stood, together, in the cellar of a house across the street from the big Emporium, which had extended until all vestige of the shop of one, Andrew Magee, had vanished.

There were a number of interesting parcels stacked upon the cellar floor, and John Vardon proceeded to unpack one of the longer packages.

John Vardon had been, as lately as the past year, a highly respected Consulting Engineer; but was now discredited, owing, to his connection with that unpleasant little affair of the Go-a-gath mines in West California. He unpacked the parcel and produced the component parts of a folding table, which he proceeded to erect. There followed further unpackings, which produced several instruments of a design familiar to mining engineers. He effected what I might term a conjunction of parts, and began to adjust the instruments.

Meanwhile, the Parson had lit up a distinctly spirited "glow" lamp, by tapping the main wire, with a confidence that would have appalled a municipal expert, and a skill that would have bewildered the head Practical Electrician of a private wiring firm.

Then the Parson and Sandy Mech began to unpack and lay out the contents of the other parcels; and while Sandy Mech gloated over ingenious little digging tools, that possessed surprising little nickel connections for electrical wiring, the Parson pored, with a grimmer appreciation, over sundries of a kind unknown outside of his own craft, and to few even who were of it.

John Vardon was busy now with a tracing of a municipal street-plan, the obtaining of which had been due to night work on the part of the Parson.

The rent of the basement in which the cellar was situated, had cost the Parson no less than £30 of his hardly saved money; this sum being three months' "advance," demanded by the City, Land and Estate agents, in the usual course.

It was impossible to occupy the basement, without some sufficient business pretext to prevent suspicions; and the Parson boldly made use of his old trade name of Andrew Magee, Bookseller, which he had painted along the "sunk" windows, in black, backed in by a light cream, which would not keep out too much daylight; yet rendered the whole premises safe from the prying of any over-curious persons.

He was able without difficulty to obtain sufficient stock on credit, owing to his having paid all his previous bills; though now, being on other Paths than those of honesty, he had not the least intention of paying.

In this way, he was able to cover securely all doubtful signs; for it was merely apparent that Andrew Magee had obtained financial backing somehow, and returned to do further battle with the huge Emporium of all stores (including books and stationery), opposite. And this, after all, is a perfectly correct description of his intention!

The tunnel under the road was commenced that night, the walls of the cellar being pierced after about two hours' work. There followed six feet of soil, and then eight feet of earth packed so hard that it was like some patent composition.

Four days, and the early portion of each night, they excavated, with Sandy Mech very earthy and damp and in his element, as he handled his pet midget drills. They did not work after the streets became still, lest the vibration of their machine should be conveyed through the earth, sufficiently to become apparent to any constable or passer-by. Moreover, the work was going forward at a speed that would enable them easily, unless something quite unexpected happened, to reach the strong-room by the eighteenth of the month. This was the date the Parson had fixed for entering the Millionaire's new strong-room, which was of the latest model, and had been elaborately and incorrectly described at great length in a score of popular journals.

The earth from the tunnel was stored in the empty rooms of the basement, which were kept locked. The sub-underground shop was very little patronised, luckily, as the Parson observed, for the wholesale book people, and this enabled Parson Guyles frequently to slip into the cellar, where he worked at carrying out the loose earth; having fixed up a temporary electric bell to warn him if anyone entered the shop.

He found it undesirable, however, to leave the shop unattended; for one day, on hearing the bell ring, he went in, to find a big constable in uniform waiting impatiently.

"You won't get no trade here, if you keeps everybody waiting half the day like this," said the big policeman. "I want a re-fill for this pocket book. I nearly went opposite, only I thought I'd patronise you; you had a shop t'other side, didn't you?"

"Yes," said Andrew Magee, tersely. "Here's your re-fill. Sixpence ha'penny, please."

"Why, I gets 'em for four an' a half, opposite!" said the policeman, aggrieved.

"Maybe," said the Parson. "But they're only straw-paper, and they ha' twenty-five leaves less in each book. Maybe, if you learnt to keep your eyes open, which I've a notion is your trade, you'd be a better policeman. You ha' na room to teach me my trade, I'm thinkin'!"

The policeman paid, grumbling, and went out.

"I don't want your sort in here," said Andrew Magee, to himself. "And I reckon you'll ha' no mind to come here at that price again! All the same, maybe, it was pryin' you were after; and I'll leave the shop no more in hours."

V

"That," said John Vardon to the Parson, on the fifth day of their work, "is the gas main." He touched with his thumb the edge of a great round of iron, that was visible through the clayey earth in the top of the tunnel. "I've run the drift straight, so the blessed main's sunk a bit. There's gravel showing here, and we'll have to line her, I'm afraid. There's been some proper municipal work in the laying of this tin pipe!"

VI

"I reckon we're across. I'm up against the wall!" said Sandy Mech, coming out of the tunnel on the evening of the eleventh day.

Five hours later, they were through the wall, and within the foundation of Millionaire Henshaw's huge Emporium.

"Six yards and twenty-seven inches more, including one division wall, and we'll be up against the strong-room," said John Vardon, after a further careful series of measurements on a tracing of the builders' secret plans of the situation of the strong-room, which tracing was, like the others, also a product of the Parson's skill in eluding those mechanical difficulties, which are presumed to ensure doors remaining closed to strangers.

VII

"We're there," said Sandy Mech's voice, in hoarse excitement, as he came out into the cellar on the afternoon of the fifteenth day. "It's cement outside. And I s'pose there'll be that everlastin' crossed railway iron to go through. How I do hate the fool as started that idee!"

"There's worse, lad," said Parson Guyles. "This is nigh the latest, and they got Anson's net wirin', running right through the cement; and the current's on all the twenty-four hours, and it's a six-inch mesh. If we snick a single wire either way, the bells in all the Police Stations for a mile round will be ringing. How would you go through that, lad?"

"Lordy!" said Sandy Mech. "Each man to his own job, Parson. I guess you'll manage. You're a holy wonder."

"I'm a mighty sinful man," said Parson Guyies, sombrely.

VIII

"The wire's laid just under a skin of the cement" said the Parson, about 11 p.m. that night; for the actual work of breaching the strong-room could not be attempted in the daytime. He fingered the stark, grey surface of cement, where the tunnel ended. "It lies in a hollow, between the main wall of the room and my finger. Hark to the hollow sound of this!" And he tapped it with a small, beautifully shaped pick-hammer, no more than two ounces in weight, that shone like silver.

With swift, light strokes of marvellous judgment and skill, he picked an oblong hole clean through the outer cement-skin, which proved to be one inch thick.

"This," muttered the Parson, as he inserted an investigating finger, "is where a rash man would spoil himsel' and ha' the constables swarming round before he knew what might be wrong—" He broke off short, and stared at Sandy Mech, as if suddenly stirred by some other thought.

"I wonder now if yon fat constable had a notion of ought," he said, pondering.

"Eh?" asked Sandy Mech, startled by the mention of so unpleasing a name. "What cop?"

But Parson Guyles merely shrugged his shoulders. "Just a notion of mine, laddie," he said. He knew Sandy Mech's cautious nature too well to explain. He had never mentioned the incident to either Vardon or Mech of the constable's brief and untimely patronage, Vardon might not have troubled unduly; but Sandy Mech was as shy as a rabbit. Perhaps his burrowing propensities had something to do with his nervous traits.

"The K wrench," said the Parson, a few seconds later. This instrument, which was made of nickel steel, and possessed extraordinarily thin jaws, covered with gutta-percha, he slipped carefully into the hole he had picked, and proceeded to break away the shell of cement. He worked with an infinite care, that showed how great he considered the risk; and presently he had laid bare a complete network of insulated wire.

"Now," said Parson Guyles, "I'll ha' yon insulation pliers an' the coil of wire. I've a real respec' for yon Anson; for it's a pretty arrangement; but the wiring should ha' been friction-spliced, an' the splices supported in the outer skin; then it would ha' been a mighty hard thing to peel away the skin, without breakin' the circuit. But he's a smart lad, is Anson, and maybe I'll give him a point or two, that'll help him to improvements. . . . Cut me a couple dozen four-foot lengths off the coil, an' peel the ends ready, Sandy, lad."

While he talked, the Parson had been working. He had removed the insulation, for a space of several inches from the lowest of the horizontal wires, and now he took a length of wire from Sandy Mech, and twisted the two bare copper ends firmly round the cleaned portion of the horizontal wire, about an inch apart. Then, with a pair of pliers, he cut the horizontal wire clean through, in the inch between the two twisted-on ends of the loop of wire.

"G' Lord! Parson!" said Sandy Mech, as Parson Guyles cut the wire. "You've sure done it now!"

"Na, lad," said the Parson, "you're a good spade and shovel man; but ye're na good at this work, I'm thinkin'! Have ye no the brains to see that yon loop of wire carries, the current from one cut end to the other. I've but lengthened the wire a wee, to give us room to put our sinful bodies through."

"If you know it's right, Parson, I'm satisfied," said Sandy, in a doubtful voice; and continued to cut lengths of wire.

Two hours later, Parson Guyles, having treated the rest of the network in similar fashion, commenced work upon the inner wall of cement.

IX

"For men wanting cash as we do, I reckon you'll say this is the finger of Providence, Parson," said Sandy Mech, three nights later, as he peered through the breach into the strong-room, on the night of the eighteenth.

"There's na finger of Providence about this, my lad," said Parson Guyles, who already stood within the strong-room. "That I ha' left the straight path, ye ken well; but I spread na honey! This is the finger o' the de'il; and if I hope to make a wee profit from the pointing thereof, I hope also to keep my brain clear to ken Satan when I see him!"

Sandy Mech grinned back silently at John Vardon, who was peering in over his shoulder. They were careful, in the main, not to "touch the Parson up" on this side of him; for he was too rough a fighter to provoke unnecessarily; and on religious subjects he was easily provoked.

"There's nothing now to stop us, but the inner circuits. They've altered them since the room was first wired, as I could see by the notes on the plan margins," said the Parson. "I couldna just put my finger on the plan of the new co-ordination; and I'll ha' to be careful, laddies, or we shall touch off one of the spring connections, and there'll be half the officers in the City round this block, before you can whistle."

"I don't like that, Parson," said Sandy Mech, in a rather grim voice. "I'd a notion you said you knowed the wirings; an' . . ."

"The old wiring, Sandy," said the Parson, smiling curiously. "The old wiring, lad. Maybe I misled you a wee; for I had need of help to get even with mine enemy; and maybe cautious Sandy Mech might ha' held back if he'd thought it wasna all cut an' dried—eh, lad?"

"Stow it!" said Mech. "Once I sees the cash winkin' up at me like this, I don't go back, not this side chokee—"

"That's how I read you, laddie," interpolated Parson Guyles, mildly.

"All the same, Parson," went on Sandy Mech, with growing wrath, "for a religious man, you ain't careful if you speaks God's trewth, or if you lies like a blame trooper; and I don't mind tellin' you so, straight,"

"You son o' the de'il—" began Parson Guyles, furiously; but John Vardon chipped in quickly.

"Drop it, for all sakes!" he said. "We're not going to mug things now by rowing like a lot of 'new pups.' Drop it, and let's get to work. I'll bet the Parson has a good notion how the new wiring is likely to be co-ordinated. He's just making you hotter than you need be!"

"You're a wise man, Vardon, in your generation," said the Parson, calming. "Put your gloves on, the two of ye, and hand me mine, and the big dividers. Then you can come in, both of you; and remember the two of ye have as much grease paint on your faces as would do for a puir de'il of an actress wench; so keep your gloves off it, or you'll smear it."

"Why ain't you made up, Parson?" asked Sandy Mech, as he began to put on a pair of good quality black kid gloves. "You need to be disguised more than me or John 'ere."

"You're a bit of a fool, Sandy, not to think before you speak; though I'm doubtin' then if ye'd ever speak at all!" said Parson Guyles, as he took his own pair from Sandy Mech. "First, ha' anyone here, or even you two ever seen my natcheral face? Don't the people round here know me as Andrew Magee! And ha' ye no' brains to see it's Andrew

Magee they'll look for! Don't they know I'm the one that took on the basement we've driven the tunnel from; not to mention the officer that came in the other night, and made belief he wanted a re-fill! Lord, I wonder if he did come in honest, or to pry?"

"What!" said the two others; both startled.

The Parson explained.

"I said nothing to the two o' ye," he continued. "What was the use of givin' you the jumps when the work had to be done. And anyway, I never notioned till to-night that he came in on the sneak; but I'm wondering now. I've got the feel in ma blood to-night that maybe yon man had designs. I'll say na mair. But if you're wantin' to go now, why I'll never stop ye."

"Now!" said both men, as one.

"Why you old—" began Sandy Mech.

"Cut it out, laddies," said Parson Guyles, cheerfully. "I'm a short tempered man, as ye ken" (the Parson grew more Scottish, as he indulged his vein). "An hour mair, if ye've the pluck o' white mice, an' ye're rich for all ye'r sinful evil lives; not but ye'll both be as poor as foolish babes a month hence. There's John Vardon now, the lusts o' the flesh, John Vardon, are the ruination of ye. The——"

"Good Lord! he's going to preach!" said Sandy Mech. "Stow it, Parson. We're with you into hell and out again. 'Ere's them dividers."

The Parson took them from him, without a word; and Sandy never knew how near he was to Eternity in that one instant; for the dividers were of steel, and heavy, and in every way adequate for so unpleasant a purpose. But John Vardon saw, and understood.

"Sandy!" he said, "shut your silly mouth. The Parson is right. We're both a pair of fools. . . . I tell you what, Parson, if I get the whack I'm looking for out of this, I'll cut the crook, and go away somewhere and live straight. I will, by the Lord, I will."

Parson Guyles' eyes gleamed with a strange and wonderful light.

"God grant it, lad," he said, with a sudden uncovering of the hidden cravings of his nature. "I wad die easier to think there had some good come out o' my sinfu' life. I haud ye to ye'r word, John Vardon, on the honour of all that you once were."

"I give you my word, Parson," said John Vardon, with perfect sincerity. "I've been a fool once; but if this comes right and we get what you think is coming to us, I'll leave England this week—"

"Not you, John!" interrupted Mech. "I've felt that way, when I first started in the perfession. It's just nerves; not funk, mind you, John; but nerves. It'll go when you handle your share of the oof."

"Sandy Mech," said Parson Guyles, in a fierce but quiet voice, "say one word mair of your de'il's talk, an' I'll wring your neck, as Samuel hewed Agag in pieces before the Lord."

And Mech, impudent, sturdy irresponsible Sandy Mech, held his tongue; for even he knew better than to cross the Parson further in that mood. But John Vardon said nothing. He fidgeted a moment or two with his gloves; and seemed as if he might be vaguely ashamed because the better side of him had so unexpectedly answered to the bizarre cry of the "lost shepherd" (bizarre because of its very sincerity) to a lost sheep.

"Come in, both of you, an' stan' by the wall, out o' my way," said the Parson.

The strong-room was different from any that John Vardon had seen, in his brief experience of the Profession; and even Sandy Mech had never seen the same inner arrangements; for the prodigious wealth was simply and neatly packed into steel trays, arranged along the floor in rows, with nothing between it and their hands, but the low steel-latticed covers, locked down with invisible locks to the floor.

Overhead, burned an electric light, and showed plainly the notes, bonds, or gold, as the case might be, in their respective numbered trays. It seemed to the two onlookers that they had nothing to do but burst the thin steel lattice-work with a crowbar, and fill their bags; but the Parson's casual remarks, showed just why the money was so stored, and the reasoning upon which it was considered safe:—

"Yon's a pretty arrangement," he said, as he spread out the plan of the old wiring, on the floor of the strong-room. "That's McLegg's invention—the idea of the 'meat-covers.' It's good points, as ye'll see. You'll perceive that a bank offecial can assure himself that things is right, without having to unlock aught; at the same time there can be na temptation to casual, honest-men's pickin' an' stealin', as you might say, on the part of any lesser offecials that ha' their occasional duties in here. . . . That was McLegg's way of looking at it. A countryman of mine, laddies, and clever; for the meat-covers are apt to trick the unwary. Henry Gably, a fair safe-blower too, was put away for a ten year spell only last month, through that same invention. He'd a notion to ha' the contents of the big Utrecht Bank, out Tallwar way. He got in through the roof; quieted the watchmen, an' made na bones about it, but just dynamited a breach clean through the wall o' the gold room. By the de'il's own luck, he wasna killed nor heard; but they had this same idea o' McLegg's inside the room, an' he thought, foolish lad, he'd naught to do, but rip the meat-covers open, an' fill his bags.

"Well, before he'd ripped off the second, the officers were mobilising, as you might say, from all round the district; for you can't touch these little grids, unless ye know the co-ordination of the wiring, without ringing up the police; and that's just the tricksiness of the notion; for they tempt a man to be done wi' fine work, and just rip them open."

Parson Guyles took the long dividers, and "set" them carefully; then he placed one point of the instrument right into the angle of the West corner of the room, and drew a segment of a circle across the corner, from wall to wall, at full radius. He did the same in the East corner; then, at each place where the segments of the circles touched the walls, he pressed a sprig into the soft rubber tiling which covered the floor. From the sprigs, he stretched two thin lines, across the room, between the rows of cages; then, with his dividers, he straddled along each of the lines, making a chalk mark at each place where the points touched.

With a knife, he cut a square clean out of the rubber tiling, round each of the chalk marks. He took a case of marvellously finished tools from his pocket, also a large horseshoe-magnet. He pressed the horseshoe-magnet against the steel floor; and lifted out of its slot in the floor, a beautifully fitting "invisible" metal plate.

"I thought so," said Parson Guyles, as he examined the terminals of the wiring, which had been so cunningly hidden under the metal cover. He went round to each of the openings in the rubber, and did the same; then he took a pair of pliers from his case, and began work upon the wiring.

"I darena cut them; for they run the main through this wiring at nights," he explained. "And the night-lights upstairs would fluff out, laddies, if I were to cut, and that would trouble the officer outside. Aye! it's a bonnie brain that thought this out."

He worked at the terminals for half an hour, crossing from opening to opening.

"I ha' small doubts but I ha' replaced the old coordination," he said, at last, standing up and stretching himself.

There were thirteen of the flat lattice cages on the floor of the room, and Parson Guyles pulled out his purse. He opened it, and took from it a bunch of minute slips of bright metal, curiously notched.

"I made these from rubbings of the firm's triplicates, when I took the chart-tracings," he said. "The whole thirteen keys are here. Aye! I put in a deal of labour to the success of this night's work!"

"You're a holy wonder, Parson!" said Sandy Mech, from where he stood, waiting by the wall. "Every man to his own job. I reckon

Providence meant you for a safe-buster, Parson."

John Vardon nudged the enthusiastic "spade and shovel" man, to be silent; but the Parson took no bitter offence.

"The ways o' the A'michty are strange an' wonderful, Sandy," he said, with a kind of sadness in his voice. "I ha' foughten oft against my weakness; but the natcheral evil that is in me, an' the bitterness o' man in general, ha' turned my feet always into the downward path. . . ." He paused, examining the keys thoughtfully. "But the desire to do battle wi' the evil that is in me, dies not, laddie, an' maybe one day I shall triumph, an' live the life I wad best like. Oh, aye, the life I wad best like. Aye me ! . . . Now," he continued, changing suddenly, "by the old co-ordination, that I trust I ha' replaced truly, the covers can only be unlocked in the following way:—To open Number 1, I must unlock Number 10 and Number 3; then return to Number 1 and lift it open; but if I attempt to open either 10 or 3, after I've unlocked them, it sets off the alarrum; also one or two other things, that maybe I'll not tell ye now, laddies. An' a likewise reasoning applies to all."

He studied some notes in his pocket book. "The numbers for unlocking the covers are according to the following:—

"Unlocking 10 and 3 unlocks 1.

"	1	"	7	"	2.
"	9	"	8	"	3.
"	6	"	3	"	4.
"	13	"	12	"	5.
"	13	"	2	"	6.
"	4	"	11	"	7.
"	5	"	12	"	8.
"	10	"	2	"	9.
"	12	"	11	"	10.
"	9	"	6	"	11.
"	8	"	2	"	12.
"	5	"	7	"	13.

"Now then, we'll make a test o' our de'il's luck that I could near pray the A'michty shall abide with us this night; for then, John Vardon, you shall go free of the chains, and I shall have vengeance upon mine enemy."

He walked quietly across to the tenth cage, and inserted one of the notched slips of metal. It turned easily, without a sound.

"That's workmanship," said the Parson, with momentary professional pride. "Good work tells." He walked over to Number 3, and the key he had made for it, fitted equally well.

"Now, for the test," he said, and stepped across to Number 1.

Sandy Mech's naturally ruddy face whitened perceptibly, and John Vardon stirred uneasily, where he stood beside Mech; but only an added touch of grimness in the lines of Parson Guyles' mouth, showed that he also felt the strain of that supreme moment.

The Parson stooped and took hold of the handle of the latticed steel cover, Number 1. He lifted gently, and the cover hinged backward sweetly and noiselessly.

"God be thankit! God be thankit!" he muttered, in a subdued outburst of relief. He stood up and beckoned to where Sandy Mech and John Vardon had leant forward simultaneously from the wall. Sandy Mech's eyes burned and glowed with the true money-greed, at the sight of the uncovered thousands in coined gold, waiting only to be lifted out; but John Vardon's eyes were eager in another way. He saw there his suddenly desired freedom from the Supreme Failure that, in his morally slackened condition, he had begun to look upon as inevitably his fate. His eyes were intense with anxiety more than desire.

The Parson, on his part, had a strange mixture of triumph and a newly born anxiety in his expression; but dominating all, in that instant, was simple thankfulness and, strangely incongruous as it must seem, a subtle consciousness of holier thoughts. Abruptly, he said:—

"John Vardon, come and take the freedom I ha' to offer ye. Fetch the bags."

As Sandy Mech and John Vardon crept down the tunnel, for the bags, the Parson rapidly unlocked 1 and 7, 9 and 8, 6 and 3, 13 and 12. 13 and 12 opened a little less easily, and the Parson stood up to examine the key. He waved a hastening hand as Vardon and Mech re-appeared with four small portmanteau-like bags and a couple of grip-sacks.

"Haste ye," he said. "Maybe, out o' evil shall come good; but I misdoubt the soundness o' it. Yet the A'michty works in various ways His Wonders to pairform— Whist! What waur that?"

In the instant that followed, they all heard it, like a knell upon their varied hopes and longings:—the sound of an alarm gong, rattling hideously in the night; the noise coming plainly down the cleverly hidden ventilation shafts. In the same instant, there came a sudden, momentary, tremendous bluish glare of light in the room, that made the interior of the strong room brighter than any day that ever shone.

"We're done!" shouted Sandy Mech, in a positive screetch. "We're found out! Scoot!"

The Parson whipped a heavy revolver out of his pocket.

"A cool head, ma laddie, or I'll drop ye here an' now," he said calmly. "John Vardon, begin to stow the gold in the bags. Sandy, lad, you hark to me. The police will be here, inside of ten minutes. What's gone wrong, I do not just know; but maybe I made some wee slip in the re-wiring. Now, hark ye; after the police are here, they can never, come at us, save through the tunnel that no one but our three selves ken of, inside of a lang half hour. They've to bring the three separate offecials that hold the three emergency keys, that are never used except in an emergency like the present. I ha' it all worked out, down to the time it will take them to get here, even if they dress in the taxi. An' it cannot take less than seven and thirty minutes from this moment, before yon door is opened. By then, we shall ha' all the gold we need, an' we'll be lang gone away through the tunnel, and out by the back passage, and away in the car of our friend, John Vardon. Now, are ye quit of your panic, laddie; for I've na more time to waste on ye?"

Sandy Mech had got hold of himself, as he realised that there was not only time to achieve the gold, but that an effectual line of retreat was ready prepared; and he nodded back, rather shame-facedly, at the Parson.

"You're boss, Parson," he said. "I'm all right now."

"That's a goodish thing," said Parson Guyles. "A very goodish thing. Get packing the gold, smart now." He opened the remaining cages, with a perfectly controlled nerve.

"Surely hath mine enemy been delivered into mine hand!" he muttered; and picking up one of the gripsacks, began to fill it rapidly with bonds.

"Nay!" he said, catching John Vardon's glance. "Just to burn, laddie, and so to repay an eye for an eye. I will take a hand with the siller in a moment."

As each of the diminutive, strongly-built portmanteaux were filled with the solid little bags of gold coin, Parson Guyles locked and strapped them carefully, his amazing coolness acting on the others in a nerve-steadying way; so that they worked with a swiftness and method that had in it no signs of the panic, that might have been expected in three burglars who knew that, already, the police were drawing a cordon round the very building which they were robbing.

As the Parson was strapping the fourth portmanteau, there came suddenly, voices, seeming far away and muffled:—

"The door's not touched." . . . "Where are they?" . . . "Inside . . ." "They've tunnelled in. . . ." And then a silence, during which there were several soft thuds on the door.

"Not a sound, either of ye!" whispered Parson Guyles. "Keep

them guessing, laddies. Keep them guessing. The longer the better!"

"... There's no one inside!" came one of the muffled voices. "The door's not touched; and they can't have tunnelled in, for this room's got an Anson's patent 'warning' incorporated in the walls. It's absolutely impossible to get in that way without ringing us. And it would take them a week after that to cut through."

Parson Guyles smiled, grimly, inside the room.

"The emergency keys will be here in less than half an hour," continued the voice, "and then we can get in. I expect some of the electrical gear has fused, or something. Anyway, it's certain there's nothing to bother about."

"That's good for us!" said Parson Guyles, still in a whisper. "Now get the bags out. And never a sound, laddies. If they knew we were here, they'd be sure we'd tunnelled, and they would ha' a cordon round all the near-bye buildings, and make immediate investigation of all likely basements and cellars."

He lifted the four, enormously heavy, small portmanteaux, one after the other into the tunnel, and John Vardon and Sandy Mech began to creep with them, with infinite difficulty, along to the cellar. They found it easiest to take only one portmanteau at a time—one of them creeping on hands and knees, with the bag on his back, and the other steadying it from rolling off.

This method required four journeys to get the portmanteaux into the cellar; and then the two returned hurriedly for the grip-sacks, one of which was filled with notes and the other with bonds.

"Darn silliness! I call it," said Sandy Mech, as he crept behind John Vardon. "You can't do nothin' with bonds; nor no wise pup ever messes with notes. They're rotten dangerous."

"Drop it!" said John Vardon. "The Boss knows what he's doing. He's a wonderful man. Come on, and get it done."

"I'm with you," said Mech, honestly. " 'E's a bloomin' wonder; but I never 'ad no use for paper trash."

They reached the strong-room again; and, silently, Parson Guyles passed out the two grip-sacks, stuffed with paper of incredible value.

"I'll be with ye in a moment," said the Parson. "Go ahead."

Sandy Mech led the way back along the tunnel to the cellar. He had the bigger of the two grip-sacks, which, though quite light, was difficult to handle, owing to its size and the way in which it kept catching the inequalities of the walls and roof of the narrow drift.

"Cuss the thing! Cuss it! Cuss it!" he exclaimed, suddenly, as the sack caught for the tenth time on a snag in the roof.

John Vardon raised his head, as he crept some feet behind Mech, to see what was wrong. He had lit the tunnel in three places with incandescent lights, that made it tolerably bright. He saw something that made him sicken; for the roof, only partly and hastily lined, was sagging perceptibly, and Sandy Mech's sack was caught by some protruding fragment of the down-sagging roof.

"Stop, Sandy!" he said, in a hoarse voice. "Stop!"

But even as he spoke, Sandy Mech lurched forward once more, dragging at his sack, and swearing. As he did so, there was a curious rending sound, as the lining-boards gave way, and then a low roar, as something like a ton of earth poured down into a tunnel, a little behind Sandy, cutting him off completely from John Vardon and the Parson.

John Vardon gasped, in an impenetrable smother of dust, and then backed rapidly, still carrying his grip-sack. His stern met the Parson's head solidly, as he backed through the opening into the strong-room.

"What the de'il's wrong?" whispered the Parson, somewhat warmly. "What the de'il—"

"The roof's fallen in, Parson," said John Vardon, husky with the dust, and the terror of the situation. "We're trapped. It's jail for us; just when I thought to win clear of all and start fresh. My goodness, Parson, we can't clear the drift in the time we've got."

"Well, laddie," said Parson Guyles, with peculiar earnestness, and growing more Scottish, "I ha' always had ma doots that good should come out o' evil; but the A'michty works in His ain way; and maybe He's but lessoning ye a bit mair, to show ye the hard and bitter path that is the lot o' the evil doer. Let us away in, an' see how the tunnel looks. The A'michty loveth a man that's na ower ready to cry 'Lord I'm beat!' He's a sight more patience wi' the weak-minded than wi' the weak-hearted. . . . I'm feared though, that yon Sandy will fall to the temptation o' the opportunity, an' to his lack o' courage, an' run off. An' the diggin'-tools is a' in the cellar, I'm thinkin'! Whist! Hark!"

The two men stood silent, John Vardon white and dust-smothered; but Parson Guyles calm, with bright, alert eyes.

"Here's the manager, with one of the emergency keys," one of the muffled-sounding voices was saying. "If the other two buck up, we shall have the door open in a few minutes."

John Vardon quivered, and stared round the steel room, madly.

"Steady, my lad! Steady!" said Parson Guyles. "We are not beat yet. Never ha' I, by the mercy of the A'michty, seen the inside o' jail yet; and never will I, while the life goes in and out between ma breast banes. . . . To work, laddie!"

He thrust himself into the low mouth of the tunnel, and John Vardon followed, desperately. They came quickly to the place where the roof had collapsed, and the Parson threw himself at the loose bank of earth in which the tunnel vanished.

"Something to shovel with?" he said. "The tools are all in the cellar. . . . Ha! thanks be, I ha' the notion. To the side, man, smartly, while I go by you."

He crept quickly past the half stupefied engineer, and so into the strong-room. In a few seconds, he was back again, carrying something.

"Here ye are, laddie. Dig now, like man never dug, or ye'll dig soon at Portland."

He had brought two of the strong metal trays, in which the gold had been stored; and excellent makeshift shovels they proved. Vardon seized his, and, side by side, the two men worked like maniacs, sending the earth back between their knees in savage showers, and so filling the low drift with dust that they were almost blinded.

For some ten minutes, they worked; and then John Vardon gasped out:—

"Go back, Parson, a moment, and see if either of the other keys has come yet. I shall break up if I go on like this, feeling that they'll open that door, and be on us any moment."

The Parson merely grunted assent; he was too breathless, and too choked with the earth-dust, to speak. But if he were going to get the best out of Vardon, right to the last bitter moment, he must ease the nerve strain from him as much as possible.

He crept rapidly into the strong-room; and there, as he stood breathing heavily, he heard a confused chorus of greeting; and then one of the muffled-sounding voices say:—

"Thank goodness! There's only the third key to come now."

There was not a moment to lose, and the Parson dived head-foremost into the tunnel again.

"God forgie me!" he muttered, "but the laddie'll drop work the instant, if I tell him the truth."

He reached Vardon, through the blinding showers of earth which the engineer was heaving back between his knees. As he came alongside of him, he inadvertently gripped the man's ankle, and Vardon whirled round on him, with a sick curse of fear.

"Whist, laddie! Whist!" said the Parson. "It is I. The second key's no arrived yet; and they've had a telephone message, saying the third man can no come for twenty minutes mair!"

"Thank God! Thank God!" said John Vardon. "I can work now."

And work he did; and the Parson beside him. But Parson Guyles worked all the time with an ear cocked down the drift, knowing full well that any minute there might arrive the third key; for the minimum time that he had calculated out for the keys to arrive, was already reached. And then there would come the opening of the door, and they would be caught, literally like human rats.

The minutes passed, like eternities, and suddenly the Parson could bear it no longer.

"I'll away back," he muttered, with breathless huskiness, "an' see if yon second key's arrived yet."

As he crept out into the clearer air of the strong-room, he heard one of the muffled voices say, in a tone of authority:—"We are all here, gentlemen. Produce each your emergency key, and insert in the electrical combination to the right of the dial, in the order that I tell you. . ."

The third key had arrived, and the officials were at that very moment proceeding to unlock the door.

A desperate feeling took the Parson for an instant, across the chest and around the heart, and he stared with a sudden fierce intensity round about the room, to see whether he might not come upon some plan to win a little more delay. Abruptly, as he stared, he noticed the lines still stretched across the floor, and the ball of cord lying in the corner.

Like lightning, an idea came to him, and he dashed at the ball; then went at a silent run to where the vast door of the strong-room fitted solidly into its rebates. It had the maker's name-plate screwed on solidly to the otherwise smooth inner side of the door, and the Parson pulled a small, beautiful turn-screw from his pocket, as he ran. He reached the door, and fitted the turn-screw into the notch of the heavy steel screw; then applied all his strength and skill, and the screw moved. In less than five, noiseless, intense seconds, the screw head was sticking out half an inch from the door. He took a swift turn with the cord round the head of the screw, and then round the metal, electric light switch-lever, which was screwed into the left wall, near to the edge of the shut door. As the Parson took the turn with the cord, he caught the final directions from the muffled voice:—

"Key 1 to the left; key 3 to the right; key 2 to the right. Withdraw Numbers 1 and 2 keys; reverse Number 3. That's right. The door is unlocked. Pull it open."

As the muffled voice gave the final direction; the Parson, sweating until he was almost blind in that horrible moment, yet kept his nerve; and his swift fingers took turn after turn of the thin strong cord, from the screw head to the switch; back and forth; back and forth.

"The door's stuck," came one of the voices. "Have we worked the combination right?"

"Yes," answered the previous voice. "Pull a bit."

"Praise be!" muttered the Parson, as he drew his sleeve across his forehead. That'll hold a while; and they'll keep guessing on the combination. Maybe, the A'michty has a mind to let us go this once mair."

He tested the tightly strung bundle of cord, with a heavy pull; then, without a second look, he dived again into the drift.

"Look out, John!" he called, softly, as he approached. "It is I. We're safe a bit mair. How goes it, laddie? How goes it?"

"We—we'll do it yet, Parson," said Vardon, between shovelfuls, gasping as he spoke.

"Whist!" said Parson Guyles, "Whist! What's yon?"

Vardon stopped, and they both listened.... Someone was digging, on the other side of the piled up obstruction.

"It's yon honest de'il, Sandy," said the Parson. "Man, I do praise the A'michty for the goodness o' that."

"He's close, Parson!" said the engineer, still gasping. "Close! Do you understand? Only a few feet . . . My God, another few minutes, and we'll be away clear."

They spoke not a word more; but dug fiercely together into the remaining mound of earth. As they threw the earth between their knees, they scrambled it backwards with their feet, in a very orgy of effort, so that it mounded up behind them, half-way to the roof of the tunnel.

Suddenly, from the strong-room, there came a single sharp sound, like a rope snapping. "It's gone!" gasped out the Parson, and whirled round. "They're into the room!"

In the same instant, John Vardon cried out, inarticulately, and Parson Guyles turned again swiftly, a thousand plans for action surging in him. He saw that a shovel, gripped by two grimy efficient hands, was stabbing through the earth that barred their escape. Sandy Mech had broken through!

From the direction of the strong-room, rose a loud incoherent outcry—a dozen men speaking at once. And then an instantaneous silence, and the flash of a bull's-eye lamp, along the drift.

"They're there, lads!" shouted a deep commanding voice. "After them! Follow me."

Sandy Mech's head and shoulders were half through from the cellar side now; and he saw their instant need.

"The roof, Parson!" he shouted. "Bring the roof down on 'em. Catch!"

He shot a short, heavy digging-spud, or flat ended bar, into the Parson's hand. Then he made another swift sweep with his shovel.

"There's room, John," he said. "Come on! Come on! Get clear out o' the Parson's road."

He literally hauled Vardon over the mound, by his head and shoulders, slithering him down on the cellar side, in a cloud of dust. Then back over the mound, to help the Parson; but the Parson needed no help. He was heaving mightily at the roof, with the spud. A big, bearded face had just loomed at him, over the mound that lay between him and the strong-room. And he had met it with all the weight of his body and fist. . . . The face had gone backwards, half-stunned; and he had attacked the roof ferociously again. Two other faces loomed, with lamps, and an automatic pistol was thrust at him.

The Parson gave a final heave; there was a roar of falling earth, and the reiterated explosion of a pistol, smothered. Then he was being hauled back by Sandy, half suffocated, over the mound on the cellar side. Between them and the strong-room, lay a barrier that would take, maybe, an hour to dig away.

"Sandy, lad," were the Parson's first words, as the three of them stood breathless and grimy in the cellar, "I owe ye apology for doubting ye. I told John, here, ye'd never ha' power to resist the temptation o' the moment. I ask pardon of ye, laddie. I'll no forget how ye proved ye'rsel' this night."

"Aw!" said Sandy Mech, "I ain't no tin god! I did think of it; but you an' me's been through some jobs together, Parson; an' I'd a' hated you to get copped. And I'd a' had a job to shunt this stuff by me lonesome."

"Now, we got to move smartly," said Parson Guyles. "They'll maybe stay diggin' in the drift awhile; but they'll sure have men into all these basements, inside ten minutes. Pick up the gold. I'll take a bag and this sack o' bonds and notes. I regret sair we're leaving one in yonder. Now follow me. . . . Whist! Hear that now! Not a sound!"

A thunderous knocking rose from the entrance door.

"The police! They're on our track a'ready!" whispered Parson Guyles.

". . . his 'ands were all earthy!" they heard a heavy voice explaining excitedly. "I thought I'd keep an eye on 'im. . . . Nothing to be suspicious about then, or I'd 'ave watched him closer. . . ."

"I was right!" whispered the Parson. "Yon fat policeman must ha' noticed things; and he's brought 'em right on our heels. Come on!"

As he spoke, there came a heavy blow on the door, that made the whole basement boom and echo.

"Quick, after me," said the Parson. "That door'll be doon in a minute."

He went swiftly through the darkness towards the rear of the basement, and the two others followed, stumbling in the gloom, with the weight of precious metal each carried.

There came the click of a lock. Then, faintly, they could see the outline of an open doorway, with the loom of the night beyond.

"Smartly now!" said Parson Guyles. "Move quiet an' noiseless as the de'il himsel. . . . Pause a wee, while I lock this door against them. . . . Hark to that!" as a crash resounded through the basement behind them. "They're in!"

He closed the door, quietly, and locked it, methodically withdrawing and pocketing the key.

"This is no' a proper way out, ye'll understan'!" he whispered. "There's no back entrances to this block; only this was a convenience that the last tenant of this basement arranged with the proprietor of the stable yard we're in now; and where I gave John the hint to keep his car. Step quiet, laddies. This way. To the left. . . . Now right. Here we are. Put the bags in, smart. I bid yon Williams lad ha' the lamps lit an' a' ready by two o'clock, an' I'm glad he's done as I told him. I explained that ma friend an' I were away to Edinboro' toon for the week end. . . . That you, Williams?" as a sleepy eyed yard-man appeared. "Here's half-a-crown, my man. Open the gates, an' let us away on oor holiday."

"Thank'ee, Sir," said the man. "I've had the lights lit this half hour."

He shambled to the gates, and began slowly to open them; while Vardon got into the driver's seat, and the Parson set the engine going.

"Throttle her, man," he said. "Not a sound more than need be. . . . What's yon man so long for!"

The man had the gates half open; but had apparently been spoken to by someone. As the car circled to approach the gates, the lamps showed something that sickened the three men in the car. Standing at the gate, questioning the man, whose replies sounded frightened and bewildered, were four big policemen, and the foremost one was the burly officer whose voice they had heard a few minutes earlier, explaining about the Parson's hands.

Abruptly, as the light showed them, the four officers barred the way.

"Pardon me, gentlemen!" said the fat policeman, raising his bull's-eye, "we shall not keep you a moment, if all is right; but— It's him!"

he ended in a shout. "Collar him! A good thing I thought to try round the back here! Shut the gates!"

The four men, in a clump, turned to do so. In that instant, the Parson stooped swiftly, and pulled a large paper bag from under the seat. He sprang upright, and dashed it at the heads of the policemen. It burst against one of their helmets, and the car's head-lights shone on a grey cloud of dust that filled the air around the police. The men in the car gasped for breath, and began to sneeze violently; but the policemen, caught literally in the thick of the cloud of pungent dust, reeled and staggered in all directions, gasping and sneezing hopelessly; for the Parson had burst a great paper bag of snuff and pepper right among them.

The Parson leaped right out among the stupefied men, hitting right and left with his fists, and clearing a path for the car in half a dozen seconds. He seized the doors, and dashed them wide open.

"Through wi' her, John!" he shouted, sneezing fiercely. "Through wi' her!"

Vardon obeyed, and the car leapt through. The Parson sprang on the foot-board, as the car swung out into the road; and as he did so, there came a thunder of blows on a door somewhere up the yard.

"To the left, John!" gasped the Parson. "Let her go!"

Ten minutes later, at a reasonable speed, the car was traversing one of the bridges over the river. Here, where they could see no one was about, they stopped the car, and John Vardon jumped out. He slipped off the number-plates, and disclosed fresh ones underneath.

"A good notion that, John," said Parson Guyles, as Vardon climbed back into his seat and re-started the car. "I flatter myself that notion o' the snuff-mixture was good, too, laddies. I've tried that trick before; and it always comes off, and no one the worse for it, either. Also, I'm thinkin' it's as well I made ye both up sae careful, too. I wonder now how ye're photos will turn out."

"What?" asked both men.

"Why!" said the Parson. "Yon box o' tricks we've just been emptyin', had a deal o' notions about it. Did ye not see yon flash, after the alarm rang? Well, I guess, laddies, that's a photograph apparatus, that one, Jamie MacAllister (they're a' Scots men, ye notice) invented; and it's to photograph any act o' irregularity that may occur. Ye micht ca' oor's some, how irregular, maybe." The two men laughed.

"The Lord forgie me," said Parson Guyles, growing more and more Scottish; "but I feel that licht hearted, I must crack a joke on ma ain sins!"

"I'm that way, always, Parson, after a job," said Sandy Mech, nodding in the darkness. "I don't reckon much of conscience when you've got the oof safe away. That's my way o' lookin' at it."

But John Vardon said nothing.

X

It was a week later, and Parson Guyles and John Vardon were walking up and down the platform of a provincial railway station.

"John Vardon," said the Parson, quietly, as the train steamed in, "I hold ye to ye're given word."

"I'll keep it, Parson," said Vardon, looking squarely at Parson Guyles. "You're a fine man, Parson—"

"Na! Na ! Man! Oh dinna shame me mair! Dinna shame me mair!" cried out the Parson, in very distress. "God go with ye an' guide ye.

"An' God help me," he muttered, as they turned, each his own way.

The Friendship of Monsieur Jeynois

CAPTAIN DROOL AND THE TWO MATES sat in the cabin and argued, gross and uncouth; but Monsieur Jeynois said nothing. Only smoked his long pipe and listened, while the bo'sun held the poop-deck! I had grown to like Monsieur Jeynois, for the brave, quiet way of him, and the calm speech that seemed so strong and wise against the rude blusterings and oathings of the captain and the mates.

The Saucy Lady was a private venture ship—in other words, an English privateer—at the time of the French war. She had been a French brig, named La Gavotte, and had been sold at Portsmouth for prize money.

Monsieur Jeynois and Captain Drool had bought her, and fitted her out against the French, with six twenty-four-pounder cannonades a side, and two long eighteen-pounders—the one mounted aft and the other for'ard, for chasers.

The brig was a matter of three hundred and fifty tons burthen, and sailed very fast, and made good weather of it.

We had ninety-six able-bodied sailors for'ard in a fine, great, new fo'cas'le, that was fitted up when Monsieur Jeynois and Captain Drool had the vessel altered. There were also six gunners, that we had helped to run free of the Royal Navy, and good men they were, but mighty opinionated, and nothing would serve them but to sneer and jeer at all and aught because we were not so fine as a King's ship. And, indeed, why they troubled to sail in us was a thing to make a man wonder!

There were, also, twelve boys in the ship. Six of these were named midshipmen, and were from rich tradesmen's families of Portsmouth Town, and paid some sort of premium to walk the lee side of the after-deck and play lob-lolly to the captain and the two mates.

I was one of the other six—just common lads off the water front at Portsmouth, though I was no Portsmouth lad, but Lancashire bred and born, but part reared on the Welsh coast and afterwards in the south, for my father had been a shipwright in Liverpool, and then went to Cardiff, and came in the end to Portsmouth, where he worked in the Royal Dockyards till the day he died, which was two years before this story. And a poor and ignorant lad I was, as I do mind me, and talked a strange mixture of dialects and rough words. But this by the way.

We wanted to fight the French, and make good prize money at brave work. And there you have the crew of us, with added thereto the bo'sun and the two carpenters.

Now, if you have never heard tell of Monsieur Jeynois, you might wonder to hear that he helped fit out a ship against the French. But, indeed, in Portsmouth Town, we had no trouble on this score, for a better hater of Frenchmen, and a greater fighter, never put a pegged boot to good deck-planks.

There were some that said he had been a great man the other side; and this I can well believe, for he was a great man, as all in that ship knew in their inwards. He had a steady, brown eye, that looked down into a man; and you knew that he feared nothing, save it might be God, which I do believe.

As for his hatred of the French, there were many tales to account for it; but none of them to the mark, as I must suppose. Yet, because he was a Frenchman, despite the many times that he had proved himself upon them, there were a thousand to hate him for no more than his name or his blood, both or either, as suited their poor brute minds. Also, while many had a deep respect for him, few loved him, because he was too quiet and aloof. And, indeed, I doubt not that, because there was something great of heart within him, there were many of the poorer souled that hated him for no other cause than that he waked in them—though scarce they knew it—a knowledge of their own inward weeviliness.

And this was the man that sat in the cabin with Captain Drool and the two mates—Hankson and Abbott—and would listen to their rude arguing, that even I, the cabin lad, could oft see the gross folly of. And then, maybe, by a dozen quiet words, he would show them their own poor selves, in a mirror of brief speech that made them and their thoughts and child's plans of no more account than they were; so that I have seen the three of them stare at him out of eyes of dumb hatred.

And then he would show them the way that the thing should be done, and they would be forced to admit the rightness of his reasoning; yet hating him the more for his constant rightness, and the way that he seemed to know all and to fear naught.

Only one thing he did not know, and that was the science to navigate; else I venture he had never sailed with any captain other than himself.

And there, in this little that I have told, you have the causes that led to the greatest fight that ever a single man put up against a multitude.

It came about in this wise. After dinner the captain and the mate that was not in charge of the deck would sit awhile and drink a sort of spiced rum-toddy. But Monsieur Jeynois drank only plain water, flavoured with molasses, and often left the table with a quiet excuse, that he would see the weather.

Then, when he was gone, the captain and whichever of the two mates that was with him, would fall to cursing him, from his keel upwards, and taking no more heed of me—whom I do venture to think they thought no more of than a wood deck-bucket!—than if I were not there; save, in truth, one of them needed the molasses or the hot water or the ground nutmeg; whereupon I was as like to get a clout as a word, to make known their wants.

And clout me they would do at any moment and were at first as handy to it if monsieur were with them as if he were on deck. Not that monsieur said ever a word, one way or the other, for he had no foolish softness about him; yet he never struck me. And once, when Captain Drool had opened my head with his pewter mug, I looked quick over at monsieur, and there was a look in his eyes that made me think he disliked to see me treated so, though he forbore to say aught, but yet I could think had come near to that point at which he might speak.

And, indeed, this is but poorly said; yet, in part, expresses the thought that came to me, before I was knocked down again, for not hastening to fetch another dipper of rum.

But late that same night, when I was lying very sick and hot-headed under the cabin table—for I was allowed no hammock—Monsieur stooped and looked under the table, and asked me how I was; and he fetched me, presently, a draught with his own hand, and afterwards put a wet cloth on my head, so that in a while I went over asleep, and woke pretty fresh in the morning.

And I found the cloth on my head to be a strip off one of monsieur's neck-clothes; and I put the thing inside my shirt, along with a big memory, as a boy will do that is badly treated, and has a great kindness where no kindness was ever expected; for I was but a common ship's boy, and monsieur a great soldier and a shipowner, as I have told.

And after that time I noticed that neither Captain Drool nor the mates touched me when monsieur was in the cabin; so that I supposed he had spoken quietly with them, when I was not there, against striking me.

Yet, when he was up on the deck, they would clout me as ever, and talk very loose and rash before me, as I have said, against monsieur. But threats are easy blows, so that I took little heed for a good while.

Then, one night after dinner, when we were heading up for the channel, they got talking in a way that set me taking sudden note of their words; for there was a real meaning and intention in what they were saying.

Presently, Captain Drool sent me to fetch aft the bo'sun to drink with them, which was a thing they had done several times of late after monsieur had gone up on to the deck.

They drank more that night than ever before, and the bo'sun so much as any. And every now and again Abbott, the second mate, would come down into the cabin and have a tot with them, and join in their talk; and me kept mighty busy, in the small pantry-place, scraping nutmeg for their spice-rum-toddy—that was the captain's own invention— and keeping water a-boil over a slush-lamp, all of which I did, despite the rolling of the ship, by holding the kettle with one hand and rubbing the nutmeg on to an iron grater with the other. And all the time I listened, so well as I could, for I had began to see that they were planning to kill monsieur quietly in the cabin, and afterwards to dump him secretly over the side, and so let it be supposed he had been washed overboard at night; for we were shipping a deal of heavy water with the strong gale that we were running before.

Then Captain Drool should have the ship entire his own, for Monsieur Jeynois was a lone man, and none in England, so it was thought, to be an heir to him and his moneys. And to pay the two mates and the bo'sun for their help in this dire and brutal murder, the captain proposed to pay them the share of the prize money that was coming to monsieur, and also a hundred golden guineas between them, each to share equal, but that they should claim no rights in the ship. And this they were well enough pleased with, being but vulgar and brutal men, and each as ignorant as the other; for it was only Captain Drool that knew the science of navigating.

And whether the man for'ard should suspect or not, seemed no great matter to these brutes as they guzzled and planned this foul deed; for there were a deal of men, I doubt not, as I have told, who could not get it out of their stomachs that monsieur was a Frenchman, and should be treated as such. There was not much love that we had those days for Frenchmen. Yet, in the main, the four men desired to keep secret the method of the end of monsieur, lest the crew should demand that monsieur's share of the prize money be distributed, which the crew might certainly have done, deeming it their right, because monsieur was French, and because they would suppose that if the captain and the mates murdered monsieur, it would be with intent to "nig" his share of the prize money. And this would most surely offend the crew, who would refuse to have them profit without the whole ship's company should profit. But, were the crew deceived in the matter, to believe that monsieur was truly washed overboard in a natural and wholesome fashion, then they would demand nothing, but expect the usual routine in such matters, which was that a man's prize-money be paid to his widow or to his heir, and this Captain Drool would provide for, by the aid of his brother who was a penman, and could write the name so clever upon the will that monsieur would think it his own were he to return again to life.

There you have it all, with the methods of their poor and brutish reasonings, which truly betray them for what they were. And I, you must picture, holding the kettle above the slush-lamp in the pantry-room off the cabin, and grinding scarce enough nutmeg to supply their needs, for the grinding of the nutmeg upon the iron scraper made a noise that prevented me from hearing them; and so I was fain to keep stopping every moment to listen. And, indeed, once I set all my sleeve alight, with the ship rolling so, for I was taking no heed of the way I held the kettle, but stopping, as I have told, to hark very desperate; and suddenly I smelled the stink of my sleeve burning in the lamp, for I had my sleeve over the flame and the kettle nowhere near.

Yet they never so much as knew, for they had drunk a matter of four dippers of rum between them, and they could think of nothing but the dreadful murder they planned so earnest.

Now, at four bells—by which I mean ten o'clock of the night—monsieur came down from the deck, and for the first time in all that voyage I heard him speak his mind to the captain, nor minded who heard him; only first he had word with the bo'sun.

"Bo'sun" he said, "you are in the wrong part of the ship. Go up on to the deck and take charge until you are relieved."

Just that and nothing more, and spoken as quiet as you like, with good English that no man could better; for monsieur was French, to my thinking, only in name.

And the bo'sun! A great hulk of a man that weighed fifteen stone as he lolled there. It was fine to watch, as you will acknowledge! I peeped out of the pantry and saw him make first as if he had heard nothing, and then in a moment, though monsieur said never another word, only looked at him, he tried to catch the eyes of Captain Drool and the two mates, smiling in a silly, ugly way as he did so; but they looked everywhere but at him, like animals that have had guilty intentions, and are full of unease when their master comes near them.

There was not a sound in all the cabin, only the cracking and groaning of the bulkheads as the ship rolled in the storm, and the shuffling of the captain's mug as he pushed it to and fro upon the table top. And still monsieur stood and looked quiet and calm at the bo'sun.

Then the bo'sun rose up slowly, looking very awkward and oafish. He made to drain his mug, to show that he was at ease, but I heard the rim of it clitter foolish against his teeth, and he slopped the half of the toddy down the front of his serge shirt.

And still monsieur never spoke, nor said a further word, only looked after him, calm and quiet as he went out on to the deck, through the cuddy doorway, which opened out of the fore-end of the cabin.

Then monsieur turned to the captain and the two mates.

"I should think shame, gentlemen," he said, "to so demean yourselves upon the high seas by this drinking and easy speech with the rough shipmen; and more than this, by the neglecting of your duties as officers, so that the ship has been the great part of this watch without an officer upon the decks."

He said never another word but what I have told, and all spoken quiet and almost gentle. And those three rough men, that had just been planning his murder, answered him nothing; nor did one of them look at him, but sat there and shuffled their mugs and looked at their hands, all like the oafs they were; only, I could tell by the purple of Captain Drool's ears, that he was like a mad beast that is like to burst with the great stress of its anger and its cowardice.

Monsieur stood a matter of a few seconds; then, saying not another word, he went into his own cabin and closed the door.

When he was gone, the three men at the table stopped playing with their mugs and looking at their great hands, and they stared at each other. Captain Drool turned, and put out his tongue at monsieur's shut door, also he put his thumb to his nose and twiddled his great, coarse fingers; then he got up and went towards the companion steps. He tip-toed as he went, as if he were afraid monsieur might hear him. He crooked his finger to the two mates to follow him. And the three of them went up the steps into the night.

Presently, when I had cleared up the odd gear upon the table, and washed all, I put out the slush-lamp in the small pantry place, for there was a lamp that hung always alight in the cabin. Then I fetched out my blanket from the locker, and hove it under the cabin table. I had no proper pillow, but used my sea-bag always, with my spare shift in it, for this purpose.

Also, it was my habit, each night when I turned in, to rig a length of spun yarn from one leg of the table to another, about a foot from the floor, so that if Captain Drool or the mates should want me in the night, I should escape being kicked in the head or face, for it was their way to wake me at any time by kicking at me under the table; but the spun yarn saved me a deal, for they never bothered to see what it was that their great sea-boots brought up against.

Now, when I had fixed all up for the night, and was rolled comfortable in the blanket, I lay a good while thinking, and half-minded to go to monsieur's door and knock gently to wake him. Yet, if they were watching the cabin from the deck—which they could do very easy without me seeing them—through the glass of the skylight, then I should be discovered, and they would, maybe, kill me when they murdered monsieur.

However, in the end, Monsieur Jeynois saved me the need of this risk, for he came out of his cabin presently, with his pea-jacket on, by which I saw that he meant to go up again on deck.

Then I put my head out a little from under the table, and said, " Monsieur!" But I was so in fear of them seeing me from the deck, that I spoke too low, and he was gone half across the cabin with his great strides—for he was a big man—before I had courage to call him proper.

But now I pushed my head out from under the table, and took my risk as I hoped a man should take it.

"Monsier! Monsieur!" I said out loud. "Monsieur!"

He stopped, and I came out clean from under the table, dropping my blanket upon the floor, and standing there in my shirt, for I had no drawers.

"What is it, boy?" he asked in his quiet way, yet seeming to smile ever so little as he looked down at me.

"You're in horful danger, sir," I told him, for that was how I spoke those days, before ever I was given the good schooling that I had later.

"How, boy?" he asked me.

"Cappen Drool an' Mestur Hankson an' Mestur Abbott an' Mestur Johns the bo'sun is going to murder you, sir. An' Cappen Drool is to have th' brig, an' he've offered t'others yourn share o' the prize money an' a hundred guineas, an' they'm not to make no claim to own the ship," I told him, getting my words out all in a heap, because of my earnestness and eagerness to warn him.

And I can vouch that I had not one thought in that one and particular moment concerning my own safety, for which I am pleased to this day to remember.

"Go on, boy," said monsieur, still in his quiet voice. "What reason have you for saying this?"

"Aa heerd 'em, sir, whiles I were boilin' yon kettle an' grindin' the nutmeg for the toddy. Aa'm feared, sir, they'm meanin' to hout you ta-neet. Doan't 'ee go up on deck, sir, but hide yere in the cabing, an' I'll load ye a mint o' pistols, sir, an' we'll blow 'em into hell when they come down to murder ye."

"Boy," he said, "I put my trust in God, clean living, and a straight sword. And by these means, and your honest warning, am I prepared; but first, before we go further, if you must kill a man, why send him down in to hell? I would rather pray, as I slew him, that he might find heaven and a gladder wisdom."

I can remember now the quaint smile, kindly and human, that he gave me as I stood there in my shirt, staring up at him, and puzzled somewhat to know all the meanings of his speech, yet not entirely to misunderstand him.

"Now," he said in a moment, and clapping me twice gently upon the shoulder, "get back into your blanket, boy, and leave me freedom to meet my kind intentioned visitors when they come."

Then suddenly I saw that he looked at my legs.

"Boy," he said, "where are your drawers?"

"Aa've got none, sir," I told him. "Maybe I'll buy two pair with my prize money for next trip when we reach port."

He looked at me for a little; then, without a word, he turned and went back into his room. He came again in a moment, with a pair of fine silk drawers in his hand, the like of which I'd never seen.

"Put these on, boy," he said, and tossed them over my shoulder.

But I feared to touch the things, they were so fine and wonderful.

"I daurna wear 'em, sir," I told him. "They'm too fine."

But he laughed quietly.

"You'll have to turn the legs up," he said, and went back into his room.

I saw then that he meant it, and I put the things on, never thinking for the moment of the captain and the mates, or whether they might be watching me through the dark skylight.

When I was into the drawers, I feared to get back into my rough blanket, lest I should dirty them; and it was while I stood there in the fine silk drawers, and looked at my old blanket, that I knew suddenly that danger was upon us, for I heard the ladder that led up to the after companion-way creak, like it always did when anyone put their weight on it. And this I heard, despite the constant creakings and groanings of the bulkheads as the ship rolled; for I knew that particular creak, having kept ears for it through many an hour at my work, to let it warn me whether any of my oaf masters were coming below. Yet whoever was on the ladder was creeping down surely in their bared feet, for there was never the sound of any clumsy boot to be heard.

I waited not a moment, but ran to the door of monsieur's room, which he had hooked open to prevent it slamming to and fro with the heavy rolling. I could see his back. He had taken off the heavy peacoat, and was priming his pistols—four brace, all silver mounted.

"Monsieur!" I said—and, maybe, I looked a little white to think that murder was even then so near. "Monsieur, they'm comin', sir! They'm comin' down th' ladder."

"Under the table, boy, and into your blanket," he said quietly, turning to the door.

"Aa'll feight 'em along with ye," I said, feeling suddenly that a man—that's how I named myself!—could die only once. "They'll get tha' behind, through yon cuddy door through the fore-cabin. Gi'e me one o' them pistols, sir. Quick, sir, I hear 'em!"

I was surprised to find myself speak so usual to monsieur. And then, to stop him thwarting me, because I feared they would stab him from behind if I did not guard the cuddy door, I stepped up close to him and said, very hasty and speaking scarce above a whisper:

"They seen me warnin' ye, sir. It ain't no use me hidin'. They'll just cut my throat after they'm done murderin' you. Quick, sir! They're into th' cabing now! Gi'e me one o' the pistols!"

He said nothing, just pointed his thumb to where three of the pistols lay. He had the fourth in his right hand, and his sword out now in his left. He fought always with his sword in the left hand, as I knew, for I had seen him before at the taking of our prizes. I made no more ado, but took up a pistol in each hand, and as I did this monsieur stepped out of his room into the big cabin.

"Well, gentlemen," I heard him say, "you see, I have done you the honour of staying out of my bunk to welcome you. Perhaps, Captain Drool, you would prefer that I take you first? Or—no, is it to be all together? Ah, Master Abbott!"

Before this I had run out into the big cabin. There had been a loud and violent thudding of bare feet as they rushed monsieur, and as I reached the doorway of his room, I had seen Captain Drool and the two mates running at him with their cutlasses out. I had seen Monsieur turn off a stab from Captain Drool with the barrel of his pistol, and then, with a wonderful quick movement of his wrist and forearm, he put his long sword right through Abbott's chest. Monsieur was wonderful with the sword.

Now, I had thought well when I had planned to guard monsieur's back; for at this moment the cuddy door, that led to the maindeck through the fore-cabin in the fore part of the poop, was hove open with a great crash, and the noise of the seas and the gale filled the cabin as the bo'sun and the chief carpenter Maull came tumbling in, each with a drawn cutlass in his hand.

There was a loud shouting from Captain Drool and the mate, and the bo'sun and Maull the carpenter answered it with other shouts as they ran aft round the big table to get at monsieur's side and back.

I heard monsieur say, in a quiet voice:

"Guard my back, boy!"

Just those words he said, and never looked round, but fenced off the mate's cutlass with the long barrel of his loaded pistol, and kept Captain Drool in play with his sword, all as easy and calm as if he were playing some game of skill for a wager rather than for his own life.

And you shall see me in that moment as proud as a young turkeycock with the trust he put in me; and full of good courage, both because of his calmness, that infected me the same way, and because of the fine pistols of two barrels each that I held ready in my hands.

"Mestur Johns and Mestur Maull," I shouted, "bide where ye are, or I shoot ye dead this moment!"

But, maybe, they thought of me as no more than a boy, and of no account, for they came with a great chare and shouting round the end of the table, to get behind monsieur. And Maull, who was first, made a great stroke at monsieur with his cutlass, but the beams of the deck above his head were a better guard than me. For I had been too late with my pistols to save monsieur, if one of the great deck beams had not caught the top of the carpenter's cutlass and stopped the blow midway.

Yet monsieur was more watchful than I knew; for he spared one brief moment of his sword-fence with Captain Drool, and cut sideway with his left hand, so that his sword shone a moment like a flame in the lamplight.

And immediately Maul loosed his cutlass, that was notched hard into the oaken beam, and clapped his hand to his neck, and went backwards into the bo'sun, singing out in a dreadful voice that he was dead. And dead he was in less than a minute after.

But before this I had loosed off twice into the bo'sun, and shot him in the arm and again in the thigh. And he also dropped his cutlass—or cutlash, as we called them—and made to reach the cuddy door, which he did in the end by creeping upon his knees and hands.

I have thought that monsieur had some notion to spare the lives of Captain Drool and the mate, for he had the loaded pistol in his right hand, and might have shot the mate at any moment; and equally he had the captain's life upon his sword point all the time, as it might be said.

But sudden the mate jumped back out of the fight, and whipped a pistol very smart out of the skirt of his blue coat that was a fancy of his from the body of a man he killed in the taking of our first prize.

Then monsieur used his own pistol in a wonderful quick way, and still fencing off Captain Drool's cutlash. As he loosed off, he called out in a low, quick voice:

"I commend you to the mercy of God, John Abbott."

And with these words he had fired, before the mate had his aim taken. I have thought often upon those words.

At this moment, and as the mate fell upon the deck of the cabin and died, there was a great shouting out upon the main deck of the brig. I caught the meaning of certain of the shoutings:

"Monsieur's killing the cap'n! Monsieur's killing the cap'n!" I heard someone sing out twice, and maybe three times. Then the bo'sun's voice: "Smart, lads! He've cut Chip's throat, an' I be all shot through an' through!"

You must bear in mind that noises came oddly to me by reason of the great excitement of the moment, and the constant skythe, skythe of Captain Drool's cutlass along the blade of monsieur's lean sword, and the stamping of the captain's bare feet. There was also the noise of the gale and the sea-thunder that beat in through the open cuddy doorway out of the black night, and all the time the creaking and the groaning of the bulkheads, and the bashing and clattering of the cuddy door as it swung and thudded to and fro with the brig's rolling.

Then, immediately, I heard the shouts rise clear and strong through the gale, and coming nearer until, in a moment, I heard the thudding of scores of feet racing aft along the decks.

And suddenly Captain Drool leaped back from his vain attacking of monsieur, and turned and ran for the cuddy door, shouting to the men to save him, though monsieur made never a step to follow.

Yet Captain Drool showed his deathly hatred of me in that moment, for he hove the cutlass out of his hand across the table in my face as he passed me.

But I stooped very quick, and the heavy blade struck the bulkhead over me. Then, stooped as I was, I shot Captain Drool in the head over the edge of the table, with no pity in me, for he had made so wantonly to kill me; also, I had been beat and kicked too oft by the brute. Moreover, while he lived to urge the men on, neither monsieur nor I might hope ever to come alive through the night.

Thus died Captain Drool, after monsieur had spared him a hundred times.

Now, in the instant after I shot the captain, I had jumped very speedy into monsieur's cabin, where I caught up his powder-flask and his bag of pistol bullets. Then I was into the big cabin again in a moment.

"Monsieur!" I called out, very breathless. "The cap'n's cabing, sir—the cap'n's cabing!"

And I ran past him into the captain's cabin, which had the door open, and was behind him as he stood there with his sword, staring very earnest and ready towards the cuddy doorway.

"Coom in, sir!" I began to call to him. "Coom in, sir!"

And then, before I could say another word, the big cabin seemed to be full of shouting men all in one moment, for they came leaping over the washboard of the cuddy alleyway, all helter-skelter, through the cuddy doorway, which was in the forepart of the cabin, as you know by this.

There were maybe twenty and maybe thirty of them; but I never had time to think how many there were, but only that they filled all the for'ard part of the big cabin.

Those that were into the cabin stopped their shouting, and seemed to hang backward when they saw monsieur standing there with his sword in his hand. But there were more in the cuddy alleyway and out on the main deck that pushed and shouted to get in, so that the men in the cabin were all a-sway, they pushing backward and the men in the alleyway and upon the main deck pushing for'ard to come into the cabin.

I saw Jenkson, Allen, Turpen, and three or four others among the men that had broke into the cabin, and all of them were of the poorer sort, being no more than the rough scum of Portsmouth Town that had come to sea along with better men to make easy money; though, truly, there was not much easy money that ever I found this way!

Now, I knew these men were among the worst in the ship, and they had never a good word for monsieur behind his back, though quiet enough to his face, but had often called him a frog-eater, and a French spy, and many another oafish name that had no base in fact; though, I doubt not, they near believed the ugly things they gave breath to.

And so you must see that last great scene, with monsieur standing there, and me behind him in the open doorway of the captain's cabin, and loading the fired-off barrels of the two fine pistols, the while that I stared at the men and monsieur. And I put a double charge of powder into each of the barrels, and upon each charge I dropped three bullets, for I saw that I should have less need of a nicety of shooting than of power to kill oft and plenty with the greatest speed.

As I have said, you must see that last great scene—how the men, though so plentiful, hung off from him, with their knives bare in their hands, ready for brutal slaughter, yet fearing him, while he stood quietly, and had no single thought to fear them, not if they had been a hundred strong. And every few moments there would fight through into the cabin another of the men, and would fall silent with the rest, staring like dumb brutes from monsieur to the dead and back again to monsieur. And all that brief while I loaded the pistols, with my hands trembling a little, though not so much with fear as might be supposed.

Now, there was hung on the bulkhead of the captain's cabin, close to my elbow, a great brass-mouthed blunderbuss, and, having a sudden thought from Providence, I stepped back, into the captain's room, and reached this down very quick. I had pushed the two pistols into the front band of my new silk drawers, and now I took monsieur's powder-flask, and near emptied it down into the blunderbuss.

There was a pair of woollen hose that belonged to Captain Drool hanging over a wood peg, and I snatched one, and pushed it down with my hand into the great barrel of the blunderbuss that was so wide I could reach my arm down it. And after that I took the bag of pistol bullets, and emptied them, every one, down into the barrel upon the powder and the woollen hose; and afterwards I thrust down the other hose upon the bullets to hold them steady in the barrel. Then, very hasty yet with a proper care, I primed the great weapon. Afterwards I cast the powder-flask on to the deck, and ran very quick with the blunderbuss to the door of the cabin.

There was scarce any shouting now, for as this man and that crowded himself into the cabin, and saw monsieur standing there with his sword and the pistol, and the dead men lying about the deck of the big cabin, they grew silent.

But suddenly some of those that were at the back began to sing out odd questions and abuse concerning me.

"What's the cub doin' wi' the blunderbuss?" shouted one.

"It aren't never loaded!" sang out another of them.

And so they began to get their courage to attack monsieur by miscalling me that they had no fear of.

"Coom back inta th' cappen's cabing, monsieur!" I kept whispering, so that he might hear me yet the men hear nothing.

In the end he heard me, for I saw him shake his head as if he were bidding me be quiet. Then in a little he spoke to the men, choosing a moment when they were silent.

"For what reason have you come aft?" he said, speaking very ordinary.

"You'm murdered cappen—all vour of 'em!" shouted a man. "We'm coom, maybe, to zee if you'm likin' to be murdered, same as poor cappen an' dree oithers!"

"They'm geet na more'n they axed for!" I shouted out. "They tried to murder monsieur—"

"Quiet, boy!" said monsieur, without looking round.

"Yes, sir," I answered him; and then, in that moment of time, I heard a sound on the companion-ladder, and I shouted out to monsieur:

"Thee's sommat coomin' down th' ladder, monsieur!"

As I shouted this, there was a slithering noise and a dull thud, as if someone had fallen, and then a low groaning. I stared hard at the doorway that led to the companion-ladder, and everyone in the cabin stared the same, save monsieur, who watched the men.

"It's the bo'sun!" shouted one of the men. "Howd'y, bo'sun!"

I saw the bo'sun's great head and face come round the edge of the doorway, about two feet from the floor. It was plain to me that he was creeping on his hands and knees, because of the wound in his leg.

Then, in a moment, he had whipped his hand in round the door, and I saw that there was a ship's pistol in his fist. He had fired before ever I could bring out a shout, and he hit monsieur somewhere, for I heard the horrid thud of the bullet, and I saw monsieur jerk his body as he was struck.

Then the bo'sun roared out in a great voice:

"On to him, lads. On to him. He's done for!"

And, at the shout, the men broke forward upon monsieur in a crowd with their knives. Yet I was to see a wonderful thing, for monsieur stood firm and swaying to the roll of the ship, despite that he was hit, as I knew, and as the men rushed upon him his sword made a dozen quick flashes in the lamplight, so that it was like an uncertain glimmer among the men; and suddenly they gave back from him, and there were four of them went thudding to the floor and five more that were wounded.

Yet they had got at monsieur; for, as I ran forward to aid him with the blunderbuss, I saw that there were three knives in his breast, though he still kept upon his feet, with his great strength of body and his greater strength of mind, or will, which are both the same thing, as I do think.

"Monsieur!" I cried out, like a lad will call out when he sees his hero all destroyed. "Monsieur!" And he looked down at me and smiled a little, steadying himself with the point of his sword upon the deck of the cabin.

There was not another sound in the place, for they saw that he was done; but, indeed, I was not yet done.

"Great men ye are!" I called out. "Forty to one, ye swine, an' him wounded dead, an' ye fear him like death—"

I'd got no further, when one of them threw a knife at me, that cut me a bit in the arm; and on that I dropped upon my knee, and lunged forward the great blunderbuss.

They gave back from it, like they might from death, which it was. But one of them called out that it was not loaded, and they came forward in a great rush once more with their knives. But I pulled the trigger of the blunderbuss, and loosed into them near half a flask of good powder and maybe two pounds' weight of pistol bullets.

The cabin was filled with the smoke of the great weapon, and out of the smoke there were dreadful screamings and the thuddings of feet; but for my part I lay flat upon my back, all shaken and dazed from the kick of the blunderbuss.

Then I rolled over and got upon my knees; and as I did so I saw that monsieur lay quiet beside me.

I dropped the blunderbuss, and caught monsieur quickly by the shoulders, and dragged him, upon his back, into the captain's cabin. Then I shut the door very hasty, and slid the bolt, and afterwards I drew and pushed one of the captain's sea-chests' up against it.

When I had done this, I felt round for the box where Captain Drool had kept his flint and steel, for there was no light in the place, now that I had shut the door upon the lamp in the big cabin.

Presently, in no more than a minute, I had the captain's lamp alight, which burned very bright with good whale oil; and I stooped then quickly to care for monsieur.

I found him lying silent where I had drawn him; but his eyes were open, and, when I knelt by him, he looked at me, quiet and natural, yet with a little slowness in the way that he moved his eyes.

"Monsieur!" I said, near sobbing because he was so near gone. "Monsieur!"

There was a minute of silence between us, and I heard the uproar ease outside the main cabin; but the door was thick and heavy for a ship's door, and deadened the sounds maybe more than I knew.

Abruptly, there came almost a stillness out in the big cabin; and then, sudden, a great blow struck upon the door, that set all the bulkheads jarring and the telescopes in the beckets leaping.

But I had them upon the hip, for I shouted out in my lad's voice, very hoarse and desperate:

"If ye break the door, I'll blow the ship to hell. Aa've geet the powder-trap oppen, an' Aa've me pistols. Sitha! If ye break in the door, Aa'll loose off me pistol into the powder!"

Just that I sung out to them; and never another blow was struck upon the door, for the powder was stored under the deck of Captain Drool's cabin, as all the ship knew, and I better than any, being the lad that had cleaned his cabin many a score of times. And this is the reason that I chose to retreat there from the men.

"Boy," I heard monsieur saying from the floor, "is the hatch open!"

"No, monsieur," I said, grinning a little at the easy way I had driven the men off.

"Open it, boy," he said gravely. "Nor tell ever a lie with a light tongue. And when you have to deal a man the bitterness of death, be not over eager to consign him to hell, but rather to God, Who understandeth all and forgiveth all."

"Yes, sir," I said; and opened the powder-hatch, with a great fear at my heart that I was truly come to the end of life.

"Am I to shoot into the powder, sir?" I asked him, all strung-up and ready to shut my eyes and fire at his bidding.

But he waved his fingers a little for me to come to him; and when I was come to him, he lay a moment and looked up at me, seeming to smile a little in spite of his pain.

"You are a strange boy," he said at last in a weak voice. "Fetch me a sheet of paper from the captain's desk—nay, fetch me the log-book and a quill and the ink."

When I had fetched these, he bid me put them upon the deck, to the left of him, and to open the log-book at the last entry, also to wet the quill ready.

"Now, boy," he whispered, "make good haste and gentle, and help me over a little upon my left side. Quick now, before I am gone, or it will be too late to do God's own justice."

His voice was very weak, and whistled thin and strange as he spoke; and when I had helped him with all my power of gentleness on to his side, I saw how he had been lying there in his blood.

"Steady me so, boy," he whispered; and I steadied him while he wrote.

And as he wrote, labouring to hold in his groans and to contain all his senses to his purpose, I could see the handles of the knives in his breast. And so he writ, and made no ado of the agony it cost him; but truly a greater victory over mortal pain I could think a man never won.

"Now, this is the letter, which I have by me to this day, though I was too ignorant at that time to know what it was that he wrote:

"To Master Alfred Sylles,

"The Corner House,

"Portsmouth Town.

"Dear Master Sylles,—I write this near death, and with no power to write much. See that justice be done me in this fashion, to wit, that the boy who bears this, John Merlyn, shall be mine heir. See that he go to a good school, well equipt. I will tell him the names of my dead lady, so that you shall know that he is indeed the youth of this my will and last testament, though none here can witness, for I am alone save for this boy, who hath fought by and for me as I could have wished mine own son to fight.

"From him will you have all the story.

"Farewell, dear Master Sylles.

"ARTOIS JEYNOIS."

When this was writ, he laid the quill down between the pages, so that the rolling of the ship should not squander it. But when I would have helped steady him again on to his back, he bid me wait and listen, for that he would certainly die with his words unsaid when he moved to lie down again.

"Remember these three names, my boy," he said; "nor tell them to any on earth save Master Sylles of the Corner House of Portsmouth Town, whom you know by repute, and to whom I have writ this letter. The names are Mercelle Avonynne Elaise. Now repeat them till you can never let them slip."

He waited while I said them over a dozen times, maybe, then he caught his breath a little, and seemed as if he were gone; but presently he breathed again, but with a louder noise and bleeding very sadly.

"To Master Sylles tell all that you know," he said; "and because you have been a brave and a faithful lad, I bequeath to you my sword, to use only with honour."

He caught his breath again, and I trembled with a strange lad's ague of pity to know how to ease him; but after a little while he began again, but whispering:

"How you shall escape, lad, I know not; but hold this cabin, for here they are in fear of you, because of the powder. Presently, when the ship is into the Channel, you may have chance to swim ashore. But wrap the letter up safe first in an oilskin. Tell Master Sylles all. Now, may God be with you, boy. Lay me down."

He sank his great shoulder against me as he spoke, and slid round on to his back with a strange, deep groan, and in that moment the light went clean out of his eyes, and I saw that he was truly dead.

And I knelt there beside him, and cried as only a lad can cry over his dead hero.

***

Of the manner of my escape, I need to tell but little here, for that night the men, being in fear of the law, ran the brig ashore below the Lizards, thinking to drown the ship and me, and so hide their foul work upon the stark rocks.

But they made a bad business of their landing, and many were drowned because of the heavy seas; but I, who stayed in the ship, was safe, for she held together until the morning, when the weather was grown fine; and I swam ashore, with monsieur's sword made fast to my back.

Yet it was a matter of twelve weary days after this before I came safe into Portsmouth Town, where I learnt from good Master Sylles that I was the heir of monsieur. And how good Master Sylles did weep—for he had loved him—when I told him all concerning the vile murdering of monsieur.

But he stayed not at weeping, being a practical man as well as a warm friend, for when the bo'sun returned to Portsmouth Town a while after, supposing me to be drowned in the brig, Master Sylles had the watch upon him within the hour, and hailed him to high justice, so that a week later the bo'sun was hanged in chains at the corner of the four roads outside Portsmouth Town, to be for a warning to shipmen and landsmen that the trade of murder shall bring eternal sorrow.

And at last I am come to an end of my telling of that dear friend of my youth, who is with me in my memory all the long years of my life. And even in that early day did his goodness and charity affect me; so that, as well I do mind me, once when I passed the dried body of the bo'sun, I must stop and loose off my cap, and set up a prayer to God for him, for I knew that Monsieur Jeynois would so have wished it.

The Inn of the Black Crow

An Extract from the Travelling Notebook of John Dory, Secret Exciseman.

JUNE 27TH.—I CANNOT SAY that I care for the look of mine host. If he tippled more and talked more I should like him better; but he drinks not, neither does he speak sufficiently for ordinary civility.

I could think that he has no wish for my custom. Yet, if so, how does he expect to make a living, for I am paying two honest guineas a week for board and bed no better than the Yellow Swan at Dunnage does me for a guinea and a half. Yet that he knows me or suspects me of being more than I appear I cannot think, seeing that I have never been within a hundred miles of this desolated village of Erskine, where there is not even the sweet breath of the sea to blow the silence away, but everywhere the grey moors, slit by the lonesome mud-beset creeks, that I have few doubts see some strange doings at nights, and could, maybe, explain the strange crushed body of poor James Naynes, the exciseman, who had been found dead upon the moors six weeks gone; and concerning which I am here to discover secretly whether it was foul murder or not.

June 30th.—That I was right in my belief that Jalbrok, the landlord, is a rascal, I have now very good proof, and would shift my quarters, were it not that there is no other hostel this side of Bethansop, and that is fifteen weary miles by the road.

I cannot take a room in any of the hovels round here; for there could be no privacy for me, and I should not have the freedom of unquestioned movement that one pays for at all inns, along with one's bed and board. And here, having given out on arriving that I am from London town for my health, having a shortness of breath, and that I fish with a rod, like my old friend Walton—of whom no man hereabouts has ever heard—I have been let go my way as I pleased, with never a one of these grim Cornishman to give me so much as a passing nod of the head; for to them I am a "foreigner," deserving, because of this stigma, a rock on my head, rather than a friendly word on my heart. However, in the little Dowe-Fleet river there are trout to make a man forget lonesomeness.

But though I am forced to stay here in the inn until my work is done, and my report prepared for the authorities, yet I am taking such care as I can in this way and that, and never do I venture a yard outside the inn without a brace of great flintlocks hidden under my coat.

Now, I have said I proved Jalbrok, the landlord of this inn of the Black Crow, a rascal. And so have I in two things; for this morning I caught him and his tapman netting the little Dowe-Fleet, and a great haul he had of fish, some that were three pounds weight and a hundred that were not more than fingerlings, and should never have left water.

I was so angry to see this spoiling of good, honest sport that I loosed out at Jalbrok with my tongue, as any fisherman might; but he told me to shut my mouth, and this I had to do, though with difficulty, and only by remembering that a man that suffers from a shortness of wind has no excuse to fight. So I made a virtue of the matter, and sat down suddenly on the bank, and panted pretty hard and spit a bit, and then lay on my side, as if I had a seizure. And a very good acting I made of it, I flattered myself, and glad that I had held my temper in, and so made them all see that I was a truly sick man.

Now, there the landlord left me, lying on my side, when he went away with all that great haul of good trout. And this was the second thing to prove the man a rascal, and liefer to be rid of me than to keep me, else he had not left me there, a sick man as he supposed. And I say and maintain that any man that will net a stream that may be fished with a feathered hook, and will also leave a sick man to recover or to die alone, all as may be, is a true rascal—and so I shall prove him yet.

July 2nd (Night).—I have thought that the landlord has something new on his mind lately, and the thing concerns me; for twice and again yesterday evening I caught him staring at me in a very queer fashion, so that I have taken more care than ever to be sure that no one can come at me during the night.

After dinner this evening I went down and sat a bit in the empty taproom, where I smoked my pipe and warmed my feet at the big log fire. The night had been coldish, in spite of the time of the year, for there is a desolate wind blowing over the great moorlands, and I could hear the big Erskine creek lapping on the taproom side of the house, for the inn is built quite near to the creek.

While I was smoking and staring into the fire, a big creekman came into the taproom and shouted for Jalbrok, the landlord, who came out of the back room in his slow, surly way.

"I'm clean out o' guzzle," the creekman said, in a dialect that was no more Cornish than mine. "I'll swop a good yaller angel for some o' that yaller sperrit o' yourn, Jal. An' that are a bad exchange wi'out robb'ry. He, he! Us that likes good likker likes it fresh from the sea, like a young cod. He, he!"

There is one of those farm-kitchen wind-screens, with a settle along it, that comes on one side the fireplace in the taproom, and neither Jalbrok nor the big creekman could see me where I sat, because the oak-screen hid me, though I could look round it with the trouble of bending my neck,

Their talk interested me greatly, as may be thought, for it was plain that the man, whoever he might be, had punned on the gold angel, which is worth near half a guinea of honest English money; and what should a creekman be doing with such a coin, or to treat it so lightly, as if it were no more than a common groat? And afterwards to speak of liking the good liquor that comes fresh from the sea! It was plain enough what he meant.

I heard Jalbrok, the landlord, ringing the coin on the counter. And then I heard him saving it was thin gold; and that set the creekman angry.

"Gglag you for a scrape-bone!" he roared out, using a strange expression that was new to me. "Gglag you! You would sweat the oil off a topmast, you would! If you ain't easy, there's more nor one as ha' a knife into you ower your scrape-bone ways; and, maybe, us shall make you pay a good tune for French brandy one o' these days, gglag you!"

"Stow that!" said the landlord's voice. "That's no talk for this place wi' strangers round. I—"

He stopped, and there followed, maybe, thirty seconds of absolute silence. Then I heard someone tiptoeing a few steps over the floor, and I closed my eyes and let my pipe droop in my mouth, as if I were dosing. I heard the steps cease, and there was a sudden little letting out of a man's breath, and I knew that the landlord had found I was in the taproom with them.

The next thing I knew he had me by the shoulder, and shook me, so that my pipe, dropped out of my mouth on to the stone floor.

"Here!" he roared out. "Wot you doin' in here!"

"Let go of my shoulder, confound your insolence," I said; and ripped my shoulder free from his fist with perhaps a little more strength than I should have shown him, seeing that I am a sick man to all in this part.

"Confound you!" I said again, for I was angry; but now I had my wits more about me. "Confound your putting your dirty hands on me. First you net the river and spoil my trout fishing, and now you must spoil the best nap I have had for three months."

As I made an end of this, I was aware that the big creekman was also staring round the oak wind-screen at me. And therewith it seemed a good thing to me to fall a-coughing and "howking," as we say in the North; and a better country I never want!

"Let un be, Jal. Let un be!" I heard the big creekman saying. "He ain't but a broken-winded man. There's none that need ha' fear o' that sort. He'll be growin' good grass before the winter. Come you, gglag you, an' gi'e me some guzzle, an' let me be goin'."

The landlord looked at me for nearly a minute without a word; then he turned and followed the creekman to the drinking counter. I heard a little further grumbled talk and argument about the angel being thin gold, but evidently they arranged it between them, for Jalbrok measured out some liquor, that was good French brandy by the smell of it, if ever I've smelt French brandy, and a little later the creekman left.

July 5th.—Maybe I have kissed the inn wench a little heartily on occasions, but she made no sound objections, and it pleased me, I fear, a little to hear Llan, the lanky, knock-kneed tapman and general help, rousting at the wench for allowing it. The lout has opinions of himself, I do venture to swear; for a more ungainly, water-eyed, shambling rascal never helped his master net a good trout stream before or since. And as on that occasion he showed a great pleasure, and roared in his high pitched crow at the way I lay on the bank and groaned and coughed, I take an equal great pleasure to kiss the maid, which I could think she is, whenever I chance to see him near.

And to see the oaf glare at me, and yet fear to attack even a sick man, makes me laugh to burst my buttons; but I make no error, for it is that kind of a bloodless animal that will put a knife between a man's shoulders when the chance offers.

July 7th.—Now a good kiss, once in a way, may be a good thing all round, and this I discovered it to be, for the wench has taken a fancy to better my food, for which I am thankful; also, last night, she went further, for she whispered in my ear, as she served me my dinner, to keep my bedroom door barred o' nights; but when I would know why, she smiled, putting her finger to her lip, and gave me an old countryside proverb to the effect that a barred door let no corn out and no rats in. Which was a good enough hint for any man, and I repaid the wench in a way that seemed to please her well, nor did she say no to a half-guinea piece which I slipped into her broad fist.

Now, the room I sleep in is large, being about thirty feet long and, maybe, twenty wide, and has a good deal of old and bulky furniture in it, that makes it over-full of shadows at night for my liking.

The door of my room is of oak, very heavy and substantial, and without panels. There is a wooden snick-latch on it to enter by, and the door is made fast with a wooden bolt set in oak sockets, and pretty strong. There are two windows to the room, but these are barred, for which I have been glad many a time.

There are in the bedroom two great, heavy, oaken clothes-cupboards, two settees, a big table, two great wood beds, three lumbersome old chairs, and three linen-presses of ancient and blackened oak, in which the wench keeps not linen, but such various oddments as the autumn pickings of good hazel nuts, charcoal for the upstairs brazier, and in the third an oddment of spare feather pillows and some good down in a sack; and besides these, two gallon puggs—as they name the small kegs here—of French brandy, which I doubt not she has "nigged" from the cellars of mine host, and intends for a very welcome gift to some favoured swain, or, indeed, for all I know, to her own father, if she have one. And simple she must be some ways, for she has never bothered to lock the press.

Well do I know all these matters by now, for I have a bothersome pilgrimage each night, first to open the great cupboards and look in, and then to shut and snick the big brass locks. And after that I look in the linen-chests, and smile at the two puggs of brandy, for the wench has found something of a warm place in my heart because of her honest friendliness to me. Then I peer under the two settees and the two beds; and so I am sure at last that the room holds nothing that might trouble me in my sleep.

The beds are simple, rustic, heavy-made affairs, cloddish and without canopies or even posts for the same, which makes them seem very rude and ugly to the eye. However, they please me well, for I have read in my time—and once I saw the like—of bedsteads that had the canopy very great and solid and made to let down, like a press, upon the sleeper, to smother him in his sleep; and a devilish contrivance is such in those of our inns that are on the by-roads; and many a lone traveller has met a dreadful death, as I have proved in my business of a secret agent for the king. But there are few such tricks that I cannot discover in a moment, because of my training in all matters that deal with the ways of law-breakers, of which I am a loyal and sworn enemy.

But for me, at the Inn of the Black Crow, I have no great fear of any odd contrivance of death; nor of poison or drugging if I should be discovered, for there is a skill needed in such matters, and, moreover, the wench prepares my food and is my good friend; for it is always my way to have the women folk upon my side, and a good half of the battles of life are won if a man does this always. But what I have good cause to fear is lest the landlord, or any of the brute oafs of this lonesome moor, should wish to come at me in my sleep, and, maybe, hide in one of the great presses or the great cupboards to this end; and there you have my reasons for my nightly search of the room.

On this last night I paid a greater attention to all my precautions, and searched the big room very carefully, even to testing the wall behind the pictures, but found it of good moorland stone, like the four walls of the room.

The door, however, I made more secure by pushing one of the three linen-presses up against it, and so I feel pretty safe for the night.

Now, I had certainly a strong feeling that something might be in the wind, as the sailor-men say, against me; and a vague uneasiness kept me from undressing for a time, so that, after I had finished making all secure for the night, I sat a good while in one of the chairs by the table and wrote up my report.

After a time I had a curious feeling that someone was looking in at me through the barred window to my left, and at last I got up and loosed the heavy curtains down over both it and the far one, for it was quite possible for anyone to have placed one of the short farm-ladders against the wall and come up to have a look in at me. Yet in my heart I did not really think this was so, and I tell of my action merely because it shows the way that I felt.

At last I said to myself that I had grown to fancying things because of the friendly warning that the wench had given me over my dinner; but even as I said it, and glanced about the heavy, shadowy room, I could not shake free from my feelings. I took my candle and slipped off my shoes, so that my steps should not be heard below; then I went again through my pilgrimage of the room. I opened the cupboards and presses, each in turn, and finally once more I looked under the beds and even under the table, but there was nothing, nor could there have been to my common-sense reasoning.

I determined to undress and go to bed, assuring myself that a good sleep would soon cure me, but at first I went to my trunk and unlocked it. I took from it my brace of pistols and my big knife, also my lantern, which had a cunning little cap over the face and a metal cowl above the chimney, so that, by means of the cap and the cowl,

I can make the lantern dark and yet have a good light burning within ready for an instant use.

Then I drew out the wads from my pistols, and screwed out the bullets and the second wads, and poured out the powder. I tried the flints, and found them spark very bright and clean, and afterwards I reloaded the pistols with fresh powder, using a heavier charge, and putting into each twelve large buckshot as big as peas, and a wad on the top to hold them in.

When I had primed the two pistols, I reached down into my boot and drew out a small weapon that I am never without; and a finely made pistol it is, by Chamel, the gunsmith, near the Tower. I paid him six guineas for that one weapon, and well it has repaid me, for I have killed eleven men with it in four years that would otherwise have sent me early out of this life; and a better pistol no man ever had, nor, for the length of the barrel, a truer. I reloaded this likewise, but with a single bullet in the place of the buckshot slugs I had put into my heavier pistols.

I carried a chair close to the bedside, and on this chair I laid my three pistols and my knife. Then I lit my lantern, and shut the cap over the glass; after which I stood it with my weapons on the seat of the chair.

I took a good while to undress, what with the way I kept looking round me into the shadows, and wishing I had a dozen great candles, and again stopping to listen to the horrid moan of the moor wind blowing in through the crannies of the windows, and odd times the dismal sounding lap, lap of the big Erskine creek below.

When at last I climbed up into the great clumsy-made bed, I left the candle burning on the table, and lay a good while harking to the wind, that at one moment would cease, and leave the big, dark room silent and chill-seeming, and the next would whine and moan again in through the window crannies.

I fell asleep in the end, and had a pretty sound slumber. Then, suddenly, I was lying there awake in the bed, listening. The candle had burned itself out and the room was very, very dark, owing to my having drawn the curtains, which I never did before.

I lay quiet, trying to think why I had waked so sharply; and in the back of my brain I had a feeling that I had been wakened by some sound. Yet the room was most oppressive quiet, and not even was there the odd whine or moan of the wind through the window crannies, for now the wind had dropped away entirely.

Yet there were sounds below me in the big taproom, and I supposed that a company of the rough creek and moor men were drinking and jollying together beneath me, for as I lay and listened there came now and then the line of a rude song, or a shouted oath, or an indefinite babel of rough talk and argument, all as the mood served. And once, by the noise, there must have been something of a free fight, and a bench or two smashed, by the crash I heard of broken woodwork.

After a while there was a sudden quietness, in which the silence of the big chamber grew on me with a vague discomfort. Abruptly I heard a woman's voice raised in a clatter of words, and then there was a great shouting of hoarse voices, and a beating of mugs upon the benches, by the sounds.

I leaned up on my elbow in the bed and listened, for there was such a to-do, as we say, that I could not tell what to think.

As I leaned there and hearkened I heard the woman begin to scream, and she screamed, maybe, a dozen times, but whether in fear or anger or both I could not at once decide, only now I drew myself to the edge of the bed, meaning to open my lantern and have some light in the room. As I rolled on to the edge of the bed, and reached out my hand, the screaming died away, and there came instead, as I stiffened and harked, the sound of a woman crying somewhere in the house. And suddenly I comprehended, in some strange fashion of the spirit, that it was because of me—that some harm was to be done me, perhaps was even then coming.

I stretched out my hand swiftly and groped for the lantern; but my hand touched nothing, and I had a quick sickening and dreadful feeling that something was in the room with me, and had taken the chair away from the side of my bed, with all my weapons.

In the same moment that thus thought flashed a dreadful and particular horror across my brain, I realised, with a sweet revulsion towards security, that I was reaching out upon the wrong side of the bed, for the room was so utter dark with the heavy curtains being across the windows.

I jumped to my feet upon the bed, and as I did so there sounded two sharp blows somewhere beneath me. I turned to stride quickly across, and as I did so the whole bed seemed to drop from under me, as I was in the very act of my stride. Something hugely great caught me savagely and brutally by my feet and ankles, and in the same instant there was a monstrous crash upon the floor of the bedroom that seemed to shake the inn. I pitched backwards, and struck my shoulder against the heavy timbers, but the dreadful grip upon my feet never ceased: I rose upright, using the muscles of my thighs and stomach to lift me; and when I was stood upright in the utter darkness I squatted quickly and felt at the thing which had me so horribly by the feet.

My feet seemed to be held between two edges that were padded, yet pressed so tight together that I could not force even my fist between them.

I stood up again and wrenched, very fierce and mad, to free my feet, but I could not manage it, and only seemed to twist and strain my ankles with the fight I made and the way I troubled to keep my balance.

I stopped a moment where I stood in the darkness on my trapped feet, and listened very intently. Yet there seemed everywhere a dreadful silence, and no sound in all the house, and I could not be sure whether I was still in the bedroom or fallen into some secret trap along with the bed when it fell from under me.

I reached up my hands over my head to see if I could touch anything above me, but I found nothing. Then I spread my arms out sideways to see whether I could touch any wall, but there was nothing within my reach.

All this time, while I was doing this, I said to myself that I must be still in the bedroom, for the taproom lay just below me; also, though the bed had fallen from under me, and I also had seemed to go down, yet I had not felt to have dropped far.

And then, in the midst of my fears and doubts and horrid bewilderment, I saw a faint little ray of light, no greater than the edge of a small knife, below me.

I squatted again upon my trapped feet, and reached out towards where I had seen the faint light; but now I could no longer see it. I moved my hands up and down, and from side to side, and suddenly I touched a beam of wood, seeming on a level with the thing which held my feet.

I gripped the beam and pulled and pushed at it, but it never moved; and therewith I put my weight on it and leaned more forward still; and so in an instant I touched a second beam.

I tried whether this second beam would hold me, and found it as firm and solid as the first. I put my weight on to it, using my left hand, and reached out my right hand, carrying myself forward, until suddenly I saw the light again, and had a slight feeling of heat not far below my face.

I put my hand towards the faint light and touched something. It was my own dark lantern. I could have cried out aloud with the joy of my discovery. I fumbled open the hinged cap that was shut over the glass, and instantly there was light upon everything near me.

A new amazement came to me as I discovered that I was yet in the bedroom, and the lamp was still upon the chair with my pistols, and that my feet had been trapped by the bed itself; for the two beams that I had felt were the supporting skeleton of one side of the heavy-made bedstead, and the mattress had shut up like a monstrous book; and what had been its middle part was now rested upon the floor of the bedroom, between the beams of its upholding framework, whilst the top edges had closed firmly upon my feet and ankles, so that I was held like a trapped rat. And a cunning and brutal machine of death the great bedstead was, and would have crushed the breath and the life out of my body in a moment had I been lying flat upon the mattress as a man does in sleep.

Now, as I regarded all this, with a fiercer and ever fiercer growing anger, I heard again the low sound of a woman weeping somewhere in the house, as if a door had been suddenly opened and let the sound come plain. Then it ceased, as if the door had been closed again.

Now, I saw that I must do two things. The one was to make no noise to show that I still lived, and the second was to free myself us speedily as I could. But first I snatched up my lamp and flashed it all round the big bedroom, and upon the door; but it was plain to me that there was no one gotten into the room, yet there might be a secret way in I now conceived, for how else should they come in to remove the dead if the door of the room were locked, just as I, indeed, had locked it before I made to sleep?

However, the first thing I shaped to do was to get free, and I caught up my knife from the chair and began to cut into the great box-mattress where the padding was nailed down solid with broad-headed clouts.

But all the time that I worked I harked very keen for any sound in the room that might show whether they were coming yet for my body. And I worked quick but quiet, so that I should make no noise, yet I smiled grim to myself to think how strange a corpse they should have to welcome them, and how lively a welcome!

And suddenly, as I worked, there came a faint creaking of wood from the far side of the big, dark room where stood one of the great clothes-cupboards. I stabbed my big knife into one of the edges of the closed mattress where it would be ready to my hand in the dark, and instantly closed the cover over my dark lantern and stood it by the knife. Then, in the darkness, I reached for my pistols from the chair seat, and the small one I stood by the knife, pushing the end of the barrel down between the mattress edges, so that its butt stood up handily for me to grip in the dark.

I caught up my two great pistols in my fists, and stared round me as I squatted, harking with a bitter eagerness, for it was sure enough that I must fight for my life, and, maybe, I should be found in the morning far out on the moor, like poor James Naynes was found. But of one thing I was determined, there should go two or three that night to heaven or to hell, and the choice I left with them, for it was no part of my business, but only to see that the earth was soundly rid of them.

Now there was a space of absolute silence, and then again I heard the creaking sound from the far end of the room. I stared hard that way, and then took a quick look round me, through the dark, to be sure that my ears had told me truly the direction of the sounds.

When I looked back again, there was a light inside the great cupboard, for I could see the glow of it around the edges of the door.

I knew now that there must be a hidden way into the bedroom, coming in through the back of the cupboard, which must be made to open; but I smiled a little to remember that I had locked the door, which had a very good and stout brass lock.

Yet I learned quickly enough that this was not likely to bother the men, for after I had heard them press upon the door, there was a low muttering of voices from within the cupboard, and then a sound of fumbling against the woodwork, and immediately there was a squeak of wood, and one end of the cupboard swung out like a door, and all that end of the bedroom was full of light from the lamp they had inside the cupboard.

In the moment when the end of the cupboard swung out there came to me the sudden knowledge that I must not be seen until the murderers were all come into the room, otherwise they would immediately give back into the cupboard before I could kill them. And I should indeed be in a poor case if they fetched up a fowling-piece to shoot at me; for they could riddle me with swan-shot, or the like, by no more than firing round the edge of the great oak cupboard; and I tethered there by the feet and helpless as a sheep the moment I had fired off my pistols!

Now, all this reasoning went through my brain like a blaze of lightning for speed, and in the same moment I had glanced round me, for the light from the cupboard was sufficient to show those things that were near me. I saw that there was half of a coverlid draped out from between the two edges of the great trap, and I snatched at it, and had it over me in a trice, and was immediately crouched there silent upon the edge of the mattress, as if I were simply a heap of the bed-clothing that had not been caught in the trap.

I had no more than covered myself and crouched still, when I heard the men stepping into the room.

"It's sure got un proper!" I heard the voice of the knock-kneed Llan say.

And he crowed out one of his shrill, foolish laughs.

"There'll be less of these king's agents an' the like after this!" I heard Jalbrok's voice growl.

"Gglag the swine!" came a familiar voice. "I'll put my knife into un, to make sure. Why, blow me if he don't know enough to gaol us all."

"There'll be no need o' knives," said Jalbrok; "an if there is, it's me that does it. He's my lodger!"

"Share plunder alike! Share plunder alike!" said another voice from the cupboard, by the sound of it.

And then there was the noise of heavy feet approaching, and the sound of scuffling in the big cupboard, as if a number of the brutish crew were fighting to get their clumsy bodies into the room, all in a great haste to see how the death trap had worked.

In that instant, and when the men were no farther from the bed than five or six paces, I hove the covering clean off me, and stood up on my trapped feet, but keeping my two great pistols behind my back, for I had them all now at my mercy.

I think they thought in that first moment that I was a ghost by the howl of terror that some of them sent up to heaven. Such a brutish crew no man need have paused to shoot down; yet I did, for I wished to see what they would do now that I had discovered myself to them.

They had, all of them, their belt-knives in their hands, as if they had meant to thrust them into my dead body rather than let no blood. The landlord carried a lantern in one hand and a pig-sticker's knife, maybe two feet long from haft to point, in the other, and his eyes shone foully with the blood-lust such as you will see once in a lifetime in the red eyes of a mad swine.

So they had all of them stopped as I rose, and some had howled out, as I have told, in their sudden fear, thinking I was dead, and had risen in vengeance, as was seemly enough to their ignorant minds.

But now Jalbrok, the landlord, held his lantern higher, and drew the flat of his knife across his great thigh.

"Good-morning, mine host and kind friends all," I said gently. "Wherefore this rollicking visit? Am I invited to join you in jollying the small hours, or does Master Gglag, you with the open mouth there, desire my help in the landing of good liquor from the sea?"

"Slit him!" suddenly roared Jalbrok, with something like a pig's squeal in the note of his voice. "Slit him!"

And therewith he rushed straight at me with the pig-sticker, and the rest of that vile crew of murdering brutes after him. But I whipped my two great pistols from behind my back, and thrust them almost into their faces; and blood-hungry though they were, like wild beasts, they gave back like dogs from a whip, and the landlord with them.

"In the name of James Naynes, whom ye destroyed in this same room," I said quietly.

And I fired my right hand pistol at Jalbrok, and saw his face crumble, and he fell, carrying the lamp, and a man further back in the room tumbled headlong. The lamp had gone out when the landlord fell, and the room was full of a sound like the howling of frightened animals. There was a mad rush in the darkness for the great oak cupboard, and I loosed off again with my left-hand pistol into the midst of the noise; and immediately there were several screams, and a deeper pandemonium. I heard furniture thrown about madly, and some of the men seemed to have lost their bearings, for I heard the crash of broken glass as they blundered into the far window.

Then I had my lamp in my hands, and my third pistol. I opened the shutter, and shone the light upon the blundering louts; and as they got their bearings in the light there was a madder scramble than before to escape through the cupboard.

I did not shoot again, but let them escape, for I judged they had seen sufficient of me to suit their needs for that one night. And to prove that I was right, I heard them go tumbling away out of the front doorway at a run. And after that there was a great quietness throughout the inn.

I threw the light upon the men on the floor. Jalbrok and his murdering helpman appeared both to be dead, but there were three others who groaned, but were not greatly hurt, for when I called out to them to go before I shot them truly dead, they were all of them to their knees in a moment, and crept along the floor into the cupboard, and so out of my sight.

I had my feet free of the trap in less than the half of an hour, and went over to the men upon the floor, who were both as dead as they deserved to be.

Then I loaded my pistols, and, with one in each hand, I entered the cupboard, and found, as I had supposed, a ladder reared up within a big press that stands in the taproom from floor to ceiling, and the top of which is the floor of the cupboard in the bedroom. So that I was wrong when I thought, maybe, that there had been a false back to it.

I found the wench locked in a small pantry place where she slept, and when she saw me alive she first screamed, and then kissed me so heartily that I gave her a good honest guinea piece to cease; also because I was grateful to the lass for her regard for my safety.

Regarding the great machine in the bedroom, I made a close examination of this, and found that the hinged centre of the monstrously, heavy mattress was supported upon a strut which went down into the taproom through the great central beam that held the ceiling up, and was kept in place by an oak peg, which passed through the beam and the supporting strut. It was when they went to knock the peg out that the wench screamed, and the two blows I heard beneath the bed were the blows of the hammer on the peg.

And so I have discovered, as I set out to do, the way in which poor James Naynes met his death, and my hands have been chosen to deal out a portion of the lawful vengeance which his murderers had earned.

But I have not yet finished with this district—not until I have rooted out, neck and crop, the ruthless and bloodthirsty band that do their lawless work in this lonesome part of the king's domain.

N.B.—This abominable bed was still to be seen as late as 1850 in the Old Black Crow Inn at Erskine, where it was shown to visitors as a relic of the past.

What Happened in the Thunderbolt

I WAS NOT WHAT ONE WOULD TERM literally hard up, for I had over fifty pounds in my pocket; yet I could see no prospect of getting more, so I thought it would be better to clear out and make a start somewhere abroad.

I had served my time—afterwards passing for second mate—some years previously, but had grown so heartily sick of the life that I had thrown it up, as I hoped then, for good. Yet, when I shipped in the Thunderbolt, I was glad enough for the chance. I little thought then to what it was going to lead.

My intention had been to leave the ship as soon as we reached 'Frisco, and I should have done so had it not been for a certain reason, of which presently I shall speak.

We had a quiet enough voyage out round the Horn. Fine weather and steady winds. The grub was good, for ship's grub, and there was nothing particular to grumble about in the treatment we received at the hands of the after crowd, though I know now that this was due chiefly to the skipper, who was a decent sort of old chap.

The second mate, for whose watch I was picked, struck me as being a fellow who would bully if he got the least encouragement. He had one of the most sensual faces I have seen. I found later that he was a fiend.

The first mate was quite a different type of man. Tall and lean, as against the second's burliness, he was mean-looking and unobtrusive in his manners. I could not stand him. Yet there was nothing I could say against him—then.

When we reached 'Frisco I went to the old man, and told him that I wanted to leave. I asked him straight whether he intended to do the right thing by me, and pay me off in full. He inquired why I was anxious to go, and I told him that I wanted to get a job ashore. He was decent enough, and suggested that I should not be in a hurry, but take time to think the matter over. And, because of this, I stayed by the ship while she was in port.

We were nearly three months before we got our grain, and then we had to go up to Crockett to finish loading. When we got down again to 'Frisco, I was surprised to hear that we were to have a passenger home—a lady.

She came off to us next day, accompanied by an awful old hag of a chaperon.

I helped to get her things aboard, and I took her portmanteau into the saloon to the cabin she was to occupy. She and her chaperon, whose name was Mrs. Wiggins, followed me, carrying various small parcels. In the doorway leading into the saloon we met the second mate coming out. I saw him look over my shoulder at Miss Vairne—so her companion had named her—and in that moment I saw the foul soul of the man flash out in his eyes. He seemed to be unconscious that he was blocking the way, so intense was his gaze. It annoyed me beyond endurance.

"Excuse me, sir," I said. "This portmanteau is heavy."

At that he stepped to one side, though with a grunt that was almost a snarl. The next instant, seeming to remember himself, he swung off his cap to the ladies, but Miss Vairne walked past him as though she were unconscious that he existed.

I carried the portmanteau into the cabin, and deposited it upon the deck of the berth; then I turned to go. The second mate had not gone on deck, but was fiddling about in the saloon. It seemed to me that he was waiting until I had gone. I had nearly reached the door opening out of the saloon, when I heard a quick patter of steps behind me, and someone touched me on the arm. I turned quickly, and saw, to my astonishment, that it was Miss Vairne.

"Thank you so much for carrying in my portmanteau, Mr.—"

She hesitated.

"My name is Kenstone," I said. "But I'm afraid you've made a mistake, I'm one of the deck-hands."

She laughed outright at that, and held out her hand to me. Over by the table I knew the second mate was glaring at me savagely.

I pretended not to see him, and shook hands with Miss Vairne.

"I'm afraid, Miss Vairne," I said, smiling, "you do not realise that I am only one of the common sailors."

She laughed—a merry little laugh. Yet there was a sense of defiant scorn in it that I knew was intended to show the lowering second mate that she would thank whom she pleased, even though he were a common sailor.

"Might I ask you, Mr. Kenstone," she said, "if you would mind just loosing the straps of my bag? The buckles are rather stiff."

"Certainly," I said; and hurried to do her request.

Yet, as I bent over it, I kept my ears open, listening intently towards where the second mate stood. I expected every instant to hear him break out, for I knew that he must be just raging at her action in shaking hands with one who was but a deck-hand, while he, the little tin god, was utterly ignored.

His anger broke bounds as I finished loosing the straps, and stood up. Miss Vairne had just given me a mischievous little smile of thanks, when he broke in:

"Here, you, Kenstone! You'd better get on deck! This ain't your part of the ship!"

I would have answered him back pretty smartly had I been still of a mind to leave the ship, but all at once I found that this was the last thing I wished to do, and so, with a slight bow to Miss Vairne, and taking no notice of the second, I went on deck.

Later in the same day I went to the old man, and told him that I had changed my mind, and would prefer to make the passage home with him, if he cared to have me. He seemed quite pleased, and told me that he had felt sure I should change my mind, as there was nothing at which to grumble in the treatment received in his ship. I assured him that I was quite satisfied with the ship and the treatment, and so nothing more was said about my leaving. This arrangement suited him all the more in that he had not, as yet, signed on a hand in my place.

Three days later we sailed. During those three days I had seen Miss Vairne several times, yet never once to speak to. On two occasions she caught me looking at her, and replied by a bright little nod. I think that she had begun to realise that it would make trouble to treat me with the open, frank friendliness of our first meeting. Nevertheless, I was more than a little anxious to speak with her again could I but manage it without the officers being aware of the fact. Also, I was desirous that none of the men should see her speak to me, for I could not stand their remarks on certain subjects.

We had got well away from the coast before I again had speech with her. It was one day in the morning watch, about seven-thirty. Seven bells had been struck some minutes. We had been washing decks, and I was coiling down the braces on the lee side of the poop, when I heard her come up out from the companionway. I knew that it was she without looking round, though I did not show my knowledge, but just went on coiling. The second mate had gone for'ard along the main-deck to see Chips, and the next thing that I knew she was there standing beside me, watching me as I flaked the ropes down upon the deck. Still, I did not take any notice of her, but pretended to be so busy at the job that I had not seen her. At that she gave her foot a stamp, which pleased me greatly, seeing that I am a man. Yet still I paid not a bit of attention to her, just went on coiling down the main topsail brace, doing it very carefully and exactly. I guessed this would make her speak, especially as she was sure to know that the second mate would be back before long. And I was not mistaken.

"You're being rude on purpose," she said.

I looked up at that, but her eyes were not in my direction; instead, she was gazing away over the lee rail with an indifferent expression on her face. This made me think that someone might be looking, and I glanced towards the fellow at the wheel, but was relieved to notice that he could not see me where I stood, owing to the companionway being between.

Then I spoke.

"I beg your pardon," I said.

At that she turned and looked at me for one short moment, and there was no anger in her eyes; nothing, it seemed to me then, save roguishness and something else that I did not then understand.

Before I could speak again, I heard the second mate coming aft from the carpenter's shop. She, too, heard him. Yet, at the risk of being seen, she bent towards me.

"Good-morning, Mr. Common Sailor," she said prettily, but in a low voice.

The next instant she was leaning over the lee rail, and looking innocently at the expanse of sea. I was conscious of a queer sense of happiness. Then, though not unpleasantly, I realised that I had omitted to wish her "Good-morning." She had intended to rebuke my forgetfulness. I wondered how she knew that I was not a common sailorman, and yet I felt that I was a wretched hypocrite to pretend to wonder. I fell to picturing myself saying "Good-mornin', Miss," and touching my forehead to her. I believe I must have laughed out loud at the thought, for the next thing the second mate sang out to know what I was making that donkey-row up on the poop for. I made no reply, though I felt angry at his cursing me before her. I felt that he was on the look-out to do a bit of showing off. He wanted to lower me in her eyes. All the same I made no reply, but finished straightening up the ropes, and then walked down on to the main deck just as eight bells went for my watch below.

I saw Miss Vairne every day after that, but somehow, one way or another, nearly a fortnight passed before I had further word with her, and then only by sheer audacity. For, though I had not been able to exchange speech with her, something in the look on her face at times had told me that she was not quite happy, nor easy in her mind—that something was troubling her. I had seen this expression of uneasiness several times. I also noticed that she had got into the way of spending the greater portion of her time on deck, and that she deliberately avoided the first and second mates on every possible occasion. I wondered how it was that her chaperon was never visible, and I took occasion once to ask the steward, but he—an evil-looking little beast—grinned and said the old lady was keeping to her bunk, as she was unwell. Even then I began to have a smattering of suspicion, but I was soon to learn for certain, more than ever I should have guessed; for on the night of the very day on which the little, lying object of a steward had told me that the ugly old chaperon was ill in her bunk, I came across the old lady herself talking to the second mate in the shadow under the break of the poop. I saw them only by chance, and I did not give any sign to show that I had spotted them, but quietly strolled forward again as though I had seen nothing.

Yet from that time forward I kept a strict watch on every possible occasion and in every possible way—even to the extent of spending much of my watch below on the fo'c's'le head, so as to be able to keep an eye on the poop. In this way I observed that Miss Vairne seemed to offer no objection to the company of the third mate. Yet, in all conscience, she must have found him monotonous enough; for he was a great, dull, fat—also good-humoured—plough-boy sort of fellow—an apprentice just out of his "time." Still, it was a comfort to me to feel that she had this friend among the afterguard, though it was poor enough when pitted against such a man as the second mate. As regards the skipper and her, I observed that they appeared to be great friends; but he was getting an old man, and turned in early and rose late—often spending his afternoons sleeping in his bunk; besides which, he was not altogether free from the friendship of the whisky bottle. Thus there were many long hours when she was absolutely companionless. This was especially evident later—I am referring now to the first mate's watch—when the first mate kept the third busy in other parts of the ship, so—as it seemed to me—to keep him away from her. This apparently purposeful keeping of the third mate from her I gathered at odd times during those portions of my watch below when I sat smoking upon the fo'c's'le' head.

As I have said, it was only by means of sheer audacity that I at last got speech again with her. It was in this wise. I had been sent up the mizzen to grease down the spanker gaff. While I was busy at this, Miss Vairne came up on deck. She did not see me, and I had time to notice how worried she looked. It seemed to me that the girl was actually looking thinner, and at the thought of this a great sense of anger rose within me. I determined I would see and speak to her in one way or another. Yet, puzzle as I might, I could not see how I was to accomplish this without attracting attention. Suddenly, when I was about half-way down the gaff, an idea came to me, and, with a view to carrying it out, I cast off the lanyard of the slush-pot from which I was dipping, and waited for the next heavish roll.

It came, and I gave a shout, and slid round on the gaff, so that my crossed feet were uppermost; at the same moment I let go the pot of grease, which fell with a bang on to the lee side of the poop, scattering grease in all directions.

Down on deck I heard Miss Vairne cry out sharply in fear, and somehow, even as I hung there feet uppermost, a feeling of pleasure filled me at the concern in her voice. The next moment I had reached up to the spanker head outhaul, and was making my way swiftly down to the deck. As I dropped on my feet I heard the second mate's voice below the break of the poop. His head came into view. When he saw me standing on the deck wiping my greasy hands on a bit of shakins, he wanted to know what the blazes I was doing there. Then his eyes caught sight of the grease-bespattered decks, and he fairly gasped.

"By gad," he roared, "you've made a mess here, d—n you! Get some waste and your knife, and get it cleaned up. You're worse than a rotten ordinary!"

I replied nothing. This was the very thing for which I had aimed in dropping the grease-pot. I knew that I should have to clean it up, and I knew that it would take time. I intended that it should take time, and during that time it would be very hard luck indeed if I did not get a chance to have a talk with Miss Vairne.

For some ten minutes I scraped away busily, without raising my gaze from the deck. Then I heard the second mate go down the poop ladder, and I knew that it would be safe to look round. I now saw that Miss Vairne was sitting on the lee side of the cabin skylight. From the wheel, neither of us could be seen, so that I felt safe in smiling and raising my cap; yet I did not attempt to rise to my feet, but kept on busily scraping. At my salutation, Miss Vairne smiled a rather wan little smile. Then she rose slowly and walked towards me. Reaching the rail, she stopped, and I spoke.

"Aren't you well, Miss Vairne?" I asked.

"Yes," she replied. "You might have been killed."

"Oh, this!" I replied. "Why, I've done it on purpose, so as to get a chance to speak to you while I am cleaning it up."

"But you slipped—you all but fell. That—that—"

"Yes," I said; "that was done purposely, so as to make the dropping of the slush-pot appear an accident."

She looked at me a moment; then, slowly, a little wave of colour passed across her face—and grew.

And at that, as it were in an instant of time, I knew, and knowing, I cried almost inanely:

"You cared?"

The colour grew gloriously in her face, and suffused her throat and temples. She turned and looked out across the sea. For my part, I was filled with a tumult of wonder and unbelief, and, deeper than these, joy.

"Miss Vairne—Miss Vairne!" I cried.

She turned now and faced me, and her eyes were like love stars.

"Eina," she said. "Call me Eina. And you?"

She paused.

"Eina! Eina! Eina!" I repeated, in a sort of delirium.

"You haven't told me yours?" she reproached.

"Mine!" I said, with a sort of little gasp. "Mine! Just John."

"John Kenstone?" she said.

"Yes," I replied stupidly.

"And you're one of the deck-hands—common sailors?" she added joyously.

"Nay," I said, gathering my wits somewhat, "but your sweetheart."

She laughed splendidly, and seemed intending to add some new impertinence; then, suddenly changing her mind, said:

"But you have not told me that you love me. You have not asked me. You—"

"You know that I do—since the very first moment in which I set eyes upon you. I believe you knew—then."

I would have stood up to embrace her there upon the poop before all, but she beckoned me with her hand not to move.

"Nay, Mr. Common Sailor," she answered. "Stay you and scrape up your grease-spots—"

She paused, caught her breath with a naughty little gurgle, and bent towards me, her eyes fairly dancing.

"John Kenstone," she said, "you're a naughty boy, and a silly boy, and you don't know one bit how to make love. You gave me a horrid fright, and you're afraid to say that you love me; but I'm not afraid. I love you. I loved you at first, and I shall always love you."

She bent lower.

"Quick!" she said. "Now!"

Something touched my lips for the briefest part of an instant, and then she was standing demurely a yard away.

She had kissed me! It had been no more than like the breath of a summer wind; yet she had kissed me, and with the very thought, almost, I was overwhelmed.

I looked up at her confusedly. She was looking back at me with a funny little droop of the lids, and round her mouth it seemed to me there lurked a shadow of tenderness that was only for me.

Abruptly her mood changed.

"What was it you wanted to say when you risked your life?"

She nodded with her head towards the gaff.

"I didn't—" I began; but she interrupted me with a queer air of sternness.

"What was it?"

I felt momentarily confused.

"Oh, lots of things!" I said. Then, remembering more particularly; "You seemed unhappy."

"I was," she put in, "but I'm not now! Oh, I have wanted you, but I've been afraid of getting you into trouble with that—that brute!"

"The second mate?"

"Yes. He seems to have kept you away from me at the other end of the ship, and I didn't know—"

"That I loved you?" I said, as she hesitated.

She nodded.

"I'm afraid of that man and the first mate! They've—they've—"

"They've not said anything?" I asked, feeling suddenly savage.

"Yes," she said simply. "I told the captain, and he's had an awful row with the second mate. I keep out of their way as much as possible."

"Your chaperon?" I questioned.

"I can't stand her!" she returned passionately. "I believe she's a bad woman. She's false to me, and she and the steward and the second mate talk together. She watches me."

I told her what the steward had said to me, and how afterwards I had seen her chaperon talking to the second mate under the break of the poop.

"You must take a stand," I said. "Ask the skipper for a cabin for yourself. Lock yourself in at nights; you'll be safe then. And, besides, there's always the skipper. He's the boss, you know."

"And now I've got you," she added.

"Yes," I said.

"What a great man you are!" she went on, looking down at me as I knelt there upon the deck.

"Only six foot," I said apologetically.

"No, not only that way—broad. And your arms; I noticed them that first day. I love your arms!"

I laughed, for I was very strong, and she seemed to sting all the virility in me to greater life.

"I do love a man!" she said, as though to herself. Then, quite gravely: "You could kill the second mate!"

I stared at her.

"I don't know," I said, with equal gravity. "He's a great, thick-set brute."

She gave a gesture of dissent, and abruptly dropped her serious air. A ripple of mischief ran across her face and stirred in her eyes. She came a step towards me, and bent her face dangerously near.

"Wouldn't you like to?" she said.

I caught her with my great hands.

"Yes," I replied; and kissed her full on the lips.

I released her, and she stood up, her hair tossing in the wind and her cheeks gloriously rosy. On my part, I knelt upon the deck almost at her feet and looked up at her manfully. Then I caught the sound of the second mate returning along the main-deck. She also heard him, and walked away to the side and leant over. I went on with my scraping.

During the rest of that watch the second mate stayed on the poop, so that I had no further chance of speaking with Eina. Yet, in spite of his presence, our eyes met more than once, and that was something.

That same night Eina and I had a long, cautious talk as I stood at the wheel. She managed it by leaning over the taffrail and staring down into the wake, as though lost in thought. Yet all the time that she kept her face turned away she was talking to me in a low voice.

My gad! I was happy. She spoke unhesitatingly, and told me that I was the one fellow on this earth, and the sea, too—I heard her laugh naughtily to herself at that—whom she should ever love. And once, when the second mate had gone down on to the main deck to give the yards a cant, she stepped swiftly over to where I stood and kissed me on the lips. I had not become inured to such surprises, and it was done so quickly that she was back again by the rail and staring down demurely into the waters before I had recovered my wits. Yet she had left me tingling, so that I was possessed with a blind desire to leave the wheel and take her into my arms.

Even as I comprehended my wish, the second mate's head appeared over the top step of the poop-ladder. He came aft and stared into the binnacle. Fortunately, the ship's head was steady on her course. As he turned away, he gave one sharp, almost suspicious glance into my face; but I was prepared for him, and my features were set in an expression of complete indifference, while my eyes bore steadily on the compass-card swaying within the lighted binnacle.

I think he was satisfied, for the next instant he went for'ard and resumed his interrupted tramp to and fro across the break of the poop.

As soon as he was gone, Eina began again to talk to me, though still taking the utmost care never to turn her face in my direction. Indeed, once she even left her place and went to sit on the saloon skylight some distance away; but presently she came back to her former post.

It was after her return that I put into execution an idea that had occurred to me since the morning. This was to take from my pocket a peculiar little whistle that I had used years previously when second mate. The tone of this whistle was extraordinarily piercing, and I knew that I should be able at any time to recognise its note were it blown.

"Eina," I said, "I've a whistle here that I'm going to throw over to you. See you catch it."

I waited until the second mate was on the opposite side of the deck; then I threw. It struck her dress and tinkled down on to the deck, but in an instant she had it.

"Look you, Eina," I called, in a low voice, "if ever you want me at any time—want me badly—blow that whistle, and I will come to you, if I am alive."

It was the following day, in the afternoon watch, that a great sensation went through the ship. This was neither more nor less than the sudden death of the captain. He had complained soon after dinner of feeling unwell, and had gone to his bunk. Then, a little before four bells, he was discovered by the steward lying there dead.

I was convinced, as soon as I heard the news, that the poor old chap had been done to death. I remembered how the steward and second mate had colloqued together. It would have been but a very simple matter for the steward—at someone's instigation—to doctor the skipper's grub. I felt sure that the second mate was not the sort of chap to stick at anything, and there had been that row between him and the skipper. I thought of Eina, and grew afraid for her, alone amongst the crowd aft. I thanked God for the thought that had prompted me to give her the whistle. At least, it gave her a means of communicating with me, should there be need. And then there was the third mate. He, I felt sure, was to be depended on. The idea came to me to try and get a few words with him, and this I managed at the end of the second dog watch that night. At first he was inclined to be on his dignity, but I showed him my second's ticket, and he came round then, I spoke of Eina, and told him how that the second mate had acted towards her in an insulting manner.

At that the good fellow's blood boiled up in a heavyish sort of way, and I knew that it would be safe to talk to him straightly. I hinted at my suspicions that the skipper's death had not been natural, but this he would not have. Yet I know that he was impressed in spite of himself, and he agreed to act with me in mounting guard as much as possible over Miss Vairne. Then I left him, and returned for'ard.

The next day the second mate started in to show the sort of stuff of which he was made. He ran the men round like a lot of slaves, and when one or two of them grumbled, came down on to the main deck, and laid them out with a belaying-pin. In his own watch, and in his own particular way, the first mate was just as bad, and for a week the ship was more like a floating prison than aught else.

At the end of that time, being a crowd of Britishers, they were just ripe for mutiny, and when at last the second struck me, and in return I laid him out upon the deck with a blow in the face, they would have torn him to pieces and mutinied outright, only that I bade them "hold on" and wait.

After that time the second went armed, though never again did he venture to touch me. I had taught him one lesson. And all these weary days I listened and listened perchance the whistle should call me to rescue my darling from vile hands.

It was two nights later, and in the middle watch, that the call came. I was lying half dressed in my bunk, and, though asleep when the note went, it thrilled in my ears like a bugle. In one instant of time I was upon the deck, and racing aft in my stockinged feet. As I ran I thought I caught a faint scream from aft. Then I was at the saloon doorway that opens on to the main-deck under the poop. The door was open, and I leapt into the short passage, my stockings making no sound. Even as I entered, from within there came a man's voice raised in anger. It was the third mate's. Then a pistol-shot, and a cry of agony from him, and a curse in the second's voice, accompanied by the colder, more deadly laughter of the first mate. Immediately afterwards there rose a short, despairing scream from Eina, and then I was among them. My gad! I am a quiet man, but then I was mad. They—the first and second mates—had hold of her. In the first mate's left hand there still smoked a revolver. Standing by, holding a candle, was the hideous steward, an evil grin on his monkey face.

He sung out something, and the mate glanced round. He saw me, and raised his revolver; but in the same instant I struck him, and his face disappeared from sight. The second mate staggered back, loosing Eina, and reaching back to his pistol-pocket. Yet he, like the mate, was too late. Once, and then again, I struck him with my clenched hands; and after that there was scarcely life, let alone fight, in him. He collapsed with a crash on to the now diddering steward, and the two rolled helplessly on to the deck.

Then I turned to her, and caught her into my arms just as she fell senseless. I carried her out on to the deck, and laid her on the after-hatch. The crew had come aft, hearing the firing and the shouts. To some of them I shouted to go into the saloon, and make the steward hustle out with brandy; yet I had scarcely spoken before the cringing object stood beside me with a decanter half full.

Presently, when my sweetheart was revived, she told me how that she had waked to find the second mate in the doorway of her berth. Evidently he must have got in by means of a master key, probably obtained from the rascally steward. She had blown her whistle, and, before she could do so again, he had snatched it from her. Then the first mate had appeared upon the scene, and almost directly the third mate. The third had interposed, but him the first had shot down like a dog without a word. Then—I had come.

The tone in which she said that thrilled me. Yet she called me to myself, by asking whether anything had yet been done for the poor third mate. I told her no, but that I would go at once. At that she said she would come with me.

We found him lying on the port side of the saloon table, and a short examination showed that he had been shot through the chest. Yet he still lived, and we carried him into his berth and laid him in his bunk, and left him in Eina's charge, while I, with some of the men, carried the second into a spare berth and locked him in; first, however, removing from him his pistol. When we came to the mate, there was need of nothing but some old canvas, for he was stone dead. I directed them to carry him out on to one of the hatches for the present. As they went, I caught a man's voice.

"My Gawd!" it said. "That's where 'e 'it 'im!"

And when they came back, quite naturally for further orders, they eyed me with awe-stricken glances.

There is little remaining to be told. I took charge of the ship, and worked her home. The third mate, under the unremitting care and attention of Eina, recovered. Indeed, he acted as my best man at a certain ceremony that Eina and I went through soon after our return. With regard to the second mate and the steward, the newspapers have already told what happened to them, and I will leave it there. There would I also leave all the flattering things that were said about my unworthy self, but that I cannot resist quoting one line:

"Mr. John Kenstone is indeed to be envied in his bonny wife."

And I am.

How Sir Jerrold Treyn Dealt with the Dutch in Caunston Cove

I

MY FATHER, SIR CHARLES TREYN, stamped his foot. "Confound the ways of the Government" he said, walking up and down the room.

He had just received a letter from my uncle (on my mother's side), who owned what is still called Ralby Common, seven miles inland from Rayle, on the South Coast, about twenty miles from Caunston.

"Hear this," said my father, and read from my uncle's letter:

" 'A Dutch frigate, Van Ruyter, landed a hundred men at Rayle yestermorn, so I have just heard. They have burned Starly Manor, and half the village, and were gone clean away before the soldiers were come from Bideford. They made their raid in their own devilish way, which is to sail in from the sea during the night, with never a light showing, and to land at daybreak. They use not the big guns, lest this bring the soldiers upon them quickly from the big towns. Likewise, their burnings are not seen so well afar in the daylight. They killed twenty-three men, of Rayle village, that opposed them, and two women, and harmed many more. They shot an herd lad in the Manor lane, where he lay dead all day; and this because he would have run off to warn old Sir James, who, by the blessing of Providence, heard that same shot, and roused his household, and escaped by the well passage.'

"He says," added my father, "that we must build more and better ships to hunt the Dutch from the sea. Everyone knows that we build no ships as good as those we take from the Dutch; but, thank God, we fight 'em as they should be fought. But we need more ships and better ships, and we need coast ships."

"We ought to have more guns, and heavier, on the Head," I told my father. "James Corby's schooner is in, and he's two guns in the hold, long thirty-two-pounders, that he lifted out of the wreck of a French frigate. They will throw a shot near two miles, and at close range would go near through the two sides of a line-of-battleship."

"I've done my duty to our cove," said my father, pinching his forehead, as is his way when vexed. "Two hundred and thirty pounds I paid in good money for the guns and the mountings and the powder and shot, and the conveying of them to the Head, and building the platform to carry them. Let Sir Beant show his loyalty, and match them with three more guns on the Lanstock cliff, and we shall be very well prepared for any of these murdering Dutch who may think they will run in here and play the Old Harry with our property and our lives."

I looked at John, my brother, and made a motion to him to keep silent. I knew that when my father had made up his mind, it was no use arguing with him, and I feared to explain the plans John and I had talked over, lest our father put a stop to all.

II

"Come down to the cove," I said later. "I believe we can buy one of those guns out of our allowance, if only Corby will not be so everlastingly greedy. Leave it to me to handle him."

"Well, Corby," I said, as we clambered aboard, "my father will not buy the guns. He has done more than his share for the cove. If anyone here is going to buy them, you'd better try Sir Beant. Or else take them up the coast as far as Mallington."

"No use, sir," said Corby, as I knew he would. "Sir Beant's as stingy as my own mother, an' that's saying a heap. He'd never pay for mounting 'em, let alone the guns themselves. And I don't want to bother takin' them up the coast. Guns is mighty rum things to market."

"I'd buy them off you myself," I said, as carelessly as I could, "but I'd have to buy out of my allowance, and I don't see why I should stint myself for the good of the cove, any more than anyone else."

"I'd cut the price for you, sir, as close as my head," he said.

And I knew, suddenly (as indeed I had half guessed) that he was mighty anxious to have them out of his vessel, so that I supposed he must have gone against the law in some way; but Corby never was a scrupulous man.

"I'll give you five guineas apiece for each gun," I said calmly, offering half of what I had meant before to offer, though my heart was beating fast, and Jack was actually pale with suppressed anxiety.

"Couldn't do it possibly, sir," said Corby. "I might, as it's you, sir, take ten guineas apiece, money down."

"I've made my offer." I said. "I don't pretend the guns are not worth more; but that's all they are worth to me." I stood up suddenly. "Come along, John," I said. "I'm sorry, Corby, we could not deal in this matter; but I don't blame you. I've no doubt you will do better up the coast."

"Master Jerrold," he said, as I reached the door of the cuddy, "they're yours, cash down. I swear I wouldn't 'a' done it for no one else in the world."

"Very well," I said easily, and pinching John's elbow to keep him from showing any excitement. "I'll pay you as soon as the two guns are on the quay,"

I looked at Corby, half minded to ask him a question or two. It was very plain that there was something funny at the back of his eagerness to sell me two thirty-two-pounders for the sum of five guineas apiece. However, I kept quiet; for, after all, I thought, the less I knew, the less I'd have to worry about.

Two hours later the guns were on the quay and I had paid Corby, who spat ruefully, I thought, on the money; but tried to appear content, which he never could be.

III

My father was called to London two days after we had bought the thirty-two-pounders, and my mother went with him.

I had told my father nothing about the guns, for I meant to have my will in the matter, and he was a little apt to forget that I was nineteen years grown, and somewhat irked to have him cross my intention more often maybe than was occasion for; though a better and more loving father no man ever had, and well I, and all of us, loved him for his solid goodness.

On the evening of the day that I had bought the guns, I had sent Mardy, one of our labourers, down to the quay with the timber-wain, and we had lifted the guns, one at a time, and taken them up into one of our fir-woods; for I thought that if Corby had come by them in some lawless manner, they should lie no longer on the quayside than might be.

Then, on the night after father was gone north to London Town, John and I went into the village, and had word with certain cronies of ours, that had been our playmates when we were boys, and were and are still our very good friends.

There were Tommy Larg, the young blacksmith; James and Henry Bowden, 'prentice wheelwrights and cart-makers, and near out of their time; and the three Cartwright brothers, young and smart fishermen, who already had their own boat. To these I explained our plans, and read to them that part of my uncle's letter which told of the burning of Rayle village, which they had heard some rumours of, but nothing certain.

When I had said all, they were as eager as John and I to strengthen our defence further; and Tom Larg, the blacksmith, and the two Bowden brothers promised there and then to make the gun-carriage for the cannon, I to pay for the material, and them to charge nothing on their labour; but to be, as we say, for love.

But before all else, then, I needed their help that night; and a solemn promise to secrecy, which they gave readily and honourably kept, I had from them, that they should give their help to get the two guns to a certain place that I had planned for them, and this must be done in the darkness, for I wished no talk or knowledge of my planning to get about.

"I'm going to mount them in the High Cave in the Winston Cliff," I told them, and smiled to myself to hear them answer on the instant that it could never be done, that the High Cave was three hundred feet above the water edge and seventy-one from the brow of the great Head, which hangs out prodigiously.

"There is no gear that us have that could lower the guns from the Head," said the elder Bowden; "nor could us ever swing 'em in."

"Wait!" I said, laughing a little. "That's the secret you've got to keep, lads. John and I have found a secret way into the High Cave, from the back, where the shoulder of the Winston comes down on to the downs, among all the big rocks up there."

There was a great exclaiming at this.

"Oft I ha' heard my old Uncle Ebenezer say as there was another way into the High Cave," said one of the Cartwrights, "but none on us ever found it, an' never ha' been in but once when I were a boy. It's a long swing into the cave, by reason o' the overhang above, and a dangerous place to come to that way."

I took the six of them up to our stable-yard, and here I had Mardy harness our biggest timber-wain to our eight big plough horses. Then I told Mardy I should not want him—for I could not trust his tongue—and John and I and our army of six set off for the fir-wood, where the guns lay hid as I have told.

It took us near until the dawn before we had the two long guns up among the rocks on the downs where we had found the secret entrance into the cave. There was a place here where a great mass of rock and earth had splitten away from the slope of the Winston, where it met the downs; and left a big scar, like an old quarry, all bracken and bramble grown.

"See, lads!" I cried.

And John and I, with the crooks of our sticks, pulled to one side a huge mass of the brambles, and there, sure enough, was a split that ran into the hillside of the Winston, so big that you could have taken a cart and horse in through it. And indeed this was so, for when we had cleared away some of the underfoot stones, and lugged back all the brambles, we drove the horses clean through and along a great twisting gallery of rock, and so to the cave, lighting them all the way with a stable lantern which I had brought.

We took the second gun in likewise, and laid it by the first; then we draped all the bracken and bramble over the hole, and you could never have guessed the things they hid so clever and natural. And afterwards to our beds, very weary and well pleased with ourselves.

IV

My brother John and I were wakened on this day (May 25th) at four in the morning, by Geels, our gardener.

"Whist, Master Jerry!" he was saying from the window. "Wake up, now, do 'ee! Wake up, Master Jerry. Wake up, do 'ee!"

John and I sat up, each in our own beds, and stared at the window.

"What's wrong, Geels?" I asked.

"There's two great frigates in the bay, Master Jerry," said Geels, "an' they'm landin' men so fast as they can. I been down to watch 'em from Sir Beant's oak-woods, an' they'm riven open the Hall an' makin' free with all."

I was out of my bed long before Geels had finished, and John with me. For now we might at last have chance to read these coast-ravaging Dutchmen a lesson, with God's aid and our own plain wit and invention.

"When did you first know they were in the bay, Geels?" I asked, as I dressed with speed.

"Half-past three they coom to anchor, by Sam Hardy's watch," said Geels. "They coom in round the point, maybe a while earlier, an' Sam Hardy, as is the coast ranger this week, waked me to watch 'em, while he went down to warn the village folk. I been that excited like, I went down to the oak-woods, so I could see 'em proper close; an' then I minded what you'd told me, to call you, Master Jerry, if they coomed, so I coom away up to the house, an' I climb the ivy to the window, same's I'm at now."

"Then they've not been ashore long?" I asked, as I pulled on my coat.

"No more than to get up to th' Hall, Master Jerry," said the old man. "A good thing Sir Beant's away to Lunnon. But I'm feard they'm been rough like with the servants. I heerd Jan Ellis, as is cook there, screetchin' fit to wake the dead; right over to the oak-woods, I heerd 'er. An' it fair made me so my blood be a-boilin' this moment. I be main glad your mother an' sister are to Lunnon Town with Sir Charles, your father. I could wish he were here now, for a fine head he have for fightin' and the like; a better I never met, Master Jerrold, though he've a timber leg. Here we are, scarce two score men in the village, what wi' pressgangin' an' the like; an' your father away, an' you but a lad as you are—not but you've the brains an' pluck of us all!—an' no offence, Master Jerrold, if so I be bound to say you'm youngish, when the like of a thing like this do happen upon us."

"Geels," I said, "get down and away to the village for Tommy Larg, the blacksmith, and James and Henry Bowden, and the three Cartwright brothers. Tell them I want them up here at once. Get back here as smartly as you can. John, come down to the armoury. Come on!"

V

I felt the blood leap in me, for here I was, nineteen years, old, and my brother sixteen and the chance to prove ourselves and to turn our plans and dreams into reality.

At the armoury I took down two swords that had belonged to our father when he was no older than I; for, as I said to John, we should bring no shame on the good blades by our attempt, and we knew that our father would have pride that we should wear them on such errand as we had in mind, if we but carried ourselves with courage and honour; for our father was a man who would see us dead with gladness, if with honour, rather than alive and backward in any time that courage of heart might be heeded.

"Now the powder," I said, for our father kept always a great stock for the three twelve-pounder cannons that he had mounted on Winston Head. He had made the villagers these two years practise with the guns, once on May Day and once on Michaelmas Day. Six men he had appointed to each gun, and a pile of twelve-pound shot to each, that he had from the Royal foundry with the guns. But the men were not very smart to hit a mark, for they fired but six shots on each day at a tub that was towed out and moored in the cove, and no man had ever hit it yet: though once James Bartlett splashed it with a round-shot, and my father was that pleased that he sent the crew down a barrel of beer to drink the health of Bartlett in.

John and I rolled out four barrels of the powder from the armoury and rolled them along the great passageway to the main hall, where we left them.

"I hope Geels will hurry," I told John "We've a deal to do. This place must be made safe, and the shot from the cannon on the Head must be carried down into the cave, and the cannon spiked—"

"Spiked?" interrupted my brother. "What for? Are not the villagers going to fire them at the frigates?"

I laughed a little.

"Don't be an ass, John," I said. "If you think but half a minute, you'll see that the Dutch would send fifty or sixty men up and just cut 'em to pieces in no time. Then they could turn the guns on to their houses. By this time, I expect, the village will be empty and everybody hiding. That's why our idea to have the guns in the cave is so good—for the Dutch cannot easily get at us, and we shall be able, to do something to-day that will teach them a lesson, and make our father proud of us. That reminds me, run down to Mardy's cottage and tell him and his father to come up at once, if they haven't gone off into the woods to hide."

While my brother was gone, I rummaged out some fuse that was kept in canisters in the armoury, and three dozen empty bombs that were made for a nine-pounder gun and bought cheap by my father, who thought to pick up a nine-pounder gun some day for a trifle from the wreckers.

These bombs I took for the two great thirty-two-pounders, having a notion how I might use them, for I had not a single shot for either of the big pieces, though we had mounted them complete more than a fortnight before.

Besides the empty nine-pounder bombshells, I found also some lengths of chain from our farmyard that were used for harrowing, also three bags of great tenpenny-nails, which pleased me a deal, and a big cake of beeswax, and all the blankets off the beds.

I got also from the armoury twelve muskets, with their flasks and bullet-bags, and a keg of ready-cast bullets.

We had already in the cave two big butts of water, with rammers and mops that the two Bowden lads had made; and Larg, the blacksmith, had fitted iron rings into the floor of the cave for the gun-tackles, which same had been fitted very cleverly by the Cartwrights.

All of this I thought over a dozen times as I ran backwards and forwards carrying things. Then I heard John at the entrance door, and Mardy and his father with him.

"Put Meg and Molly in the shafts and fetch round the firewood trolly," I called to them.

And, when it was brought, I set them to loading all the gear into it, and made them lash it all secure. After which, I sent John up to the roof to see if he could discover any signs of Geels or the Dutch.

He came down, very excited, in a minute to tell me that Geels was running along the green walk towards the house with the six others, and a dozen Dutch sailors after them with their cutlasses drawn and carrying muskets.

"The muskets, John!" I said quietly, and had one up in my hand as I spoke. I snapped open a powder-flask, and, by all good mercies, there was powder in it. I caught a bunch of the weapons up in my left hand by the muzzles and snapped a charge into each. "The bullets, John!" I said very quick, but still quietly, so us not to fluster him. "Don't wait to wad. Drop two into each!"

I whipped out a ramrod and plunged it into each barrel, as my brother dropped in the bullets. As I rammed home the last, I laid the whole lot down and began to prime them, one at a time, handing them out to John and Mardy and his father as I did so. I loaded six in all in less than one full minute, and no man can say I was slow.

"Now follow me," I said, and ran through the great door and down into the shrubbery that bordered the green walk.

There was a thudding of running feet, and then the crash of a musket near by. Someone in the green walk cried out, and immediately I heard Larg, the blacksmith, shout out:

"Ey, the murderin' swine! I'd gie my hand for a good musket!"

I peered through the bushes, and saw the Dutchmen to our right, kneeling, to steady their aim.

"Quick!" I said to the others. "Stick your guns out and shoot! Same as if you were at your poaching tricks, Mardy!"

The man grinned, licking his lips a little. He never bothered to set the musket to his shoulder, but fired with the butt on his thigh. By Jove, but he killed two Dutchmen with that one shot. And then John and I opened fire.

I killed one with my first, and John wounded one, who lay on his face and kicked, screaming like any woman. That stopped John, and Mardy's father just snatched his other musket from him, and loosed it again from his thigh. I never saw the like of such shooting;

I fired my second musket and wounded one Dutchman slightly; but already Mardy had killed seven outright, for his son had never even attempted to fire, but just handed his two weapons over to his father.

"Charge them!" I shouted. "Use the butts!" And I burst through the hedge into the green walk, with the three others after me. But the Dutchmen that remained alive ran, throwing away their muskets.

"Stop!" I said to my army.

As we all stopped, I noticed that Mardy's father was laughing silently. A curious man. I had heard rumours of his gun shooting and his coolness, and I never saw the equal before or since.

Geels and the six others had stopped when they saw the Dutchmen begin to fall, and now they came running back round us, with Larg supporting Oliver Cartwright, the youngest of the fishing brothers, who had been shot in the thick of the lower leg, but nothing much of a wound, as it proved.

"A'm thankin' God ye coomed, Master Jerry," said Geels, panting for breath. "They was agoin' to fire just as ye fired, an' I do reckon they'd 'a' had every one of us through the back."

"Come on, all!" I said. "No, Larg, don't cut that poor wounded devil's throat! Leave him. I'll give you killing enough presently. Pick up their muskets, and bring their ammunition. Hurry, all of you! We're going to give these beggars a lesson that will make them shy of visiting Caunston Cove again in a hurry."

They did as I bade them, and we hastened back to our house, which is named Caunston Tower, and has its own moat, forty feet broad; and glad was I then to think of the moat (though my mother always said it made the house damp), for I feared that the Dutchmen who escaped might return with others—but not many, if our plan carried out properly.

The moat was crossed by one oak-timbered bridge to the great entrance door, and there was still the chains attached and the windlass in the cellar by which the bridge might be hoisted up in front of the doorway as in past times, though we never used them except once each year to test the bridge, which idea was a whim of my father's.

As we came back into the big hall there were four of the maids crowded there, pale and shivering with terror, and Alice, our cook (and a big woman she was), trying to get them back to their own part of the house.

"The Dutchmen!" screamed out the four servant-maids as we ran in through the big doorway.

"Dutchmen, ye idiots!" said Alice. "Drat ye! Saw ye ever Dutch loons like yon?"

"Be quiet, all of you, please," I said. "There is not the least danger. Sam Hardy's away nearly an hour ago for the soldiers, and they should be here within four or five hours. Alice, if there's any shooting, keep all your lot in the cellars. Do try to get them out of our way now."

"Ess, Master Jerry," said Alice.

And without a word more she slipped an arm each round the waists of two of the maids, and half carried and half dragged them out to their own quarters, with the other two following quietly enough.

"Now, Geels," I said, "we're going to see what we can do with these Dutchmen. I'm leaving you in charge here, with Mardy and his father under you. As soon as we're across the bridge hoist it clean up before the door, and then close all the heavy outer shutters. Load all the muskets, and for the rest trust to Heaven, or to the quick eye of Mardy here, who is worth any three men I ever saw with a musket. I'm leaving young Cartwright with you. He can fire a musket, but he'll be no good for walking for a while yet, I fancy."

Geels started some kind of remonstrance, as did the Cartwright boy at being left, but I just signed to my men to slip their Dutch bandoliers over their heads and follow me to the loaded trolly.

"Now," I said, "lead off smart for the Winston before those Dutchmen get over on this side of the cove."

I turned to Geels, who stood, still gesticulating, in the entrance.

"Get that bridge up, right away!" I shouted. "If you need help, ask Alice. Tell her I said she would give a hand. I'm trusting you, Geels, to do nothing to-day that would displeasure me or my father. God be with you!" I said, and began to run after the others, who were already gone forward a hundred yards or more.

VI

We came up on to the downs among the Winston rocks at the back of the Winston in about half an hour, and in that time we saw not a single Dutchman; only, across the cove, from the direction of Sir Beant's place, we could hear far-off cries and shouts coming through the still air.

In the shallow gully, where lay the landward entrance to the cave, we found everything undisturbed and the cave in order, with the two long, grim guns staring down silent out of the shadows of the cave into the cove.

I had the lads unload the stuff smartly, and dump it just within the cave; for I wished to have the guns above safely spiked and the round-shot in our possession. As soon as the trolly was empty we set off up over the landward shoulder of the Head until we came to where the gun platform lay, with the three guns on it and the mounds of shot stacked up snugly in piles on each side of the guns, the whole very nicely surrounded by sturdy oak palings, which my father had put up to keep the children from playing on the guns or rolling the shot down the hill.

"Now," I said, as I unlocked the door in the palings with my father's key, "smartly all of us, and get this shot into the trolly. I'm glad we brought the two mares, for it will weigh a deal. There's some powder, too, in the locker here with the rammers that we'll take down with us."

"Can't we fire the guns once, Jerry?" asked my brother. "Father would like to think they were used once against the frigates."

I thought a moment, and made up my mind.

"Quick, then!" I said. "We'll fire a shot each. Larg, give Jack and me a hand here with the guns. Go on loading the trolly, you others."

In ten minutes the trolly and the guns were loaded.

"Start down with the trolly," I said to the others. "Get the shot into the cave as quickly as you can. Then drive the trolly out on to the downs, and unharness the mares and let them run. Here, Larg, and you, Jack, give me a hand to get the three guns all bearing on the outside frigate. They won't depress enough to touch the inside ship."

As we finished training the guns my brother called out suddenly:

"Look! They've fired the Hall! The brutes! And see, down there, below the oak-woods, there's about a hundred of them on the way to our place! Fire the guns, Jerry! Do something to stop them!"

As he spoke there came the far-away bang of a musket from the lower Head across the cove.

"They've sure a man there keepin' a watch as sees us, Master Jerrold," said Larg. "Fire off the guns, do 'ee, an' let's away down to the cave an' start with the big guns."

"Here!" I said, as a sudden idea came to me. "Slue this gun round. I'm going to send a shot among that lot going up to our place."

"You'll never hit—not a one of 'em," said Larg.

But both he and my brother worked eagerly with me to get the gun round. I knocked out the wedge, and elevated the gun to about twenty-five degrees, for the shot was a long one for a small piece.

"Now, watch!" I said, and set the tow, which Larg had lit, to the touch-hole.

The powder flashed up into my hair, singeing it, and there was a great belch of fire from the muzzle and a stunning report. The three of us ran to the side to watch the effect of the shot. And truly, so great was the distance, we seemed to wait half a dozen seconds before a sudden burst of white splinters from a young oak-tree on the near side of the road showed where the ball had struck.

The tree was about opposite to the middle part of the long line of men marching along the road, and Larg cried out that two of them were down, struck with the splinters; but neither Jack nor I could be sure of this, only that there was certainly some confusion in the ranks, near where the shot had struck the tree.

"Look at 'em in the frigate!" said Larg.

I turned and stared down at the two powerful war vessels, and saw that a file of men were drawn up across the quarter-deck of the nearer one, with an officer, who was pointing up at us. Immediately afterwards there came a dozen little flashes and puffs of smoke, and an irregular volley of bullets went all round us, sounding like the drone of a swarm of hornets. A most uncomfortable sound! One bullet struck the muzzle of the middle gun, and flew off, with a strange pinging sound, but not one of us was hit.

"Quick, Larg!" I shouted. "Spike the fired one!"

And I jumped to the breeches of the two loaded guns, and clapped the burning tow to the touch-hole of each, one after the other. There were two large, bright bursts of flame, and two heavy bangs, and, under the smoke, as I stared down at the decks of the far frigate, I saw a curious thing. One of the upper-deck guns had jumped clean on end with its muzzle to the sky. And a shower of splinters was spraying out in a great fan from the mainmast.

"Good!" shouted Jack, slapping his thigh. "Oh, good! You've knocked the breech clean off one of the guns, and you've gouged a piece right out of one of their masts, and made a hole clean through the deck. Father will be pleasured."

"Quick, Larg!" I called. "They're sending a boatload of men. Look out! They're going to shoot again!"

We dodged down, as the ripple of flashes came from the near frigate; then, as the bullets whoozed by, over us, we sprang up, and Larg spiked the two other guns, by driving a brittle piece of iron into the touch-holes, and breaking it off short.

"That'll sure take a mint o' drillin' out, Master Jerrold," he said. "Look at yon men on the other frigate! They'm like bees as you've prodded."

VII

When we reached the cave, we found that they had already done as I told them, and the bushes and creepers were dropped back again over the entrance, hiding it perfectly. One of the Bowden boys was inside, behind the growths, standing guard with his musket, and when we had entered, he rearranged the creepers, while we ran through to the guns.

"We must, get them going," I said, "as quickly as possible, to bring them back from attacking the house. Open out the gear, quick, Larg; open one of the powder-barrels; roll it well back from the guns. James Bowden, give me a hand here with these bombs. Harry Cartwright, light Larg's hand-forge. We left it up here when we finished mounting the guns. It's in one of the recesses there, up to the left. There's wood and small coals there, and the flint and steel's on the top of the bellows.

"Jack, you and Tom Cartwright get the rammers down and wipe out the guns, and dip some water out of the tubs into the buckets, ready for sponging them out."

Ten minutes later we were all furiously busy. In the heart of the forge fire there were two cylinders of solid iron, that Larg had forged out to fit the bores of the guns, and now we were heating them red-hot; for I meant to fire them down through the decks of the frigate. Larg was busy ramming down a charge of powder, and on the top of it a great wail of torn-up blanket. Then he passed in a length of the chain I had brought; first putting a knot in each end. Afterwards he rammed home a bucketful of broken flints, and then stepped back and primed the gun.

"It's all ready for laying, Master Jerrold," said Larg. "Shall us run her out a bit?"

"Yes," I said; and we all went over to give him a hand with the tackles. "That's right," I said. "No, don't wedge her up. It's his rigging I want to cut up with the chain and stones. Get on with the other gun. Give her a full measure and a quarter of powder, then a wad, and three of the twelve-pounder shot, with earth round each one, rammed hard. Soften that beeswax over the forge-fire, Harry; and, John, go on filling those bombs with powder, then stuff in one of the cut lengths of fuse into each, and fill in the hole solidly with beeswax. Right, Larg, give me the tow and stand to the side."

I spied along the big gun, aiming at the maintop of the nearer frigate. Then I touched the burning tow on the priming and jumped to the side as the great gun roared down at the frigate.

"By George, Master Jerry!" said the oldest of the Cartwrights, "you fair cut clean through all her riggin' on the starboard side o' the main! Her can never go to sea till her's rigged up preventers, or her'd lose the whole stick."

The fisherman had said right, for the length of chain had hit the rigging on the starboard side, just below the bolsters, and smashed them as clean away as a great knife might have done. The chain itself had ripped a gouge in the mast, for the scar showed plainly. For the rest, there was a good matter of flying ends of the running gear both to starboard and larboard; for the broken flints had spread like shot from a fowling-gun.

My brother and the rest had run to the mouth of the cave to see the damage, and Jack pointed across the cove.

"Look!" he said. "They've set the whole village on fire. Look, there's your house, Cartwright, near the jetty; they've just fired it, and Bowden's house has got the thatch alight."

Jack was right; the Dutch had fired the village, as was their way in these small wanton raids that the Government would never bother to take any notice of; and now the brutes, after having killed a number of harmless villagers, would retreat to their ships and get away. But I vowed aloud that they should never leave the cove unharmed; and Bowden and Cartwright swore in the simple, brutal fashion of their class, to split the two warships asunder, or sink them.

There was the crash of a volley, three hundred feet below us, and splinters of stone flew in all directions from the rock of the cave-mouth. I stepped forward a pace, and stared down. The file of men across the quarter-deck of the nearer frigate were reloading, and the officer was staring up at the cliff.

On the deck of the frigate farther out there were a number of men clustered round one of the long stem-chasers—a sixteen-pounder, I supposed it might be, by the look of it at that distance.

"They can never get the elevation," I said. "All of you haul in the gun. That will do. Now, Jack, sponge her out. All of you get to work again. Larg, I will help you load."

"There's two boatloads of Dutchmen coming out to the ship," said my brother, with the sponge-stick in his hand. "Hark to the musketry firing from above Sir Beant's oak-woods. It's our house, Jerry! They've not come back. They're— Look at the smoke over the trees!"

"We can do nothing," I said; "only we can smash up their ships, and then they'll have to recall all hands. Keep on with your work."

"I got 'arf a doz'n of them bomb things filled, Master Jerrold," said

Bowden. "Will you take a look at 'em to see if they're as you want 'em?"

I took a bomb to the light and found he had packed it solidly with powder, and inserted a fuse, and then rammed sand and melted beeswax in all round the fuse, hiding the powder completely.

"Perfect!" I said. "Let me have what you've done, and go ahead with the others."

"She's loaded," said Larg, as he threw down the rammer. As he spoke, there came the thud of a heavy gun in the cove, and then a dull blow sounded somewhere below us.

"They'm shooted at us!" said Larg, "and they'm hit the cliff, near two hundred feet down. Do 'ee let 'em have this dree-shotted charge, an' show 'em what for, Master Jerrold."

"All of us on the tackles!" I called out; and we hauled out the gun that Larg had just loaded with three twelve-pound shot. "The handspike!" I said. "Heave her round. Right! Now depress!"

It took us maybe ten minutes to get the big gun laid, for we lacked practice, and a long thirty-two-pounder is a monstrous big gun to move.

"Now," I said, "stand by the tackles to snub her."

As I spoke, there came a second far-off crash of musketry that made me set my teeth, for I knew they must be firing at our home. Then there came a heavy volley of small arms from both of the frigates, the musket-balls striking the cave-mouth in scores of places, and chipping off pieces of rock; but not one of us was touched.

As I took a final sight along the gun, I saw that many of her men had already come off from the shore, and the whole of the stern part of her was taken up with a swarm of men working at some contrivance to obtain a sufficient elevation for their stern guns to be able to bear on us.

There came again the rolling of heavy musketry firing from above the woods, and I clenched my teeth as I lifted the burning tow.

"Now!" I said, standing to the side and clapping it to the touch-hole.

The heavy gun literally jumped clean off her two front wheels, and reared up, almost on end, with the effect of the recoil; for Larg had exceeded my instructions, and put two measures of powder, and his packing of the round-shot had been done with savage vigour.

Even before the cloud of smoke that rolled and eddied over the cave mouth had cleared, I knew I had done some surprising damage, for there were shouts and a terrible screaming of injured men, and a strange, crashing sound, all of it rising up strangely blended.

"By George, Master Jerrold, you sure hit 'em hard that time!" said Larg.

And we all crowded nearer to the cave mouth to try to see through the smoke; even the younger Bowden running from his place (on guard behind the creepers over the land entrance) to ask what execution had been done. But I sent him back on the instant, with a sharp reprimand for leaving his post.

As the smoke finally cleared away, there was an amazing sight. The mizzenmast of the outside frigate had been hit—for my shots had gone nowhere near where I had thought to strike—one of the shots having struck it where the mast went through the deck, and ripped a surprising great hole, splitting the mast up near three fathoms. A second of the three shots had smashed the carriage of a gun on the larboard side, and the gun had been thrown among the men, crushing several, as I judged. But it was the third shot that had pleased me, for it had struck outside the stern of the vessel altogether, and made a great white scar of splintered wood in the trunnion of the rudder:

There were cheers from the lads about me, but I bid them save their wind, and hasten. Already the near frigate was shortening her cable, and the boats were passing between her and the shore. Then she fired two guns quickly together; and, after a pause, two more together; and then, after a pause, two more in the same fashion, so that I knew she was recalling the body of sailors who were firing up beyond the oak woods.

"Haul in the gun and get her sponged out. Give her two measures and a half of powder, then a wad of dry blanket. Then sponge out every grain of loose powder from the bore, and give her a wad of wet blanket on top of the dry. I'm going to try one of those red-hot shot, and see if I can set the frigate on fire. God help us if the gun bursts!"

Twice while I spoke the Dutch in the near ship had loosed off their muskets at the cave-mouth, to try to keep us from working the guns. It was plain they saw they could never come at us, and they were anxious only to have their men aboard and get away before we did them greater harm. But this was just what I did not mean to let be.

I helped Larg load the right-hand gun with six of the bombs that I cut the fuses off very short with my knife. I put no more than one measure of powder in this gun, and then a wad of our good blankets, and after that the six bombs, and a matter of a dozen pounds of broken flints on the top, and a final wad to hold all in.

Before we could run this gun out, the outside frigate gave us a bad surprise, and showed there were men of good resource in her;

for Jack, who was ever on the stare, shouted out suddenly that they'd boats out astern of her, and were towing her round, broadside on.

"Try them with a musket-shot or two," I bid my brother, which he did; but though he hit the boat twice, he did no harm, and got his ear clipped by a ball, through going too near the mouth of the cave.

They had the frigate round pretty smart, and no sooner was she part round than they loosed off at us six of their guns, each as it came to bear, and then twelve in a clump, for I counted the flashes, and a terrible noise they made; but not one of their round-shot hit us, though there went many a ton of good honest rock and stone tumbling down the cliff-face into the sea, where the broadside had struck.

"They weren't twenty yards below us," said Larg.

"Look!" said my brother. "She's leaning over!"

And truly she was. Even as we watched her, she canted over more and more, until her gun-ports seemed to grin right up at us.

"That's ugly," I said. "Stand by to get into the sides of the cave if I tell you."

"By George! Her's shifted most of her guns over to larboard!" said Larg. "That's how hers done it, an' a mighty cute notion, too, if she don't capsize."

As the blacksmith said, it was a clever notion, and it put us in real danger; but if most of her guns were down on the larboard side, there would not be many starboard to train on the cave.

The big vessel was already a long way over, showing a full fathom of the bright copper on her bottom. And then suddenly I got an idea.

"Hurry now with the other gun!" I said. "All of you lend a hand!"

"The powder's in, two and a half measures, and them two wads as you wanted in, one on 'em dry an' one on 'em wet," said Bowden.

"Jack," I said, "keep an eye on the frigate, and shout the moment you see a gun hauled out. Larg, get your tongs, and I'll help you with the shot. It's red-hot."

We lifted it out of the hand-forge with two big tongs that he had made at the smithy, and in a minute we had it into the gun and well-rammed down, and a ring wad on top of it.

"Out with her, before the shot burns through to the powder!" I shouted. "Hasten, all! Hasten, all!"

We hove the gun out with a will, and a burst of musket-balls came all over the mouth of the cave as the long muzzle showed.

We depressed the big gun until it bore direct on the bright copper.

"They've pushed out six guns on the main deck," said my brother. "Look out!"

"Into the side of the cave, all of you!" I shouted.

As I spoke there came six flashes, and a great thud of sound as the six reports made one, and, blending with them, there was a horrible splintering and crashing of heavy shot on rock all about us, and the thud of masses of rock falling from the roof of the cave. And in the midst of the uproar I dashed down my burning tow on the touch-hole and leaped right away from the gun.

The bang was enormous, and the great gun flung herself right up on end, and came down on her side with a crunch, just missing crushing me to death as I jumped again.

The cave-mouth was full of smoke, and I could not see whether my shot had succeeded. I stared round.

"Is anyone hurt?" I asked.

I felt hoarse, and I realised my shoulder hurt badly. A falling lump of rock had struck it, but I had scarcely noticed it in that supreme moment.

"I'm all right," said Jack.

But Larg was lying senseless. The three others had obeyed me and got away safely to the side.

I ran across to Larg and looked at him. He was not dead, for he breathed heavily, and I felt his head. There was a great lump on it, full as big as my fist, but no other hurt about him, so far as I could see.

"Get some water and bathe his face," I told my brother. I stood up and ran to the mouth of the cave. "Dear Lord!" I shouted. "She's sinking fast!"

At my cry they all left Larg and came crowding to the edge of the cave-mouth.

"Back!" I shouted.

As I spoke a musket volley came from the nearer frigate, and three of us were struck by that one volley; yet not a wound to count more than a bad cut or a graze, only it was a good lesson to us all to keep in shelter.

As for the outer frigate, my eyes never looked with fiercer gladness on any sight than that of the despoiler, sinking helpless away below us. For my last shot had struck her low down on her copper, as she lay over. She had rolled under the concussion of her own gun-fire, and this is what I had waited for when I fired; and my shot had ripped clean through her far under the water-line, just on the bend of the stern run. The blow had smashed clean through the outer skin and one of her great ribs, and a butt had started, so that a fathom of one of her planks had sprung off from the ribs, and the water was rushing into her in tons. As she rolled a little, the place where the shot had struck showed, and it was plain to us that she could not float many minutes.

Twenty minutes later she sank, rightly and going down on a level keel, until only her topsail-yards showed above water. We saw at least fifty of her men drown before our eyes; for the other frigate could not pick them up, most of her boats being ashore, wailing for the recalled sailors.

These were even then on the beach, and, so evil was their mood, we saw them deliberately shoot with their muskets four of the village men they had caught among the woods, one of them being an uncle by marriage of the Cartwrights, as they could tell even at that distance by the make of his smock,

"The other gun now!" I said. "We will pay them for that!"

We trained the gun down on their one vessel, which was busy receiving the boats of the sunk frigate, crowded with men. Then, as the shore boats arrived and clustered alongside, we slued the gun a little, in spite of a heavy musketry fire, and I touched her off. Two of the shore boats were blown literally to pieces by the bombs, and the broken flints must have spread over boats and ship like a hail of death; for I saw dozens of men fall about the decks of the frigate.

VIII

With all her boats towing, she went out of the cove, and we fired one more charge of chain-shot at her rigging as she went. Three lengths of chain I fired, and there was scarce a sound piece of gear aloft in her after that last shot. And so she passed out into the Channel; and as she went, filled with her dead and her wounded, with her gear shot to pieces, we stood there in the mouth of our lofty cave (the Gun Cave they call it these days) and cheered the Dutch.

Much had we to sorrow for—poor Larg dying, as we found later, many killed, our village burned, and my father's house sorely injured by the fire of a boat-gun that the Dutch had taken ashore with them, as we learned later.

But in all this sorrow we had no cause for shame, for only to remember that proud ship of war being towed out, laden with her dead and her dying, was a balm for all who had lost or suffered in that raid. And those three masts that stood up above the waters of our cove were a sight to ease the whole angry countryside for many a long day.

But one more thing there is to tell, and I had it from a man that saw it all. The good ship Henry Bolt, a small English frigate, met the Dutch frigate Van Ruyter outside in the Channel and gave her lather, and sank her in two hours, she having more than a hundred wounded men in her, and so much cut about in her top hamper that she could sail neither to fight nor run.

And this is the true history and telling of that day of adventure in our cove, and a thing I remember often, though now I am old.

Jem Binney and the Safe at Lockwood Hall

"DRAT IT!" MUTTERED JEM, AS A BIG THORN scratched his face in the darkness. Jem Binny, the dandy Anglo-American cracksman, was doing some cross-country work in a manner that might have excited the professional poachers of the district to envy. Silence and speed marked his progress as masterly, so that the dark October night saw no more than a swift shadow that passed from hedge to hedge.

Binny had left his lodgings at the White Lyon, in the little Kentish village of Bartol, by the window, and was "stretching himself"—as he would have phrased it—to reach the railway embankment at the Lower Bend, where the ten o'clock express was forced to slow down to some five miles per hour for a few hundred yards. His intention was to board the train during those seconds of lagging, and so reach town both quickly and secretly.

Yet you must not suppose that Jem Binny was doing anything so vulgar as a "bunk" from his lodgings because of an uncomfortable cash shortage, or for any other reason. It was very much the other way. In fact, his one desire was to get back as smartly as possible; for he was working what Mr. Weller would have termed "a halibi."

You see, Jem had a little bit of "business" on hand which must be begun and concluded between dusk and dawn. It included this flying visit into town to make certain arrangements with men whose business was done—shall we say?—on the shady side of the fence.

He had to return by the Boat Express, which passed the Lower Bend at precisely 3 a.m., as he had taken good care to ascertain. Here, once more, he intended to avail himself of that convenient "five-mile limit" round the curve, and disembark himself and gear as inconspicuously and speedily as possible.

Then would follow two miles of cross-country work in the dark, preceding the little "operation" which he—as an expert—contemplated upon the safe at Lockwood Hall, where were stored some very remarkable solid items of gold and silver that no melting-pot need turn up its nose at.

The business of the night would end in the corner of a certain field, where a large stone already concealed a hole prepared. The "goods" would be afterwards removed as circumstance and caution decided.

Meanwhile, Jem Binny would have done a further mile and a half to his lodgings in the White Lyon, where, having ascended via the window to his virtuous couch, he would contemplate affectionately a certain wax phonograph record within the machine that stood beside his bed.

It may be wondered wherein lay the "halibi," and I would reply: "In that same record," which was entirely a notion of the sagacious Binny; for the record gave a very fair reproduction of Binny's cough, which had earned for him at the White Lyon much sympathy, and the name of "that young fellow with the cough."

Now, normally—that is, when engaged upon his nocturnal trade—Binny was not given to coughing. He would have considered it unprofessional, as being something of a physical trait inclined to hamper him in climbing to the proudest heights of his career. In fact, he never coughed except at the White Lyon, or when in the company of the villagers.

Yet this wise conserving of his vocal efforts was his own secret, and, had you ventured to suggest the truth to any of the customers of the White Lyon, you would have been disappointed in its reception.

They had all heard him cough. Did he not cough between drinks, or would not the point of many a somewhat racy tale be unduly delayed by the inevitable paroxysm? Finally, was not the landlady of the White Lyon often awakened in the night-time by the distressful throat of her lodger?

"Poor lad!" she would mutter sleepily; and fall again into the pit of slumber. And next morning she would ask Binny how he felt, and assure him—to his enormous gratification—that she had heard him in the night, and pitied him.

I have said that the news proved gratifying to Binny. You will the better understand this when I tell you that Jem Binny refused to lie awake and cough in the night, even to have the pleasure of disturbing the rest of the landlady. He invariably slept, or just as invariably opened his bedroom window and slipped out into the darkness.

Yet, all through his absences, or his sleep, there would come at pleasingly regular intervals, the well-known "A-haa! A-haa! A-haa!" which told all the world—in the shape of his wakeful landlady—of his whereabouts.

This was, as will be now understood, a convenient kind of thing to occur in the case of a man who designed to earn for himself the reputation of extreme regularity of habit, and an "early-to-bed-fear-the-night-air-y'-know" kind of disposition. He could take his night walks and investigations in peace, assured that he had left his cough behind him to signify his innocence. For it was clear that if a man lay coughing in his bedroom he could not be confounded with some unknown law-breaker who may have had a penchant for safe-testing in other peoples' houses.

And the way of it all was so delightfully simple, a constant mark of exclamation to the sagacity of Jem Binny's character. All the village knew that he had a phonograph. All the village—that is, all those who came in for their malt extract—had heard many of his records, yet none of them—knowingly— had heard one in particular; for that was reserved for the nightly concert of which the landlady—and occasionally her husband— formed, in their innocence, the audience.

Neither, I may add, had anyone any knowledge of a neatly designed piece of clockwork which, when attached to the phonograph o' nights, allowed that machine to run only in little jerks, spaced twenty minutes apart, so that a portion of the unknown record would be played thrice in the hour thus: "A-haa! A-haa! Humm!" Then the twenty minutes' pause, and repetition. It was really most ingenious. And it was doing its work faithfully enough on this night when its owner and constructor was bent on boarding the London express at the sharp curve in the Lower Bend.

Binny reached the Bend some minutes ahead of the train, and sat down on the embankment to wait. He was feeling very fairly contented with himself, for he had that evening concluded the exhaustive survey of the fine piece of "property" which was to be the scene of his operations that night.

As I have remarked, Binny was in a contented and self-satisfied frame of mind, which was marred only by one trifle of anxiety, that he kept pushing into the background.

"Not 'im—'e never saw me!" he muttered to himself once or twice, with the intent to assure himself. "Too bloomin' slow, these folk, to see a 'ouse! Guess it's all right, anyway."

Yet it was obvious, from Binny's recurring to the subject, that he was not absolutely assured on the point.

His thoughts and comments referred to a trifling incident of the evening, just as the dusk had begun to come down on the countryside. He had been scouting through the shrubberies at the rear of the big hall that he had arranged to "investigate," and behind him there had been an old, long-disused quarry, lying at the back of the laurels. It was fenced off artistically, so that it formed a great, rough, basin-like depression in the grounds, all boulder bestrewn and grown with rough bushes, and made an excellent foil of natural wildness to the more cultured beauty of the surrounding gardens und estate.

It was here that, suddenly, Binny had seen a man, dressed something like one of "them gamekeeper fellers," who seemed to be striving to keep himself out of sight in a rather suspicious fashion; yet to be staring in his direction.

"Blow me, if I don't reckon 'e ain't trailin' me!" Jem had muttered, after a cautious survey rearwards from the security of a thick laurel-bush. He had found cause—in the process of his varied "investigations"—to distrust and dislike all men who were dressed after the fashion of the man he was watching. "Gamekeeper fellers!" he called them, with something of a snort; for, whilst he resented and was wary of them, he had no respect for their abilities to trail him. "Nothin' to do but loaf round in the blessed grounds!" had been his comment

This was his distinctly incorrect description of a gamekeeper's duties; but then it must be remembered that Jem Binny had on several occasions, as I have hinted, been in danger of discovery at inoppor tune moments by one of the prowling men in knickers and gaiters. Yet, on each occasion, his ability as a woodsman was such that he had managed to evade an actual meeting, and had crept away, sneering contemptuously; yet gradually the warning of their constant proximity had become impressed upon him, so that he found himself always alert—though with a jeer in his heart—for the approach of these "paid loafers," as he imagined them truly to be.

On this particular evening he had sat and watched the man for several minutes, as he moved stealthily from bush to bush in the quarry, always seeming to be making in his—Binny's—direction, so that at last the cracksman had considered the advisability of a retreat.

" 'E can't see me," he had assured himself; "but then 'e may 'ave seen me. I'll get a move on. Guess 'e thinks I'm after the chickens!"

This was said with the air of a dynamiter who knows he is suspected of wishing to steal a halfpenny bun. Thereafter, Jem Binny made himself scarce in a very speedy and effective manner peculiar to his character and to his woodcraft; the second of these having been obtained in the course of years upon the borderlands of the great prairies.

Jem Binny, as I hope you have now begun to understand, was really a very smart young man—almost as smart as he believed himself to be, and, indeed, this is very high praise, of a sort. By birth he was a Cockney, and by upbringing a Canadian, and that means much to those who know. And now, as he sat waiting on the embankment, he gave himself a final shake—mentally—and dismissed from his mind, for the time being, the vague wonder and uneasiness that had possessed him lest, after all, the man in the knickers and gaiters had seen him, and suspected his true intentions.

Presently, away in the night, sounded the distant thunder of the express, laughing noisily over the miles. He walked to and fro, searching for a sound place from which to take his spring, then waited, looking to his right. The train drove into view, slowing evenly for the Bend, and Binny stepped back into a bush until the engine had passed him, for he had no intention to be seen, and possibly recognised later, by the driver or his man.

The big express went by, running smooth and slow; then Binny leapt to the place that he had decided would do for his purpose, and the next instant was crouching on the footboard. Very cautiously he raised his head and peeped into the window of the carriage; but it would not suit his purpose, for there were people inside. He moved carefully along from carriage to carriage, searching for the inevitable empty, and holding on strongly, for the big engine was once more taking up its mile-devouring song. At the sixth carriage, which happened to be a first-class, he had a nasty and violent shock, of one sort, which was changed to an even more painful shock of another kind, after he had gazed into the carriage for a few moments.

The cause of the first shock was simple, and nowise complex. For there, sitting in the corner of the carriage, was the identical man who had been tracking him in the quarry earlier in the evening.

"Goin' up ter town fer ther bloomin' 'tecks!" was Jem's mental lightning-like thought, as he dropped swiftly and coolly from eight. "Guess 'e saw me, after all. But I'm on the right side of the 'edge, I am, every time, you bet!"

He stole another cautious look at the man, and therewith got his second shock. By the man's side stood a small grip-sack, stuffed to bursting, and his hand rested upon it in a way that betrayed very plainly he was conscious of the contents.

"My gord!" said Binny. "My gord!" And studied the man's face and clothes with a keen scrutiny, his hands shaking with the excitement which had suddenly affected his hitherto cool and well-balanced nervous system.

" 'Course 'e ain't no bloomin' keeper-man," he said presently, with a temporary but bitter scorn of himself. " 'E's a blessed trike, same as me—same as me! And 'e's done me one in the eye, proper! Just nipped in an' lifted the 'ole blessed cabosh! Guess 'e saw I was onter it, an' moved in ter night, w'ile 'e 'ad the charnce!"

He ducked again, and squatted on the footboard, thinking hard and savagely.

"I'll do 'im! I'll do 'im yet, you'll see!" he assured the passing night landscape. "Let me think!"

He sustained his incredible position for a while longer, quite oblivious to the fierce, steady rush and screech of the wind as the express beat onward across the night. And suddenly he saw how he might even matters up in the neatest way possible.

"Ha!" he said, breathless with delight, and slipped his hand back to his hip-pocket.

The next instant he had entered the carriage, revolver convenient, and seated himself calmly in the opposite corner. He made no attempt to speak to the other man, but sat quietly for some minutes, without appearing even to look at him. Then, calmly and assuredly, he turned and stared at him, with all the composed sternness of the law.

The man opposite looked guilty; what is more, he sat guiltily, and his eyes were two silent witnesses of the consciousness of guilt and a temporarily paralysed nervous system.

"It's all up, my lad," remarked Binny, after a duly impressive pause, during which, however, he had held his pistol handy in his side coat pocket, to which he had conveniently transferred it. "We've been watchin' you all ther evenin'. You'll 'ave ter come along of me."

"I—I—my—" said the man, with a grotesque, nervous puckering of his features.

"Ain't got much bloomin' nerve!" was Binny's caustic mental comment. Aloud, he continued:

"We meant ter 'ave you. We was all round you in that there quarry, if you'd only 'ad eyes!"

"I—saw you!" the man got out with a jerk. "I knew it was you when you came in here. I had hoped you hadn't seen me. I—I—"

"That'll do, my lad," said Binny, who wanted to think. "What you says now 'll be used against yon; so shut up!"

"It's the first time I've ever done such a thing!" said the man entreatingly.

"An' a bloomin' mess I 'spect you've made of it!" replied Binny, with professional scorn, as he realised that, after all, the man was only an amateur who had been blessed by incredible luck. "It's people like you as spoils the perfession! I've a good mind—"

He paused abruptly, realising that this was hardly the point of view of the Law. Then, still looking across at the other, he clinked a couple of drills in his pocket in a suggestive fashion, and stood up.

"D-don't handcuff me!" said the other man, his face grown suddenly whiter, as he realised in very truth that the "clutch of the law" was a phrase of which he was at last to know the true inward meaning. "D-don't handcuff me!" he begged, with a frantic note coming into his voice. "I'll be quiet. I'll do anything—anything, only don't handcuff me."

Jem remained upon his feet, appearing to consider and reconsider the point.

"I'll give you my word, I'll not even attempt to escape, if you'll spare me that," interpolated the man, very earnestly. "You know I couldn't escape, anyway," he continued. "You've got those other men of yours. What could I do?"

It seemed to Binny that there was a faint note of hope in the man's tones, and in the uncontrolled eyes, as he suggested that the other officers—to whom Jem had vaguely referred—were with him. Binny smelt something of a question in the remark, and settled the answer with characteristic promptitude and calmness.

"Very good, my lad," he said, nodding. "As you say, there ain't no chance for you, seein' as there's three of us on this train." He saw the vague hope go out of the man's eyes as he said that, and realised that he had read his intention aright. "But I'll just take charge of that there grip, seein' it's important evidence. An' if you forgets what you've promised, you'll 'ave the handcuffs on you in two jiffies, an' a broke 'ead to keep 'em company."

As he made known this more humane side of the law, he took hold of the grip-sack, to move it across to his own side of the carriage.

"This 'ere's wot I call bein' caught red-'anded, my lad," he remarked. "I guess—"

But what it was he guessed he never made known, for he broke off short in his speech, nearly gasping with delight as he felt the weight of the gold and silver in the sack. It was so much in excess of what he had ever dared to hope. He experienced the dim beginnings of a belated respect for this amateur who had forestalled him.

"Guess you must have cleaned the place out," he remarked, weighing the tightly crammed bag in his hand.

"No, indeed!" exclaimed the other, eager to prove at least this much in his favour. "Indeed, I left far more than I—I—er— brought away. I left some of the best—I hadn't the heart to take them. I—I regretted it even then. I assure—"

"Wot!" shouted Binny, his half-respect for the amateur lost utterly in a fierce disgust. "Wot! You left more 'n 'arf? You left more 'n 'arf? You left mor 'n 'arf? Wot!" His anger choked him temporarily. "You've bloomin' well ruined the cop. You've—"

He realised suddenly what he was saying, and forced himself into silence; but his thoughts grew even more bitter because of the dumbness that he laid upon them.

The man attempted further to assure the law that he had truly taken but a portion of what there had been to take; but the Law quietened him effectually with the stem order to "Shut his face up tight and padlock it." Mean while, the Law mourned in silence awhile; but gradually adjusted itself to the inevitable, and became virulently official.

Presently, as the train began to draw up into one of the big stations, Mr. Binny stood up and chinked the bits again in an unpleasant fashion in his pocket.

"Now, my lad," he said. "Am I to 'and-cuff you, or am I to trust your word? It just lies with you. You be'ave, and you can go through 'ere like a toff; but try 'anky-panky, an' I guess I'll 'ave to fix you up like a bloomin' convic'!"

The man assured him abjectly that he would not stir, or do any other thing that might annoy the Law, if only the Law would be merciful in this one case.

Said Mr. Binny:

"I'll try you, my lad. I've to 'and this evidence over to my two men. If I see you move a 'and, it'll be the last time this side o' Holloway!"

As he finished speaking, the train drew up alongside the lighted platform, and Jem Binny lifted the grip-sack, and descended in search of his "men"—his investigations taking him directly and without pause to the exit, where, upon paying his fare—in place of a ticket—into the collector's hand, he was allowed to pass through. He turned to the left, for he knew the place, and strode rapidly, down the empty street. Half an hour's hard walking brought him into the suburbs, and another half-hour saw him well into the country.

Once or twice, as he went, he ruminated comfortably upon the position of the amateur cracksman, and concluded that he was enough of a softy to be likely to make no attempt to "do a bunk" until the next station, by which time even the nervous amateur would surely have discovered that he had been "done" in a brilliant and variegated fashion. Yet whether the "muff" left immediately or postponed his attempt for freedom had no longer any interest for Mr. Jem Binny. He knew that the man dare not attempt to put the police upon him, and he judged, truly enough in some ways, that the amateur would be so overjoyed to find himself free that he would bother about nothing except to get home—wherever that might be—and leave burglary to more daring spirits for the rest of his life.

Jem felt almost virtuous as this side of the case presented itself to him. He had turned one pair of erring feet from the difficult path that the successful cracksman has to tread, and, as is ever the case with virtue, he had his reward—in his fist!

Presently Jem turned in at a gate of a big pasture upon the right-hand side of the road. The gate was locked, and he passed the gripsack over, dropping it as easily as possible on the other side. Then, catching hold of the top bar, he vaulted; but miscalculated the height in the dark, caught the toe of one boot, and pitched heavily clean over the gate, wrenching and spraining his ankle badly.

"Oh, lor'!" he said. "Oh, lor'!" And fell to nursing his swelling ankle with his hands. " 'Ow 'll I get the express back?" was the thought that came to him during a little respite from the pain, some minutes later. "Might get a cart," he decided, after due and anxious thought. "Must get this oof buried safe an' smart, an' get back onter the road again."

The following morning the landlord of the White Lyon was much exercised by the news which the village doctor brought at an early hour. The doctor was returning from Lockwood Hall, where he had been called hurriedly to attend Sir Harry Lockwood. He had found the old knight suffering from a stroke, brought on by the improper excitement attending the discovery that his big safe had been burgled at some time during the previous night. An enormous amount of very valuable gold and silver work had been stolen, though enough had been left to suggest that the thief had taken sudden fright, and left hastily with but a portion of his intended haul. All this the doctor imparted with unprofessional gusto over a glass of gin and water, in which the fat landlord felt that the occasion demanded his accompanying him.

"That'll put a stop proper to them fossil 'unters, an' such like, I'm thinkin'!" remarked the landlord mournfully. "Sir 'Arry give orders last week as no strangers was to be allowed in the privit grounds. 'E'll be very perticler now. Bad for trade, doctor. They was a dry lot, mostly like!"

The doctor nodded, and the two of them renewed, with a little more gin this time. From the neat little bed-sitting-room, which lay to the right of the bar-parlour, there came distinct the recurrent

"A-haa, a-haa, a-haa! Humm!" which betokened the presence of Mr. Jem Binny. The landlord nodded, and indicated the shut door of the bed-sitting-room with his thumb.

"Remarkable nice young man, that Mr. Binny, doctor," he said. "Got a turrible cough, like. 'E's like that all the night long. You'll 'ear 'im again, doctor, in a bit. 'E's as reg'lar as a clock."

The doctor discoursed learnedly with the stout landlord upon the peculiarities of coughs, and the landlord nodded a constant assent, as in duty bound. Meanwhile, they renewed, and the landlord grew more than ever human.

"I'd like you just to 'ark a moment at 'is door, doctor," he said presently. " 'E's about doo now. P'r'aps you could ease it for 'im, doctor."

The doctor agreed, and the two of, them, each with a steaming glass of toddy in hand, adjourned to the outside of Mr. Binny's door. They stopped, listening, very hushed and sober, at whiles straightening momentarily to imbibe; then again to listening. It came in a little while:

"A-haa, a-haa, a-haa! Humm!"

"Ah!" said the doctor gravely. "Bronchial, without a doubt. Bronchial, Mr. Thiggs. D'you notice the wheeze in it?"

"Ay," agreed the landlord; and they straightened their backs again, preparatory to a return to the bar-parlour.

This would have inevitably been their next action, but that, in that very moment, there raced into the White Lyon the village policeman, accompanied by a sergeant of police. They wasted no words, but ran straight to the door and hammered upon it with their fists.

"Open, in the king's name!" roared the sergeant.

But no one hastened to oblige, whereupon the sergeant said:

"In with it!"

And they "inned" with it. But there was no Mr. Jem Binny there, neither had his bed been slept in. The two policemen made a hurried search, and rushed out again, the sergeant shouting to the landlord to see that no one entered the room until he returned.

"It's the phonygraff!" said the landlord, twenty minutes later, to the doctor, after they had guarded the room together, aided by further refreshment.

They stared gravely at the machine, and then at one another. Afterwards they sat down and waited for a repetition of the noise. But before it came the doctor was called away, and the landlord sat on, keeping guard and waiting, like a fat, expectant child.

"It's goin' to do it again!" he said delightedly, as the machine gave a little preliminary clicking.

He leant forward and stared, watchful.

"A-haa, a-haa, a-haa! Humm!" said the phonograph faithfully.

"Ha, La!" roared the landlord, his fat quivering. "Dod!" he whispered huskily, as the laughter eased from him, leaving his eyes full of tears. "Dod, that's cute—that's cute! An' 'e paid 'is week advance like a gentleman!"

The landlord filled his pipe and began to smoke, awaiting the inevitable music which appeared so to charm him. But far away up the line, in a field, near a gate, Jem Binny, dandy Anglo-American cracksman, sat with a badly sprained ankle and an opened gripsack, which displayed to all and any who might choose to be interested nothing more formidable than a collection of varied fossils embedded in the coating of their almost original chalk.

Mr. Binny had ceased all attempts to express himself some hours earlier. He had made his discovery when he took a glance into the grip-sack before burying it. Since that time he had largely lost interest in most things, except a curiosity as to what the other man's "game" had been.

You see, fossils were a little below his horizon, and he had no conception that an enthusiast might venture into forbidden places in pursuit of his hobby. Neither could he conceive that, having once gotten "a lot o' muck like that," the getter thereof might hasten away, pursued by a guilty conscience—especially when that same conscience had been previously stirred into being troublesome by the knowledge that someone else had been there in the quarry, maybe spying upon the luckless fossil hunter.

None of these things did Mr. Binny know, nor would he have been easy to put into the right focus to see these things as the milder sinner saw them. Therefore, Mr. Jem Binny had still a certain curiosity to salt his sudden lack of interest in life. For the rest, he had to get to the station and away to the shelter of London, as by now his "patent cough-producer" would have certainly exceeded its object, and the White Lyon, and all the district around Bartol, would be, to put it mildly, unhealthy.

There had been too many little "affairs" in the neighbourhood for which he would be now considered responsible, and the safe at Lockwood Hall was to have been the last of a glorious series done "under the halibi." Poor Binny! He never learned—and I doubt whether it would have comforted him if he had—that there had been a third factor in the history of that night, and that the safe at Lockwood Hall had been actually burgled, by a professional, evidently, who had chosen the psychic moment that should fix for ever on to the shoulders of Jem Binny a crime of which he could, for once, plead truthfully innocent—at least, in the act.

Who the third man was, who got the profits whilst the other two shared the pain of this triangular muddle, I do not know. Nor, up to the present, do the police.

Diamond Cut Diamond with a Vengeance

"WELL, MR. MOSS," SAID HARRISON at the end of the interview, "do you feel comfortable about putting cash into a big operation?"

"Certainly," replied the Jew. "If you and Miss Gwynn will come round to my lawyer's to-morrow at eleven, we'll get the agreement drawn up and signed."

"Miss Gwynn and Tony Harrison could both see that the big Jew knew what he was doing; and when he had pronounced the results of their work, a diamond of very fair colour, though small, but still a diamond by every known test, they turned naturally to each other and shook hands in silence and mutual congratulation.

Both of them were Americans, who had met in London at the same chemistry class, and in the course of time had grown so well acquainted that Mr. Cupid had finally stepped their way and linked them conclusively with an engagement ring. Money was, however, unfortunately scarce with the two of them, and at first they had looked forward to their marriage as a sacrament that lay very far in the future. Yet now, suddenly, it loomed close; for a piece of curious experimental work which they had carried out during the last six months had resulted in a success far beyond anything that they had dared to expect.

The Jew-man, as Tony called him, was a Mr. Moss, a noted dealer in precious stones. Tony had managed to interest him in the experiment, and had extracted an informal promise from him to finance a big experiment on similar lines should a diamond truly result from the first tentative attempt. And now the diamond lay there, a potent fact, in the fat palm of the Jew, whilst the young man and woman shook hands joyfully at the prospective nearness of their happiness-to-be.

On the following day, after a couple of hours spent over the discussing and signing of the necessary papers, Nell Gwynn and Tony Harrison left the Jew and his man of business, carrying their copy of the agreement, duly signed and witnessed. Yet, though everything had been done squarely, had it not been for Miss Gwynn's quickness the two young people would certainly have put their names to one or two clauses that might have proved disastrous in the future. But she made it clear that they were going to have what they had stipulated for, and, as a result, they came away with a fair and satisfactory agreement; though the girl said she wished they could have got someone for partner in whom she could feel more confidence than in Mr. Moss. But, as Tony pointed out to her, so long as the agreement was right they could not go very far wrong.

During the next month Harrison and Miss Gwynn prepared for the big experiment. They were both chemists, and had gone considerable distances along certain lines of thought and research. But it was not until after their engagement that each had confided to the other the results of their labours, and how each had come to precisely the same conclusions on the subject of Urfur's experiments, in which, as most of the world knows, he produced a sort of coarse diamond powder. Following this had come the attempt in which Harrison had managed to interest the Jew. In this experiment they had used an explosive to get the necessary pressure, and then kept the "pressure-box" hot for six months, slowly cooling it by infinitesimal degrees, and so produced the small diamond on the strength of which Mr. Moss had agreed to finance a big operation.

As I have said, during the next month Harrison and Nell had made their preparations, and at the end of that period Tony was installed in a small house off Cheyne Walk, with a huge "pressure-box" in a properly constructed gas furnace, with everything in train for what he called a "year's sit-down" to tend it. Briefly, their theory was that, given a certain latitude of time, temperature of a certain exact ratio of gradations of diminishment was the surest way to success. They had broken free from Jarnock's and Urfur's theory of a very protracted period of time for this phase of the experiment, and believed entirely, with Mr. Laodwen, in an exact ratio of diminishing temperatures; though, of course, Laodwen was never more than a theorist, and his statement had yet to be tested.

When the explosion was made in the "pressure-box," both Miss Gwynn and Harrison stayed in to watch the result. Luckily their calculations had been made with a sufficient margin of safety; for the pressure came on without a burst, which would possibly have wrecked the place. And after that, as I have said, Harrison settled to his year's "sit-down" to tend the apparatus—a lime-jet furnace, the lime packed about the clay-covered, cylindrical "pressure-box," and the jet passing through the lime.

It was arranged between the two of them that Nell Gwynn should come down every day and tend the furnace for a few hours in the afternoon whilst Harrison got out for fresh air. This she did, bringing her young sister with her for company, and possibly as a sort of chaperon, which arrangement Harrison thought very sensible, particularly when he found that the Jew was developing a habit of coming down to have a look in for a moment during the times when Nell was on watch.

Previously, that is during the preliminary stages, Mr. Moss had been rigorously excluded, for, as Harrison told him, "The secret is our secret, and we're not giving it away. We've agreed with you to give a half-share of the results; but we do not intend to tell you our secret. You must be content, and keep your part of the agreement."

The Jew had grumbled loudly at this; but had finally assented, and they had seen no more of him until the business was well under way, and Harrison had written to tell him that he might pay a visit of inspection any time that pleased him. This he had done, and was now following it up by a series of "casual" visits during Miss Gwynn's watch, as I have said. At first he had grumbled at the presence of Nell's sister, saying that it would get all round the place that they were making diamonds; but this proved to be chiefly an excuse to get the younger girl away so that he could talk to Miss Gwynn.

It was three months later that the Jew had a conversation with Nell which she kept entirely to herself; for she did not want to worry her lover, nor to have any trouble before the great experiment was concluded.

The Jew began the talk by saying that nothing could come of the attempt, that he had financed it merely to please her; that Harrison was poor, whilst he—Mr. Moss—was rich, and loved her. Would she marry him? In short, it was a proposal, approached delicately and strategically from the Jew's way of looking at things, and certainly it ticketed his character rather neatly. He took her refusal with a fat, unbelieving, smile, and told her to "think it over," which offer she briefly but firmly declined.

It took the man a week of steady refusals to make him realise that the girl meant what she said. "But he's poor, and this'll come to nothing," he assured her a dozen times, as if no more fatal argument could be used against Harrison and favour his own suit. Finally, when at last he did realise that she would not have him at any price, he became rude, and said several things for which next day he came back to tender a heavy and cunning apology.

"We can still be friends," he said, after he had explained his lapse of manners. "No use not to be friends."

And he insisted on her shaking his big, fat, flabby hand. And the girl, disliking him heartily, agreed to consider him as such, for the sake of the well-being of the great experiment.

From then onwards through a great many days his visits were very regular, and the girl observed that he seemed to examine the fittings of the furnace in a constant and rather furtive manner. She noticed also that his talk now centred very much around the making of diamonds, and this suited her very well; for she could talk by the hour on such a subject, and so keep him from his objectionable attitude of a badly used lover. At the end of a fortnight, however, she realised that he was no longer talking and questioning in a general way about their work, but was attempting to "pump" her. She grew a little suspicious, and evaded straight answers; and had finally to tell him directly in so many words that he must not ask too much, as she could not answer some of his questions without making known some of their secrets. At this the disappointment was plain for a moment on the man's coarse, fat face; but he hid it, and turned the conversation. After that day for a week he stayed away altogether.

From that time onward Mr. Moss ceased to bother Miss Gwynn with his presence to any great extent. He took, however, to calling on Tony Harrison, possibly to find out whether the girl had said anything about his offer of marriage; but whether this was one reason or not, it was soon obvious to Harrison that the Jew was on the search for information, particularly with regard to the ratio of diminishment of the temperatures and concerning the minimum length of time necessary to complete the cooling.

Because of these questions Harrison grew suspicious, but instead of saying flatly that he would not give the information, and so, perhaps, having trouble which he wished to avoid, he supplied the Jew with a great deal of inaccurate data, which that gentleman digested with a smiling and contented face.

At odd times the Jew offered to relieve Harrison for a few hours from his constant watch, so that he might take advantage of the fine weather and go for a walk. Once or twice Harrison accepted the service, and went for a trip into the country with Nell, though she, for her part, was not truly happy on such occasions, feeling that something might be "done" or "happen" whilst they were away. But Tony laughed at her fears.

"It's all right, my dear," he told her. "He won't meddle, not yet awhile. If he's any thought of that it'll be later, when things are approaching the end. He's simply paving the way for some notion he has for the future, and I don't see why we shouldn't take advantage now of his offer to watch. We can be sure he sees no one touches anything or comes in, and the 'ratio' hasn't to be varied until eight to-night, long after we're back and he's gone."

And so it proved at that time. The Jew kept a faithful enough watch, and Harrison always made an examination of everything on returning, only to find all in order; though once he fancied that his cupboards had been visited, as if someone had been prying or searching for something. But if the Jew had been looking for papers or formulas he had been disappointed, for those were kept at the bank under Miss Gwynn's and Harrison's joint signatures.

It was in this eighth month that Tony discovered that the house was being watched. He had seen the man before, in a sub-conscious fashion; but on this night, happening to look out of the window just before he drew down the blind, he caught sight of the fellow standing opposite, under the glare of the street lamp.

The man was obviously looking across at the house, and Harrison paused, with the blind half down, watching him. He remembered suddenly that he had seen him several times before, and always in the vicinity. Abruptly the fellow seemed to have become aware that he had attracted attention, for he turned and walked awkwardly up the street in a self-conscious manner. Harrison noted him carefully as he went, and realised that he was a big, hulking man, likely to be dangerous if it were made worth his while. Then he drew the blind and went back to his work, wondering whether he was getting fanciful.

Three nights later, having to run out for something he wanted, he saw the same man again, this time talking to someone just in the mouth of a side street, from where he could see the house. A sudden suspicion came to Harrison as to the personality of the man to whom the rough was talking, and he turned quickly and walked past the entrance of the side alley. As he cleared the corner he saw Mr. Moss, apparently shrinking back to avoid observation.

He said nothing to show that he had seen the Jew; instead, he went into the first shop he came to. When he returned a few minutes later the Jew had gone, and the big rough was slouching in an unconcerned fashion down the street, where presently he came to a pause, and began to retrace his steps, evidently patrolling the front of the house.

Harrison knew now without any doubt that the house was being watched, and more, that the Jew was the instigator of the watching.

All of which made him very uneasy, so that the nest day he had a long talk with Nell Gwynn on the matter, and she in return told him all that she had hitherto kept back.

"What's he up to? That's what bothers me!" said Harrison. "Does he think we're going to run away with the red-hot cylinder in our pockets, or has he some dirty scheme in his mind? I wish it was all over."

That night when the alarm clock called Harrison, at 2 a.m., to take a look at the furnace, he had a queer and unpleasant surprise. The furnace was dead out. That is to say, the lime was hot but the jet had gone out, and there was gas on.

He caught up a box of matches and applied a light to make sure; but there was no sound anywhere of gas escaping. He ran to the meter and found it full on, as ordinary, then he tried the other gases in the house, but none of them would light. He looked out at the street gas-lamps, and found them all burning as usual, and ran back to his furnace in despair. What devilment was on? If the gas did not come on soon, the whole experiment and all those months and months of weariful watching would be spoilt and lost.

He stood there, in his stockinged feet, and listened. Far away it seemed to him that he could hear a faint sound. He ran to the door of the room, and put his head out, but the noises were not in the house. He returned hurriedly to the furnace, and listened. He heard it again—a slight sound of tapping, and then an odd, chinking sound, as of steel, and immediately the low, vague murmur—so he thought—of men's voices, but he could not be sure. He struck a match and stared round the room. There was nothing.

He caught up a spare length of iron pipe for a weapon, and stared round again. Then the match burnt his fingers, and he dropped it. He caught the faint noises again. They seemed to come from the direction of the furnace, and he stepped close to it. He heard the sounds very distinctly now, though very low and distant seeming. They appeared to come from somewhere behind the furnace—from beyond the furnace. But the wall was there, and only an empty house lay on the other side. He knew it, for he had been through it himself before he took the one in which he stood.

Abruptly he realised that there were men in the other house, on the other side of the wall, and they were doing something. They it must be who had cut off his gas supply, and were ruining the great experiment. He grasped his iron pipe and turned hastily to the door. And in that minute the gas came on with a rush, hissing vigorously through the big jets. He applied a match to the furnace, then settled down to think it all out, with the result that he decided to do nothing until the morning, but to sit up the rest of the night and get the temperature of the furnace correct again.

In the morning he went out, back and front, and had a look at the next-door house, but it stood untenanted as usual, the windows dirty, and the notice, "THIS HOUSE TO LET," still in the windows. After that, he returned to his watching.

When Nell came in the afternoon to relieve him, he told her what had happened in the night. After he had finished she was silent a minute, then she said, abruptly:

"I should like you to go right out now, Tony, and buy a revolver. I'm not a bit happy. There's something going to happen, and I want you to be led by me in this."

As a result, an hour later, Harrison, armed with a licence, went into a gunsmith's, and came out with a fine, heavy Smith and Wesson in his pocket, along with a box of fifty cartridges.

"Nell's right," he said to himself. "I shall feel happier to-night."

Having procured the weapon he paid a visit to the landlord of the house next door, who was also the landlord of the one he was inhabiting. Here he made inquiries as to whether he could go through the other house; but was told that it had been let for the past three weeks. This certainly made things look a bit more definite, and Harrison, began to see a possible explanation. He resolved, if he could to find out who were the queer tenants who took a house and left the windows uncleaned and the notice up, and who, moreover, at two o'clock in the morning, meddled with the gas to such a tune that they had put out his furnace.

He walked back to his own house and asked Nell whether she had seen Mr. Moss. She told him that the Jew had just gone down the street in company with another man, who was dressed in blue overalls.

"Then I'll bet there's no one in next door now," he replied, for he had given her all his news. "I'm going to try the back way."

To his delight he found the back door merely on the latch. He opened it quietly and stepped inside. He tiptoed into the kitchen and then along the little passage into the front apartment. Here he found a plumber's lamp and a bag of tools, down by the door, but no one in the house. He went down the passage again, and entered the little, middle room. There was a smell of white lead and burnt gas, and here it was that he found an explanation of all that bothered him.

In the far corner, against the wall where—on the other side—was built his own furnace, stood one in every way similar. On the floor, in front of it, was a heap of wet fire clay, and by this was a massive, new-seeming metal cylinder which Harrison recognised at once as being a "pressure-box," identical with the one in his furnace. Evidently both furnace and cylinder had been made by the same firms to whom he had gone.

He went to the door and listened, then back and across to the cylinder. The head was loosely screwed in, and with a twist or two he had it free. Inside, there was a quantity of crude carbon, whereat he smiled rather grimly, for now he perceived the whole plot. He screwed back the head of the cylinder, and went quickly into the kitchen, for the Jew and his man, or men, might return at any moment. As he passed out through the back door, he heard the rattle of the front handle, and knew that he had not been a moment too soon in making his escape. He put a hand on the low dividing wall between the two diminutive yards, and vaulted over into his own, then hurried in to tell all that he knew to Nell.

"You see how Moss means to jew us," he concluded. "He'll come in one of these days soon, and offer to take my watch for a bit whilst I take you for a run round. While we're gone he'll bring in his cylinder, which he's stuffed with carbon and some other rubbish, and put it in our furnace, in the place of the genuine cylinder which holds the diamonds. That he'll cart into his own, and grade down the temperature according to some rather picturesque formulæ I gave him months ago, and which he's probably noted carefully for the occasion. I tell you, Nell, he's a hog of the very first water, if there is such a thing! He means not only to rob us of our share of the diamonds, but to rob us of our chance of marrying soon. I suppose the brute thinks you might look at him if the experiment turns out a failure, as he means to make it appear!"

He stopped, breathless with anger and bitterness, and the girl nodded, with a little scornful laugh at the futility of the Jew's mean schemes.

"The beauty of it is," continued Harrison, "that I'll let him do all that he's meaning to do, only there'll be one little alteration which will make just a slight difference. I'll fake up a dummy cylinder, fireclay it, and put it in the top of the furnace, and have the genuine one right down out of sight at the bottom. "What do you think of the notion?"

"Splendid!" said the girl, delighted. "It's just a splendid idea. We shall have him all along the line, sha'n't we? And he won't dare say a word afterwards, when he finds out how we've got back on him, as we say at home,"

"Yes, I think we've got him all right." said Harrison. "He'll take the visible, dummy cylinder, and leave his own in place of it. Then he'll put the dummy to bed in his own furnace, believing that it contains the diamonds. Meanwhile we'll remove his, and hide it until we need it, and bring the genuine one up to its proper place again. In a month from to-day we'll open the real one; and get the diamonds, if there are any, without saying a word to Moss. Then we'll shove the faked cylinder back into the furnace, and invite him to come in and see it opened, telling him we've been cooling down for days, and that it is now ready. As soon as we get it open, he'll shake his head, and say that he feared the experiment could hardly come to anything—just a matter of chance and luck. Then he'll go away hugging himself with the belief that he has the real cylinder safe in his own furnace—see?"

Harrison proved something of a prophet; for in no single thing was he wide of his mark. The Jew did offer to take his watch one day soon, whilst he took Miss Gwynn for an outing. When he returned, a very brief examination showed him that the Jew had effected the exchange. When the two lovers wore assured of the fact, they looked at each other, and laughed heartily. Afterwards they hoisted the faked cylinder out of the furnace, and hid it away at the bank.

"Three weeks later Harrison removed the genuine cylinder from the furnace and replaced it with the faked counterpart. Then he put the real one into hot sand to cool off. At the end of another week, he judged it would be safe to venture upon opening it.

Yet when they came to open it, they found that the screwed head was hopelessly fused solid with the remainder of the cylinder. Harrison, however, had foreseen this, and had provided himself with a suitable hacksaw and a plentiful supply of spare blades. Yet, before he attempted to do anything else, he drilled a small hole in the side of the steel case to let off the imprisoned gases. As the drill bit through the last fraction of steel, there came a sharp report and a shrill whistling of rushing gas. The drill was blown clean out of Harrison's hand, and rang against the opposite wall; but, fortunately, neither he nor Nell was hurt.

Directly afterwards he set to with the saw, working feverishly; but it was late on in the evening before they were able to get at the contents of the cylinder. When they did, they found a mass of slag and vitreous matter, which Harrison examined carefully, and afterwards broke cautiously to pieces.

Bit by bit they examined: but never a sign of a diamond could they see, and they were beginning to grow sick with disappointment;

for they had built so many hopes upon the success of the great experiment. Then, just as they were making up their minds to utter disappointment, Harrison saw something, and gave out an excited little yell. Immediately he held up a three-cornered fragment of the slag, in which was embedded three fair-sized objects, which both he and Nell at once identified as diamonds.

They searched on; but found nothing more, though they reduced the whole of the contents to fine powder, to ensure that they missed nothing. After all, they had not done so badly; for the three diamonds later realised a total of £4,700, which, though not an enormously large sum, was yet sufficient to provide a very comfortable start in life to the two impecunious Americans.

There is little left to be told. The next day, Mr. Moss was invited in to the formal opening of the faked cylinder, which, of course, he imagined they supposed to be the genuine one. When it was finally opened, and nothing but a mixture of clinkers and coarse carbon discovered, he waxed somewhat sarcastic, and pointed out the very considerable expense to which he had been put. He suggested, with a great deal of rudeness, that Tony should pack up his traps and remove himself, for his acquaintanceship had been entirely a losing concern. Then he went out and left the two of them, staring at each other, both very angry.

"I must punch his head, before I say goodbye!" said Tony at last. "One good, comfortable punch!"

"Don't," said the girl. "Let's get out of here after we've buried the real cylinder. We mustn't leave that, it might tell him the truth."

This they did, and meanwhile the Jew had gone off down the street metaphorically patting himself on the back with both hands. A little later, Harrison and Nell came out of the house in which they had spent so many hours of watching.

"Well, that's over!" Tony said, as he locked the door.

Then he took the key across to the landlord, and said good-bye.

"He'll open the dummy to-night," said Harrison later that evening over their dinner at a good restaurant. "I vote, when I've got a room for to-night, that we go that way when I take you home. We'll have a glance over the back wall, and find out whether he's there. It would be lovely to see his face when he pulls the fireclay off that dummy and finds what sort of a diamond cartridge he's got. It makes me feel virtuous to think that we've got the best of a brute like that!"

It was dark long before eight o'clock, so that Tony Harrison and Nell Gwynn had no difficulty in taking up a stand, unnoticed, which enabled them to see over the low wall, and across the tiny strip of yard into the back room where the furnace was erected.

The gas was lit, and they could see that the Jew was stooping over something on the floor, which he was tapping with the hammer.

"He's at it! We're just in time!" said Tony, with a thrill of delight in his voice. "He's knocking off the fireclay."

Abruptly there came a roar of blasphemy, muffled and vague, because of the intervening window, and they saw the Jew commence to beat the thing upon the floor, madly, with his hammer. Harrison leaned against the wall and shook with laughter.

"Crikey!" he gasped. "He's got at it at last!"

The girl also was breathless with laughter. They stood for a minute longer, watching the frantic Jew, then Harrison drew Miss Gwynn's arm within his.

"Come along, Nell," he said. "He's learning his lesson good!"

And the two of them turned and went towards the girl's home, leaving a fat, furious Jew-man beating a two-foot lump of pig iron savagely with a hammer.

Eloi, Eloi, Lama Sabachthani

DALLY, WHITLAW AND I WERE DISCUSSING the recent stupendous explosion which had occurred in the vicinity of Berlin. We were marvelling concerning the extraordinary period of darkness that had followed, and which had aroused so much newspaper comment, with theories galore.

The papers had got hold of the fact that the War Authorities had been experimenting with a new explosive, invented by a certain chemist, named Baumoff, and they referred to it constantly as "The New Baumoff Explosive".

We were in the Club, and the fourth man at our table was John Stafford, who was professionally a medical man, but privately in the Intelligence Department. Once or twice, as we talked, I had glanced at Stafford, wishing to fire a question at him; for he had been acquainted with Baumoff. But I managed to hold my tongue; for I knew that if I asked out pointblank, Stafford (who's a good sort, but a bit of an ass as regards his almost ponderous code-of-silence) would be just as like as not to say that it was a subject upon which he felt he was not entitled to speak.

Oh, I know the old donkey's way; and when he had once said that, we might just make up our minds never to get another word out of him on the matter, as long as we lived. Yet, I was satisfied to notice that he seemed a bit restless, as if he were on the itch to shove in his oar; by which I guessed that the papers we were quoting had got things very badly muddled indeed, in some way or other, at least as regarded his friend Baumoff. Suddenly, he spoke:

"What unmitigated, wicked piffle!" said Stafford, quite warm. "I tell you it is wicked, this associating of Baumoff's name with war inventions and such horrors. He was the most intensely poetical and earnest follower of the Christ that I have ever met; and it is just the brutal Irony of Circumstance that has attempted to use one of the products of his genius for a purpose of Destruction. But you'll find they won't be able to use it, in spite of their having got hold of Baumoff's formula. As an explosive it is not practicable. It is, shall I say, too impartial; there is no way of controlling it.

"I know more about it, perhaps, than any man alive; for I was Baumoff's greatest friend, and when he died, I lost the best comrade a man ever had. I need make no secret about it to you chaps. I was 'on duty' in Berlin, and I was deputed to get in touch with Baumoff. The government had long had an eye on him; he was an Experimental Chemist, you know, and altogether too jolly clever to ignore. But there was no need to worry about him. I got to know him, and we became enormous friends; for I soon found that he would never turn his abilities towards any new war-contrivance; and so, you see, I was able to enjoy my friendship with him, with a comfy conscience—a thing our chaps are not always able to do in their friendships. Oh, I tell you, it's a mean, sneaking, treacherous sort of business, ours; though it's necessary; just as some odd man, or other, has to be a hangsman. There's a number of unclean jobs to be done to keep the Social Machine running!

"I think Baumoff was the most enthusiastic intelligent believer in Christ that it will be ever possible to produce. I learned that he was compiling and evolving a treatise of most extraordinary and convincing proofs in support of the more inexplicable things concerning the life and death of Christ. He was, when I became acquainted with him, concentrating his attention particularly upon endeavouring to show that the Darkness of the Cross, between the sixth and the ninth hours, was a very real thing, possessing a tremendous significance. He intended at one sweep to smash utterly all talk of a timely thunderstorm or any of the other more or less inefficient theories which have been brought forward from time to time to explain the occurrence away as being a thing of no particular significance.

"Baumoff had a pet aversion, an atheistic Professor of Physics, named Hautch, who—using the 'marvellous' element of the life and death of Christ, as a fulcrum from which to attack Baumoff's theories—smashed at him constantly, both in his lectures and in print. Particularly did he pour bitter unbelief upon Baumoff's upholding that the Darkness of the Cross was anything more than a gloomy hour or two, magnified into blackness by the emotional inaccuracy of the Eastern mind and tongue.

"One evening, some time after our friendship had become very real, I called on Baumoff, and found him in a state of tremendous indignation over some article of the Professor's which attacked him brutally; using his theory of the Significance of the 'Darkness', as a target. Poor Baumoff! It was certainly a marvellously clever attack; the attack of a thoroughly trained, well-balanced Logician. But Baumoff was something more; he was Genius. It is a title few have any rights to; but it was his!

"He talked to me about his theory, telling me that he wanted to show me a small experiment, presently, bearing out his opinions. In his talk, he told me several things that interested me extremely. Having first reminded me of the fundamental fact that light is conveyed to the eye through the means of that indefinable medium, named the Aether. He went a step further, and pointed out to me that, from an aspect which more approached the primary, Light was a vibration of the Aether, of a certain definite number of waves per second, which possessed the power of producing upon our retina the sensation which we term Light.

"To this, I nodded; being, as of course is everyone, acquainted with so well-known a statement. From this, he took a quick, mental stride, and told me that an ineffably vague, but measurable, darkening of the atmosphere (greater or smaller according to the personality-force of the individual) was always evoked in the immediate vicinity of the human, during any period of great emotional stress.

"Step by step, Baumoff showed me how his research had led him to the conclusion that this queer darkening (a million times too subtle to be apparent to the eye) could be produced only through something which had power to disturb or temporally interrupt or break up the Vibration of Light. In other words, there was, at any time of unusual emotional activity, some disturbance of the Aether in the immediate vicinity of the person suffering, which had some effect upon the Vibration of Light, interrupting it, and producing the aforementioned infinitely vague darkening.

" 'Yes?' I said, as he paused, and looked at me, as if expecting me to have arrived at a certain definite deduction through his remarks. 'Go on.'

" 'Well,' he said, 'don't you see, the subtle darkening around the person suffering, is greater or less, according to the personality of the suffering human. Don't you?'

" 'Oh!' I said, with a little gasp of astounded comprehension, 'I see what you mean. You—you mean that if the agony of a person of ordinary personality can produce a faint disturbance of the Aether, with a consequent faint darkening, then the Agony of Christ, possessed of the Enormous Personality of the Christ, would produce a terrific disturbance of the Aether, and therefore, it might chance, of the Vibration of Light, and that this is the true explanation of the Darkness of the Cross; and that the fact of such an extraordinary and apparently unnatural and improbable Darkness having been recorded is not a thing to weaken the Marvel of Christ. But one more unutterably wonderful, infallible proof of His God-like power? Is that it? Is it? Tell me?'

"Baumoff just rocked on his chair with delight, beating one fist into the palm of his other hand, and nodding all the time to my summary. How he loved to be understood; as the Searcher always craves to be understood.

" 'And now,' he said, 'I'm going to show you something.'

"He took a tiny, corked test-tube out of his waistcoat pocket, and emptied its contents (which consisted of a single, grey-white grain, about twice the size of an ordinary pin's head) on to his dessert plate. He crushed it gently to powder with the ivory handle of a knife, then damped it gently, with a single minim of what I supposed to be water, and worked it up into a tiny patch of grey-white paste. He then took out his gold tooth-pick, and thrust it into the flame of a small chemist's spirit lamp, which had been lit since dinner as a pipe-lighter. He held the gold tooth-pick in the flame, until the narrow, gold blade glowed white hot.

" 'Now look!' he said, and touched the end of the tooth-pick against the infinitesimal patch upon the dessert plate. There came a swift little violet flash, and suddenly I found that I was staring at Baumoff through a sort of transparent darkness, which faded swiftly into a black opaqueness. I thought at first this must be the complementary effect of the flash upon the retina. But a minute passed, and we were still in that extraordinary darkness.

" 'My Gracious! Man! What is it?' I asked, at last.

"His voice explained then, that he had produced, through the medium of chemistry, an exaggerated effect which simulated, to some extent, the disturbance in the Aether produced by waves thrown off by any person during an emotional crisis or agony. The waves, or vibrations, sent out by his experiment produced only a partial simulation of the effect he wished to show me—merely the temporary interruption of the Vibration of Light, with the resulting darkness in which we both now sat.

" 'That stuff,' said Baumoff, 'would be a tremendous explosive, under certain conditions.'

I heard him puffing at his pipe, as he spoke, but instead of the glow of the pipe shining out visible and red, there was only a faint glare that wavered and disappeared in the most extraordinary fashion.

" 'My Goodness!' I said, 'when's this going away? And I stared across the room to where the big kerosene lamp showed only as a faintly glimmering patch in the gloom; a vague light that shivered and flashed oddly, as though I saw it through an immense gloomy depth of dark and disturbed water.

" 'It's all right,' Baumoff's voice said from out of the darkness. 'It's going now; in five minutes the disturbance will have quieted, and the waves of light will flow off evenly from the lamp in their normal fashion. But, whilst we're waiting, isn't it immense, eh?'

" 'Yes,' I said. 'It's wonderful; but it's rather unearthly, you know.'

" 'Oh, but I've something much finer to show you,' he said. 'The real thing. Wait another minute. The darkness is going. See! You can see the light from the lamp now quite plainly. It looks as if it were submerged in a boil of waters, doesn't it? that are growing clearer and clearer and quieter and quieter all the time.'

"It was as he said; and we watched the lamp, silently, until all signs of the disturbance of the light-carrying medium had ceased. Then Baumoff faced me once more.

" 'Now,' he said. 'You've seen the somewhat casual effects of just crude combustion of that stuff of mine. I'm going to show you the effects of combusting it in the human furnace, that is, in my own body; and then, you'll see one of the great wonders of Christ's death reproduced on a miniature scale.'

"He went across to the mantelpiece, and returned with a small, 120 minim glass and another of the tiny, corked test-tubes, containing a single grey-white grain of his chemical substance. He uncorked the test-tube, and shook the grain of substance into the minim glass, and then, with a glass stirring-rod, crushed it up in the bottom of the glass, adding water, drop by drop as he did so, until there were sixty minims in the glass.

" 'Now!' he said, and lifting it, he drank the stuff. 'We will give it thirty-five minutes,' he continued; 'then, as carbonization proceeds, you will find my pulse will increase, as also the respiration, and presently there will come the darkness again, in the subtlest, strangest fashion; but accompanied now by certain physical and psychic phenomena, which will be owing to the fact that the vibrations it will throw off, will be blent into what I might call the emotional-vibrations, which I shall give off in my distress. These will be enormously intensified, and you will possibly experience an extraordinarily interesting demonstration of the soundness of my more theoretical reasonings. I tested it by myself last week' (He waved a bandaged finger at me), 'and I read a paper to the Club on the results. They are very enthusiastic, and have promised their co-operation in the big demonstration I intend to give on next Good Friday—that's seven weeks off, to-day.'

"He had ceased smoking; but continued to talk quietly in this fashion for the next thirty-five minutes. The Club to which he had referred was a peculiar association of men, banded together under the presidentship of Baumoff himself, and having for their appellation the title of—so well as I can translate it —'The Believers And Provers Of Christ'. If I may say so, without any thought of irreverence, they were, many of them, men fanatically crazed to uphold the Christ. You will agree later, I think, that I have not used an incorrect term, in describing the bulk of the members of this extraordinary club, which was, in its way, well worthy of one of the religio-maniacal extrudences which have been forced into temporary being by certain of the more religiously-emotional minded of our cousins across the water.

"Baumoff looked at the clock; then held out his wrist to me. 'Take my pulse,' he said, 'it's rising fast. Interesting data, you know.'

"I nodded, and drew out my watch. I had noticed that his respirations were increasing; and I found his pulse running evenly and strongly at 105. Three minutes later, it had risen to 175, and his respirations to 41. In a further three minutes, I took his pulse again, and found it running at 203, but with the rhythm regular. His respirations were then 49. He had, as I knew, excellent lungs, and his heart was sound. His lungs, I may say, were of exceptional capacity, and there was at this stage no marked dyspnoea. Three minutes later I found the pulse to be 227, and the respiration 54.

'You've plenty of red corpuscles, Baumoff!' I said. 'But I hope you're not going to overdo things.'

"He nodded at me, and smiled; but said nothing. Three minutes later, when I took the last pulse, it was 233, and the two sides of the heart were sending out unequal quantities of blood, with an irregular rhythm. The respiration had risen to 67 and was becoming shallow and ineffectual, and dyspnoea was becoming very marked. The small amount of arterial blood leaving the left side of the heart betrayed itself in the curious bluish and white tinge of the face.

" 'Baumoff!' I said, and began to remonstrate; but he checked me, with a queerly invincible gesture.

" 'It's all right!' he said, breathlessly, with a little note of impatience.

'I know what I'm doing all the time. You must remember I took the same degree as you in medicine.'

"It was quite true. I remembered then that he had taken his M.D. in London; and this in addition to half a dozen other degrees in different branches of the sciences in his own country. And then, even as the memory reassured me that he was not acting in ignorance of the possible danger, he called out in a curious, breathless voice:

" 'The Darkness! It's beginning. Take note of every single thing. Don't bother about me. I'm all right!'

"I glanced swiftly round the room. It was as he had said. I perceived it now. There appeared to be an extraordinary quality of gloom growing in the atmosphere of the room. A kind of bluish gloom, vague, and scarcely, as yet, affecting the transparency of the atmosphere to light.

"Suddenly, Baumoff did something that rather sickened me. He drew his wrist away from me, and reached out to a small metal box, such as one sterilizes a hypodermic in. He opened the box, and took out four rather curious looking drawing pins, I might call them, only they had spikes of steel fully an inch long, whilst all around the rim of the heads (which were also of steel) there projected downward, parallel with the central spike, a number of shorter spikes, maybe an eighth of an inch long.

"He kicked off his pumps; then stooped and slipped his socks off, and I saw that he was wearing a pair of linen inner-socks.

" 'Antiseptic!' he said, glancing at me. 'Got my feet ready before you came. No use running unnecessary risks.' He gasped as he spoke. Then he took one of the curious little steel spikes.

" 'I've sterilized them,' he said; and therewith, with deliberation, he pressed it in up to the head into his foot between the second and third branches of the dorsal artery.

" 'For God's sake, what are you doing!' I said, half rising from my chair.

" 'Sit down!' he said, in a grim sort of voice. 'I can't have any interference. I want you simply to observe; keep note of everything. You ought to thank me for the chance, instead of worrying me, when you know I shall go my own way all the time.'

"As he spoke, he had pressed in the second of the steel spikes up to the hilt in his left instep, taking the same precaution to avoid the arteries. Not a groan had come from him; only his face betrayed the effect of this additional distress.

" 'My dear chap!' he said, observing my upsetness. 'Do be sensible. I know exactly what I'm doing. There simply must be distress, and the readiest way to reach that condition is through physical pain.' His speech had becomes a series of spasmodic words, between gasps, and sweat lay in great clear drops upon his lip and forehead. He slipped off his belt and proceeded to buckle it round both the back of his chair and his waist; as if he expected to need some support from falling.

" 'It's wicked!' I said. Baumoff made an attempt to shrug his heaving shoulders, that was, in its way, one of the most piteous things that I have seen, in its sudden laying bare of the agony that the man was making so little of.

"He was now cleaning the palms of his hands with a little sponge, which he dipped from time to time in a cup of solution. I knew what he was going to do, and suddenly he jerked out, with a painful attempt to grin, an explanation of his bandaged finger. He had held his finger in the flame of the spirit lamp, during his previous experiment; but now, as he made clear in gaspingly uttered words, he wished to simulate as far as possible the actual conditions of the great scene that he had so much in mind. He made it so clear to me that we might expect to experience something very extraordinary, that I was conscious of a sense of almost superstitious nervousness.

" 'I wish you wouldn't, Baumoff!' I said.

" 'Don't—be—silly!' he managed to say. But the two latter words were more groans than words; for between each, he had thrust home right to the heads in the palms of his hands the two remaining steel spikes. He gripped his hands shut, with a sort of spasm of savage determination, and I saw the point of one of the spikes break through the back of his hand, between the extensor tendons of the second and third fingers. A drop of blood beaded the point of the spike. I looked at Baumoff's face; and he looked back steadily at me.

" 'No interference,' he managed to ejaculate. 'I've not gone through all this for nothing. I know—what—I'm doing. Look—it's coming. Take note—everything!'

"He relapsed into silence, except for his painful gasping. I realised that I must give way, and I stared round the room, with a peculiar commingling of an almost nervous discomfort and a stirring of very real and sober curiosity.

" 'Oh,' said Baumoff, after a moment's silence, 'something's going to happen. I can tell. Oh, wait—till I—I have my—big demonstration. I'll know—that—brute Hautch."

"I nodded; but I doubt that he saw me; for his eyes had a distinctly in-turned look, the iris was rather relaxed. I glanced away round the room again; there was a distinct occasional breaking up of the light-rays from the lamp, giving a coming-and-going effect.

"The atmosphere of the room was also quite plainly darker—heavy, with an extraordinary sense of gloom. The bluish tint was unmistakably more in evidence; but there was, as yet, none of that opacity which we had experienced before, upon simple combustion, except for the occasional, vague coming-and-going of the lamp-light.

"Baumoff began to speak again, getting his words out between gasps. 'Th'—this dodge of mine gets the—pain into the—the—right place. Right association of—of ideas—emotions—for—best—results. You follow me? Parallelising things—as much as—possible. Fixing whole attention—on the—the death scene—'

"He gasped painfully for a few moments. 'We demonstrate truth of—of The Darkening; but—but there's psychic effect to be—looked for, through—results of parallelisation of—conditions. May have extraordinary simulation of—the actual thing. Keep note. Keep note.' Then, suddenly, with a clear, spasmodic burst: 'My God, Stafford, keep note of everything. Something's going to happen. Something—wonderful—Promise not—to bother me. I know—what I'm doing.'

"Baumoff ceased speaking, with a gasp, and there was only the labour of his breathing in the quietness of the room. As I stared at him, halting from a dozen things I needed to say, I realised suddenly that I could no longer see him quite plainly; a sort of wavering in the atmosphere, between us, made him seem momentarily unreal. The whole room had darkened perceptibly in the last thirty seconds; and as I stared around, I realised that there was a constant invisible swirl in the fast-deepening, extraordinary blue gloom that seemed now to permeate everything. When I looked at the lamp, alternate flashings of light and blue—darkness followed each other with an amazing swiftness.

" 'My God!' I heard Baumoff whispering in the half-darkness, as if to himself, 'how did Christ bear the nails!'

"I stared across at him, with an infinite discomfort, and an irritated pity troubling me; but I knew it was no use to remonstrate now. I saw him vaguely distorted through the wavering tremble of the atmosphere. It was somewhat as if I looked at him through convolutions of heated air; only there were marvellous waves of blue-blackness making gaps in my sight. Once I saw his face clearly, full of an infinite pain, that was somehow, seemingly, more spiritual than physical, and dominating everything was an expression of enormous resolution and concentration, making the livid, sweat-damp, agonized face somehow heroic and splendid.

"And then, drenching the room with waves and splashes of opaqueness, the vibration of his abnormally stimulated agony finally broke up the vibration of Light. My last, swift glance round, showed me, as it seemed, the invisible aether boiling and eddying in a tremendous fashion; and, abruptly, the flame of the lamp was lost in an extraordinary swirling patch of light, that marked its position for several moments, shimmering and deadening, shimmering and deadening; until, abruptly, I saw neither that glimmering patch of light, nor anything else. I was suddenly lost in a black opaqueness of night, through which came the fierce, painful breathing of Baumoff.

"A full minute passed; but so slowly that, if I had not been counting Baumoff's respirations, I should have said that it was five. Then Baumoff spoke suddenly, in a voice that was, somehow, curiously changed—a certain toneless note in it:

" 'My God!' he said, from out of the darkness, 'what must Christ have suffered!'

"It was in the succeeding silence, that I had the first realisation that I was vaguely afraid; but the feeling was too indefinite and unfounded, and I might say subconscious, for me to face it out. Three minutes passed, whilst I counted the almost desperate respirations that came to me through the darkness. Then Baumoff began to speak again, and still in that peculiarly altering voice:

" 'By Thy Agony and Bloody Sweat,' he muttered. Twice he repeated this. It was plain indeed that he had fixed his whole attention with tremendous intensity, in his abnormal state, upon the death scene.

"The effect upon me of his intensity was interesting and in some ways extraordinary. As well as I could, I analysed my sensations and emotions and general state of mind, and realised that Baumoff was producing an effect upon me that was almost hypnotic.

"Once, partly because I wished to get my level by the aid of a normal remark, and also because I was suddenly newly anxious by a change in the breath-sounds, I asked Baumoff how he was. My voice going with a peculiar and really uncomfortable blankness through that impenetrable blackness of opacity.

"He said: 'Hush! I'm carrying the Cross.' And, do you know, the effect of those simple words, spoken in that new, toneless voice, in that atmosphere of almost unbearable tenseness, was so powerful that, suddenly, with eyes wide open, I saw Baumoff clear and vivid against that unnatural darkness, carrying a Cross. Not, as the picture is usually shown of the Christ, with it crooked over the shoulder; but with the Cross gripped just under the cross-piece in his arms, and the end trailing behind, along rocky ground. I saw even the pattern of the grain of the rough wood, where some of the bark had been ripped away; and under the trailing end there was a tussock of tough wire-grass, that had been uprooted by the towing end, and dragged and ground along upon the rocks, between the end of the Cross and the rocky ground. I can see the thing now, as I speak. Its vividness was extraordinary; but it had come and gone like a flash, and I was sitting there in the darkness, mechanically counting the respirations; yet unaware that I counted.

"As I sat there, it came to me suddenly—the whole entire marvel of the thing that Baumoff had achieved. I was sitting there in a darkness which was an actual reproduction of the miracle of the Darkness of the Cross. In short, Baumoff had, by producing in himself an abnormal condition, developed an Energy of Emotion that must have almost, in its effects, paralleled the Agony of the Cross. And in so doing, he had shown from an entirely new and wonderful point, the indisputable truth of the stupendous personality and the enormous spiritual force of the Christ. He had evolved and made practical to the average understanding a proof that would make to live again the reality of that wonder of the world—CHRIST. And for all this, I had nothing but admiration of an almost stupefied kind.

"But, at this point, I felt that the experiment should stop. I had a strangely nervous craving for Baumoff to end it right there and then, and not to try to parallel the psychic conditions. I had, even then, by some queer aid of sub-conscious suggestion, a vague reaching-out-towards the danger of "monstrosity" being induced, instead of any actual knowledge gained.

"Baumoff!' I said. 'Stop it!'

"But he made no reply, and for some minutes there followed a silence, that was unbroken, save by his gasping breathing. Abruptly, Baumoff said, between his gasps: 'Woman—behold—thy—son.' He muttered this several times, in the same uncomfortably toneless voice in which he had spoken since the darkness became complete.

" 'Baumoff!' I said again. 'Baumoff! Stop it!' And as I listened for his answer, I was relieved to think that his breathing was less shallow. The abnormal demand for oxygen was evidently being met, and the extravagant call upon the heart's efficiency was being relaxed.

" 'Baumoff!' I said, once more. 'Baumoff! Stop it!"

"And, as I spoke, abruptly, I thought the room was shaken a little.

"Now, I had already as you will have realised, been vaguely conscious of a peculiar and growing nervousness. I think that is the word that best describes it, up to this moment. At this curious little shake that seemed to stir through the utterly dark room, I was suddenly more than nervous. I felt a thrill of actual and literal fear; yet with no sufficient cause of reason to justify me; so that, after sitting very tense for some long minutes, and feeling nothing further, I decided that I needed to take myself in hand, and keep a firmer grip upon my nerves. And then, just as I had arrived at this more comfortable state of mind, the room was shaken again, with the most curious and sickening oscillatory movement, that was beyond all comfort of denial.

" 'My God!' I whispered. And then, with a sudden effort of courage, I called: 'Baumoff! For God's sake stop it!'

"You've no idea of the effort it took to speak aloud into that darkness; and when I did speak, the sound of my voice set me afresh on edge. It went so empty and raw across the room; and somehow, the room seemed to be incredibly big. Oh, I wonder whether you realise how beastly I felt, without my having to make any further effort to tell you.

"And Baumoff never answered a word; but I could hear him breathing, a little fuller; though still heaving his thorax painfully, in his need for air. The incredible shaking of the room eased away; and there succeeded a spasm of quiet, in which I felt that it was my duty to get up and step across to Baumoff s chair. But I could not do it. Somehow, I would not have touched Baumoff then for any cause whatever. Yet, even in that moment, as now I know, I was not aware that I was afraid to touch Baumoff.

"And then the oscillations commenced again. I felt the seat of my trousers slide against the seat of my chair, and I thrust out my legs, spreading my feet against the carpet, to keep me from sliding off one way or the other on to the floor. To say I was afraid, was not to describe my state at all. I was terrified. And suddenly, I had comfort, in the most extraordinary fashion; for a single idea literally glazed into my brain, and gave me a reason to which to cling. It was a single line:

" 'Aether, the soul of iron and sundry stuffs' which Baumoff had once taken as a text for an extraordinary lecture on vibrations, in the earlier days of our friendship. He had formulated the suggestion that, in embryo, Matter was, from a primary aspect, a localised vibration, traversing a closed orbit. These primary localised vibrations were inconceivably minute. But were capable, under certain conditions, of combining under the action of keynote-vibrations into secondary vibrations of a size and shape to be determined by a multitude of only guessable factors. These would sustain their new form, so long as nothing occurred to disorganise their combination or depreciate or divert their energy—their unity being partially determined by the inertia of the still Aether outside of the closed path which their area of activities covered. And such combination of the primary localised vibrations was neither more nor less than matter. Men and worlds, aye! and universes.

"And then he had said the thing that struck me most. He had said, that if it were possible to produce a vibration of the Aether of a sufficient energy, it would be possible to disorganise or confuse the vibration of matter. That, given a machine capable of creating a vibration of the Aether of a sufficient energy, he would engage to destroy not merely the world, but the whole universe itself, including heaven and hell themselves, if such places existed, and had such existence in a material form.

"I remember how I looked at him, bewildered by the pregnancy and scope of his imagination. And now his lecture had come back to me to help my courage with the sanity of reason. Was it not possible that the Aether disturbance which he had produced, had sufficient energy to cause some disorganisation of the vibration of matter, in the immediate vicinity, and had thus created a miniature quaking of the ground all about the house, and so set the house gently a-shake?

"And then, as this thought came to me, another and a greater, flashed into my mind. 'My God!' I said out loud into the darkness of the room. It explains one more mystery of the Cross, the disturbance of the Aether caused by Christ's Agony, disorganised the vibration of matter in the vicinity of the Cross, and there was then a small local earthquake, which opened the graves, and rent the veil, possibly by disturbing its supports. And, of course, the earthquake was an effect, and not a cause, as belittlers of the Christ have always insisted.

" 'Baumoff!' I called. 'Baumoff, you've proved another thing. Baumoff! Baumoff! Answer me. Are you all right?'

"Baumoff answered, sharp and sudden out of the darkness; but not to me:

" 'My God!' he said. 'My God!' His voice came out at me, a cry of veritable mental agony. He was suffering, in some hypnotic, induced fashion, something of the very agony of the Christ Himself.

" 'Baumoff!" I shouted, and forced myself to my feet. I heard his chair clattering, as he sat there and shook. 'Baumoff!'

An extraordinary quake went across the floor of the room, and I heard a creaking of the woodwork, and something fell and smashed in the darkness. Baumoff's gasps hurt me; but I stood there. I dared not go to him. I knew then that I was afraid of him—of his condition, or something I don't know what. But, oh, I was horribly afraid of him.

" 'Bau—' I began, but suddenly I was afraid even to speak to him. And I could not move. Abruptly, he cried out in a tone of incredible anguish:

" 'Eloi, Eloi, lama sabachthani!' But the last word changed in his mouth, from his dreadful hypnotic grief and pain, to a scream of simply infernal terror.

"And, suddenly, a horrible mocking voice roared out in the room, from Baumoff s chair: 'Eloi, Eloi, lama sabachthani!'

"Do you understand, the voice was not Baumoff's at all. It was not a voice of despair; but a voice sneering in an incredible, bestial, monstrous fashion. In the succeeding silence, as I stood in an ice of fear, I knew that Baumoff no longer gasped. The room was absolutely silent, the most dreadful and silent place in all this world. Then I bolted; caught my foot, probably in the invisible edge of the hearth-rug, and pitched headlong into a blaze of internal brain-stars. After which, for a very long time, certainly some hours, I knew nothing of any kind.

"I came back into this Present, with a dreadful headache oppressing me, to the exclusion of all else. But the Darkness had dissipated. I rolled over on to my side, and saw Baumoff and forgot even the pain in my head. He was leaning forward towards me; his eyes wide open, but dull. His face was enormously swollen, and there was, somehow, something beastly about him. He was dead, and the belt about him and the chair-back, alone prevented him from falling forward on to me. His tongue was thrust out of one corner of his mouth. I shall always remember how he looked. He was leering, like a human-beast, more than a man.

"I edged away from him, across the floor; but I never stopped looking at him, until I had got to the other side of the door, and closed between us. Of course, I got my balance in a bit, and went back to him; but there was nothing I could do.

"Baumoff died of heart-failure, of course, obviously! I should never be so foolish as to suggest to any sane jury that, in his extraordinary, self-hypnotised, defenseless condition, he was "entered" by some Christ-apeing Monster of the Void. I've too much respect for my own claim to be a common-sensible man, to put forward such an idea with seriousness! Oh, I know I may seem to speak with a jeer; but what can I do but jeer at myself and all the world, when I dare not acknowledge, even secretly to myself, what my own thoughts are. Baumoff did, undoubtedly die of heart-failure; and, for the rest, how much was I hypnotised into believing. Only, there was over by the far wall, where it had been shaken down to the floor from a solidly fastened-up bracket, a little pile of glass that had once formed a piece of beautiful Venetian glassware. You remember that I heard something fall, when the room shook. Surely the room did shake? Oh, I must stop thinking. My head goes round.

"The explosive the papers are talking about. Yes, that's Baumoff's; that makes it all seem true, doesn't it? They had the darkness at Berlin, after the explosion. There is no getting away from that. The Government know only that Baumoff's formulae is capable of producing the largest quantity of gas, in the shortest possible time. That, in short, it is ideally explosive. So it is; but I imagine it will prove an explosive, as I have already said, and as experience has proved, a little too impartial in its action for it to create enthusiasm on either side of a battlefield. Perhaps this is but a mercy, in disguise; certainly a mercy, if Baumoff's theories as to the possibility of disorganising matter, be anywhere near to the truth.

"I have thought sometimes that there might be a more normal explanation of the dreadful thing that happened at the end. Baumoff may have ruptured a blood-vessel in the brain, owing to the enormous arterial pressure that his experiment induced; and the voice I heard and the mockery and the horrible expression and leer may have been nothing more than the immediate outburst and expression of the natural "obliqueness" of a deranged mind, which so often turns up a side of a man's nature and produces an inversion of character, that is the very complement of his normal state. And certainly, poor Baumoff's normal religious attitude was one of marvellous reverence and loyalty towards the Christ.

"Also, in support of this line of explanation, I have frequently observed that the voice of a person suffering from mental derangement is frequently wonderfully changed, and has in it often a very repellant and inhuman quality. I try to think that this explanation fits the case. But I can never forget that room. Never."

The Room of Fear

1

WILLIE JOHNSON LAY IN THE BIG BED very quiet and rigid. He had that day come upon his eighth birthday, and in consequence thereof—beginning to be, as his father had told him at breakfast that morning, a big boy—had been promoted from the night nursery and the company of his little sister Jenny and the baby, to the lonely state of a bedroom all to himself.

He had begged hard to be allowed to stay in the night nursery; but his father had teased him for his babyishness, and his mother had negatived his desire with a few curt words. His nurse, Nanny Josephs, had sat with him for some time to keep him company; for she knew something of the fear of the dark in which the little man had lived all his short days; but his mother, chancing to come in to see how he liked his new bedroom, had ordered her out, telling her that she was but pandering to the cowardice of the boy, which he would have to learn to outgrow, and that she considered nurse's conduct as nothing more or less than encouraging the boy to rebel against the wishes of his parents.

His mother had stayed with him some few minutes after Nanny had gone, and she had improved the time with some sharp remarks upon her little son's lack of courage, the which, indeed, hurt her in a very tender place; for, above all sins, she held none so vile as that of cowardice. Then she had given him a cold, reproveful, duty kiss—and gone out into the light of the big corridor, closing the little man in alone with the darkness. Yet she was a good woman, somewhat cold-blooded it is true; yet by no means lacking in steady affection. But she was also a very proud woman, and neither the Johnsons nor the Lemots—her own family—had ever numbered the fear-vice among their many others. And now, here had she given birth to a son who was a coward to his little marrow. Yet he should be cured, or—what! I doubt if she gave even a thought to the alternative. He should be cured. There was nothing more. Certainly he should be cured!

She went downstairs and came presently to her husband. To the big, ruddy man she told in a few words her reprehension of nurse's conduct, and quoted a fragment of conversation that had passed between them:

"I asked her if she thought Willie would grow into a manly boy if she pandered to him in that manner; and what do you think, John, the foolish woman said: 'I'm thinkin', Ma'am, as children do see things as we carn't.' I ordered her out of the room instantly. No wonder Willie is afraid to go to bed if she talks after that fashion in his hearing."

Upstairs, alone in the dark bedroom, Willie lies in the coldness of the big bed—a little rigid, human atom, too frozen by fear even to pull the clothes over his face. He is watching with wide-opened, fixed eyes a great shadow against the lofty, invisible ceiling. It is shaping and shaping in hideous convolutions into the form of a vast hand. The four gigantic fingers are completed, and now the huge thumb sprouts of the, as yet, indefinite palm. And the little man alone in the darkness, seeming a thousand miles from all human comradeship, grows yet more rigid, and his eyes become the more fixedly open and staring. Suddenly, he realizes that the still uncompleted hand has moved downwards bodily, and the fingers are crooked towards him. The whole thing comes lower by perhaps a whole foot and pauses. The child is scarcely breathing, and his feet, spine, hands and forehead are sweating coldly. His senses seem to have become preternaturally sharp, and he hears, unconsciously, a dull regular booming in his ears that seems to fill, and throb through, the great dark room. In his little heart is one vast desire—prayer, that he might get the bed clothes over his head; but he knows that the crooked hand will pounce the instant he moves even one tiny inch. Sixty seconds pass—sixty minutes of immortal agony—such agony as only the fresh nerves of a fearful child can know. Then the staring eyes note a slow movement in the overhanging mass of shadows. It is—receding, slowly, slowly, withdrawing into itself, shrinking, fading; but all the while in constant movement—convoluting. It has risen near to the ceiling, and is become little more than a small shadow. The child on the bed gives a terrific, spasmodic movement, and is under the clothes. The little, relieved heart is sledge-hammering against the frail ribs, so that the curtains of the great bed quiver to each throb. Truly he shall be cured!

Down in the servant's hall cook and nurse are talking:

"They're a plucky family is the Missus's," cook is saying. "I b'lieve she don't scarce know what it is to be frightened. An' I've 'eard 'er say as she's sooner 'ave a thief than a coward."

"Master Willie ain't a coward. He's always been a sensitive child, and I'll admit he's afraid of the dark; but all children are. I've thought sometimes as they could see more than us grown up. But they grow out of it, an' so will he if the Missus 'll give him time."

"The Missus ain't one 's 'll give time. It's kill or cure with 'er, an' always 'as been. She's more down on cowardice in 'er own flesh an' blood 'n she would be if 'twas a stranger; but she's fair an' straight in 'er dealin's with folk, an' kind enough in 'er own fashion."

"I'm not sayin' as she ain't; but she don't understand Master Willie. Ther's not a sweeter child anywhere, an' he's pluck enough in his own way. It's not only the dark as he's frightened of. He's feared of that there West bedroom in which the Missus has put him. I said to 'er that if he couldn't stay in the night nursery he never seemed to mind much being in the little room in the East wing. He slept there the time as Miss Jenny had measles. But she told me to hold my tongue, an' sent me out of the room. She's got a pretty temper she has when she starts!"

"I don't see," remarked cook, "as it matters which room 'e's in, so long as it's the dark as 'e's feared of."

"I've told you, it ain't only the dark as he's frightened of. He's afraid of that there West room, an' always has been. I don't know why, I'm sure. It's a beautiful room; but it seems to me there's some rooms as children seem to be feared of as soon they put foot inside. I daresay too, it isn't always without reason. I tried to tell that to the Missus; but it wern't no good."

"I don't know as ever I wer' feared of a room when I wer' a young un," remarked the cook, reflectively, and polishing her red face with her apron.

"Yet you daren't go down the cellars of this very house unless you've someone with you—and you going on for forty-five!" And with this as a parting word, the nurse turned and left her.

2

At breakfast next morning, Willie was quiet and pale; but then he was naturally quiet, and usually pale, so that this attracted no particular notice. His father bantered him good-humouredly upon his lack of appreciation of his new bedroom, and asked him how he would have managed in the old days, if he had wished to be a knight, considering that he would have to have undergone a whole night's vigil in a great church alone? To which Willie replied simply and truthfully that he would not have liked it, and that he thought he would sooner not have become a knight at all. At this reply, his mother turned and stared at him steadily; but said nothing for some moments. Then:

"I would far sooner see you dead than a coward, Willie!" she remarked with a quiet simplicity. "There has never been a coward in our family on either side till now—" And she paused a moment significantly; then continued: "Can you understand that, Willie? All our men have been famous for their bravery as far back as the Conqueror—Is it not so, John?" she concluded, turning to her husband.

Sir John nodded slowly for reply, and a look of mingled pride and regret came into his eyes—the pride was for his race—the regret that he had lacked chance in his quiet, country life to add to the family traditions of great deeds. Yet, in a moment he was busy again at his breakfast; for he was a hearty, healthy man, fond of sport and outdoor life, and not over given to sentiment. Occasionally, in the course of the meal, he touched genially on his little son's weakness; but to his direct questions the boy replied no more than "Yes, Sir," or "No, Sir." For he was busied with strangely bitter thoughts for so young a child. His mother's cold, sincere remark had bitten into the brain and heart of the boy, and had roused more than his pride; for Willie loved the somewhat stern woman in a passionate, quiet manner, and with a curious element of reverence, which latter might have been less developed had she shown him more of the mother-side. And because of his love for her, that remark: "I would far sooner see you dead than a coward, Willie," had, as I have said, roused more than his pride. It had waked a great resolve within him to win her approbation by conquering his fear of the dark and of that room. And if he could not do this, at least, he would hide from her for the future that he was any longer afraid.

And presently, breakfast being ended, he went to his governess.

***

All through the day, the boy has the fear of the night oppressing him, and though he tries manfully to put it from him, and pretends to himself that he is no longer afraid, he is in a tensely nervous state when the evening comes.

Later, when with his nurse he enters the big bedroom, he gives a little shiver of sheer apprehension, and his gaze sweeps quickly round, the action being so full of fear that nurse gives a little start, and steps back a pace.

"How you did startle me, Master Willie!" she remonstrates, as she proceeds to help him into bed. "I thought sure you'd seen something."

When he is in the big bed, a kindly thought comes to her, and she makes the round of the room, peeping into the great wardrobes, behind the curtains, and under the bed itself! Then she assures him that he has nothing of which to be afraid, that she has been all round, and after that, with a kiss, she leaves him; but purposely leaves the door a little ajar, so that a little light from the lamp outside creeps into the darkness of the room. Yet Willie has no knowledge of this; for, the instant she has started to pull the door behind her, he has dived beneath the clothes, and there his mother finds him, very silent and frightened and wide awake when she comes up to say goodnight to him. She is cross with him, and a little scornful; telling that it is bad for his health, and that he is no safer from his bogy (which is simply cowardice) under the clothes than outside of them. After that, having turned the clothes down so as to leave his face exposed, she kisses him without emotion and goes from the room, shutting the door behind her.

For a time after she has gone, the boy lies there quietly, his eyes tightly closed. Presently, he is tempted to open them; but resists. Yet the temptation becomes stronger, so that he has to screw them up tight to keep them shut, and so a few short, painful minutes pass; then, abruptly, he has opened his eyes and is staring up into the darkness above him. Right above him near to the ceiling there seems a slightly darker patch amid the darkness. As he stares at it with unwilling eyes, it begins to move—convoluting slowly at first; then rapidly. It grows larger and begins to take shape. Again he sees the giant hand form slowly finger by finger. The huge thumb protrudes out from one side of the mass; then the whole thing sinks bodily toward him; but stops with a jerk, maybe, halfway between the ceiling and the bed.

The boy has gone rigid, and his heart is failing in its action. Again there comes that dull booming sound that fills the dark room. Above him the great fingers are all of a-waver. Then, suddenly, the four of them and the huge thumb crook down towards him; and the hand itself drops bodily lower with a jerk. The child is soaked in a cold sweat; but has no knowledge of it; all his faculties are concentrated to keep perfectly still—not to move and bring THAT down upon him. He is pressing down hard against the bed with a fierce, rigid terror, to get as far away from the thing as possible. The booming sound fills the room like thunder, and the child begins to catch for breath. He struggles to keep silent—immovable. If he could only get the clothes over his face! The booming is more persistent. He begins to see two hands—hands everywhere, all blurred and great. Then he sinks down through the bottom of the bed, and the hands have gone.

3

Through all the following day, it is plain to nurse and his governess that Willie is not himself. He is pale and nervous, jumping when a door is banged, and makes but a poor fist of his lessons.

At breakfast even his father has noticed his increased pallor and mentions it; but his wife chimes in, perhaps a little sharply, that it is due to Willie's having taken to sleeping under the bed clothes, and that she had to uncover him by main force when she went in the previous evening.

That night, when nurse takes him to bed, she repeats her kindly search of the previous night, assuring him afterwards that he has nothing of which to be afraid, to which he replies, his courage at twanging pitch, that he is not going to be frightened any more. And so she leaves him.

Now in this night, for some reason, perhaps because the child is so thoroughly worn out by the strain of the two previous nights, he goes off to sleep, untroubled by any phantasm, and wakes near to being himself in the morning, and with a new and strange sense of confidence in his courage. Strong in this feeling, he approaches his mother after breakfast, when his father has gone out.

"Mother," he says shyly, "I've stopped being a coward. I never felt afraid at all last night, and I never pulled the clothes over my head all the night."

"I'm pleased to hear it, Willie," she replies; but without much enthusiasm; for, to her, pluck over such a thing is so trifling a matter that she would rather almost that her little son had said nothing, than put forward so small a thing as proof of courage. For his part, the boy feels repulsed. He feels that he has achieved a gigantic victory, and cannot understand her utter inability to appreciate it. It is beyond his imagination that anyone should have never known his enemies.

That night, his new-found confidence in himself is smashed. He sees the giant hand form, as on the previous occasions, and come towards him, sinking so near that he seems like to die of suffocation. The room is filled with the same dull thunder, and, at last, the poor child swoons outright, coming to at intervals through the night. This is the second time that Terror has gone so far with him towards the Land of Shadows; though Willie does not know but that he has had a "horrid" sleep.

At breakfast the following morning, his pallor and general look of ill-health provoke remark; but the boy denies that he has been sleeping with his head beneath the clothes, when his mother taxes him with so doing, and there is something of unconscious pride in his denial that puzzles her faintly.

4

That night, when nurse takes Willie to bed, his terror is so palpable, that she is near to going down to her mistress and giving her, as she puts it, "a piece of her mind." Yet, after a little, the boy calms down and presently assures her in a somewhat strained little voice that he isn't really afraid. At this, having twice made search through the room, and stayed beside him so long as she dare, she has to leave him, closing the door after her; for her mistress has spoken to her about leaving it open a couple of nights previously.

Then begins for the little, nervous man, a time of torture grim and terrible. He tries to obey his mother, and keeps the clothes below his chin; but he shuts his eyes hard and determines not to open them; yet, despite his determination, within ten minutes he is staring frightenedly up at a convoluting mass of shadow near the ceiling. The great hand is forming steadily. He sees the vast fingers grow and waver about in the darkness overhead. Then he makes a huge attempt, and closes his eyes; yet, now that he knows the thing is there, it is worse to have them shut than open; for he imagines that it has come down close to him—that it is touching his face, and so, with something near to a cry, he opens his eyes and looks. The hand has grown whilst his eyes have been closed, and even as he stares, the thing comes down with its accustomed jerk. He tries to gather sufficient courage to grab at the clothes and get them over his head; for his fear has mastered his power to obey. Yet, already, he is past the ability to move and can only lie there, rigid and pressing madly and silently back against the bed.

The booming has come again in the room, throbbing solemnly, and growing louder. Above him the hand is lying motionless in the darkness; yet only for a second; then it begins to move from side to side with a peculiar waving motion, the great fingers twirling and twirling rapidly. Suddenly it stops, and the vast forefinger is reaching down toward him—down, down, down. . . . The booming noise ends suddenly, and then the finger is withdrawn. For a little the hand is very indistinct. Then it becomes plainer to his sight, and the booming noise re-echoes once more through the room; but more irregularly. For a time, the child is scarce conscious of anything save a deadly sick feeling, and behind that the overmastering fear. The sense of sickness goes, and the fear predominates nakedly. The hand is nearer, and now, for the first time, it is plain seen even to the gigantic wrist. For a while it remains motionless; then again is the long, shadowy forefinger reached down to him; but only to be withdrawn immediately, and after that, for a little, the hand remains quiet. . . . Suddenly, Willie is aware that it is sinking down upon him, slowly, imperceptibly almost . . . down . . . down . . . down. The booming noise dies out as he stares at the great shadowy mass coming down upon him. Without moving, he yet crouches backward down against the bed a little further. A cold sweat is running off his face. He sees the four vast fingers and the thumb come down right on to his face. In the same instant he screams out and then something goes snap, and he stops screaming. . . .

5

Downstairs in the big dining room Sir John and his lady are finishing dinner. Doctor Lubbock is at the table with them, and he is listening attentively to the lady. She has asked him to come to dinner, because she is wishful to have a little talk about Willie; for she has felt a little uneasy about the child's pallor and look of ill-health in the morning. Lady John ceases to explain, and the Doctor commences to speak:

"I shouldn't trouble about him. He's a nervous child and will grow out of it; but I should be inclined to let him go back to the night nursery. Plenty of time, you know; plenty of time. I will slip in tomorrow and have a look at the young man. You say . . ." At this instant he is interrupted by a loud scream in the room overhead, and then the noise of something striking the floor with a distinct soft thud. Sir John starts to his feet, but his lady is before him, and is at the door, her face somewhat pale. There are running footsteps on the front stairs, and nurse bursts in upon them, her hair flying, her eyes wild and bright in the lamplight.

"In—in Mas-ter Willie's roo-om!" she gasps, and then the mother has flung her to one side, and is racing for the stairs, her husband behind. The Doctor follows, without a word. He catches them at the door of Willie's room. Lady John has got the corridor lamp. She turns the handle and enters. The bed is empty, the bedclothes thrown all on one side. They stand and stare around; then the mother gives out a cry of "Willie!" and runs forward to the wash-hand stand. Crouched beside it, cowering back in the corner, is a little white-robed figure, shivering and silent. The light from the lamp shines on uncomprehending eyes.

6

Three years have passed—three years in which the stern hand of sorrow has dealt with Willie's mother. Yet now she is by no means a sorrowful looking woman as she watches a lean, sunbrowned, healthy-looking boy come bounding across the beach to her. It is Willie—Willie whom at one time she had thought gone from her forever; but, by the grace of God, the shadow has passed from the child, and now he is winning back to all of that for which she prayed so despairingly in those first two years. More, with greater health, the boy has come to courage such as would have warmed her heart in the older days; but now, though it does not fail to do so, the delight is ever tinctured by the memory of a certain night of terror, on which, for the first time, she met face to face the grim spectre—FEAR, and came to know something of the agony through which the child, her son, has passed.

Tomorrow they return to Blakenhouse Hall; they have not been near it since that night when she found her son, a little mad thing, crouched beside the wash handstand. But there is a certain room of fear into which neither he nor she will ever enter again; for the masons have walled up the doorway. And terror may hold its grim reign there undisturbed and harmless.

The Promise

I, JACOBEOUS DEACON, TELL THIS THING, unshaken in my faith—as becometh a true believer—yet as one humanly wondering and fearful.

On the thirteenth of January—now one month gone—I kneeled by the bedside of my young brother, Josephus; he no more than sixteen years in this world, and dying of the hectic fever. I held his hands when he passed, wasted and thin were they, and my promise I gave to him in the moment he died that I, who had loved him so surely, should watch by his body until such time as he should be commit to the earth, from whence we are come.

And so died my brother whom I loved before all others; and through three nights and three days (he having passed upon the evening of the ninth day) I strayed no whither from kneeling beside him; tasting neither food nor water, which is ever my drink, in all that space. And my mother who bore me, and the father from whose loins I am descended, and the children of these twain who call me brother, came many times and besought me that I would take some food, even though a little, and sleep for a while in the room which lay next, and which was mine. But I took no heed; being, it might be, stone-like with the excess of my grief.

Then, on the fourth night, being as I have said, the thirteenth of the month, I must have broken my promise with the dead lad upon the bed; for my nature weakened, and I fell upon so profound a sleep that I heeded not that they, my people, carried me hence into the next room, and there, having laid me upon my bed, did lock me in—being determined for my reason's sake, that I should no more come anigh the dead lad until my sanity of spirit was something restored within me.

And so for a space I slept there, all unknowing; and, presently, waked. And knowledge came to me, as I lay a moment to gather my witlessness, how that I had fallen from my sure self-respect, and slept when I should surely have watched. And in that moment I would gladly have died that this thing might have been undone.

And I got me slowly and wearifully from the bed, with sickness and desperateness in my soul that I had broken word with the dead lad; and I passed through the darkness to the door—meaning to complete my poor and scattered task in deep and humble shame. For, until that time, I, Jacobeous Deacon, had broken not my word in all my twenty years of life—counting no dishonour so great; and holding in contempt the weakness that bade the flesh fail to perform that which the spirit had laid its seal upon.

But when I was come to the door, I perceived that it was secured upon me, and my shame bade me to make no unseemly outburst. And as I stood there, unknowing for the while how to guide my actions, there came from the wall which divided my brother's room from mine, a slight noise as though a cat scratched thrice. At this, a sudden sweat broke out upon me, and I shook a little with a sudden newly-known fear, that was yet not all clear to my consciousness; for the sound was the signal that my brother had used, in the years of his weakness, to make to me when he desired my presence in the night-time to company and cheer him. Yet was my brother dead upon the bed; and none other knew the signal. And so the strangeness that took me so coldly about my heart as with a half-knowing.

Then I had come to the wall and, pulling aside a little picture, I disclosed the hole which we had made years gone, that we might speak with one another, without need to come from our rooms. And through this hole I spied swiftly and saw my brother quiet upon the bed; and the wind, blowing gently, brought a little of the smell of the room to me; for my brother was to have burial upon the morrow.

Now, there burned three candles on each side of my brother; and he lay alone, and all the room seemed full of a dreadful stillness. And I let my gaze go about the room and come back again to the bed. But my brother was not there; and my heart dulled and sickened within me, and set thence to a mad beating; for there was no one in the room to move my brother.

Then something touched the wall upon the other side, and the hole gave to me a sudden greater smell of the room so that I was aware that I smelled. Then something came against the hole upon the other side and darkened it. And I fell backward from the hole, for some terrible thing, my spirit told to me, lay against it upon the other side, and looked at me through the darkness. And the smell of the dead spread around me; and there was a coldness upon my face.

And presently I knew that I pressed at the wall, and my cries filled the house, save when I fought to breathe. And then my people came to me, and unfastened the door, and brought lights. But I heeded them not as my friends; but cried out continually that the dead lad peered at me through the wall. And they, think me mad, and seeking to reassure me, went into the next room and returned to tell me that my brother lay all undisturbed. And they seeked to take me to him, to still my shiverings; but for a great while I was fearful, through all my being, to go. Yet, in time, they took me; their assurances having calmed my spirit. And it was as they had told to me. The boy lay quiet upon the bed, and ready for his burial.

But I, going at last to his side, saw that the rose I had placed above his hands was no longer there. And I turned me about and looked towards the wall, and so I found the rose upon the floor below the hole. But, by the grace of God, I calmed my spirit, and gat me to my knees, and they, seeing me thus, must have gone quietly from me; but I heard them not, for I prayed for the soul of my brother. And through all that remained of that night, prayed I, out of an humble heart; and my brother moved not, neither was I harmed.

And this I have set down under the seal of my faith in God, knowing that I have not wittingly writ aught but that which my soul knoweth to be of verity.

Unto God I give thanks for His Graciousness to my brother and to me; in that He stayed my spirit in that moment to fight for the soul of my brother. Unto God I give praise, out of an humble and contrite heart.

Set out this day of grace, in the year of our Lord 1733, being the thirteenth day of February.

Captain Dang

(An account of certain peculiar and somewhat memorable adventures.)

No. 1

"The Ship in the Lagoon"

ST. MARZAIRE WAS THE NAME UPON THE BOWS of the splendid, great steel, four-masted barque lying alongside in the East India dock.

I stared at her longingly, and wandered slowly aft along the quayside, as far as her gangway, noting the perfectness of her equipment of deck furniture and the number of "patents" in evidence.

"Guess they'll run her short-handed, with all that lot of fakements!" I thought, looking at the topsail-haulyard winches.

Then I saw something that made me start, with a great waft of hopeless longing; for at the inner end of the gangway was a notice:

"WANTED—A SECOND MATE"

I had just passed for Second Mate, and I was only twenty-one. My virgin "Ticket" (i.e., Certificate) was even then in my inner breast pocket, and I had already boarded over twenty vessels in my truly hopeless search. For who wanted a young, untried Second Mate when old and experienced men could be had for the asking at the same figure? You perceive my position?

This clipper of steel and shining paint-work wanted a Second Mate, and would surely get the pick of "sailing-ship-men" at the shipping office. Mind you, if I had been a fo'cas'le shellback, I should have steered clear of this vessel; for she was too clean, too spick and span. She shouted suji-muji fore and aft, with a constant minor key of swabbing paint-work and brass-cleaning. But as Second Mate, I viewed things from an extraordinarily different standpoint. It would be my pride to see that she was kept even more spick and span than she looked at that shining moment. Thus human nature!

Not, as I have endeavoured to impress upon you, that there was ever much expectation that I, young and callow and but new "Ticketed," should ever pace that shimmering poop. . . . Yet I went aboard to offer myself. I don't know whether it was sheer desperation at the foolish hopelessness of my desire, or something that I saw in the face of a short, stern, powerfully-built man, immaculately dressed in frock-coat and top-hat, who was pacing the far side of the poop in company with one whom I took to be the First Mate.

I crossed the gangway, almost at a run; down onto the main deck, and away up what I might term the "lee" ladder to the poop; the presence of the Captain and Mate giving to the one upon their side the temporary honour of being the "weather" steps—sacred to authority.

Now, it is a curious thing that I knew the short, broad, stern-faced man, in the immaculate morning suit, to be the Captain; for never a note of the sailor was there in him, from knight-heads to half-round, as one might say nautically; though not, perhaps, with perfect modesty. In short, so far removed was he from the "odour of salt" that, but for his stern face, I should have named him as a frequenter of Bond Street and other haunts, in Piccadilly and elsewhere, of the Smart and Fashionable.

As I came near to him, he turned and faced me, and somehow I knew—suddenly—that he had been watching me all the time. I looked at him, and his face seemed none the less stern for being nearer; but he had an understanding look in his eyes that heartened me wonderfully.

"So," he said, in a curious, terse way, "you want to be my Second Officer, do you?"

"I never said so, Sir; but I do, for all that, with all my heart."

There came the faintest easing of the sternness out of what I supposed then to be his habitual expression, and I thought the shadow of a smile touched the corners of his mouth; but his eyes looked at me, emotionless, though full of a peculiar sense of understanding me far more thoroughly that I did myself.

"Your papers," he said suddenly, holding out an extraordinarily muscular, but most beautifully kept hand, quite white and free from sunburn, and like no sailor's hand I have ever seen before or since.

I pulled out my little japanned case, containing my discharges, characters, and my precious Ticket. I was about to open it; but he made a quick gesture, signifying that he wanted it in his own fist. He took it, opened it, and emptied all the papers into his other hand; then, putting the case in his pocket, went quietly and methodically through all my discharges, folding each one up as he finished with it; and so until he came to my brand-new Certificate. This he opened slowly and with a quite curious carefulness; read it through, apparently word for word; then refolded it, and began to replace it and my discharges back in my little case, which he drew from his pocket.

He handed me back the case, looking intently for a moment at my eyes, nose, mouth, jaw, chin. . . . I could feel his glance wander from feature to feature. It shifted down to my chest, my hands, my thighs, knees, feet.

"You're something of an athlete as well as a sailor-man, Mister Morgan," he said. "What can you lift with your right?"

"Three fifty-sixes, when I'm feeling fit, Sir," I answered, surprised and a little bewildered.

He nodded.

"Active too, I fancy," he said, as if to himself. "Done much boat work?"

"Yes, Sir," I answered. "I was senior 'prentice the two last trips, and since then I've been a trip to 'Frisco as acting Third. Had a good deal of boat-work all three trips."

He nodded again and turned to the First Mate—a big, gaunt-looking man. "I shall be down again tonight, Mister," he said. "Tell the steward not to turn in till I come." He turned to me.

"Come up to the shipping office, Mr. Morgan."

I saw the First Mate frown angrily. I guessed that he did not relish having a mere lad of twenty-one as a brother officer, who would literally have to be taught his job. I did not blame him; but I thought to myself that he might find I had less to learn than he feared. Anyway, I did not dislike the look of him and felt we would be likely to grow friendly enough in a day or two.

All this, in a flash through my brain, as I turned and followed my future Captain, my heart thumping a merry tune with the joy of this unexpected success, and a fierce determination to show myself fully capable of filling the post I was so tersely and unexpectedly offered.

The business at the shipping office was soon completed, and Captain Dang (as I learned was my new master's name) told me to get my gear aboard that night, as we sailed in the morning.

When I got down aboard, Mr. Darley, the First Mate, was still pacing the poop. He watched me moodily as I was helping the cabby to get my chest aboard; then, seeming to have made up his mind to make the best of things, he came across and shook hands with me, and bellowed an order to a couple of the hands to come and get my stuff aboard and down to my cabin.

I gave the men a couple of bob, and then joined the Mate on the poop where he gave me a half-whimsical, half-rueful look up and down.

"I know how it seems to you, Mister Darley," I said, laughing. "You feel I'm a kid, and you expect you'll have two men's work to do. I don't blame you. Only, you know, somehow I think you'll not find me as bad as you think. You see, I've done one 'Frisco trip as acting Third; and all the way home the Second was laid up, and I had to take his watch."

"Oh!" said the gaunt Mate, evidently greatly relieved. "I guess you're all right, Mister. We'll do fine; an' th' Old Man's a good sort, right down to th' keelson, an' no mistake. Shake!"

And therewith we shook and became very sound friends indeed.

The next morning, a little after six o'clock, the tug took us in charge, and we began our trip down the river. There's one thing I do like about sailing from London; the river trip gives one time to get settled a bit before getting out into broken water. But if you sail from Liverpool or any of those sea-board ports, you're right out in the smother before you know where you are, and everything adrift, and a regular bunch o' buffers if there's any sea on.

The Mate took her out; and I never so much as saw the Captain until evening, after the tug had cast us off, and we were bowling down Channel under all sail, with a splendid fair wind. The Mate had just sung out for all hands to muster aft to pick the watches, and I was leaning over the rail, across the break of the poop, looking up at the drawing canvas.

"There's poetry in canvas, laddie, when the wind gets into it," said a half-familiar voice in my ear.

I turned my head quickly and looked at the speaker. I saw a short, stout-seeming, enormously broad, unshaven man, dressed in heavy, blue pilot-cloth, with a peak-hat pushed well back on his head. I give you my word, I never recognized who it was for quite half a minute; but just stared stupidly, with a feeling that was only part uncanny oppressing me. Then, suddenly, I knew—

"Captain Dang!" I said with something that approached a gasp. "Captain Dang!"

"The same, laddie. The very same," he replied, his face widening grotesquely in a smile of enormous good humour.

I never saw such a change in a man. His very voice was different. It had lost it's note of culture and its crispness. It sounded deeper, more mellow, slacker—if I might so describe it. His shoulders were rounded; his face had broadened, and might never have looked stern. His walk had lost its swift precision and had given place to a careless roll that yet had a cat-like note of quickness in it.

I had stepped back a little from him, and was staring, like the bewildered lad that I was. Then I saw his eyes, and felt I recognized him fully once more—they were the same steadfast, grey, understanding eyes that had looked at me so inscrutably the previous day.

"It is Captain Dang!" I said aloud, involuntarily.

The burly, rounded shoulders heaved, and the face hid itself once more in a vast smile; the mouth opened and bellowed laughter.

"The very same, laddie; the very same," it succeeded in explaining in a husky whisper, as the laughter died away. He fumbled for and produced an enormous red handkerchief, with which he mopped his somewhat red face. I saw then that his hands were encased in the very smartest, lavender kid gloves. Picture the man—broad, roughly clothed, unshaved, full of gorgeous laughter, wearing long gum-boots up to his thighs, a great chew of plug tobacco in his mouth; homely, almost to roughness of speech, and wearing smart kid gloves.

Do you wonder that I stared afresh.

And Captain Dang, for his part, just leaned back against the harness-cask and roared afresh. Then, suddenly, he bent towards me.

"You'll be pickin' your watch, laddie, in a moment; be sure to pick Turrill, that lanky, daft lookin' devil for our side. I want him in our watch."

"Very good, Sir," I replied. "I know the man you mean. He's a good sailorman, I fancy, too."

"Maybe, laddie. Maybe," said Captain Dang, and he turned and walked aft, chaunting in a deep voice, not a song of a Chauntey; but what I recognized later to be Mendelssohn's "But the Lord is Mindful"—a thing which I found he was always bumming and humming, as he paced the poop.

I stepped back again to the break of the poop, and looked down to where the Mate was sitting on the hatch, waiting whilst the men mustered aft. He saw me and glanced up and grinned, as if something tickled his fancy; then took his pipe slowly from his mouth:

"Come along down, Mister," he said, beckoning with the pipe to the assembling men. "We'll get this job done, an' then settle the watches for the night." As I reached him, he stood up from the hatch, and leaned towards me:

"You've met th' Old Man at sea now," he said. "Almighty strange card, ain't he? A downright good sort, Mister; but don't you make any bloomin' error; he's a devil when he wants to be."

"I believe you," I said frankly. "He makes me feel as if he were my own father; and yet I'm hanged if I know whether he's good or bad. I don't know whether I like him or funk him. But I think I do like him."

"I know," agreed the Mate. "But you'll find he's all right; only he's up to any damned devilment that hits him. I'll give you one tip, though, Mister; never say a word again' wimmin where he can hear you, or he'll plug you sure as fate. No good your argying; you're a strong lad, I can see; but he's as strong again as you. You be told in time. Now then, Mister, we pick our watches an' be damned to 'em!"

Which we did, I securing the lanky, leathery-looking, daft-faced seaman Turrill as my first choice, with the result that his somewhat expressionless eyes lit up for a moment with surprised pleasure.

For a few days at this, I saw very little of Captain Dang, that is to say, intimately. He kept to his cabin a good deal in the day time, and from a glance or two I had through the open doorway, I saw that he was busy with some chart-work. At night, however, he would come up on deck about four bells (ten o'clock), and pace noiselessly but swiftly up and down for maybe an hour, bumming away eternally at his favourite selection from Mendelssohn. Then, quite suddenly, as though an idea had come to him, he would make a bolt for the companionway, and down out of sight, without a word, and I would, like as not, never see him again that watch.

A night or two later, however, we had a long talk, and he took me into his confidence in the following way. I had been down on the main-deck, slacking off the braces, a little after five bells. When I finally returned to the poop, I found the Old Man pacing fore and aft, to windard, bumming away as usual at his classical selections.

For my part, as it seemed to me that he wished to be alone, I walked thwart ship, to and fro across the poop break, arranging my journeys so as not to meet the Captain, as he came forrard. Suddenly, however, he left his regular beat and came across to me, where I had paused a moment, staring away to leeward.

"Laddie," he said, speaking in a quieter voice than usual, "I want you to take the wheel from yon Turrill, and send him forrard to me. I want a word with him without the crowd knowing. Away with you now, smart, laddie. I've a yarn for you later, maybe."

"Aye, aye, Sir," I said and went away aft to relieve the A.B., telling him the Skipper wanted a word with him, which news the man received without comment, and walked forrard to the break.

For some time they stood and talked, a little foreside of the jigger-mast; then Captain Dang took the man below into his cabin, and for quite half an hour the low murmur of their voices came up to me, mingled with the odd, faint sounds of papers rustled, by which I surmised that the Captain was handling an unmounted track-chart, and tracing out something that had to do with their talk.

Now, what I have recorded is not exactly orthodox. It is not usual for the Master of a vessel to indicate to his officer that any particular A.B. shall be placed in any particular watch; it is still less usual for a ship-master to follow up such an action by inviting the A.B. down into his cabin, to some conference connected, presumably, with chart-work of any form or description. All this was, obviously, intruding itself upon me. I could neither fathom it, nor yet push it out of my thoughts. I found myself conjuring up a wild romance of mystery, for which I called myself a fool immediately. Yet, as it chanced, nothing that had flashed through my puzzling brain, was half so extraordinary as the actual strangeness towards which we were heading; as I think you will acknowledge, eventually.

Seven bells struck forrard, and I answered them with the bell on the wheel-box; for I had told the 'prentice who was time-keeping that he could go down for a smoke. The ring of the bell had hardly died away, before Captain Dang emerged from the companionway, followed by Turrill, who came immediately to relieve me at the wheel. As soon as I had given him the course, the Old Man told me to light up and come for a turn along the poop, as he wanted to have a talk.

"Laddie," he said, after we had done the distance fore and aft a couple of times, "yon Turrill's the devil of a lad."

He stopped and fumbled for his matches, and I found myself nibbling mentally at the fact that he spoke with something of a Scotch tang. Yet there had been no suggestion of any kind of tang in the speech of the well-dressed man I had applied to for a billet only a few days before. However, I had almost ceased to wonder at any new side to his character that my Captain chose to turn up.

He lit his pipe methodically and walked slowly to leeward to dump the burnt-out match into the sea. There he stood for some minutes, as if he had entirely forgotten me and the thing he had meant to talk about. Abruptly, he turned and beckoned to me through the gloom to join him, which I did.

"Hark to it, laddie," he said and bent now over the lee rail, staring down into the sea. "Hark to it."

I bent also, in doubt as to what he meant; but all that I could hear was the strange, keening hiss of the foam to leeward, as the ship drove easily along with the light breeze upon our beam.

"Yon's the sea an' the ship talkin', laddie," he said at last, showing me again that half-poet side that he had uncovered in that former remark, days before, when I was looking up at the canvas.

I made no reply, being young; and indeed there was nothing I could say. Once Captain Dang spoke: "And the wind, laddie! And the wind, laddie! Hark to it talkin'!" he said.

I heard it then, though I had not noticed it before—the low musical booming of the wind emptying itself out of the lee of the cross-jack. And, listening, you know, I began dimly to appreciate. But I was, as I have said, something young as yet.

Captain Dang returned to wind'ard, and we resumed our traipse fore and aft.

"Yon Turrill was in a whalin' packet, laddie," he said abruptly. "She foundered, so he says, in a little bit of the Pacific Ocean that I happen to be uncommon well acquainted with. Ran on to a spike of rock and went down in two minutes, more or less. That's the beginning of it, laddie; an' there's no such rock marked in any chart of those seas, as well I know; though, mind you, it's an uncommon lonesome patch he'd got into. There's a few hundred miles that way, laddie, North an' South, East an' West, that's precious little known, even to the whale-ships; an' they go mostly everywhere, an' to the devil in the end, like the rest of us.

"That's, as I was saying, laddie, only the beginnings. Yon Turrill got away in one of the boats with the Mate and three of the hands. They were, I should say, uncommon lucky; for it was all so sudden that there was only two other boats got afloat, and a rare throat-cuttin' to get into 'em, with the result they was both capsized, and the contents went to D.J., which is short for Davy Jones."

He stopped and chuckled at me through the darkness; and in the pause that followed, I found myself puzzling, almost half irritably why he did these things—why he talked like that; why—oh, a hundred things! It was the irritation and puzzlement of Youth that cannot put one of its limited supply of labels on some newly found object; and is therefore troubled.

"As I was sayin', laddie, for the third time isn't it? all this was only the first lap, as you might say. Presently, after a little spell of something like fourteen days in the boat—five of 'em without grub or drink—they drifted in sight of a great big lagoon; mind you that, laddie—a thunderin' big one; no five-shilling-piece reef; but a good fifteen miles long, so the man says, an' always has said, even in the papers, way back. You may remember reading something about it?"

"No, Sir," I said. "I never read the papers."

"Well you should, laddie," he replied. "If I didn't read 'em, I should never have come across this. It was that way I found out Turrill and signed him on. We're out for something this trip, I'm hoping; an' maybe we shall be a bit overdue—from the freighters' point o' view; dam 'em; the Lord help 'em!

"Well, as I was saying, they discovered this big lagoon, away down on the horizon; and that put some spunk into them; an' they out oars and pulled for it until they came to one of the openings and put the boat in through, with a great deal of misdirected energy in the shape of Thanksgiving; so I gathered from Turrill."

He paused again to chuckle; and I smiled to myself, to notice how the wording of the last part of his yarn had betrayed the man of culture, with its accompanying touch of cynicism, peeping out unwittingly through the rind of rough, pilot-clad sailorman.

"Now, laddie," he continued, after an almost imperceptible little pause of silence following his laugh, and with something in his voice and words that stirred me to a sense of coming adventure and mystery: "there's no such lagoon marked on any chart of that part of the great big Pacific Ocean. Moreover, and what is more, I've never run against it; and, as I've hinted already, I happen to know that patch pretty well; for I've done some hanky-panky down there that would prove interestin' telling, laddie. Yet, mind you, it's an almighty big patch, as I do admit; an' a ship or two, or an island, for that matter, might be lost there for an odd century or so without much trouble.

"Now they found three islands in the lagoon, laddie, and an old-time wooden, 'Merican sailing-ship. Think of it! An' these five blessed shipwrecked mariners, of course, away for the ship an' hailed her; but never no answer." He chuckled inaudibly. "So they up an' hailed her again; but still no answer; then the Mate an' Turrill shinned up the cable (chain it was, so the miracle wasn't complete, laddie!) and got aboard. There was no one in that vessel, fore or aft; and Turrill says she had a queer, desolate sort of feel to her. Yet she wasn't rotted, an' her paint-work was good, as I made him remember. What do ye think o' that, laddie? But there was no water in her—leastways, the two of 'em couldn't find the water bar'l." Again Captain Dang chuckled silently to himself as he discovered himself overdoing his language. At least that is what I supposed; though I don't know whether he had discovered the infusion of Americanism that was now in evidence. He paused for quite a minute; so that I prompted him; for I was impatient to hear more:

"Yes, Sir," I said.

"So they went down again into the boat, My Son," said Captain Dang in his queer, whimsical fashion. "And they went ashore then on the middle island, which was the nearest, and in a biggish hurry, I fancy, having something of a thirst on 'em; though weakish, you know. Bound to have been—hey?"

I began to perceive that Captain Dang was quite prepared to find Turrill's story all moonshine. His manner told me so much; yet he was plainly not entirely of this mind.

"They found some bananas ashore," continued Captain Dang, knocking out his pipe. "That should tell you something about the climate, sonny. Also, there was plenty of water. They filled the boat's breaker, took some big bunches of the fruit, and went back to the old ship. What did they do that for when they had a chance to have a run ashore!

"They slept aboard that night, the whole five of them in the big poop-cabin. And this is where the yarn comes a bit thicker than ever. Turrill says he woke up sometime in the night with a feeling that something was wrong. There was a good moon shining, and he lay still and took a careful look round the big cabin; but the men were snoring away in their bunks, and everything just quiet and ordinary. Yet, all the same, yon man says he felt there was something queer about. He's daft lookin' enough, anyway! He lay still as a mouse, just harking for all he was worth. Then he thought he heard a faint, wee sound on deck, and the next moment there came something up against the window that looked over his bunk. He swears it was the most lovely lookin' face ever he'd seen, but it gave him the horrors, worse than if it had been a tiger lookin' at him.

"An' then, so it seems, the thing went away from the port, or window, as I should say, and the next instant it came back, laddie, an' looked at him again. But now it was a huge, great face, like a monstrous great hag's. An' the thing just looked at him, so he has it, and looked at him until he woke up and found that it was morning, and the sun shining in through the window on his face, and he pretty sure then that it must have been a dream—only it seems he was to know different in a bit.

"They went ashore in the morning onto the middle island for some more fruit, and to see whether they couldn't put their hands on something better to get their teeth into. An' well I know the feelin', laddie! One of the men stayed aboard an' said he'd have another root round in the ship to see whether there weren't nothin' fit to eat somewheres.

"Turrill says they'd meant to split up when they got ashore, go different ways, and all meet again at the boat with anything they might have found. They did this, too, at least at first. But in awhile the three men all drifted together, an' they kept together after that, except the

Mate was away off somewhere by himself, laddie."

He paused again here to fill his pipe, and I gave way to a silly temptation to say something:

"You've altered again, Sir," I said, meaning that what I considered was his assumed 'rough speech' was not homogenous but hybrid. I grinned slyly to myself.

"What's that, laddie?" he asked, in a simple seeming sort of way. But somehow there was something at the back of his tone that warned me I'd made a mistake to venture what I had said. So I made as if I had not heard him, which was the wisest thing I could have done; for he went on in a minute, as if neither of us had spoken.

"They'd gone maybe half round the island, laddie, keeping together like this for company's sake, when they heard a most horrible scream away up in the woods to their left; for it seems that all three of the islands were middlin' well wooded, some places right down to the water. Now when they heard this scream, they were all struck in a heap; you see, they'd been feelin' lonesome like; for there was a queer, quiet way about the island that gave 'em all the hump, so yon Turrill says, laddie; an' that's why they'd all come together again so soon as the Mate had left 'em. And now, when they heard this scream away up among the trees, they were fit to run.

"And then the scream came again, laddie, and a nasty, hoarse sort of dying away note to it. 'That's the Mate, lads!' shouts Turrill, and away up into the wood he went, with a whale-lance that he'd brought out of the boat. He run on a bit, an' then stops to shout. But there was no answer, only all the wood seemed extra still like. And yon Turrill, so he says, lookin' everyway at once over his shoulder, for what might come out at him.

"He sung out then to the two others to come along up after him, and they shouted back that they were coming; and at that he calls again to the Mate, an' thought he heard something away among the trees to his left. He went that way, with his whale-lance handy, an' lookin' all about him. He saw something move behind a tree trunk, a bit off from him; but whether it was aught or a shadder, he couldn't say, laddie; but away to it, holding the whale-lance to the ready, as it were. An' then, when it got close, it being a bit dark there, he stops and shouts the Mate's name again. An', on that, something poked out from behind the tree, and yon Turrill swears it was that same wonderful lovely-lookin' face he'd seen in the night, staring in at him through the cabin window.

"Now, yon Turrill man says he knows it was a devil; and he up with the whale-lance and hove it at the thing; an' then round the back of the tree, with his sheath-knife out in his fist; but there was nothing there, only his big whale-lance stuck fast into a bush, an' the side of the tree all blazed where the lance had skinned off the bark.

"Now that's all queer telling, laddie. But I do believe yon man when he says he got the trembles, and just caught up the whale-lance out of the bush, and away anyhow through the trees, shoutin' an' yellin' for his two mates. An' then he outs into a bit of glade among the trees, and tumbles and falls bang over something that makes him squeal worse than ever; for 'twas the Mate's body, all torn, like as never a wild beast tore a human body yet, laddie; though how yon man knows so much neither you nor me knows.

"An' then there was shoutin' from the other end of the bit glade, and in comes his two mates, and stopped and stiffened up, to see the Mate dead and all tore like that, laddie; as well I should think."

Captain Dang paused a moment or two and drew hard at his pipe, staring away to wind'ard. "Wonderful purty night, laddie," he said, apropos of nothing at all. "I do think the big, big sea's God's own bath-tub, these sorts o' nights, laddie. Are ye too young to feel the mystery o't—aye, it's weel said, laddie—the mystery o't—the mystery o't. There's ought might happen out in all that; any-thin'; anythin'! It's juist an unknown world, laddie . . . a place where God goes playin', maybe o' nights, laddie, like some bit wonderfu' lonesome Chiel o' Wonder . . . aye, aye . . . an' the devils an' monsters of the sea crowdin' out on to the lonesome islands, that neither you nor me nor any other man ever sees in all our wanderings. Aye, the mystery o't. . . !"

And then suddenly, and in an entirely different tone and speech:

"Mr. Morgan, what does it mean! Is the man mad! Or did he see something of all this! Or is there Pearls or Piracy at the bottom of it—aye, Pearls and Piracy! Pearls and Piracy! Or is he just telling the perfect, simple truth, and the truth is too great for our unbelieving little souls to grasp!"

The whole thing was so evidently an unconscious outburst, requiring no attempt at answering, that I said nothing, but just waited, full of newly stirred thoughts and newly-born beliefs. . . . What if there were truth in all this half-told, extraordinary story! You get something of the feelings that crowded in on me, standing there in the quiet night by that strange man who, for once, was so unaccountably stirred out of himself. Do you—eh? Do you get it at all?

"An' there's more to it, laddie," said Captain Dang, reverting suddenly to pilot-cloth talk and manners, as I might phrase it. "Yon Turrill an' the two others got the Mate down to the beach someways; and good pluck to them that they did it, with the terror and the shakes that was on 'em. They buried him there in the sand, usin' the oars for spades and the boat's dipper; and afterwards made a bit cross along the top of it, laddie, with white stones and shells. And so away aboard again in a hurry, with some nuts and plantains that they had got.

"When they came alongside, yon Turrill swears he felt there was something wrong aboard. He jumps away up the ladder before ever the boat was made fast and sings out: 'Jensen!,' that being the name, laddie, of the man they'd left aboard, a Dutchman by the sound of it. Turrill got a sick feelin' when there was no answer, an' sung out to the others to hurry. They went away after to the poop-cabin, which was entered from the after end, laddie, with a narrow runway of deck on each side, as maybe you've seen. When they got aft, they found a litter of stuff on the deck outside of the companionway—a beef-bucket still headed up, sailcloth, an' a small keg of spirits, laddie, an suchlike.

"They puts their heads down the companionway an' sings out the man's name again; but there was no answer and somehow, none of them wanted to be the first down. Yon Turrill says it was terrible quiet seeming down there. They sings out Jensen's name again an' got the echo of it back at them, so that yon man says they near run, an' small blame to them, laddie, feelin' as they would ha' felt—eh?

"Then Turrill jumps down the three-step way and goes in through the cabin doorway with his sheath-knife out in his hand, ready. 'Je—' he shouts as he steps into the cabin and finishes short. For there was no Jensen there, only a terrible mess o' blood on the floor, laddie.

"Yon Turrill says he just turned his head over his shoulder, quiet like, and bid the two others come down an' look. I guess, laddie, if that's so, he'd about come to the tail end of the rope. When his mates saw the cabin, they just did a run for the deck, an' yon man had the devil's job to stop 'em goin' right off with the boat, all unprovisioned, laddie. He held 'em to sense, though, an' made 'em help him search the ship which they did, as the saying goes, from truck to keelson; though there weren't any trucks with her having lost her upper spars. Nor was there any sign of Jensen except what was in the cabin.

"Afterwards, Turrill made them put in the galley fire, using bulk-sheadin' for fire-fodder, and he broaches the old beef bucket an', when the worst of the stink had gone, he shoves all the beef in one of the coppers so as to have it cooked for the boat voyage that they was in for, laddie.

"Meanwhile, he goes down an' gets the cabin clean an' straight, an' looks under all the bottom bunks: for it was gettin' on towards evening, and he didn't expect to get away til the morning. Then he sets the men stowing the canvas an' oddments in the boat, an' meanwhile, he cleans out the water bar'l in the galley, meaning to fill it for the trip.

"By the time this was done, the beef was cooked, an' he gets it into the boat, copper an' all, saving a piece that he keeps back for their supper. Then he sees the boat good and fast, and gets his mates down into the cabin, it being just on the dusk, an' they fixes up the door good an' solid, and lights up the boat's lamp which Turrill had brought up out of the boat for that one night."

Captain Dang stopped and looked up, for away up in the night the royals were slatting back against the masts.

"Keep her full, my lad, keep her full!" he sang out to Turrill at the wheel, and stepped over to the binnacle to see how she was heading. "Full an' bye! Keep her full an' bye!" he said.

"Aye, aye, Sir," replied the man at the wheel, and Captain Dang rejoined me in our walk fore and aft, just as one bell went, and we heard the familiar bellow forrard, of: "Show a leg; show a leg there! Rise and shine, My Bullies! Rise and shine! Rise and see the broad daylight! Show a leg; show a leg there!" The other watch was being called.

"Who wouldn't buy a farm!" muttered Captain Dang whimsically at my elbow, and therewith concluded his retelling of Turrill's history:

"Yon Turrill's two mates had taken the brandy-keg down into the cabin, an' they started whackin' at it as soon as they'd done their supper. Yon man says he tried to get 'em off it, for he felt there might anything happen that night. But they only turned nasty an' told him to come and drink with them or leave it alone, which he did.

"Presently the two fools turned into their bunks, pretty fuddled, I'm thinking, laddie, an' yon man sits down on a locker with his whale-lance across his knees. You see, it'd been shortened, an' it's a pretty handy kind of weapon, laddie, as I will know, an' I may tell you why some day, my son.

"Turrill, you see, laddie, meant to sit up all the night to keep watch, for he knew there was some dreadful kind of monstrous thing knockin' around. He says . . ."

Captain Dang broke off suddenly and stepped aft to the helmsman, returning to me after a moment's talk.

"Yes, laddie," he said, "I've thought yon Turrill said as much. He says there was never a living bird that flew over that lagoon, nor yet a fish in the waters underneath. And if that's so, then I that knows what life there is round an' above a coral reef, am just fair flummoxed, laddie. I am that.

"I am that," he continued, after a moment's pause. "Why, laddie, as you sure know, a reef s just a fair hot-bed of life, top an' bottom an' all ways. I tell you laddie, this yarn o' yon man's just hits me everyway. It's just as queer as the divvil's hind leg!

"An' we're not done yet. Yon Turrill turns the lamp well up an' sits there, eyes forrard an' eyes astern, every other moment, an' ready to shove the whale-lance through his own shadow when it moved. He sat a mighty long time like that, listening to the others snorin'. An' then, you know, laddie, like we've all done in our time, he wakes up . . . Which shows he must have gone over asleep! The lamp had burnt low, an' there was the queerest kind of silence in the cabin, which he didn't account for at first. The whale-lance had rolled down on to the deck of the cabin, an' he stoops for it an' gets it safe back into his hands. Then he steps over to the lamp and gives it a turn up so that he can get a good look round.

"Everythin' looked right enough, laddie—at first. And then, sudden, he saw that something was at the windows over the men's bunks. Two of those wonderful lovely faces was there, starin' in at him an' the men in the bunks. He stood there, solid; and then there was nothing, and he was fit to swear he had dreamed it. An' then, in a moment, there come at the nearer window that same mighty, great Hag-face that he knew of. He ups with his great whale-lance, an' heaves it at the thing; and the weapon smashes clean through the window, out into the sea. But there was nothin' there. An' there was he standin' there with no weapon except his knife, though one of the men had the iron of a new whale harpoon, which is a good enough weapon, laddie, at a pinch.

"And so yon Turrill man stood lookin' at the smashed window, an' wonderin' what the devil was goin' to happen in a moment. An' then he found himself harking to the silence of the cabin; and suddenly he knew why it was so damned quiet—the two men in the bunks had stopped breathin'. He knew then they'd stopped a good while since. He knew there was devilment about then, you bet, laddie. Just you try to figure out his feelins, my son, in that moment.

"He was stiffened a moment, an' no wonder—by the Lord, laddie, if he's tellin' the truth it beats all Creation!—and then he takes one step to the table an' catches hold of the lamp. He turns up the burnt wick till it's all aflame, an' goes over careful an' cautious to the near bunk, holding his knife ready. For yon man says he didn't know but it might be some monster he'd find there in the bunk in place of his mate. That's a queer thing to say, laddie, ain't it, but I had the very same feelin' it might be somethin' bad when he was tellin' it to me.

"But there was nothin' extaordinair." Captain Dang smothered a half-chuckle that I feel sure was his overdoing the Scots. "In the bunk was only the stiffened corpse of the man, an' a queer, awful set look in the open eyes of him, as yon Turrill tells. An' then he away to the other bunk; and the other man set out stiff there also, as if, yon man, he'd looked at some almighty horrid kind o' thing, laddie. And never a mark of vi'lence was there on 'em, laddie, so far as he could see, though he was that in fear that maybe he missed as much as he saw. I reck'n, laddie, yon Turrill man must have had a bad hour, waitin' for the dawn to come along an' let some healthy light into all that nasty quiet, eh, laddie?"

Just then eight bells went, and Captain Dang knocked out his pipe finally, and concluded what he had to tell:

"That's about the lot, laddie," he said. "Yon man cleared out of the cabin so soon as the daylight was come proper; an' away down into the boat, never waiting' for nothin'; cuts her adrift and pulls like mad to get away from the old ship.

"There was a nice bit of a mornin' breeze, an' presently he steps the mast, and up with the lug, an' away he goes, laddie, out through one of the openings in the Reef, away into the everlastin' blue av the sea. Aye, aye, an' well I know the feelin' of eternity that it gives to put a boat like that away an' away out into the almighty mystery av the waters, laddie . . . the almighty, lonesome mystery of the waters . . . aye . . . aye . . ."

He had plainly lost himself in soliloquy so that I ventured to prompt him:

"Yes, Sir," I said. "And Turrill . . . ?"

He took off his cap and polished his face with his big red handkerchief.

"Oh, aye," he said. "Yon Turrill, he was picked up, laddie, a matter of some twenty-three days later by one of the Castle boats—the Birkley Castle. His water, yon man says, had been done five days, an' he was in a bit of a fever that near finished him. That's all, laddie. That's all."

He yawned and spoke suddenly in an entirely different fashion:

"Mr. Morgan," he said, "that's a very curious little bit of history or romance that I've just given to you. Either the man is mad or else there is something quite peculiar at the back of it all; quite peculiar, Mr. Morgan.

"Supposing," he said slowly, apparently to himself, "supposing that there is something more than the obviously possible in it—supposing it is the one odd case where the existence of the Unknown Octaves of LIFE justify our reasoning that they exist by manifesting . . . "

He broke off, seemingly carrying the theme forward in thought regions not easily translatable into words. Here was the other man in Captain Dang speaking—the man of culture, with a vengeance. I stood waiting for him to break out again into speech. Abruptly, I heard Turrill speaking to me. He had just been relieved at the wheel, and was giving me the course:

"Full an' bye, Sir," he said.

"Full and bye," I repeated, glancing at him through the darkness, with more than a touch of interest, bred of his peculiar adventure. He passed on, and I heard his footsteps echoing away forard, crossing those of the "relieved" lookout, coming aft to report:

"Saxon's relieved the lookout, Sir. Lamps is burnin' bright," came a hoarse voice from somewhere between me and the lee ladder.

"Very good," I said, and the man retreated down the ladder to the maindeck and stumbled away forrard.

"An' we're goin' there, laddie," said Captain Dang suddenly, reverting at that moment to his other method and manner. "Accidental like, so as to make no silly talk among the hands, damn their souls. We'll in for water, maybe, hey laddie?" And he shook with easy and uncalled-for laughter. "Maybe the freighters 'll think we're a bit overdue this trip, laddie, I'm thinkin'," he added, shaking again like a great boy stuffed with high spirits.

I suspected then that he must have a very great deal of influence with his company, else surely he would never dare to delay the ship, as was plainly his intention.

"An' maybe we'll find out a thing or two, laddie," he concluded. "Maybe we shall have something to remember. It's a mighty strange place, the sea. Aye, a mighty strange place is the great big, blue, blue sea, laddie—a mighty strange big unknown place. An' no one knows better just how little known it is, laddie. I could tell you things, sonny, I could that; I could that . . . "

He broke off into a momentary silence; then turned abruptly from me.

"Good night, laddie," he said, as he moved aft to go below. "Tell Chips in the morning to rig my punch-ball ring in the old place; he knows. I shall want it by seven o'clock. Good night, laddie."

"Good night, Sir," I said to this extraordinary man, and therewith he left me, just as the First Mate—who was a little late in turning out—came up to relieve me.

It was, of course, my morning watch from four to eight; and at four bells (six o'clock) I sent word along to Chips that the Old Man wanted his punch-ball ring rigged by seven, which message brought master Chips aft in a great fluster, for he would have to stretch his lazy bones to do the job in the time. He had, I regret to say, the impudence to assert that I ought to have told him earlier, and as I perceived that his attitude to me was plainly indicative of his belief that I was but a callow youth, I stepped up to him, and assured him that I would pull his nose out long enough for a muffler, if he tried that kind of thing with me. At which, Chips, being an uncommon big man, became even more violently rude, which ended in my hitting him once, a little harder than was perhaps considerate, for which I can only plead the youth of which the Carpenter suspected me; but certainly not the callowness.

My blow was certainly a good one, and it drove big Mister Chips stern foremost down the lee ladder, howling strangely. His noise was answered by a bellow of enormous laughter from the companionway, and turning, I saw that Captain Dang was standing in the companionway in his flannel drawers and shirt, shaking with a huge delight at the Carpenter's sudden and shocked removal.

Chip's face appeared once more into view as he came up the lee ladder, blustering vengeance in a half-frightened fashion, but at sight of the Captain, he silenced in the strangest and most cringing fashion and went instantly to work at rigging the punch-ball ring.

"Chips! Chips!" said Captain Dang, chuckling hugely. "You made a wee mistake that time, my mannie. Mister Morgan is no very big, but he's uncommon well made, Chips my lad. Use your eyes more, my mannie. It's the well-made ones that can hit the hardest." Then, suddenly changing his tone in the most extraordinary fashion, he said slowly and grimly: "Mr. Morgan is one of my officers, my lad. If that ring isn't rigged by six bells, God Almighty help you, for I'll show you your place in this packet, my lad, as I've shown it to you once before." And with and without a word further, he turned slowly and descended into the cabin, moving, as I remember noticing, like a great cat, more than a human. And it was this unusual quality of movement in Captain Dang that gave me some inkling of how enormously high must be his nerve vitality and his muscular development.

Chips completed the rigging of the ring by five minutes to seven, working with trembling, feverish hands, and the sweat running down his face, all of which told to me that there was a grimmer side to Captain Dang than any that I had seen prior to the last hour. Punctual to the stroke of the bell, Captain Dang appeared in a huge, checked dressing gown. In his right hand he carried a huge, leather punching-ball, and in his left a pair of very strongly made punching-bag gloves.

He walked up to where the ring was fixed by an iron bracket to the fore-side of the jigger-mast, and reaching up to the heavy teak ring, struck it violently with his open hand, nodding approvingly on discovering that Chips had done his work thoroughly. Then he bent the ball on to the ball joint and, stepping back, slipped off his dressing gown. My word! What a gladiator of a man he was! I have never seen a man quite like him, anywhere. The arms were nothing short of miracles; but even more astonishing was the state of development to which he had brought the vast masses of his trunk muscles. And with it all, considering his lack of height, he was most amazingly shapely.

He put on the gloves, and then stepping up to the ball, hit it a gentle-seeming tap with his left; but the tremendous sound of the impact of the ball on the teak ring, showed both how powerful had been the blow and how heavy the tightly blown bag must be. He caught the ball, with a full swing with his right as it came back, and therewith the whole length of the jiggermast vibrated with the thud of the ball upon the ring; whilst I stood off from him a few paces, lost in an utter delight of the trained coordination of his muscles and resultant perfect movements, and the play of the multitudinous muscles themselves beneath his slightly sun-bronzed skin—a colour that showed how often he must have trained in the open air in his present attire, which consisted of nothing but a pair of black running-drawers.

For half an hour he punched the ball, using not only his hands, elbows and head; but also his shoulders, and showing in a very vivid manner the tremendous and dreadful blow that can be given by the shoulder in a close rough-and-tumble. The movement of his shoulders was astonishing. At the conclusion of his bout, he stripped off his running-drawers and rubbed down, after which he had the bo'sun play the hose over him for quite five minutes.

"That's the way, laddie, to keep fit," he said to me, as he finally finished towelling. He proceeded to throw half a dozen back-springs fore and aft along the weather side of the poop—a truly extraordinary but physically splendid sight, the great muscles working and rippling and bunching marvelously under his perfect skin. He walked up to me and told me to put my hand on his naked chest in order to feel his heart.

"Runnin' sweetly, laddie," he said. "That's what comes of right livin', in the main, laddie, in the main! We're none of us always able to win over the flesh and the natural desires."

He went across and picked up his big dressing gown. As he slipped into it, he beckoned towards the punch-ball.

"Off with your coat an' shirt, laddie, an' let's see how you shape." At which invitation, being in no wise loath to show that I also had some claim to be counted strong, I off with my upper gear and stripped to the waist. Then, going up to the ball, I gave it a light, preliminary blow, and was astonished to find how heavy it was. Indeed, I saw that if I hit it full strength a few times without some protection, I should bruise my hands badly. Captain Dang realized the same thing and tossed me his gloves; whereupon I put in ten minutes creditable work at the ball; for I had trained many an hour with one.

"Very good, laddie," said Captain Dang from where he had taken a seat on the skylight to watch me. "You've a pretty way with your hands, an' you strip surprisin' well. You'll be a hefty lad in a few more years, though you'll always lack weight. I'd back you now again any man aboard, savin' maybe that big Russian. I'm not countin' the Mate or me, laddie. The Mate's surprisin' well-made for such a long devil, sonny."

And with that he left me.

As it chanced, that very day I had opportunity to see another side of Captain Dang that was yet connected with the above. It was in the end of the second dog-watch, and I had been down taking a pull on the braces. Captain Dang and the Mate were walking the poop. Whilst I was slacking off the fore-braces, I caught a mutter of grumbling from the men to leeward, sufficiently loud to tell me that it was an intentional impertinence aimed at me. I knew then that my time had come—the moment every youthful officer in the merchant service has face to face, when his men will definitely test his power to maintain his authority. In plain English, they will be insolent, and if he takes it "lying down," then he had better be dead than aboard that vessel for the rest of the voyage. And these men knew, what all the world could see; that I was young; but maybe they underrated my experience and—may I say it—my sand.

I looked across at the men and noticed that Jarkoff, the big Russian mentioned by Captain Dang, was the man at the front of the rope. And he was the man who was "doing the grumble," in a nasty, sulky, insolent growl, looking sideways to wind'ard at me.

I took a turn with the braces and sung out to the men to leeward to belay; then I walked across to them.

"Jarkoff," I said quietly, "what is the matter with you?"

The great hulking brute turned and glowered down at me, sneering in all his bulk at the youth in me.

"You vas sweat us for noding on der braces!" he said at last with a surly growl. "You vas vish to show you vas Second Mate, He!

He!" He laughed, sneering, and one or two of the men joined in, half-hesitatingly.

I know now that it was no use hesitating or talking any more. They had got to learn something immediately; and I had got to do the teaching. That something was that I was Master, with a big "M," in spite of the sin of my youthfulness. I took two quick steps up to the big Russian, and as he swung to meet me, insolently careless, I hit him hard in the neck, and then, instantly, twice on the mark. I got the blows home good and solid, and the man went down on to the spare topmast with a most comfortable little moaning. He rolled from there to the deck, quite inert. I never managed a better knockout in my life.

"Pick him up and put him on the hatch!" I said, and two of the men jumped to do what I directed. There was no longer any thought of insolence. My lesson was given and already learnt.

As I returned again to the weather braces, I noticed that Captain Dang was leaning over the rail across the break of the poop, looking quietly down on to the main-deck. Yet he made no sign to show that he had been watching anything out of the ordinary, nor, when I returned to the poop in a few minutes, did he make any reference to the affair.

But for all that, Captain Dang made no comment. Presently I had sufficient proof that he had seen the whole business, for a certain exhilaration seemed to be in his blood, stirring him to little acts of vigour—a symptom that I have often observed in very vigorous men after witnessing a fight. It is the fighting-part of them waked . . . the fighting-pride of the cock, that knows it is truly cock of the walk.

So it was with Captain Dang. His step was lighter and more cat-like than usual in its easy, muscular litheness. From time to time he would grip at belaying-pins in the pin-rails, as he passed, pulling them. Every action was an unconscious expression of the additional fuel being burned within him—of the extra energy thus liberated. He felt his upper arms, hardening them time after time, and walked with his chest thrown out, as was his habit when dressed for the shore.

This continued until eight bells, when the roll was called and my watch relieved. The Mate came up a little late, as usual, and we stood talking for a time. All the while Captain Dang walked springily up and down the weather side of the poop, feeling first one enormous biceps and then the other in the most sublimely unconscious fashion possible. I saw the Mate watching him in a way that he suggested he recognized the symptoms. Yet he made no comment to me except that he gave me a sudden look and a suppressed, curious smile, continuing his talk the while.

Suddenly, Captain Dang ceased his walk near to me and began methodically to take off and fold his coat, which he put on the top of the sail-locker hatch.

"Laddie," he said, and I saw the Mate glance quickly at me, "yon's stirred the blood in me," and I knew he referred to my trouble with the big Russian. "I must go forrard an' have a word with the men."

He went down the weather ladder onto the main-deck, rolling up his shirt sleeves carefully, and began to go forrard, bumming away cheerfully at "But the Lord is Mindful." Presently I heard his voice forrard in the fo'cas'le, the words floating aft plainly:

"If there's any of you lads thinks himself a likely man, just step out on deck here with me."

Captain Dang paused.

"Any two of you."

Captain Dang paused again.

Then an enormous bellow of delight came from him, and the sounds of a rush of heavy feet out on deck. There came a tremendous noise of scuffling, blows, shouts of pain and anger from some of the crew, a further exultant bellow from Captain Dang, and the sounds of more feet rushing out of the fo'cas'le.

I turned, meaning to run forrard, but the Mate caught me by the arm, grinning.

"Let it be, Mister," he said. "Th' Old Man don't need you, an' he don't want you. He'll feel more comfortable after this. I guessed he'd got the fit on him. He spoils for a bit of rough an' tumble once in a way. . . . My word, Mister!" he added. "You've got a rare good arm on you for a youngster."

As he spoke, there came Captain Dang's voice again:

"You three go aft to the steward, lads, an' get him to fix you up. Tell him I said you was to have a tot each."

I leant forward over the break and saw three men come aft through the dusk. And pretty woeful looking objects they seemed, so far as I could judge in the gathering darkness. Evidently Captain Dang had "done himself proud," as a coster might have expressed it.

A few seconds later, I heard the Captain shout the cheeriest of good nights to the men in the fo'cas'le, the same being answered with the utmost heartiness and respect. Then his footsteps came lightly and trippingly aft, the while that he broke out joyously into his favorite: "The Lord is Mindful of His Own," repeating and repeating the words with immense gusto. Singing thus, he reached the poop again and resumed his coat without a word of reference to what had transpired forrard. Yet, even in the gloom I noticed that his new kid gloves were all burst and split to pieces.

The Mate pinched me slyly:

"Ain't he a corker, Mister!" he said in a low tone. And therewith I went below to turn in, agreeing profoundly.

From then onwards, Captain Dang put in his morning's half hour at the punch-ball, which I found to be his invariable rule on all trips, once the ship was well away in the open; and each morning, when it was my watch on deck, I would follow-on at the ball, with the result that it helped me to keep splendidly fit.

From that time onward, we made fair wind of it, right down across the Line, where we picked up the Trades again finely, and ran bang away south for the Horn. Our luck in fair holding until we hammered into a "Southerly Buster" that went round to the West'ard and held us up off the Horn for six bitter weeks of snow and ice, until we looked more like a ghost ship of snow, heading into the enormous, grey, desolate seas round the Cape.

No one who has not faced continuous head gales off Cape Horn for a matter of several weeks on end can have any idea of what the sea presently becomes. In the gales themselves, the splendid wrathful wildness of the smoking mountains of water is a thing never to be forgotten, with the sails booming the damp wind out of their leeches, and everything dripping and glistening with the incessant flog of the countless tons of water that are hove aboard, hour after hour, through the long, bitter, wind-tanged watches. And then come the periods of calm between the constant succession of the head gales that are the trial of all vessels rounding the Horn the "wrong way."

I think, in some ways, the hours of calm—that is freedom from wind but not from the sea—is the thing that always leaves the deeper impression upon me—the memory of a shifting world of eternal grey desolation of waters; the sky a perfect grey canopy of gloom, shedding yet a stern, cold light down upon the wandering mountains of grey brine, shifting, shifting eternally. The strange silence of the hours of no-wind that is yet no silence, but only apparently so, because then one may hear the incessant noise of the gear, slatting, the creak of the spars, the dulled, wet rustle of the heavy canvas; and outside of the ship, the enormous slop, slop of the windless sea, striking the steel side of the ship, and the occasional iron clang of some tumbling, clumsy, vast mound of water striking the steel side of the ship and slamming the iron water-doors in the bulwarks that supplement the scuppers in bad weather.

"Eh, laddie," said Captain Dang to me during one of these strange times of windlessness, "could ye not think to near see the grey Babes o' Death in the sma' hollows that go sa canny in the tops o' the seas, like as they was cradles o' water." I stared at him, for the idea was so unexpectedly quaint, and to me so unmeaning. Then I looked out at the slow moving seas and saw what he meant.

He was silent for a little, his glance going away over the miles, and mine likewise, noting many a thing that until then I had not "wakened" to see. Here and there an odd, strange mounding of foam would be thrown up, like a dome of white out of the greyness:

"The domes av th' sea-palaces, laddie," he said suddenly. "They're all about here, laddie. . . . A strange place to be drowned . . . a strange place to be drowned!" he muttered to himself, the while that I just listened as a young man will, stumbling on the borders of thoughts and fancies that had never come to me before. There followed a little space of silence, and Captain Dang spoke again:

"I do like mushrooms, Mister," he said suddenly. "Don't you?"

I stared at him, bewildered a little, whereat he grinned enormously.

"Yes, Sir," I said, "but I can't say I've had much of that kind of thing at sea."

"We're having 'em for tea tonight, laddie," he said, chuckling. "I've been experimenting with a bed of them down in the lazarette."

And thus the unexpected conclusion of his strangely poetical and imaginative previous remarks!

As I have said, we were six bitter weeks of storm and desolate windless spells before we came round upon the Eastern side of the old Cape of Lonesomeness; and then, to reward us, we got a splendid fair breeze that hove us Northward at the rate of X knots. Yet, even with this we could not make the best of it, as Captain Dang wanted to sweep a big surface of the little known portion of the Pacific. And so, in a few days' time we were literally beating to leeward, if one can make use of so paradoxical a term. That is to say that we had a fair wind, but the Captain hauled us up and made a beam wind of it, letting us to leeward about fifty miles each tack of three hundred miles; and this way quartering the ocean like a giant dog, searching for the mysterious lagoon with the three islands and the strange olden ship that the A. B. Turrill had told about in his most improbable yarn.

Each night, Captain Dang hove the ship to as soon as night was fully come, commencing the search again with the first glimmer of dawn. I got a better notion those days of the fund of vast, almost grim, determination that lay beneath his frequent bellows of laughter and his quaint moods of meditation or audible ponderings.

"You mean to find that lagoon, Sir," I said to him one night, when he had come up to join me in the middle watch. It was a thing that he had begun to do quite frequently of late.

"I do that, laddie," was his reply, spoken quite normally and without any suggestion that the man thought he was saying anything to display forcefulness. "While there's bread in the biscuit tanks we'll look for her, laddie, if she's above water—meanin' in this case, my son, the Waters o' Reality."

I knew him well enough now to be aware that he truly meant that nothing short of proof that the unknown lagoon either existed or did not exist would now put him off the search, short of actually running short of provisions.

"And the freighters, Sir?" I asked.

"Damn the freighters, laddie," he said genially.

"And the Company?" I ventured.

But this received no reply, and I knew that I had presumed a little beyond the line with which this seemingly free-and-easy man defined our relationship.

"Do you think there is really any such lagoon, Sir?" I asked after a moment, covering up my unanswered question.

"The Lord, He knows, laddie," was all that Captain Dang said, and he turned and put his hands on the rail, staring dreamily away through the dark miles to wind'ard. Presently he began bumming away softly at his favorite tune, and I, thinking that maybe he wanted to be alone, began to walk the poop by myself. But he called me to him softly as I passed.

"Laddie," he said, "the sea-life's just hell! But oh, the Sea's no less itself than the gateway o' Eternity, laddie. 'Tis just that, laddie, an' no less . . . a place where a man may find his God with nought of shame or insufficient words, laddie. Do ye look now away out on the beam, into the almighty mystery. Look! Can ye no' see the mystery on mystery—eh, laddie? Or are ye blind like the rest—are ye?" He was silent a moment, staring and muttering gently. And suddenly I caught the words that he was saying over and over to himself: "I was born in the froth of thy mountains."

He seemed to be almost tasting and flavoring the words with his tongue, as if he had been an epicure with some much-appreciated dainty. It was a new experience to me . . . it opened yet another door of the unopened Doors of Youth that shut me out from the knowledge-of-life. I got a glimpse, fleeting, of a form of enjoyment and actual happiness that had hitherto been outside of my awareness. I wonder whether I make myself clear.

"And if there's beauty, there's deviltry out there, laddie," he said suddenly. "Eh, but I could tell you things, I could tell you things. . . . Look you, laddie," he added, turning suddenly on me; "there's places out there so strange"—and waved his arm around at the surrounding grey gloom of the sea—"that I should be laughed at ashore, if I was to say one word of the truth. It's just because I've seen things myself that I know yon Turrill man may ha' told the truth, the whole truth an' nothin' but the truth, my son."

"Yes," I said, rather ineffectually.

"All the same," he added, "yon man's told a damned funny yarn; an' whether it's Gospel, or whether it's fever-fancies that he got in the boat, I don't know. Maybe we'll know in a day or two. Maybe we've somethin' queer ahead. By the Lord, Mister, I hope so!" The last words came out with an intensity of expression that almost startled me, and they showed the volcano of a man that he was when the mood for adventure was upon him.

He turned from me abruptly and began to pace the poop alone, muttering from time to time some half-spoken words that I judged to be the line I had heard: "I was born in the froth of thy mountains." And so he went, pacing and dreaming from time to time, sniffing at the night wind, or pausing to lean his elbows on the weather rail and stare away to wind'ard. . . . "I was born in the froth of thy mountains!"

I never met any other man to whom it might so well apply.

For seventeen days we tacked steadily across the great strip of ocean that we were searching, heaving-to at nights. The light, fair breeze held with wonderful steadiness, but never a sign of anything did we see. Once I asked Captain Dang whether he did not think this proof that the A.B. Turrill must truly have mistaken his delirium for reality.

"Wait, laddie, wait," was his reply. "There's nought done in this world, my son, by impatience. Wait till I've beat up this part of the blessed Pacific for another three months. No one knows better'n me how a tidy big thing can get lost surprisin' easy in these parts."

And so we continued for a space of eleven days further, narrowing the distance between out beats from fifty to thirty miles, with two men at the mastheads the whole long day. Yet, curiously enough, they were not the first to see it.

It came about in the dawn of the twelfth day. I was walking the poop in the middle watch, with the vessel hove to, and a light, steady breeze blowing. Away Eastward there was just the first faint loom of the dawn, which slowly strengthened into a pale, uncertain light that showed the sea vaguely.

Suddenly I heard Captain Dang's voice to my back.

"Where are your eyes, Mister! Where are your eyes!" he was saying, and turning, I saw that he was pointing away to leeward. . . .

[UNFINISHED]

Captain Dan Danblasten

This story concerns the treasure of a certain Captain Dan Danblasten, known in his youth as merely Dan Danblasten, in the village of Geddley, on the south coast.

With the youth of Captain Dan Danblasten, which occurred, if I may so phrase it, prior to 1737, I have little to tell, except that being "wild like" and certainly lacking in worldly "plenishings," he was no credit to the respectability of that quiet seaport village.

In consequence of this double stigma of commission and omission, he went away to sea taking his wildness and his poverty along with him; on which it is conceivable that the respectable matrons and maidens of Geddley sighed; though, possibly with different feelings.

There you have the whole tale of Dan Danblasten's youth in a few words; that is, so far as Geddley is concerned.

Twenty years later he returned, with an ancient and ugly scar from right eyebrow to chin, and two enormous iron-bound chests, whose weight was vouched for by the men he hired to carry to the old Tunbelly Hostel, that same Tunbelly Inn being fronted on the old High Street Alley, which has been done away with this twenty years, and more.

Now, if young Dan Danblasten had lacked of friends and kindliness in his wild and youthful days of poverty, the returned Captain Danblasten had no cause for complaint on such score. For, no sooner had he declared his name and ancient kinship to the village, than there were a dozen to remember him and shake him by the hand, in token of those older days, when—as they seemed strangely to forget—there had been no such general desire to grip hands and invite him to sundries of that which both cheers and inebriates.

Yet, at the first of it, there seemed to be every reason to suppose that Captain Danblasten had forgotten the slights and disrespect that had been put upon the onetime Dan; for he accepted both the hands and the liquors that were offered to him; and these, I need scarcely say, were not stinted, when word of those weighty iron-bound chests had gone through the little port; for there was scarcely a man who could refrain from calling in the Tunbelly to welcome "old Dan, coom back agen. Cap'n Dan, sir, beggin' your pardin'."

As that first evening of warm welcoming of the returned and now respectable citizen of Geddley wore onward, Cap'n Danblasten warmed to the good liquor that came so plentiful and freely, and insisted on dancing a hornpipe upon the bar-table. At the conclusion of the warm applause which followed this feat, he declared his intention of showing them that Cap'n Danblasten was as good as the best: " 's good asser besht," he assured the barroom generally a great many times; and finally shouted to some of them to bring in his two great chests, which was done without argument or delay; a thing, perhaps, easy to understand. They were set in the middle of the floor, and all the men in the room crowded round, with their beer mugs, to watch. But at this point Cap'n Danblasten proved he was quite uncomfortably sober; for he ordered every man to stand back, enforcing his suggestion with a big brass-mounted pistol which he brought very suddenly out of a long pocket in the skirts of his heavy coat.

Having assured himself of a clear space all around his precious chests, Cap'n Danblasten pocked the big, brass-mounted pistol, and pulled out a big snuff-box, from which he took ample refreshment. He then dug in amid the snuff, with one great powder-blackened forefinger, and presently brought out to view two smallish keys. He replaced the snuff-box in his vest pocket, and set the keys against the side of his big nose, exclaiming with a kind of half-drunken knowingness, in French:

"Tenons de la verge d'une ancre!" which most of those present understood, being sailormen and in the free-trade, to mean literally the "nuts of the anchor"; but used at that time as a marine catch-phrase, as much as to say "the key of the situation"; though often used also in a coarser manner.

"Tout le monde à son poste!" he shouted, with a tipsy laugh, and turned to unlock the nearer chest. There were two great locks on each chest, and a separate key was used for each; and the interest was quite undoubted, as the cap'n turned back the bolts, and lifted the lid of the chest. Upon the top of all, there were four long wooden cases containing charts. Those he lifted out, and put with surprising care upon the floor. Afterwards, there came a quadrant, wrapped in an old pair of knee-breeches; then a compass, similarly wrapped in an old body-vest. Both of these he put down upon the four chart-cases with quite paternal tenderness.

He reached again into the chest, lurching, and hove out on to the floor a pile of heavily braided uniforms; a pair of great sea-boots with iron leg-guards stitched in on each side of the tops; a couple of heavy double-barrelled French pistols; a big Navy cutlass, and two heavy Malay knives without sheathes. And all the time, as he ladled out these somewhat "tarry" treasures, there was no sound in the big, low-ceilinged room, except the heavy breathings of the interested men-folk of Geddley.

Cap'n Danblasten stood up, wiped his forehead briefly with the back of his hand, and stooped again into the chest, seeming to be fumbling around for something; for the sound of his rough hands going over the wooden inside of the chest was plain to be heard. Presently he gave a satisfied little grunt, and immediately afterward there was a sharp click, which, as the landlord of the Tunbelly told certain of his special cronies afterwards, was a sure sign of there "bein' a secrit lock-fast" within the chest. Be this as it may, the next instant Cap'n Danblasten pulled a thick wooden cover or partition, bolted with flat iron-bands, out of the chest, and hove it with a crash to the floor. Then he stooped, and began to make plain to the men of Geddley the very good and sufficient reason for the immense weight of the two great chests; for he brought out a canvas bag, about the size of a man's head, which he dropped with a dull ringing thud on to the floor. Five more of these he brought out, and threw beside the first; and all the time, no sound, save the breathing of the onlookers, and an occasional hoarse whisper of excited suggestion.

Cap'n Danblasten stood up as he threw the sixth bag upon the others, and signed dumbly for his brandy-mug, with the result that he had half a score offered to him, as we say these days, gratis. He took the first, and drained it; then threw it across the room, where it smashed against the far wall. Yet this provoked no adverse comment, even from the fat landlord of the Tunbelly; for those six, bulging, heavy bags on the floor stood sponsors for many mugs, and it is to be supposed, the contents thereof.

It will be the more easily understood that no one bothered to remark upon Captain Danblasten's method of disposing of his crockery-ware, when you realise that the cap'n had squatted down upon the floor beside his bags, and was beginning to unleash the neck of one. There was not a sound in the room, as he took off the last turn of the spunyarn stopper; for each man of Geddley held his breath with suspense and expectation. Then Cap'n Danblasten, with a quite admirable unconcern, capsized the bag upside down upon the floor, and cascaded out a heap of coins that shone with a dull golden glitter.

There went a gasp of astonishment, echoing from man to man round the room, and then a chorus of hoarse exclamations; for no man there had ever seen quite so much gold at one time in his life. Yet, Cap'n Danblasten took no heed; but with a half-drunken soberness, proceeded to unlash the necks of the five other bags, and to empty them likewise upon the contents of the first. And by the time that the gold from the sixth bag had been added to the heap, the silence of the men of Geddley was a stunned and bitter and avaricious silence; broken at last by the fat landlord of the Tunbelly, who with a nice presence of mind, came forward with the brandy keg under his arm, and a generous sized beer-mug, which was surely a fit spirit-measure for the owner of so prodigious a fortune.

Yet, Captain Danblasten was less appreciative of this tender thought-fulness than might have been supposed; for with a mixed vocabulary of forceful words, chosen discriminately from the French and English, he intimated that the landlord of the Tunbelly should retire, possibly with all the honours of war, but certainly with speed. And as the stout proprietor of the Tunbelly apparently failed to grasp the full and imperative necessity of speed, Cap'n Danblasten plucked his big brass-mounted pistol from the floor beside him, and let drive into the brandy-keg which reposed, as you know, under the well-intending arm of the fat Drinquobier; this being, as you may as well learn here, the landlord's name. The bullet drove through the little keg, and blew out the hither end, wasting a great deal of good liquor, and scored the head of Long John of Kenstone, who came suddenly into a state of fluency; but was unheeded by the majority of the men of Geddley, who were gathered round the stout landlord of the Tunbelly, where he lay like a mountain of flesh upon the floor of the tap-room, shouting at the top of his fat and husky voice that he was shot, and shot dead, at that—which seemed to impress his customers with a conviction of truth. But as for Cap'n Danblasten, he sat calmly upon the floor, beside his heap of gold coinage, and began unemotionally to shovel it back into the six canvas bags, lashing each one securely as it was filled. Presently, still unheeding of the death cries of the very much alive landlord, he rose slowly to his feet, and began to replace the gold in the big chest, replying to Long John of Kenstone's rendering of the commination service, merely by drawing forth a second heavy pistol, laying it ready to his hand across a corner of the chest.

In course of time, the fat landlord having discovered that he still breathed, and Long John of Kenstone having considered discreetly the possibilities of the second pistol, there was a period of comparative quiet once more in the big tap-room, during which Cap'n Danblasten methodically completed his re-stowage of his goods in the chest, and presently locked it securely with the two keys.

When this was finally achieved, a sudden silence of renewed interest came down upon the men of Geddley, as the cap'n proceeded to unlock the second chest, which though somewhat smaller than the other, was yet considerably the heavier. Cap'n Danblasten lifted back the ponderous lid, and there, displayed to view, was the picture of an enormous skull, worked in white silk on a background of black bunting. It was evident that the cap'n had forgotten in his half-drunken state that this lay uppermost in the chest; for he made now a hurried and clumsy movement to turn back the folds of the flag upon itself, so as to hide the emblem which was uncomfortably familiar in that day. Yet, that the men of Geddley had seen, was obvious; for there came a general cry from the mariners present, some of whom had been privateersmen, and worse, of: "The Jolly Roger! The Jolly Roger!"

Cap'n Danblasten stood a moment, in a seeming stupid silence, with the flag all bunched together in his hand; then suddenly, he turned, and flirted it out wide across the floor, so that the skull and the crossed bones, surmounted by a big D, showed plain. Underneath the D there was worked an hourglass in red wool. The men of Geddley crowded round, handling the flag, and criticising the designs, with something of the eyes of experts; some of them, and notably Long John of Kenstone, saying it was no proper Jolly Roger, seeing that it held no battle-axe. And on this, a general and forceful discussion ensued, which ended in a physical demonstration of their views, on the part of Long John of Kenstone, and a squat, heavy privateersman, during which Captain Danblasten hauled the flag out of the midst of the discussion, and began to bundle it back into the chest, which he did so clumsily that he disturbed a layer of underclothing which covered the lower contents, and displayed to view the chest nearly two thirds full of smashed and defaced gold and silver work of every description, from the gold-hilts of swords and daggers, to the crumpled golden binding of some great Bible, showing the burst jewel-sockets from which precious stones had been roughly prised.

At the sight of all this new treasure, the value of which was plainly enormous, a great silence came upon the room, broken only by the scuffling and grunting of the two who were setting forth their arguments upon the floor of the tap-room. So marked was this silence that even the latter at last became aware of something fresh, and scrambled to their feet to participate. And they, also, joined in the general hush of astonished awe and avarice, and—what cannot be denied—renewed and intense respect for this further proof of the desirable worth of the returned citizen of Geddley. And the cap'n, realising in his half-drunken pride, the magnitude of the sensation he had created, and the supremeness of the homage that he had won, shut down the lid of the chest, and locked it with the two keys, which he afterwards returned to the snuff-box; bedding them well down into the snuff, and shutting the box with a loud snap, after he had once more refreshed his nose sufficiently.

"Be you not goin' to turn out t'other, cap'n?" asked Long John of Ken-stone, in a marvellously courteous voice—that is, considering the man!

"Non," said Captain Danblasten, with that brevity of courtesy so admired in the wealthy; and truly Cap'n Danblasten was indeed wealthy; for it is likely enough that the wealth contained in those two great chests was sufficient to have bought up the whole of the port of Geddley, and a good slice of the country round about it lock, stock and barrel, as the saying goes.

Now, when the captain had so wittily described his intention, he pulled out a small powder flask from his side pocket, and proceeded, in a considerable silence, to recharge the fired pistol, which he did with a quite peculiar dexterity, speaking of immense practice, and this despite his half-drunken condition. When he had finished ramming down a couple of soft-lead bullets upon the charge of powder, he primed the lock, replaced the flask, and announced his intention of turning-in (i.e. going to bed), which he achieved with remarkable speed, by dragging the two chests together in the middle of the tap-room and using them as a couch, with his rolled up coat for a pillow; and so in a moment he composed himself with a grunt, his loaded pistols stuffed in under the coat, and his great right hand resting on the butts.

And so he seemed to be instantly asleep; yet it is a curious thing that once, when Long John stepped over towards him, after a bout of hoarse whispering with several of the men in the room, Cap'n Danblasten opened one bleary eye, and—without undue haste—thrust out one of his big pistols in an indifferent manner at the body of Long John, whereat that gentleman stepped back without even attempting to enter into any argument on the score of intention.

After this little episode, the cap'n once more returned to his peculiar method of slumbering; but there was no longer any whispering on the part of Long John Kenstone and his mates. Instead, a quite uncomfortable silence reigned in the tap-room, broken presently by the departing feet of this man and that man, until the place was empty, save for the fat landlord who leaned against the great beer-tub, and regarded the sleeping captain in a meditative and puzzled fashion.

The landlord's pondering was interrupted disagreeably; for slowly one of the sleeping captain's eyes opened, and a curiously disturbing look was fixed silently upon the fat landlord, for the space of perhaps a full minute. Then Captain Danblasten extended a great hand towards the landlord, and in the hand was one of his big brass-bound pistols, the muzzle towards the Master Drinquobier. For a little space the captain directed the pistol thus, whilst the landlord shrivelled visibly in a queer speechless fashion.

"Tenons de la verge d'une ancre!" said Captain Danblasten, even as he had said it once before that evening. He tapped the pistol with his other hand, to emphasise his remark; and sat up on the bigger chest, still looking at the landlord.

"So," he said, at last, speaking in English, "you're thinkin' to go halves with Long John o' Kenstone, ye gowk tunbelly. You'm waitin' now, beer-hog, to give them the signal to enter when I'm gone over, ye swine; and think to fool Dan Danblasten easyways; and I knowin' what ye meant, an' they only without in the enter-porch, ye fat fool. Out with you, smartly! Out, I say!" And therewith he flung the leaded pistol at the landlord's head; but he dodged, quite cleverly for so fat a man, and the weapon exploded against the wall with a great crash of sound; whilst Drinquobier ran heavily for the door, tore it open, and fell headlong out into the passage-way, whilst within the empty tap-room, the captain sat on the chest and shook with a kind of grim laughter.

Presently, he rose from the chest, after he had heard the landlord go scrambling away in clumsy fright upon his hands and knees. He stood a few moments, listening intently; then, seeming to hear something, he ran with surprising nimbleness to the door, pushed it silently to, and set down the socket-bar across from side to side, so that the door would have to be broken down before anyone could enter. Then he bent forward to listen, and in a little while, heard the faint sound of bare feet without in the passage, and soon a soft, gentle fumbling at the door.

"Dépasser!" he shouted, roaring with a kind of half-laughter, half-anger. Then, in English: "You've over-run your reckoning, my lads! Get below an' turn in!" And with the word, he turned unconcernedly from the door, and went back to his rough couch, and presently was sleeping unemotionally, whilst without the door, the men who had come with some hope of surprising him, departed with muffled but considerable fluency, and an unabated avarice.

And thus, and in this manner exactly, was the home-coming of Captain Danblasten, Pirate (presumably), and now (certainly) a most desirable citizen of the Port of Geddley.

Captain Danblasten waked early, and rolled off his uncomfortable bed. He walked across to the shelf where the brandy-kegs were stored, and helped himself to a generous tot; after which he went over to the door, unbarred and opened it, and bellowed the landlord's name, calling him also old tunbelly and beer-hog, and cursing him between whiles in both French and English until he came tumbling down the creaking stairs, in a very fluster of dismay.

Breakfast, was Cap'n Danblasten's demand. Breakfast, and speedily and plentifully; and if the maids were not up yet, then it was time they turned out, or old tunbelly could prepare the meal himself and serve it to him there in the tap-room, upon one of his big chests. Meanwhile, he applied himself methodically to the brandy-keg, varying his occupation by occasional bellows through the quiet of the inn, for the breakfast he had ordered.

It came presently, and, squatted sideways upon the narrower chest, he set to work. As he ate, he asked the landlord questions, about this and that woman of the port, who—when he had gone off to sea all those twenty years gone—had been saucy maids, but were now mostly mothers of families, if he could believe all that the fat Drinquobier told him.

"Eh," said Cap'n Danblasten, wiping his mouth with the back of his hand, "there was some saucy young ones among that lot, when I was a younker. An' how's young Nancy Drigg doin'?"

"She be Nancy Garbitt these thirteen year, Cap'n Danblasten, sir," said the landlord. Whereat the cap'n ceased his eating, a moment, to hark the better.

"Eh?" he said, in a curious voice, at last. "Married that top o' my thumb, Jimmy Garbitt? Dieu! but I'll cut the throat of him this same day of our Lord! Dieu! The sacre man-sprat! The blandered bunch o' shakin's! Dieu!"

"He'm dead these yere two years, cap'n," said Drinquobier, staring hard at Captain Danblasten, with half-frightened and wholly curious eyes. "I heard oncest 's ye was sweet-ways on Nancy. No offence! No offence, cap'n! Seven, Jimmy left be'ind, an' all on 'em maids, at that."

"What!" cried Captain Danblasten, with a sudden, strange anger, and threw his brandy-mug at the landlord's head. But afterwards he was silent for a time, neither eating nor speaking; only frowning away to himself. "An' Nancy Drigg, herself?" he asked, at length. "How'm she lookin' these days, ye old tunbelly? Seven on 'em! Seven on 'em, an' to that blandered bunch o' shakin's.... Why don't ye answer, you bilge-guzzlin' beer-cask! Open your face, ye—ye—"

"Fair, cap'n, sir; fair an' bonny like, Cap'n Danblasten," old Drinquobier interjected with frightened haste, his frontal appendage quivering like a vast jelly, until the form shook on which he sat.

"Ah!" said the captain, and was quiet again; but a minute afterwards he made it pointedly clear to the landlord that he needed a timber-sled to be outside of the inn speedily. "An' half a dozen of thy loafer lads, tunbelly, do ye hear! An' smart, or I'll put more than beer betwixt thy wind and water, ye old cut-throat, that must set a respectable townsman to sleep with his pistols to hand all the long night in this inn o' yours, lest ye an' your louts do him a mischief! Smartly, ye beer-swiller, wi' yon sled, an' smartly does it, or I'll be knowin' the why!"

And evidently smartly he did do it, as we say; for in a very few minutes Captain Danblasten was superintending, pistol in hand, the transferring of his two great chests to the sled, by the hands of a dozen brawny longshore men, who had been fished out of various handy sleeping places, by the fear-driven landlord.

Cap'n Danblasten sat himself down upon his chests, and signalled to the horse-boy to drive on. But as he started to move, the fat landlord discovered somewhere in his monstrous body the remnant of a one-time courage, and came forward towards the sled, crying out that he would be paid for his liquor, bed and board. At this, Cap'n Danblasten raised one of his pistols, evidently with the full intention of ending—once and for all—the entire agitation of the landlord's avaricious soul; but suddenly thinking better of it, he drew out a couple of guineas, which he hove in among the little crowd of shore-boys, shouting to them to get their fill of good beer at the hatchways, and the change might go to pay his debts to Drinquobier. This he did, knowing full well that no change would the landlord ever see out of those two guineas; and so sat back, roaring with laughter, and shouting to the horse-boy to "crack on sail an' blow the sticks out o' her!" Which resulted in the lad laying his cudgel repeatedly and forcibly across the hindquarters of the animal, which again resulted in the beast changing its walk to a kind of absurd amble, which in its turn resulted in the sled bounding and bumping along down the atrociously paved street, dignified by the name High Street Alley, so that the last the group around the doorway of the Tunbelly saw, was the broad heavy figure of Cap'n Danblasten jolting and rolling on the top of his great chests, and trying to take aim at the horse-boy with one of his big brass-bound pistols, the while he bellowed to the lad to shorten sail, and likewise be damned, as before.

And so they went rattling and banging round the corner, out of sight, the clatter and crashing of the heavy sled punctuated twice by the reports of the cap'n's pistols; after which he was content to hold on, and curse the boy, horse, sled, the landlord of the Tunbelly, and the road, all with equal violence, until in a minute the lad had once more got the horse controlled to a walk, and was cursing back pluckily at the cap'n for loosing off his pistols at him. And this way they came presently to a little house in the lower end of the alley, where the boy stopped the sled and his cursing all in the same moment, and pointed with his horse-cudgel to the door of the little house, meaning that they had come to the place.

At this, Cap'n Danblasten got down lumberingly from the tops of his big chests; and suddenly, before the boy knew his intention, he had caught him by the collar of his rough jacket and hoist him bodily from the ground; whereupon the lad, full as ever of his strange pluck, set-to to curse him again (so well he might, being half-strangled) and to striking at him with the horse-cudgel. Immediately, the captain plucked the cudgel from him, and then, setting the lad's feet to the road again, he hauled forth a great handful of gold-pieces, which he crammed forcibly down the back of the boy's neck, shaking with queer, noiseless laughter all the while.

"A good plucked un, Dieu! A good plucked un!" he said, and loosed the lad suddenly, applying one of his big sea-boots with indelicate dexterity to intimate that he had no further need of his services. Whereupon the lad, who had ceased now to curse, ran off down the alley a little way, and commenced to shake himself, until all the gold had come through; after which he gathered it up, and calling to his horse, mounted the sled, and away so fast as the brute could go.

Meanwhile, Cap'n Danblasten was pounding at the door of the house, and shouting lustily the name of Nancy Drigg, outside the door of Nancy Gaddley (Garbitt); until presently a startled feminine face came out of a lattice above, and, seeing him, she screamed suddenly:

"Dan! Da-an!" And withdrew hurriedly from sight.

"What do you want?" she asked presently, from within the room, and not showing herself.

"Open!" shouted the cap'n, "afore I has the door down. I'm coom to board wi' ye, Nance. Open! I say!" And he commenced to kick at the door with his great sea-boots.

"Husht now, Dan! You've the drink in you, or you'd no think to shame a lone woman in this fashion. Husht now, an' I'll coom down and let 'ee in."

Whereupon the cap'n ceased from his kicking, and turned round to survey the various heads that had been thrust from the casements of the alley about, to discover the cause of the disturbance.

"Bon quart! Bon quart!" he called, at first good humouredly; but changing his tone, as he saw they still continued to stare at him. "Bon quart! Bon quart!!" he roared angrily, and aimed with one of his discharged pistols at the head of the nearest. The flint snapped harmlessly, and the head dodged back; but the captain hauled a fresh weapon from the skirts of his long coat, and seeing that he was still spied upon from a window higher up, he let drive in sound earnest, and very near ended the life of the onlooker; after which the alley might have held only the dead, for all of the living that displayed themselves to his view. He turned again, and commenced to kick upon the door, shouting.

And in the same instant, it was opened by Nancy, hurriedly wrapped about with her quilt.

"Husht now! Husht now, Dan, an' coom in sober-like," she said, "or 'tis only the outside of the door I'll have to 'ee."

The cap'n stepped inside, and turned on her:

"Nice wumman, ye, Nancy Drigg, to splice that blandered bunch of shakin's, Jimmy Garbitt. An' seven ye've had to him; an' not a man in the lot; an' little wonder; ye that could not wait for y'r own man to come home wi' the fortun' I promis'd ye; but must take a top-o-my-thumb to bed-mate. Shame on ye for a poor sperreted wench; an' me this moment wi' the half o' oor silver penny to my knife-chain, that we broke all them years gone; an' never a throat I cut, but I ses: 'there be another gold piece to my Nancy. An' you to go brood-mare to that blandered—'"

"Husht, Dan!" said Nancy, at last; not loudly, but with surprising firmness. "You be proper an' decent ways wi' me, Dan, an' good care I'll take of 'ee, an' put up wi' 'ee, so well as I may, fr owd sake's sake. But no word at poor Jimmy, an' nowt to trouble my maids, or out ye go to the sharks o' Geddley, an' clean they'll pluck ye, as well ye know."

"An' well they fear me, an' well can I mind my own helium!" said the captain warmly; yet unmistakably more civil in his manner, for he felt that if Nancy Garbitt would take him in, then at least he need fear no "traitors in the camp," as the saying goes.

"I'm troubled wi' a sick pain in th' heart, Nancy, an' can't last long," he said, after a little pause. "Will I pay ye a gold piece every week-ending, or will I pay ye nothin', an' you have the will of me when I go below?"

"I'll trade on no man's death, Dan; an' least on yours," said Nancy. "Pay me the guinea-piece each week, an' well I'll do by 'ee as you know, Dan. An' do 'ee be easy with drinkin' an' ill-livin', an' many a year you'm boun' to live yet."

And so it was arranged.

"An' you keep the seven — brats out o' my course—!" said the cap'n. "Dan!" said Nancy.

"Pardieu, Nance! No ill to it! No ill to it!" apologised Cap'n Danblasten. "You're pretty-lookin' yet, wi' the sperret that's in ye, Nance," he concluded. At which complement Nance's eyes softened a little, so that it was like enough she had still in a corner of her heart a gentle-feeling towards this uncouth sea-dog of a man, who had been her lover in her youth.

And this way came, and settled, and presently died, Captain Dan Danblasten, and with his death there arose the seven-year mystery of die treasure, which to this day may be read in the Records of the Parish of Geddley, by John Stockman, 1797.

And regarding the length of life still coming to him, Cap'n Danblasten was right; for he lived no more than some eighteen or nineteen months (date uncertain) after the arrangement mentioned above. And these are the concluding details of his life:

For some months he lived quietly enough with Nancy Garbitt, paying her regularly, and amenable to her tongue, even in his most fantastic fits of humour, whether bred of drink, or of his state of health. Eventually, however, his little room was broken into one dark night, whilst he slept. But the cap'n proved conclusively that he was well able to defend both life and fortune; for he used his pistols, and—later—his cutlass, to such effect that when the raiders drew off, there lay three dead and one wounded on the floor of his room, whose groans so irritated Cap'n Danblasten that he went over to him, and picking up one of their overturned lanterns from the floor, passed his cutlass twice or thrice through him, to quieten him, remarking as he did so: "I knew I'd ha' to fix 'ee, tunbelly, afore I was done wi' ye." (For he recognised the landlord's corporation, despite the masks which he and all the robbers had worn.) "An' here's luck—an' you'm sure goin' easy." And he jabbed him, conscientiously, for the last time.

The direct result of this raid was that Captain Danblasten resolved to build himself a house that would make him and his treasure secure in future from an attack of this sort. To this end, he had masons by coach from a great distance—as distances were counted great on those days—and acting as his own architect, he planned out a strange great house in the form of a ship, in masonry, with a double tier of iron-barred windows in place of ports, and three narrow towers, like modern lighthouses, to take the place of masts, with stairs inside, so that they could be used for lookout posts. There was one great door in the stern, which was hung on pintles, from the sternpost, like a huge and somewhat abnormally-shaped rudder. Somewhere below this ship-house, there was built a strong room: though this was not known until later; for as soon as the masons had done their work, they were sent back to their own towns, and in this way the secrets of the house were hidden from the men of Geddley. It may be as well to say here that this peculiar house, minus its three towers, which had long since been removed, was to be seen almost intact, as late as 1874. It had become built in, 'bow-and-stern' into a terrace of houses which still form what is known as Big Fortune Terrace, and was then an inn, run by one Thomas Walker, under the name of The Stone Ship Inn. . . . "Very much in!" used to be the local and extraordinary witty joke, according to the New Records of Geddley, which we owe to Richard Stetson, a citizen, I imagine, of that same quaint seaport.

To revert to Cap'n Dan Danblasten, as I have said, he "concluded" his house, and "shipped back" his masons to their varied and distant homes; by this means hiding from the men of Geddley all possible details concerning the construction of his stronghold.

Presently, he removed, with his two great chests of treasure, to his new house, and thereafter very little of his doings appear to have been worthy of remark; for, saving an odd walk down to Nancy Garbitt's little cot, or a still rarer visit to the Tunbelly (now under the care of a new landlord), Cap'n Danblasten, sir, as he was latterly always addressed, appeared but little beyond his own great rudder-door.

After his removal, he still continued to pay Nancy her guinea per week, and often assured her that when he died, she should own the whole of his treasure.

And presently, as I have intimated, he died. And certain grave lawyers, if that be the right term, came all the way from Bristol to read his will; which was quaint, but simple. The whole of his wealth he left to Nancy Garbitt and her seven daughters; the one condition being that they must first find it; one day in each year being allowed only for the search; and if they had no success within and including seven years from his death, then the whole of the treasure, when found, must be handed over entire to a certain person named in the codicil to the will, which was not to be read, save in the event of the gold not being found within the said seven years.

As may be imagined, the sensation which this will provoked was profound, not only within the Parish of Geddley, but throughout the whole county, and beyond. Eventually, certain of the masons who had assisted in the building of the Stone Ship House heard of the will, and sent word that there was a specially built strong room under the foundations of the house, very cunningly hidden, and under it, again, there was a sealed vault. For a remuneration, one of their number would come by coach, and assist the locating of the place. This, of course, increased the excitement and general interest; but it was not until the twenty-seventh day of September of that year, that the search might be made, between the hours of sunrise and sunset; the Stone Ship House being occupied, meanwhile, by the lawyers' caretakers, and seals liberally spread about.

On September 26th, the mason arrived, accompanied by two of his fellows—the three of them being hired by Nancy Garbitt to act as expert searchers on their behalf. For, very wisely, she had steadfastly refused the enormous amount of "free" aid that had been tendered by the men of Geddley, collectively and singly from day to day.

The 27th dawned; the anniversary, had Nancy but remembered, of that day, so many years gone, when she and young Dan had broken their silver penny. Surely the date was significant!

Nancy Garbitt and her seven daughters and the men of Geddley stood near the door of the Stone Ship House, with the three masons. As the sun rose into sight, the lawyer knocked on the door, and the caretakers opened and stood back for Nancy, her daughters and the three masons to enter. But the men of Geddley had to remain outside, and there waiting, many of them remained the whole of that livelong day, if we are to believe the worthy John Stockman.

Within the house, the masons went confidently to work; but at the end of a short time, had to acknowledge themselves bewildered. There had been surely other masons to work, since they had been sent away; or else the grim old sea-dog himself had turned mason in those last months of his life; for no signs of the hidden entrance to the strong room could they discover.

At this, after some little discussion, it was resolved to break down through the stone-built floor, direct into the strong room, which the masons asserted to be immediately below a certain point which they had ascertained by measurements. Yet, the evening of that day found them labouring, still lacking the whereabouts of the strong room. And presently sunset had put an end to the search for a year; and Nancy Garbitt and her seven daughters had to return treasureless to their small cot in the alley.

The second and the third and the fourth years, Nancy and her daughters returned, likewise lacking in treasure; but in the fifth year, it was evident to Nancy and her maidens that they had come upon signs of the long lost strong room. Yet the sunset of the "day of grace" cut short their delving, before they could prove their belief.

Followed a year of tense excitement and conjecture, in which Nancy could have married off her daughters to the pick of the men of Geddley; for to every sanguine male it was apparent that the treasure was almost in sight.

Some suggestion there was of carrying the Stone Ship House by assault, and prosecuting the search to its inevitable end without further ridiculous delay; but this Nancy would not listen to. Moreover, the strength of the building, and the constant presence of the armed legal guardians thereof forbad any hope of success along these lines.

In the sixth year Nancy Garbitt died, just before sunset on the day of the search. Her death was possibly due, in part at least, to the long continued excitement, and the nearing of the hour when the search must be delayed for another whole year. Her death ended the search for that time; though a portion of the actual built-in door of the strong room itself had been uncovered. Yet, already, as I have said, it had been close to the time when the search must cease.

When the twenty-seventh day of September in the seventh year arrived, the men of Geddley made a holiday, and accompanied the seven Misses Garbitts with a band to the door of the Stone Ship House. By midday the door of the long-shut strong room was uncovered, and a key the lawyer produced was found to fit. The door was unlocked, and the seven maidens rushed in—to emptiness.

Yet, after the first moment of despair, someone remembered the sealed vault which lay under the strong room. A search was made, and the covering stone found; but it proved an intractable stone, and sunset was nigh before it was removed. A candle was lowered into the vault and a small chest discovered; otherwise the vault was as empty as the strong room.

The box was brought out into the light and broken open. Inside was found nothing but the half of a broken silver penny.

At that moment, watch in hand, the lawyer decreed that the hour of sunset had arrived, and motioned for silence where was already the silence of despair. He drew from his pocket the package that held the codicil, broke the seal, and proceeded to read to the seven maidens its contents. They were brief and startling and extraordinary in the revelation of the perversity of the old sea-dog's warped and odd nature. The codicil revealed that the gold for which they had so long searched was still left to Nancy; but that it lay under the stone flags of their own living-room, where the captain had buried it at nights, all the long years gone when he had lived at Nancy's, storing the removed earth in the chests in place of the gold.

"Seven children have you had, Nancy Drigg, to that top-o'-my-thumb, Jimmy Garbitt," the codicil concluded, "and seven years shall you wait—you that could not wait!"

That is all. The money went to the children of Nancy Garbitt; for by the whimsy of Fate, the woman for whose reproval all this had been planned was never to learn, and the bitter taunt of the broken silver penny was never to reach its mark; for Nancy, as you know, was dead. And so ended the seven years' search. And likewise this history of the strange and persistent love affair of Captain Dan Danblasten, sea-dog and pirate.

Copyright Versions

The Ghost Pirates

The Figure Out of the Sea

HE BEGAN WITHOUT ANY CIRCUMLOCUTION.

"I joined the 'Mortzestus' in 'Frisco. I heard, before I signed on, that there were some funny yarns floating round about her; but I was pretty nearly on the beach, and too jolly anxious to get away to worry about trifles. Besides, by all accounts, she was right enough, so far as grub and treatment went. When I asked fellows to give it a name, they generally could not. All they could tell me was that she was unlucky, and made thundering long passages, and had more than a fair share of dirty weather. Also that she had twice had the sticks blown out of her, and her cargo shifted. Besides all these, a heap of other things that might happen to any packet, and would not be comfortable to run into. Still, they were the ordinary things, and I was willing enough to risk them, to get home. All the same, if I had been given the chance, I should have shipped in some other vessel, as a matter of preference.

"When I took my bag down, I found that they had signed on the rest of the crowd. You see, the 'home lot' cleared out when they got into 'Frisco; that is, all except one young fellow, a cockney, who had stuck by the ship in port. He told me afterwards, when I got to know him, that he intended to draw a payday out of her, whether anyone else did or not.

"The first night I was in her I found that it was common talk among the other fellows that there was something queer about the ship. They spoke of her as if it were an accepted fact that she was haunted; yet they all treated the matter as a joke, all, that is, except the young cockney—Williams—who, instead of laughing at their jests on the subject, seemed to take the whole matter seriously.

"This made me rather curious. I began to wonder whether there was, after all, some truth underlying the vague stories I had heard; and I took the first opportunity to ask him whether he had any reasons for believing that there was any truth in the yarns about the ship.

"At first he was inclined to be a bit offish; but presently he came 'round and told me that he did not know of any particular incident which could be called unusual in the sense in which I meant. Yet, at the same time, there were lots of little things which, if you put them together, made you think a bit. For instance, she always made such long passages and had so much dirty weather—nothing but that, and calms and head winds. Then other things happened—sails that he knew himself had been properly stowed were always blowing adrift at night. And then he said a thing that surprised me.

" 'There's too many bloomin' shadders about this 'ere packet; they gets onter yer nerves like nothin' as ever I seen before in me nat'ral.'

"He blurted it all out in a heap, and I turned 'round and looked at him.

" 'Too many shadders!' I said. 'What on earth do you mean?' But he refused to explain himself, or tell me anything further—just shook his head stupidly when I questioned him. He seemed to have taken a sudden, sulky fit. I felt certain that he was acting dense purposely. I believe the truth of the matter is that he was, in a way, ashamed of having let himself go like he had in speaking out his thoughts about 'shadders.' That type of man may think things at times; but he doesn't often put them into words. Anyhow, I saw it was no use asking any further questions, so I let the matter drop there. Yet, for several days afterward, I caught myself wondering at times what the fellow had meant by 'shadders.'

"We left 'Frisco next day, with a fine, fair wind that seemed a bit like putting the stopper on the yarns I'd heard about the ship's ill luck. And yet—"

He hesitated a moment, and then went on again:

"For the first couple of weeks out nothing unusual happened, and the wind still held fair. I began to feel that I had been rather lucky, after all, in the packet into which I had been shunted. Most of the other fellows gave her a good name, and there was a pretty general opinion growing among the crowd that it was all a silly yarn about her being haunted. And then, just when I was settling down to things, something happened that opened my eyes no end.

"It was in the 8-to-12 watch, and I was sitting on the steps on the starboard side leading up to the fo'cas'le head. The night was fine and there was a splendid moon. Away aft I heard the timekeeper strike four bells, and the lookout—an old fellow named Jaskett, answered him. As he let go the bell lanyard, his eye caught sight of me, where

I sat, quietly smoking. He leant over the rail, and looked down at me.

" 'That you, Jessop?' he asked.

" 'I believe it is,' I replied.

" 'We'd 'ave our gran'mothers an' all the rest of our petticoated relash'ns comin' to sea, if 'twere always like this,' he remarked, reflectively—indicating, with a sweep of his pipe and hand, the calmness of the sea and sky.

"I saw no reason for denying that, and he continued:

" 'If this ole packet is 'aunted, as some on 'em seems to think, well, all as I can say is, let me 'ave the luck to tumble across another of the same sort. Good grub, an' duff fer Sundays, an' a decent crowd of 'em aft, an' everythin' comfertable like, so as yer can feel yer knows where yer are. As fer 'er bein' 'aunted, that's all nonsense. I've comed 'cross lots of 'em before as was said to be 'aunted, an' so some on 'em was; but 'twasn't with ghosteses. One packet I was in they was that bad yer couldn't sleep a wink in yer watch below, until yer'd 'ad every stitch out yer bunk an' 'ad a reg'lar 'unt. Sometimes—'

"At that moment the relief, one of the ordinary seamen, went up the other ladder onto the fo'cas'le head, and the old chap turned to ask him 'why the 'ell' he'd not relieved him a bit smarter. The ordinary made some reply, but what it was I did not catch, for, abruptly, away aft, my rather sleepy gaze had lighted on something altogether extraordinary and outrageous. It was nothing less than the form of a man stepping inboard over the starboard rail, a little abaft the main rigging. I stood up and caught at the handrail and stared.

"Behind me, someone spoke. It was the lookout, who had come down off the fo'cas'le head, on his way aft to report the name of his relief to the Second Mate.

" 'What is it, mate?' he asked, curiously, seeing my intent attitude.

"The thing—whatever it was—had disappeared into the shadows on the lee side of the deck.

" 'Nothing!' I replied, shortly, for I was too bewildered then at what my eyes had just shown me to say any more. I wanted to think.

"The old shellback glanced at me; but only muttered something, and went on his way aft.

"For a minute, perhaps, I stood there, watching; but could see nothing. Then I walked slowly aft, as far as the after end of the deckhouse. From there I could see most of the main deck; but nothing showed, except, of course, the moving shadows of the ropes and spars and sails, as they swung to and fro in the moonlight.

"The old chap who had just come off the lookout had returned forrard again, and I was alone on that part of the deck. And then, all at once, as I stood peering into the shadows to leeward, I remembered what Williams had said about there being too many 'shadders.' I had been puzzled to understand his real meaning then. I had no difficulty now. There were too many shadows. Yet, shadows or no shadows, I realized that, for my own peace of mind, I must settle, once and for all, whether the thing I had seemed to see stepping aboard out of the ocean had been a reality or simply a phantom, as you might say, of my imagination. My reason said it was nothing more than imagination, a rapid dream—I must have dozed; but something deeper than reason told me that this was not so. I put it to the test, and went straight in amongst the shadows. There was nothing.

"I grew bolder. My common sense told me I must have fancied it all. I walked over to the mainmast, and looked behind the pinrail that partly surrounded it, and down into the shadow of the pumps; but here again was nothing. Then I went in under the break of the poop. It was darker under there than out on deck. I looked up both sides of the deck and saw that they were bare of anything such as I looked for. The assurance was comforting. I glanced at the poop ladders, and remembered that nothing could have gone up there without the Second Mate or the timekeeper seeing it. Then I leant my back up against the bulkhead, and thought the whole matter over, rapidly sucking at my pipe and keeping my glance about the deck. I concluded my think, and said 'No!' out loud. Then something occurred to me, and I said 'Unless—' and went over to the starboard bulwarks, and looked over and down into the sea; but there was nothing but sea; and so I turned and made my way forrard. My common sense had triumphed, and I was convinced that my imagination had been playing tricks with me.

"I reached the door on the port side leading into the fo'cas'le, and was about to enter, when something made me look behind. As I did so I had a shaker. Away aft, a dim, shadowy form stood in the wake of a swaying belt of moonlight that swept the deck a bit abaft the mainmast.

"It was the same figure that I had just been attributing to my fancy. I will admit that I felt more than startled; I was quite a bit frightened. I was convinced now that it was no mere imaginary thing. It was a human figure. And yet, with the flicker of the moonlight and the shadows chasing over it, I was unable to say more than that. Then, as I stood there, irresolute and funky, I got the thought that someone was acting the goat, though for what reason or purpose

I never stopped to consider. I was glad of any suggestion that my common sense assured me was not impossible; and, for the moment, I felt quite relieved. That side to the question had not presented itself to me before. I began to pluck up courage. I accused myself of getting fanciful; otherwise I should have tumbled to it earlier. And then, funnily enough, in spite of all my reasoning, I was still afraid of going after to discover who that was standing on the lee side of the main deck. Yet I felt that, if I shirked it, I was only fit to be dumped overboard; and so I went, though not with any great speed, as you can imagine.

"I had gone half the distance, and still the figure remained there, motionless and silent—the moonlight and the shadows playing over it with each roll of the ship. I think I tried to be surprised. If it were one of the fellows playing the fool, he must have heard me coming, and why didn't he scoot while he had the chance? And where could he have hidden himself before? All these things I asked myself, in a rush, with a queer mixture of doubt and belief; and, you know, in the meantime, I was drawing nearer. I had passed the house, and was not twelve paces distant when, abruptly, the silent figure made three quick strides to the port rail and climbed over it into the sea.

"I rushed to the side and stared over; but nothing met my eyes except the shadow of the ship, sweeping over the moon-lit sea.

"How long I stared down blankly into the water it would be impossible to say; certainly for a good minute. I felt blank—just horribly blank. It was such a beastly confirmation of the unnaturalness of the thing I had concluded to be a sort of brain fancy. I seemed, for that little time, deprived, you know, of the power of coherent thought. I suppose I was dazed—mentally stunned, in a way.

"As I have said, a minute or so must have gone, while I had been staring into the dark of the water under the ship's side. Then I came suddenly to my ordinary self. The Second Mate was singing out: 'Lee fore brace.'

"I went to the braces, like a chap in a dream.

The Search for Stubbins

"And then, on the fourth night, something fresh happened, for about two bells that night the fore t'gallant sheet carried away, and Williams and I went up to fix it. We did this, and I went down to give a hand with the haulyards, whilst Williams stayed up to light up the gear. And then, suddenly, when the yard was nearly mastheaded,

Williams started to sing out something queer, and a minute later he came down with a crash, and smashed upon the deck.

"Jove! We were shaken, and the second sent Tammy (our first-voyage 'prentice) up to take the wheel, to be out of the way. When we'd cleared up the ropes and things we went into the fo'cas'le, and had a long yarn about it; but no one, 'cept, perhaps, Stubbins, seemed to have any idea of the way to look at things. And so the conversation slacked off. He were all so moody and shaken.

"Presently I heard the second whistling for someone to relieve the wheel, and when I got aft I found he'd kicked Tammy away from the wheel, because Tammy thought he'd seen a man climbing aboard out of the sea, and had, consequently, bunked away from the wheel. I had a long talk with Tammy, over the wheel-box, after the Second Mate had gone forrard to the break, and he told me all about it, and I explained to him that I was growing pretty certain that the ship was open to be boarded by these strange shadow-men; and then the Second Mate came aft again, and we had to shut up.

"We buried Williams next day, about midday. And after that came the mist, which I always hold brought a queer, invisible atmosphere about the ship, which made other ships invisible to us and, I believe, even the natural sea, though all looked to us as usual, except that we could not see other vessels any longer, though I found out afterwards, as you know, that they could see us. When I say we couldn't see other ships, I mean only in odd flashes, and then gone in a minute. I know I got kicked away from the wheel and off the lookout for seeing another vessel and lights, which no one else could see. Though I wasn't the only one.

"It was on the following night that something further happened. Just at the beginning of the middle watch one of the men, called Svensen, fell from aloft and killed Jock, who was passing underneath. And then we heard Jacobs, who had been aloft with Svensen, singing out like mad on the royal yard. When we got up to him he seemed to be fighting with someone or something; but what it was we couldn't see. And he went quiet when we got to him, and so we got him down on deck and into his bunk. After that we took in the main royal, and the Second Mate came with us, to keep us company, because he knew there was something very wrong aloft.

"When we got down again the Old Man sung out to call all hands, and we set to to shorten her down; but up aloft we were all attacked by invisible things that pulled at us, and the whole crowd simply bunked down on deck.

"When the attack began, Jaskett was just below me in the

foregging; but whether I slid over him, or he gave way, I don't know one bit. I only know that I reached the decks, at last, among a crowd of shouting, half-mad sailor men.

"In a confused way, I was conscious that the Skipper and the Mates were down among us, trying to get us into some state of calmness. Eventually they succeeded, and we were told to go aft to the saloon door, which we did in a body. Here the Skipper himself served out a large tot of rum to each of us. Then, at his orders, the Second Mate called the roll.

"He called over the Mate's watch first, and everyone answered. Then he came to ours, and he must have been agitated, for the first name he sung out was Jock's.

"Among us there came a moment of dead silence, and I noticed the wail and moan of the wind aloft, and the flap, flap of the three unfurled t'gallan's'ls.

"The Second Mate called the next name, hurriedly.

" 'Jaskett,' he sung out.

" 'Sir,' Jaskett answered.

" 'Quoin.'

" 'Yes, Sir.'

" 'Jessop.'

" 'Sir,' I replied.

" 'Stubbins.'

"There was no answer.

" 'Stubbins,' again called the Second Mate.

"Again there was no reply.

" 'Is Stubbins here? Anyone: the second's voice sounded sharp and anxious.

"There was a moment's pause. Then one of the men spoke.

" 'He's not here, Sir.'

" 'Who saw him last?' the second asked.

"Plummer stepped forward into the light that streamed through the saloon doorway. He had on neither coat nor cap, and his shirt seemed to be hanging about him in tatters.

" 'It were me, Sir,' he said.

"The Old Man, who was standing next to the Second Mate, took a pace towards him, and stopped and stared; but it was the second who spoke.

" 'Where?' he asked.

" ' 'E were just above me, in ther crosstrees, when, when—' the man broke off short.

" 'Yes—yes!' the Second Mate replied. Then he turned to the Skipper.

" 'Someone will have to go up, Sir, and see—' he hesitated.

" 'But—' said the Old Man, and stopped.

"The Second Mate cut in:

" 'I shall go up, for one, Sir,' he said, quietly.

"Then he turned back to the crowd of us.

" 'Tammy!' he sung out. 'Get a couple of lamps out of the lamp-locker.'

" 'Aye, aye, Sir,' Tammy replied, and ran off.

" 'Now,' said the Second Mate, addressing us. 'I want a couple of men to jump aloft along with me, and take a look for Stubbins.'

"Not a man replied. I would have liked to step out and offer, but the memory of that horrible clutch was with me, and for the life of me I could not summon up the courage.

" 'Come—come, men!' he said. 'We can't leave him up there. We shall take lanterns. Who'll come now?'

"I walked out to the front. I was in a horrible funk; but, for very shame, I could not stand back any longer.

" 'I'll come with you, Sir,' I said, not very loud, and feeling fairly twisted up with nervousness.

" 'That's more the tune, Jessop!' he replied, in a tone that made me glad I had stood out.

"At this point Tammy came up with the lights. He brought them to the second, who took one, and told him to give the other to me. The Second Mate held his light above his head, and looked 'round at the hesitating men.

" 'Now, men,' he sung out, 'you're not going to let Jessop and me go up alone? Come along, another one or two of you. Don't act like a damned lot of cowards!'

"Quoin stood out and spoke for the crowd.

" 'I dunno as we're actin like cowyards, Sir; but just look at 'it!' And he pointed at Plummer, who still stood full in the light from the saloon doorway.

" 'What sort of a thing is it as 'as done that, Sir?' he went on. 'An' then yer arsks us ter go up agen! It aren't likely as we're in a 'urry.'

"The Second Mate looked at Plummer, and surely, as I have before mentioned, the poor beggar was in a state; his ripped-up shirt was fairly flapping in the breeze that came through the doorway.

"The second looked; yet he said nothing. It was as though the realization of Plummer's condition had left him without a word more to say. It was Plummer himself who finally broke the silence.

" 'I'll come with yer, Sir,' he said. 'Only yer ought ter 'ave more light than them two lanterns. 'Twon't be no use, unless we 'as plenty 'er light.'

"The man had grit; I was astonished at his offering to go, after what he must have gone through. Yet I was to have even a greater astonishment; for, abruptly, the Skipper—who all this time had scarcely spoken—stepped forward a pace, and put his hand on the Second Mate's shoulder.

" 'I'll come with you, Mr. Tulipson,' he said.

"The Second Mate twisted his head 'round, and stared at him a moment in astonishment. Then he opened his mouth.

" 'No, Sir; I don't think—' he began.

" 'That's sufficient, Mr. Tulipson,' the Old Man interrupted. 'I've made up my mind.'

"He turned to the First Mate, who had stood by without a word.

" 'Mr. Grainge,' he said, 'take a couple of the 'prentices down with you and pass out a box of blue-lights and some flare-ups.'

"The Mate answered something, and hurried away into the saloon with the two 'prentices in his watch. Then the Old Man spoke to the men.

" 'Now, men,' he began, 'this is no time for dilly-dallying. The Second Mate and I will go aloft, and I want about half a dozen of you to come along with us, and carry lights. Plummer and Jessop here have volunteered. I want four or five more of you. Step out, now, some of you!'

"There was no hesitation whatever now, and the first man to come forward was Quoin. After him followed three of the Mate's crowd, and then old Jaskett.

" 'That will do—that will do,' said the Old Man.

"He turned to the Second Mate.

" 'Has Mr. Grainge come with those lights yet?' he asked, with a certain irritability.

" 'Here, Sir,' said the First Mate's voice, behind him in the saloon doorway. He had the box of blue-lights in his hands, and behind him came the two boys, carrying the flares.

"The Skipper took the box from him, with a quick gesture, and opened it.

" 'Now, one of you men come here,' he ordered.

"One of the men in the Mate's watch ran to him.

"He took several of the lights from the box and handed them to the man.

" 'See here,' he said, 'when we go aloft, you get into the fore-top, and keep one of these going all the time. Do you hear?'

" 'Yes, Sir,' replied the man.

" 'You know how to strike them?' the Skipper asked, abruptly.

" 'Yes, Sir,' he answered.

"The Skipper sung out to the Second Mate:

" 'Where's that boy of yours—Tammy—Mr. Tulipson?'

" 'Here, Sir,' said Tammy, answering for himself.

"The Old Man took another light from the box.

" 'Listen to me boy!' he said. 'Take this, and stand by on the forrard deckhouse. When we go aloft, you must give us a light until the man gets his going in the top. You understand?'

" 'Yes, Sir,' answered Tammy, and took the light.

" 'One minute!' said the Old Man, and stooped and took a second light from the box. 'Your first light may go out before we're ready. You'd better have another in case it does.'

"Tammy took the second light and moved away.

" 'Those flares all ready for lighting there, Mr. Grainge?' the captain asked.

" 'All ready, Sir,' replied the Mate.

"The Old Man pushed one of the blue-lights into his coat pocket and stood upright.

" 'Very well,' he said. 'Give each of the men one apiece. And just see that they all have matches.'

"He spoke to the men particularly:

" 'As soon as we are ready, the other two men in the Mate's watch will get up into the crane lines and keep their flares going there. Take your paraffin tins with you. When we reach the upper topsail, Quoin and Jaskett will get out onto the yardarms and show their flares there. Be careful to keep your lights away from the sails. Plummer and Jessop will come up with the Second Mate and myself. Does every man clearly understand?'

" 'Yes, Sir,' said the men, in a chorus.

"A sudden idea seemed to occur to the Skipper, and he turned and went through the doorway into the saloon. In about a minute he came back, and handed something to the Second Mate that shone in the light from the lanterns. I saw that it was a revolver, and he held another in his other hand; this I saw him put into his side pocket.

"The Second Mate held the pistol a moment, looking a bit doubtful.

" 'I don't think, Sir—' he began. But the Skipper cut him short.

" 'You don't know!' he said. 'Put it in your pocket.'

"Then he turned to the First Mate.

" 'You will take charge of the deck, Mr. Grainge, while we're aloft,' he said.

" 'Aye, aye, Sir,' the Mate answered, and sung out to one of his 'prentices to take the blue-light box back into the cabin, and led the way forrard. As we went the light from the two lanterns shone upon the decks, showing the litter of the t'gallant gear. The ropes were foul of one another in a regular bunch o' buffers. This had been caused, I suppose, by the crowd trampling over them in their excitement when they reached the deck. And then, suddenly, as though the sight had waked me up to a more vivid comprehension, you know, it came to me, new and fresh, how damned strange was the whole business. I got a little touch of despair and asked myself what was going to be the end of all these beastly happenings.

"Abruptly I heard the Skipper shouting, away forrard. He was singing out to Tammy to get up onto the house with his blue-light. We reached the fore rigging, and the same instant the strange, ghastly flare of Tammy's blue-light burst out into the night, causing every rope, sail and spar to jump out weirdly.

"I saw now that the Second Mate was already in the starboard rigging, with his lantern. He was shouting to Tammy to keep the drip from his light clear of the staysail, which was stowed upon the house. Then, from somewhere on the port side, I heard the Skipper shout to us to hurry.

" 'Smartly, now, you men!' he was saying. 'Smartly, now.'

"The man who had been told to take up a station in the foretop was just behind the Second Mate. Plummer was a couple of ratlines lower.

"I caught the Old Man's voice again.

" 'Where's Jessop with that other lantern?' I heard him shout.

" 'Here, Sir,' I sung out.

" 'Bring it over this side,' he ordered. 'You don't want the two lanterns on one side.'

"I ran 'round the fore side of the house. Then I saw him. He was in the rigging and making his way smartly aloft. One of the Mate's watch and Quoin were with him. This I saw as I came 'round the house. Then I made a jump, gripped the sherpole, and swung myself up onto the rail. And then, all at once, Tammy's blue-light went out, and there came what seemed by contrast a pitchy darkness. I stood where I was—one foot on the rail and my knee upon a sherpole.

The light from my lantern seemed no more than a sickly yellow glow against the gloom; and higher, some forty or fifty feet, and a few ratlines below the futtock rigging on the starboard side there was another glow of yellowness in the night. Apart from these, all was blackness. And then from above—high above—there wailed down through the darkness a weird, sobbing cry. What it was, I don't know; but it sounded horrible.

"The Skipper's voice came down jerkily.

" 'Smartly with that light, boy!' he shouted. And the blue glare blazed out again, almost before he had finished speaking.

"I stared up at the Skipper. He was standing where I had seen him before the light went out, and so were the two men. As I looked, he commenced to climb again. I glanced across to starboard. Jaskett and the other man in the Mate's watch were about midway between the deck of the house and the foretop. Their faces showed extraordinarily pale in the dead glare of the blue-light. Higher I saw the Second Mate in the futtock rigging, holding his light up over, the edge of the top. Then he went further and disappeared. The man with the blue-lights followed, and also vanished from view. On the port side, and more directly above me, the Skipper's feet were just stepping out of the futtock shrouds. At that I made haste to follow.

"Then, suddenly, when I was close under the top, there came from above me the sharp flare of a blue-light, and almost in the same instant Tammy's went out. I glanced down at the decks. They were filled with flickering, grotesque shadows cast by the dripping light above. A group of the men stood by the port galley door—their faces upturned and pale and unreal under the gleam of the light. Then I was in the futtock rigging, and a moment afterwards standing in the top, beside the Old Man. He was shouting to the men who had gone out on the crane lines. It seemed that the man on the port side was bungling; but at last—nearly a minute after the other man had lit his flare—he got his going. In that time the man in the top had lit his second blue-light, and we were ready to get into the topmast rigging. First, however, the Skipper leant over the after side of the top, and sung out to the First Mate to send a man up onto the fo'cas'le head with a flare. The Mate replied, and then we started again, the Old Man leading.

"Fortunately, the rain had ceased, and there seemed to be no increase in the wind; indeed, if anything, there appeared to be rather less; yet what there was drove the flames of the flare-ups out into occasional, twisting serpents of fire at least a yard long.

"About half-way up the topmast rigging the Second Mate sung out to the Skipper to know whether Plummer should light his flare; but the Old Man said he had better wait until we reached the crosstrees, as then he could get out, away from the gear, to where there would be less danger of setting fire to anything.

"We neared the crosstrees, and the Old Man stooped and sung out to me to pass him the lantern by Quoin. A few ratlines more and both he and the Second Mate stopped almost simultaneously, holding their lanterns as high as possible, and peered into the darkness.

" 'See any signs of him, Mr. Tulipson?' the Old Man asked.

" 'No, Sir,' replied the second. 'Not a sign.'

"He raised his voice.

" 'Stubbins!' he sung out. 'Stubbins! Are you there?'

"We listened; but nothing came to us beyond the blowing moan of the wind, and the flap, flap of the bellying t'gallant above.

"The Second Mate climbed over the crosstrees, and Plummer followed. The man got out by the royal backstay and lit his flare. By its light we could see plainly; but there was no vestige of Stubbins, so far as the light went.

" 'Get out onto the yardarms with those flares, you two men!' shouted the Skipper. 'Be smart, now! Keep them away from the sail!'

"The men got onto the footropes—Quoin on the port and Jaskett on the starboard side. By the light from Plummer's flare I could see them clearly as they lay out upon the yard. It occurred to me that they went gingerly—which is no surprising thing. And then, as they drew near to the yardarms, they passed beyond the brilliance of the light, so that I could not see them clearly. A few seconds passed, and then the light from Quoin's flare streamed out upon the wind; yet nearly a minute went by, and there was no sign of Jaskett's.

"Then out from the semi-darkness at the starboard yardarm there came a curse from Jaskett, followed almost immediately by a noise of something vibrating.

" 'What's up?' shouted the Second Mate. 'What's up, Jaskett?'

" 'It's ther footrope. Sir—r—r!' He drew out the last word into a sort of gasp.

"The Second Mate bent quickly with the lantern. I craned round the after side of the topmast and looked.

" 'What is the matter, Mr. Tulipson?' I heard the Old Man singing out.

"Out on the yardarm, Jaskett began to shout for help, and then, all at once, in the light from the Second Mate's lantern, I saw that the starboard footrope on the upper topsail yard was being violently shaken—savagely shaken, is perhaps a better word. And then, almost in the same instant, the Second Mate shifted the lantern from his right to his left hand. He put the right into his pocket and brought out his gun with a jerk. He extended his hand and arm, as though pointing at something a little below the yard. Then a quick flash spat out across the shadows, followed immediately by a sharp, ringing report. In the same moment I saw that the footrope ceased to shake.

" 'Light your flare! Light your flare, Jaskett!' the second shouted. 'Be smart, now!'

"Out at the yardarm there came the splutter of a match, and then, straightaway, a great spurt of fire as the flare took light.

" 'That's better, Jaskett. You're all right now!' the Second Mate called out to him.

" 'What was it, Mr. Tulipson?' I heard the Skipper ask.

"I looked up, and saw that he had sprung across to where the Second Mate was standing. The Second Mate explained to him; but he did not speak loud enough for me to catch what he said.

"I had been struck by Jaskett's attitude, when the light of his flare had first revealed him. He had been crouched with his right knee cocked over the yard and his left leg down between it and the footrope, while his elbows had been crooked over the yard for support as he was lighting the flare. Now, however, he had slid both feet back onto the footrope, and was lying on his belly over the yard, with the flare held a little below the head of the sail. It was thus, with the light being on the fore side of the sail, that I saw a small hole a little below the footrope, through which a ray of light shone. It was undoubtedly the hole which the bullet from the Second Mate's revolver had made in the sail. Then I heard the Old Man shouting to Jaskett:

" 'Be careful with that flare, there!' he sung out. 'You'll be having that sail scorched!'

"'He left the Second Mate, and came onto the port side of the mast.

"To my right Plummer's flare seemed to be dwindling. I glanced up at his face through the smoke. He was paying no attention to it; instead he was staring up above his head.

" 'Shove some paraffin onto it, Plummer,' I called to him. 'It'll be out in a minute.'

"He looked down quickly to the light, and did as I suggested. Then he held it out at arm's length, and peered up again into the darkness.

" 'See anything?' asked the Old Man, suddenly observing his attitude.

"Plummer glanced at him, with a start.

" 'It's ther r'yal, Sir,' he explained. 'It's all adrift.'

" 'What!' said the Old Man.

"He was standing a few ratlines up the t'gallant rigging, and he bent his body outwards to get a better look.

" 'Mr. Tulipson!' he shouted. 'Do you know that the royal's all adrift?'

" 'No Sir,' answered the Second Mate. 'If it is, it's more of this devilish work!'

" 'It's adrift, right enough,' said the Skipper, and he and the second went a few ratlines higher, keeping level with one another.

"I had now got above the crosstrees, and was just at the Old Man's heels.

"Suddenly he shouted out:

" 'There he is! Stubbins—Stubbins!'

" 'Where, Sir?' asked the second, eagerly. 'I can't see him!'

" 'There—there!' replied the Skipper, pointing.

"I leant out from the rigging and looked up along his back in the direction his finger indicated. At first I could see nothing; then, slowly, you know, there grew upon my sight a dim figure crouching upon the bunt of the royal, and partly hidden by the mast. I stared, and gradually it came to me that there was a couple of them, and, further out upon the yard, a hump that might have been anything, and was only visible indistinctly amid the flutter of the canvas.

" 'Stubbins!' the Skipper sung out. 'Stubbins, come down out of that! Do you hear me?'

"But no one came, and there was no answer.

" 'There's two—' I began; but he was shouting again:

" 'Come down out of that! Do you damned well hear me?'

"Still there was no reply.

" 'I'm hanged if I can see him at all, Sir!' the Second Mate called out from his side of the mast.

" 'Can't see him!' said the Old Man, now thoroughly angry. 'I'll soon let you see him!'

"He bent down to me with the lantern.

" 'Catch hold, Jessop,' he said, which I did.

"Then he pulled the blue-light from his pocket, and as he was doing so, I saw the second peek round the back side of the mast at him. Evidently, in the uncertain light, he must have mistaken the Skipper's action; for, all at once, he shouted out in a frightened voice:

" 'Don't shoot, Sir! For God's sake, don't shoot!'

" 'Shoot be damned!' exclaimed the Old Man. 'Watch!'

"He pulled off the cap of the light.

" 'There's two of them, Sir,' I called again to him.

" 'What!' he said in a loud voice, and at the same instant he rubbed the end of the light across the cap, and it burst into fire.

"He held it up so that it lit the royal yard like day, and straightaway a couple of shapes dropped silently from the royal on to the t'gallant yard. At the same moment, the humped something, midway out upon the yard, rose up. It ran in to the mast, and I lost sight of it.

" '—God!' I heard the Skipper gasp, and he fumbled in his side pocket.

"I saw the two figures who had dropped on to the t'gallant run swiftly along the yard—one to the starboard and the other to the port yardarms.

"On the other side of the mast, the Second Mate's pistol cracked out twice, sharply. Then, from over my head the Skipper fired twice and then again; but with what effect, I could not tell. Abruptly, as he fired his last shot, I was aware of an indistinct Something gliding down the starboard royal backstay. It was descending full upon Plummer who, all unconscious of the thing, was staring towards the t'gallant yard.

" 'Look out above you, Plummer!' I almost shrieked.

" 'What? where?' he called, and grabbed at the stay, and waved his flare excitedly.

"Down on the upper topsail yard, Quoin's and Jaskett's voices rose simultaneously, and in the identical instant their flares went out. Then Plummer shouted, and his light went utterly. There were left only the two lanterns, and the blue-light held by the Skipper; and that, a few seconds afterwards, finished and died out.

"The Skipper and the Second Mate were shouting to the men upon the yard, and I heard them answer, in shaky voices. Out on the crosstrees I could see by the light from my lantern that Plummer was clinging in a dazed fashion to the backstay.

" 'Are you all right, Plummer?' I called.

" 'Yes,' he said, after a little pause; and then he swore.

" 'Come in off that yard, you men!' the Skipper was singing out. 'Come in! Come in!'

"Down on deck I heard someone calling, but could not distinguish the words. Above me, pistol in hand, the Skipper was glancing about, uneasily.

" 'Hold up that light, Jessop,' he said. 'I can't see!'

"Below us, the men got off the yard, into the rigging.

" 'Down on deck with you!' ordered the Old Man. 'As smartly as you can!'

" 'Come in off there, Plummer!' sung out the Second Mate. 'Get down with the others!'

" 'Down with you, Jessop!' said the Skipper, speaking rapidly. 'Down with you!'

"I got over the crosstrees, and he followed. On the other side, the Second Mate was level with us. He had passed his lantern to Plummer, and I caught the glint of his revolver in his right hand. In this fashion we reached the top. The man who had been stationed there with the blue-lights had gone. Afterwards, I found that he went down on deck as soon as they were finished. There was no sign of the man with the flare on the starboard craneline. He also, I learnt later, had slid down one of the backstays on to the deck, only a very short while before we reached the top. He swore that a great black shadow of a man had come suddenly upon him from aloft. When I heard that, I remembered the thing I had seen descending upon Plummer. Yet the man who had gone out upon the port craneline—the one who had bungled with the lighting of his flare—was still where we had left him, though his light was burning now but dimly.

" 'Come in out of that, you!' the Old Man sung out. 'Smartly now, and get down on deck!'

" 'Aye, aye, Sir,' the man replied, and started to make his way in.

"The Skipper waited until he had got into the main rigging, and then he told me to get down off the top. He was in the act of following, when, all at once, there rose a loud outcry on deck, and then came the sound of a man screaming.

" 'Get out of my way, Jessop!' the Skipper roared, and swung himself down alongside of me.

"I heard the Second Mate shout something from the starboard rigging. Then we were all racing down as hard as we could go. I had caught a momentary glimpse of a man running from the doorway on the port side of the fo'cas'le. In less than half a minute we were upon the deck, and among a crowd of the men who were grouped around something. Yet, strangely enough, they were not looking at the thing among them, but away aft at something—in the darkness.

" 'It's on the rail!' cried several voices.

" 'Overboard!' called somebody, in an excited voice. 'It's jumped over the side!'

" 'Ther' wer'n't nothin'!' said a man in the crowd.

" 'Silence!' shouted the Old Man. 'Where's the Mate? What's happened?'

" 'Here, Sir,' called the First Mate, shakily, from near the centre of the group. 'It's Jacobs, Sir. He—he—'

" 'What!' said the Skipper. 'What!'

" 'He—he's—he's dead—I think!' said the First Mate, in jerks.

" 'Let me see,' said the Old Man, in a quieter tone.

"The men had stood to one side to give him room, and he knelt beside the man upon the deck.

" 'Pass the lantern here, Jessop,' he said.

"I stood by him, and held the light. The man was lying face downwards on the deck. Under the light from the lantern, the Skipper turned him over and looked at him.

" 'Yes,' he said, after a short examination. 'He's dead.'

"He stood up and regarded the body a moment, in silence. Then he turned to the Second Mate, who had been standing by during the last couple of minutes.

" 'Three!' he said, in a grim undertone.

"The Second Mate nodded, and cleared his voice.

"He seemed on the point of saying something; then he turned and looked at Jacobs, and said nothing.

" 'Three,' repeated the Old Man. 'Since eight bells!'

"He stopped and looked again at Jacobs.

" 'Poor devil! Poor devil!' he muttered.

"The Second Mate grunted some of the huskiness out of his throat, and spoke.

" 'Where must we take him?' he asked, quietly. 'The two bunks are full.'

" 'You'll have to put him down on the deck by the lower bunk,' replied the Skipper.

"As they carried him away, I heard the Old Man make a sound that was almost a groan. The rest of the men had gone forward, and I do not think he realized that I was standing by him.

" 'My God! O, my God!' he muttered, and began to walk slowly aft.

"He had cause for groaning. There were three dead, and Stubbins had gone utterly and completely. We never saw him again.

The Shadow in the Sea

"When eight bells went, at four o'clock, and the other watch came on deck to relieve us, it had been broad daylight for some time. Before we went below, the Second Mate had the three t'gallants set; and now that it was light, we were pretty curious to have a look aloft, especially up the fore; and Tom, who had been up to overhaul the gear, was questioned a lot, when he came down, as to whether there were any signs of anything queer up there. But he told us there was nothing unusual to be seen.

"At eight o'clock, when we came on deck for the 8-to-12 watch, I saw the Sailmaker coming forward along the deck from the Second Mate's old berth. He had his rule in his hand, and I knew he had been measuring the poor beggars in there for their burial outfit. From breakfast time until near noon he worked, shaping out three canvas wrappers from some old sailcloth. Then, with the aid of the Second Mate and one of the hands, he brought out the three dead chaps, upon the after hatch, and there sewed them up, with a few lumps of holy stone at their feet. He was just finishing when eight bells went, and I heard the Old Man tell the Second Mate to call all hands aft for the burial. This was done, and one of the gangways unshipped.

"We had no decent grating big enough, so they had to get off one of the hatches, and use it instead. The wind had died away during the morning, and the sea was almost a calm—the ship lifting ever so slightly to an occasional glassy heave. The only sounds that struck on the ear were the soft, slow rustle and occasional shiver of the sails, and the continuous and monotonous creak, creak of the spars and gear at the gentle movements of the vessel. And it was in this solemn half-quietness that the Skipper read the burial service.

"They had put the Dutchman first upon the hatch (I could tell him by his stumpiness), and when at last the Old Man gave the signal, the Second Mate tilted his end, and he slid off, and down into the dark.

" 'Poor old Dutchie,' I heard one of the men say, and I fancy we all felt a bit like that.

"Then they lifted Jacobs on to the hatch, and when he had gone, Jock. When Jock was lifted, a sort of sudden shiver ran through the crowd. He had been a favourite in a quiet way, and I know I felt, all at once, just a bit queer. I was standing by the rail, upon the after bollard, and Tammy was next to me; while Plummer stood a little behind. As the Second Mate tilted the hatch for the last time, a little, hoarse chorus broke from the men:

" 'S'long, Jock! So long, Jock!'

"And then at the sudden plunge, they rushed to the side to see the last of him as he went downwards. Even the Second Mate was not able to resist this universal feeling, and he, too, peered over. From where I had been standing, I had been able to see the body take the water, and now, for a brief couple of seconds, I saw the white of the canvas, blurred by the blue of the water, dwindle and dwindle in the extreme depth. Abruptly, as I stared, it disappeared—too abruptly, it seemed to me.

" 'Gone!' I heard several voices say, and then our watch began to go slowly forward, while one or two of the other started to replace the hatch.

"Tammy pointed, and nudged me.

" 'See, Jessop,' he said. 'What is it?'

" 'What?' I asked.

" 'That queer shadow,' he replied. 'Look!'

"And then I saw what he meant. It was something big and shadowy, that appeared to be growing clearer. It occupied the exact place—so it seemed to me—in which Jock had disappeared.

" 'Look at it!' said Tammy again. 'It's getting bigger!'

"He was pretty excited and so was I.

"I was peering down. The thing seemed to be rising out of the depths. It was taking shape. And as I realized what the shape was, a queer, cold bunk took me.

" 'See,' said Tammy. 'It's just like the shadow of a ship!'

"And it was. The shadow of a ship rising out of the unexplored immensity beneath our keel. Plummer, who had not yet gone forrard, caught Tammy's last remark, and glanced over.

" 'What's 'e mean?' he asked.

" 'That!' replied Tammy, and pointed.

"I jabbed my elbow into his ribs; but it was too late. Plummer had seen. Curiously enough, though, he seemed to think nothing of it.

" 'That ain't nothin', 'cept ther shadder er ther ship,' he said.

"Tammy, after my hint, let it go at that. But when Plummer had gone forrard with the others, I told him not to go telling everything round the decks, like that.

" 'We've got to be thundering careful!' I remarked. 'You know what the Old Man said last watch!'

" 'Yes,' said Tammy. 'I wasn't thinking; but I'll be more careful next time.'

"A little away from me, the Second Mate was still staring down into the water. I turned and spoke to him.

" 'What do you make it out to be, Sir?' I asked.

" 'God knows!' he said, with a quick glance round to see whether any of the men were about.

"He got down from the rail, and turned to go up on to the poop. At the top of the ladder, he leant over the break.

" 'You may as well ship that gangway, you two,' he told us. 'And mind, Jessop, keep your mouth shut about this.'

" 'Aye, aye, Sir,' I answered.

" 'And you too, youngster!' he added, and went aft along the poop.

"Tammy and I were busy with the gangway, when the Second came back. He had brought the Skipper.

" 'Right under the gangway, Sir,' I heard the Second say, and he pointed down into the water.

"For a little while, the Old Man stared. Then I heard him speak.

" 'I don't see anything,' he said.

"At that the Second Mate bent more forward and peered down. So did I; but the thing, whatever it was, had gone completely.

" 'It's gone, Sir,' said the Second. 'It was there right enough when I came for you.'

"About a minute later, having finished shipping the gangway, I was going forrard, when the Second's voice called me back.

" 'Tell the captain what it was you saw just now,' he said in a low voice.

" 'I can't say exactly, Sir,' I replied. 'But it seemed to me like the shadow of a ship, rising up through the water.'

" 'There, Sir,' remarked the Second Mate to the Old Man. "Just what I told you.'

"The Skipper stared at me.

" 'You're quite sure?' he asked.

" 'Yes, Sir,' I answered. 'Tammy saw it too.'

"I waited a minute. Then they turned to go aft. The Second was saying something.

" 'Can I go, Sir?' I asked.

" 'Yes, that will do, Jessop,' he said, over his shoulder. But the Old Man came back to the break, and spoke to me.

" 'Remember, not a word of this forrard!' he said.

" 'No, Sir,' I replied, and he went back to the Second Mate; while I walked forrard to the fo'cas'le to get something to eat.

" 'Your whack's in the kid, Jessop,' said Tom, as I stepped in over the washboard. 'An' I got your limejuice in my pannikin.'

" 'Thanks,' I said, and sat down.

"As I stowed away my grub, I took no notice of the chatter of the others. I was too stuffed with my own thoughts. That shadow of a vessel rising, you know, out of the profound depths, had impressed me tremendously. It had not been imagination. Three of us had seen it—really four; for Plummer distinctly saw it, though he failed to recognize it as anything extraordinary.

"As you can understand, I thought a lot about this shadow of a vessel. But, I am sure, for a time, my ideas must just have gone in an everlasting, blind circle. And then I got another thought; for I got thinking of the figures I had seen aloft in the early morning; and I began to imagine fresh things. You see, the first thing that had come up over the side had come out of the sea. And it had gone back. And now there was this shadow vessel-thing—ghost-ship I called it. It was a damned good name, too. And the dark, noiseless men—I thought a lot on these lines. Unconsciously, I put a question to myself, aloud:

" 'Were they the crew?'

" 'Eh?' said Jaskett, who was on the next chest.

"I took hold of myself, as it were, and glanced at him, in an apparently careless manner.

" 'Did I speak?' I asked.

" 'Yes, mate,' he replied, eyeing me, curiously. 'Yer said sumthin' about a crew.'

" 'I must have been dreaming,' I said; and rose up to put away my plate.

The Great Ghost Ship

"Next morning, when we were called again, at a quarter to four, the man who had roused us out, had some queer information.

" 'Toppin's gone—clean vanished!' he told us as we began to turn out. 'I never was in such a damned, hair-raisin' hooker as this here. It ain't safe to go about the bloomin' decks.'

" ' 'Oo's gone?' asked Plummer, sitting up suddenly and throwing his legs over his bunk-board.

" 'Toppin, one of the 'prentices,' replied the man. 'We've been huntin' all over the bloomin' show. We're still at it—but we'll never find him,' he ended with a sort of gloomy assurance.

" 'Oh, I dunno,' said Quoin. 'P'raps 'e's snoozin' somewheres 'bout.'

" 'Not him,' replied the man. 'I tell you we've turned everythin' upside down. He's not aboard the bloomin' ship.'

" 'Where was he when they last saw him?' I asked. 'Someone must know something, you know!'

" 'Keepin' time up on the poop,' he replied. 'The Old Man's nearly shook the life out of the Mate and the chap at the wheel. And they say they don't know nothin'.'

" 'How do you mean?' I inquired. 'How do you mean, nothing?'

" 'Well,' he answered. 'The youngster was there one minute, and then the next they knew, he'd gone. They've both sworn black an' blue that there wasn't a whisper, he's just disappeared off of the face of the bloomin' earth.'

"I got down on to my chest, and reached for my boots.

"Before I could speak again, the man was saying something fresh.

" 'See here, mates,' he went on. 'If things is goin' on like this, I'd like to know where you an' me'll be befor' long!'

" 'We'll be in 'ell,' said Plummer.

" 'I dunno as I like to think 'bout it,' said Quoin.

" 'We'll have to think about it!' replied the man. 'We've got to think a bloomin' lot about it. I've talked to our side, an' they're game.'

" 'Game for what?' I asked.

" 'To go an' talk straight to the bloomin' Capting,' he said, wagging his finger at me. 'It's make tracks for the nearest bloomin' port, an' don't you make no bloomin' mistake.'

"I opened my mouth, to tell him that the probability was we should not be able to make it, even if he could get the Old Man to see the matter from his point of view. Then I remembered that the chap had no idea of the things I had seen and thought out; so, instead, I said:

" 'Supposing he won't?'

" 'Then we'll have to bloomin' well make him,' he replied.

" 'And when you got there,' I said, 'What then? You'd be jolly well locked up for mutiny.'

" 'I'd sooner be locked up,' he said. 'It don't kill you!'

"There was a murmur of agreement from the others, and then a moment of silence, in which, I know, the men were thinking.

"Jaskett's voice broke into it.

" 'I never thought at first as she was 'aunted—' he commenced; but Plummer cut in across his speech.

" 'We mustn't 'urt anyone, yer know,' he said. 'That'd mean 'angin', an' they ain't been er bad crowd.'

" 'No,' assented everyone, including the chap who had come to call us.

" 'All the same,' he added. 'It's got to be up helm an' shove her into the nearest bloomin' port.'

" 'Yes,' said everyone, and then eight bells went, and we cleared out on deck.

"Presently, after roll-call—in which there had come a queer, awkward little pause at Toppin's name—Tammy came over to me. The rest of the men had gone forrard, and I guessed they were talking over mad plans for forcing the Skipper's hand, and making him put into port—poor beggars!

"I was leaning over the port rail, by the fore brace block, staring down into the sea, when Tammy came to me. For perhaps a minute he said nothing. When at last he spoke, it was to say that the shadow vessels had not been there since daylight.

" 'What,' I said, in some surprise. 'How do you know?'

" 'I woke up when they were searching for Toppins,' he replied. 'I've not been asleep since. I came here, right away.' He began to say something further; but stopped short.

" 'Yes,' I said encouragingly.

" 'I didn't know—' he began, and broke off. He caught my arm. 'Oh, Jessop!' he exclaimed. 'What's going to be the end of it all! Surely something can be done?'

"I said nothing. I had a despairing feeling that there was very little we could do to help ourselves.

" 'Can't we do something?' he asked, and shook my arm. 'Anything's better than this! We're being murdered!'

"Still, I said nothing; but stared moodily down into the water. I could find nothing convincing to tell him.

" 'Do you hear!' he said. He was almost crying.

" 'Yes, Tammy,' I replied. 'But I don't know! I don't know!'

" 'You don't know!' he exclaimed. 'You don't know! Do you mean we're just to give in, and be murdered one after another?'

" 'We've done all we can,' I replied. 'I don't know what else we can do, unless we go below and lock ourselves in, every night.'

" 'That would be better than this,' he said. 'There'll be no one to go below, or anything else, soon!'

" 'But what if it came on to blow?' I asked. 'We'd be having the sticks blown out of her.'

" 'What if it came on to blow now?' he returned. 'No one would go aloft, if it were dark. Beside, we could shorten her right down first. I tell you, in a few days there won't be a chap alive aboard this packet, unless they jolly well do something!'

" 'Don't shout,' I warned him. 'You'll have the Old Man hearing you.' But the young beggar was wound up, and would take no notice.

" 'I will shout,' he replied. 'I want the Old Man to hear. I've a good mind to go up and tell him.'

"He started on a fresh tack.

" 'Why don't the men do something!' he began. 'They ought to damn well make the Old Man put us into port! They ought—'

" 'For goodness' sake shut up, you little fool!' I said. 'What's the good of talking a lot of damned rot like that? You'll be getting yourself into trouble."

" 'I don't care,' he replied. 'I'm not going to be murdered.'

" 'Look here,' I said. "I told you before that we shouldn't be able to see the land, even if we made it.'

" 'You've no proof,' he answered. 'It's only your idea.'

" 'Well,' I replied. 'Proof, or no proof, the Skipper would only pile her up, if he tried to make the land, with things as they are now.'

" 'Let him pile her up,' he answered. 'Let him jolly well pile her up! That would be better than staying out here to be pulled overboard, or chucked down from aloft!"

" 'Look here, Tammy—' I began; but just then the Second Mate sung out for him, and he had to go. When he came back, I had started to walk to and fro, across the fore side of the mainmast. He joined me, and after a minute he started his wild talk again.

" 'Look here, Tammy,' I said once more. 'It's no use your talking like you've been doing. Things are as they are, and it's no one's fault, and nobody can help it. If you want to talk sensibly, I'll listen; if not, then go and gas to someone else.'

"With that I returned to the port side, and got up on the spar again, intending to sit on the pin rail, and have a bit of a talk with him. Before sitting down, I glanced over into the sea. The action had been almost mechanical; yet, after a few instants, I was in a state of the most intense excitement, and without withdrawing my gaze, I reached out and caught Tammy's arm to attract his attention.

" 'My God!' I muttered. 'Look!'

" 'What is it?' he asked, and bent over the rail beside me. And this is what we saw: A little distance below the surface there lay a pale-coloured, slightly-domed disk. It seemed only a few feet down. Below it we saw quite clearly, after a few moments staring, the shadow of a royal yard, and below it the gear and standing-rigging of a great mast. Far down among the shadows, I thought, presently, that I could make out the immense, indefinite stretch of vast decks.

"Tammy gave out a short exclamation, as though an idea had come to him; and got down off the spar, and ran forrard on to the fo'cas'le head. He came running back, after a short look into the sea, to tell me that there was the truck of another great mast coming up there, a bit off the bow, to within a few feet of the surface of the sea.

"In the meantime, you know, I had been staring like mad down through the water at the huge, shadowy mast just below me. I had traced out bit by bit, until now I could clearly see the jackstay, running along the top of the royal mast; and, you know, the royal itself was set.

"But, you know, what was getting at me, more than anything, was a feeling that there was movement down in the water there, among the rigging. I thought I could actually see, at times, things moving and glinting faintly and rapidly to and fro in the gear. And once, I know, I was practically certain that something was on the royal yard, moving in to the mast; as though, you know, it might have come up the leech of the sail. And this way I got a beastly feeling that there were things swarming down there.

"Unconsciously, I must have leant further and further out over the side, staring; and, suddenly—good Lord! how I yelled!—I overbalanced. I made a sweeping grab, and caught the fore brace, and with that I was back in a moment upon the spar. In the same second, almost, it seemed to me that the surface of the water above the submerged truck was broken, and I am sure now I saw something a moment in the air against the ship's side—a sort of shadow in the air, though I did not realize it at the time. Anyway, the next instant, Tammy gave out an awful scream, and was head downwards over the rail in a moment. I had an idea then that he was jumping overboard. I collared him by the waist of his britches and one knee, and then I had him down on the deck and sat plump on him, for he was struggling and shouting all the time, and I was so breathless and shaken and gone to mush I could not have trusted my hands to hold him. You see, I never thought then it was anything but some influence at work on him, and that he was trying to get loose to go over the side. But I know now that I saw the shadow-man that had him. Only, at the time, I was so mixed up and with the one idea in my head, I was not really able to notice anything properly. But, afterwards, I comprehended a bit (you can understand, can't you?) what I had seen at the time without taking in.

"And even now, looking back, I know that the shadow was only like a faint-seen greyness in the daylight, against the whiteness of the decks, clinging against Tammy.

"And there was I, all breathless and sweating and quivery with my own tumble, sitting on the little, screaching beggar, and he fighting like a mad thing, so that I thought I should never hold him. And then I heard the Second Mate shouting, and there came running feet along the deck. Then many hands were pulling and hauling to get me off him.

" 'Bl—dy cowyard!' sung out someone.

" 'Hold him! Hold him!' I shouted. 'He'll be overboard!'

"At that, they seemed to understand that I was not ill-treating the youngster, for they stopped mishandling me and allowed me to rise, while two of them took hold of Tammy and kept him safe.

" 'What's the matter with him?' the Second Mate was singing out. 'What's happened?'

" 'He's gone off his head, I think,' I said.

" 'What?' asked the Second Mate. But before I could answer him Tammy ceased suddenly to struggle, and flopped down upon the deck.

" ' 'E's fainted,' said Plummer, with some sympathy. He looked at me with a puzzled, suspicious air. 'What's 'appened? What's 'e been doin'?'

" 'Take him aft into the berth!' ordered the Second Mate, a bit abruptly. It struck me that he wished to prevent questions. He must have tumbled to the fact that we had seen something, about which it would be better not to tell the crowd.

"Plummer stooped to lift the boy.

" 'No,' said the Second Mate. 'Not you, Plummer. Jessop, you take him.' He turned to the rest of the men. 'That will do,' he told them, and they went forrard, muttering a little.

"I lifted the boy, and carried him aft.

" 'No need to take him into the berth,' said the Second Mate. 'Put him down on the after hatch. I've sent the other lad for some brandy.'

"When the brandy came we dosed Tammy, and soon brought him 'round. He sat up, with a somewhat dazed air. Otherwise he seemed quiet and sane enough.

" 'What's up?' he asked. He caught sight of the Second Mate. 'Have I been ill, Sir?' he exclaimed.

" 'You're all right now, youngster,' said the Second Mate. 'You've been a bit faint. You'd better go and lie down for a bit.'

" 'I'm all right now, Sir,' replied Tammy. 'I don't think—'

" 'You do as you're told!' interrupted the second. 'Don't always have to be told twice. If I want you, I'll send for you.'

"Tammy stood up, and made his way, in rather an unsteady fashion, into the berth. I fancy he was glad enough to lie down.

" 'Now, then, Jessop,' exclaimed the Second Mate, turning to me. 'What's been the cause of all this? Out with it now—smart!'

"I commenced to tell him; but almost directly he put up his hand.

" 'Hold on a minute,' he said. 'There's the breeze!'

"He jumped up the port ladder, and sung out to the chap at the wheel. Then down again.

" 'Starboard fore brace!' he sung out. He turned to me. 'You'll have to finish telling me afterwards,' he said.

" 'Aye, aye, Sir,' I replied, and went to join the other chaps at the braces.

"As soon as we were braced sharp up on the port tack, he sent some of the watch up to loose the sails. Then he sung out for me.

" 'Go on with your yarn, now, Jessop,' he said.

"I told him about the great shadow vessel, and I said something about Tammy—I mean, about my not being sure now whether he had tried to jump overboard. Because, you see, I began to realize that I had seen the shadow; and I remembered the stirring of the water above the submerged truck. But the second never waited, of course, for any theories; but was away, like a shot, to see for himself. He ran to the side and looked down. I followed and stood beside him; yet, now that the surface of the water was blurred by the wind, we could see nothing.

" 'It's no good,' he remarked, after a minute. 'You'd better get away from the rail before any of the others see you. Just be taking those haulyards aft to the capstan.'

"From then until eight bells, we were hard at work netting the sail upon her, and when at last eight bells went I made haste to swallow my breakfast and get a sleep.

"At midday, when we went on deck for the afternoon watch, I ran to the side; but there was no sign of the great shadow ship. All that watch, the Second Mate kept me working at my paunch mat, and Tammy he put on to his sinnet, telling me to keep an eye on the youngster. But the boy was right enough, as I scarcely doubted now, you know; though—most unusual thing—he hardly opened his lips the whole afternoon. Then, at four o'clock, we went below for tea.

"At four bells, when we came on deck again, I found that the light breeze which had kept us going during the day had dropped, and we were only just moving. The sun was low down and the sky clear. Once or twice, as I glanced across the horizon, it seemed to me that I caught again the odd quiver in the air that had preceded the coming of the mist; and, indeed, on two separate occasions, I saw a thin wisp of haze drive up, apparently out of the sea. This was at some little distance on our port beam; otherwise, all was quiet and peaceful, and, though I peered into the sea, I could make out no vestige of that great shadow ship in the deep.

"It was some little time after six bells, that the order came for all hands to shorten sail for the night. We took in the royals and t'gallants, and then the three courses. It was shortly after this that a rumour went 'round the ship that there was to be no lookout that night after eight o'clock. This naturally created a good deal of talk among the men; especially as the yarn went that the fo'cas'le doors were to be shut and fastened as soon as it was dark, and that no one was to be allowed on deck.

" ' 'Oo's goin' ter take ther wheels?' I heard Plummer ask.

" 'I s'pose they'll 'ave us take 'em as usual,' replied one of the men. 'One of ther officers is bound ter be on the poop, so we'll 'ave company.'

"Apart from these remarks, there was a general opinion that—if it were true—it was a sensible act on the part of the Skipper. As one of the men said:

" 'It ain't likely as there'll be any of us missin' in ther mornin' if we stays in our bunks all ther blessed night.'

"And soon after this, eight bells went.

The Ghost Pirates

"At the moment when eight bells actually went I was in the fo'cas'le, talking to three or four of the other watch. Suddenly, away aft, I heard shouting, and then on the deck overhead came the loud thudding of someone pomping with a capstan-bar. Straightaway, I turned and made a run for the port doorway, along with the four other men. We rushed out through the doorway onto the deck. It was getting dusk, but that did not hide from me a terrible and extraordinary sight. All along the port rail there was a queer, undulating greyness, that moved downwards inboard, and spread over the decks. As I looked, I found that I saw more clearly, in a most extraordinary way. And, suddenly, all the moving greyness resolved into hundreds of strange men. In the half-light they looked unreal and impossible, as though there had come upon us the inhabitants of some fantastic dream-world. My God! I thought I was mad. They swarmed in upon us in a great wave of murderous, living shadows. From some of the men, who must have been going aft for roll-call, there rose in the evening air a loud, awful shouting.

" 'Aloft!' yelled someone; but, as I looked aloft, I saw that the horrible things were swarming there in scores and scores.

" 'Jesus Christ!' shrieked a man's voice, cut short, and my glance dropped from aloft, to find two of the men who had come out from the fo'cas'le with me, rolling upon the deck. They were two indistinguishable masses that writhed here and there across the planks. The brutes fairly covered them. From them came muffled, little shrieks and gasps; and there I stood, and with me two other men. A man dashed past us into the fo'cas'le, with two grey men on his back, and I heard them kill him. The two men by me ran, suddenly, across the fore hatch, and up the starboard ladder onto the fo'cas'le head. Yet, almost in the same instant, I saw several of the grey men disappear up the other ladder. From the fo'cas'le head above, I heard the two men commence to shout, and this died away into a loud scuffling. At that I turned to see whether I could get away. I stared 'round hopelessly, and then, with two jumps, I was on the pigsty, and from there upon the top of the deckhouse. I threw myself flat, and waited, breathlessly.

"All at once, it seemed to me that it was darker than it had been the previous moment, and I raised my head very cautiously. Then I saw that the ship was enveloped in great billows of mist, and then, not six feet from me, I made out someone lying face downwards. It was Tammy. I felt safer, now that we were hidden by the mist, and I crawled to him. He gave a quick gasp of terror when I touched him; but when he saw who it was he started to sob, like a little child.

" 'Hush!' I said. 'For God's sake, be quiet!' But I need not have troubled, for the shrieks of the men being killed, down on the decks all around us, drowned every other sound.

"I knelt up and glanced round, and then aloft. Overhead I could make out dimly the spars and sails, and now, as I looked, I saw that the t'gallants and royals had been unloosed and were hanging in the buntlines. Almost in the same moment the terrible crying of the poor beggars about the decks ceased, and there succeeded an awful silence, in which I could distinctly hear Tammy sobbing. I reached out and shook him.

" 'Be quiet! Be quiet!' I whispered, intensely. 'They'll hear us!'

"At my touch and whisper he struggled to become silent, and then, overhead, I saw the six yards being swiftly mast-headed. Scarcely were the sails set when I heard the swish and flick of gaskets being cast adrift on the lower yards, and realized that ghostly things were at work there.

"For a minute or so there was silence, and I made my way cautiously to the after end of the house, and peered over. Yet, because of the mist, I could see nothing. Then, abruptly, from behind me, came a single wail of sudden pain and terror from Tammy. It ended instantly in a sort of choke. I stood up in the mist and ran back to where I had left the kid; but he had gone. I stood dazed. I felt like shrieking out loud. Above me, I heard the flaps of the courses being tumbled off the yards. Down upon the decks there were the noises of a multitude working in a weird, inhuman silence. Then came the squeal and rattle of blocks and braces aloft. They were squaring the yards.

"I remained standing. I watched the yards squared, and then I saw the sails fill suddenly. An instant afterwards the deck of the house upon which I stood became slanted forrard. The slope increased, so that I could scarcely stand, and I grabbed at one of the wire-winches. I wondered what was happening. Almost directly afterwards, from the decks around, rose a loud, simultaneous, hoarse crying. This grew into an intense screaming that shook my heart up. Then a breath of cold wind seemed to play in the mist, and I could see down the slope of the deck. I looked below me, towards the bows. The jibboom was plunged right into the water, and as I stared the bows disappeared into the sea. The deck of the house became a wall to me, and I was swinging from the winch, which was now above my head. I watched the ocean lip over the edge of the fo'cas'le head, and rush down onto the main deck, roaring into the empty fo'cas'le. And still all around me came the crying of the lost sailormen. I heard something strike the corner of the house above me, with a dull thud, and then I saw Plummer plunge down into the flood beneath. I remembered that he had been at the wheel. The next instant the water had leapt to my feet; there came a drear chorus of bubbling screams, a roar of waters, and I was going swiftly down into the darkness. I let go of the winch and struck out madly, trying to hold my breath. There was a loud singing in my ears. It grew louder. I opened my mouth. I felt I was dying. And then, thank God!, I was at the surface, breathing. For a moment I was blinded with the water, and my agony of breathlessness. Then, growing easier, I brushed the water from my eyes, and so, not three hundred yards away, I made out a large ship, floating almost motionless. At first, I could scarcely believe I saw aright. Then, as I realized that indeed there was yet a chance of living, I started to swim towards you.

"You know the rest—"

Carnacki, the Ghost Finder

"NOW," SAID CARNACKI REMINISCENTLY, "I'll tell you some of my experiences. In that case of 'The House Among the Laurels,' which was supposed to be haunted, and had a 'blood-drip' that warned you, I spent a night there with some Irish constabulary. Wentworth, who owned the place, was with me, and I drew a pentacle round the lot of us in the big hall and put portions of bread and jars of water and candles round it. Then I fixed up the electric pentacle and put a tent over us, and we waited with our weapons. I had two dogs out in the hall with us, and I had sealed all the doors except the main entrance, which I had hooked open. Suddenly I saw the hook of the door slowly raised by some invisible thing, and I immediately took a flashlight photograph. Then the door was slowly closed. Perhaps an hour and a half of absolute silence passed, except when once in a while the dogs would whine distressfully. Then I saw that the candle before one of the sealed doors had been put out, and then, one after another, every candle in the great hall was extinguished, except those round the pentacle.

"Another hour passed, and in all that time no sound broke the stillness. I was conscious of a sense of awful strain and oppression, as though I were a little spirit in the company of some invisible brooding monster of the unseen world who, as yet, was scarcely conscious of us. I could not get rid of this sense of a presence, and I leaned across to Wentworth and asked him in a whisper whether he had a feeling as if something was in the room. He looked very pale and his eyes kept always on the move. He glanced just once at me and nodded, then stared away round the hall again. And, when I came to think, I was doing the same thing. Abruptly, as though a hundred unseen hands had snuffed them, every candle in the barrier went dead out, and we were left in a darkness that seemed, for a little, absolute, for the fire had sunk into a low, dull mound of red, and the light from the pentacle was too weak and pale to penetrate far across the great hall. I tell you, for a moment, I just sat there as though I had been frozen solid. I felt the 'creep' go all over me, and it seemed to stop in my brain. I felt all at once to be given a power of hearing that was far beyond the normal. I could hear my own heart thudding most extraordinarily loud. I began to feel better after a little, but I simply had not the pluck to move. Presently I began to get my courage back. I gripped at my camera and flashlight and waited. My hands were simply soaked with sweat. I glanced once at Wentworth. I could see him only dimly. His shoulders were hunched a little, his head forward, but, though it was motionless, I knew that his eyes were not. The other men were just as silent. And thus a while passed.

"A sudden sound broke across the silence. From three sides of the room there came faint noises. I recognized them at once—the breaking of sealing wax. The sealed doors were opening. I raised the camera and flashlight, and it was a peculiar mixture of fear and courage that helped me to press the button. As the great flare of light lit up the hall, I felt the men all about me jump. It was thoughtless of me perhaps to have fired it without warning them, but there was no time even if I had remembered. The darkness fell again, but seemingly tenfold. Yet, in the moment of brightness, I had seen that all the sealed doors were wide open.

"Suddenly, upon the top of the tent, there sounded a drip, drip, drip, falling on the canvas. I thrilled with a queer, realizing emotion and a sense of very real and present danger—imminent. The 'blood-drip' had commenced. And the grave question was, would the pentacles and the circles save us?

"Through some awful minutes the 'blood-drip' continued to fall in an ever-increasing rain. Beyond this noise there was no other sound. And then, abruptly, from the boarhound farthest from the entrance there came a terrible yelling howl of agony followed, instantly, by a sickening, snicking, breaking noise and an abrupt silence. If you have ever, when out shooting, broken a rabbit's neck, you'll know the sound—in miniature. Like lightning the thought sprang into my brain: it has crossed the pentacle. For, you will remember that I had made one about each of the dogs. I thought instantly, with sickening apprehension, of our own barrier. There was something in the hall with us that had passed the barrier of the pentacle about one of the dogs. In the awful succeeding silence, I positively quivered. And suddenly one of the men behind me gave out a scream, like any woman, and bolted for the door. He fumbled and had it open in a moment. I yelled to the others not to move, but they followed like sheep. I heard them kick the water jars in their panic, and one of them stepped on the electric pentacle and smashed it. In a moment I realized that I was defenceless against the powers of the unknown world, and with one leap I followed, and we raced down the drive like frightened boys.

"Well, we cooled down in a bit, and I went to the inn where I was staying and developed my photos. Then, in one of them, I saw that a wire was juggling with the hook of the entrance door, so I went back to the house and got in quietly through a back window and found a whole lot of chaps who had just come out of a secret doorway. They proved to be members of a secret society. They all escaped, but I guess I laid the ghost. You see, they were trying to keep the house empty for their own uses.

"Then in that business of 'The Gateway of the Monster' I spent a night in the haunted bedroom alone in the electric pentacle, and very nearly got snuffed out, as you'll see. I had a cat die in the room. This is what happened: I had been in the pentacle some time, just like in the last business, only quite alone, when, suddenly, I was aware of a cold wind sweeping over me. It seemed to come from the corner of the room to the left of the bed—the place where both times I had found the bedclothes tossed in a heap. Yet I could see nothing unusual—no opening—nothing. And then, abruptly, I was aware that the candles were all aflicker in the unnatural wind. I believe I just squatted there and stared in a sort of horribly frightened, wooden way for some minutes. And then flick! flick! flick! all the candles round the outer barrier went out, and there I was locked and sealed in that room, and with no light beyond the queer weakish blue glare of the electric pentacle. Still that wind blew upon me, and then, suddenly, I knew that something stirred in the corner next to the bed. I was made conscious of it rather by some inward, unused sense than by the sight or sound, for the pale, short-radius glare of the pentacle gave but a very poor light to see by. Yet I stared and stared, and abruptly it began to grow upon my sight— a moving something, a little darker than the surrounding shadows. I lost the vague sight I had of it, and for a moment or two I glanced swiftly from side to side with a fresh new sense of impending danger. Then my attention was directed to the bed. All the coverings were being drawn steadily off with a hateful, stealthy sort of motion. I heard the slow, dragging slither of the clothes, but I could see nothing of the thing that pulled.

"The faint noises from the bed ceased once, and there was a most intense silence. The slurring sound of the bedclothes being dragged off recommenced. And then, you know, all in a moment, the whole of the bed coverings were torn off with extraordinary violence, and I heard the flump they made as they were hurled into the corner.

"There was a time of absolute quietness then for perhaps a couple of minutes, and none can imagine how horribly I felt. Then, over by the door, I heard a faint noise—a sort of crickling sound, and then a patter or two upon the floor. A great nervous thrill swept over me, for the seal that secured the door had just been broken. Something was there. And then it seemed to me that something dark and indistinct moved and wavered there among the shadows. Abruptly, I was aware that the door was opening. I reached out for my camera, but before I could aim it the door was slammed with a terrific crash that filled the whole room with a sort of hollow thunder. There seemed such a power behind the noise, as though a vast, wanton force were 'out.' The door was not touched again, but directly afterwards I heard the basket, in which the cat lay, creak. I tell you I fairly pringled. Now, at last, I should learn definitely whether whatever was abroad was dangerous to life. From the cat there rose suddenly a hideous caterwaul that ceased abruptly, and then—too late—I snapped on the flashlight. In the great glare I saw that the basket had been overturned and the lid was wrenched open, with the cat lying half-in and half-out upon the floor. I saw nothing else. But I was full of the knowledge that I was in the presence of some being or thing that had power to destroy.

"I was half-blinded because of the flashlight. Abruptly I saw the thing I was looking for close to the 'water-circle.' It was big and indistinct and wavered curiously, as though the shadow of a vast spider hung suspended in the air just beyond the barrier. It passed swiftly round the circle and seemed to probe ever toward me, but only to draw back with extraordinary jerky movements, as might a living person if he touched the hot bar of a grate. Round and round it moved, and round and round I turned. Then, just opposite to one of the 'vales' in the pentacles, it seemed to pause, as though preliminary to a tremendous effort. It retired almost beyond the circle of the pentacle's glow and then came straight toward me, appearing to gather form and solidity as it came. I got a most terrible feeling of horror, for there seemed such a vast malign determination behind the movement that it must succeed. I was on my knees, and I fell over onto my left hand and hip in a wild endeavor to get back from the advancing thing. With my right hand I was grabbing madly for my revolver, though, as you can imagine, my look never left the horrible thing. The brutal thing came with one great sweep straight over the garlic and the 'water-circle' right almost to the pentacle. I believe I yelled. Then, just as suddenly as it had swept over, it seemed to be hurled back by some mighty invisible force. I'd learnt something. I knew now that the grey room was haunted by a monstrous hand!

"Suddenly I saw what had so nearly given the monster an opening through the barrier. In my movements within the pentacle I must have touched one of the jars of water for, just where the thing had made its attack, the jar that guarded the 'deep' of the 'vale' had been moved to one side, and this had left one of the five 'doorways' unguarded. I put it back quickly and felt almost safe again. The 'defense' was still good and I began to hope again I should see the morning come in.

"For a long time I could not see the hand, but presently I thought I saw, once or twice, an odd wavering over among the shadows near the door. Then, as though in a sudden fit of malignant rage, the dead body of the wretched cat was picked up and beaten with dull, sickening blows against the solid floor. A minute afterwards the door was opened and slammed twice with tremendous force. The next instant, the thing made one swift, vicious dart straight at me from out of the shadows. Instinctively I started sideways from it, and so plucked my hand from upon the electric pentacle where, for a wickedly careless moment, I had placed it. The monster was hurled off from the neighborhood of the pentacles, though, owing to my inconceivably foolish act, it had been enabled for a second time to pass the outer barriers. I can tell you I shook for a time with sheer funk. Then I moved right to the center of the pentacles and knelt there, making myself as small and compact as possible.

"I spent the rest of that night in a haze of sick fright. At times the ghastly thing would go round and round the outer ring, grabbing in the air at me, and twice the dead cat was molested. Then the dawn came and the unnatural wind ceased. I jumped over the pentacles, and in ten seconds I was out of the room and safe. That day I found a queer ring in the corner from which the wind had come, and I knew it had something to do with the haunting, so that night I stayed in the pentacle again, having the ring with me. About eleven o'clock a queer knowledge came that something was near to me, and then an hour later I felt the wind blow up from the floor within the pentacle, and I looked down.

"I continued to stare down. The ring was there, and suddenly I was aware that there was something queer about it—funny, shadowy movements and convolutions. I stared stupidly, though alert enough to fear, and then abruptly I knew that the wind was blowing up at me from the ring. A queer, indistinct smoke became visible, seeming to pour upward through the ring. Suddenly I realized that I was in more than mortal danger, for the convoluting shadows about the ring were taking shape and the death-hand was forming within the pentacle. It was coming through, pouring through into the material world, even as a gas might pour out from the mouth of a pipe. With a mad awkward movement, I snatched the ring, intending to hurl it out of the pentacle; yet it eluded me, as though some invisible, living thing jerked it hither and thither. At last I gripped it, yet in the same instant it was torn from my grasp with incredible and brutal force. A great black shadow covered it and rose into the air and came at me. I saw that it was the hand, vast and nearly perfect in form. I gave one crazy yell and jumped over the pentacle and the ring of burning candles, and ran despairingly for the door. I fumbled idiotically and ineffectually with the key, and all the time I stared with a fear that was like insanity toward the barriers. The hand was plunging toward me; yet, even as it had been unable to pass into the pentacle when the ring was without, so, now that the ring was within, it had no power to pass out. The monster was chained, as surely as any beast would be were chains riveted upon it. I got the door open at last and locked it behind me and went to my bedroom. Next day I melted that thing, and the ghost has never been heard of since. Not bad, eh?

"Another case of mine—'The Horse of the Invisible'—was very queer. It was supposed, according to tradition, to haunt the daughter of a certain house during courtship. This began happening with the present generation, so they sent for me. After a lot of queer hauntings and attacks, I had decided to guard the girl closely and get the marriage performed quickly. On the last night, as I, with a Mr. Beaumont, was sitting outside of her door keeping guard, my companion motioned suddenly to me for absolute quiet. Directly afterward I heard the thing for which he listened—the sound of a horse galloping out in the night. I tell you, I fairly shivered. Some five minutes passed, full of what seemed like an almost unearthly quiet. And then suddenly, down the corridor, there sounded the clumping of a great hoof, and instantly the lamp was thrown down with a tremendous smash, and we were in the dark. I tugged hard on the cord and blew the whistle, then I raised my camera and fired the flashlight. The corridor blazed into brilliant light, but there was nothing, and then the darkness fell like thunder. >From up the corridor there came abruptly the horrible gobbling neighing that we had heard in the park and the cellar. I blew the whistle again and groped blindly for the cord, shouting in a queer, breathless voice to Beaumont to strike a match before that incredible, unseen monster was upon us. The match scraped on the box and flared up dully, and in the same instant I heard a faint sound behind me. I whipped round, wet and tense with terror, and saw something in the faint light of the match—a monstrous horse head—close to Beaumont.

" 'Look out, Beaumont!' I shouted in a sort of scream. 'It's behind you!'

"The match went out abruptly, and instantly there came the huge bang of a double-barreled gun—both barrels at once—fired close to my ear. I caught a momentary glimpse of the great head in the flash, and of an enormous hoof amid the belch of smoke, seeming to be descending upon Beaumont. There was a sound of a dull blow, and then that horrible, gobbling neigh broke out close to me. Something struck me and I was knocked backward. I got on to my knees and shouted for help at the top of my voice. I heard the women screaming behind the locked door, and directly afterward I knew that Beaumont was struggling with some hideous thing, near to me. I squatted there half an instant, paralyzed with fear, and then I went blindly to help him, shouting his name. There came a little choking scream out of the darkness, and at that I jumped plunk into the dark. I gripped a vast furry ear. Then something struck me another great blow, knocking me sick. I hit back, weak and blind, and gripped with my other hand at the incredible thing. Abruptly I was aware that there were lights in the passage and a noise of feet and shouting. My hand grips were torn from the thing they held. I shut my eyes stupidly and heard a loud yell above me, then a heavy blow, like a butcher chopping meat, and something fell upon me.

"I was helped to my feet by the captain and the butler. On the floor lay an enormous horse head, out of which protruded a man's trunk and legs. On the wrists were fixed two great hoofs. It was the monster. The captain cut something with the sword that he held in his hand and stooped and lifted off the mask—for that is what it was. I saw the face of the man then who had worn it. It was Parsket. He had a bad wound across the forehead where the captain's sword had bit through the mask. I looked stupidly from him to Beaumont, who was sitting up, leaning against the wall of the corridor.

"That's all there is to the yarn itself. Parsket was the girl's would-be lover, and it was he who had been doing the haunting all this time, trying to frighten off the other man by acting the ghost, dressed in a horse mask and hoofs. So I cleared that up all right.

" 'The Whistling Room,' one of my later cases, was a disagreeable business and nearly finished me. Tassoc, the chap who owned the place, sent for me. He half-thought it was some of the wild Irish playing a trick on him, for it was generally known that one of the rooms gave out a queer whistling. I searched a lot, but found nothing, and I'd begun to think it must be the Irishmen after all, only the whistling wouldn't stop. So one night, when it was whistling quietly, I got a ladder and climbed up gently to the window. Presently I had my face above the sill and was looking in alone with the moonlight.

"Of course, the queer whistling sounded louder up there, but it still conveyed that peculiar sense of something whistling quietly to itself. Can you understand? Though, for all the meditative lowness of the note, the horrible, gargantuan quality was distinct—a mighty parody of the human, as if I stood there and listened to the whistling from the lips of a monster with a man's soul.

"And then, you know, I saw something. The floor in the middle of the huge empty room was puckered upward in the centre into a strange, soft-looking mound that parted at the top into an ever-changing hole that pulsated ever to that great, gentle hooning. At times, as I watched, I saw it gape across with a queer inward suction, as with the drawing of an enormous breath; then the thing would dilate and pout once more to the incredible melody. And suddenly, as I stared dumbly, it came to me that the thing was living. I was looking at two enormous blackened lips, blistered and brutal, there in the pale moonlight. . . .

"Suddenly they bulged out to a vast, pouting mound of force and sound, stiffened and swollen, and hugely clean cut in the moonbeams, and a great sweat lay heavy on the vast upper lid. In the same moment of time the whistling had burst into a mad, screaming note that seemed to stun me even where I stood, outside of the window, and then the following moment I was staring blankly at the solid, undisturbed floor of the room, smooth polished oak flooring from wall to wall, and there was an absolute silence. Can't you picture me staring into the quiet room and knowing what I knew? I felt like a sick, frightened kid, and wanted to slide quietly down the ladder and run away. In that very instant I heard Tassoc's voice calling to me, from within the room, for help! help! My God, but I got such an awful dazed feeling and such a vague, bewildered notion that, after all, it was the Irishmen who had got him in there and were taking it out of him! And then the call came again, and I burst the window and jumped in to help him. I had an idea that the call had come from within the shadow of the great fireplace, and I raced across to it, but there was no one there.

" 'Tassoc!' I shouted, and my voice went empty sounding round the room; and then, in a flash, I knew that Tassoc had never called. I whirled round, sick with fear, toward the window, and, as I did so, a frightful, exultant whistling scream burst through the room. On my left, the end wall had bellied in towards me in a pair of gargantuan lips, black and utterly monstrous, to within a yard of my face. I fumbled for a mad instant for my revolver—not for it, but myself, for the danger was a thousand times worse than death; and then suddenly the unknown last line of the Saaamaaa Ritual was whispered quite audibly in the room. Instantly the thing happened that I have known once before—there came a sense as of dust falling continually and monotonously, and I knew that my life hung uncertain and suspended for a flash, in a brief, reeling vertigo of unseeable things. Then that ended, and I knew I might live. My soul and body blended again and life and power came to me. I dashed furiously at the window and hurled myself out head foremost; for I can tell you I had stopped being afraid of death. I crashed down onto the ladder and slithered, grabbing and grabbing, and so came some way or other alive to the bottom. And there I sat in the soft, wet grass, with the moonlight all about me, and far above, through the broken window of the room, there was a low whistling.

"That's the chief of it. I was not hurt. So, you see, the room was really haunted after all and we had to pull it down and burn it. That's another business I managed to clear up."

"The Dream of X"

Edited by

William Hope Hodgson

(Note:—The charred fragments of "The Dream of X" were discovered in an iron box, after the burning of his ancient country residence at Z., where he had lived many years alone after the death of his wife, the "Mirdath" mentioned in the following pages. Through these fragments, which I as Editor have striven to piece and unify into a comprehensible "whole," we get glimpses of a stupendous Dream of the Future of this World, and of X's imagined or real meeting with his wife again in that far off age, with a new name and a new body; but possessed of the olden soul of the woman whom he had plainly loved so madly.)

The Preface Appended by "X" To His Dream

"This to be Love, that your spirit to live in a natural holiness with the Beloved, and your bodies to be a sweet and natural delight that shall be never lost of a lovely mystery. . . . And shame to be unborn, and all things to go wholesome and proper, out of an utter greatness of understanding; and the Man to be an Hero and a Child before the Woman; and the Woman to be an Holy Light of the Spirit and an Utter Companion and in the same time a glad Possession unto the Man. . . . And this doth be Human Love. . . ."

". . . for this to be the especial glory of Love, that it doth make unto all Sweetness and Greatness, and doth be a fire burning all littleness; so that did all to have met The Beloved, then did Wantonness be dead, and there to grow Gladness and Charity, dancing in the years."

("And I cannot touch her face
And I cannot touch her hair
And I kneel to empty shadows
Just memories of her grace;
And her voice sings in the winds
And in the sobs of Dawn
And among the flowers at night
And from the brooks at sunrise
And from the sea at sunset. . . .
. . . .")[1]

[1] A reference by "X" to his loss.—Ed.

The Rescued Fragments of "The Dream of X"

Edited by William Hope Hodgson

Since the time when Mirdath, my Beautiful One, died and left me lonely in this world, I have visited in my dreams those places where in the womb of the Future she and I shall come together, and part, and again come together—breaking asunder most drearly in pain, and again re-uniting after strange ages, in solemn wonder.

And some shall read and say that this was not, and some shall dispute with them; but to them all I say naught, save "Read!" And having read that which I set down, then shall one and all have looked towards Eternity with me—aye, unto its very portals. And so to my telling:—

To me, in this last time of my visions, it was not as if I dreamed; but, as it were, that I waked there into the dark, in the future of this world. And the sun had died; and for me thus newly waked into that Future, to look back upon this our Present Age, was to look back into dreams that my soul knew to be of reality; but which to those newly-seeing eyes of mine, appeared but as a far vision, strangely hallowed with peacefulness and light.

Always, it seemed to me when I awaked into the Future, into the Everlasting Night that lapped this world, that I saw near to me and girding me all about a blurred greyness. And presently this, the greyness, would clear and fade from about me, even as a dusky cloud, and I would look out upon a world of darkness, lit here and there with strange sights. And with my waking, I waked not to ignorance; but to a full knowledge of those things which lit the Night Land; even as a man wakes from sleep each morning, and knows immediately he wakes, the names and knowledge of the Time which has bred him, and in which he lives. And the same while a knowledge I had, as it were sub-conscious, of this Present—this early life, which now I live so utterly alone.

In my earliest knowledge of that place, I was a youth, and my memory tells me that when first I waked, or came, as it might be said, to myself, I stood in one of the embrasures of the Last Redoubt—that great Pyramid of grey metal which held the last millions of this world from the Powers of the Slayers. And so full am I of the knowledge of that Place, that scarce can I believe that none here know; and because I have such difficulty, it may be that I speak over familiarly of those things of which I know; and heed not to explain much that it is needful that I should explain to those who must read here in this our present day. For there, as I stood and looked out, I was less the man of years of this age, than the youth of that, with the natural knowledge of that life which I had gathered by living all my seventeen years of life there; though, until that my first vision, I knew not of that other and Future existence; yet woke to it so naturally as may a man wake here in his bed to the shining of the morning sun, and know it by name, and the meaning of aught else. And yet, as I stood there in the vast embrasure, I had also knowledge of memory, of this present life of ours, deep down within me; but touched with a halo of dreams; and yet with a conscious longing for One, known even there in a half Memory as Mirdath.

As I have said, in my earliest memory, I mind that I stood in an embrasure, high up in the side of the Pyramid, and looked outwards through a queer spyglass to the North-West. Aye, full of youth and with an adventurous and yet half-fearful heart. And in my brain was, as I have told, the knowledge that had come to me in all the years of my life in the Redoubt; and yet until that moment, this Man of this Present Time, had no knowledge of that future existence; and now I stood and had suddenly the knowledge of a life already spent in that strange land, and deeper within me the misty knowings of this our present Age, and, maybe, also, of some others.

To the North-West I looked through the queer spy-glass and saw a landscape that I had looked upon and pored upon through all the years of that life, so that I knew how to name this thing and that thing, and give the very distances of each and everyone from the "Centre-Point" of the Pyramid, which was that which had neither length nor breadth, and was made of polished metal in the Room of Mathematics, where I went daily to my studies.

To the North-West I looked, and in the wide field of my glass, saw plain the bright glare of the fire from the Red Pit shine upwards against the underside of the vast chin of the North-West Watcher—The Watching Thing of the North-West... "That which hath Watched from the Beginning, and until the opening of the Gateway of Eternity" came into my thoughts, as I looked through the glass . . . the words of Aesworpth, the Ancient Poet (though incredibly future to this our time). And suddenly they seemed at fault; for I looked deep down into my being, and saw, as dreams are seen, the sunlight and splendour of this, our present Age. And I was amazed. And here I must make it clear to all that, even as I waked from this age, suddenly into that life, so must I—that youth there in the embrasure—have awakened then to the knowledge of this far-back life of ours . . . seeming to him a vision of the very beginnings of eternity in the dawn of the world. Oh! I do but dread I make it not sufficient clear that I and he were both I . . . the same soul. He of that far date seeing vaguely the life that was (that I do now live in this present age); and I of this time beholding the life that I yet shall live. How utterly strange! And yet, I do not know that I speak holy truth to say that I, in that future time, had no knowledge of this life and Age, before that awakening; for I woke to find that I was one who stood apart from the other youths, in that I had a dim knowledge—visionary, as it were, of the past, which confounded, whilst yet it angered, those who were the men of learning of that age. But this I do know, that from that time, onwards, my knowledge and assuredness of the Past was tenfold; for this my memory of that life told me. And so to further my telling. Yet before I pass onwards, one other thing is there of which I shall speak. . . . In the moment in which I waked out of that youthfulness into the assured awaredness of this life, in that moment the hunger of this my love flew to me across the ages; so that what had been but a memory-dream, grew to the pain of reality, and I knew suddenly that I lacked; and from that time onwards, I went, listening, as even now my life is spent. And so it was that I, (fresh-born in that future time), hungered, strangely for my Beautiful One; with all the strength of that new life, knowing that she had been mine, and might live again, even as I. And so, as I have said, I hungered, and found that I listened.

And now, to go back from my digression, it was as I have said, I had amazement at perceiving in memory the unknowable sunshine and splendour of this age breaking so clear through my hitherto most vague and hazy visions; so that the ignorance of Aesworpth was shouted to me by the things which now I knew. And from that time onward, for a little space, I was stunned with all that I knew and guessed and felt; and all of a long while the hunger grew for that one I had lost in the early days—she who had sung to me in those faery days of light, that had been in verity. And the especial thoughts of that age looked back with a keen regretful wonder into the gulf of forgetfulness.

But, presently, I turned from the haze and pain of my dream-memories once more to the inconceivable mystery of the Night Land, which I viewed through the great embrasure. For on none did it ever come with weariness to look out upon all the hideous mysteries; so that old and young watched from early years to death the black monstrosity of the Night Land, which this our last refuge of humanity held at bay.

To the right of the Red Pit there lay a long, sinuous glare, which I knew as the Vale of Red Fire, and beyond that for many dreary miles the blackness of the Night Land; across which came the coldness of the light from the Plain of Blue Fire. And then, on the very borders of the Unknown Lands, there lay a range of low volcanoes, which lit up, far away in the outer darkness, the Black Hills, where shone the Seven Lights, which neither twinkled nor moved nor faltered through eternity; and of which even the great Spy Glass could make no understanding; nor had any adventurer from the Pyramid ever come back to tell us aught of them. And here let me say, that down in the Great Library of the Redoubt were the histories of all those, with their discoveries, who had ventured out into the monstrousness of the Night Land, risking not the life only, but the spirit of life.

And surely it is all so strange and wonderful to set out, that I could almost despair with the contemplation of that which I must achieve; for there is so much to tell, and so few words given to man by which he may indicate that which lies beyond his sight and the present and general knowings of Peoples.

How shall you ever know, as I know in verity, of the greatness and reality and terror of the thing that I would make clear to all; for we, with our puny span of recorded life must have great histories to tell, but the few bare details we know concerning years that are but a few thousands in all; and I must set out to you in the short pages of this my life there, a sufficiency of the life that had been, and the life that was, both within and without that mighty Pyramid, to make clear to those who may read, the truth of that which I would tell; and the histories of that great Redoubt dealt not with odd thousands of years; but with very millions; aye, away back into what they of that Age conceived to be the early days of the earth, when the sun maybe still gloomed dully in the night sky of the world. But of all that went before, nothing, save as myths, and matters to be taken most cautiously, and believed not by men of sanity and proved wisdom. And I, . . . how shall I make all this clear to they who may read? The thing cannot be; and yet I must tell my history; for to be silent before so much wonder would be to suffer of too full a heart; and I must even ease my spirit by this my struggle to tell to all how it was with me, and how it will be. Aye, even to the memories which were the possession of that far future youth, who was indeed I, of his childhood's days, when his nurse of that Age swung him and crooned impossible lullabies of this mythical sun which, according to those future fairytales, had once passed across the blackness that now lay above the Pyramid.

Such is the monstrous futureness of this which I have seen through the body of my far-off youth.

And so back to my telling. To my right, which was to the North, there stood, very far away, the House of Silence, there upon a low hill. And in that House were many lights and no sound. And so had it been through an uncountable eternity of years. Always those steady lights, and no whisper or sound—not even such as our distance-microphones could have discovered. And the danger of this House was accounted the greatest danger of all those Lands. And round by the House of Silence, wound The Road Where The Silent Ones Walk. And concerning this Road, which passed out of the Unknown Lands, nigh by the Place of the Ab-humans, where was always the green, luminous mist, nothing was known, save that it was held that, of all the works about the Mighty Pyramid, it was, alone, the one that was bred, long ages past, of healthy human toil and labour. And on this point had a thousand books, and more, been writ; and all contrary, and so to no end, as is ever the way in such matters. And as it was with The Road Where The Silent Ones Walk, so it was with all those other monstrous things. . . . whole libraries had there been made upon this and upon that; and many a thousand million mouldered into the forgotten dust of the earlier world.

I mind me now that presently I stepped upon the central travelling roadway which spanned the one thousandth plateau of the Great Redoubt. And this lay six miles and thirty fathoms above the Plain of the Night Land, and was somewhat of a great mile, or more, across. And so, in a few minutes, I was at the South-Eastern wall, and looking out through The Great Embrasure toward the Three Silver Fire Holes, that shone before the Thing that Nods, away down, far in the South-East. Southward of this; but nearer, there rose the vast bulk of the South-East Watcher—the Watching Thing of the South-East. And to the right and to the left of the squat monster burned the Torches; maybe half-a-mile upon each side; yet sufficient light they threw to show the lumbered-forward head of the never-sleeping Brute.

To the East, as I stood there on the quietness of the Sleeping-Time of the One Thousandth Plateau, I heard a far, dreadful sound, down in the lightless East; and, presently, again, a strange, dreadful laughter, deep as a low thunder among the mountains. And because this sound came odd whiles from the Unknown Lands beyond the Valley Of the Hounds, we had named that far and never-seen Place "The Country Whence Comes The Great Laughter." And though I had heard the sound, many and oft a time, yet did I never hear it without a most strange thrilling of my heart, and a sense of my littleness, and of the utter terror which had beset the last million of the world. Yet, because I had heard the Laughter oft, I paid not over-long attention to my thoughts upon it; and when, in a little it died away into that Eastern Darkness, I turned my spy-glass upon the Giants' Pit, which lay to the South of the Giants' Kilns. And these same Kilns were tended by the giants, and the light of the Kilns was red and fitful, and threw wavering shadows and lights across the mouth of the pit; so that I saw giants crawling up out of the pit; but not proper seen, by reason of the dance of the shadows. And so, because ever there was so much to behold, I looked away, presently, to that which was plainer to be examined.

To the back of the Giants' Pit was a great, black Headland that stood vast, between the Valley of the Hounds (where lived the monstrous Night Hounds) and the Giants. And the light of the Kilns struck the brow of this black Headland; so that, constantly, I saw things peer over the edge, coming forward a little into the light of the Kilns, and drawing back swiftly into the shadows. And thus it had been ever, through the uncounted ages; so that the Headland was known as The Headland from which Strange Things Peer; and thus it marked in our maps and charts of that grim world.

Before me ran The Road Where The Silent Ones Walk; and I searched it, as many a time in my earlier youth had I, with the spy-glass; for my heart was always stirred mightily by the sight of those Silent Ones. And, presently, alone in all the miles of that night-grey road, I saw one in the field of my glass—a quiet, cloaked figure, moving along, shrouded, and looking neither to right nor left. And thus was it with these beings ever. It was told about in the Redoubt that they would harm no human, if but the human did keep a fair distance from them; but that it were wise never to come close upon one. And this I can well believe. And so, searching the road with my gaze, I passed beyond this Silent One, and past the place where the road, sweeping vastly to the South-East, was lit a space, strangely, by the light from the Silver Fire Holes. And thus at last to where it swayed to the South of the Dark Palace, and thence Southward still, until it passed round to the Westward, beyond the mountain bulk of the Watching Thing in the South—the hugest monster in all the visible Night Lands. My spyglass showed it to me with clearness—a living hill of watchfulness, known to us as the Watcher of the South. It brooded there, squat and tremendous, hunched over the pale radiance of the Glowing Dome.

Much, I know, had been writ concerning this Odd, Vast Watcher; for it had grown out of the blackness of the South Unknown Lands a million years gone; and the steady growing nearness of it had been noted and set out at length by the men they called Monstruwacans; so that it was possible to search in our libraries, and learn of the very coming of this Beast in the olden-time. And, while I mind me, there were even then, and always, men named Monstruwacans, whose duty it was to take heed of the great Forces, and to watch the Monsters and the Beasts that beset the great Pyramid, and measure and record, and have so full a knowledge of these same that, did but one but sway an head in the darkness, the same matter was set down with particularness in the Records.

And so to tell more about the South Watcher. A million years gone, as I have set out, came it out from the blackness of the South, and grew steadily nearer through twenty thousand years; but so slow that in no one year could a man perceive that it had moved. Yet it had movement, and had come thus far upon its road to the Redoubt, when the Glowing Dome rose out of the ground before it—growing slowly. And this had stayed the way of the Monster; so that through an eternity it had looked toward the Pyramid across the pale glare of the Dome, and seeming to have no power to advance nearer. And because of this, much had been writ to prove that there were other forces than evil at work in the Night Land, about the Last Redoubt. And this I have always thought to be wisely said; and, indeed, there to be no doubt to the matter, for there were many things in the time of which I have knowledge, which seemed to make clear that, even as the Forces of Darkness were loose upon the End of Man; so were there other Forces out to do battle with the Terror; though in ways most strange and unthought of by the human soul. And of this I shall have more to tell anon.

And here, before I go further with my telling, let me set out some of that knowledge which yet remains so clear within my mind and heart. Of the coming of these monstrosities and evil Forces, no man could say much with verity; for the evil of it began before the Histories of the Great Redoubt were shaped; aye, even before the sun had lost all power to light; though, it must not be a thing of certainty that even at this far time the invisible, black heavens held no warmth for this world; but of this I have no room to tell; and must pass on to that of which I have a more certain knowledge. The evil must surely have begun in the Days of the Darkening (which I might liken to a story which was believed doubtfully, much as we of this day believe the Story of the Creaton). A dim record there was of those olden sciences (that are yet far off in our future) which, disturbing the unmeasurable Outward Powers, had allowed to pass the Barrier of this Life some of those Monsters and Ab-human creatures, which are so wondrously cushioned from us at this normal present. And thus there had materialized, and in other cases developed, grotesque and horrible Creatures, which now beset the humans of this world. And where there was no power to take on material form, there had been allowed to certain dreadful Forces to have power to affect the life of the human spirit. And this growing very dreadful, and the world full of lawlessness and degeneracy; there had banded together the sound millions, and built the Last Redoubt; there in the twilight of the world (so it seems to us, and yet to them bred at last to the peace of usage) as it were the Beginning; and this I can make no clearer; and none hath right to expect it; for my task is very great, and beyond the power of human skill. And when the humans had built the great Pyramid, it had one thousand three hundred and twenty floors; and the thickness of each floor was according to the strength of its need. And the whole height of this pyramid exceeded seven miles, by near a mile, and above it was a tower from which watchmen looked (these being called the Monstruwacans). But where the Redoubt was built, I know not; save that I believe in a mighty valley of which I may tell more in due time.

And when the Pyramid was built, the last millions, who were the Builders thereof, went within, and made themselves a great house and city of this Last Redoubt. And thus began the Second History of this world. And how shall I set it all down in these little pages! For but my task, even as I see it, is too great for the power of a single life and a single pen. Yet, to it!

And, later, through hundreds and thousands of years, there grew up in the Outer Lands, beyond those which lay under the guard of the Redoubt, mighty and lost races of terrible creatures, half men and half beast and evil and dreadful; and these made war upon the Redoubt; but were beaten off from that grim, metal mountain, with a vast slaughter. Yet, must there have been many such attacks, until the electric circle was put about the Pyramid, and lit from the Earth

Current. And the lowest half-mile of the Pyramid was sealed; and so at last there was a peace, and the beginnings of that Eternity of quiet watching for the day when the Earth Current shall become exhausted. And, at whiles, through the forgotten centuries, had the Creatures been glutted time and again upon such odd bands of daring ones as had adventured forth to explore through the mystery of the Night Lands; for of those who went, scarce any did ever return; for there were eyes in all that dark; and Powers and Forces abroad which had all knowledge; or so we must fain believe.

And now to continue my telling concerning the Night Land. The Watcher of the South, was as I have set to make clear, a monster differing from those other Watching Things, of which I have spoken, and of which there were in all four. One to the North West, and one to the South East, and of these I have told; and the other twain lay brooding, one to the South West, and the other to the North East, and thus the four watchers kept ward through the darkness, upon the Pyramid, and moved not, neither gave they out any sound. Yet did we know them to be mountains of living watchfulness and hideous and steadfast intelligence. I passed now to the South Western side of the Pyramid and looked out at the tower that stood on the far edge of the Deep Valley of the Red Smoke.

Beyond these, South and West of them, was the enormous bulk of the South West Watcher, and from the ground rose what we named the Eye Beam—a single ray of grey light, which came up out of the ground, and lit the right eye of the monster. And because of this light, that eye had been mightily examined through unknown thousands of years; and some held that the eye looked through the light steadfastly at the Pyramid; but others set out that the light blinded it, and was the work of those Other Powers which were abroad to do combat with the Evil Forces. But however this may be, as I stood there in the embrasure, and looked at the thing through the spy-glass, it seemed to my soul that the Brute looked straightly at me, unwinking and steadfast, and fully of a knowledge that I spied upon it. And this is how I felt.

To the North of this, in the direction of the West, I saw the Place Where the Silent Ones Kill; and this was so named, because there, maybe ten thousand years gone, certain humans adventuring from the Pyramid, came off the Road Where the Silent Ones Walk, and into that place, and were immediately destroyed. And this was told by one who escaped; though he died also very quickly: for his heart was frozen. And this I cannot explain; but so it was set out in the Records.

Far away beyond the Place Where The Silent Ones Kill, in the very mouth of the Western Night was the Place of the Ab-humans, where was lost the Road Where The Silent Ones Walk, in a dull green, luminous mist. And of this place nothing was known; though much it held the thoughts and attentions of our thinkers and imaginers; for some said that there was a Place of Safety, differing from the Redoubt (as we of this day suppose Heaven to differ from the Earth), and that the Road led thence; but was barred by the Ab-humans. And this I can only set down here; but with no thought to justify or uphold it.

Later, I travelled over to the North Eastern wall of the Redoubt, and looked thence with my spy-glass at the Watcher of the North East—the Crowned Watcher it was called, in that within the air above its vast head there hung always a blue, luminous ring, which shed a strange light downwards over the monster—showing a vast, wrinkled brow (upon which an whole library has been writ); but putting to the shadow all the lower face; all save the ear, which came out from the back of its head, and belled towards the Redoubt, and had been said by some observers in the past to have been seen to quiver: but how that may be, I know not; for no man of our days had seen such a thing.

And beyond the Watching Thing, was The Place Where The Silent Ones Are Never, close by the great road; which was bounded upon the far side by The Giant's Sea; and upon the far side of that was a Road which was always named The Road by the Quiet City; for it passed along that place where burned forever the constant and never moving lights of a strange city; but no glass had ever shown life there; neither had any light ever ceased to burn. And beyond that again was The Black Mist. And here, let me say, that The Valley of The Hounds ended towards the Lights of the Quiet City.

And so have I set out something of that land, and of those creatures and circumstances which beset us about, waiting until the Day of Doom, when our Earth Current should cease, and leave us helpless to the Watchers, and the abundant terrors. And there I stood, and looked forth composedly, as may one who has been born to know of such matters, and reared in the knowledge of them. And, anon, I would look upward, and see the grey, metalled mountain going up measureless into the gloom of the everlasting night; and from my feet the sheer downward sweep of the grim, metal walls, four full miles, or more, to the plain below.

And one thing (aye! and I fear me, many) have I missed to set out clearly. There was all around the base of the Pyramid, which was five and one-quarter miles every way, a great circle of light which was set up by the Earth Current, and burned within a transparent tube; or had that appearance. And it bounded the Pyramid for a clear mile upon every side, and burned forever; and none of the monsters dared ever to pass across, neither had the Evil Powers ability to cause harm to any within; yet there were some dangers against which it might not avail; but these had no cunning to bring harm to any within the Great Redoubt, who had wisdom to meddle with no dreadfulness. And so were those last millions guarded until the Earth Current should be used to its end. And this circle is that which I have called the Electric Circle; though with failure to explain. But there it was called The Circle.

And thus have I, with great effort, made a little clear that grim land of night, where, presently, my listening heard one calling across the dark. And how that this grew upon me, I will set out forthwith.

Now, oft had I heard tell, not only in that great city which occupied the thousandth floor, but in others of the one thousand, three hundred and twenty cities of the Pyramid, that there was somewhere out in the desolation of the Night Lands a second Place of Refuge, where had gathered, in another part of this dead world, some last millions of the human race, to fight unto the end. And this story I heard everywhere in my travels through the cities of the Great Redoubt, which travels began when I came upon my seventeenth year, and continued for three years and two hundred and twenty-five days, being even then but one day in each city, as was the custom in the training of every child. And truly it was a great journey, and in it I met with many whom to know was to love; but whom never could I see again; for life has not space enough; and each must to his duty to the security and well-being of the Redoubt. Yet, for all that I have set down, we travelled much, always; but there were so many millions, and so few years.

And, as I have said, everywhere I went there was the same story of this other Place of Refuge; and in such of the Libraries of those cities, as I had time to search, there were great numbers of works upon the existence of this other Refuge; and some, far back in the years, made assertion with confidence that such a Place was in verity; and, indeed, no doubt did there seem in those by-gone ages; but now these very records were read out by Scholars, who doubted, even whilst they read. And so is it ever.

Now below the Great Redoubt lay the Underground Fields. And of the Underground Fields (though in that age we called them no more than "The Fields") I should set down a little; for they were the mightiest work of this world; so that even the Last Redoubt was but a small thing beside them. An hundred miles deep lay the lowest of the Underground Fields, and was an hundred miles from side to side, every way; and above it there were three hundred and six fields, each one less in area than that beneath; and in this wise they tapered, until the topmost field which lay direct beneath the lowermost floor of the Great Redoubt, was but four miles every way. And thus it will be seen that these fields, lying one beneath the other, formed a mighty and incredible Pyramid of Country Lands in the deep earth, an hundred miles from base to the topmost field. And the whole was sheathed in at the sides with the grey metal of which the Redoubt was builded; and each field was pillared, and floored beneath the soil, with this same compound of wonder; and so was it secure, and the monsters could not dig into that mighty garden from without. And all of that Underground Land was lit, where needed, by the Earth Current, and that same life-stream fructified the soil, and gave life and blood to the plants and to the trees, and to every bush and natural thing. And the making of those fields had taken maybe a million years, and the "dump" thereof had been cast into the "Crack," whence came the Earth Current, and which had bottom beyond all soundings.[2]

Now there was presently, in the Garden of Silence, which was the lowermost of all the Underground Fields, the Ending of those seventeen hundred heroes, and of the Youths that they saved and slew. And the Garden was a great country, and an hundred miles every way, and the roof thereof was three great miles above, and shaped to a vast dome; as it had been that the Builders and Makers thereof did remember in their spirits the visible sky of this our Present Age. And the making of that Garden was all set out in a single History of

[2] There follow many pages of obliterated MS.; but here and there a legible line or word has pointed the way, and I gather that X., in his Dream, has got into communication with the Lesser Redoubt, and had speech through the night of the world with a maid named Naani, whom he believes to be the olden Mirdath. Disaster comes upon the Lesser Redoubt, in the form of an attack by monsters and by the failure of their Life Current. The communications come to an end, leaving all the people of the Great Redoubt full of sympathy and horror. One night certain youths of the Great Redoubt steal out into the Night Land, to attempt to find and rescue the other Humans and Naani; but fail, and some are brought back dead to the Pyramid by a number of men who go out to their rescue, many of whom get killed by a terrible attack from the Night Hounds. Follows the gigantic burial scene, almost intact.—Ed.

Seven Thousand and Seventy Volumes. And there were likewise seven thousand and seventy years spent to the making of that Country; so that there had unremembered generations lived and laboured and died, and seen not the end of their labour. And Love had shaped it and hallowed it; so that of all the wonders of the world, there had been none that shall ever come anigh to that Garden of Silence—an hundred miles every way of Silence to the Dead.

And there were in that roof seven moons set in a mighty circle, and lit by the Earth Current; and the circle was sixty miles across, so that all that Country of Quiet was visible; yet to no great glare, but a sweet holy light; so that I did always feel in my heart that a man might weep there, and be unashamed. And in the midst of that silent Country, there was a great hill, and upon the hill a vast Dome. And the Dome was full of a Light that might be seen in all that Country, which was the Garden of Silence. And beneath the Dome was the "Crack," and within it the glory of the Earth-Current, from which all had life and light and safety. And in the Dome at the North, there was a gateway; and a narrow road went upwards to the gateway, and the Road was named The Last Road, and the Gateway was named by no name; but known to all, as The Gateway.

And there were in that mighty Country, long roadways, and hidden methods to help travel; and constant temples of rest along the miles; and groves; and the charm of water, falling. And everywhere the Statues of Memory, and the Tablets of Memory, and the whole of that Great Underground Country full of an echo of Eternity and of Memory and Love and Greatness; so that to walk alone in that Land was to grow back to the wonder and mystery of Childhood; and presently to go upwards again to the Cities of the Mighty Pyramid, purified and sweetened of soul and mind. And in my boyhood, I have wandered oft, a week of days in that Country of Silence, and had my food with me, and slept quietly amid the memories; and gone on again, wrapped about with the quiet of the Everlasting. And the man-soul within would be drawn mightily to those places where the Great Ones of the past Eternity of the World had their Memory named; but there was that within me which ever drew me, in the ending, to the Hills of the Babes; those little Hills where might be heard amid the lonesomeness of an utter quiet, a strange and wondrous echo, as of a little child calling over the hills. But how this was I know not, save by the sweet cunning of some dead Maker in the forgotten years. And here, mayhaps by reason of this Voice of Pathos, were to be found the countless Tokens of Memory to all the babes of the Mighty Pyramid, through a thousand ages. And, odd whiles, would I come upon some Mother, sitting there lonely, or mayhaps companied by others. And by this little telling shall you know somewhat of the quietness and the wonder and the holiness of that great Country hallowed to all Memory and to Eternity and to our Dead.

And it was here, into the Country of Silence, that they brought down the Dead to their Burial. And there came down into the Country of Silence, maybe an Hundred Million, out of the Cities of the Pyramid, to be present, and to do Honour.

Now they that had charge of the Dead, did lay them upon the road which ran up unto The Gateway, even that same road which was named The Last Road. And the Road moved upwards slowly with the Dead; and the Dead went inward through the Gateway; first the poor Youths, and afterward they that had given up life that they might save them. And as the Dead went upwards, there was a very great Silence over all the miles of the Country of Silence. But in a little while there came from afar off, a sound as of a wind wailing; and it came onwards out of the distance, and passed over the Hills of the Babes, which were a great way off. And so came anigh to the place where I stood. Even as the blowing of a sorrowful wind did it come; and I knew that all the great multitudes did sing quietly; and the singing passed onwards, and left behind it an utter silence; even as the wind doth rustle the corn and pass onwards, and all fall to a greater-seeming quietness than before. And the Dead passed inward through The Gateway, into the great light and silence of the Dome and came out no more. And again from beyond the far Hills of the Babes there was that sound of the millions singing; and there rose up out of the earth beneath, the voices of the underground organs, and the noise of the sorrow passed over me, and went again into the distance, and left all hushed.

And lo! as there passed inward to the silence of the Dome the last of those dead Heroes, there came again the sound from beyond the Hills of the Babes; and as it came more nigh, I knew that it was the Song of Honour, loud and triumphant, and sung by countless multitudes. And the Voices of the Organs made an honour to the dead.

[3]And, in a while, I found the Road where the Silent Ones Walk, to bend inward at the North of the House of Silence; so that it came

[3] Evidently X, in his Dream, has now ventured out alone into the Night Land; presumably, from sense of mutilated contest, in search for the Lesser Pyramid, and to rescue Naani.—Ed.

right horridly close unto the House; for here the hill on which the House did stand, was very abrupt and fell steeply unto the Road. And so was that Dreadful House stood up there above me in the Silence, as that it did seem to brood there upon the Land. And this side did seem truly as the other; and equal lone and dreadful.

And the House was monstrous and huge, and full of quiet lights; and it was truly as that there had been no Sound ever in that House through Eternity; but yet was it as that the heart did think each moment to see quiet and shrouded figures within, and yet never were they seen; and this I do but set down that I bring all home unto your hearts also, as that you crouched there with me in those low moss-bushes, there beside the Great Road, and did look upward unto that Monstrous House of Everlasting Silence, and did feel the utterness of silence to hang about it in the night; and to know in your spirits the quiet threat that lived silent there within.

And so shall you have mind of me, hid there among the bushes, and sodden and cold; and yet, as you will perceive, so held in my spirit by an utter terror and loathing and solemn wonder and awe of that Mighty House of Quietness loomed above me in the Night, that I wotted not of the misery of my body, because that my spirit was so in terror for the life of my Being[4] that the Master-Word did beat softly about me, out of all the night of the world. And all mine heart did throb with great glowings of joy; yet was the beat of the Word unsure, so that I knew not truly whether my Spirit had indeed heard aught, for there was immediately a silence, as ever, about mine inward being. Yet, as you shall believe, there was a new hope and strength of courage in all my body and soul.

And I went forward very swift, and all renewed, as it were; and my strength and hope did make naught of any terror that should lie to bar my way, neither did I have further heed of the boulders that lay always upon my path, but did go over them with quick leapings, and a wondrous and thrilling eagerness of the heart within me.

And, sudden, in the end of the tenth hour, I perceived that the mighty walls of blackness that made the sides of the Gorge be no more there, and that I was come truly upon the end of the Gorge. And I near trembled with hope and astonishment; for when I was gone a little way on, I had ceased to go upward any more, and was

---

[4] Here we have X in a great Gorge, further upon his journey. Evidently the Master Word is a sign sent through the aether by Naani.—Ed.

come clear out from the mouth of the Gorge, and did peer forth across a mighty country of night. And it did seem to me as that I was come to a second Land of strange matters, even as the Night Land where did lie the wonder of the Mighty Pyramid. And surely, I did think within mine heart that I was come at last to that far and hidden place of the world where did be the Lesser Redoubt. But yet was there no place in all that night where did tower the shining lights of the Lesser Pyramid, the which I did hope vainly to perceive. And a new despair came upon me; for indeed, it seemed I was come all astray in the night of the World, and did nowise have any knowing whether I stood near to the Country of the Lesser Redoubt, or whether that I was gone half across the World unto a strange place.

And, then, as the despair troubled my spirit and dulled the beating of mine heart, a sudden thought did light up a fresh hope within me; for, indeed, as you do know, I was come upward of a great height, and did surely have a huge view over all that Land; and mayhaps the Lesser Pyramid did lie somewhere in a valley, if, in verity, it did be anywheres at all in that Country. And I turned me from the cliffs, and lookt backward over all the night of the Land; but there was nowhere in all that Country the shining of the Lights of the Lesser Pyramid.

And lo! of a sudden I did know that there was something in the night. And I stared, with a very keen and anxious look. And behold there was the black shape of a great pyramid afar off in the night, that did show against the shining of the distant light; for it did stand between me and the far off fires. But until I was come to that place, whence I did look, I had not stood to have it plain against the shining upon the other side of that Land. And how I did feel in that moment, I have no words to set out unto you. But surely was mine heart gracious with thankfulness, and I ready to leap with joy and hope, and all my body thrilled with an excitement that would not have me to be silent; so that, suddenly, I began to shoot foolishly across the night. But came soon to wisdom and silence, as you shall think. And I ran down into the Land, and many hours I went; and presently I sat me down to rest.

And, after that I had sat there awhile, I did mind me suddenly that I should send the Master-Word through the night; for, indeed, how else might I ever know whether Naani did yet live; though, in truth, I had little, save desperate hope, in this matter; but yet did remember how that I had seemed odd times of my journey to hear the beat of the Master-Word with my spirit, out of all the dark of the world. And, in verity, if Naani answered not, but there came instead an Evil

Power to destroy me, I should but cease me of mine utter misery the more speedy.

And I stood me upon my feet, and looked outward about me into the blackness of that Land. And I sent the Master-Word with my brain-elements; and immediately I called Naani, thrice, sending the call with my brain-elements.

And lo! in a moment, as it did seem, there broke around me out of all the mystery of night, low and solemn, the Master-Word, beating in the night. And immediately there did sound within my brain a far, small voice, very lone and faint, as that it had come from the end of the world. And the voice was the voice of Naani and the voice of Mirdath, and did call me by mine olden love-name.

Then, indeed, I did near to choke with the utter affright of joy that did take me in the heart, and also I was shaken with a mighty excitement, and my despair was gone, as that I had never known it. For, in verity, Naani did live and did call unto me with her brain-elements; and surely I had not heard the voice of mine Own for an utter age of grim labour and dread.

And the voice was, as I did say, as that it came from one that did be in a far place of the earth. And, in verity, whilst I stood dazed with a great joy that the Maid did live, I knew within me, concerning the fear that she was utter far off; and what peril might come anigh to her, before that I should stand to her side, to do battle for her life and well-being and mine own joy.

And lo! in the same moment, and before that I made further speech unto Naani, I did wot that some one did be a little way off from me, in the bushes, where a fire hole did burn anigh to me; and it was as that my spirit knew this thing, and told of it unto my brain. And I made no answer unto the Maid, across all the dark of the world; but went very swift into a great bush that was nigh to the fire-hole, upon this side. And I lookt through, into the open space that did be about the fire-hole. And there was a little figure that did kneel, sobbing, upon the earth, beside the fire-hole; and truly it was a slim maid, and she did seem as that she harked very desperate, even whilst yet she did sob. And surely, mine own soul did Know, all in one white moment of life. And she there, unknowing, and harking unto a cry of the spirit, that she did think to come through all the desolation of the night—even from the Mighty Pyramid. For oft, as I did perceive, had she cried unto me in all that lonesome month, and known no answer; neither that I was making a desperate way unto her; for, indeed, her weakness was great, so that she had no power to throw the Word strongly afar, neither to make plain her spiritual cryings through any mighty space of the aether.

And lo! I drew in my breath, and set my teeth a moment, to steady my lips; and I said:—"MIRDATH," out of the bush where I did be, and using natural human speech. And the Maid ceased from her weeping, and lookt this way and that, with an utter new fear, and with a frightened hope that did shine with her tears in the light from the fire-hole. And I divided the bush before me, and went through the bush, so that I came out before her, and did be there in my grey armour; and I did pause then, and was all adrift in myself; for mine heart said that I should take this Maid into mine arms again; for that I was come again to be with Mirdath after an utter lost Eternity. But yet was I all paused; for truly she was Naani and she was Mirdath, and she did be a stranger in mine eyes, and very dainty and pretty and shaken with woe and sore trouble and grief.

And in that same moment of my coming unto her out of the bush, she screamed and fell back from me, and strove weakly to gain unto the hither bushes; for, truly, she knew not what was come upon her in that first little moment. And immediately she saw that it did be an human man, and no monster to slay her, and in that instant I said the Master-Word unto her, aloud, that she should have knowledge of peace and help. And I told my name, and said I am That One.

And she knew this thing, even as my lips made the sounds. And she cried out something in an utter broke voice, and ran unto me, and thrust her two small hands into my charge and keeping, and fell thence into a great sobbing and shaking, so that I was all in trouble to ease her; but did keep a silence and held fast her hands, for I had not on mine armoured gloves. And she leaned against me, very weak, and seeming wondrous like to a child. And lo! in a while she ceased to sob, and did but catch her breath this time and that, but said no word. And I bethought me that she did suffer of hunger, for I perceived that she had been long wandering and alone, and was come unto the end of hope, when that I did come.

And the Maid stood there yet silent, for she might not yet command her mouth to speak. And she trembled as she stood. And I opened my left hand, and lookt at the hand within my palm, and surely it was utter thin and wasted. And I made no more pause, but lifted mine Own and set her easy upon the earth, with an hump of smooth rock unto her back. And I stript off my cloak very quick, and put it about her, for she was scarce covered with her clothes that had been all torn among the bushes; so that part she shook with an utter chill, and part because of weakness, for she was nigh to be starved unto her death, and destroyed with her grief and lonesomeness.

And I took from my back the scrip and the pouch, and I gat a tablet from the scrip, and brake it into my cup, and with the water I made a little broth very swift upon an hot rock that was to the edge of the fire-hole. And I fed the broth unto the Maid; for truly her hands did shake so that she had spilt it all, if that I had done otherwise.

And she drank the broth, and was so weak that presently she did fall again to sobbing, yet very quiet; so that I strove not to be troubled in the heart; for, indeed, this thing was but reasonable, and not cause for me to have an anxiousness. But I put mine hands under the cloak and took her hands into mine and held them strong and firm; and that did seem to bring something of peace and strength unto her; so that presently the trembling and the weeping went from her. And, indeed, the broth was surely helpful in this matter.

And presently, I knew that her hands did stir a little within mine, and I loosed somewhat of my grip; and immediately she did graspt mine hands with a weak and gentle grasp; but lookt not yet at me; only did stay very quiet, as that she did gather her strength within her. And, indeed, I was content: save that an anxiousness of the heart did stir me this time and that, lest some monster should come upon us. And because of this trouble, I did hark about me, now and oft, and with a new and strange fearfulness of danger, because that now mine Own was given unto my charge; and surely mine heart would break, if that there came any hurt unto her.

Now, of a sudden, the Maid did make as that she would rise, and I loosed free from her, to give help. And she gat me by the hand, and slipt sudden to her knees, and did kiss mine hand, and did begin again to weep. And surely I was so utter abashed that I stood very stupid and let her do this thing. But in a moment I drew free from her; for this thing might not be. And I gat me to my knee likewise before her, and took her hands, and kist them once, newly humbled, as it were, very humbly; and thus should she know all that was in mine heart, and of mine understanding. And she did but sob the more; for she was so weak, and utter moved unto me, because that I had come to her through the night of the world. And this thing I knew, though no speech had yet past between us. And I gave up her hands, lest she need them for her tears; but she left them to lie in my palms, as she did kneel there; and she bowed her head a little over her weeping; but did show that she was mine, in verity, unto the very essence of her dear spirit.

And I took her into mine arms, very gently and without caress; but presently I stroked her hair, and called her Naani and Mirdath, and said many things unto her, that now I scarce do wot of, but she did know them in the after time. And she was very quiet in mine arms, and seeming wondrous content; but yet did sob onward for a great time. And oft did I coax her and say vague things of comfort, as I have told. But truly she did ask no more comfort at that time than that she be sheltered where she did be. And truly she had been lonesome and in terror and in grief and dread, a great and horrid time.

Now, presently, she was grown quiet; and I made to put her comfortable in the cloak against the rock that I should have freedom to make her more of the broth. But yet she did nestle unto me, with a little sweet wistfulness, that made warm mine heart in a most wondrous fashion; for surely she was mine Own. And she to begin to say odd words to me. And so to have gentle obedience to me, and to rest quiet against the rock, the while that I did make the broth. Yet ever her gaze did follow me, as I knew; for I must look oft her way.

And I took the broth to her, and she drank it, using her own two hands; and I sat by, and eat three of the tablets and drank some of the water, for truly it was a foolish great time since last I had eat.

Now, in a while, the broth did make bright the eyes of the Maid, and she did begin to talk; and at whiles had pauses, because that she lacked of strength, and there was more to be told than an human may have the heart-strength and cunning to make plain. And twice she did come again to sobbing; for, truly, her father was dead and the Peoples of the Lesser Redoubt all slain and dispersed through that Dreadful Land.

And so we two set out presently, after a great sleep, to the return journey. And made the whole way in a matter of maybe a month more, and so were come at last to the top of the mighty slope, and had sight of the Great Redoubt.

And, in verity, I did stare with a fierce eagerness unto the far off place in the middle part of the Night Land, where did be the Mighty Pyramid; and surely it there to shine in the midst of the land, and did be mine Home, where never had I dared hope I should return. And I set mine arm very swift and eager about the Maid, and pointed, so that she see quickly the wonder and safe Mightiness of that which did be our Refuge for all our life to come, if but that we to win unto it. And the Maid to look with a great and earnest soberness and a lovely gladness and utter soul and heart interest, unto that Place that bare me, and where I to have come from, and now to take her. And long and long she lookt; and sudden came round unto me, and set her arms quick about my neck, and burst unto a strange and happy weeping. And I to hold her gentle to me, and let her cry very natural, until that she was something unpent.

And lo! when that she was eased, she to stand close beside me, and to look again unto the Mighty Pyramid; and afterward, as she to steady, she to ask an hundred questions, so utter eager and so to thrill with joy and excitement, as that she did be a glad child. And an hundred questions I answered, and showed her new things and Wonders uncounted. And of all strangeness that she then to see, there did none so to shake her in the spirit with terror as did that Dreadful and Horrid House, which did be the House of Silence. And it was as that her very being did know and be repulsed of some Horror that did concern and be in that House; so that she to want to hide in the bushes that did be anigh to the Road; and truly, I to think this wise, and to remember that we did be come into the Power of Monstrosity that was forever abroad in that Land. And so we to begin to go forward; but always in hiding.

And in the tenth hour were we come something nigh unto the House; for truly, we to be off from the Road Where The Silent Ones Walk, and so to go more straightly, and always to save distance. And we kept so far outward from the House as we might; but could pass it not more than a great mile off, because that the bushes did have their margin near upon our left, as we went; and there to be bareness of rock beyond; and fire-holes in this place and that amid the starkness of the rocky places; that should be like to show us very plain, if that we came outward from the bushes. And moreover, there went upward into the everlasting night one of those Towers of Silence, which did be in this part and that part of the Land, and were thought to hold Strange Watchers. And the Tower stood great and monstrous afar off in the midst of the naked rocks, showing very grey and dim, save when the flare of some great fire did beat upward in the Land, and sent huge and monstrous lights upon it. And we to have need always now to remember this Tower, and to keep the more so to the sheltered hiding of the bushes. Yet, in verity, we to have little thought of aught, save of the grim and threatening terror and monstrousness which did stand forever upon that low hill, and did be the House of Silence.

And in the eleventh hour, we did go creeping from bush unto bush, and did be as shadows that went in the mixt greyness and odd shinings of that Land. And the grim and dreadful House did be now unto our right, and did loom huge and utter silent above us in the night.

And the lights of the House did shine steadfast and deathless with a noiseless shining, as that they shone out of the quiet of Eternity. And there did a seeming of Unholiness to brood in the air, and a sense of all and deathly Knowledge; so that, surely, our hiding did seem but a futile thing unto our spirits; for it was to us as that we did be watched quiet and always by a Power as we slipt gentle from bush unto bush.

And when the twelfth hour did be nigh, we to begin to draw clear of the House; and surely there to come somewhat of ease into my brain and heart, for it did be as that we should come clear of all harm. And I turned to the Maid, that I whisper gentle and loving encouragement unto her. And lo! in that moment, Mine Own gave out a sudden low sobbing, and was gone still upon the earth. And, truly, mine heart did seem to die in me! for I knew that there did be directed a Force out of the House of Silence, which did be aimed unto the Spirit of Mine Own Maid. And I caught the Maid instant into mine arms, and I set my body between her body and the dreadness of the House; and surely, my spirit to perceive that there beat out at her a dreadful Force, which did have in it an utter Silence and a bleakness of Desolation. And lo! I saw in a moment that the Force had no power to slay me; but did surely make to slay the Maid. And I set my Spirit and my Will about her, for a shield, if this might be, and I had her to mine arms as that she did be mine own babe. And I stood upright, for there did be no more use to hide; and I knew that I must walk forever until that I have Mine Own to the Shelter of the Mighty Refuge, or to walk until I die; for only with speed might I save her from the dread and horrid Malice of this Force.

And I set free the Diskos from mine hip, and had it in mine arms beside the Maid, and I strode forward out of the bushes, and put forth my strength that I journey with an utter speed. And ever my spirit did know of that monstrous Force which did be direct upon us, to the Destruction of Mine Own Maid. And odd whiles, as I walkt, I called Mine Own by her olden love name, and by the new name of Naani; but never did she move or seem even that she lived; and surely mine heart sickened within me with a mighty despair, so that a constant madness did begin to thrill in me and to make me something monstrous in strength, with my fierce agony and intentness to save. And one hope only had I, that I bring her yet living into the Shelter of the Mighty Refuge; and so, swift, to the care of the Doctors.

And lo! I did strive to be wise in my despair; for I made a quick halting soon, and I warmed a broth of the tablets and water upon a hot rock, and strove that I set some of the broth between the closed lips of Mine Own Maid; yet did it be useless, as I to have known before in my heart. And always I kept my body and my Will and my Spirit and my Love between the Maid and the dreadfulness of the House. And I made some of the water, and dasht it upon the face of Mine Own, and I chafed her hands; but truly it to have no use; neither did I truly to think it should be like to. And I wiped her face then, and harked to her dear heart; and surely it did beat, very slow and husht. And afterward, I wrapt her in the cloak and I lifted her and set forward. And surely no man did ever go so fast, on his feet for an eternity.

And three days I went thus; and then as I drew nigh to the Pyramid, I heard, afar off, the baying of the Night Hounds and knew a monstrous pack was out and they came nearer; so that I called out in vain despair and to no end, why that none come to give me aid in this extremity; for the Hounds did bay now but the half of a great mile, upon my left, and did surely have scent of me, by the way of their dreadful baying.

And, truly, the Millions to have an anguish of sympathy for me; for the spiritual noise of their emotion did be plain unto my spirit; and they surely to have seen and to have interpreted the way that I did look about me and affear call out in despair; for there came all about me in a moment the companioning of a great and sweet spiritual force, which I did be bred of their quick going with me in their understanding and love; and they to have perceived how that I did be unto the end of hope; and the Hounds to be almost upon me.

And in this moment, there came to mine hearing the shaking beat of the Earth Current; so that I knew the Humans to take desperate means to save. And there came to my view a vast pack of the Hounds unto my left, and they came running at a great pace, and their heads did be low, and they to be so great as horses; and seen plain, and again in shadow, all in the same moment, as they did come.

And, in verity, I knew that we two to be dead indeed ere a minute be gone, if that the Humans not to haste. And I stood where I did be; for there was no more use to run; and I lookt from the Hounds unto the Mighty Pyramid, and again to the Hounds. And again I lookt with mine hope gone, unto the Pyramid; for the Hounds did be scarce two hundred fathoms off from me; and there did be hundreds of the mighty beasts. And lo! even as I lookt that last time unto the Pyramid, there brake out a monstrous bursting flame, that did rush downward from the Sealed lower part of the Mighty Pyramid. And the flame smote downward upon the Land where the Hounds did run, and all the Night to be lost from my sight in the brightness and strangeness of that mighty flame; so that I saw no more the Pyramid, or aught; but only the shining and dreadful glory of that flame. And the Flame made a blast in the Night, and a hotness that did seem to wither me, even where I did be from it. And I perceived that the Humans had truly turned loose the Earth Current upon the Hounds, that I be saved. And there went a constant great thundering over the land, because that the Earth-Force did rend and split the air, and did tear up the earth. And the roaring of the Monsters did be husht and lost in that mighty sound; and I to see no place where the Hounds did be; but only flames and broken lands where the Earth-Force did strike; and great rocks did be hurled all whithers, with a vast noise; and truly it did be a mercy that I was not slain an hundred times, if this might be, by the fallings and burstings of great rocks and boulders.

And lo! in a moment the Humans did cut off the Earth-Force, and had it again to their control. And there to seem now a great quietness upon the Land, and an utter dark; save that flames and noise came from that part where the Current did strike. And I very speedy to come free of the dazedness that had me, and made again to my running; for, in truth, it to seem now that I should yet be let to win unto safety with Mine Own.

And mine eyes did grow presently unto their accustomed using; and I saw there went living things, creeping, between me and the light of the Circle. And I to know that I yet to have to fight bitter, if that I would bring the Maid safe. And I swung the Diskos free, and ran on.

And sudden my Spirit to know that I did be warned of some new peril; and I to look upward into the night, that the Master Monstruwacan should mayhap to tell me the danger, by the Set Speech. But, in truth, there came not the quick flashings of the Set Speech; but only an upward stillness, and a dimness of the lights of the Mighty Pyramid. And afterward, I to learn that the dear Master Monstruwacan made to warn me of danger; but that all the instruments of the Tower of Observation to fail to work, and likewise all the machinery of the Pyramid to cease, even unto the moving of the great lifts, and the moans of the air Pumps; and all to have been this way for nigh a great hour, until that the Earth Current did flow again more full. And surely, this doth show that Death did nigh to come unto all the Millions, because of the great trial that did be made to save us.

But, truly, my spirit did be warned by the trouble of the Millions; so that I went ever more warily, and did look all ways. And lo! sudden I to stare above me into the night; and there to be a pale circle, very quiet and steadfast that did go alway over the twain of us. And I saw that this did be surely one of those sweet Powers of Holiness, that did stand between our souls and some dread Power that came anigh to work our Destruction. And I to have no overfear; but did put my trust in the Force of Holiness, and went forward, running warily.

And surely, I came mayhap so nigh as to within four hundred paces of the Circle; and I to think that I yet to win Mine Own safe and undelayed within the guarding of the Circle. And the light of the Circle did burn dim; so that I had sudden fear whether that it be any more use for a Guard, until that the Earth Current to come more free. And all this as I ran, swift and weary and utter anxious.

And lo! in that moment in a dim place there rose up three beast-men from the earth, and came at me growling. And the first did be so close that I had no room to the Diskos; but beat in the head of the man with the haft-part. And I leaped unto the side then, and swung the Diskos, and did be utter mad, yet chill, with fury; so that the Maid did be no more than a babe in the crook of mine arm. And I came in sudden to meet the two beast-men as they ran at me; and I cut quick and light with the great Weapon, and did have that anger upon me which doth make the heart a place of cold and deadly intent; so that I had a wondrous and brutal judgment to the slaying. And, truly, I slew them as that they had been no more than mice; and I had no harm, neither so much as a touch from them. And, behold! in that moment there came a great Shout of wonder and of welcome from within the Circle. And I lookt swiftly, and began again to run; for there did be men in grey armour all within the Circle; yet came they not to mine aid. And lo! in a moment I knew why that the Hundred Thousand did have held off from me in mine extremity; for, behold! there did be monstrous Black Mounds all along without of the Circle, and did rock and sway with a force of strange life that did set an horror into my soul as I ran; for truly they did be the visible signs of monstrous Forces of Evil. And did any Human have ventured outward beyond the Circle, then had that man been Destroyed in the spirit, and lost utterly; so that none had dared to come; neither had it been of use if any had made themselves to be a sacrifice to aid me; for, truly, they to have been of no use when dead, as you shall say.

And there came a constant shouting from the Hundred Thousand to me, that I haste, and indeed to haste. And truly I did haste with all my strength. And I lookt unto the dear Circle of Holiness that did be above us twain; and it to go steadfast over us; so that I saw we to be surely saved.

And lo! I to be no more than an hundred paces now from the

glowing of the Circle. And behold! even in that instant, there must come brutal things to destroy us; for there came an herd of squat and brutish men all about me in a moment from the shadows, where they had been hid. And they caught at me, and caught at the Maid to tear her from mine arm. And truly, it did be as that they surely to have success; for I could nowise in a moment free myself, and yet to guard the Maid and to use the Diskos. And lo! I kickt with my metal boots, and gave from them, and turned all ways in a moment, and wrenched free; and I leaped back; and the herd of horrid brutes after me. And now I to have space for the Diskos, and a grimness in mine heart; and I came round very sudden, and ran in among the men, smiting. And I hit very swift from right to left, and to and fro with a constant quick circling. And the Diskos did spin and roar, and made a strange light upon the faces of the men; and they to have tusks like to the tusks of pigs. And surely I did rage through them, smiting; and they to seem without end. But I made alway forward unto the glowing of the Circle; and the night be full in that place of the fierce shoutings of the Hundred Thousand; and many—as I did learn—to have tried to come unto me, but that their comrades held them from so useless a dying.

And, in verity, I to be now scarce fifty paces from the glowing of the Circle; and did be night to fall; for I did be all wounded with the fight, and ill with a vast weariness and the despair and madness of my journey; and moreover, as you do know, I not to have slept, but to have carried the Maid forever through days and nights, and to have fought oft. And lo! the Hundred Thousand stood just within the Circle, and they that were to the front did swing each man the Diskos; and they hurled each the Diskos in among the herd of tuskt men that did make to slay me. And surely this to save me; for the herd did thin to my front; and I to gather my strength, and to charge with despair and to smite and never be ceased of smiting; so that there did be dead creatures all about. And behold! I brake through the herd, with Mine Own, and did be upon the Circle. And lo! I stept over the Circle; and a thousand hands did come forward to give me help; yet did none touch me, but gave back from me; for there did be that about me which held them off, as with an awe; for I to be strange unto them. And I stood there in a great silence, and the Diskos in mine hand ran blood to the haft. And maybe I rokt as I stood; for many again did put out their hands, as to hold me, and again drew back, and were silent. And I lookt unto them, and they lookt back at me; and I did gasp awhile, and was strangely dazed, and did try to tell them that I had need of the Doctors for the Life of Mine Own Maid, that did be dying in mine arms. And behold, in that moment, there did be a sound of giants running out in the night. And some then to cry out different matters, to aid me, and to beware of the giants, and to bring the Doctors to attend me on the instant. And other voices did call that the Holy light was gone from above; and likewise the Black Mounds from the outer part of the Circle. And there did be a monstrous noise of roarings in the Land, and all to come bewildered unto my brain, which did surely fail now with the grim and utter stress which had been mine so long. And there to be also a constant noise that came from near and from upward; and truly I to know, as in a dream, that it did be made of the shouting of the countless Millions, that did make an eternal and vague roaring-sound upward in the night, that did come down from the upper heights, no more loud than a strange and continued murmuring out of the lofty miles.

And surely, I to find my voice in a little minute, and did ask a near man whether there be any Doctors with the men. And in that moment there came forward a Master of the Diskos, which doth be as a Commander of this age. And he made the Salute of Honor with the Diskos, and would have eased the Maid from me; but I to ask again, very slow, whether that there was a Doctor a-near. And he on the instant to give an order; and the great thousands begin to shape, and did make a mighty lane unto the great Gateway of the Mighty Pyramid. And the Master of the Diskos made a sign to certain of they that did be near; and they stood about me, as I to know dully, lest I fall; but they not to touch me; for I did be as that I must not be laid hand upon; for I did near to choke with despair lest I to have come Home too late; and surely, also, the men to seem as that I did be strange unto them.

And there went orders swift and constant this way and that; and lo! in a little while, there came two big men of the Upward Cities, running; and they had a little man between them upon a sling. And the little man did be a Master of the Doctors; and he aided me gentle to lay Mine Own Maid upon the earth. And the Master of the Diskos made a sign, and the men that did be near, turned each his back; and the Doctor to make examination for the life of Mine Own.

And there to come about that time a seeming of silence in the land. And truly the Hundred Thousand did be utter quiet; and a great quiet in the Mighty Pyramid; for in truth, all to know, by this, that there to be a fear that the Maid I did bring out of the night, did be slain by the Evil Forces.

And sudden the little man that did be the Master Doctor, lookt up quiet and piteous at me; so that I knew in a moment that Mine Own Maid did be dead. And he to see that I knew; and he covered the face of Mine Own, and stood up very speedy; and he called softly to the men that did be to my back, and he signed to them that some to support me, and some to lift Mine Own Maid, and bare her unto the Great Gateway. And he lookt keen at me; and I to fight a little that I breathe; and afterward did make with mine hands, that the men not to come near me, neither to touch Mine Own. And the Master Doctor to understand that I did be truly strong until I die, and did beckon the men from me, and from the Maid.

And I stoopt, in a little, and I lifted Mine Own Maid into mine arms for that last journeying.

And I came down the mighty lane of the Hundred Thousand, all in their grey armor. And they did make silent salute with the Diskos reversed, each man as I past him, and did be utter silent. And I scarce to wot of aught, save that all the world did be quiet and emptied, and my task to have failed, and Mine Own to lie dead in mine arms. Yet, truly, did it to have failed utter? For I had surely saved Mine Own from the terror of the Second Night Land, and she not to have come alone and with madness unto her death; but to have died in mine arms; and she surely to have been comforted within her spirit, because that my love did be so utter about her. And I to think vaguely and terribly on an hundred sweet love actions that she to have shown unto me; and sudden I did remember with a dreadful pain how that I never to have waked to discover Mine Own Maid kissing me in my sleep, as I to have meant. And a madness of anguish did flash sudden through the numbness upon my brain; so that I did be blinded a little, and surely went crooked in my walk; for I to know, sudden, that the Master Doctor steadied mine elbow for a moment; but afterward did leave me be, as I to have again control of my spirit.

And lo! as I drew nigh unto the Great Gateway, the lights of the Pyramid to begin to glow again more strong, and the machinery of the Lifts and the Air Pumps to work, because that now the Earth Current did grow once more to natural strength. And they to have power now to open the Great Gates, which did be done by great machines. And there to come forth to meet me a number of the Masters of the Mighty Pyramid; and the dear Master Monstruwacan did come before them all, so eager as that he did be mine own Father. And he to have heard somewhat, vaguely, that there to have been a fear for the life of the maid that I did bring. And surely, he did be told by one near to the

Gateway, that the Maid did be dead in mine arms; for he and all the Masters did pause and stand silent for me to go by, and did reverse each his Diskos; and this to have been an Honour shown, than which there did be scarce any greater.

And there went a constant murmuring up in the night, which did be the speech of the Millions, questioning. And the news that the Maid did be dead, went upward through the miles. And my spirit to know, as in a dream, of the spiritual noise which did go outward through all space, and did be the grief of the Multitudes, as they did hear this thing. Yet, truly, there did nothing comfort me anywise; neither I proper yet to know the verity of my loss; for I did go stunned.

And I came in through the Great Gateway, and the Full Watch did stand there silent in their armour; and they made the Salute of Honour. And I went onward with the dead Maid that I did bring out of Eternity.

And presently, they that were around, did guide me, with the Maid in mine arms, unto the Great Lift. And I took Mine Own Maid into the Great Lift; and the Masters came with me, and did be in their armour; and none did speak to me. And the Master Monstruwacan and the Master of the Doctors stood silent to the side of me. And there did be everywhere great Multitudes, that I did see vaguely; but my spirit not to wot of them.

And lo! I stood very quiet and dumb as we did go upward through the miles; and the Millions of the Cities stood about the Great Lift, and there did be a great silence upward and downward through the strange miles; save for the weeping of women that did sound far and low and constant.

And presently I to know that the Master Monstruwacan and the Master of the Doctors did look one to the other; and I to be aware sudden that I stood in my blood; for I did be wounded in an hundred parts, and the blood to go alway from me. Yet did the Master Doctor be slow to do aught for me, because that he to perceive that I did be slain in the heart; and there to be no pain so dreadful as that he should be like to wake me unto, if that he went hastily.

Yet, presently, there did come whirlings into mine head; and someone did surely make to ease Mine Own Maid from mine arms. But I held her, dumbly; and the blood to go the more from me; and they not to know what should be done. And I to look at them. And the dear Master Monstruwacan did be saying somewhat unto me, that I did have no power to hear; but only to know that his face did be human. And there went a strange noise all about me; and the Master

Monstruwacan to seem to hold me up, and to beckon to some that did be to my back. And lo! there came a blackness, and the gentleness of arms about mine armour. . . .

And I to come presently to quietness and to half-dreams; and did alway to seem that I carried Mine Own Maid in mine arms. But truly there did pass three great days, whilst that I did be thus. And I all that while to be laid quiet, and to be tended by the Master Doctor, and aided by all knowledge that did be known of the humans.

And on the third day, as it might be called, I to come full unto my senses; and the pain to take me in the breast; and the Master of the Doctors did be with me, and they that nurst me; and the Master Doctor watched me very keen and gentle.

And I did be in a bed of the Health Room of mine own city. And I gat from the bed, and the Doctor to say naught; but only to watch me. And I walkt to and fro a little, and he alway to watch me; and presently he gave me somewhat to drink; and I drank. And I was gone soon from all knowledge.

And I to come again unto a knowing that I yet to live; and there went a certain strength in my body. And lo! the first that I did see, was the Master of the Doctors; and I to perceive in a moment that he had wakened me, and had nurst my strength for that moment, that I live through the Burial. For he to be very wise, and to have known from that first seeing of me, that I not to live after that Mine Own did die.

And there was brought to me a loose garment; but I to refuse the garment, dumbly, and did look about me, very troubled and forgetting. And the Master Doctor lookt alway at me; and lo! in a moment he called one, and gave an order. And there was brought in then my broken armour, and a garment to wear below. And I then to know that I did be content in this matter; and the Doctor alway to watch me. And they drest me in my broken armour. And surely, as they drest me, my spirit to hear the sorrow and sympathy of the Multitudes, and did know that they went downward by millions, unto the Country of Silence. And lo! in that moment when I near to be in mine armour, I to mind sudden again that I never to have waked to discover Mine Own Maid kissing me in my sleep. And the Pain gat me in the breast, so that I had surely ended then, but that the Master Doctor set somewhat to my breath, that eased me, and gave something of dullness unto my senses for a while.

And I did be carried then in a sling unto the Great Lift, and there did be a bed in the lift, and the Doctor to have me to lie upon the bed; and I to know that he also to know that I never to need a bed any more; neither should I ever to come upward again in the Lift.

And truly the Mighty Pyramid did be an emptyness; for there did seem to be left only the Stress Masters that did arrange the moving of the Millions. And the Stress Masters did stand about the Lift, as we dropt downward through the great miles unto the Underground Fields.

And we came downward in the last unto the Country of Silence, which did lie an hundred miles deep in the world, and did be an hundred miles every way of Silence unto the Dead.

And they that were with me, gat me from the Lift, and did mean to carry me in the sling unto The Last Road. But I stood upon my feet, and made that I should walk, and I held out mine hand for the Diskos, which one did carry. And the Master Doctor signed that they should obey me, as my spirit to know. And I walkt very steadfast down the Way that did lead unto The Last Road; and the Master Doctor walkt behind me, a little space off. And surely, there did be all the Peoples of the World in that great Country; and the Peoples did be spread out forever, so far as my seeing did go; and they to have sight of me; and all the aether did be stirred with the humanness of their sorrow and their kind sympathy. And there grew a murmur, which did be like to a low rolling thunder, and did be the voices of the Peoples. And the rolling of that great husht Sound went to and fro across that mighty Country of Quiet; and there to be afterward an utter silence.

And I saw below me the place of the Last Rest, where did be the beginning of The Last Road; and there did lie there a little figure, covered with a white robe, that did glimmer with the beauteous work of women that had stitcht love and honour into that Last Garment. And surely, I to rock upon my feet, and to steady myself with the Diskos; and the Master Doctor to be unto my side in a moment, and gave me again something that I breathe-in. But, indeed, I to refuse, after that I had taken one breath of the drug; for I to be able to bear my pain the little time that I now to have to live; and I to mean that I have no dimness of my senses for those short minutes that I should have yet near unto Mine Own. And truly the Master Doctor did not press me anywise, but had a perfect understanding, and went quiet again to my rearward.

And I came soon to that place where Mine Own Dead One did lie; and the Master Monstruwacan stood to her feet, and did be clothed in grey armour, and had the Diskos reversed; and this to be for an Honour unto My Dead Maid. And there kneeled two maids in white, one to the right and one to the left of Mine Own, and they to be for

Faithfulness, and did be maids, because that they watched by a maid; and had likewise been matrons, if that the Dead had been wife unto any. And the place at the Head of the Last Rest did be empty, and did be for me; and he that stood to the head, did be for Love; for it did be the chief, and did hold dominion over and did make to live both Faithfulness and Honour. And this to be the way of the Burial alway.

And lo! I took my courage into my heart; and I stood to the head of Mine Own Maid; and I lookt down upon the wondrous white glory of the garment, which did be white because that Mine Own did be a Maid; yet did be worked with yellow Flowers of Weeping, as we did call them, because that she had died in love. And I to know that no hand had toucht that wonderful garment, save the hands of maidens.

And behold! as I stood there, from far away over the Land, there did come a far and faint sound; and the sound did come more nigh, so that I knew that afar off, beyond the Hills of the Babes, the Millions did begin to sing the Calling Song, where Million did call husht unto Million, and the sound did come onward toward where we did be, and did go over us, and pass onward in a husht and wondrous breathing of sound, as that all the Love that did be ever in this world, did call in a low anguish unto a lost Beloved. And the sound to pass away and away over that mighty Country in the deep world, and did hush and hush unto a great and utter silence, save for faint murmur of countless women weeping, that did be in the air of that Land of Quiet.

And there to be a space of silence, and again the silence to be broke by a far sound; and there to come again from beyond the far Hills of the Babes a strange and low sound, and did be as of a wind wandering through damp forests. And the sound grew, and came across the Hills of the Babes, and did be breathed forth by Million after Million, so that in a little I to hear the Song of Weeping sung very low and sorrowful by the multitudes. And the Song came onward over all that great Country, and past over us, and went onward into the far Land beyond the Dome, and did be caught by the voices of Millions that did be hid in great distances, and so to go onward forever, and to die at last unto a mighty silence.

And the Master Monstruwacan lookt at me from the feet of Mine Own Maid, and I to know that the moment did be come when I to part from the maid Naani forever and forever, even though I to live in some strange future, and to find her soul in some other sweet child. And I stoopt and laid the Diskos beside Mine Own Maid there upon the Last Rest; and the two maids drew back the light wonder of the Garment, and showed me the face of Mine Own, and she to sleep there forever so sweet and husht as a child, and as oft I to have seen her to sleep. And I lookt a little while, and the pain of mine heart did be sufficient, so that I knew I died as I lookt. And once more I lookt, and I set my soul about Mine Own. And I fought with myself, and stood upward, and the maids did cover the face of Mine Own Maid.

And the Master Monstruwacan commended Naani unto Eternity. And he raised the Diskos reversed; and lo! the Road did begin to move upward unto the Dome, and Mine Own Maid did be upon the Road; and I to fight that I keep breathing; so that I not to die before she be lost utter to my sight.

And there did rise now a sound from all that Country that had no order in it; and did be like to a low moaning that did fill all the air of the Land; and there to be also a constant sound, as of a little whistling dree wind that did be in all that Country of Quiet; and truly this to be more than any singing; for it to be the true weeping of multitudes, that did sorrow from the heart, with the grief of this thing that did be.

And I stood utter still, and did draw my breath very even, and lookt unto that small form that did be now afar off where it did lie upon the moving Roadway. And I gazed, as that my soul and all my being did have no power else, even as a man that dies, doth set all his power to a last movement. And I not to wot that the Master Monstruwacan and the two maids did hold me up, because they to perceive that I did be dying; for I only to see Mine Own Little One lying afar off upon the moving of the Last Road.

And the maid in that moment to come to the place where the Road did pass into the strange and luminous vapour of the Earth Current, which did lie all about the base of the Dome; and the vapour to be only as a faint shining smoke, scarce seen, yet to be enough to give something of uncertainty to the Dead, when that they did have past inward of it.

And I stared, with all that did be left of my strength; for Mine Own to be gone utter and forever in but a little minute. And the uncertainty of the luminous vapour did cling about her, and to make her to seem unreal to my gaze; for the vapour did be in constant movement, and to give a seeming of shifting to and fro of all that did be in it.

And behold! as I did stare, with my dreadful pain, there did be sudden a strange hoarse noise from the nearer Millions. And lo! in an instant there came a mighty SHOUT out of all that Country; and the shout did be made again, and did grow into a mighty hoarse roaring from the Millions, so that all that great Country did be filled with the monstrous sound. And, in verity, I to have seen the thing likewise;

but to have set it to the madness of longing of mine heart and to that desperate and dreadful pain which did make me to be crazed and lost from all sane thinking.

And the thing that I did see, had been that the Maid did seem to move there upon The Last Road, where she did lie; but indeed, this to have appeared only to be the stirring of the luminous vapor of the Earth Current, which did seem to make things shift, as I have told.

And lo! I now to see truly again that the Maid did move where she laid afar off upon the Road; and I now to know, and to believe that she did indeed live. And my life came into me within a bounding; yet did mine heart seem to be a moment stilled in my breast. And the Master Monstruwacan to have signed already that the Roadway be stopt, and brought backward; but I to be now upon the Last Road, and did run as a madman, shouting vainly upon the name of Mine Own. And I to learn afterward that there to have been a dreadful peril that all the near Millions to rush toward the Last Road, and so, mayhap, to have caused the death of many, and to have been like to have crusht Mine Own. But this danger to have been eased, because that the Watch Master did act very prompt, and set the great regiments of his men to keep back the Millions, and did send a signal abroad over all the Country, that there to be calmness, for that the Maid should be succoured. And alway, whilst this to be, I did run staggering most strangely upward of the Last Road; and surely that great roof did ring and boom with the constant and mighty shoutings of the Millions.

And there did run others also along the Road, to my back; but I to have been the first, and to make a good speed, though I did stagger and rock so strange upon my feet; and the Road always to be moving backward under me; and so I to be come wonderful soon unto where the Maid did be. And she to be upon her back, and to have pusht the Garment from her face, and did be lying with her eyes open, and a look of gentle wonderment upon her dear face. And she then to see me, and her eyes did smile at me, very glad and quiet; for there to be yet an utter weakness upon her.

And lo! I came with a falling beside her, and I gat upon my knees and upon mine hands, and mine heart did shake my lips to dry whisperings. And she to look weak and steadfast unto me, and I to look forever at her; and I did always try to say things unto her; but my mouth to refuse me.

And understanding did come into her, as a light; and she to know that instant that she to be truly come into the Mighty Pyramid, and I to have gat her there somewise; and she to wake sudden in her body, and set her hands forth all a-trembling from the garment, and in dreadful trouble. And I to see then that the blood did go from me, constant; and the Maid to have perceived this thing, so that she was waked the more proper in a moment from her death-swoon. And surely, I did bleed very dreadful; for all my wounds did be opened with my running. And I to have sudden power with my lips, and did say unto her, very simple, that I loved her. And she to be all in an haze from me; and I to know that she to have come likewise unto her knees, and did have mine head upon her breast; and there to be an utter shaking of the air with some great sound, and a mighty spiritual stirring of the aether of the world. And there to be then the voice of the Master Monstruwacan very dull in mine ears; and the low voice of the Master Doctor; but I never to hear what they did be saying; and did know only that Mine Own Maid did live; and I not to mean to die, but to fight unto living. And even whilst that I made this resolving, I was gone into an utter blackness.

The Love Days

Now, when that I gat back unto life, I to know that I went upward in the Lift, and did be upon that same bed, where I to think I never to need a bed any more, neither to come upward again from out of the Country of Silence.

And I to know vague and strange, that there rose up from out of the mighty depths of the world, the deep thunder of the Underground Organs, and did sound as that they made a strange and utter distant music beyond death; and there to go alway a rolling chaunting, as that multitudes did sing beyond far mountains, and the sound to be somewhiles as a far-blowing wind low in the deep; and again to come clear and to be that great olden melody of the Song of Honour. And I knew, as in a dream, that the Millions in that deep Country made an Honour and a Rejoicing over this Wonder of Joy which did be come. But yet all to be faint and half hid from me, and mine eyes to be as that they had no power to open, and I to seem to be lifting alway upon strange waters of unrealness. And there to be sweet and lovely odours, and these to be of reality, and to come from the great Fields, where the flowers did alway to grow about the passage ways of the Lifts; for the Lift even then to be going upward through the great miles.

And mayhap I moved a little; for there came the voice of the Master Doctor low and gentle to me; and bid me rest; for that all did be well with the Maid. And surely, afterward, I did be gone into an haze, and there to be then a seeming of days in which I half to live and half to sleep, and to wonder without trouble whether I did be dead.

And then there to come days when I lay very quiet, and had no thought of aught; and the Master Doctor oft to bend over me in this hour and that hour, and to look keen into my face. And in the end, after strange spaces, there bent over me another, and there lookt down upon me the dear and lovely face of Mine Own, and the eyes did speak love into my soul; yet did she be calm and husht. And I to begin again to live in my body; and I made, mayhap, a little fumbling with mine hands; for she to take and to hold them; and life to come from her to me; and she to be ever wordless and gentle; and contentment to grow in me, and presently a natural slumber.

And there came a day when I did be let rise, and they that tended me, carried me to one of the Quiet Gardens of the Pyramid; and they set me there, and they did seem to leave me alone. And there came One then around a bush, and lookt at me a moment, as with an half shyness; only that the love that did shine in her eyes, made the shyness to be a little thing. And, truly, I knew that it did be Mine Own Maid; but I never before to have seen Naani drest pretty as a maid. And I lookt to her, and knew that she did be more dainty than even I to have known. And sudden I made that I rise to come unto her; but she to run quick to me, that she stop me of this natural foolishness; and she then to sit beside me, and to take mine head against her breast, and she not to deny me her lips; but to both a maid and a mother to me in the same moment.

And afterward, she had me to be very still; and we to sit there in an utter dumb happiness, until they that did attend me, were come again. And the Master of the Doctors did be with them, and I to see that there went something of satisfaction in his face.

And after that day I saw Mine Own Maid every day; and I gat better unto health with a wondrous quickness; for Love did mend me. And soon I did be let go downward unto the Fields; but yet to go by private ways, because that the Multitudes should be like to follow me alway; and I to need to be quiet.

And the Maid to be with me; for the Master Monstruwacan and the Master of the Doctors did agree upon this matter, and had an Officer of Marriage to wed us; and we to be married very quiet and simple; for I yet to be over-weak for the Public Marriage, which we to have later; when, truly, the Millions made us a Guard of Honor eight miles high, from the top unto the bottom of Mighty Pyramid. But this to have been later, as I do tell, and did be a Ceremonial of the Peoples, because that they not to be denied that they give me an Honour.

And surely the Maid to be with me alway, and did be now my wife, and my strength to come alway upon me, and Mine Own to grow again unto a perfect health. And, in verity, we did be now in the Love Days which do be the most beauteous if that the Love to be True.

And we did wander through the mighty Fields at our will, and walkt in the Love Paths of the Fields, which did be alway anear to those places where did be the villages. And I to hide our name, lest we to be beset by any, out of natural curiousness and kindliness; for we to need to be utter together and quiet. And we to chose those places for our slumber where beauty of flowers did be most wondrous; and we to carry somewhat of food with us; but also to eat when we came unto the villages which did be here and there in the Fields, which were truly so huge as Countries. And Mine Own did make good her promise an hundred times, as you shall say, and did prepare me a great and hearty meal; and did tease me utter, that I be a glutton, as I did eat, and kist me lest that I have ever a chance to say aught in mine own defense. And truly, she did be all that mine heart and my spirit did desire; and she to have companioned me with Love, and to have entered my spirit into Joy.

And once we to go downward unto the Country of Silence; but not to stay very long at that time, because that my Memory did return upon me. Yet in the after time, we to wander there oft with Memory, and Holiness of great Thinkings, and with Love which doth hold all. And as we to leave that Country, I to tell Mine Own how that when she had been suspend of her life by the Horrid Force of the House, I to have minded me with a dreadful pain that I never to have waked to discover her kissing me when that I did sleep. And surely Mine Own Dear One did blush most lovely, and had never known that I did be aware of her sweet naughtiness; and she then to have all thought for mine agony, when that she did be dead, ere the Vapour of life of the Earth-Force did set her spirit free of the Silence. And she to come unto me, and set her arms about me in utter love and dear understanding.

And she then to tell me that the Doctors to say that she had been, as it were, stunned and froze of the Spirit, and all her Being and Life suspend; and the great life-force of the Earth-Current to have waked her spirit, and her body then to live and her blood to flow proper again. And the Doctors had talkt much and searched much of late in the olden Records of their Work; and they to have found somewhat of one such happening in the olden time; but truly, naught such to have been ever through a mighty age of years.

And whilst that we to wander and to rest in the Fields, I oft to tell Mine Own of this matter and that matter; and I to know that she had learned somewhat of odd things, ere I did be come to health; but not overmuch; for she also to have been utter alack, as you shall think; and to have come from her bed, when that I did lie so still, for the Master Doctor to have ordained this, because he to fear that I to be going truly to die, if that he not to do somewhat to awaken my spirit. And in verity, you shall think upon the deepness of my love, as I to know that she did have held mine hands so brave and gentle, whilst that she to have scarce power to her feet. And I to say a little holy praise of Mine Own; and did have her loving unto mine arms, that I hold her to me.

And so do I come to mine ending; and have but one more thing that I tell. And this to happen a while later; after that Mine Own and I had gone through the second marriage which did be the Public Marriage. For it did be, that one day My Wife, that did be Mine Own, did take me with a sweet cunning unto the Hall of Honour. And surely, when I was come there, I to see that many of the Peoples did be in that great Hall, and did stand about in a silence; yet as that they had no meaning to do aught; but yet to be that they did wait upon somewhat.

And My Wife did go forward with me unto the centre place of the Hall; and sudden I saw why that she did bring me so cunning sweet; for there did stand in the midst of the Hall of Honour, in the Place of Honour, a Statue of a man in broken armour, that did carry a maid forever.

And I did be dumb; and how of this Age shall you to know the Honour that this to mean in that; for it did be an Honour that was given only to the Great Dead; and I to be but a young man, and did be so utter far off from greatness; save that I to love with all mine heart and with all my spirit, and therefore death to be but a little thing before love. And you to know how Love doth make sweet and brave the heart; and to have understanding with me in mine humbleness and my wonder and my natural pride that there did any so think to honour me. And Mine Own did be weeping with joy and honest pride of her Man, beside me. And there to be an utter silence of dear sympathy in all the great Hall of Honour. And they that did be there, to let me go in quietness, with Mine Own, which did be a lovely thing of understanding.

And I to go loving and thoughtful with Mine Own Wife; and she to be very nigh to me. And I to have gained honour; yet to have learned that Honour doth be but as the ash of Life, if that you not to have Love. And I to have Love. And to have Love is to have all; for that which doth be truly LOVE doth mother Honour and Faithfulness; and they three to build the House of Joy.

Senator Sandy Mac Ghee

"YES, I ONCE MET A MAN NEAR AS SMART at jewel running as I myself," Captain Gault went on:

Sandy Mac Ghee, the Senator, you know. He was doing it to smash the jewel tariff. He was out to show that the Customs simply can't stop a smart man getting the stuff past them. And he was right. He knew there was a spy aboard, and one day, in the first class smoke room, he got all the passengers to trust him to run their jewelry through for them, duty free. Then he pointed out to the Chaplain how free from jewelry, and all such "heathenish charms," the passengers were; and of course, the fool of a parson must go and preach a sermon on that heading, in which he thought he was smoothing 'em down, I suppose!

Well, this is how Sandy did it. I was Captain of the ship, and I watched it all, and was up to my neck in it, as you might say. When the chief searcher and his men came aboard, Sandy was talking to a new pal of his, a Miss Macleoid, and he jumped suddenly to the rail and dumped a packet into the sea. Miss Macleoid called out "oh!" for she guessed he'd dumped something valuable. The Chief searcher then produced from his coat a brace and bit, and from his pocket several dowels (pieces of round wood) used as plugs to fit into holes in the deck-planks, over the heads of the holding-down bolts.

"Do you happen, Mister Mac Ghee, to recognize these?" he asked, with a grin of somewhat savage triumph; for he felt himself at last within touch of "putting away" Mac Ghee; and he knew that his superiors would count it in heavily for promotion; for the Treasury was sore, from top to bottom, as one might say, with the way that Sandy Mac Ghee's publicly successful jewel-runnings had given the opposition press a chance to be scathing in cutting headlines.

Sandy Mac Ghee stared, in a dumb, stupid kind of way at the dowels and the brace and bit. Then, he shrugged his shoulders, and attempted a laugh.

"You'll laugh better in a minute, I'm thinking," said the chief searcher. "Perhaps you'll come this way, Sir. We've already located the dowels you've hid the stuff under." He beckoned his men up. "Stand back there! Stand back!" he shouted in true official fashion, at the passengers, who had begun to crowd round—Many of them exceedingly anxious. One of the men, who appeared to be a carpenter, was down on his knees, working at the dowels in the deck-planks. Presently, he lifted one out, and it proved to be no more than a thin disk of wood, scarce a quarter of an inch thick, instead of a couple of inches or so. And in the hollow, between it and the bolt-head, there were three magnificent diamond rings. "There!" said the head searcher, unable to hold back his triumph. "There's no hiding places aboard ship, that we don't know of. You can't put that sort of trick over on us! Open up the others, Jim."

In half an hour, they appeared to have collected all the surplus rings and valuable jewels that had been missing since the day when Mac Ghee had explained to the men in the First Class smoke-room, the Custom's Jewel tariff. There was little, the head searcher felt, to add to his triumph, except the fixing of the crime upon Mac Ghee. But this, he could not do yet; for though the spy had found, and handed on to him, the dowels and the brace and bit; yet he had collected no evidence that would actually associate Mac Ghee with the hiding, and he knew it; and hence his attempt to bluff Mr. MacGhee into admitting that he knew where the stuff had been hid.

"Now," said the officer, to the passengers, as he collected his men, "if any of you ladies and gentlemen want your jewelry, you'll have to come up to the office to claim it, and pay the duty and fines, or else lose it!" Then he went; but as Mac Ghee walked ashore, later, he knew perfectly well that a Treasury detective tracked him all the way to his hotel. Perhaps the following cutting, which Sandy Mac Ghee enclosed with a note to his new friend, Miss Macleod, concludes this tale as effectively as anything I could add. The cutting is headed:

"SANDY PUTS ANOTHER OVER ON THE TREASURY"

"Sandy, Or His Ghost, Puts The Dowels Over The Diamonds"

Then followed much that I have told, in fluent and flowery journalese. "Only," it concluded:

"the diamond rings and the other gew-gaws that someone (was it you, Sandy dear?) had put under the deck dowels, weren't gen-u-ine at all, at all. (Sandy may have bought a little cheap jewelry in Brummagem!) Anyway, it was Brummagem trash the Head Searcher got swelled head over. And, of course, after this bully clean-up, the

Customs never bothered to frisk anyone in the covered hall adjoining the wharf; and Sandy and the passengers walked ashore with their fal-lals in their pockets, as happy as you please; and poor Uncle Sam has never touched a cent. Honest Sandy must go as usual for his Treasury Receipt, to add to his little collection that's going to knock the Jewel Bill out of time, before he's finished. Well done, Sandy! Go to it again; We're watching out for you!"

Sandy sent this note with the cutting:

Dear Miss Macleoid,

I heard you say, "oh!" when I dumped that package. It contained nothing but what was left over of the false Brummagem jewelry, that I bought in London; for I had planned out everything, before the trip across. If they'd caught me with that they might have been able to trace the dowel mystery to me. You will, I know, feel relieved to hear that, as usual, the Treasury will benefit to the full amount of what I smuggled. The sermon the Chaplain preached, was due to me, I'm afraid. You see, I guessed there was a Treasury spy somewhere in the ship; and I wanted to make sure he tumbled to the fact of the passengers' abstinence from what the Chaplain called "heathenish charms." So I got talking to the Chaplain about the way people were developing, these days, and I instanced that point in particular, and wondered why no one ever seemed to remark on these "upward tendencies." He fell at once for my plan, like a useful innocent!

I hope to see you next time I cross. I know your father makes the trip every month, and if you are with him, it will be a great pleasure to look forward to.

Yours faithfully,
Sandy Mac Ghee.

P.S. It was rather neat, don't you think so, leaving the brace and the odd dowels where the spy could find 'em!

P.P.S. By the way, I slipped a small parcel into your bag, when I was talking to you, just before the search officer came up. Take care of it for me, won't you. It contains 100,000 dollars worth of cut stones. I thought it better not to have it on me, in case the Treasury forced matters a bit, and detained me. S. MG.

The Last Word in Mysteries

"OH, YES, I'VE HAD MY SHARE of 'amoorus' adventures, too," asserted the Captain:

Why, my own sweetheart was once kidnapped up in 'Frisco, though she carried a gun; and I near went dotty till we traced her. We suspected old Tim Murgan's wood shanty, that was built out on wooden piles, over the river, and searched it through and through—a matter of two or three separate times; but we couldn't find her. Well, we watched the house day and night, and at last, one night, we saw three men with a big package enter the house. The police surrounded the house and entered it; but never a sign was there of the three big men and the big package. It was the last word in mysteries.

We had to give it up; but we still watched the house. And later, to crown the mystery, we saw the three men come out of that same house, that we had searched every nook of. It left us guessing. Only we did more. The police officer meant to take no chances this time, and, after having stationed his men, bid eight of the biggest pick up an old pile that lay along the side of the jetty. With this, they smashed in the door of the house, with a single quick run. Then, whilst two stood on guard in the doorway, the rest rushed inside. I heard the Officer order two of the men to "look after" Murgan, and they ran up the steep little stairway, and there was immediately a sound of pistol shots above.

But I was otherwise interested; for I had run into the kitchen; and there, in the middle of the floor, where the butt-ends of the floor-boards joined, the boards had been slid endwise apart, showing a small hole, just about big enough for a man to enter.

In the mouth of this hole, a small electric fan was whirling round silently. That was all; but it was the solution of the mystery. We lifted out the fan, and there below us went a deep, narrow shaft. At the bottom, there was a dim light.

"By George!" muttered the Officer, looking down. "It's the inside of one of the piles. Don't you see? It's a big iron pipe, covered, I expect on the outside with wood, so as to look like the rest."

And so it proved. When the men had lowered us down, I found that we had come into a long, round iron structure, lighted by a single small electric lamp.

"An old biler—sunk. Do you see?" said the Officer. "Lord! What a cute idea!"

One end of the sunk boiler was curtained off, and behind that curtain, there was a low camp-bed, and on the bed lay my sweetheart, sleeping quietly. Beside her, lying upon the floor, evidently her gaoler and attendant, and like her fast asleep, lay Mrs. Tim Murgan. That is about all.

There is little to explain. My sweetheart had been surprised by two men during a walk, and before she could get her gun free, they had a sponge of chloroform over her mouth and nostrils.

When she woke up, she found herself lying on a bed, in the big sunk boiler, with Mrs. Tim in attendance. She had been treated with a certain rough care and consideration; and had only been kept there, as was apparent to me, because her disappearance had created such a tremendous stir and commotion that they had been afraid to risk moving her, or even to attempt any overtures for a ransom.

The reason we did not discover her hiding place, is obvious; for it had never occurred to us that any of the piles supporting the house might be hollow, and the way the floor-boards met naturally and irregularly over the end of the hollow pile (there were really two of them, so as to have an up-draught and a down-draught), was so cunning that none of us had seen anything to make us suspicious.

There is one other thing. Down in the boiler was discovered an immense amount of stolen property, which helped to send Mr. and Mrs. Tim Murgan to the Penitentiary for quite a long period. And it was down there, with their big package of stolen goods, that the three strange men had hidden, whilst we searched so intently for some hidden compartment, big enough to hold them and the package they had carried.

The Dumpley Acrostics

YES, I ONCE DID QUITE A BIT of smart, detective work. I cleared up that affair of that valuable book, the "Dumpley Acrostics." There was only one copy in existence, so that Messrs. Malbrey and Jones, Editors of the "Bibliophile and Booktable" were astonished and sceptical when a Mr. Ralph Ludwig walked into their office with a second copy—a "find." They, Professor Wagflen, the great Bibliophile, and Mr. Neuls, chief librarian of the Caylen Museum (where reposed the supposed "one and only" copy of the "Dumpley Acrostics") all examined Ralph Ludwig's "find"—and pronounced it unmistakable genuine. Malbrey and Jones, however, smelt a rat, and put me on the job, and this is what I unearthed and told them in their office, after I had gathered all the characters there to hear my tale:

"Gentlemen," I began, "I went first to the Caylen Museum and asked questions. I found that "Rare Editions," such as the Dumpley, are never loaned out. An examination of the signatures in the registers showed that the book had been consulted only three times, by three separate people, Charles, Nolles, and Waterfield, in the last two years, and always in the presence of an attendant. Expert examination, showed, however, that the three signatures were in the same handwriting, and that they were identical with a specimen I had of Mr. Ralph Ludwig's writing. The next step is deduction on my part, and is indicated by reasoning as the only possible lines on which Mr. Ludwig could have worked. I can only suppose that Mr. Ludwig must, in some way or other, have come into possession of a dummy copy of the Acrostics. This blank-paper dummy of the book, would he made up by the printer and bookbinder, so as to enable Lord Wellbeck, who published the book, to see how the "Acrostics" would bind up and bulk out. The method is common in the publishing trade; and though the binding of a book may be exactly a duplicate of what the finished binding will be, yet the inside is nothing but blank paper of the same thickness and quality as that on which the finished hook will be printed. In this way, a publisher is enabled to see beforehand how the book will look.

"I am quite convinced that I have described the first step in Mr. Ludwig's ingenious little plot; for he made only three visits to the Museum; and as you will see in a minute, if he had not been provided already with a facsimile in binding of the "Acrostics," on his first visit, he could not have carried out the plot under four. Moreover, unless I am wrong in my psychology of the incident, it was through becoming possessed of this particular dummy copy, that Mr. Ludwig thought out his scheme.

"Well, the rest is simple. He went the first time to the Museum, and after appearing to study the Museum copy deftly replaced it with the dummy, which he had brought in, hidden about him. The attendant took the dummy (which was externally identical with the printed copy) in place of the genuine article which Mr. Ludwig had secreted somewhere on him. This was, of course, the one big risk in his little plot; also that someone might call to see the "Acrostics" before he could replace it again with the original; for this is what he meant to do, and did, after he had photographed each page. It must have been a deal of work, Mr. Ludwig!

"This accounts for his second visit, after which he printed the retrieved dummy copy, on a hand press, with the photographic blocks which he had prepared. And after he had done that, he returned to the Museum, and once more exchanged the copies, taking away now for 'keeps' the Museum copy, and leaving the most excellently printed 'dummy' in its place.

"Each time, as you know, he used a new name and a new handwriting, and probably disguises of some kind; for he had no wish to be in any way connected with the Museum copy. Also, if the blank dummy had been discovered between the first and second visits, then on his second visit, unless disguised, he would most certainly have been arrested.

"Now let us look at the lessons his little plot has for us. He realized that, if he stole the book frankly, he could never sell it in the open market. He would have to sell it secretly to some unscrupulous collector, who would of course (knowing it was stolen) give him next to nothing for it; and might indeed hand him over to the police; though as we are speaking of collectors, I don't think he feared much on that head.

"But if he could arrange so that the Museum still had its copy, he might sell his own without fear in the open market to the highest bidder. But, and here comes the lesson some of you ought to take to heart. Mr. Ludwig realized that his copy of the "Acrostics" would be mercilessly challenged and examined. And this is why he made his third exchange, and once more left his dummy (now printed as you know) and took away with him the authentic copy. He knew that the copy at the Museum would not be suspiciously examined; therefore his must be the genuine thing. If the three famous experts had given the same suspicious attention to the false copy at the Museum, which they took to be the original, this little, shall I call it comedy, would have been nipped right off in the bud! By the way, do comedies have buds? Summed up briefly, Mr. Ludwig's course of action has been: A. First visit to Museum to obtain the book, replacing it by his own blank "dummy" copy. B. Second visit, to return the book and take back his "dummy." C. Third visit, to exchange his now printed "dummy" for the authentic Museum copy. Is that clear to all of you? I need say little more. Mr. Neule, you hold in your hands what does not belong to your library. The copy which belongs to your Institution is in Messrs. Malbrey and Jones's safe, over there."

Alternate Versions

An Adventure of the Deep Waters

THIS IS AN EXTRAORDINARY TALE. We had come up from the Cape, and owing to the Trades heading us more than usual, we had made some hundreds of miles more westing than I ever did before or since.

I remember perfectly the particular night of the happening. I suppose what occurred stamped it solid into my memory with a thousand little details that in the ordinary way I should never have remembered an hour. And, of course, we talked it over so often among ourselves that this no doubt helped to fix it all past any forgetting.

I remember the Mate and I had been pacing the weather side of the poop and discussing various old shellbacks' superstitions. I was third mate, and it was between four and five bells in the first watch (i.e. between ten and half-past). Suddenly, he stopped in his walk and lifted his head and sniffed several times.

"My word, Mister," he said, "there's a rum kind of stink somewhere about. Don't you smell it?"

I sniffed once or twice at the light airs that were coming in on the beam; then I walked to the rail and leaned over, smelling again at the slight breeze. And abruptly I got a whiff of it, faint and sickly, yet vaguely suggestive of something I had once smelt before.

"I can smell something, Mr. Lammart," I said. "I could almost give it name; and yet, somehow I can't." I stared away into the dark, to windward. "What do you seem to smell?" I asked him.

"I can't smell anything now," he replied, coming over and standing beside me. "It's gone again—No! By Jove! there it is again. My goodness! Phoo—"

The smell was all about us now, filling the night air. It had still that indefinable familiarity about it, and yet it was curiously strange; and, more than anything else, it was certainly simply beastly.

The stench grew stronger, and presently the Mate asked me to go forward, and see whether the lookout man noticed anything. When I reached the break of the forecastle head, I called up to the man, to know whether he smelled anything.

"Smell anything, sir!" he sang out. "Jumpin'larks! I sh'ud think I do. I'm fair p'isoned with it!"

I ran up the weather steps, and stood beside him. The smell was certainly very plain up there; and after savouring it for a few moments, I asked him whether he thought it might be a dead whale. But he was very emphatic that this could not be the case; for, as he said, he had been nearly fifteen years in whaling ships, and knew the smell of a dead whale "like as you would the smell of bad whisky, sir," as he put it. " 'Tain't no whale, yon; but the Lord He knows what 'tis. I'm thinkin' it's Davy Jones come up for a breather."

I stayed with him some minutes, staring out into the darkness, but could see nothing; for, even had there been something big close to us, I doubt whether I could have seen it, so black a night it was, without a visible star, and with a vague, dull haze breeding an indistinctness all about the ship.

I returned to the Mate and reported that the lookout complained of the smell; but that neither he nor I had been able to see anything in the darkness to account for it.

By this time the queer, disgusting odour seemed to be in all the air about us, and the Mate told me to go below and shut all the ports, so as to keep the beastly smell out of the cabins and the saloon.

When I returned he suggested that we should shut the companion doors; and after that we commenced to pace the poop again, discussing the extraordinary smell, and stopping from time to time to stare through our night glasses out into the night about the ship.

"I'll tell you what it smells like, Mister," the Mate remarked, once, "and that's like a mighty old derelict I once went aboard in the North Atlantic. She was a proper old-timer, an' she gave us all the creeps. There was just this funny, dank, rummy sort of smell about her, sort of century-old bilge-water and dead men an' seaweed. I can't stop thinkin' we're nigh some lonesome old packet out there; an' a good thing we've not much way on us!"

"Do you notice how almighty quiet everything's gone the last half hour or so?" I said, a little later. "It must be the mist thickening down."

"It is the mist," said the Mate, going to the rail and staring out. "Good Lord, what's that?" he added.

Something had knocked his hat from his head, and it fell with a sharp rap at my feet. And suddenly, you know, I got a premonition of something horrid.

"Come away from the rail, sir," I said, sharply, and gave one jump, and caught him by the shoulders and dragged him back. "Come away from the side!"

"What's up, Mister?" he growled at me, and twisted his shoulders free. "What's wrong with you? Was it you knocked off my cap?" He stooped and felt around for it; and as he did so I heard something unmistakably fiddling away at the rail, which the Mate had just left.

"My God, sir!" I said, "there's something there. Hark!"

The Mate stiffened up, listening; then he heard it. It was for all the world as if something was feeling and rubbing the rail, there in the darkness, not two fathoms away from us.

"Who's there?" said the Mate quickly. Then, as there was no answer: "What the devil's this hanky-panky? Who's playing the goat there?" He made a swift step through the darkness towards the rail, but I caught him by the elbow.

"Don't go, Mister!" I said, hardly above a whisper. "It's not one of the men. Let me get a light."

"Quick, then!" he said; and I turned and ran aft to the binnacle and snatched out the lighted lamp. As I did so I heard the Mate shout something out of the darkness, in a strange voice. There came a sharp, loud, rattling sound, and then a crash, and immediately the Mate roaring to me to hasten with the light. His voice changed, even whilst he shouted, and gave out something that was nearer a scream than anything else. There came two loud, dull blows, and an extraordinary gasping sound; and then, as I raced along the poop, there was a tremendous smashing of glass, and an immediate silence.

"Mr. Lammart!" I shouted. "Mr. Lammart!" And then I had reached the place where I had left the Mate, not forty seconds before; but the Mate was not there.

"Mr. Lammart!" I shouted again, holding the light high over my head, and turning quickly to look behind me. As I did so my foot glided on some slippery substance and I went headlong to the deck, with a tremendous thud, smashing the lamp and putting out the light.

I was on my feet again in an instant. I groped a moment for the lamp, and as I did so I heard the men singing out from the main-deck and the noise of their feet as they came running aft. I found the broken lamp and realised it was useless; then I jumped for the companionway, and in half a minute I was back, with the big saloon lamp glaring bright in my hands.

I ran forward again, shielding the upper edge of the glass chimney from the draught of my running, and the blaze of the big lamp seemed to make the weather side of the poop as bright as day, except for the mist, that gave something of a vagueness to things.

Where I had left the Mate there was blood upon the deck, but nowhere any signs of the man himself. I ran to the weather rail and held the lamp to it. There was blood upon it; and the rail itself seemed to have been wrenched by some huge force. I put out my hand and found that I could shake it. Then I leaned out-board and held the lamp at arm's length, staring down over the ship's side.

"Mr. Lammart!" I shouted into the night and the thick mist. "Mr. Lammart! Mr. Lammart!" But my voice seemed to go lost and muffled and infinitely small away into the billowy darkness.

I heard the men snuffling and breathing, waiting to leeward of the poop. I whirled round to them, holding the lamp high.

"We heard somethin', sir," said Tarpley, the leading seaman in our watch. "Is anything wrong, sir?"

"The Mate's gone," I said blankly. "We heard something, and I went for the binnacle lamp. Then he shouted, and I heard something smashing things; and when I got back he'd gone clean." I turned and held the light out again over the unseen sea; and the men crowded round along the rail, and stared, bewildered.

"Blood, sir," said Tarpley, pointing. "There's something almighty queer out there!" He waved a huge hand into the darkness. "That's what stinks—"

He never finished; for, suddenly, one of the men cried out something in a frightened voice: "Look out, sir! Look out, sir!"

I saw, in one brief flash of sight, something come in with an infernal flicker of movement; and then, before I could form any notion of what I had seen, the lamp was dashed to pieces across the poop deck. In that instant my perceptions cleared, and I saw the incredible folly of what we were doing; for there we were, standing up against the blank, unknowable night; and out there in the dark there surely lurked some thing of monstrousness; and we were at its mercy. I seemed to feel it hovering, hovering over us; so that I felt the sickening creep of gooseflesh all over me.

"Stand back from the rail!" I shouted. "Stand back from the rail!" There was a rush of feet as the men obeyed, in sudden apprehension of their danger; and I gave back with them. Even as I did so I felt some invisible thing brush my shoulder; and an indescribable smell was in my nostrils, from something that moved over me in the dark.

"Down into the saloon, everyone!" I shouted. "Down with you all! Don't wait a moment!"

There was a rush along the dark weather deck, and then the men went helter skelter down the companion steps, into the saloon, falling and cursing over one another in the darkness. I sung out to the man at the wheel to join them, and then I followed.

I came upon the men huddled at the foot of the stairs, and filling up the passage, all crowding each other in the darkness. The Skipper's voice was filling the saloon, and he was demanding in violent adjectives the cause of so tremendous a noise. From the steward's berth there came also a voice, and the splutter of a match; and then the glow of a lamp in the saloon itself.

I pushed my way through the men and found the Captain in the saloon, in his sleeping gear, looking both drowsy and angry, though perhaps bewilderment topped every other feeling. He held his cabin lamp in his hand, and shone the light over the huddle of men.

I hurried to explain, and told him of the incredible disappearance of the Mate, and of my conviction that some extraordinary thing was lurking near the ship, out in the mist and the darkness. I mentioned the curious smell, and told how the Mate had suggested that we had drifted down near some old-time, sea-rotted derelict. And, you know, even as I put it into awkward words, my imagination began to awaken to horrible discomforts—a thousand dreadful impossibilities of the sea became suddenly possible.

The Captain (Jeldy was his name) did not stop to dress, but ran back into his cabin, and came out in a few moments with a couple of revolvers and a handful of cartridges. The second mate had come running out of his cabin at the noise, and had listed intensely to what I had to say. Now he jumped back into his berth and brought out his own lamp and a large-pattern revolver which was evidently ready loaded.

Captain Jeldy pushed one of his revolvers into my hands with some of the cartridges, and we began hastily to load the weapons. Then the Captain caught up his lamp and made for the stairway, ordering the men into the saloon out of his way.

"Shall you want them, sir?" I asked.

"No," he said. "It's no use their running any unnecessary risks." He threw a word over his shoulder: "Stay quiet here, men; if I want you, I'll give you a shout; then come spry!"

"Aye, aye, sir," said the watch, in a chorus; and then I was following the Captain up the stairs, with the second mate close behind.

We came up through the companionway on to the silence of the deserted poop. The mist had thickened up, even during the brief time that I had been below, and there was not a breath of wind. The mist was so dense that it seemed to press in upon us; and the two lamps made a kind of luminous halo in the mist, which seemed to absorb their light in a most peculiar way.

"Where was he?" the Captain asked me, almost in a whisper.

"On the port side, sir," I said, "a little foreside the charthouse, and about a dozen feet in from the rail. I'll show you the exact place."

We went forward along what had been the weather side, going quietly and watchfully; though, indeed, it was little enough that we could see because of the mist. Once, as I led the way, I thought I heard a vague sound somewhere in the mist; but was all unsure because of the creak, creak of the spars and gear as the vessel rolled slightly upon an odd, oily swell. Apart from this slight sound, and the far-up rustle of the canvas, slatting gently against the masts, there was no sound at all throughout the ship. I assure you, the silence seemed to me to be almost menacing, in the tense, nervous state in which I was.

"Hereabouts is where I left him," I whispered to the Captain, a few seconds later. "Hold your lamp low, sir. There's blood on the deck."

Captain Jeldy did so, and made a slight sound with his mouth at what he saw. Then, heedless of my hurried warning, he walked across to the rail, holding his lamp high up. I followed him; for I could not let him go alone; and the second mate came too, with his lamp. They leaned over the port rail, and held their lamps out into the mist and the unknown darkness beyond the ship's side. I remember how the lamps made just two yellow glares in the mist, ineffectual, yet serving somehow to make extraordinarily plain the vastitude of the night, and the possibilities of the dark. Perhaps that is a queer way to put it, but it gives you the effect of that moment upon my feelings. And all the time, you know, there was upon me the brutal, frightening expectancy of something reaching in at us from out of that everlasting darkness and mist that held all the sea and the night, so that we were just three mist-shrouded, hidden figures, peering nervously.

The mist was now so thick that we could not even see the surface of the water overside; and fore and aft of us the rail vanished away into the fog and the dark. And then, you know, as we stood here staring, I heard something moving down on the main deck. I caught Captain Jeldy by the elbow.

"Come away from the rail, sir," I said, hardly above a whisper; and he—with the swift premonition of danger—stepped back and allowed me to urge him well inboard. The second mate followed, and the three of us stood there in the mist, staring round about us and holding our revolvers handy, and the dull waves of the mist beating in slowly upon the lamps in vague wreathings and swirls of fog.

"What was it you heard, Mister?" asked the Captain, after a few moments.

"S-s-s-t!" I muttered. "There it is again. There's something moving, down on the main-deck!"

Captain Jeldy heard it himself, now; and the three of us stood listening intensely. Yet it was hard to know what to make of the sounds. And then, suddenly, there was the rattle of a deck ringbolt, and then again, as if something or someone were fumbling and playing with it.

"Down there on the main deck!" shouted the Captain, abruptly, his voice seeming hoarse close to my ear, yet immediately smothered by the fog. "Down there on the main deck! Who's there?"

But there came never an answering sound. And the three of us stood there, looking quickly this way and that, and listening. Try to imagine how we felt! Abruptly the second mate muttered something: "The lookout, sir! The lookout!"

Captain Jeldy took the hint, on the instant.

"On the lookout there!" he shouted.

And then, far away and muffled-sounding, there came the answering cry of the lookout man from the fo'cas'le head:

"Sir-r-r?" A little voice, long drawn out, through unknowable alleys of fog.

"Go below into the fo'cas'le, and shut both doors, and don't stir out till you're told!" sung out Captain Jeldy, his voice going lost into the mist. And then the man's answering: "Aye, aye, sir!" came to us faint and mournful. And directly afterwards the clang of a steel door, hollow-sounding and remote; and immediately the sound of another.

"That puts them safe for the present, anyway," said the second mate. And even as he spoke, there came again that indefinite noise, down upon the main deck, of something moving with an incredible and unnatural stealthiness.

"On the main deck there!" shouted Captain Jeldy, sternly. "If there is anyone there, answer, or I shall fire!"

The reply was both amazing and terrifying; for, suddenly, a tremendous blow was stricken upon the deck, and then there came the dull rolling sound of some enormous weight going hollowly across the main-deck. And then an abominable silence.

"My God!" said Captain Jeldy, in a low voice, "what was that?" And he raised his pistol, but I caught him by the wrist. "Don't shoot, sir!" I whispered. "It'll do no good. That—that—whatever it is—I—I mean it's something enormous, sir. I—I really wouldn't shoot—" I found it impossible to put my vague idea into words; but I felt there was a Force aboard, down on the main-deck, that it would be futile to attack with so ineffectual a thing as a puny revolver bullet.

And then, as I held Captain Jeldy's wrist, and he hesitated, irresolute there came a sudden bleating of sheep, and the sound of lashings being burst and the cracking of wood; and the next instant a huge crash, followed by another and then another, and the anguished m-a-a-ma-a-a-ing of the sheep.

"My God!" said the second mate, "the sheep pen's being beaten to pieces against the deck. Good God! What sort of thing could do that!"

The tremendous beating ceased, and there was a splashing overside; and after that a silence so profound that it seemed as if the whole atmosphere of the night was full of an unbearable, tense quietness. And then the damp slatting of a sail, far up in the night, that made me start—a lonesome sound to break suddenly through that infernal silence, upon my raw nerves.

"Get below, both of you. Smartly now!" muttered Captain Jeldy. "There's something run either aboard us or alongside; and we can't do anything till daylight."

We went below, and shut the doors of the companionway, and there we lay in the wide Atlantic, without wheel or lookout or officer in charge, and something incredible down on the dark main-deck.

II

For some hours we sat in the Captain's cabin, talking the matter over, while the men slept, sprawled in a dozen attitudes on the floor of the saloon. Captain Jeldy and the second mate still wore their pajamas, and our loaded revolvers lay handy on the cabin table. And so we watched anxiously through the hours for the dawn to come in.

As the light strengthened, we endeavoured to get some view of the sea from the ports; but the mist was so thick about us that it was exactly like looking out into a grey nothingness, that became presently white, as the day came.

"Now," said Captain Jeldy, "we're going to look into this." He went out through the saloon, to the companion stairs. At the top he opened the two doors, and the mist rolled in on us, white and impenetrable. For a little while we stood there, the three of us, absolutely silent and listening, with our revolvers handy; but never a sound came to us except the odd, vague slatting of a sail, or the slight creaking of the gear as the ship lifted on some slow, invisible swell.

Presently the Captain stepped cautiously out on to the deck; he was in his cabin slippers, and therefore made no sound. I was wearing gum-boots, and followed him silently, and the second mate came after me, in his bare feet. Captain Jeldy went a few paces along the deck and the mist hid him utterly. "Phoo!" I heard him mutter, "the stink's worse than ever!" His voice came odd and vague to me through the wreathing of the mist.

"The sun'll soon eat up all this fog," said the second mate, at my elbow, in a voice little above a whisper.

We stepped after the Captain, and found him a couple of fathoms away, standing shrouded in the mist in an attitude of tense listening.

"Can't hear a thing!" he whispered. "We'll go forrard to the break, as quiet as you like. Don't make a sound."

We went forward, like three shadows, and suddenly Captain Jeldy kicked his shin against something, and pitched headlong over it, making a tremendous noise. He got up quickly, swearing grimly, and the three of us stood there in silence, waiting lest any infernal thing should come upon us out of all that white invisibility. Once I felt sure I saw something coming towards me, and I raised my revolver; but saw in a moment that there was nothing. The tension of imminent, nervous expectancy eased from us, and Captain Jeldy stooped over the object on the deck.

"The port hencoop's been shifted out here!" he muttered. "It's all stove!"

"That must be what I heard last night, when the Mate went," I whispered. There was a loud crash, just before he sang out to me to hurry with the lamp."

Captain Jeldy left the smashed hencoop, and the three of us tiptoed silently to the rail across the break of the poop. Here we leaned over and stared down into the blank whiteness of the mist that hid everything.

"Can't see a thing," whispered the second mate; yet, as he spoke, I could fancy that I heard a slight, indefinite, slurring noise somewhere below us, and I caught them each by an arm to draw them back.

"There's something down there," I muttered. "For goodness' sake, come back from the rail."

We gave back a step or two, and then stopped to listen; and even as we did so there came a slight air playing through the mist.

"The breeze is coming!" said the second mate. "Look, the mist is clearing already!"

He was right. Already the look of white impenetrability had gone; and suddenly we could see the corner of the after hatch coamings through the thinning fog. Within a minute we could see as far forward as the mainmast, and then the stuff blew away from us, clear of the vessel, like a great wall of whiteness, that dissipated as it went.

"Look!" we all exclaimed together. The whole of the vessel was now clear to our sight; but it was not at the ship herself that we looked; for after one quick glance along the empty main-deck, we had seen something beyond the ship's side. All around the vessel there lay a submerged spread of weed, for maybe a good quarter of a mile upon every side.

"Weed!" sung out Captain Jeldy, in a voice of comprehension. "Weed! Look, by Jove! I guess I know now what got the Mate!"

He turned and ran to the port side and looked over. And suddenly he stiffened and beckoned silently over his shoulder to us to come and see. We had followed, and now we stood, one on each side of him, staring.

"Look!" whispered the Captain, pointing. "See the great brute! Do you see it? There! Look!"

At first I could see nothing except the submerged spread of the weed into which we had evidently run after dark. Then, as I stared intently, my gaze began to separate from the surrounding weed a leathery looking something that was somewhat darker in hue than the weed itself.

"My God!" said Captain Jeldy. "What a monster! What a monster! Just look at the brute! Look at the thing's eyes! That's what got the Mate. What a creature out of hell itself!"

I saw it plainly now. Three of the massive feelers lay twined in and out among the clumpings of the weed; and then, abruptly, I realised that the two extraordinary round disks, motionless and inscrutable, were the creature's eyes, just below the surface of the water. It appeared to be staring, expressionless, up at the steel side of the vessel. I traced, vaguely, the shapeless monstrosity of what must be termed its head. "My God!" I muttered. "It's an enormous squid of some kind! What an awful brute! What—"

The sharp report of the Captain's revolver came at that moment. He had fired at the thing; and instantly there was a most awful commotion alongside. The weed was hove upward, literally in tons. An enormous quantity was thrown aboard us by the thrashing of the monster's great feelers. The sea seemed almost to boil in one great cauldron of weed and water all about the brute, and the steel side of the ship resounded with the dull, tremendous blows that the creature gave in its struggle. And into all that whirling boil of tentacles, weed and sea water, the three of us emptied our revolvers as fast as we could fire and reload. I remember the feeling of fierce satisfaction I had in thus aiding to avenge the death of the Mate.

Suddenly the Captain roared out to us to jump back; and we obeyed on the instant. As we did so the weed rose up into a great mound, more than twenty feet in height, and more than a ton of it slopped aboard. The next instant three of the monstrous tentacles came in over the side, and the vessel gave a slow, sullen roll to port, as the weight came upon her; for the monster had literally hove itself up almost free of the sea against our port side, in one vast, leathery shape, all wreathed with weed fronds, and seeming drenched with blood and some curious black liquid.

The feelers that had come inboard thrashed around, here and there, and suddenly one of them curled in the most hideous, snake-like fashion around the base of the mainmast. This seemed to attract it; for immediately it curled the two others about the mast and forthwith wrenched upon it with such hideous violence that the whole towering length of spars, through all their height of a hundred and thirty feet, were shaken visibly, whilst the vessel herself vibrated with the stupendous efforts of the brute.

"It'll have the mast down, sir!" said the second mate, with a gasp. "My God! It'll strain her side open! My—"

"One of those blasting cartridges!" I said to Captain Jeldy almost in a shout, as the inspiration took me. "Blow the brute to pieces!"

"Get one, quick!" said the Captain, jerking his thumb toward the companion. "You know where they are."

In thirty seconds I was back with the cartridge. Captain Jeldy took out his knife and cut the fuse dead short; then, with a perfectly steady hand he lit the fuse and calmly held it until I backed away, shouting to him to throw it, for I knew it must explode in another couple of seconds.

Captain Jeldy threw the thing, like one throws a quoit, so that it fell into the sea, just on the outward side of the vast bulk of the monster. So well had he timed it that it burst, with a stunning report, just as it struck the water. The effect upon the squid was amazing. It seemed literally to collapse. The enormous tentacles released themselves from the mast and curled across the deck helplessly, and were drawn inertly over the rail as the enormous bulk sank away from the ship's side out of sight into the weed. The ship rolled slowly to starboard and then steadied. "Thank God!" I muttered, and looked at the two others. They were pallid and sweating, and I must have been the same.

"Here's the breeze again," said the second mate, a minute later. "We're moving." He turned, without another word, and raced aft to the wheel, while the vessel slid over and through the weed field.

Meanwhile, Captain Jeldy had sung out to the men, who had opened the port forecastle door, to keep under cover until he told them to come out. Then he turned to have a look at the vessel itself.

"Look where that brute broke up the sheep-pen!" cried Jeldy, pointing. "And here's the skylight of the sail locker smashed to bits!"

He walked across to it and glanced down. And suddenly he let out a thunderous shout of astonishment:

"Here's the Mate, down here!" he shouted. "He's not over board at all! He's here!"

He dropped himself down through the skylight on to the sails, and I after him; and, surely, there was the Mate, lying all huddled and insensible on a hummock of spare sails. In his right hand he held a drawn sheath knife, which he was in the habit of carrying, A.B. fashion, while his left hand was all caked with dried blood where he had been badly cut. Afterward we concluded he had cut himself in slashing at one of the tentacles of the squid, which had caught him round the left wrist, the tip of the tentacle being still curled, cruelly tight, about his arm, just as it had been when he hacked it through.

For the rest, it will please you, I am sure, to know that he was not seriously damaged; the creature having obviously flung him violently away, as he slashed at it, so that he had fallen in a stunned condition on to the pile of sails.

We got him on deck and down into his bunk, where we left the steward to attend to him. When we returned to the poop, the vessel had drawn clear of the weed field, and the Captain and I stopped for a few moments to stare astern over the taffrail. The second mate turned also, as he stood at the wheel, and the three of us looked in a silence at that Death Patch lying so quiet and sullen in the dawn.

As we stood and looked, something wavered up out of the heart of the weed—a long, tapering, sinuous thing, that curled and wavered against the dawn-light, and presently sank back again into the demure weed—a veritable spider of the deep, waiting in the great web that Dame Nature had spun for it, in the eddy of her tides and currents.

And we sailed away northward, with strengthening Trades, and left that patch of monstrousness to the loneliness of the sea.

Captain Gunbolt Charity and the Painted Lady

S.S. Boston.
April 2nd. Evening.

I HAD A SPLENDID OFFER MADE ME TO-DAY. A man came aboard, with what looked like a drawing-board, wrapped in brown paper.

He had a letter of introduction from a man who knows me.

"My name's Black, as I guess Mr. Abel's told you in the letter," he said. "I want to talk business with you, Cap'n Charity."

"Go ahead!" I said.

"What I say, goes no further, that's understood, I guess?" he asked. "Mr. Abel gave you a good name, Cap'n, an' he told me a thing or two about you that sounded pretty safe to me."

"I'm mum!" I told him. "If you've murdered someone, it's no concern of mine, and I don't want to hear about it. If it's anything clean, get it off your chest. You'll find me a good listener."

He nodded.

"You know about that Mona Lisa bit of goods?" he asked me.

"The picture?" I said.

He nodded again.

"Well," he said, "they got the wrong one. That's a copy that's been made from the original. It's a mighty good copy. It should be; it cost me over twenty thousand dollars, before it was finished.

"It's so good, you couldn't make 'em believe it isn't the original. I got the original, though, safe and sound; and a patron of mine's mad for it. That's what I came to see you about. I've got to get it taken across and through the U.S.A. Customs."

"But you don't tell me that a copy could fool all the art experts who've seen the recovered Mona Lisa?" I said. "Why the old canvas—"

"Wood, Cap'n," he interpolated.

"It's on wood, is it? " I said. "I'd never realised that. Well you don't tell me they don't know the kind of wood, and the smell and the general oldness and the seasonedness, and all the rest of it, of a panel of wood as old as that must be. The very smell of it would be enough to tell them whether it was the original or not.

"And that's not all! Why the pigments they used; they can't be matched to-day, so I understand. And how'd you get the 'time tone,' the 'time surface'—? Why, man, any one of these things could never be faked properly—not well enough to deceive an expert who knew his business. And then, I shouldn't think it would be possible for any man alive to even imitate the feeling of the picture—that is, if it's anything like I'm inclined to believe it must be.

"Don't you see, your tale won't wash. All these things put together, make a picture as famous as the Gioconda absolutely un-forgable—that is, of course, to an expert."

"Now, Cap'n," he said, "you've had your say, and I'll have mine."

"First of all, to get a panel that could not be pronounced anything but genuine, Cap'n, I had the Mona Lisa panel split, using a special machine-saw for the purpose. It was an anxious job, I can promise you. The man who cut it was an expert at his job, and the saw was a specially made ribbon-saw, with hair-fine teeth.

"He practised on a dozen model panels, before I'd let him split the Mona. Then he put the picture flat on the steel saw-table, and he just skinned off the Mona with no more than a sixteenth of an inch of wood under her. He did it as easy and smooth as skimming milk; but I just stood and sweated till it was done.

"He got a hundred dollars for that ten minutes' bit of work, and I guess I got a hundred extra grey hairs.

"Well, Cap'n, then I took the Mona, and mounted her on a brand new panel, for she was on a layer of wood so thin that she bent just with picking her up.

"That's how we got the panel for the copy. The copy's painted on the old Mona Lisa panel. Smart, wasn't it? I guess the Experts couldn't get past that—what! Not much, Sir!

"Queer, when you come to think of it, Cap'n, that if those Frenchmen only thought to notice it (not that they could, after not seeing the lady for a couple of years!) they'd the clue right there, in the thinner panel, that the Mona's been doctored!

"Great, I call it! And she'll hang there all through the ages; and people'll come from all parts and stare and gasp and go away, feeling they've seen the only Genuine! And all the time she'll be where all the real stuff's going—in God's own country, Sir— U.S.A. That's her.

"And to think a pair of calipers would give the whole show away, if only they'd taken the thickness of the panel, before a 'friend' of mine lifted her out of the Louvre!"

"That was smart, certainly," I said. "You can spin a good cuffer. What about the old pigments and all the rest of the impossible things—eh?"

"The pigments, Cap'n, cost me exactly fifteen thousand dollars in cold cash. I bought old canvasses of the same period—some of them were not bad either, and I scraped 'em, Sir. Yes I did, for the pigments that were on 'em. Nearly broke my heart! But this is a big business. Then an old painter I know, got the job of his life. He's as clever a man as ever stole a canvas, 'cause he hadn't money to pay for it.

"I got hold of him and locked him up in a room for three months, to get the drink out of him. If someone'd done that for him regular, and given him paint, brushes and canvas, he'd have been pretty near as big a man as the Master himself; but he never could keep his elbow down.

"At the end of the three months, when I'd all my pigments re-ground and mixed ready for use, I showed him the Mona and the empty panel. He went down on to his blessed knees to the thing, and pretty near worshipped.

"I told him there were five thousand big fat dollars for him, the day he'd finished a copy of her, on the wooden panel; that's if the copy were so good, I couldn't tell one from t'other.

"Well, Cap'n, he did it. And he did it properly, like a monk might pray. Four months he took; and when it was finished, I couldn't have told one painting from the other except that the new one wanted 'sunning'—that's a little secret of my own. I do part of it with a mercury lamp, and part of it with the sun and coloured glass. I gave her a solid year of that treatment, while she was drying and hardening. Then I'd have defied L. da V. himself to tell one from t'other!"

"And the chap who painted the copy" I asked.

"He got his five thousand bucks," he said, casually. "There's a lot of absinthe in five thousand dollars."

"Poor devil," I said. "What was the idea of getting this copy made for twenty thousand dollars, when you had the real thing?"

"It was for the French Government to sneak," he told me.

"What?" I said.

"It was for a plant!" he explained. "It was going to be 'planted'; and then an agent of mine was going to approach the picture-dealers and offer to sell it, as the real thing, you know.

"And of course, I knew no dealer on the East side the duck-pond would look at it. No use to anyone this side, except to get 'em into bad trouble. I knew the next thing they'd do, would be to lay information, for the sake of the reward and the press notices."

"Well," I asked, "what had you to gain by all that, and what did you gain by getting your agent into the hands of the police?"

"He bungled things!" he told me. "It wasn't my fault he got nabbed. However, he don't matter. He'll be made for life, when he comes out clear of all the bother. I'll see to that; and he knows he can trust me, so long as he holds his tongue."

"But the reason you wanted the authorities to cop the copy you'd spent twenty thousand dollars on?" I asked again. "If you were so anxious for them to have a copy, why didn't you offer to sell it back? They'd have paid a decent sum—quite decent, I should imagine—that's if they couldn't get their hands on you first!"

"That's just the point," he explained. "If I'd offered to sell back the picture, they'd have approached it in a more suspicious spirit; and I want no blessed suspicions at all, Cap'n. If they thought I was trying to get rid of the original, secretly to a dealer, and that they had dropped on me unexpectedly, then their whole frame of mind would be the way I want it to be—see?

"You see, Cap'n, I paid twenty thousand dollars odd to get that copy made, simply for a blind. I'm taking the original out to U.S.A. where I've got a patron for it at five hundred thousand dollars, as I've told you; or anyway as I'm telling you now.

"But he won't even look at it, if there's going to be any bother attached. I've to clean up behind me. I'd to let the French Government have back what they think is their picture; and then my patron can hang the original in his private gallery, without fear of trouble.

"He's a real collector, and it's sufficient for him to know he's got the original, under his own roof-slates, without wanting to shout the song half across the world, like a society hostess.

"If there are any comments, he'll acknowledge it to be what it isn't—and that's a copy. This is bound to go down, as people are convinced the original is clamped up good and solid, back in its old place in the Louvre. Thank God for that sort of collector, I say." They make living possible for people in my business. Now, have you got all the points, Cap'n?"

He grinned so cheerfully, that I had to do the same thing.

"But all the same," I told him, "I'm not available for handling stolen goods, Mr. Black. You'll have to try further up."

"Come now, Cap'n Charity," he said; "and you a good American, too! I guess we got to have this bit of goods in little old U.S.A. It's too fine for any other nation on earth. You mustn't think it's only the dollars I'm thinkin' of. Why, Cap'n, there's a patron of mine, right here in England, that will give me ninety thousand pounds for it, now that I've made it safe; and that's only fifty thousand dollars under what I'm to get across the water. And out of that fifty thousand I've to pay you, and all expenses, and run the risk of the U.S.A. Customs dropping on it, and all my work going up in a flare!

"No, Sir! If it were just the dollars only I'm after, I'd sell it right here, within twenty-four hours, and be shut of all trouble and risk; but it's got to go over to our country, Cap'n, and stay right there, till it's acclimatised."

I couldn't help liking the man for that. But I had to stare at him a bit, to size up how much he was honest and how much I was dreaming: but he was honest, right enough; and I felt I'd got to look good and hard; so that I'd not forget what an honest picture-dealer looked like.

"What about the French?" I asked him. He shrugged his shoulders.

"I guess I'm not French, Cap'n," he said. "Anyway, they've got a fine copy, and you couldn't persuade them, not with a hammer, that it wasn't the real one; not unless you showed 'em the original. I'll agree then they might grow suspicious; but there's not got to be any suspicions set going. That's what all my work's been to stop."

"Look here," I said; "for all I know, this one you want me to put through, may be the copy, that you're going to palm off on your customer!"

"No, Sir!" he replied, very wrathy in a moment. "No, Sir ! I never try that sort of thing. No double-crossing for me! I've never done a patron yet. That's how I've built up my business. I'm known to be honest."

"It's a pity you can't put it through, openly, as the original," I said. "You'd have no duty at all to pay then, seeing that it's more than a hundred years old. Anyway, why don't you put the thing through yourself, as a copy? If your customer's going to manage to palm it off to his friends (and there's likely to be some experts among 'em) as a copy, why don't you put it through the Customs, frankly, as a copy? There'll be nothing much to bother about in the duty-line on a mere copy by an unknown artist. Shove a fairly good price on it, so they won't think you're trying to jew them, and there you are. Anyway, Mister, that'll come a heap cheaper than paying me what I should need, before I'd even look at a job of this sort."

He put his finger to the side of his nose, in French fashion.

"Don't you worry, Cap'n," he replied. "That picture's worth five hundred thousand dollars; and I guess I'm taking no chances at all.

You must reckon there's others that guess things about this, besides me, and it ain't only the Customs I'm bothering about, but it's a little bunch of crooks that have got to suspecting more than's good for them. And I guess if they can't get a finger in the pie, they're capable of dropping a hint to the New York Customs, just for spite.

"If the Customs put their eyes on the picture, after a hint like that, they'd hold it and communicate with the French authorities, and it'd be all U-P then, once the two pictures were put together and compared.

"And, anyhow, Cap'n, I reckon there may be a bit of trouble, going across; for the gang'll never drop trying, until it's 'no go' for them. They'll sail with the picture and me, on the chance of nipping in before we get to the other side. I'd not be surprised if they came across with a proposal to go shares or split. If they can't do me in any other way.

"Now, what's it to be, Cap'n Charity—are you on, or is it no go?"

I thought for a few seconds, then I answered him:—

"I'll do it," I said. "I guess I'd like it to go across to God's country; and I suppose it's about as much right in the Louvre, as Cleopatra's needle has on the Embankment. Doesn't it belong by rights to Italy?"

He winked at me, and shrugged his shoulders, in a grotesque fashion.

"I guess, Cap'n," he told me, "we won't go into that now, or the Lord knows where the complications are going to end. It's going to belong in little old U.S.A., and that's good enough for me. . . . What'll your figure be, Cap'n?"

"Five per cent," I told him. "That'll be twenty-five thousand dollars."

"Very good, Cap'n," he agreed. "It's a good tough price; but I'll come across all right. I reckon the more you stand to make out of it, the more like you are to do your best! And just what that is, I guess every Customs official each side of the pond knows! If you do up to your usual, the New York Customs'll never even smell it. That's why I've come to you; and that's why I don't kick at your figure.

"You're a dandy, Cap'n ! You're IT! I heard about the way you ran that cargo of smokes into Liverpool. That was smart now! That must have taken a bit of planning!"

"Where's the picture?" I asked him.

"Here!" he said, almost in a whisper, and patted the wrapped up drawing-board affair, that he held under his arm.

"Bring it along into my cabin, and let's have a look at it," I told him. "I want to see this smile that won't come off, that I've heard so much about. Is it anything wonderful?"

"Cap'n," he said, with extraordinary earnestness, "it is wonderful! It's as if one of the old gods had got in some mighty fine work on the panel."

We went along to my cabin, and I shut and locked both doors. Then he unwrapped the thing, on the table. It was painted on what appeared to be a solid panel of hard wood, about three quarters of an inch thick. I looked at it for a good bit. It was certainly fine and strange.

"It's got something about it that looks as if a clever devil had painted it," I told him. "She's got no eyebrows. That makes her look a bit peculiar and, somehow, slightly abnormal. But it doesn't explain what I mean. It's as if the elemental female smiled out in her face—not what we mean now-a-days by the word woman; but all that is the essential of the female, as opposed to the essential of the male—not the man, you know! The smile is conscienceless; not consciously so, but naturally. . . . It's as if the unrestrained female—the 'faun' in the woman—the subtle licence in her—the subtle, yet unbridled, goat-spirit in her, were spreading out over her face, like a slow stain. It's the truth about that side of a woman that the best part of a man insists on turning his blind eye to. The painting ought to be called:—'The Uncomfortable Truth!'"

"Cap'n," he said, "for a man that pretends not to understand pictures, you're doing mighty well! I guess you've just put into words, a bit that I've felt, but couldn't ever get unmuddled into plain talk. I've felt that, many and many a time, since—well since she came into my hands. It isn't that she's bad, so much as that she's not good! It's as if she's got a throwback fit on. I guess women get that sometimes—more often than we think!"

"They're primitive things," I said. "Nature keeps them too close to her, to let them be anything else, at bottom. A woman's as primitive as a savage—whether she's cultured or uncultured. Just notice, for instance, her idea of repartee! It is to be crudely insolent in a modulated voice, if she's cultured, and otherwise if she isn't! Her desires are more moderate than a man's, only in those things she doesn't want. When she wants a thing, she's no more sense of moderation than a child or a savage. Look at her immoderate notions of dressing herself, or undressing herself, perhaps is what I ought to call it! She's no sense of moderation, except about the things she doesn't want! And even then she's immoderate not to want 'em!"

"Cap'n", he said, "you've sure been hit sometime by a woman, and I reck'n she wasn't much good to God or man. I guess I recognise the symptoms!"

I had to laugh at his cuteness; but I didn't add up the particulars for him!

"All the same," I said, nodding at the Mona, "it's a good painting and clever insight; but it's rotten bad art. It's unmoral!"

"Lord, Cap'n Charity, don't talk like that!" he said, genuinely distressed. "I'd begun to think I'd met a man that understood things my way of looking at 'em. An' then you go and blow off like that!"

"Art's not got the right to be a vehicle for unwholesomeness!" I said, smiling a bit at his earnestness.

"I guess, Cap'n, you're wrong, all the way there!" he asserted. "Art's the right to do and say and be what it likes, so long as it's clever and wonderful enough."

"No," I said. "Have a cigar. It's not worth talking about, anyway; but you can take it from me that when Art claims only its Privileges, and shirks its complementary Responsibilities, it is bound to become as undesirable as any other irresponsible force."

"I quit, Cap'n!" he said, biting off the end of his cigar. "You out-argue me. The chief thing that counts just now, is there's five hundred thousand dollars on the table there; and twenty-five thousand of them are yours, the day you hand me the painted lady, safe and sound, in Room 86 of the Madison Square Hotel, New York.

"I guess you got that all plain, Cap'n. Meanwhile, I'll book my passage across with you. I reckon I shall feel easier, sleeping in the same ship with her."

"That's all right, Mr. Black," I told him. "If you've got an hour or two to put in, you'll find that chair's comfortable, and that's my brand of whisky in the rack, and there's Perrier and Soda, whichever you fancy."

"Right you are, Cap'n," he said; and while he was making himself comfortable, I began to get out my colours, palette and brushes.

"You paint, Cap'n?" he asked, over the top of his glass. He seemed surprised.

I nodded towards the oils and water-colours, round the bulksheads. He got up with his glass of whisky, and began to go the round, sipping, and muttering some astonishment, as he journeyed.

"My word, Cap'n!" he said at last, facing round at me. "You sure can paint some! And I guess I'm slinging no cheap flattery. What you going to do now?"

"I'm going to do an oil sketch of the Mona as a keepsake, right now, and before I hide her for the voyage," I told him. I hauled out a sheet of prepared cardboard from my portfolio. "I guess I'd like to remember I once handled the original," I went on. "And I'd like to have a shot at that smile. The trick of it catches me."

"Good for you, Cap'n," he said, quite interested, and set down his whisky, while he propped up the Gioconda, in a good light from the glazed skylight, above. Then he came round behind me, to watch.

I finished the thing, a rough sketch, of course, in about an hour and a half; and Mr. Black seemed to be genuinely impressed.

"Cap'n," he said, "that's good work, you know! You're a mighty queer sort of sea-captain!"

"Mr. Black," I said, as I fetched out my pipe, "you're a mighty queer sort of picture-dealer!"

But he couldn't see it.

April 8th. At sea.

Mr. Black's an interesting man to talk to; but he's got the itch to know where I've hidden his blessed picture. I've explained to him, though, that when a secret has to be kept, it's better kept by one head than by any other number you could think of in a month.

He's had to agree that my method's the right one; but, every time I ask him up to my chart-room for a smoke and a yarn, he has a try to wheedle out of me whereabouts I've stowed away his five hundred thousand dollar lady.

Meanwhile, I've found that he's a good taste for other things besides pictures. As he put it:—

"Cap'n, I'm no one-horse show, in the matter of liking good things. A pretty woman I like, and if they're good, so much the better—"

"They're rare!" I told him.

"I grant you that, Cap'n," he said. "As rare as a high-pressure man with a sound temper. That's why they're some worth finding. Well, I like a pretty woman, a good violin solo, a good whisky, a good picture, and a good patron of art. And I reckon the five mean life!"

I smiled, and I said nothing; but when he came up to my chart-room to-day, I introduced him to a pretty young American, of the name of Lanny, who has made a point of pall-ing on with me, and has come up to look at my pictures.

When he came in, she was criticising my copy of the Gioconda, on cardboard, which I had pinned up on the bulkshead; and after I had introduced him, she hauled him into the discussion, willy-nilly.

"I think that's a fine piece of work of the Captain's," she said. "But you sure ought to see the original in the Louvre, Mr. Black. Captain Charity's done fine; but the original just gives you shivers all down your spine."

"I've seen it, Miss Lanny," he assured her, "and I agree with you. It's a mighty wonderful thing. But Cap'n Charity don't reckon it's good art!"

"What!" said Miss Lanny. "Captain Charity, you don't tell me that?"

"It's not good art, Miss Lanny," I said. "It's true; but it shows the ugly side of a woman's character."

"That's downright insulting, Captain," she said, warmly. "I reckon it shows what the great artist meant it to show. It shows the delicate subtlety and refined spirituality of woman. There's more in La Gioconda's smile than in the laughter of a hundred men."

"I hope you're right, Miss Lanny," I said. "For the sake of the hundred men. In fact, I'm sure you are right, supposing that the hundred men are good average, clean, wholesome citizens."

This talk occurred this morning; and I put the stopper on then, for it was getting a bit too serious. I felt if the young lady came out with any more of that cheap Suffragette I'm-better-'n-any-man-that-steps-the-earth kind of thing, I should begin to feel like the giant, when the boy slapped him with his own hair-brushes. And when I get feeling like that, I never know whether I'm going to turn rude or over polite; and either way is not the method, when there's a pretty girl in one's chart-room, who looks as if she's good as gold and chock full of hell-fire, all in one and the same moment.

But they seldom are either, let alone both; not when it comes to the pinch. They so often talk big, and then fizzle out into silly viciousness, or else you find the gold's only gilding on top of a deal of petty thoughts on things in general and men in particular! Lord! doesn't that sound narky!

April 10th. Night. Late.

Great excitement. At least. Mr. Black's in a state.

He's spent most of the last two days spooning Miss Lanny, in my chart-house, while I've made shots at doing sky effects in water-colours.

I call that cool, to try to cut me out with the young lady; though I can't say that she's seemed backwards! But I've had my revenge! I've made a set of six caricatures of the two of 'em looking generally spoony and absolutely loony!

However, this sort of thing has to be paid for!

About an hour ago, Mr. Black sent word by a steward, would I come along to his cabin. Lord! The mess! Someone, or several, I should think, had been through his place, and left it like a wooden township after a cyclone.

His box lids had all been ripped off; his bed had been pulled to pieces, and his mattress had been cut open; his wardrobe (he's got a suite de luxe, off the saloons) was ripped away from the bulkshead, and was lying on its side, and the mirror had been broken clean out and lay on the carpet.

The marble top had been lifted off the wash-stand, and the carpet had been pulled up in several places and was ripped across, as if with a pair of shears.

In his dining room, the Louis sixteenth sofa had met bad trouble, and yielded up its springs, much tapestry and the ghost, all at once. The writing table had its top lifted off, and another table had evidently seen trouble. The heavy pile carpet here was divorced both from itself and the floor, and lay in heaps, literally cut to pieces.

In the bathroom, some of the tiles had been forced out, as if the human cyclone had meant to make sure of what lay below; and in the dressing-room, things had equally not been neglected.

I sat down on the wreckage of Mr. Black's bed, and roared. He just stood and stared.

"You sure see the funny side of a thing, Cap'n!" he said at last.

"This'll pay you for cutting me out with my lady friends!" I told him, when I could breathe again. "I suppose you been up, spooning on the boat-deck, instead of coming down and turning-in at a reasonable hour, like a Christian."

He looked sheepish enough to please me.

"Providence, Mr. Black," I told him, "is always careful to leave the dustpan on the stairs, when it sees we're getting too 'aughty." Then I got serious. "Missed anything?" I asked him.

"Not a thing yet," he said; "but it'll take a bit of straightening out."

I rang for his servant, and sent a message to the chief steward.

Fortunately the next suite was empty, and we moved Mr. Black's gear into it. Just the three of us; for I want no talk among the passengers until the trip is finished. That sort of thing is better kept quiet.

The chief steward locked up the whole suite, and we knew then there could be no talk; for Black's servant had not been allowed in to see the place, since the trouble.

"Now, Mr. Black," I said, "come along up to my place for a talk."

When we reached my cabin, Mr. Black had a whisky to pick him up; and we talked the thing over; though I saw he didn't see as far into it as I had done already.

"Anyway," I told him, "you've lost nothing; and now they'll leave you alone. They've proved the thing isn't in your possession. If it had been, they'd sure have had it—eh?"

"Sure!" he said, soberly. "Are you mighty certain it's safe where you've put it?"

"Safe till the old ship falls to pieces!" I told him. "All the same, they must be a pretty determined lot, whoever they are; and I expect they'll be paying my quarters a visit if they get the half of a show. By the Lord! I'd like 'em to try it on!"

April 11th. Afternoon.

Mr. Black and Miss Lanny spent the morning up with me in my chart-room. The talk turned on a water-colour I was making of the distant wind-on-spray effects, and I hit out once or twice at Miss Lanny's critical remarks.

"That's pretty good, Cap'n Charity," she said, looking over my shoulder; "but I like your copy of the Gioconda better; though you haven't got the da Vinci ability to peep underneath, and see the abysmal deeps of human nature."

"Dear lady," I said, "may I light a cigarette in your presence, and likewise offer you one?"

She accepted, and Mr. Black also.

"Da Vinci was a great painter!" I said.

"I'm sure," she answered.

"But he wasn't a great artist. . . . Understand, I'm judging him just on the Mona, which is the only thing of his I've seen; but which is supposed to be his greatest work."

"That's a wicked thing to say, Cap'n!" she interrupted. "The whole world acclaims him great!"

"He's one more proof," I said, "of the truth of my contention that a man may be a 'great painter' or a 'great sculptor' without being a great artist; in other words a man of great feeling, and intellectuality combined—that is to say, a Compleat Personality.

"I admit that a great artist does occasionally happen to be a 'great painter' or a 'great sculptor'; and as a result his sculpture or painting, as the case may be, is vastly more complete, perfect, great, (call it which you like) than the work of the other sort; but, so far, the 'other sort' seems able to dispense with the greatness of personality, which is the 'bricks' of the great artist. . . . This quality doesn't appear to be necessary to their 'greatness,' any more than greatness of Personality is necessary to the making of a great singer. A great singer may be (and sometimes is) a human pig, into whose larynx has been inserted the throstle of an angel; but he's still what he'd be if you took the tune-pipe out of his throat—and that's plain unadulterated, unintellectual, unfeeling p-i-g. I don't mean to say they're unemotional. They're generally emotional enough, the Lord knows! So's a congenital idiot, a drunken man, a woman of easy virtue, or a certain type of actor when he's just been told he's outtopped old Garrick!"

She was gasping now in her attempts for words suitable to my eternal quenching. She got some of them out; but they cut no ice! Finally, she demanded fiercely, in so many words:—"What do you mean?"

That was a plain question; and I answered it plainly:—

"The da Vinci johnny was too busy looking out for his abysmal deeps of human nature, to remember the heights!" I told her. "He was like a painter, with his eye glued into a sewer, painting and sweating himself into eternal fame—that is in the eyes of other Perverts like himself; and in the eyes of the big blind, indiscriminative, unmeaning crowd that follows the shouting of the Perverts, because they don't know enough to shout tosh frankly.

"Now, the value of the Mona must be put at a high figure, maybe ten million dollars in the open market." (I grinned cheerfully at the back of my mind.) "But if it's worth that, it's worth it as a painting—not as a compleat work of art!"

"You're mad, Cap'n; either mad or ignorant, or both!" she slammed out at me, and I could see that Mr. Black wanted to say much the same thing.

"St. Paul is my brother, dear lady," I said; "only he was accused of achieving his through much learning!

"Meanwhile, I assert that our friend da Vinci was not a great artist—not if you judge him on the merits of the Mona as a compleat work of art. (Fine word compleat. Means just what I want it to mean!)"

"Why? Why? Why?" she broke out again, reduced once more to blank questioning.

"Yes," joined in Mr. Black, beginning to show warmth, "I'd just like to know, Cap'n, how you make out da Vinci's not a great or compleat, or whatever you like to call it, artist?"

"Because," I said, "Art is personality expressed in and through the 'artist's' subject. If the artist's personality is a great personality and a balanced one, it will express itself in and through his subject in a great and balanced way. And the greater and more balanced the personality, the more the artist's work will approximate to perfect art—Great Art; always supposing that the man is a master craftsman, which, of course, is understood.

"The Great Art is the great, wise, compleat human personality, vital and therefore creative, expressing itself through some medium; inevitably a 'handicraft.' I'm using the word widely.

"If, however, the artist has a twisted personality, the twist will express itself in and through his work, and the work will be as much out of perspective in its deviation from compleat sanity and truth, as it would be technically, were the artist an indifferent craftsman.

"You see, sound art is a true, personal expression of anything, in its general relationship to human nature. If a man's art produces results which are not coupled up with human nature, it becomes non-intelligible to the human; as much so, as are the X rays to the human retina!

"And it is because of all these things that I condemn the Mona as a work of the highest art. It is the product of a twisted art and a very great handicraft."

"It is a perfect work of great and wondrous art!" said Miss Lanny. "I like to see how piffly little amateurs, try to teach the Master!"

I laughed at her bad temper.

"Dear lady," I said, "you admit my copy of the Gioconda is not so bad," and I beckoned to where I had pinned the picture on the bulkshead, under the skylight.

"By the side of the original," she smiled at me, "it is as a ginger-pop bottle beside a Venetian glass wonder. You sure got a healthy conceit of yourself, Cap'n!"

"Mea culpa, dear lady!" I murmured, holding out my case of gold-tips. "I suppose you'll deny next the truth of my contention that all art must say something, or it's nothing?"

"Art needn't say a thing, and you know it, Cap'n!" she said.

"Just so," agreed Mr. Black. "It's sufficient to be just what it is! A picture isn't meant to be a book!"

"Quite so!" I told him. "It takes a certain amount of brains and mental energy, that is, personality, to write even a moderately good book! And a book is great or not, in so far as it says much or little, and says it truly or askewly, completely or incompletely. And that simple little test is the test for all art—painting, sculpture, prose, poetry, music—all of it; for if a 'work of art' says nothing, it is nothing.

"The matter with the Mona is that it says only part of what it should say; and the part that it does say is no more a compleat measure of a woman, than a pint-measure approximates to a furlong, in any sense. He has seen only the female in the woman, and painted it in the 'moment of gratification.' It no more approximates to a normal or compleat human woman, than a male, portrayed in a moment of murderous fight, approximates to a normal or compleat human man.

It is simply an abnormality—showing nothing beyond what is painted! As abnormal as if the artist had drawn, shall we say, one enlarged nostril of an ape-man, and handed that down to posterity as a compleat work of art. But it is wonderful handicraft; and does not forget the shaven eyebrows—"

"Why, Cap'n, you've painted your copy with eyebrows!" interrupted Miss Lanny.

"Yes," I said. "I like the effect better. I've no use for those abnormal effects. Besides, it's more decent!"

"Lord!" muttered Mr. Black, "you sure are cracked to-day, Cap'n."

"The Mona," I asserted once more, "is a twisted fragment of a woman—the produce of a twisted nature. As opposed to this inadequacy, the Greatest Art is complete, in the sense that it shows a Man or a Woman or a Moment in such a way that you see, with the great and particular insight of the artist who created the work, the thing you are shown, plus all the rest, which it makes or aids you to comprehend also. It portrays the Man, the Woman, or the Moment, in such a way that you realise, as you look, all the potentialities of the Man, the Woman, the Moment—The greatness and absurd weakness of the Man; the infinite tenderness and incredible meanness of the Woman; and the æons of Eternity that lie in wait behind the Moment.

"The Gioconda is, as I've said, a small Art and a very great Handicraft; that is, if it is anything at all! It's abnormal—a fine handicraft and a cute brain used to give out to the world the twisted freakishness of the biassed soul, that could not see the woman as a complete whole! I understand, I guess, because I'm a bit twisted myself; it's only in odd moments that I can fight down the twist in me, which makes me see every woman worse even than she is.

"There, you see! I can't stop slamming at 'em; not even when I'm out to explain!"

I had to laugh at myself; and the tension eased out of the two of them. I had watched the softer look of capable feminine interest, supersede the incapable critical light in Miss Lanny's eyes, as I had explained my own short-comings.

"Cap'n Charity's sure running amock, every time a woman's on the carpet!" said Mr. Black. "I guess, Miss Lanny, he's like a number of men, he's gone and got fond of a bad 'un, some time or other, and she's scorched the youngness out of his soul. I know!"

He wagged his head at me.

"The only reason he'll talk about the Mona, is because she's a woman, bless her," he said. "But, you know, Cap'n, you'll sure have to quit going on the rampage like that, or it'll be getting a habit. I once got a bit like that myself, and I guess I know! It was some fight I had to break from it."

Miss Lanny reached out her hand for another cigarette, and then bent towards me, for a light.

"Was she a very bad woman, Captain Charity?" she said, under her breath. "She must have been!" She looked up into my eyes, through the smoke of her cigarette. "I'm sorry you've had that sort of experience of women," she went on, still in an undertone, and still looking up into my eyes. "You ought sure to know a really nice woman; she would heal you up."

"Why?" I asked. And then:—"Do you reckon you're qualified to act the part of kind healer, dear lady?"

"I'd not mind trying," she said, still in a low tone.

"Why," I said, out loud, so that Mr. Black could hear, where he sat, over by the open doorway, "in your way, you're just as bad! You say a thing like that, in a tone to make me think you're a stainless Angel of Pity and Compassionate Womanhood; and at bottom you're just another of them! You may be virtuous, I don't say you aren't. I believe you are; but you're up to all the eternal meanness and everlasting deceit of the woman! You come here, posing as my friend; as the friend of Mr. Black, chummy and friendly with us, even to the point of losing your temper; and all the time you're one of a gang of thieves aboard this ship, trying to diddle Mr. Black or me out of a picture you and your pals think is aboard!"

As I spoke, she had whitened slowly, until I thought she must surely faint. And she sat there, without saying a word, the smoke curling up from her cigarette, between her finger-tips, and her eyes looking at me dumbly, and big and dark through the thin smoke.

Mr. Black had stood up, and taken a quick step towards me, an incredulous anger in his face, as I had proceeded to formulate my charge against Miss Lanny; but he had checked, at my mention of the picture, and now he was staring in a stunned sort of way at the girl. We were both looking at her: but she never moved, and she never ceased to look at me in that speechless fashion.

"You allowed Mr. Black to make love to you last night, late, so that you could keep him up on the boat-deck, while your friends ransacked his suite. And now, as you realise that Mr. Black has not got the picture, you and your friends suppose that I must have it; and you have been directed to divert your valuable attentions to me. . . . If necessary, I don't doubt that you meant to encourage a little love-making on my part, up on the boat-deck or elsewhere to-night, while an attempt was made on my cabin.

"But I assure you, dear Madam, that, where a lady is concerned, it has been my rule in life to avoid making one of a crowd. Also, as Captain of this vessel, I have facilities for keeping an eye on things which might surprise you and your friends.

"In proof of this, let me mention the names of your gang. . . . They are Messrs. Tillosson, Vrager, Bentley and finally Mr. Alross, your husband.

"I had the names of three of them before we had been at sea twenty-four hours; and now I think I may say I can put my finger on the whole lot of you.

"It is quite within my power to cause the arrest of you and your party; but there is no need.

"Neither Mr. Black nor I have any fear of what your friends can do; for let me tell you, the only Mona Lisa on view aboard this ship, is the copy which you see hanging up there on the bulkshead.

"Surely you did not suppose that if Mr. Black has or had a valuable picture to transmit to New York, he would advertise the fact to people of your sort, by travelling in the same vessel with it!

"That is almost all I have to say. You had better go now. Provided I receive from your party before to-night, the sum of one hundred and two pounds, fifteen shillings (which is the chief steward's estimate of the damage done to Mr. Black's suite last night), I shall allow affairs to pass; and your party may land free in New York.

"But, if the money is not delivered before six o'clock to-night, and if afterwards I have any further trouble with Messrs. Tillosson, Vrager, Bentley, Alross or yourself, I shall order the arrest of the entire party, and shall hand you all over to the police, when we enter New York."

She had spoken not a single word; only once had she shown any sign of feeling, and that was when I announced my knowledge of her relationship to Mr. Alross, a tall, thin, blond man, of quiet manners and an unhappy skill at cards. Then the hand which held the cigarette had begun to shake a little; but, beyond this, never a sign of the shock, except the absolutely ghastly whiteness of her face. She certainly is a woman of nerve, and a good pluck too, I grant her.

Then she stood up suddenly, and what do you think she said?

"Cap'n, your cigarettes are as treacherous as you seem to imagine all women to be. See how it's burnt me, while I was listening to your scolding. . . . I must run away now."

And she turned and walked out of the chart-house, as calmly as if she had just been in for one of her usual chats.

"How's that for 'some'!" I said to Mr. Black. "Let me tell you, man, I respect her courage. She's got the real female brand of pluck, and full strength at that. She's stunned half dead at the present moment, yet she carried it off! But, Lord! She's a conscienceless creature."

Mr. Black was all questions; and he wanted to know why I'd tried to make them think the picture wasn't aboard.

"I told them what I told 'em," I said, "in the gentle hope that they may try to believe it, and so not consider it worth while to lay information with the Customs, which is a thing they'd do in a moment, as you mentioned, just to make things ugly for us, and to ease their own petty spite."

"Why not arrest them?" he asked.

"Don't want any unnecessary Mona Lisa talk in New York, do you?"

"My hat! No!" he said.

"And now they know I'm on to the crowd of them, they're bound to walk a bit like Agag—eh?" I said. "No, I guess we'll have no more trouble with 'em, this side of New York. And I bet they pay up within the hour."

April 12th. Night.

I was wrong in one respect, and right in the other. The money was sent up to me by a steward, inside of half an hour; and I sent back a formal receipt.

But we have not seen the end of our troubles about the picture; for the gang approached Mr. Black quite openly, last night, and told him that if he'd let them come in on a quarter-share of the profits, they'd hold their tongues, and give him all the assistance they could. If he said no; then the New York Customs were going to get the tip, as soon as ever the search officers came aboard.

They told him quite plainly that they knew the picture was aboard; and that they were satisfied I was the one who had it hidden away. But, as they put it to him, it was one thing to hide contraband Jewels, like small packets of pearls, of which a hundred thousand dollars worth could go into one cigar; but that I could never hope to hide from the Customs, if they were put on the scent, a thing the size of the Mona, which being painted on a panel of wood, could not be rolled up small, like a picture on canvas, etc., etc.

They quite worked on poor old Mr. Black's feelings. I guess he may be some expert at picture stealing, like any other dealer; but he's out of it when it comes to real nerve—the kind that's wanted for running stuff through the Customs!

However, I've got him pacified; and I guess he'll manage now to keep a stiff upper lip. I pointed out to him that a twenty-thousand-ton ship is a biggish affair, and there are quite some hiding places aboard of her; and that I know them all.

I told him, in good plain American, that the picture would not be found.

"You needn't fear they'll start to break the ship up, looking for it!" I told him. "Ship-breaking is an expensive job. Don't you get fretful. They'll never find her, where I've put her!"

April 13th. Evening.

We docked this morning, and the gang did their best to do us down.

I reckon they'd guessed I wasn't keen to arrest them; and they just put the Customs wise to the whole business, before they went ashore, that is, as far as they had it sized up.

Well, next thing I knew, the chief searcher was in my place, demanding Mona Lisas, as if they were stock articles; but I disabused him, to the best of my ability.

"No, Sir!" I told him. "The only Mona Lisa picture we've got on exhibition in this gallery, is the one there on the bulkshead; and I guess you can have that for fifty dollars, right now, and take it home. I reckon that's a good painting now, don't you, Mister, for an amateur?"

But I couldn't enthuse him; not up to a sale! He was out for big things it seemed, by his talk; so I let him search. . . .

They're still at it, and Mr. Black, last I saw of him, as he went ashore, was looking about as anxious as a man who's bet someone else's last dollar on a horse race!

April 14th.

Still searching.

April 15th.

Still searching.

April 16th. Afternoon.

Mr. Black sent a messenger down aboard this morning, to ask when 'it' was going to come.

I swore; for if that note had got into the wrong hands, the game would have been all up. I've warned him to keep away from the ship, and not to communicate with me, in any way. I'll act as soon as it's safe.

I decided to give him a heart-flutter, as a lesson to be patient.

"Look here," I said to the hotel messenger; and I pulled down the cardboard on which was my painted version of the Mona. I rolled it up and handed it across to him. "Take this ashore," I told him. "Go to a picture dealer's, and tell them to frame it in a cheap frame, and send it up to A. Black, Esq., Room 86, Madison Square Hotel, with the compliments of Captain Charity. Tell them to wrap it up well; as if it were something valuable. Here's a dollar for you, my son. Tell them he'll pay! When you see Mr. Black, tell him that 'it'—mind you say 'it'—is coming! . . . It is! . . . When I say so! And not before!"

When he had gone, I sat down and roared at poor Black's digestion, when he found what 'it' amounted to. I guess I'll not be bothered with him now, until I'm ready to see him.

April 16th. Night.

I went ashore to see Mr. Black this evening. The Customs nabbed me en route, as usual, and I had a search that would have unmasked a blushing postage stamp. But they needn't fear. I'm not carting Mona Lisas ashore in the thick of this hue and cry!

When I saw Mr. Black, it was for the first time since he left the ship, and he rushed at me.

"Where is it?" he asked. He looked positively ill.

"Dear man," I said, "I don't hawk the Mona around with me. Perhaps that's what you want," and I pointed to the caricature of the Mona, in its cheap frame, which stood on the top of a book-case.

"Quit it!" he snapped, almost ugly; but I only laughed at him.

Then I took out my hanky, and a bottle of solution. I lifted the picture down and put it on the table; I wet my hanky with the solution, and wiped the picture over gently but firmly.

The eyebrows came away; also one or two other parts where I had laid my fake paint on pretty thick.

"There's the Mona, Mr. Black," I said; "and I guess you owe me twenty-five thousand dollars."

He looked; then he yelled; yes, he fairly yelled; first his delight, then his questions. I endured the first, and answered the second.

"You saw me paint a picture, didn't you?" I asked.

"Sure!" he said.

"Well, I did that, as I told you, for a keepsake," I said. "Afterwards, I took the Mona, soaked her off the board-backing you had glued her to, and remounted her on cardboard. Then I painted her a pair of eyebrows with fake paint, and touched up one or two other parts of the picture; and you and Miss Lanny spent most of the voyage criticising the immortal da Vinci. You see, I hung my own copy on the bulkshead first; but afterwards replaced it with the Gioconda.

"Miss Lanny called her even worse things than I did. She told me, if I remember right, that the painting was like a ginger-pop bottle compared with Venetian glass!

"I think I said he was not a big artist; and as for you, you looked as if you backed up what Miss Lanny said. Altogether, poor old da Vinci had a lot of hard things said against him. And all the time, his masterpiece, plus a pair of eyebrows, and some surface polish, was looking down at us from the bulkshead. I offered her to the Customs officer for fifty dollars; but I couldn't get him to bid.

"Yes, Mr. Black, I've enjoyed myself this trip, That's what I call doing the thing in style.

"Thanks, yes, twenty-five thousand dollars is the figure. I guess we've got to celebrate this!"

The Storm

"Look where you're going, man, or you'll have us by the lee! Where the hell are you running her off to?" The burly mate grasps the spokes of the big wheel, and puts forth all his strength to assist the weary helmsman in heaving it down.

They are off Cape Horn. Midnight has passed and the murderous blackness of the night is slit at times with livid gleams that rise astern, and hover, then sink with a sullen harsh roar beneath the uplifted stern, only to be followed by others.

The straining helmsman snatches an occasional nervous glance over his shoulder at these dread monstrous spectres. It is not the foam-topped phosphorescent caps he fears; it is the hollow blackness that comes beneath. At times as the ship plunges, the binnacle light flares up, striking a reflected gleam from that moving mass, and showing the curved, furious living walls of water poised above his head.

The storm grows fiercer, and hungry winds howl a dreadful chorus aloft. Occasionally comes the deep hollow booming of the main lower topsail.

The man at the wheel strains desperately. The wind is icy cold and the night full of spray and sleet, yet he perspires damply in his grim fight.

Presently the hoarse bellow of the mate's voice is heard through the gloom:

"Another man to the wheel! Another man to the wheel!"

It is time. Unaided the solitary, struggling figure guiding the huge plunging craft through the watery thunders is unable to cope longer with his task, and now another form takes its place on the lee side of the groaning wheel, and gives its strength to assist the master hand through the stress.

An hour passes, and the mate stands silently swaying nearer the binnacle. Once his voice comes tumultuously through the pall:

"Damn you! Keep her straight!"

There is no reply, none is needed. The mate knows the man is doing his utmost; and knowing that, he struggles forward and is swallowed up in the blackness.

With a tremendous clap the main top sail leaves the ropes and drives forward upon the foremast, a dark and flickering shadow seen mistily against the deep, sombre dome of the night.

The ship steers madly in swooping semi-circles, and with each one she looks death between the eyes. The hurricane seems to flatten the men against the wheel, and grows stronger.

The night becomes palpably darker, and nothing now can be seen except those foamy giant shapes leaping up like moving cliffs, then sweeping forward overwhelmingly.

Time passes, and the storm increases.

A human voice comes out of the night. It is the mate standing unseen close at hand, hidden in the briny reek.

"Steady!" It rises to a hoarse scream. "For God's sake! Steady!"

The ship sweeps up against the ocean. Things vast and watery hang above her for one brief moment. . . .

The morning is dawning leaden and weary—like the face of a worn woman.

The light strikes through the bellying scum overhead, and shows broken hills and valleys carven momentarily in liquid shapes. The eye sweeps round the eternal desolation.

The Crew of the Lancing

"COME OUT ON DECK AND HAVE A LOOK, Darky," shouted Jepson, rushing into the berth. "The Old Man says there's been a submarine earthquake and the sea's all babbling and muddy."

Out I ran to find the everlasting blue of the sea mottled with splotches of a muddy hue, and the water disturbed by huge bubbles floating about and bursting with a hissing pop.

The skipper and the three Mates were all on the poop with their glasses, staring out at this strange phenomenon. Far away to windward something like a mass of seaweed hove up into the evening air, and fell back into the sea with a sullen splash. Then the tropical sun fell and in the afterglow things grew shadowy. The wind which had been fresh during the day was gradually dropping and the night was becoming oppressively hot.

The First Mate called to me from the poop to dip a bucket of water and bring it to him. I did, and he put the thermometer into it.

"Just as I thought," he muttered, taking it out and showing it to the Skipper. "Ninety-nine degrees! Why, the sea's hot enough to make tea with!"

"Hope it won't get any hotter," growled the Captain. "We shall be boiled alive if it does."

I took the bucket and, after emptying it, put it back in the rack, then I went to the side while the Skipper and the Mate paced the poop together. The air grew hotter and hotter, and an hour or so passed in silence, broken only by the pop of some bursting gas bubble.

The moon rose and showed watery through a warm fog of vapour which had risen from the heated sea, enveloping the ship in a moist shroud that penetrated to the skin.

Slowly the interminable night rolled away and the sun rose dimly through the steam. From time to time we tested the temperature, but found only a slight increase in heat. No work was done. A general feeling of something impending was over the whole ship. The ship's bell was kept going constantly, while the lookout-man peered uselessly into the wreathing mists, and the Captain and Mates kept an anxious watch.

There was evidently some difference of opinion amongst them for I heard the Second Mate say, "That's all rot. I've seen things in fogs before today and they've always turned out to be nothing."

The Third Mate made some reply which I couldn't catch, and the matter dropped.

When I came on deck at eight bells after a short sleep, the steam still held us, and if anything it seemed thicker. Hansard, who had been taking the temperature at intervals while I was below, told me that it had gone up three degrees, and that the Old Man was getting into a rare old state.

About three bells I went forrard to have a look over the bows.

As I leaned on the rail Stevenson, whose lookout it was, came and stood by me.

"Rum go, this," he grumbled.

Suddenly there appeared up out of the water a huge, black face, like a monstrous caricature of a human face.

I grasped his arm and pointed. "Look!" I whispered, "Look!"

Stevenson turned quickly and stared down. "Lord!" he said, and bent over more to see the thing. "It's the devil," he cried, and as he spoke the thing, whatever it was, disappeared. Blankly we both looked down into the dark water. When I glanced up at him, his face wore a puzzled, startled look.

"Better go aft and tell the Old Man," he said, and I nodded and went.

On the poop I found the Skipper and First Mate pacing moodily. To them I told what I had seen.

"Bosh!" sneered the Captain, "You've been looking at your own ugly reflection in the water!" Yet in spite of his sneers, he questioned me, and finally the Mate went forrard himself to have a look, but returned in a few minutes to say that he could see nothing.

Four bells went, and we were relieved for tea. After that I went on deck again, I found the men clustered together forrard. They were talking about the thing Stevenson and I had seen. Several questioned me, and I told them all I knew.

"I suppose, Darky," said one of the older men, "it couldn't by any chance have been a reflection? Johnson, here, says as he heard the Old Man tell yer as how you'd been alookin' at yer own face in the water."

I laughed. "Ask Stevenson," I replied, and went away.

At eight bells I made my way aft. So far nothing further had appeared.

About an hour before midnight the Mate called out for me to bring him up a match to light his pipe. He struck a light and handed me back the box, and as he did so, there rose far out in the night, a muffled screaming, and then a clamour of hoarse braying like an ass's, only deeper, and with a horribly suggestive human note ringing through it.

"Did you hear that, Darky?" asked the Mate sharply.

"Yes, sir," I answered. I was listening intently for a repetition of the sounds, and scarcely noticed his question. Suddenly the noise came again and other voices took it up. It sounded away on our starboard bow. The Mate's pipe dropped with a clatter to the deck.

"Run forrard!" he shouted. "Quick now, and see if you can see anything!"

I flew forrard, and there I found the lookout man and all the watch gathered in a clump.

"Have you seen anything?" I called out as I reached the fo'cas'le head.

A frightened voice answered me. "Listen!"

The sound rose again. It seemed closer and almost ahead, though the fog confused one and made it impossible to tell for certain.

Undoubtedly the noises were nearer, and I hurried aft to the Mate. I reported that there was nothing to be seen but that the sounds seemed considerably closer and to come from more ahead. On hearing this he told the helmsman to let the ship's head go off a couple of points.

A minute later, a shrill screaming tore its way through the mists, followed by the braying sounds again.

"It's close on the starboard bow," muttered the Mate, as he beckoned the helmsman to let her head go off a little more.

A minute passed and then another, yet the silence was unbroken.

Then, overpoweringly, the sounds recommenced, and so close were they that it seemed they must be right aboard of us.

I noticed a strange booming note that mingled with the asinine brays, and once or twice there came a sound which can only be described as a sort of "gug, gug, gug." Then would come a wheezy whistling, for all the world like an asthmatic person breathing.

The moon shone dimly through the steam which seemed to me somewhat thinner. Once the Mate gripped my shoulder tightly as the noises rose and fell. The sounds were coming from right opposite us. I was staring hard into the gloom when I saw something—something long and black, which was sliding past us into the night. Out of it rose indistinct towers which gradually resolved into masses of ropes and sails. Thus I saw it, spectrally and unreal.

"A ship! It's a ship!" I cried, excitedly. I turned to Mister Grey. He too had seen something and was staring after the thing fading away into our wake.

Then our sails gave a sudden slat and the Mate glanced aloft.

"Wind's dropping," he growled, savagely. "We shall never get out of this infernal place at this rate."

Gradually the wind fell until not a breath stirred, and the steamy mists closed in thicker than ever.

Hours passed. The watch was relieved and I went below.

At seven bells we were called again. As I went along the deck to the galley, I noticed that the steam-fog was much thinner, and the air felt cooler.

At eight bells I went on deck to relieve Hansard at coiling down the ropes. From him I learned that the steam had started to clear about four bells, and the temperature of the sea had fallen ten degrees.

It must have been some half hour later that the dissolving mists gave us a glimpse of the surrounding sea. It was still mottled with darker patches but the bubbling and popping had ceased. Such of the ocean as I could see had a peculiar desolate aspect. At times a wisp of steam would float up from the nearer sea and roll undulatingly across its silent surface until it was lost in the vagueness that still held the horizon hidden. Here and there columns of steam rose up in pillars of mist which gave me the impression that the sea was hot in patches.

I crossed to the starboard side and looked over. It was the same there. The sea preserved a forlorn, deserted look that impressed me with a feeling of chilliness, though the air was quite warm and muggy.

"Get me my glasses, Darky" I heard the Mate speak up on the poop.

I ran to his berth and then up on the poop with them. He walked aft to the taffrail and took a look astern. Here the mists seemed to be gathered more thickly, though the water was much heated thereabouts.

I stayed up on the poop a minute looking in the same direction as the Mate. Presently something shadowy grew on my vision. Steadily I watched it until I distinctly saw the ghostly outline of a ship within the mists.

"See!" I cried, but even as I spoke a lifting wreath of mist had disclosed to view a great four-masted barque lying becalmed with all sail set a few hundred yards astern of us. Then the mist fell again and the strange ship lay hidden.

The Mate was all excitement, taking quick jerky strides up and down the poop, only to stop every few minutes to have another peer through his glasses. Gradually, as the mists dispersed, the vessel became more plainly seen, and it was then we got an inkling of the cause of those dreadful noises in the night.

For some time we watched her silently, the conviction growing on me that, in spite of the steam, I could distinguish some sort of movement aboard her. In a little while the doubt became a certainty; and also I could see, hazily, a continuous splashing and churning of the water round about her hull.

Suddenly the Mate dropped the glasses from his eyes. "Fetch me the speaking trumpet," he called quickly, without looking round.

In a moment I was back with the instrument. He gave me his glasses to hold while he raised the trumpet to his mouth and sent a loud "Ship Ahoy" across the water to the stranger. We waited intently for an answer.

A moment later came a deep hollow mutter out of the mist that rose quickly into the asinine bellowing of the previous night. Higher and louder drove the horrid sounds, and then they sank and died away amongst the further mistiness.

At this unexpected answer to his hail the Mate stood amazed. Now he turned sharply and told me to call the Old Man at once.

The watch had come aft, attracted by the noise, and were now climbing into the rigging to get a view over the stern. After calling the Captain, I returned to the poop where I found the Second and Third Mates standing by the First, all engaged in trying to pierce the clouds of steam. A minute later the Skipper appeared, carrying his telescope. The Mate gave him a short account of the state of affairs and handed him the trumpet. Putting his telescope down, the Captain raised the trumpet to his mouth and hailed the shadowy craft.

We all listened breathlessly. Again came that distant mutter, and again it rose into that ass-like bellow through which rang that terrible, half human note, rising and falling in the dreadful cadence.

The Skipper lowered the trumpet, and stood for a moment with an expression of astonished horror on his face.

"Lord!" he exclaimed. "What an ungodly row!"

Suddenly the Third Mate, who had been spying through his binoculars, broke the silence.

"Look!" he exclaimed. "There's a wind coming up astern." At his words the Captain looked up quickly, and we all watched the ruffling water.

"That packet yonder is bringing up the wind with her," said the

Skipper. "She'll be alongside in a few minutes if this cat's-paw lasts."

Some minutes passed and the bank of fog had come to within a hundred yards of our taffrail. The strange ship could be seen distinctly just within the fringe of driving wisps. Then the wind died away. A minute passed, then another, and the water became faintly ruffled astern of us. At the same time the stranger vessel neared us steadily. Quickly the seconds passed, and she was within fifty yards; then the wind reached us and blew clammily through our rigging. Our sails filled and we started to forge ahead. The strange barque came on rapidly; she had the wind before us, and consequently, had better way through the water.

Just as her bows came abreast of our quarter she yawed sharply and came up into the wind with her sails all a-flutter. I looked towards her wheel, but could see it only dimly through the mistiness. Slowly she fell off again and started to go through the water.

We, meanwhile, had gone ahead; but it was soon evident that she was the better sailer, for she came up to us hand over fist. The wind freshened and the fog began to clear quickly so that each moment the detail of her spars and cordage showed more plainly.

The Skipper and the Mates were watching her closely through their glasses when an almost simultaneous exclamation of fear broke from them.

"My God!"

Crawling about the decks now visible in the thinning mist, were the most horrible creatures I had ever seen. In spite of their unearthly strangeness I had a feeling that there was something familiar about them. They were like nothing so much as men. They had bodies the shape of seals, but of a dead unhealthy white colour. The lower part ended in a sort of double curved tail on which they had two long, snaky feelers, and at the ends a very human-like hand with talons instead of nails—fearsome parodies of humans.

Their faces, which, like their arm-tentacles, were black, were the most grotesquely human things about them, and save that the upper jaw shut into the lower—much after the manner of the jaw of an octopus—I have seen men amongst certain tribes of natives who had faces uncommonly like theirs; yet no native I have ever seen could have given me the extraordinary feeling of horror and revulsion that I experienced towards those brutal looking creatures.

"What devilish beasts!" burst out the Captain in disgust.

He turned to look at the Mates and, as he did so, the expression on their faces told me that they had all realised what the presence of those bestial looking brutes meant.

If, as was doubtless the case, these creatures had boarded this vessel and destroyed the crew, what was to prevent them from doing the same with us? We were a smaller ship and a small crew, and the more I thought about the matter the less I liked it.

Her name, Lancing, could be read easily on her bows with the naked eye, while the lifebuoys and boats had the name bracketed with Glasgow painted on them, showing that she hailed from that port. At times the derelict would yaw wildly, thus loosing so much ground that we were able to keep some distance ahead of her.

Then, as we gazed at her, we noticed that there was some disturbance aboard, and several of the creatures started to slide down her side into the water.

The Mate pointed and called out excitedly.

"See! See! They've spotted us. They're coming after us!"

It was only too true. Scores of them were sliding into the sea, letting themselves down with their long arm-tentacles. On they came, slipping by scores into the water and swimming towards us in great bodies. The ship was going some three knots an hour, otherwise they would have caught us in a very few minutes. As it was they came on, gaining slowly but surely, nearer and nearer. Their long tentacle-like arms rose out of the water in hundreds, and the foremost ones were already within a score of yards of us before the Captain bethought himself to shout to the Mates to fetch up the half dozen cutlasses comprising the ship's armoury. Then, turning to me, he bade me go below and bring him the two revolvers out of the top drawer of his cabin table, also a box of cartridges that was there.

When I returned with the weapons he handed one to the Mate, keeping the other himself. Meanwhile the pursuing creatures were getting steadily closer, and soon a half dozen of the leaders were right under our stern. Immediately the Captain leaned over the rail and discharged the weapon amongst them; but without apparently producing any effect whatever. I think he realised how puny and ineffectual all efforts against such an enemy must be, for he did not trouble to reload his pistol.

Some dozens of the brutes had reached us, and the arm-tentacle rose into the air and caught at the rail. I heard the Third Mate scream suddenly as he was dragged violently against the taffrail. Seeing his danger, I snatched one of the cutlasses and made a fierce cut at the thing that held him, severing it clean in two. A gout of blood splashed me in the face, and the Third staggered and fell to the deck. A dozen more of those grasping arms rose and wavered but they seemed to be some yards astern. A rapidly widening patch of clear water appeared between us and the foremost of the monsters and I gave a crazy shout of joy, for we were leaving them behind. The cause was soon apparent; the wind, now that it had come, was freshening rapidly and the ship was running some eight knots through the water.

Away in our wake the barque was still yawing. Presently we hauled up on the port tack and left the Lancing running away to leeward, with her devilish crew of octopus-beasts aboard her.

The Third Mate was struggling to his feet with a dazed look. Something fell from him as he rose and I stooped to pick it up. It was the severed portion of the talon-like hand that had gripped him.

***

Three weeks later we anchored off 'Frisco'. There the Captain made a full report of the affair to the authorities with the result that a gunboat was dispatched to investigate.

Six weeks later she returned to report she had been unable to find any signs, either of the ship herself, or of the fearful creatures that had attacked her. And since then nothing as far as I know has ever been heard of the four-masted barque Lancing, last seen by us in the possession of creatures which may be rightly called the demons of the sea.

Whether she still floats occupied by her hellish crew, or whether some storm has sent her to her last resting place beneath the waves is purely a matter of conjecture. Perchance, on some dark, fogbound night, a ship in that wilderness of waters may hear cries and sounds beyond those of the wailing of the winds. Then let them look to it; for it may be that the demons of the sea are near them.

Counterfeits

The Raft

by C. L.

"PUSH OFF!" SAID THE MATE HOARSELY. The raft glided into the gloom, to lay motionless within a biscuit toss of the doomed brig. At her taffrail a lamp hung still and brilliant. Aloft, her canvas, pearly-hued in the gloaming, wore an aspect ghostlike and unreal.

In the silence the four occupants of the raft bent an expectant and fascinated gaze upon the vessel they had just quitted. Suddenly a hideous chatter pierced the sombre stillness, bringing the boy lounging upon the chest to his feet with a vigour that made the raft sway ominously.

"Jack! Jack!" he cried. And as if in answer to his call the clamour on the brig redoubled in volume. "Let's take him off," entreated the boy tearfully to the mate, who stood staring sullenly over the glassy surface towards the ship. "There's plenty of time. I don't believe she'll sink any—"

"Curse your bird!" returned the other savagely. "Sit still or—"

The chattering ceased with a squeal as the brig gave a sudden horrifying lurch to starboard, a movement followed by the muffled rumble of shifting cargo. Again she swooped. For one brief instant her stern hung ludicrously in the air, then she plunged with a curious slithering movement beneath the surface of the smooth water. A couple of cough-like explosions, as the inrushing sea expelled the air from her hull, ruffled the slow swell, and the next moment the raft, with its awe-stricken watchers, was alone on the ocean.

With his face buried in his hands the boy sat whimpering softly to himself over the loss of his parrot. Karl Bronson, cook of the late "Cissie Williams," leaning with one enormous hand on the stump mast, reflectively and without emotion revolved a quid in his heavy jaws. Tasker, a consumptive-looking man, the brig's carpenter, seated on the end of the chest plucked with purposeless fingers at a hank of yarn.

With a deep sigh the mate turned to his companions. "There

goes £20 worth of kit, to say nothing of the best billet this side the Horn." If he expected an answer he received none, each of his hearers being deeply preoccupied with his own thoughts. The cook expelled his "chew" with violence, produced a length of twist, and measured a fresh quid with bovine placidity. The boy, rubbing his wet cheeks with grimy hands, stared resentfully at the spot where the brig had disappeared, while Tasker, intent upon his rope's end, did not deign to raise his lack-lustre eyes from the job.

With the suddenness common to the tropics night had fallen, and the mate, after a few minutes spent in anxious speculation, wearily extended his length on the rough logs, braced his back against the chest, and presently repose fell upon the survivors of the brig. Seven men and her captain had been lost in the terrific storm which had driven the little vessel some hundreds of miles from her course and started her planks in a leak, which, after three days of weary pumping, had vanquished the herculean efforts of the four occupants of the raft.

When morning broke it revealed to the sleepy eyes of the mate, who woke first, a strange scene. He glanced at his fellows in misfortune, still sleeping the sleep of exhaustion, the fierce rays of the morning sun streaming on their distorted, sweating features. A steady snore from the wide-open mouth of the "Dutchman" was the only sound which broke the oppressive stillness as the mate rose wearily to his feet with the intention of inspecting the contents of the provision chest, which had been securely lashed to the centre of the stable but unwieldy craft. As he looked from under his shading hand a cry broke from him—a cry that brought his companions, sleep-sodden and yawning, back to realities.

"The Sargasso, by God!" On every hand, save for the narrow ribbon of open water by which the raft had made its entrance, the bosom of the ocean was brown with weed, carpeted in places so thickly as to present an almost solid surface to the mate's astonished gaze. Not a mile from the raft lay the dismasted hull of a large wooden ship, bluff-bowed, and with the high poop and low waist of a Spanish man-of-war of a long bygone age. Huge barnacles, or what the mate took for such, covered the hull in grotesque protuberances, while festoons of seaweed hung luxuriantly from her bulwarks and streamed defiantly from the huge lantern which swung at her stern.

In every direction, as far as the eye could see, dismal derelicts of a similar nature, from galleons, hundreds of years old, to small brigantines, some fully rigged, and modern steam vessels, dotted the seascape, each locked, as if for eternity, in the dreadful embrace of the Gulf weed.

There was something hideous and awful in that broad, brown expanse, which undulated almost imperceptibly with a slow, rolling motion; and with a gesture of loathing, the mate tore down the rude sail, which was stealthily drifting the raft further and further into the weedy wilderness. The others surveyed the scene with dull eyes.

"Rum start this!" commented Tasker, and burst into a fit of coughing which choked further utterance. The boy rose owlishly to his feet, opened the locker, and revealed a well-stocked larder, so far as tinned beef, water, and ship's biscuit went. Mechanically and silently he set out four pannikins of water, opened a tin of meat, and carved rude lumps with his clasp knife. Tasker and the cook looked on with lack-lustre eyes. Inertia seemed to have fallen on the raft, each of its occupants holding aloof from his fellows as well as the restricted space allowed. Bronson was the first to shake off the mysterious lethargy. He seized his portion of the rations, retired to the end of the raft, and fell to with the avidity and gusto of a wild beast.

They breakfasted in silence. Presently the carpenter threw down his platter with a clang, and proceeded to arrange the discarded sail so that it afforded a grateful refuge from the sun's rays, now beginning to grow unpleasantly hot. He coughed furiously at short intervals.

"Do you happen to know where we are?" he said presently to the mate, who had also sought the shelter of the sail.

"Yes," was the reply. "We happen to be in the last spot in the world I ever expected to bring up in. This is the Sargasso"—he vaguely indicated the expanse about them—"and the storm of the past week must have blown us something like five hundred miles from our course. All hands must fall to presently and warp the raft out the way she came in. And the sooner we're out of this muck the better I, for one, shall like it. As for our chances afterwards—" He shrugged his shoulders and sat thinking, his eyes fixed upon the narrow ribbon of clear water on which the raft lay motionless.

With pole and kedge the four laboured well into the evening in their efforts to win blue water. The task of forcing the raft along the tiny channel proved interminable and, apparently, well-nigh fruitless, progress being so imperceptible. The mate's plan, and the only plan possible in such a strait, was to hurl the little anchor as far as the length of rope attached allowed into the weed. Then all hands strained on the rope, and thus the unwieldy craft crawled towards the open sea. Oars they had none, these having been lost with the boats in the late storm.

Late towards the evening a calamity befell them with appalling suddenness. The little anchor parted while the raft was still some hundred or more yards from the point where the ocean lapped the weed. The full meaning of the disaster struck, perhaps, the mate with greater force. The carpenter realised in a lesser degree that a crowning blow had befallen them, but neither Bronson nor the boy seemed affected by what had happened. The raft was stocked with provisions and water was plentiful!

Utterly exhausted, the quartette sprawled under the star-powdered sky wrapped in sleep. A sudden movement of the raft woke the mate, whose repose herculean labours has rendered fitful. Broad awake in an instant, he shifted to his elbow to peer into the blue gloom. He saw what froze the blood in his veins and set his brain whirling.

On one side the raft lay cradled in the weed. On the other, something like a gigantic whip, studded with bud-like excrescences, and tapering from the thickness of a man's leg to a finger-tip, rose from the turgid depths, and searched with a blind but devilish certainty of purpose for something on the raft.

Sick from inexpressible fear, the watcher sank back with closed eyes, and simultaneously a shrill scream of agony clove the night. As if depressed by a giant hand the raft sank on the one side almost to the water's edge; the mate opened his eyes in time to catch a brief glimpse of something being dragged overboard with a strangling, gurgling cry—and all was again still.

With incoherent cries of fear, Tasker scrambled on his knees to where the mate lay.

"Gawd! What was that?" he gasped, vainly endeavouring to repress a fit of coughing.

"I don't know. Don't know, I tell you! Keep quiet—it'll come back," exclaimed the mate in a hoarse whisper.

Bronson, crawling noiselessly, installed himself close to his companions, and presently, judging from the steady snore he emitted, was asleep again. Fearfully, the other two lay watching the edge of the raft, momentarily expecting to see the terrible feeler reappear; and presently—after an eternity of waiting—the sun rose.

It was the signal for commencing another day of Sisyphean labour. The kedge gone, nothing remained but the pole, which had augmented their efforts of the previous day, but the progress made by forcing it against the weed and pushing was heart-breaking in its results. And yet, when the mate, late that afternoon, by means of a match held at arm's length, measured the distance from the open sea, he saw that progress had been made.

The three men refreshed themselves at intervals almost without speech. Bronson seemed to regard the position, as he did the disappearance of the boy, with stolid indifference, performing his share of the labour with the unquestioning obedience of a horse. He had but little English at his command, if any, a fact which caused neither himself nor companions many regrets.

So the work went on, with intervals of escape from the burning sun beneath the awning—and again night fell upon the raft, and for two of the occupants the dying rays of the sun were fraught with horror.

The mate lay down to rest with a small hatchet close to his hand, while Tasker, spent with coughing and labour, sought the drowsy goddess with an open clasp-knife in his fingers. Long before either of them closed their eyes, the resonant snore of the "Dutchman" boomed a deep diapason on the fœtid air.

The mate had dosed off when a light touch caused his fingers to close fiercely upon the halt of his weapon.

"Look!" hissed the voice of the wakeful Tasker in his ear, and the mate followed the direction of the outstretched, trembling finger, with difficulty repressing a cry. With a movement which reminded him dully of the fluttering of a moth, he saw a horrible tentacle, leather-hued and lithe, appear from the gloom beyond the raft, and whip-like dart hither and thither among the rude logs at the opposite end to where he and the carpenter lay. Then, as the shaking Tasker crouched against him, his livid brows streaming with terror-sweat, and vainly trying to repress his uncontrollable cough, the tentacle touched the sleeping Bronson on the ankle. It instantly whipped round his calf like a lash; with a hoarse, animal-like cry the cook awoke, stiffened, and turned half over on his face, clutching with frenzied fingers at the interstices in the planks beneath him.

At the sight something seemed to snap in the mate's brain. He hurled his strangling shipmate from him with a yell, and with Berserker rage leaped towards the Thing, brandishing the axe. Even as he did so, like a straw, Bronson arose from the raft into the air, rigid and helpless, his right leg and thigh and his left ankle encircled in the clutch of the devil-fish.

The mate aimed a savage blow at the murderous feelers, at the same moment grasping the wretched man by the collar of his open shirt. Instantly the water was churned into foam by the rapid appearance of half-a-dozen of the horrible tentacles, which proceeded to fasten with silent ferocity upon the body of the doomed man, tearing him from the mate's grasp with irresistible force. A tentacle slipped round the mate's leg. He aimed at it a frenzied blow, and stood for a moment gazing stupidly upon the severed piece of leather-like flesh at his feet.

Then, as the body of the cook disappeared into the sea in a swirl of foam, he pitched forward on his forehead in a dead faint.

The sun was high in the heavens when he again opened his eyes. He found his companion in misfortune capering about like a madman, signalling to something on the horizon by means of the shirt he had taken off.

There was no sign of the dreadful octopus, save that planks at the end of the raft were covered with slime and gore. The mate's head ached intolerably, and, putting his hand to his forehead, he discovered, a tremendous bruise—a discovery which brought the events of the previous night crowding back.

"A ship!" screamed Tasker, in an ecstasy. "They're putting about—they see us—" waving the shirt frantically. Painfully, the mate rose to his feet, and saw, perhaps two miles off, a ship, evidently a small barque, almost becalmed.

Anxiously they watched the tiny ship grow slowly larger, while the blazing sun reached its meridian and began to sink lower in the heavens. At times the barque was quite motionless. At others, it seemed to the castaways that she contemplated turning back upon them and leaving them to their fate. Their frantic signals had apparently no effect upon the men who were bearing down upon the weed which imprisoned them.

The afternoon passed, and night was rapidly falling upon the scene when a boat put off from the barque, whose sails flapped idly in the catspaw breezes which disturbed the awful calm. The rescuing boat touched the weed nearly half a mile from where the raft lay. Frantically the two men, who had watched every movement with starting eyes, noted the halt, and frantically waved signals of direction to the boat.

Again the four rowers bent to their oars, driving their craft rapidly through the water to the entrance of the tiny creek. Again they paused doubtfully, and a moment later those on the raft could no longer see, even dimly, what was happening. A deep voice came booming over the weed. "Lay to, mates! We'll fetch you off at daylight. Cheero!" The carpenter and the mate replied with a volley of frantic, incoherent cries, but when, exhausted and hopeless, they lapsed into silence, the dull thump of oar upon rowlock told them that the boat was on its way back to the barque. As they stared into the darkness a light sprang into being on the distant ship, and its steady effulgence smote like a pang of despair into the hearts of the men on the raft.

The mate was the first to rouse himself to action. He threw back the lid of the larder and began to tumble provisions and water-beaker out upon the rude deck. The carpenter watched him with a hard, curious gaze.

Mentally each man measured the capacity of the locker. Then their eyes met.

"There's only room for one of us," said the mate in a low tone, "and the devil-fish gets the other!" The carpenter nodded, and began to cough.

Far across the impenetrable waste a bright eye blinked a message of hope—for one man!

R.M.S. "*Empress of Australia*"

THE EARTHQUAKE

I DO NOT INTEND WRITING AN ACCOUNT to cover the whole scene of the appalling disaster which completely destroyed the whole City of Yokohama, the greater part of Tokio, the base of the Japanese Navy at Yokoseeka (Yokosuka), Kamura, and also doing much damage in the districts to the east of Fugiyama. This is to give an account, partly in the form of a Log, of some of my own experiences and the part played by the Empress of Australia during her stay in Yokohama from August 31st to September 7, 1923.

AUGUST 31st.

We arrived in Yokohama, homeward bound, and berthed, starboard side to, alongside the Custom's Wharf. This wharf was under construction, the parts built of wood were being rebuilt of re-inforced concrete. It was to have accommodated four of the largest vessels at a time, two on each side of the wharf. It had two large freight sheds built of wood, with upper stories in the form of semi-open cafes, which are popular places for people to gather to see the ships depart.

SEPTEMBER 1st.

We were all ready for sailing at noon. The weather was fine and clear, with a light, southerly breeze. At one and one-half minutes to noon, we felt the ship vibrating, and wondered what was wrong, as the engines had not yet moved. After a few seconds the vibration became terrible; the whole ship seemed to jump and bend. In the engine room the engineers reported that the steam pipes were working at the expansion joints as much as a foot.

From the bridge I saw the wharf from end to end rolling like a wave. The usual large crowds were gathered to see the ship go out. Down on the wharf there was terrible confusion; people were being thrown down in all directions. Then, with a rending crash, the whole wharf opened up. Down with the wreckage went all the crowds of struggling people, with numbers of horses, vans and motor cars. We threw over numbers of linen and rope ladders to those who were left on the narrow strip of wharf which remained standing. But at that time we were unable to render very much assistance, as the wind had suddenly increased to gale force, and the ship was being thrown away from the wharf as much as twenty feet, then back towards it again, by the extraordinary upheaval of the water. Several of our moving lines had carried away, it being impossible to slack them away in time. The atmosphere was rapidly becoming dark with dust from the fallen masonry on shore. I have a hazy recollection of seeing the buildings along the Bund collapsing, and the noise was terrible. No description can give any idea of the inferno. It seemed that this was the end of everything. The panic-stricken people on the wharf were trying to make their way to the shore over pieces of wreckage which still showed above water. Our Shanghai pilot (Kent) was about the first to go through the wharf. I saw him in the water with a motor car sliding in on top of him, and that was the last I saw of him until he appeared over the ship's side, hauled up on a rope.

The two tugs that were standing by to tend the ship had both cleared off in a hurry. Astern of us was an American freighter, Steel Navigator, and on our port side, moored to a buoy, was another steamer that had dragged her moorings and struck us on the quarter, smashing in the rail round the poop, and damaging some of the light plates on the counter, which was not serious. With the ship astern, we were able to get away. The Japanese pilot boat (a motor sampan) came off to us after a time and, after great efforts, succeeded in carrying out a 9" Manila to the buoy. This line parted, however, as we attempted to heave the ship out. We had just to hold on where we were.

12:15 p.m. Fires could be seen through the smoke to be breaking out all over the city.

12:30 p.m. We asked the ship astern to move out so that we could get away to an anchorage—that sportsman wouldn't move, although the wind had eased off considerably, and the sea was back to normal.

1:30 p.m. The whole of the wrecked city was now one enormous fire. The wind was blowing strong towards the harbour, driving the flames towards us. The heat and smoke were now getting terrible, and clouds of ashes were flying over us. All hands now, together with several volunteers from the passengers, were working at the fire service. We had thirty fire hoses in operation, throwing water over the whole of the outside of the ship. A number of cargo lighters in the harbour had already taken fire, and having burned through their moorings, were drifting about the harbour with the tide, igniting the other lighters as they came together. The freight sheds on the wharf, although they had collapsed, were still above water, and it was now only a matter of time before they took fire. We again made an unheeded appeal to the Steel Navigator to get away and let us out of the danger. They had let go an anchor which was leading close under our stern. Instead of heaving up and clearing out, they slacked away, still holding on to the wharf.

2:00 p.m. The freight shed right off our starboard bow took fire and went up like matchwood. Things were looking very serious now. All hoses were directed towards the fore part of the ship and on to the wharf. We hauled astern until we were close up to the Navigator's bows. They could see the imminent danger we were in, of taking fire, and they refused to move for us! The burning lighters were now moving round us, several having worked their way in between us and the wharf.

When the Germans built this boat, they did not design her for speed, but they certainly gave us a good fire gear. Nothing less could have saved the ship.

Towards 3 o'clock the fire on the wharf began to burn itself out, and for the present the worst of the fire was over, and no part of the ship had taken fire. The Municipal Building was still standing. All the windows were spouting flames, and from the two high towers the fire was leaping as from a huge blast furnace.

We were now able to get the boats away and pull in shore to bring off refugees who, to escape from the fire, had crowded down to the water, many having waded out up to their necks. We continued backwards and forwards between the ship and the shore, bringing off great numbers, many of whom were in a very bad state, and had to be carried down on improvised stretchers. All these cases were being treated on board. Under the supervision of the ship's doctor, one part of the ship was being set aside for a hospital. The stewardesses and lady passengers and a number of the men were doing great work among the injured. Towards night the ship was becoming very crowded. Being impossible to take everyone, we had to limit our numbers to Europeans and Chinese, all injured cases and women with children. (Europeans meaning all white people and British subjects.) Out of all the ships in the harbour, most of which were Japanese, we only saw boats put off from two of them: The Dongola (P & O), the only other British ship in port, and the Andre Lebon, (French Mail).

The Japanese, during that Saturday night, seemed to take no notice at all of the terrible suffering on shore.

The most pressing need of those on shore was the lack of fresh water. The earthquake had broken all the mains leading into the city, and in that terrible heat the people were dying of thirst.

When we stopped taking off the Japanese, we started a station on shore for distributing water, and had two life boats carrying off large quantities of water, which a party of us on shore served out in bowls.

Towards 4:00 p.m. The people were coming down in only small numbers, and hearing that a number of Europeans were sheltering in the Park, which lies in the centre of the city, I decided to go up there and try to find them.

The first great flood of the fire had passed over this part of the city, and it was impossible to make one's way through. On shore the sight was appalling. There was not one building standing. Everywhere was a mass of burning ruins. Although the glare of the fire made it as bright as day, I had difficulty in finding my way, for little over half a mile of streets I knew very well. In places they were so covered in ruins as to be quite unrecognizable as roads. Deep crevices had broken the surface of the earth in all directions. In some places the roads had sunk and were three feet under water, which made dangerous going, as the holes were not visible. Tangles of twisted wire from telephones and tramways lay everywhere. Here and there were twisted pieces of metal which were once street cars. There was no sign at all of the rails. Wherever one looked, there was to be seen the inevitable of such a disaster—the burnt and charred remains of what were once human beings.

I found the Park—or what was once the Park. It now resembled a lake, with islands of mud. On these mud islands were huddled together thousands of poor people who had lost everything, with no food to eat. Some had small bundles representing their worldly possessions. Amongst them were a few horses and cows. There was no distinction now between human beings and animals; all were in the same plight. It was very quiet. I was not there very long; it was getting rather too much for one's nerves. I know I felt that any kind of noise would be more bearable than that awful stillness, after what had gone before. The only sounds one heard were a few wanderers floundering through the mud, crying out names of people they hoped to find.

We got one or two more injured people and, at 4:30 a.m., we were all returned to the ship.

SEPTEMBER 2nd.

On trying out our engines, we found that our port engine would not turn. The ship astern of us, at some time, must have tautened up her cable, which was now foul of our propeller. That hero then slipped his cable, leaving us with 75 feet of cable, and his lower anchor round our port propeller. Our pilot boarded her, passed us a wire, and towed us astern, clear of the wharf, where we anchored.

We had so far come through with no harm to the ship, except for our now disabled port engine and the damage on our poop, only to be faced by a far greater danger. During the night, some of the large oil storage tanks had taken fire and burst. Now from one end of the harbour came a huge pool of blazing oil. We were anchored where the set of the tide would bring this oil right down on us. Everyone saw it coming, but there was no panic.

There was no chance of getting towed out of the harbour as we had only one engine and all that cable and anchor dragging from the other propeller. Captain Robinson then took his one chance and got under weigh with his one engine.

It was a triumph of fine seamanship, how he manoeuvered the ship clear of the oil, turned her in the harbour, and headed her up for the breakwater entrance. The whole evolution took about an hour. There was no accident or mishap of any kind. Then, clear of the breakwater, we anchored. During the afternoon a pool of oil had drifted to the north end of the breakwater within the harbour, and was burning furiously. Watching this, we perceived that the fire had jumped the breakwater and set fire to some wharves along the north shore, and was now rapidly spreading towards a Japanese oil station where there were three 10,000-ton storage tanks close to the waterfront. If these tanks caught, we should probably find ourselves in a dangerous position.

7:00 p.m. The Dutch oil tanker Iris, took us in tow, and towed us right out, clear of everything, where we at last anchored in safety. I should say here that when the Dutchman saw our lame duck manoeuvering in the harbour, he shewed good sportsmanship by offering, over the wireless, to come into the harbour and tow us out.

That night the oil tanks caught fire. The sky in the north still shewed red with the glare from the fire at Tokio.

By this time there were nearly three thousand people on board, two thousand of whom were refugees from the shore. Launches were coming off all through the day and night, bringing off others. There were a great number of injured, many of them serious cases.

SEPTEMBER 3rd.

Several Japanese destroyers arrived with relief stores. The military arrived from Tokio and established camps in the reclaimed land.

Japanese battleships arrived in the morning and sent off a quantity of medical supplies. They later sent a diving party who did very well to clear the cable off our propellers and reported that the propellers appeared to have sustained only slight damage.

The Empress of Canada also arrived this morning outward bound. We were busy all day transferring refugees to her in the ship's lifeboats. She took several hundred people and as many injured cases as were safe to be moved.

SEPTEMBER 4th.

In the morning we made an expedition ashore in two parties to look for survivors around the European settlement. We landed on the reclaimed land and proceeded towards the Bluff. The Bluff was one of the prettiest parts of Yokohama where about 1,000 Europeans had their homes—beautiful places, some of them.

In daylight we were able to see what a state of absolute destruction the whole city was in. The Grand Hotel was a heap of ruins which had fallen right across the Bund. There were only about three burnt out frame works of buildings standing. Every other building in the city was flattened to the ground and burnt in the great fire. The canals which subdivide the city were full up with dead bodies. How many lay under the ruins, we shall probably never know. The whole disaster was so sudden that it does not seem possible that very many had a chance to escape. Everywhere we went was nothing but destruction and death.

For the last two days the military had taken charge of things, but very little seemed to have been done. Close around their headquarters, dead bodies still lay around, and even on their landing steps they had made no attempt to move them. If something was not done soon, disease would be sure to be breaking out. Difficulties facing them were having no means of transport. All trucks and wagons were burnt, the roads leading in from the country were impassable, and all the bridges were down. As all the towns and villages for miles round had also suffered, the nearest relief town was Kobe, which is 360 miles by sea.

During the morning whilst on shore, we felt another very pronounced shock.

The Empress of Australia was the headquarters for Europeans in Yokohama. The British Consul (Mr. Boulter) and the American Vice-Consul were on board. Refugees were brought off to the ship and kept on board until we were able to transfer them to other vessels leaving for Kobe or America.

Four American destroyers also arrived during the day and sent over large quantities of medical stores.

At noon on the same day, the H.M.S. Dispatch arrived from Shanghai. She at once sent over doctors, sick-bay attendants, and four signalmen.

The British and American ships were all assisting in transferring refugees from ship to ship.

Dense clouds of smoke were still rising up from Yokosuka, where the huge naval oil reserve tanks and coal supply were stored.

We have since heard that the explosions which took place during that Saturday afternoon, were the ammunition dumps blowing up.

By now considerable numbers of refugees were arriving from Tokio.

SEPTEMBER 5th—5:00 p.m.

Went for a trial run in the Gulf. Both engines were working satisfactorily, although there was much vibration. Returning, we anchored close to the Dispatch. She sent over a diving party to survey our propellers and found three turns of wire round boss of starboard propeller, which they were able to clear.

SEPTEMBER 6th—Thursday.

Today transferred 450 passengers, mostly Chinese, to West O'rore, We had by now only about 400 left on board.

The consul releases the Australia tomorrow.

SEPTEMBER 7th—Friday.

We had a busy day exchanging refugees, passengers and baggage, with Andre Lebon. We took all who wished to get to Kobe. The British consul left in the last boat in the evening, transferring his quarters to the French ship.

A number of business people were remaining behind in hopes of salvaging safes and business records left undestroyed.

11:00 p.m. Sailed for Kobe with a very crowded ship.

SEPTEMBER 9th—7:00 a.m.

Arrived Kobe. The ship was met by parties from the American and Japanese hospitals and parties from various relief societies of different nationalities.

SEPTEMBER 11th—Noon.

Sailed for Yokohama to fill up with oil from oil tank steamers. In the vicinity of the Gulf of Tokio, there was only one lighthouse in service. All the others were wrecked. The two big forts built out in the middle of the bay were completely wrecked. Gun turrets were twisted on their sides, and the other parts had caved in or sunk altogether out of sight.

SEPTEMBER 12th—7:48 p.m.

Ship once more back to normal, and we sailed for Vancouver.

A Note on the Texts

Whenever possible, texts for this series have been based on versions that were published in book form, preferably during Hodgson's lifetime. The major exceptions to this rule are the stories that appear in volumes edited by Sam Moskowitz. Moskowitz was known to have access to original manuscripts and other source materials. Some stories were published only in serial form, and have been taken from those primary sources.

Over the years, many of Hodgson's stories have appeared under variant titles, which are noted below. As a rule, the titles used in this series are based on the first book publication of a story, even if it previously appeared under a different title, in serial form.

Specific textual sources are noted below. The only changes that have been made to the texts have been to correct obvious typographical errors, and to standardize punctuation. British and archaic spellings have been retained.

"The Valley of Lost Children" is based on its appearance in *The Haunted "Pampero"* (Donald M. Grant, 1992). It originally appeared in *Cornhill*, Feb. 1906.
"Date 1965: Modern Warfare" is based on its appearance in *The Haunted "Pampero"* (Donald M. Grant, 1992). It originally appeared in *New Age*, 24 Dec. 1908.
"My House Shall Be Called the House of Prayer" originally appeared in *Cornhill*, May 1911. Text provided by Douglas A. Anderson.
"Judge Barclay's Wife" is based on its appearance in *Adventure*, Oct. 1912. It originally appeared in *London Magazine*, July 1912.
"The Getting Even of Tommy Dodd" is based on its appearance as "The Apprentices' Mutiny" in *Sea Stories*, Oct. 20, 1923. It originally appeared in *The Red Magazine*, Aug. 15, 1912.

"Sea Horses" is based on its appearance in *Men of the Deep Waters* (Eveleigh Nash, 1914). It originally appeared in *London Magazine,* March 1913.

"How the Honourable Billy Darrell Raised the Wind" originally appeared in *The Red Magazine,* Mar. 15, 1913.

"The Getting Even of 'Parson' Guyles" is based on its appearance in *Luck of the Strong* (Eveleigh Nash, 1916). It originally appeared in *The Red Magazine*, Nov. 1914.

"The Friendship of Monsieur Jeynois" originally appeared in *The Red Magazine*, Aug. 1, 1915.

"The Inn of the Black Crow" originally appeared in *The Red Magazine,* Oct. 1, 1915.

"What Happened in the Thunderbolt" originally appeared in *The Red Magazine,* Jan. 15, 1916.

"How Sir Jerrold Treyn Dealt with the Dutch in Caunston Cove" originally appeared in *The Red Magazine,* May 1, 1916.

"Jem Binney and the Safe at Lockwood Hall" originally appeared in *The Red Magazine,* Oct. 16, 1916.

"Diamond Cut Diamond with a Vengeance" originally appeared in *The Red Magazine,* Jan. 1, 1918.

"Eloi, Eloi, Lama Sabachthani" (aka "Baumoff's Explosive") is based on its appearance in *Out of the Storm* (Donald M. Grant, 1975). It originally appeared in *Nash's Illustrated Weekly*, Sep. 20, 1919.

"The Room of Fear" is based on its appearance in *Terrors of the Sea* (Donald M. Grant, 1996).

"The Promise" is based on its appearance in *Terrors of the Sea* (Donald M. Grant, 1996).

"Captain Dang" is based on its appearance in *Terrors of the Sea* (Donald M. Grant, 1996).

"Captain Dan Danblasten" is based on its appearance in *The Wandering Soul* (Tartarus Press, 2005).

"The Ghost Pirates" is a 1909 abridgment of *The Ghost Pirates* (*The Collected Fiction of William Hope Hodgson Volume 3: The Ghost Pirates and Other Revenants of the Sea*), and is based on its appearance in *The Haunted "Pampero"* (Donald M. Grant, 1992).

"Carnacki, the Ghost Finder" is a 1910 condensation of several Carnacki stories (*The Collected Fiction of William Hope Hodgson Volume 2: The House on the Borderlands and Other Mysterious Places*), and is based on its appearance in *Spectral Manifestations* (Bellknapp Books, 1984).

"The Dream of X" is a 1912 abridgment of *The Night Land* (*The Collected Fiction of William Hope Hodgson Volume 4: The Night Land and*

Other Perilous Romances), and is based on its appearance in *The Dream of X* (Donald M. Grant, 1977).

"Senator Sandy Mac Ghee" (1914) originally published in U.S. copyright pamphlets. Text provided by Douglas A. Anderson.

"The Last Word in Mysteries" (1914) originally published in U.S. copyright pamphlets. Text provided by Douglas A. Anderson.

"The Dumpley Acrostics" (1914) originally published in U.S. copyright pamphlets. Text provided by Douglas A. Anderson.

"An Adventure of the Deep Waters" is an expanded variant of "The Thing in the Weeds" (*The Collected Fiction of William Hope Hodgson Volume 1: The Boats of the Glen Carrig and Other Nautical Adventures*). It originally appeared in *Short Stories*, Feb. 1916.

"Captain Gunbolt Charity and the Painted Lady" is a May 1916 variant of the Captain Gault story "The Painted Lady" (*The Collected Fiction of William Hope Hodgson Volume 1: The Boats of the Glen Carrig and Other Nautical Adventures*). It is based on its appearance in *Luck of the Strong* (Eveleigh Nash, 1916).

"The Storm" is a variant of "By the Lee" (*The Collected Fiction of William Hope Hodgson Volume 3: The Ghost Pirates and Other Revenants of the Sea*). It originally appeared in *Short Stories,* Dec. 1919, and is based on its appearance in *The Haunted 'Pampero'* (Donald M. Grant, 1992).

"The Crew of the Lancing" is a variant of "Demons of the Sea"(*The Collected Fiction of William Hope Hodgson Volume 3: The Ghost Pirates and Other Revenants of the Sea*). It originally appeared in *Over the Edge,* (Arkham House, 1964), and is based on its appearance in *Deep Waters* (Arkham House, 1967).

"The Raft" is an Oct. 1905 counterfeit by C. L. Text provided by Douglas A. Anderson.

"R.M.S. 'Empress of Australia'" is a 1923 counterfeit. It is based on its appearance in *Terrors of the Sea* (Donald M. Grant, 1996).

The Complete Fiction of William Hope Hodgson is published by Night Shade Books in the following volumes:

The Boats of the "Glen Carrig" and Other Nautical Adventures
The House on the Borderland and Other Mysterious Places
The Ghost Pirates and Other Revenants of the Sea
The Night Land and Other Perilous Romances
The Dream of X and Other Fantastic Visions